Bellosguardo

The Lives of Anna & Huguette Clark
by Marjorie A. May

Book Cover: Hay River Press

Cover painting: *Carnation, Lily, Lily, Rose* by John Singer Sargent (1895-96), Tate Britain

First edition 2024

Contents

To my parents,

Wayne & Kristine

Le grillon

Un pauvre petit grillon
Caché dans l'herbe fleurie
Regardait un papillon
Voltigeant dans la prairie.
L'insecte ailé brillait des plus vives couleurs;
L'azur, la pourpre et l'or éclataient sur ses ailes;
Jeune, beau, petit maître, il court de fleurs en fleurs,
Prenant et quittant les plus belles.

Ah! disait le grillon, que son sort et le mien
Sont différents! Dame nature
Pour lui fit tout, et pour moi rien.
Je n'ai point de talent, encor moins de figure.
Nul ne prend garde à moi, l'on m'ignore ici-bas:
Autant vaudrait n'existait pas.

Comme il parlait, dans la prairie
Arrive une troupe d'enfants:
Aussitôt les voilà courants
Apres ce papillon dont ils ont tous envie.

Chapeaux, mouchoirs, bonnets, servent à l'attraper;
L'insect vainement cherche à leur échapper,
Il deviant beintôt leur conquête.

L'un le saisit par l'aile, un autre par le corps;
Un troisième survient, et le prend par la tête:
Il ne fallait pas tant d'efforts
Pour déchirer la pauvre bête.
Oh! oh! dit le grillon, je ne suis plus fâché;
Il en coûte trop cher pour briller dans le monde.
Combien je vais aimer ma retraite profonde!
Pour vivre heureux, vivons caché.

—Jean-Pierre Claris de Florian
Fables (1792)

The Cricket

A poor little cricket,
Concealed in grass flower-strewn,
Watched in a thicket
A butterfly hover at noon.
The winged insect shone with the brightest of hues,
Purple, gold and blue its wings elaborate.
Young, handsome, little master, it hurries to choose
All the finest blooms to take and pollinate.

"Ah!" said the cricket. "How his fate and my fate
Are different! Mother Nature did her best,
Did everything for him, but for me it's too late.
I have no great talent, beauty even less.

No-one takes notice of me. They resist.
I might as well just not exist."

As he was talking, down in the meadow
A troupe of children out of nowhere come
And right away they break into a run.
After the butterfly all want to follow.
Hat, hankies, bonnets serve to hold it fast.
The insect's attempts to escape do not last.
It soon their thirst for conquest slakes.

One grabs it by the wing, another by the thorax,
A third child comes up and by the head it takes.
It did not need an ax;
The tearing of it sates.

"Oh! Oh!" said the cricket. "By anger I'm not driven.
Making much of oneself's no easy requirement.
How much I'll enjoy my total retirement."
In order to live happily, live hidden.

—Jean-Pierre Claris de Florian

Intreat me not to leave thee, or to return from following after thee:
for whither thou goest, I will go; and where thou lodgest, I will lodge:
thy people shall be my people, and thy God my God:
Where thou diest, will I die, and there will I be buried:
the Lord do so to me, and more also, if ought but death part thee and me.

Ruth 1: 16 – 17 KJV

March 1991
907 Fifth Avenue, New York City

Twelve years since she had faced someone. Perhaps longer. She couldn't quite recall. Time meant little; the hour barely regarded. Only a noted day of the month piqued interest: Rich memories bound to the calendar's seasonal rhythm. She lived largely without time in the most famous city in the world notorious for grasping and groaning after it.

Huguette sat expectant, ears perked. She held a worn Yves Delorme hand towel to a painfully raw mouth wound, her other hand gripped the olive-green receiver. She lowered the towel, "I think he's here, Simone. *Salut!*"

Lacking lip tissue, Huguette's words slurred. Simone Pierre was accustomed and could pick up Huguette's meaning with little trouble.

"*Je suis très contente* you will be seeing Dr. Townsend!" said Simone. "Call me later to let me know the diagnosis. So, I don't worry."

Trembling, Huguette said goodbye again and pressed an index finger with a dirty fingernail onto the clear plastic button to cut off the line. She inhaled deeply, not wanting to go through with the appointment but knowing it was vital. Her will to live was stronger than the pressing demand for privacy. She set the receiver onto the phone cradle.

Earlier in the day in the doormen's office, Rocco Marino immediately recognized Mrs. Clark's high-pitched, slurry voice. He loved to tell stories about co-op owners' eccentricities and outlandish requests. Mrs. Clark was a favorite easy target. In New Jersey during holiday parties, Marino's punch line was: "And me never seeing her, that's sayin' somethin', cuz I've worked in that building for over sixteen years!"

Marino explained to the new guy as they stood in the break room, "You've got to know old lady Clark in 8W gives a very generous Christmas tip, which ain't like everybody around here, let me tell you! And she's *easy*. I only bring up deliveries twice a week maybe. A few bags here and there from Winter's Market. No big deal! Flowers or boxes a few times a month, *maybe*." He gestured widely with meaty hands and head cocked back. "Not much these days! Used to be a whole lot more comin' and goin' from her place."

Marino prided himself on excellent communication skills. He slowed his rate of speech and winked at the new guy next to him listening in. "How can I help you on this beautiful day, Mrs. Clark?"

"Mr. Marino, I have a medical appointment. Please check the doctor's I.D. before admitting him into 8W. He will be coming at one o'clock."

"Sure thing, Mrs. Clark! I—"

Marino's thick black eyebrows flew up and then went down again as quickly as the line went dead. He rubbed his large nose and hung up as the new guy was called to the front door.

The broad never seemed to go nowhere, like, no matter what! Man, some peoples make no sense. Today could be the day I catch a glimpse of her. Wouldn't that be a scoop!

Several hours later, Marino escorted the doctor onto the elevator, then faced his captive audience. "I've worked here many years, Doctor, but I ain't never seen this lady you're about to visit. I hope she's okay!" Marino nodded vigorously.

Mark Townsend gave a polite nod in return and then ignored the doorman. Imposing in long camel hair overcoat, cashmere plaid scarf, and leather case, he was accustomed to making house calls. He never made the mistake of engaging staff in conversation.

The elevator softly shuddered to a stop. As the doors eased open, Marino attempted again: "I heard Clark owns 8E too, but that ain't common knowledge. All I knows is, no one ever goes in or out! Reminds me of Wonka in 'Charlie and the Chocolate Factory.' Ever seen that movie?"

Townsend ignored him so Marino walked to 8W, and using a master key, opened it wide.

Marino raised his voice purposely, as instructed, "Here you are, Dr. Townsend!" He leaned inside, but only the long gallery lit up by the soft yellow hallway light could be seen. "Have a good day!"

Faint rustlings and men's voices at the faraway front door. *Oh, dear!*

With one wasted arm, Huguette wrestled aside layers of Pendleton blankets, down comforters, and a threadbare Frette sheet. She was unaware of the cloying scent of shut-in that had settled like noxious dust in the tiny bedroom with a kitchenette. Before the early sixties, the bedroom had once been half the size and occupied by a maid.

They must be inside already. I hope Mr. Marino remembers my instructions. It's so bothersome when the doormen don't remember exactly what I've told them...

Swinging matchstick legs off the twin bed, Huguette pressed the towel to her mouth to relieve pain. The aged mattress squeaked as she eased downward, retrieving slippers with a practiced foot. With her free hand, she attempted to close a thin silk kimono robe over a cotton nightgown. She gave up to shuffle hastily down the hallway past the kitchen and breakfast room.

Huguette's heart pounded and she felt light-headed. She almost forgot the throbbing pain as she halted momentarily to steady herself. *This is entirely disagreeable, but like most disagreeable things in life, it must be done.* Allons-y!

Hearing her name called by a masculine voice, she felt a pang of regret agreeing to Simone's urging. Rounding the corner, she almost collided with a tall man. *I think I'm going to faint!* Huguette's eyes squeezed shut, which stung a raw eyelid.

"Hello! Mrs. Clark? I'm Dr. Townsend from Doctor's Hospital. Nice to meet you. We spoke earlier today."

Huguette peeked to see the doctor extending a large hand. She recoiled.

I should have turned on the lights!

She inhaled before moving the towel, squeaking, "Nice to meet you, Dr. Townsend. Shall we sit in there?"

She pointed in the direction he should go. Out of professional habit, Townsend reached to grasp the elderly woman's arm. He was shocked at Mrs. Clark's appearance.

The woman looks like an advanced leper patient! I need good light to examine her. Where is a light switch?

"I can walk, Dr. Townsend." Huguette shook free and advanced into the drawing room. She had no trouble in the darkened rooms and sat primly on a red damask chair before motioning for the doctor to do the same. "Thank you for coming."

Townsend noted the patient's anxiety. *Most likely from having a stranger in her home. That's normal.* At first glance, she was a commonplace, elderly waif in a filthy robe, recently out of bed with wispy white hair smashed to her skull. One would see her like repeated in every nursing home in America. *Where the heck is the staff?*

"Excuse me while I take the liberty to turn on a few more lights, but I must see you clearly."

He switched on lamps and moved aside heavy silk curtains and thick blinds. *There's the park!* While removing his overcoat, in seconds Townsend scanned the surroundings. The parquet de Versailles flooring needed polishing. Out in the gallery, matching Louis XV console tables and Qing Dynasty vases flanked the doorway. Chippendale chairs lined up. World class art. Custom dust covers on most furniture. The enormous ivory and red Aubusson carpet in excellent condition. Waterford chandelier.

Mrs. Clark is clearly not a typical Chanel-wearing, Fifth Avenue doyenne despite what appears to be quite a large apartment facing Central Park. In this pre-war building, even if she merely had a smaller apartment with no view, she would be rich.

At his request, Huguette lowered the saliva and blood encrusted towel. Eyelids, cheek, and mouth throbbed with jolts of exposed nerve pain. Townsend knelt to take stock.

The woman's eyes are sharp; she's unbathed, slight body odor. Normal issues of dementia, obesity, gout, or diabetes clearly not an issue; rather, it's probably cancer eating away at the flesh, deforming lips and eyelids. Dark spots and mottling from obvious sun damage on all exposed tissue. In need of dental care.

Townsend cupped Huguette's face, gently lifting it to the right and left examining the extent of the damage.

About five six, less than eighty pounds, dehydrated, in need of immediate medical attention. She'll require multiple surgeries.

Huguette watched the doctor's grey-blue irises dart over her face again and again. He was silent for several minutes, his facial expression concerned.

Oh dear, it's probably worse than I suspected. Simone is correct, of course. Dr. Townsend seems an okay man, even handsome. Some tension eased, and she breathed more freely. A hand went up to hair: *I must look terrible at the moment!*

Townsend sat back on his haunches. "It must be very difficult for you to eat and drink with so much of your lower lip eaten away by what appears to be skin cancer."

Tentatively, Huguette tried a small joke. "Yes, and I love to eat so it's been difficult!" She laughed lightly, wary eyes taking in the doctor's smile. "Skin cancer... I've been reading reports in *The New York Times*, as now suddenly the sun is the enemy! Well, I'll have you know I spent half my life getting brown as a berry! I was a lizard in the summertime, as was everyone else. We all *worshipped* the sun!"

The sudden chatter surprised Townsend. *A good sense of humor indicates health; she'll probably be fine in the long run. However, the right eyelid, right cheek, and nose have what appear to be red actinic keratoses. What causes most concern is the missing section of lateral lower lip, most likely due to rampant squamous cell carcinoma.*

"I want to be honest with you; your condition is very serious, Mrs. Clark. You need to be operated on immediately. I would give a preliminary estimate of at least two to three surgeries. Some plastic surgery will be required to restore normal facial features, such as your lower lip, but not much. I admit I'm *very* surprised you haven't requested medical care before now. With these types of sores, your pain and discomfort must be intense." The doctor smiled encouragement.

"Yes, the sores have worsened over the past twelve months. Lately I've been reduced to eating what amounts to baby food: mashed bananas, buttermilk, ice cream, yogurt. Any foods needing to be chewed thoroughly will either be too painful or fall out of my mouth. Plop! Even drinking water is awkward. I've been craning my neck back to drink nourishment. Like a bird! Despite all this, I'm still alive!"

"You're quite the trooper."

"Yes, but I'm okay, Doctor, as you can plainly see. I merely need a bit of fixing up. It can't be done here?" She stopped talking to catch her breath, feeling light-headed again.

Townsend shook his head. "I need you to come today to Doctor's Hospital. With these types of cancerous wounds, I cannot properly examine or treat you in your home. Your body is dehydrated, and you have lost too much weight for proper healing to occur. I won't mince words: your body is fighting to stay alive at the moment. It's critical you're treated in a hospital as soon as possible."

"Oh, I see." Huguette looked down with displeasure, stiffening up again.

"I sympathize you want to be treated here, in your home where you feel most comfortable. But as your doctor, I insist on us going to the hospital today for treatment. Do you consent to surgery? You will need it very soon. This week in fact."

"This week? Well, I hadn't realized I was so bad off!" Huguette's hands wrung the towel. The overwhelming thought of leaving caused her to pull back against the chair, shutting eyes. In a firm tone of voice that slurred only occasionally, she said, "Dr. Townsend, if I were to pay you more, substantially more, could you not set up some sort of small clinic here? To treat me privately?"

Townsend paused. In his most serious tone, he said, "Mrs. Clark, it's my strongest professional opinion you *must leave immediately* for treatment. To the hospital where every medical emergency can quickly be dealt with if there are complications. Your life is at stake! I implore you to reconsider."

Huguette's eyes popped back open. Her voice faltered, "Right now...?"

Townsend, seated on a chair close by, nodded.

I don't think I can handle the pain any longer. It upsets me terribly to not be able to eat and drink properly. I very much want to be healed. Huguette could tell her normally energetic body was giving out from prolonged lack of nourishment. *I dislike feeling cooped up in the bedroom in pain and fatigue. It's been many months since I've lived normally. Frankly, I think I'm losing the battle.*

Huguette made up her mind in a moment. Cornflower blue eyes bored into the doctor's, French accent more pronounced. "Dr. Townsend, I was prepared for this to happen, as of course I comprehend I need serious medical care. Please call an ambulance with the phone in the library. However, I have something I *must insist on.* I don't want to be seen by anyone while I leave. How can you make that happen?"

"I'll try." He rummaged in his bag for a medicated skin salve.

"No, I demand it happen!"

"Okay, no one will see you."

He dabbed on salve and put bandages on Huguette before exiting the room. Fielding odd requests from eccentric Upper East Side patients was his specialty. He assumed the patient's vanity was revealing itself. Such requests didn't faze in the least; it was part and parcel of his job making house calls. If it would help save the patient's life, he was game.

Returning from the library, he said, "The ambulance will be here in less than ten minutes. How about we find a scarf and a coat to put on?"

"Not good enough, I'm afraid. I'm adamant I want no one to even see me lying on the gurney. I cannot stand the thought of my privacy being invaded by prying eyes. I will not be gawked at. It's embarrassing!" Huguette's chin lifted obstinately and eyes became sharp.

Townsend hesitated. The EMTs wouldn't be happy with superficial requests interfering with set procedures. "Okay, we'll figure something out."

Huguette's youthful training demanded she remain soft-spoken and polite, but trepidation and arrogance longed to lash out at any denial of her wishes. *I will not leave if they don't cover me completely and lift me high up!*

While waiting for the ambulance, Townsend attempted to appease his new patient by chatting about the spring weather and Mayor Dinkin's promise to clean up New York's streets. Meanwhile, he continued to tacitly note his surroundings, admiring Impressionist paintings in antique frames.

Soon 8W's door was thrown wide and all the lights turned on. The apartment bustled with EMTs carrying a gurney and various medical bags. There hadn't been such a commotion in the apartment in many a year. Huguette shrank from it all, wrapping up in several thick cashmere shawls and shutting eyes tight. She swayed on the gurney as they easily hoisted her.

Huguette departed 907 Fifth Avenue like a modern-day Cleopatra, swaddled out of recognition and transported aloft on the EMT's muscled shoulders. Bound for Doctor's Hospital a short ambulance-drive away, she would never return despite living over twenty more years.

Within a week, Huguette underwent two surgeries and recuperated in a private room. She was no longer in pain, able to drink copious amounts of water, eat soft meals, and sleep soundly. With round-the-clock care reinstated, she was ecstatic. Despite all this, Huguette was in sore need of a friend in the unfamiliar hospital environment. She relented, consenting for Simone to visit.

The women gazed at each other fondly while holding hands. Conversing in French, no one else could follow. "It is good to finally see you in person! And, as promised, Madame Clark, I've brought delicious *brioche*, artichokes, and chicken soup to heal you up. You cannot eat awful hospital food while you are here. What is this, this ridiculous red Jell-O and spongey bread? Send it back!"

Simone requested the nurse remove the tray as she set down a Gristedes paper sack. She slid off a Max Mara wool coat to reveal a pink St. John tweed suit and Chanel heels.

"Ah, how wonderful! You're so thoughtful, Simone. And how lovely you look. I must look a sight! Come sit down by me." She patted the bed, but Simone brought over a chair.

Huguette watched with anticipation as the chicken soup was placed before her. "Isn't this wonderful? I'm well taken care of, healing fast. At night, I even have warmed milk before bed. It's been so long since I've enjoyed that!" She smiled like a little girl. The hospital bed seemed to swallow her up.

"Wonderful! I'm happy to hear you're doing so well. You need fattening though. I was very worried for you. Very worried! You let it go on for far too long. One needs to care for oneself." Simone smiled, eyes trained on her long-time friend to ascertain any desire.

"You're a choice friend, Simone. I owe you my life, you know."

"Nonsense. You would've done the same for me."

"*Oui,* I would've!"

Despite constant interruptions by a variety of medical professionals attempting to enter the room *without* Huguette's permission—who were yelled at and thrown out on the instant—she felt more relaxed than she had in years. She relished peaceful days in a modern hospital. *Where else can I be this safe from outsiders and germs? This well cared for?*

After long discussions with a baffled Townsend, Huguette got her wish to stay as a resident. With Simone's help to interview candidates—"Because *of course* that will not be left for Madame Clark to do!"—a private day nurse and night nurse were found. Only those women were permitted to care for Huguette. Hospital staff were not admitted into the room unless strictly necessary.

Requiring little physical care, she preferred to dress, bathe, and cut nails and hair herself. Beyond that, she wanted to never worry about bothersome daily tasks. She never saw chores as her responsibility; never thought to do those activities herself. She wouldn't know how to go about completing them in the first place. The nurses merged seamlessly with doting servants who had cossetted Huguette since a baby. She knew no other life than one of devoted staff performing every desire.

For the next two decades, prohibitive hospital bills and private nursing care were paid in cash. Huguette's world hovered far above the classes who concerned themselves with various insurances. These products staved off financial disaster for tens of millions of Americans. Huguette, on the other hand, had never considered so-called necessities such as health, life, accident, or dental insurance. She knew to insure houses and valuables. That went without saying. But she required no other insurance. She had no driver's license because she had never driven a vehicle. Nor had she attended college or ever earned wages. She had no use for a FICO score and was laughably ineligible for Social Security or Medicare.

Within forty-eight hours of being admitted to Doctor's Hospital, Huguette gave the name of her attorney. Less than an hour after the call by the billing department, an overweight man in a Sear's suit and a beat-up briefcase appeared out of breath in the hallway.

That Mrs. Clark was in the hospital, given her advanced age, Joshua Schwartz was not surprised by. But he was shocked his client appeared in public. He hurried across town with the hope of finally meeting face-to-face. He wanted to assess Clark's physical condition, then ask to visit again another day, very soon. He had a lot of highly sensitive, important pending legal and financial paperwork she had long neglected.

Schwartz had spoken with Mrs. Clark on the telephone many times over the years, but she was very strange when he attempted a visit over ten years ago.

"Mrs. Clark would only talk to me on the other side of a cracked door!" he wailed to his boss.

She's my nuttiest but kindest client. In fact, she could be the craziest client in the entire firm.

Mrs. Clark was also the most demanding client when she wanted something. She might call three times a day if an issue concerned her. But she never raised her voice. Regardless, Schwartz knew when she was keen he do something immediately.

She could surprise you how savvy and strong-willed she was behind that polite, upper-crust French accent.

He stood prepared, almost with boyish excitement, but the prim-mouthed nurse came out and shut the door firmly. His hope faded.

"Mrs. Clark instructed earlier you be called regarding the hospital billing, and that was sufficient. She does not need your services today. She would prefer to be left alone. If you need to talk with her in future, please call. Thank you for coming." The nurse took the bouquet and turned away.

He rolled bulbous eyes while ambling back down the squeaky linoleum smelling of disinfectant. He didn't doubt for a second the nurse was repeating verbatim what Mrs. Clark said. On the street, he eased into a taxi, all excitement and adrenaline evaporated.

This client is a pain in the neck. What will I tell my boss this time about the unsigned will and other overdue estate and tax documents? Schwartz sighed and loosened his silk tie. His suits were off-the-rack, but he liked expensive ties.

How long will I be allowed to be the lead for this client if I'm not able to make any headway signing a current will? He was out of ideas; it was a stalemate. *She's been thwarting me for years!*

Unbelievably, Mrs. Clark's will was sixty years old. And she was worth major money from significant real estate holdings in three states, tens of millions in accounts at multiple banks, investments, dozens of pieces of fine art, Stradivari instruments, and millions in gold and jewels in safe deposit boxes.

Some of the bank accounts and safety deposit boxes stretched back to 1925. From her mother, Anna Clark, who died in the early sixties. Incredibly, Schwartz had recently learned about an account set up in 1908 by Senator and Mrs. William Clark. By the mid to late-1980s, two of the banks in question had no record of any recent communication regarding several large safety deposit boxes affiliated with the account. Somehow the annual fee lapsed, or, at least, that's what the banks reported...

Schwartz thought otherwise. *But how am I to intervene in a client's affairs when I'm not privy to all the information?*

Belatedly, he learned the safe deposit boxes were dealt with per each bank's normal procedures for unclaimed property. They were last opened *so many decades ago* the banks assumed, understandably, the original owner was deceased. The fabulous 22-karat gold and jeweled contents were auctioned off quietly. The banks kept the millions.

By the time Mrs. Clark learned of the errors, it was too late. Her mother's cherished property was long gone. Lost to collectors' clutches from London to Singapore.

What did Mrs. Clark do? Nothing.

"I implore you to sue, to counter, to get back at least *some* of the millions owed! Don't ignore this crime!" Schwartz spat into the phone.

"My privacy is paramount to lost property, however much I have agonized about my mother's missing possessions."

Then Mrs. Clark stopped talking to him for a month.

What was I supposed to do about it if decades went by and Mrs. Clark never went to check on the safe deposit boxes, never asked my firm to check on them, never called the banks herself?

After Schwartz discussed the situation with the banks, sweating all the while, *it must have been Mrs. Clark's mother and father who had set up the safe deposit boxes before World War I, for cryin' out loud, not Mrs. Huguette Clark!* He had to show the documentation to his partners, it was almost too incredible to be believed. Before World War I!

No one had been in to look at them since before 1955! And that visit was by Anna Clark. Her daughter would've been early middle-aged. Why didn't she ever go along with her mother? Why didn't she care about millions in gold and jewels sitting around...?

He sniffed, then groaned. The driver had lit a cigarette.

It's asinine to not care about money when money is everything. You get so rich and then boom! You become eccentric and make zero sense. It's like a disease.

Talking on the phone was fine with Mrs. Clark, but more than that she refused. Documents sent over were rarely returned; she would ignore requests to meet. If it had to do with her will, he heard nothing back. Schwartz guessed this client was overwhelmed with her vast fortune.

And her way of dealing with it is not to deal with it! Maybe she thinks she won't die? Ridiculousness...

In the backseat, Schwartz slumped. *I'm being slowly killed off by a woman in her eighties, I just know it.*

He heard the Jamaican driver swear as a Cadillac black stretch limousine cut him off in Midtown's thick traffic. With tired eyes, he watched the driver's multi-colored knit hat encasing thick dreads bob up and down and up and down as the driver slammed on the brakes. The bobbing hat and the cigarette smoke were a hypnotic combination.

The driver threw up large brown hands in consternation, the cigarette scissored delicately by two long fingers. "Watch yo'self, man!" he said out the open window.

Feeling tempted by the second-hand smoke, Schwartz took out a small blue bag of Planter's. His wife made sure he always had multiple bags in his briefcase; chewing kept him from chain-smoking.

His thoughts went automatically back to the task at hand. The way Mrs. Clark acted since he had taken over, none of her wealth mattered anyway. Yet she wouldn't update her will to protect her fortune from shirttail relations. Instead, as a precaution, she repeatedly advised to never divulge her address or phone number to anyone for anything. Ever.

On that point, Mrs. Clark was adamant and crystal clear: "I have no family I'm close to. Absolutely no one has a right to claim a relationship without my prior approval."

No matter how he tried, he couldn't make out her motives regarding the hundreds of millions in the estate that would need to be dealt with upon her demise. The media went bananas for philanthropists like Brooke Astor. But he personally knew Mrs. Clark had well over triple the assets in comparison. *Yet no one's heard of her!*

My client is now in her mid-eighties. What if she dies soon? I don't have the foggiest idea what she wants me to do with the grossly outdated will at this, no doubt, the end of her life. It'll probably turn into a mess of legal and IRS paperwork someday very soon. At least I can bill the estate with the time...

The taxi stopped, and he groped for his wallet. Counting out the cash, he couldn't turn off his brain. *What will I tell my boss...?*

He could already hear Jameson, an obnoxious colleague two doors down, taunting softly as Schwartz passed by in the hallway: "Schwartzy-baby strikes out again! Clark 100, Schwartz 0!"

He knew others were jealous. There were no clients in their white shoe law firm, or in any of their competitor's firms, for that matter, worth as much as Mrs. Huguette Marcelle Clark.

July 4, 1893
Butte, Montana

Anna dripped with sweat. *My mouth feels like sawdust!*

She scratched the toga's soggy waistline before resuming position as Lady Liberty. Her costume was a white bedsheet slung over a sprigged muslin dress with sleeves rolled up, secured with a leather belt. Anna smiled broadly at thick holiday crowds. It was a rare day with almost clear skies. Despite the unrelenting rays causing beads of sweat to drip into her eyes, she was thrilled to have a starring role.

I need to take every opportunity to be noticed. I will be on the stage someday—singing and dancing for adoring audiences—and today is a step in the right direction!

With one arm held aloft with a gilded torch—thankfully not lit—Anna felt the wagon bed sway awkwardly. Sometimes she began to lose her balance on the stacked hay bales when nervous horses reacted to jubilant crowds.

Normally she would be wearing a bonnet and holding a parasol. It was brutal in the unrelenting sun under a gilt crown borrowed from the Butte Drama Club's costume box. The force of the heat on bare flesh shocked. *How awful will my sunburn be tomorrow?*

Drunken hoots of admiration increased as the float approached the main blocks of downtown. Anna's costume highlighted svelte curves and smooth skin. She tried not to react when men called out. Once, she even heard her name yelled. With chagrin, she immediately recalled what Sally Smith warned earlier that morning: "It's *very brash* to volunteer yourself for such an immodest part!"

Anna had clambered into the wagon's flatbed without replying. Sally continued with a serious expression.

"Staying on the sidelines in the shade is what a well-bred young lady does during public events. She doesn't literally *parade herself* before hundreds of men! You're only fifteen! What's gotten into you?" Her small pink mouth pouted disdain.

Anna laughed gaily, "You sound like a schoolmarm!" She arranged herself on hay bales decorated with red, white, and blue bunting. "Sally dear, it's only for fun, and my papa gave his permission. So, leave me alone!"

"I hope turning red from too much sun is the only problem stemming from this indecent behavior! If you go through with this, I don't know how I can be seen with you in public!" Sally whirled around, lace parasol erect, and stalked off.

She's becoming a stick in the mud who'll never leave Butte! Anna figured Sally would probably marry that ridiculous Tom Jenkins whose father owned the hardware store. *And then Sally will be here the rest of her life, in dusty, boring Butte with gallows frames outlined against the smoky sky. Richest Hill on Earth, my foot... It isn't rich for me!*

To remain in Butte wasn't an option, even though Anna wasn't quite sure how escape would play out. *Remember, Maman says the influence of others rubs off on us. Sally is no longer the kind of girl I plan on surrounding myself with. I won't apologize for my ambition.*

She threw her best self into directing the crowd's energy into a frenzy of patriotism as she embodied Lady Liberty rolling slowly past. When the wagon lurched and the flimsy crown threatened to topple again, Anna smiled widely while raising a quick arm to catch it. Onlookers laughed good-naturedly. Then Anna would smile and wave enthusiastically, even blowing kisses, and the crowd cheered louder. Relishing the attention, she urged them on louder as the band behind played "Yankee Doodle" and "Battle Hymn of the Republic."

Above the main float, a man in an expertly cut white linen suit and straw boater seemed amused by the scene. He attentively watched Lady Liberty approach while standing with a group of men on a shaded second-story hotel balcony off to the right. As Anna was five feet six, and standing on straw bales, she could clearly see the distinguished man from her vantage point. *He must be important to be up there*!

When the float was adjacent to the building, the man doffed his straw boater and smiled at the precise point the girl could see him best. She smiled widely back, exuding youthful confidence and a fun nature. He was immediately attracted to her big smile and dancing eyes.

William Andrews Clark Sr. was a short, slight man with auburn hair and whiskers. He was a diehard capitalist and titan of business in a country that positively begged for development. At fifty-four, he was one of the most famous bosses in Butte, owning much of the mining, banking, real estate, and utilities. If Butte was a dirty, smoky city famous for copper, Clark was chief among those who made it so. He was a ruthless, ambitious entrepreneur with an empire built on mining copper, railroads, real estate, banking, farming, and utilities in a handful of states stretching across enormous western swathes of the United States.

Clark was becoming one of the top three richest men in the United States with an annual income of millions of dollars. Year after year, profits increased at record pace. In modern-day valuations, he was a billionaire. And that summer's day he took notice of Anna precisely as he had taken notice of other lucrative opportunities: He knew a good prospect when he saw one.

I'll find out who that attractive, young woman is and see if she's worth my time.

Turning to the men beside him, Clark joined the heated conversation on local politics.

Days later, Anna's youth, pretty face, good sense of humor, and strong desire to pursue musical performance on the stage thoroughly charmed Clark. In fact, his attraction was enough that after meeting in a hotel restaurant, he was pleased to discover Miss La Chappelle—accompanied by Mrs. Pierre La Chappelle—was a bright young woman.

"I wish to be an actress. However, a more practical desire is to study singing and piano. I could use those talents to teach others when I need to support myself." She almost blushed under Clark's direct gaze.

"Well, Miss La Chappelle, I think we need to raise your sights a bit higher, if you don't mind me saying. I might have a different idea for you, a better idea perhaps... If Mrs. La Chappelle agrees with me, of course." William nodded at Philomene La Chappelle who only smiled weakly.

Anna La Chappelle's ambition and independence Clark could certainly comprehend. The next week, he called to offer sponsorship at the Ladies Seminary.

"It will be for one academic year on probation." Clark sat with legs crossed and hat off at the simple wooden table in the rear kitchen. "And what's more, if Miss La Chappelle studies hard and makes sufficient progress, I will sponsor the other children as well. That way, the entire family will benefit and rise together." Clark steepled thin fingers.

In heavily accented English, Pierre La Chappelle said, "Mr. Clark, what do we say to such a generous offer...? We can hardly refuse! In fact, Anna already agrees. As her parents, we know how well-deserving she is of this opportunity. We will miss our daughter, but we will allow her to go with our best wishes."

Philomene sat quietly, hardly daring to believe. *What a fine education she will receive!* She was privately relieved Anna would not have to face the drudgery and indignities of working at the boarding house. *With an education the seminary provided, she could be a teacher. It's a far better job and will allow her to meet suitable men.*

The parents exchanged glances. From Montreal, they emigrated soon after marriage. The family joined the throngs headed west after a better life. Pierre had been a practicing doctor in Quebec but was unable to renew his medical license in the United States; the family fortunes suffered, and he worried about the future.

"Mr. Clark, you honor our eldest daughter. I'm delighted you see her talent and potential as we do. I thank you most generously." Pierre shook Clark's hand.

"My good man, your eldest's talent shines brightly, and it costs me very little to educate her at the school I sponsor. Miss La Chappelle is a fine young woman raised by respectable parents. And a man of my means wants to help others to better themselves. Allow me the honor of serving your family in this way. I'm grateful for my own education which has helped me become successful."

Clark's normally stern visage smiled widely at the awestruck couple. A meticulous dresser, he wore a bespoke, three-piece, ivory linen suit with a pearl stick pin in the yellow silk tie. Slightly greying at the temples, auburn hair and beard were still abundant. The unrelenting stare of blue eyes indicated an intense personality. However, Clark's words were warm and his manner kind.

Philomene looked down from appraising the most famous man in Butte. *Mr. Clark is a curious blend of cold sternness and intensity of feeling. How can we tell this man no? It's impossible.*

She knew her girls were listening on the other side of the door. *Anna will insist on going, that's for certain. As he travels so extensively—everyone knows the Clark mansion is empty for long stretches—and Anna will be studying safely far away at Deer Lodge, perhaps nothing will come of the attention?*

Philomene stood, feeling more in control on her feet. "I'm most grateful to you, Mr. Clark. May I offer you more coffee?"

"No thank you, Mrs. La Chappelle. I must be going. I'll have my secretary draw up the school documents to sign. Classes begin mid-September. As my ward at the seminary, I feel it imperative I provide for all Miss La Chappelle's needs. Clothing, books, and supplies, what have you. I'll send adequate funds. Oh, and one more important point."

Clark rose from the round-backed wooden chair. "Please impress upon Miss La Chappelle if she does not perform, all will be rescinded. I will not tolerate sloth!"

"Anna will perform well; I will make sure of it," Pierre said.

Anna burst through the door, eyes shining and breathing shallowly. "Mr. Clark, I'm very grateful! You're making my dreams come true!"

Clark chuckled, delighted by Anna's passionate reaction, and placed a straw boater carefully on his head. As the front door closed, Anna and Amelia raced to the front windows to observe a tall, burly man in a charcoal grey suit and bowler hat open the carriage door. After securing it shut after Clark, the severe-looking man jumped onto a small step, hanging on to a leather strap. His cool eyes never stopped scanning both sides of the busy street. Two more men were at the front of the fine black carriage, one of which held the reins to four gleaming, black horses.

"I wonder what he's doing?" Anna said while examining the man at the rear as the carriage rolled away.

"He must not mind eating dust!" Amelia giggled.

That night, Anna went to bed late after hours of grueling chores. She was tired, but when she lay down her head filled happily with possibilities and dreams. *When I'm a student at the seminary, no man will be able to disrespect me there. The men here assume I'm for the taking!*

The memory of the man who grabbed her as she mopped the floor of a hallway last month came to mind. With a sickening fear, she had felt rude hands grasp her arm and waist. Anna froze as he pulled her roughly to his chest. She could smell fetid breath before he pressed lips on hers.

Instant revulsion canceled fear. She dropped the mop and began to fight, screaming loudly for help.

The man attempted to drag her into a nearby bedroom. He would have been successful if another guest had not intervened. An older man rushed down the hall.

"Hey, what do you think you're doing? She's not a whore! This is a boarding house!" The older man yanked the larger, younger man away.

"Leave me be!" The young man said while hitting the wall with a muffled grunt.

"Get out of here! Go to the red-light district, man!" The older man motioned for Anna to get behind him.

"We *are* in the red-light district!"

It's hard having no solid prospects. Anna sighed, her head turning on the pillow to gaze out the sheer curtains to the summer night sky. Only scattered stars could be seen. Amelia breathed deeply in the next bed.

Men I meet are rough and tumble, not educated like Father. What would have happened to me if that man hadn't heard me? Anna shuddered. *Don't worry, as* Maman *always says. I'm going to be a young lady of worth someday. At the moment, it's all in my head, but that will have to change somehow...*

Two weeks later, Philomene entered the kitchen with hat on and beaded purse in hand. "I've received a note from Mr. Clark. We had best get to the dressmaker he recommends. Although, it's not the type of shop I would've chosen."

"Why *Maman*? Is there something wrong with it?" Anna looked up from darning socks.

"Put your hat on. *Allons-y!* I've got a little money for two new dresses and shoes."

"Oh *Maman*, two new dresses?" Anna jumped up, beaming at the unexpected windfall.

"You must look presentable. Now let's hurry before it gets too hot out."

As the La Chappelles entered the elegant store, they were immediately accosted. Two sets of dark eyebrows flew up as several women rushed over.

The best dressed woman launched into a sing-song tone, hands beckoning. "Please come in, come in, come in, Mrs. La Chappelle and Miss La Chappelle! We've been expecting you! We've received orders from Mr. Clark for his new ward. And you, young lady, *must be her*! What a *lucky young lady* you are, my dearie!"

Mrs. Penelope Anderson put a thick arm through Anna's to escort her through the store. A few other female customers gawked.

"Yes, indeed. A *lucky* young woman! Please come to the back by the mirrors; we'll take your measurements, dearie."

While Anna was all but pushed behind a pink velvet curtain, Philomene said, "I would like to order two dresses—"

"Oh no. Never you mind, my good woman. We have it all here." Anderson pointed with a wink to a paper on the counter. Philomene requested to see it, soon becoming transfixed by the unbelievable number of items listed. *Everything a young lady could ever want is accounted for! How am I to pay for all this?*

Anderson zoomed around the counter to whisper, "Clark has a wife and two daughters of his own. He knows! I used to dress them. A *wonderful* woman. But she's long gotten all her gowns in Paris, I dare say!" The woman laughed heartily while eyeing up her assistant's measuring technique.

Philomene set the list on the counter. From the purse dangling at her wrist, she took out ten dollars. "I want to add my contribution to the final bill."

Anderson looked down at the cash and made a dismissive gesture. "Mr. Clark expressly stated you weren't to pay one penny. In fact, I've already sent the bill, as I'm *well versed* in what things cost from so many years in business. Take no thought of it, Mrs. La Chappelle! Be grateful your daughter is now Mr. Clark's ward! She's a *lucky* girl!" The woman winked at Anna.

Philomene nodded weakly. *How much money does this list represent? Well over fifty dollars, for sure.* She sank down on a yellow velvet loveseat with gold tassels while Anna's measurements were completed. *What does this portend?*

They arrived home to complete chores by the six o'clock supper hour. After eating a late dinner, Anna washed stacks of dirty dishes, endless silverware, and mucky pots and pans. Her fingertips became whizzled and rolled up sleeves soggy from standing so long at the washbasin.

Amelia dried and put dishes away. She giggled, nudging Anna, and then danced off before repeating the teasing. Anna shooed her and kept head down while trying not to smile.

"Does this mean I get your pink muslin?"

"Oh, go away, silly goose! You've got plenty of dresses!" Anna good-naturedly pointed to dishes needing drying.

When they finished an hour later, Anna went into the dining room and sat down with Philomene who looked over account books.

"Young single women have to be on their guard in the presence of men, married or not, rich or poor."

Anna pulled at wet sleeves, trying to dry them with a towel. "Oh, *Maman*! I know all about what men do to single women. We live close to a neighborhood which has taught us all about that!"

"*Je sais, ma petite*. Oh, don't remind me..." Philomene stopped writing to look at her eldest. "If we could've afforded a house in a better neighborhood, we would've moved years ago. *Ma petite fille*, I only want you to take advantage of this marvelous opportunity without compromising yourself with a married man, however rich and powerful. Say your rosary. Look for a man who'll marry you, not a man with a family of his own."

"*Maman, bien sûr*... And besides, I have no desire to marry young and burden myself with a family too soon! I'll complete my education when I'm seventeen and then see what's in store for me. Never fear, I'll stay out of the clutches *des tous les hommes*, not merely Mr. Clark."

Anna reached to give a reassuring hug before beginning to iron. While Anna's hands were busy with a well-known task, she had time to reflect. The powerful way Clark looked at her made her heart race. *Mr. Clark does interest me a little, but I'm glad he'll rarely visit Deer Lodge.*

Anna did not intend to do as some urged. Her long-time friend, Becky Tomkins, was incredulous when she found out.

Standing in front of the post office, Becky gushed, "What! By thunder, Anna! You're Mr. Clark's new ward? He's the richest man in Butte!" Her mouth gaped. "Oh, *my!* Well now, look at you, fine little miss!" Then her eyes widened salaciously. "He'll want a kiss his first visit to Deer Lodge, mark my words! And you'd better let him, payin' all that money fer ya."

"For shame! That's enough, Becky! How indecent!" Anna hissed, grasping her friend's arm to turn away from passersby. "I'll not tell you anything if that's how you're going to react to my personal business. And I certainly have no intention of ever getting involved improperly with any man. You know me better than that! And you'd better not be spreading your thoughts around as gossip, because if you do, our friendship is *over*!"

Anna departed quickly down the crowded street. Normally high-spirited but sweet, Anna's vehemence left Becky confused. The girls had met by chance, which normally would have led to soon spending more time together; however, that day Anna hurried home without extending an invitation.

Being gossiped about by everyone learning of my good fortune is upsetting. I didn't bargain on Mr. Clark's magnetic name. Now mine is coupled with his!

Anna entered the house and collected herself before saying, "*Maman*, when will the order be delivered? Did the dressmaker say?"

"About three weeks, plenty of time for you to leave by the second week of September. Keep all the items packed away though, *ma petite*. It's too much for your father. Take out only one new dress to wear. I'm sure I don't have to remind you to take good care of everything, as I cannot afford to replace it."

Mrs. La Chappelle nodded pointedly at Anna before looked ruefully at the account book. The boardinghouse barely made a profit, and she struggled getting men to pay in full. Her husband was too gentle to stand up to the rough miners and workmen, and Arthur too young to help.

Amelia burst in, "Oh Anna, I want some new clothes too! *Maman*, can I have a new dress, *s'il te plaît*?"

"You've been listening behind doors again, *ma petite*! No more!" Philomene good naturedly admonished. "When you're mature enough, you can have some fine things. At twelve years old, you're not ready."

"*Mais, Maman, je voudrais une nouvelle robe!*" Amelia twirled around the table in fantasy of wearing it to a ball. Her dark brunette braids secured with pink ribbons fanned out.

"You can have my blue muslin gown when you're old enough to fit into it," Anna promised.

"*Ç'est vrai?*" Amelia stopped with arms akimbo and grinned. "That one is so pretty on you. I won't forget!"

Sunday evening was the only night Anna and Amelia were able to take a walk. Instinctively, their feet took them to the better part of town where they could look at beautiful houses and dream of an easier life. Neither child wanted to offend by discussing grand plans of a future far away; they confided only in each other.

"Oh Amelia, I hope Deer Lodge is a town that has no mining in it whatsoever."

"Can you believe all this is happening to you? *C'est un rêve!*"

"I can't...! It's as if all my prayers are coming true at once. Sally told me in no uncertain terms I was very immodest for being in the parade but look what's happened now! Soon, I'll be going to school as the ward of the richest man in Butte! So there, Sally! That's what modesty does for you! Well, I mean, I would never be as immodest as the, uh, 'ladies,' shall we say, of the district where we live..."

Both girls laughed, which was a relief. Anna had secured Clark's favor, which meant Amelia had a chance to escape. Even at the tender age of twelve, Amelia felt the confining pressure of class differences.

"Very soon there won't be any laundry days for me either!" Amelia stooped to pluck a yellow rose dangling through a white picket fence onto the packed dirt of the street. "But wait, in only a few weeks I'll have to do dishes all by myself!" Her mouth turned down in a pout.

"Let's feel worse for *Maman*, who will be without both of us within two short years," Anna admonished. "She'll have to hire on help then."

In the twilight, they moved along the residential street lined with trees. Anna took a deep breath of the cleaner air. "Never fear, Amelia, I'm going to study very hard and do my best so we will both end up graduating from the Ladies Seminary. *Je te le promets!* And I'll help you out any way I can. *D'accord?*"

"*Oui, oui, oui!* Oh, Anna...," Amelia's hazel eyes opened wide, "with all those pretty dresses you're going to have a lot of *beaux*! You'll be the *prettiest* girl in puffed sleeves and yards of lace, dancing at balls. And wait until they see you've two different colored eyes!" Amelia giggled, twirling the rose in her hand.

Anna tugged at the loose ribbons of Amelia's bonnet, then she winked first one light brown eye then the blue-grey one. She didn't bother explaining to her romantic little sister she didn't want to find any *beaux* in Butte, or all of Montana, for that matter. The day after she graduated, she would leave on the first train out east to look for work.

Marriage won't trap me under a man's thumb before I'm ready!

In Butte, Clark was something of a feared figure. He was everywhere, knew everyone. He made the toughest deals, squeezing profit at every turn. He had hands on literally every aspect of frontier life that generated profits. A respected businessman who toiled brutally long hours and thrived on it, life for Clark had worked out supremely well. He had risen without pause from one peak to another.

Clark sponsored wards now and then when a young man or woman proved to be worth his time. To those enquiring, he would defend the practice: "I enjoy encouraging young adults in life, paving their way, if need be, when they interest me. I think a man a mean-spirited fool who refuses to lift the hard-working and appreciative if one has the means to do so!"

For twenty-four years, Clark had been happily married to Katherine Louise Stauffer. They had seven children, five living. Clark had met the vivacious, well-educated, younger Katherine in Pennsylvania in his early twenties. Upon earning enough money to support a family by 1869, he wrote of his intentions. The newlyweds settled in Deer Lodge in a white clapboard, six-bedroom house.

Less than a decade later, the prosperous family traveled extensively in Europe. Now mingling closer to the environs of the upper class, the young couple attempted to make up for deficiencies in middle class education. They studied German, French, and *les Beaux-Arts*. Back in America, William took university classes, studying minerals, among other useful subjects.

By the 1880's, Kate's entire focus was on securing her children's future. She bore the distasteful title of *nouveau riche* with grace because it was undeniable in the eyes of those included in Mrs. Astor's 400. She needed society women; they did not need her. She could have retaliated with growing economic assets at her disposal. It was obvious particular women in the Social Register had a priceless surname but not much in the bank. At the opening night of the opera, some of the best families wore well-worn Worth gowns with yellowing lace and faded velvet. Around necks and wrists, paltry jewels set in unfashionable settings. However, these lucky women were accepted in the highest reaches of society due to their family's long-standing reputation as Old New York. The Clarks—for all their Parisian *haute couture* and mountain of cash—were never invited.

Fashionable public events, concerts, the best restaurants, and popular plays the Clarks could and did attend. And while there, they could feel as if they were a part of upper-class society. They certainly seemed so to impoverished outsiders looking in. However, the tell-tale sign of true acceptance was perpetually closed. In other words, a coveted invitation by one of the fashionable grand dames *after* the public entertainment.

Edith Bend, Kate's old friend, had explained how it worked when they met for tea at a Manhattan hotel. "The *crème de la crème* arrive to the seemingly quiet façade of a private brownstone. In actuality, Kate, the well-concealed interior boasts a spacious gilded ballroom and sumptuous reception rooms behind the plain front. For example, I've heard that Mrs. Astor's accommodates many hundreds of guests reasonably well. I'm invited next month, so I shall see then."

Kate leaned forward in eagerness. "Are you *really* invited? My, how you've shot up."

"Yes, yes, but it's all because of my husband, George. Without him, you know, I would be in your shoes." Edith patted her hand.

Kate sat back with a weak smile. *Unassailable respectability is something William can never give me.*

Edith selected a small chocolate cookie. "I'm sure Mrs. Astor's will be the height of elegance and beauty. But as for some other brownstones, it's shocking, Kate, how drab and dark they can be! Take a recent social visit as an example of my point. The poor lady in question, who, albeit from a venerable family line, will remain nameless, did not study the domestic arts in the least. I was *decidedly* not impressed with her forty-year-old interiors."

Bend munched thoughtfully. "As for Mrs. Astor's ball, even if I were on my deathbed I would attend. If one isn't seen at these balls and parties at least a few times during the season, *at minimum*, then one is a nobody." Her fleshy hand bladed and cut across the air.

"There's no escaping reality, my dear." Edith looked with pity at Kate before popping another dainty cookie in her mouth.

Kate set down her teacup. "Forgive my candor, but as we've known each other since we were girls, you will understand. Due to my husband's business acumen and wealth, I can overtake them all. But, dear Edith, I will forbear. It's for the children's futures, I remind myself on particularly tough evenings socially sidelined once again." She shook her head mournfully.

Edith nodded in sympathy. "Yes, it was that way for me as well until my Mr. Bend rescued me. Thank heavens you can escape to Europe. I hardly go on account of my husband's recent poor health."

Kate shifted in her seat, suddenly animated. "In Europe it's much easier to blend in and be accepted if one finds the right circle, as all Americans are somewhat at a social disadvantage there. It depends on the mix of company. But here, the sobering social truth of maximum exclusion is very apparent to me and my husband."

In 1888, Clark moved himself into a thirty-four-room Victorian mansion on West Granite Street in Butte which cost $250,000 to build. The ornate house was designed to confer social status, with room after room of polished wood, stained glass, and a sixty-two-foot ballroom on the third floor. However, it was in a town known for mining. Kate never had to explain why she rarely stayed a night in it; Clark understood. He bought her a Long Island mansion instead.

Clark was doing what he could to heighten the family status through business. Kate knew the children were as important to the long-term social equation. *My children's social lives will be above and beyond my own.*

The master plan worked very well after patient years of lock-step behavior. Kate kept the same fashions and customs as her peers. She followed the same routine of New York in the fall to winter season and Europe in the spring to summer season. As the years passed, Kate favored Dresden, London, and Paris, which was still within the bounds of the cultural customs of the day. This preference gave the Clark children even more polish in languages, art, and culture.

Then, as her husband's reputation, money and power strengthened enormously, Kate was accepted by a few women who weren't so rigidly bound by Old New York. Which opened the way by 1889 or so for other women to acquiesce. An invitation to a tea party here, a garden party there, and finally an invitation to an important ball in January.

"Perhaps we'll see each other in Paris?" a high-born, elderly woman wearing a decrepit fox stole said to Kate at the end of the season.

Another beside her in a flowered bonnet casually remarked, "Will you be in Florence this summer, Mrs. Clark? I would enjoy inviting you to luncheon at my villa."

After the group of women rolled away in their landau, Kate and Bend were alone on the sidewalk outside a long row of brownstones in Lower Manhattan. Kate turned to her old friend to marvel: "Five years ago they would have utterly shunned me!"

Clark relinquished familial control to Kate while frequently away, crisscrossing the country from Los Angeles to Salt Lake City to Butte to Chicago to New York and then back again in a private Pullman rail car. It was done up in oak paneled walls, burgundy velvet furniture trimmed with gold tassels, European masterpieces on every wall, and the bathroom in green marble with gold fixtures. He incessantly toiled away with ledgers, letters, and reports for long hours, seven days a week as his train chugged along from one state to the next.

On a rare night Clark wasn't working, he and Kate sat before a fire at Navarro Flats on Central Park South at Fifth Avenue discussing their children's private school education. He changed the subject abruptly.

"I want to build a house in the city. The neighborhood in question is quickly becoming the most fashionable and exclusive."

Kate glanced up from a floral needlepoint. "And where would you like this brownstone to be?"

He smiled at her assumption. "Further up Fifth Avenue."

Kate put her needlepoint down slowly. "Why there?"

Clark ignored her. "The house will replace both the Long Island mansion and Navarro Flats." He gestured around him. "This double-floor apartment seemed grand with 7,000 square feet when we first chose it. However, I'm convinced the mere seven bedrooms are insufficient for my family's burgeoning needs."

"Insufficient? The drawing room is so large we can have a range of instruments at one end. And there's the library and billiards room. We've never lacked for accommodating visiting family..." Kate's gentle eyes looked perplexed.

He waved a hand at her impatiently. "Kate darling, it's my dream to build a private house with an entire floor of art galleries to showcase our treasures we've collected for the past decade. It'll rival aspects of the Metropolitan Museum of Art, I know it! I could end up on the board someday, my love. What a thrill!"

Clark stood to pace in energetic anticipation before the blaze in the green marble fireplace. A blizzard hummed outside the thick stone walls while he went back and forth repeatedly. "I have it all worked out! Socially, it's the most advantageous move we can make!"

"William, darling, may I remind you, in that location our neighbors would by that future date all belong to a level of society which, I hate to admit, we're not a part of... I know you've told me Fifth Avenue is constantly discussed as *the* area. But are you sure this is in our family's best interest?"

"My dear wife, the design of the house—at least what I have in my head—would outdo every structure currently built on Fifth Avenue. It would *surely* aid our entrée into the best of society!"

"May I remind you a private house there will attract too much negative attention. We already have multiple lovely residences, don't we?" Kate paused for effect, looking demurely at her hands before slowly lifting long eyelashes over expressive brown eyes. *It will not do to challenge directly.* "Oh, my darling husband, I worry it would be unseemly to flaunt ourselves in a grand house on Fifth Avenue as if we were the Vanderbilts or the Astors."

Clark remained unaffected. *That is precisely the point! It's surprising she's resisting me. Kate always accepts whatever I want. She's supported every dream and risk I've taken.*

"My future political ambitions demand I run with the most powerful men in America. I'm not to be left behind. Ever." Clark stared pointedly at his wife, who instantly averted her eyes.

"But that will entail a move to Washington..." Kate whispered.

Her heart dropped and tears formed. *If William says he's running, it's only a matter of time before he wins.* This development put a serious wrench in her plans.

"I believe further discussion would distress you. Let's save it for another time. I'll be leaving for Montana after breakfast. I would like to see you then. Goodnight, my darling." Clark bent to kiss Kate's forehead, dismissing her.

As Clark watched Kate leave the library with bowed head, his mind was made up. He would begin making inquiries to his lawyer about buying property as close as possible to the Metropolitan Museum of Art. *I'm not in a hurry. It'll be accomplished slowly and surely, every aspect completed to perfection. On the largest scale possible! I will stun New York!*

Soon after, Clark's eldest, Mary Joaquina Clark, gleefully seized her big chance. The top society wedding in the summer of 1891 was her own. The week after ringing in the 1890 New Year with fabulous parties all over the eastern seaboard, Mary became engaged to Dr. Everett Mallory Culver. He was a respected man from a family well ensconced in the Social Register. It was a social triumph.

Families began debating in drawing rooms up and down the East Coast whether the Clarks were up to the Culver's level. The gossip on both sides of the Atlantic assured an invitation to this society wedding would be something to aspire to. Although people were quick to reference the Culver name over Clark: "Are you attending the Culver wedding on Long Island in June?"

Kate had a wonderful time planning the three days of elaborate wedding festivities. This was one occasion she had permission to set aside discretion, planning as if her eldest daughter were royalty. It was off to Paris for the Clark women to check into their suite at *Hôtel Westminster* on 13, *rue de la Paix*. They walked directly over to *La Maison Worth* at 7, *rue de la Paix* to seek an exclusive design from the aging *couturier*, Charles Frederick Worth. He had superbly dressed empresses and queens. Why not Miss Mary Joaquina Clark?

Two thousand guests delighted in the young bride in a Worth off-white silk satin gown with a sixteen-foot, handmade lace veil, acres of flowers, and a champagne fountain splashing away. The guests gorged themselves on: Beluga caviar, oysters, Maine lobster, salmon with aspic, venison, beef roast, pheasant with truffle sauce, Cornish hen, Kentucky ham, turtle soup, French cheeses, and mandarin sorbet. The gilded white and pink wedding cake festooned with thousands of sugar roses and candied violets was twelve layers high. Two orchestras played Strauss for hundreds of waltzing couples until the last stragglers climbed wearily into carriages at dawn.

Clark assumed all his children would benefit from his savvy wife's careful planning regarding weddings. However, in October 1893, Clark was in his Butte office when he received a telegram that unnerved. He raced to his rail car to head east. "Don't stop for anything! We're to go straight on to New York City!"

Addressing the butler who opened the front door at Navarro Flats, Clark raged as he passed: "My perfectly healthy wife was touring the World's Fair in Chicago where she contracted typhoid fever? I can't believe this!"

He didn't stop to take off top hat and coat, scaling the steps of the grand staircase two and three at a time. He tore open the master bedroom door. His heart clenched at the body on the canopy bed with its bloodless face and still, white hands. Clark rushed over to sob on the cold chest before tearing himself away, unable to accept he was too late. Hands raked through hair as eyes saw nothing.

The elderly doctor stood apart in the large, wood paneled room with black top hat in hand, bag long packed. "By the time I was called to examine your wife, it was too late. I could not halt the fever. She died at quarter past ten this morning. I offer my heartfelt condolences, Mr. Clark."

Dr. Scott held out a hand, but Clark didn't notice. Clark automatically nodded, shaking out a handkerchief to wipe wet eyes. He dared to look back at the bed and the still form.

"Thank you for waiting to inform me... Dr. Scott, could this have been prevented? My wife should have lived many more years. This is a severe blow to me and my children!"

Scott hesitated. He didn't want to further upset the man. "Typhoid fever is contagious, yes. Such a large, public event would of course spread contagion through food or drink, possibly. I'm very sorry, Mr. Clark."

"So, with proper precautions and protections, this could've been prevented?"

"Yes, sir." Scott nodded deferentially and moved to exit the room.

To allay grief, Clark sought something grand to distract. He honored his wife by commissioning a $150,000 neoclassical mausoleum in the most prestigious section of Woodlawn Cemetery in the Bronx. The interior was decorated in the ancient tradition with a gold-inlaid ceiling, a beige marble altar, and beige marble mosaics. Eighteen steps led up to a massive bronze portal set in an exterior of white granite. A young, promising, American sculptor in Paris, Paul Wayland Bartlett, used a portrait of Kate to sculpt face and figure to grace the 10-foot high, 5-foot wide bronze door. Cast by the Henry-Bonnard Bronze Company in New York, Clark readily agreed to display it publicly until it was set permanently in place.

A month after the funeral, Clark gathered his children at the Navarro Hills flat for a Sunday dinner. During the dessert course which he didn't touch, he rashly promised, "I'll never remarry."

Charlie, Will Jr., and Paul were silent before an overbearing father, but Mary and Katherine whispered about the sensitive subject. A typical threat in a fragile world: An energetic father could remarry a younger woman and produce more heirs.

Both of Clark's daughters embodied the spirit of the age. When money and status were linked, there was little kindness involved. The winter after their mother's demise, neither had ever heard the name Anna La Chappelle—who had recently begun the Ladies Seminary in far-away Montana—or comprehended much about their father's activities and private passions. They had a common refrain: "A wonderful father but endlessly working!" Clark's daughters had no time to keep up with his frenetic schedule when their own social lives beckoned with far greater urgency.

Indeed, after their father's repeated promise in genuine tones of melancholy—"I assure you all, children, I'll remain faithful to my beloved Katherine's memory."—they assumed he would continue grieving while living a widower's celibate life.

After dinner, Mary sang, and eighteen-year-old Katherine played a Brahms piano concerto. Clark and his sons clapped politely.

"Children, I'm grateful to have seen you this evening, and I hope we can meet another Sunday very soon. Do well in your studies while I'm away. Boys, I don't want to hear negative reports from any of your schools. I'll excuse myself. I've some work that must be completed tonight."

Once he knew his father was out of earshot, twenty-two-year-old Charlie sneered, "He'll be an abstemious monk for life, I assure you, May! All he cares about is business."

He snapped fingers in a habitual gesture, which caused her eyes to narrow at him.

"Don't be so peevish, my *darling, sweet* May! Cheer up!" Charlie grinned widely and winked, which produced snickerings of laughter from Will Jr. and Paul.

The slight Paul stood erect and pursed his mouth while wagging a stiff forefinger. "Boys, hear me out. High living eventually leads to financial ruin and an early grave! Practice temperance!"

His brothers laughed harder, and Paul relaxed to crack a grin.

"Silence! We've only recently lost our dear mother. I've no intention of being cheerful, you brutes," hissed Mary while rising. Her embroidered Worth satin and velvet gown swished richly as she moved to the center of the drawing room.

"Hey, come now, May. Lighten up! Marriage is turning you into a battle-axe. I loved Mother too. I'm only laughing at Father," said Charlie, flopping lengthwise on a Louis XVI sofa in bespoke white tie while settling black patent-leather boots on piled up embroidered silk pillows.

He grabbed a gold tasseled pillow to toss repeatedly in the air. "I fancy a game of poker tonight. Anyone game? I've got three hundred to burn."

Charlie sat up to wriggle eyebrows enticingly at his brothers.

"At Father's age, he's *far too busy* with politics and business to worry about women!" said Will Jr., only sixteen but soberly shaking his head. "Trust me! Chuck, I'll play you, you lunkhead. I've got three fifty."

"Do you really believe so, Will?" said Katherine from beside him.

She closed a book of Wordsworth with eyes on Mary across the room. Will Jr. ignored her.

"I've got one fifty."

"That all, Pauly?" said Charlie. "What's a thirteen-year-old, pimply guy doing with his money these days?"

"Never you mind!" said Paul, unwilling to lose his entire allowance to his wily, older brother once again.

Speaking imperiously over everyone, as was her wont, Mary said, "Well, I certainly hope my brothers are correct, as I know precious little of Father's private habits. You must keep me apprised of what occurs."

She motioned with a frown to her drunk husband sitting by himself in a corner. "It's time I departed for the evening."

In little more than a decade, the Clark children would comprehend how misled they had all been.

August 1895
The Atlantic Ocean off the North American Continent

Wearing only a chemise and petticoats, Anna stood fidgeting beside a brass bed in the largest first-class suite on a White Star passenger liner. Annoyed, she kept flicking loose, brunette locks past white shoulders.

No doubt it's taking so long because the maids are kept busy with that demanding woman! Anna's attention strayed to the new gown laid out on the gold satin quilt. *The character failing of vanity will have to be mentioned the next time I go to confession.* Anna smirked. *No doubt that too will turn out to be a key difference between me and my new chaperone.*

The older woman had already moaned on two separate occasions: "Piety drives me to distraction!"

An hour earlier, Anna watched while a maid released the gown from layers of cushioning tissue. The lavender gown with heavy jet beading along the neckline, skirt, and cap sleeves was new. Dozens of black lace ruffles cascaded down the voluminous satin. It was the most expensive gown offered by Mrs. Anderson's. Anna had been saving it for the first night on board.

I'm on a steamship bound for La France et la Conservatoire de Musique!

Anna twirled around the room, allowing the pent-up excitement to swell within. On the long train trip from Butte to Chicago to New York City, she remained calm, pushing her own situation out of mind to be deferential to her chaperone, Mrs. Abascal, and two daughters, Anita and Mary. Anna was determined to make this opportunity work, regardless of the sacrifice.

Before leaving her hotel room for breakfast each day, Anna stood for a moment at the closed door. She shut eyes tight rehearsing the mantra: Suppress silly and unladylike desires. Be kind and patient.

On their arrival in Chicago, Anna held back from whooping with joyous excitement at the largest city she ever beheld. Or at the gracious hotel filled with magnificent large bouquets of flowers, gleaming marble in a variety of hues, gilt mirrors, and staff virtually everywhere. She wrote to Amelia:

The wealthy people which now surround me—there are so many!—are so well-dressed it's mystifying anyone has that much money. And tomorrow and the day thereafter and then again at dinner, the gowns and suits and hats will change again!

Anna had only been on board since noon. The boarding process was far more chaotic than expected. Excitement hummed in the humid air. In the heat, it stank of dead fish, dank salt water, and horse manure. The wharf teemed in every direction, making a tremendous racket. People thronged the streets and alongside the enormous ship. Family members saying goodbye; sailors shouting and jumping on and off massive gangways; a hundred different merchants loading massive crates or boxes; deliverymen with wooden boxes or burlap bags of potatoes or onions slung on shoulders hurriedly moving along; journalists calling out while scribbling in small notebooks.

Held up in traffic, the rented carriage crawled forward only slightly once every few minutes. Despite hordes of servants, stern signage, and thick cords roping off the first-class arrival point, hoi polloi swarmed. Inquisitive boys in ragged clothing scurried every which way. People became argumentative in the heat, noise, and confusion. Policemen honked on whistles or brandished billy clubs at those interfering with the ship's processes.

Clark's intrepid sister, Mrs. Elizabeth "Lizzie" Clark Abascal observed the crowds with energetic interest. She grinned with auburn eyebrows raised high. "All this traffic means the ship is a good one. Popular is always good, my dears, take note! The ship is obviously full to bursting. Which means we'll have a splendid voyage across with loads of people to meet! Nothing is worse than sailing on an unpopular ship only half full."

Bernie, a Maltese sitting on Mary's lap, panted furiously.

"Mommy, our tickets say departure is at ten o'clock in the morning on August the second, and now it's quarter to ten. We'll not make it," wailed Anita. She closely examined the first-class ticket on ecru linen paper with her name elegantly written, intending to keep it pristine to glue into a travel journal.

"So, we can't go now?" said Mary with a furrowed brow.

"What a notion you two have. The ship won't leave without first-class passengers who are merely caught up in traffic, no matter *how late* we board. The captain can observe from his great height above and witness the people attempting to board. He's no fool. He'll wait for us, my loves. *We* are first-class passengers. No worrying your pretty little heads." Abascal reached to tenderly stroke fourteen-year-old Anita's cheek.

The younger daughter, Mary, sat beside Anna, happily smiling while petting Bernie. She was easy to please and get along with. They quietly resumed watching the crowds while wafting lace fans over flushed cheeks.

Two hours later they boarded. Anna's back was drenched in sweat and her legs needed stretching. After a short period of exploration—standing with Anita and Mary to wave to those left behind on the docks—with the deep horn blasts resounding in their ears, the great ship pulled away. They stayed to watch North America recede into the horizon.

Anna smiled with wonder. *I'm surrounded by water!* Then, glancing at her new young friends leaning on the metal railing: *I can't believe I'm standing here with Mr. Clark's nieces on my way to France!*

For twenty years Mrs. Joaquín Abascal had been married to a California business-man. Her husband was an associate of the successful Clark brothers, which led Lizzie to meet Joaquín at a Clark family ball in Los Angeles. The Abascal family resided in a new mansion in the toniest neighborhood in Los Angeles. However, Abascal's wealth did not compare *in the least* to her much older brother. This she knew all too well; it privately grated.

When Abascal's older brother offered the opportunity to chaperone his ward to Paris for six months (*What a do-gooder! What on earth does he have in mind with this young woman?*), she jumped at the chance. She would force William to pay for every penny of first-class travel and living expenses. To her surprise, William acquiesced without any of the normal quibbling or bargaining he was notorious for.

Clark knew his youngest sister was a stickler for society norms, which was why he gave such generous financial terms. "I want Miss La Chappelle well taken care of. Guided by the right hands, one could say," as Clark explained to the secretary who dictated the letter:

Dear sister, always keep uppermost in mind Miss La Chappelle is only seventeen and not born in the best circles. She is, in fact, learning important etiquette alongside my own dear nieces. Please pay the closest of attention. Likewise, you will always ensure the reputation and physical safety of Miss La Chappelle while she attends lessons and learns to go about in Parisian society. Learning the language will not be a problem, as Miss La Chappelle is already fluent. In fact, she may tutor your daughters in the language, much like a governess.

I would be most grateful for accommodating my ward in these matters while you reside gratis under my Parisian roof. I am aware of the increased social standing you will enjoy as chatelaine of such a fashionable address, dear sister.

Your elder brother, W.A.

I can almost hear the sarcasm in the last line! Abascal lounged in an overstuffed, velvet chair in the pink chintz morning room. Balmy air blew back lace curtains on the fourth story of a Victorian mansion. She clicked her tongue with both amusement and annoyance at his cleverness. *He knows me too well. And William always gets what he wants by paying attention to the details.*

The letter dropped to her lap as head leaned back against rose velvet. *What's in it for me...? The deal is fair. Easy to perform, as I'll already be doing all that for Anita and Mary... Miss Anna La Chappelle, only seventeen, and Montana! A backwater... Oh, my goodness, she must have a great deal to learn. How very taxing...*

Abascal's slender fingers squeezed her nose bridge in a familiar gesture of exasperation. *It'll work out easily if the girl isn't a complete dolt. I can't imagine she is, as William wouldn't associate with that sort.*

Educating her daughters within high-class society was a great expense which could not be avoided. Once debutantes, it would practically be a blood sport to acquire the best marriage offers. There was nothing else that would suffice for Abascal's ambition.

I don't want them stuck here as I've been all these years. My husband's business affairs demand I remain, but not so my children. Oh no, a husband from the east or a European husband... A baron, perhaps? My precious babies will live in England or France, not California! How William's ward is going to help or hinder my plans remains to be seen.

She rose with purpose to ring her maid.

While Anna waited, she pointed toes and stretched legs in wide arcs. Her thoughts wandered back to worries which repeated endlessly. *Who knows what Mrs. Abascal really thinks of me?*

The middle-aged woman's shrewd eyes sometimes betrayed studying Anna with a questioning glance. And then the dreaded question: *What if Mr. Clark asked her to assess me?* She chided herself: *I'm a mere ward, nothing more. I merely happen to be the particular favorite, obviously, as I'm headed to Paris with Mr. Clark's own sister.*

An unbelievable coup announced at graduation by Clark himself. It had shocked some of her enemies into submission. Not one of them was doing anything as spectacular.

Absolutely nothing in my behavior can ever betray the dislike of being watched in what I consider to be an intrusive manner. It grated on Anna to feel her chaperone's gaze. She knew she was an outsider, but that status was reinforced daily. If Abascal reported Anna was unfit for Clark's eyebrow-raising generosity in *any* way, then the dream of Paris would be snuffed out!

How to rise to this extreme height again, even as a mere ward of Mr. Clark's? Never! Anna knew it instinctively. *This is a once in a lifetime opportunity. The risk of losing Mr. Clark's patronage could not happen for at least a year more, not with my siblings benefitting as well.*

Arthur she wasn't as concerned with. He already had plans to complete high school early. Amelia, however, had years of schooling to complete. *Therefore, I must be the perfect ward. Mr. Clark never forgets any detail I tell him. He'll be paying close attention to progress reports in my letters.*

Night after night as they traveled east, Anna lay in bed energized with whirling thoughts. Eyes wide open in the dark with hands splayed with the effort of reminding: *I'm not a member of the family. I must remember that every day! Remember, remember! Smile, be gracious, and befriend Anita and Mary. It shouldn't be too difficult, but I mustn't jeopardize this opportunity with my big mouth full of jokes at the wrong moment... Perhaps I could find employment in Paris? Perhaps I'll meet a man I'll marry?*

Anna had no confidant save Amelia. She would never lay her fears on her poor father and mother. In letters home, everything was gaiety, thrills, and working hard. They had been through too much to deserve any complaining. Amelia received the truth:

With you dear sister, I know we share the same goals and values. You will support me through anything, won't you? From what I've experienced, we're helping each other through the labyrinth of American society.

Your loving sister, Anna

She became wary of others. She had learned through hard experience many socially polished women were privately small-minded, prideful, and jealous. Girls who were introduced smiling and speaking softly while adults were present at the opening social quickly turned cruel in the dormitory.

"Don't you speak to me, you Butte gutter-trash. If it weren't for Mr. Clark's seat on the board, you would *never* be here. I want nothing to do with you!" sneered Delia Vandemeer two years ago. Brown eyes contrasted beautifully with blonde hair, and her imposing height intimidated younger students. Delia's father was a prominent banker. She ruled the most prestigious social set due to beauty, intelligence, and connections. If Delia rejected Anna, most other girls would follow suit.

Anna shrunk away from such unwelcome pronouncements. Shunned, she became vulnerable. That first year, her spirits plunged, and a more serious side emerged. It wasn't until her second year that things improved. It helped enormously that Delia's cohort graduated. By the fall of 1894, Anna's burgeoning musical talent, goofy humor, and kind nature aided her assent. She refused to let bad memories cloud her thoughts, but she did not make the mistake to chase popular girls. She largely kept to herself, not retaliating after unkind remarks. Instead, she threw herself into academic studies, voice lessons, and piano practice.

In the long run, being an outsider helped Anna in nonobvious ways. She studied with great interest privileged students' deportment, speech patterns, dress, and table manners. It became an unconscious habit to study high class women to make up for the first fifteen years of an impoverished life. Anna desired to eradicate all offensive behavior, habits, and speech. She was nervous of unconsciously committing an error, which was easy to do with a slap-dash upbringing.

Initially, there had been much suppressed laughter directed at her. However, Anna had no one to turn to for advice. She soldiered on, promising herself while weeping, *I'll learn to mask my upbringing so no one will ever, ever suspect I wasn't born into a well-to-do family!*

At balls, Anna noticed which young men the popular girls would dance with, and which they avoided. She was frequently asked to dance, but never pursued by any serious *beaux*. She perceived how the most intelligent and successful older girls made choices which influenced their future prospects. Many would not consider accepting a *beau* from Montana.

"Mr. Jake Preston is the handsomest young man in Butte, I dare say, and he asked me *twice* to dance. However, when I graduate and am of age, I am heading straight for Philadelphia or Boston to whichever granny will take me in!" tossed off Violet Meyer Watson with a smug laugh while brushing light brown hair two hundred strokes. "Both families are very well set up out east. I would never consider Jake Preston's or Andrew Knutson's offers to ride in their buggies!"

Laughter from the girls perched on Violet's bed. Anna hesitated for a moment in the dormitory hallway, pretending to be digging in a basket of toiletries. She noted how the other girls reacted. *They're all so sure of themselves, of their futures.*

"No matter how handsome Jake Preston is, or however well Andrew Knutson waltzes, none of us will ever allow ourselves to be found alone with either. Right, girls?" urged Violet while nodding with big eyes.

"Then a proposal's bound to come, for sure!" said Laura, Violet's best friend.

Before Anna's second year began, she was invited to a friend's house for several weeks in August. *They reside in Mr. Clark's neighborhood*, Anna realized with awe after descending from the carriage and looking up at the ten-bedroom Victorian mansion.

Aurelia Allsbury had been kind to Anna if somewhat reluctant to make a blatant show of it. She held out eager hands that morning. "Welcome, Anna! I'm delighted to have you for a visit. We've only just arrived from New York. I can't tell you how happy I was that you accepted my invitation. I'm bored of my mother's friends already!"

"Thank you for the kind invitation. Your house is beautiful!"

"Oh yes, it's Father's favorite. Mother prefers our house in South Carolina," Aurelia said in an off-hand manner, completely unaffected by wealth. She shrugged. "Come inside and have some lemonade with me. Then we can play a duet together. I've missed playing with you all these months."

Mrs. Abigail Allsbury led an active social life, and there seemed to be one or two daily events to attend. She included the girls at every opportunity. Meanwhile, surrounded by Butte's upper class, Anna experienced a crash course in etiquette, speech, wardrobe, and conversation. Her quick eyes were opened to the fashions from Europe. It was now obvious to Anna what to select for the fall order at the dressmaker's. *So that's the difference in quality, print, and cut. The loud prints, deep colors, and embroidery the seamstress recommended for my gowns last year were not fashionable. No wonder I was an object of derision!*

One quiet afternoon during the third week of her visit, Anna said, "Mrs. Allsbury, if you don't mind me asking, I notice you deal with your servants in a particular manner which interests me. As you know, I do not come from a household that employs servants. Would you mind explaining your philosophy?"

"Certainly, Ms. La Chappelle. Servants are an absolute necessity. However, they can idly spread malicious gossip, or even worse, betray their employers to make quick money. I keep my family's affairs as private as possible. I avoid gossip; I do not confide in my servants.

"In this competitive mining town, newspapers are always looking for a new story to spread slander. And they will pay handsomely for it. My husband must continually protect his business interests and family from those who would do him ill, whether at home or at his place of business."

"Oh, I see. You're wise to be aware. I've seen many such headlines in the newspapers but was ignorant how it affected private households."

Aurelia took a sip of tea, unsure why Anna would be interested in such a topic. Aurelia rose from the green damask seat and held out a slim hand, "Would you like to play a duet with me, Anna? We've not played enough today."

"I'm not very good on the piano yet. But of course."

The girls sat on the embroidered bench at the Steinway concert grand. It was placed along the bank of large windows in the spacious, cool room. They played quite some time for a doting Mrs. Allsbury. Anna let the talented Aurelia take the lead.

While playing, Anna was acutely aware of a strong sense of well-being in the calm room. A light green, yellow and ivory botanical fabric print decorated the walls and furniture, with towering ferns in several corners. Family oil portraits in gilded frames hung from long wires. A massive chandelier in the center threw off crystal rainbows if any reflected sunlight hit it. An ivory Spanish shawl with red roses and delicate fringe was draped over the Steinway; family photographs in silver frames scattered on top. A green and red stained-glass Tiffany lamp was set in between easy chairs near the carved white marble fireplace.

The wide bank of windows with white lace curtains behind Anna overlooked the back yard. The heady scent of the large rose garden floated in on the warm breeze. *How clever. The roses cover the acrid smell of smoke.*

The girls' duet created a perfect accompaniment to the tune of contentment which prevailed in the house. *How beautiful and comfortable life can be when sheltered from the harsh reality of scrabbling for a dollar. The Allsbury's house is like another world, yet my parents are merely a buggy ride away.*

The few times Anna returned home, she understood instinctively she no longer belonged there. In the past year of new experiences, Anna had grown into a different creature. She did not socialize with former friends. She helped her mother with the boarding house upkeep or read, returning to the sanctuary of school as soon as possible.

During each visit, *Maman* reminded, "Anna, enjoy every privilege offered to you by Mr. Clark's generosity. Don't worry about us one bit! Amelia and Arthur are following in your footsteps and your father and I are very proud."

"Are you sure, *Maman*? I feel I'm neglecting you."

"Nonsense!" said Philomene, hugging Anna close. "You run off and secure your future. Remember Mass on Sundays. Don't worry, *ma petite*. Your brother will take care of us."

The lady's maid still had not arrived. Anna twirled again and reached for the ceiling to gently stretch slim arms and back, feeling the great ship hum. *My eighteenth birthday is next year. If all goes well, an extended estimate is two years of study in Paris as Mr. Clark's ward. It's inevitable Mr. Clark will move on. I must be ready to accept harsh reality. Once I'm nineteen, perhaps? I can't return to Butte. However, merely being a teacher—full of rules, loss of independence, and vigilant eyes—doesn't please either.*

Anna whispered, "I'm resolved to not focus on the unknown. It'll spoil my present pleasure."

There was a light tap on the door before it began to open. Anna whirled around. The Irish maid, Meredith Murphy, stuck her head in and said, "Are you ready, miss?"

Anna nodded eagerly to be dressed before sitting at the vanity. Hair combs with seed pearls would be the finishing touch. Her only other jewelry was a set of black jet. Within minutes, the maid transformed her into an elegant young woman.

"Would you like me to put on the powder and rose balm, Miss La Chappelle?" Murphy gestured toward unopened boxes of cosmetics.

Anna hesitated, biting her lower lip. "Do you think it would be appropriate?"

"Absolutely, Miss La Chappelle. Many fine ladies use them."

As Murphy began to pat on rice powder, Anna remembered it was this past April, once the plan to study in Paris had been settled, that Clark's generosity increased. When the hat boxes and steamer trunks monogrammed with Anna's initials were delivered, she gasped. Inside were dozens of garments of every type, plus hats, shoes, and accessories. Most surprising, a small parcel of perfumes, rice powder, and rose scented pink lip balm was discovered. Anna only knew what they were because of fashionable friends.

"The balm imparts a lovely pink if you put it plumb on your cheeks, like so," demonstrated Lavinia Drake, whose father was a lawyer employed by Clark. "And rice powder takes away the nose and forehead's shine!" Lavinia touched her round nose. "But don't overdo it. Only a whisper. My mother says not to admit I've used it to *anyone*. It's a lady's beauty secret," she said, nodding matter-of-factly.

"But I've never seen you wear powder. How vile," said Sarah Hancock. With a well-worn teddy bear cradled in fleshy arms, she flounced on the bed beside Anna.

Lavinia retorted, "Oh, you can say that now, Sarah. I have *dozens* of cousins in New York and Boston who go to Europe. They're fashionable and aren't afraid to powder their nose or wear rouge or do ever more daring things like smoke French cigarettes. But don't tell my father if you want me to live past my eighteenth birthday!"

"I'm finished, ma'am. You look beautiful." Murphy brushed a little more powder on Anna's décolletage.

"Oh, thank you, Ms. Murphy. I'm nervous!"

"Don't be. You'll do wonderful out there in that grand dining room with all them old folks." Ms. Murphy smiled encouragingly before carefully reinserting a pearl comb.

Anna was about to ask for another curl on her temple, but the petite, auburn-haired Abascal blew into the room. Anna jumped up.

Abascal stopped short in her quick, energetic way, shrewd green eyes rapidly scanning. "Darling girl, that dress is *at least* a year out of fashion! From smoky Butte, of course? Well, we'll have to take you to a *couturier* immediately upon arrival. I'll send the bill to poor William. He started this! I have no pity... And no jewelry besides, I suppose?"

She clucked her tongue, placing hands on plum satin clad hips. "That won't do. I can't stand jet! It reminds me of cheap stage women. I don't want you standing out in a negative way. Come along!"

Anna stood in Abascal's stateroom while her chaperone examined velvet-lined cases laid on the bed. The older woman's hand reached for a necklace. "Why on earth this was packed, I couldn't say. It's only opals, so it won't attract attention. You can keep it for the duration of the voyage. I have a pearl set you can wear as well."

As the maid put the opal and gold necklace, bracelet, and earrings on Anna, Abascal said, "You have a lot to learn, and dressing appropriately for dinner is a perfect place to begin. Pay close attention, following what we've practiced." Abascal pointed a forefinger. "Ask for my help when you are unsure. I'm treating you as if you were my daughter. Be attentive tonight but *silent*! Do not embarrass me under any circumstances. If you do, you'll be dining in your stateroom *alone* for the duration of the voyage."

"Yes, Mrs. Abascal. I realize I have much to learn."

Anna averted her eyes and pressed lips together to hide a smile. *Is a curtsy required after these lectures?*

After an astonishing number of courses, which Anna studied repeatedly on the printed menu to have something to do, no one regarded her. The dinner felt interminable; she picked at the food after the sixth course. By eleven o'clock, she was utterly exhausted. The table still buzzed with conversation and laughter.

"I want nothing more than to retreat to my room and relax uncorseted in a nightgown in bed with a book," she whispered in an unguarded moment.

Immediately, the young man beside her turned his body only slightly to her without making direct eye contact. While abstractly twirling his goblet, he said, "What? Did you say something amusing?"

"No, nothing!" Anna's eyes flared. The young man did not lift his eyes to meet hers. She turned away from his half-hearted attempt, blushing.

An hour later, Abascal stopped dead inside their suite, gloved hands to temples. "Oh, my head. French champagne... Oh, my! Ah, wait... William wanted me to give you something... If I don't do it now, I'll forget... And then he'll lecture me."

Anna soon clutched the bills in her hand and thanked Abascal before going to her stateroom. When the maid left, she retrieved the money from a vanity drawer and took out an embroidered purse. She hadn't had any time to count what was casually stuffed into her hand.

Twenty dollars more. *So much! Did the Clarks comprehend themselves in comparison to the average person on the street?*

Moving to the bed, from the purse she took out her savings. She organized the bills on the satin bedspread. After two years, it amounted to $135. A small fortune!

Anna knew the only way she was able to save anything came down to Clark's patronage. Even at fifteen, she knew she needed a nest egg for the day Clark withdrew patrimony. An uncertain future forced maturity beyond her years, and she had denied herself many times.

Once he forgets me, I'll have to live off this money. Anna rolled the bills to be secured away once more.

Lying in the brass bed in the dark, the double-berth stateroom barely betrayed it rode magisterially on a frigid, gently rolling Atlantic. Drifting off to sleep, she focused on good things to come.

Dear God, please don't wake me from this fairy-tale life...

The women arrived in Paris during the height of *La Belle Époque*. Years of economic prosperity, industrial progress, regional peace, and colonial expansion had strengthened France. Despite crushing poverty for many in the urban slums, the *haute bourgeoisie* and royalty enjoyed unparalleled luxury. The sciences and the arts flourished, pushing boundaries. Many eyes looked to Paris as the world's greatest, most beautiful city.

London had undeniable power, but Paris had glamorous charisma. To resounding acclaim, it hosted the World's Fair in 1889 with the newly completed Eiffel Tower (costing five Francs to climb). Millions of tourists flooded the city and helped pull France out of an economic recession.

For decades, the nighttime burlesque entertainment was the most risqué in the world. The cabarets *Folies Bergère* had successfully rebranded itself in 1872, and *Le Moulin Rouge* opened for business in 1889 as the place for the rich to go slumming. The exclusive bistro Maxim's opened in 1893. All over the city, once squirreled-away mistresses were delighted to be escorted there by bold male companions. The seductive *demimondaines* notoriously ruled lofty social circles and titled men. The wisest ones learned to grow immensely rich off patrons. Painters begged to immortalize the beauties, knowing a successful portrait would secure their career.

In 1895, Paris was a mere handful of years from undergoing the social and cultural transformations the proliferation of motorcars, the creation of the subway system, and artistic revolutionaries such as Isadora Duncan, Rodin, Toulouse Lautrec, Proust, Picasso, and Gauguin would have on French society, culture, and art. Many people were optimistic of the future; apart from those who mourned the decadence prevalent during *le fin de siècle*.

It was the golden period of innocence and beauty before the unimaginable horrors wrought by the Great War. Such mechanically impersonal and brutal death tactics—trench warfare, gas masks, automatic weapons, tanks, flame-throwers, and fighter planes dropping bombs—were entirely incomprehensible in an age which rashly celebrated its own omnipotent civilization and innate honor.

Blissfully unaware of the powerful empires which monitored each other covetously, and of much of the notoriety and social dealings of Paris, Anna stepped into Clark's large, recently renovated flat with wide eyes. It was so breathtaking she forgot to not openly marvel. *Numéro 6 avenue Mac-Mahon* of the seventeenth *arrondissement* was a revelation. Anna had never been in a more luxurious private household. She had no presentiment she would live this way the rest of her life.

Clark lavished his residences with the best of everything. Maintaining multiple households on two continents cost peanuts in comparison to his overall fortune. When Anna agreed to live in the Paris flat, she never dreamed of such beauty and refinement. She had heard he was the richest man in Butte, but now it seemed he was the richest man *in the entire world*.

"Marie Antoinette or Queen Victoria would be at home here...," Anna marveled in the gold drawing room to Mary.

"Do you think so?"

Mary looked innocently on the assembled treasures and fine fabrics. She saw nothing out of the ordinary in Uncle's flat.

Anna had visited Clark's Butte mansion with hundreds of other holiday guests, but the grand house with carved woodwork, stained-glass windows, and burgundy velvet furniture did not overwhelm. This Parisian household did! Each room was perfection, a feast for the eyes with the best of French, English, and Italian design and art in profusion.

Led to her bedroom by the housekeeper, Anna was gobsmacked. The suite had twelve-foot ceilings and multiple, long windows opening onto charming wrought-iron balconies. Voluminous yards of blue and white striped or blue silk damask were used on bed, pillows, and furniture. Curtains of the same silk fabric flowed down from the gilded half-tester and windows. The suite's walls were covered in rose or blue damask and punctuated with paintings of dogs, horses, and flowers. Chandeliers and crystal sconces provided light and decoration.

Anna's delighted eyes immediately fell on the tall, gilded harp wrapped with a red bow. Clark planned to have two harps waiting, delivered weeks earlier from *Érard et Cie*, on *13, rue du Mail*, Paris's premier harp shop.

"There is a second harp in the music room," said the housekeeper.

Anna whirled around; she had forgotten about the woman. Francine Marie Bouchard had greying hair pulled severely into a chignon. The simple gold jewelry and cameo brooch she wore daily did not betray how much money she had amassed in a long career with room and board included on top of a generous salary. She was tightly corseted, which showed off a slender waist. Invariably, she dressed in a long, black wool gown relieved by small bits of white lace at the neck and wrists.

"Oh! I can keep this one in here?" Anna blurted out with wide eyes.

Bouchard nodded. She noted with interest that Clark's ward was not yet spoiled.

Anna circled the harp, put a graceful finger out to lightly touch a chord, and then sat down on the blue velvet stool. She examined the student compositions on the bronze and wood music stand. *Mr. Clark thinks of everything*.

Anita and Mary came through the door in time to hear, "How lovely of Mr. Clark! He is too good!"

The amiable girls smiled and clapped, and Anna beamed before bursting out in joyous laughter as she removed the bow. While Bouchard retreated, Abascal stepped into the room to discover the source of the commotion.

"Now I can learn a new piece to play for you all soon. And I can practice every day! I'm determined to become an accomplished harpist." Anna picked up a piece of music to gauge the difficulty.

"That's a worthy goal, dear," Abascal said, biting her tongue to complain aloud no such marked attention had been paid to William's nieces. Her eyes narrowed, scanning her daughters. "Now, how about my girls deciding on an instrument to dedicate themselves to, hmm? It would be proper for you three to play for guests. Remember, we're going to have lots of company!"

Anita and Mary watched their mother depart, and then smiled sheepishly.

"Anna, is the harp as hard to play as the piano?" said Mary, eyeing the enormous harp with its many strings.

"Not really. Although I'm only proficient on the piano. Which is why I'm here to study at the conservatory. You both will have to come to my recital. Perhaps by November?"

"Will we still be here then?" said Mary, dismay crossing her face.

"Mary, stop worrying. Mother will never last, you know her!" said Anita, running fingers across taut strings.

The first day, the small party of American women looked over every room as they moved about shadowed by Bouchard. The housekeeper felt protective of both the property and of her late mistress's memory. *Thank heavens this brash American mistress is merely temporary!*

Abascal smiled serenely as she entered the master suite trailed by the girls. *How well my new Worth couture will shine in these interiors. My almost half-year reign as one of the season's social queens of Paris begins now.* The venerable address on calling cards would be sweet revenge on those who snubbed her as a West Coast parvenu.

Abascal rang the bell pull beside the black marble fireplace. Bouchard immediately appeared; Anna suspected the housekeeper of eavesdropping.

"Madame Bouchard, I would like tea served immediately in the gold drawing room." Abascal motioned to her daughters. "Now come along, girls!"

In Anna's opinion, late September was all too soon for conservatory classes to begin. To prepare, she practiced daily, waking up hours earlier to avoid her chaperone. A celebrated harp professor, Alphonse Hasselmans, began coming several days a week for private lessons.

"I will ensure you are prepared for the musical courses you will soon undertake."

"*Merci*, Monsieur Hasselmans. That appeases my fears somewhat."

"And you should fear, Mademoiselle La Chappelle. We have a demanding curriculum!"

• • •

Like a lightning rod, Abascal could sense all Paris was aglow with entertainments and dizzying frivolity. She wanted a slice of the fun. As soon as they arrived, she ran to *La Maison Worth* to view the live models in the showroom. Reams of new *couture* clothing and accessories began arriving. As her mania for shopping increased, a guest bedroom was converted into a second dressing room. Bouchard privately dubbed the new mistress "Madame Bovary."

For Anna, life became a blur of social calls, shopping, and sitting demurely and perfectly outfitted in a landau pulled by the finest horses. The object was to see and be seen by the never-ending society parade in the spacious Bois de Bologne and along the packed Champs-Elysées. Amongst juggling demanding classes at the conservatory and private lessons, Anna's time was devoted to keeping up with her chaperone's frenetic social schedule. It was tiresome.

By late September, the first of what would turn out to be frequent dinner parties, luncheons, and regular Thursday salon times from four to seven o'clock were given at *6, avenue Mac-Mahon*. It was obvious by the formality demanded during a party *chez Clark* the quality of guest had risen sharply. The girls minded themselves in the extreme when the lower orders of European aristocracy were mixed in. It became harder to secure an invitation. If you had a title, you were guaranteed admittance, no matter how tight the squeeze in the drawing room.

Mrs. Joaquín Clark Abascal's guests fawned over the overt display of wealth; they were shocked into temporary submission by this American queen. The décor and art were divine, the conversation and music sublime, and the champagne and food the finest. One never suffered a dull moment with the vivacious hostess.

One evening, the celebrated dancer and *demimondaine La Belle Otero* appeared with an elegant hand on the arm of a young Austro-Hungarian prince. He had recently given *La Belle Otero* a necklace with emeralds the size of eggs—which she wore that evening, *bien sûr*— which caused consternation amongst conservative guests. The glamorous pair commanded the attention of the room, but only stayed for twenty minutes. In the meantime, the hostess had to ostensibly snub the famous woman's presence as best she could—despite a delighted smile of triumph—as the more prudish ladies' quivering fans and widened eyes betrayed only one opinion of the prince's effrontery.

Outwardly, Abascal went along with the prevailing social opinion. She was aware of what was and wasn't *bon goût*, but privately she was over the moon. She held head high while gliding to her seat, sycophants grouped nearby. To have a prince appear with a notorious *demimondaine* secured her brief reputation as a hostess of some of the most fascinating *soirées* for *Le Tout-Paris*.

Tomorrow, this will be talked about at the horseraces and Maxim's, thought Abascal.

Anna watched the proceedings with a cast of mind which took in all that was offered socially and rejected it. The superficiality did not satisfy. She observed the women largely fell into two camps: Those who genuinely liked Abascal and the larger group that seemed to merely be using the American hostess for their own interests. Anna inherently avoided such false society.

At these various entertainments, Abascal and Bouchard were indeed reporting on Anna's behavior. Clark had ordered:

Write to me about my ward's reaction to Parisian temptations, if you will. She is very young and naïve. I would like to try her character while she is there. To ascertain if she is worth my while. On another note, as it has been reported you are abusing some aspects of my goodwill, I ask, dear sister, after your departure, will any vintages of note be left in my wine cellar?

Your loving elder brother, W.A.

Day to day, Anna was dependable and mature; soon she became a social secretary to Abascal. From the successful run as one of the premier American hostesses of the season, Abascal now had so many irons in the fire she needed help. It was a never-ending round of organizing appointments, writing letters, dealing with bills and accounts, accepting or declining invitations—"I won't step one foot in that undeserving woman's home!" Abascal proclaimed at one card, tossing it at Anna who knelt to scoop it up—planning entertainments, reviewing menus, and tackling the obligatory round of social calls.

"This is exhausting!" Abascal said, slumping on a chaise. "Are we done?"

"We need to finish these letters, and we have an appointment at Worth at four o'clock," said Anna.

"Must we? I'd rather have tea..."

While Abascal barely paid attention to any of the girls—caught up in her own heady Parisian world of horse races, balls, gambling, and parties as she was—Anna had much opportunity to observe the various women who called. It was quite the eye-opening education in cosmopolitan society.

Anna perceived many of the intimidating girls at the seminary were, in fact, not as well-bred as the internationally educated women she now encountered. Paris was a magnet for the wealthiest and most aristocratic of people in the world. Once introduced as Clark's ward—"or in other words, as a nobody," she later explained to Anita and Mary—Anna was dismissed. Relegated to the background, she played the harp or sat demurely on the fringes.

Due to this sidelined position, she was able to minutely observe the women. In the late evenings, she returned to her bedroom to jot down notes in a journal. Back in the U.S., she wanted to remember everything she was experiencing. A clever remark or how a woman deflected gossip or how she reacted when someone undesirable approached. She heard the speech patterns and vocabulary of upper-class Parisian French, how aristocrats behaved, and how an elegant woman ate ortolan or caviar. And Anna recorded it all.

Soon, cold winds blew harshly through the streets and parks on Anna's daily walks. Even in the decay of fall, she thought Paris beautiful. The girls went out together often, enjoying the late fall weather and fading light. Afterwards, they might go ice skating at the *Palais de Glace* near the Champs Elysées, and then to a nearby café for hot chocolate. They were never alone, as at a bare minimum, the girls' governess and nanny hovered.

Anita said, "It's as if Mother's never attended a party in her life! Which is silly. In Los Angeles, Mommy and Daddy are always attending events with gobs of people." She quickly pulled delicate lips back from scorching hot chocolate and set the porcelain cup on its saucer.

"Mother wants me to keep the count in mind for an option in future! Uck! Marrying an old man of forty-five, with *big bushy whiskers*—which only old men have!—and gout. I heard Mommy discussing remedies when he was last over for luncheon. Revolting! He simply needs to eat less rich food and stop getting drunk. Uncle Clark discussed it last Easter, remember Mary? He said many of his associates eat and drink too much. It causes an early grave. I remember Uncle's words precisely."

"No, I don't remember... What's gout?" Mary said. She flicked a long black curl behind a shoulder and looked out the window. High in the grey sky, thousands of birds migrated south.

"*En français...*" Anna chided. "She means well, Anita. Madame Abascal wants the best for you both. Never mind the old count; it won't happen. Now what *I* want is for you two to practice your French with me far more often! What will your uncle say when he next visits and queries you? I'll be blamed for your lack!"

"Oh, Uncle isn't fluent either!" Mary said in English. "He speaks French better than I do, but his accent is atrocious. *Très américain!*" All three girls giggled.

Outside the café, the wind picked up and desiccated leaves swirled around black leather boots. The girls wore wool capes and cashmere berets to ward off the chill. They walked slowly down the street, stopping outside a park to watch squirrels gathering acorns and listening to geese honking far above. The nanny bade them hurry into the waiting carriage, knowing they had to eat a meal and then wash and dress for the opera that evening.

The girls looked forward to the opera. It meant they wouldn't have to endure another party. The running joke *"chez Clark"* became a warning of hard times ahead. Whether it was dealing with a rattled, over-excited Abascal or parading in their best dresses in front of leering guests commenting on rose-petal skin, thick hair, and bright eyes, it was all torture.

"As if we were prize piglets at the fair!" muttered Anita with a scowl.

Attending classes at the *Conservatoire de Musique* in eighteenth century buildings at the junction of *rue Bergère* and *rue de Faubourg Poissonnière* was the highlight of Anna's day. Unlike other outspoken students desiring change, she didn't chafe against the conservative leadership of Ambroise Thomas. She attended while celebrated musicians—Charles de Bériot, Maurice Revel, César Frank, and Claude Debussy, among many others—were also teaching or studying at the school.

Weekday mornings, she bundled herself in a fur-lined wool cape and raced down stone steps to the waiting carriage. She all but pressed her nose against the glass to see the streets and bridges over the Seine go by as she traveled to and from school or to other engagements. The intense musical practice and demanding atmosphere thrilled her more and more. Even Hasselmans shaking his head when she failed to impress did not trouble Anna for long.

"Silly girl, the wrong notes in measures forty-one through forty-five *again*! I thought you practiced enough. Apparently not!" he said with a stern look.

"Oh, I assure you, I did, Monsieur Hasselmans! My fingers are a little stiff today from the cold weather. I do apologize."

The drafty, unheated classrooms were almost intolerable; Anna wore black wool gloves with the tips removed. Only when Hasselmans came to *avenue Mac-Mahon* for private lessons did they have a large fire lit, ordered by Bouchard well before the lesson. Then Anna played with few mistakes. Bouchard was vigilant Clark's ward had nothing to complain about.

Many evenings, as a storm rattled the wood shutters, Anna wrote grateful letters:

Mr. Clark, I do believe I am in love with music! I adore it! I can never seem to get enough. The best part of my day is leaving to attend classes at the Conservatory. The hours in classes pass too quickly. I do my best to please the demanding professors. Then I hurry home to practice for as many hours as I can steal from social duties or writing letters home.

I do enjoy spending time with your nieces as well. They are good friends. I will sorely miss them. I am most obliged for allowing me to be educated in Paris and live in your beautiful flat.

Sincerely yours, Anna

On a Friday morning soon after, Hasselmans commented, "I am pleased with the demonstration of your talent up to this point. You have *much* to learn, but you have done well this week."

At the rare compliment from the celebrated master, Anna smiled. Hasselmans was not an effusive man; he demanded her best efforts.

Anna's harp playing became the quiet, soothing background to many a social intrigue and slandered reputation during Abascal's parties. Not a few of the guests were surprised to learn Hasselmans was the young harpist's private instructor, and she would attend the *Conservatoire National de Musique* until the coming spring. While apprising the facts of this young girl's situation—ascertaining correctly she would continue living at the flat after Abascal's departure—Parisians tacitly assumed Anna was the natural daughter of William A. Clark.

That suspicion and the young lady's fluency in French (if tainted with traces of Québécois, "*Quel dommage!* Nevertheless, vastly superior to many Americans.") bolstered her reputation.

Abascal eyeballed a letter from a larger packet of material recently arrived. Her brother's French agent, Jean Paul Pelletier, had sent steamer tickets and other necessary travel papers for a mid-December voyage to London. "It's just as well, my lovies. I'm finally tiring of Paris. I have *such* a headache! I wonder if Father will allow us to linger for the start of the London season...?"

The breakfast table was set with Limoges porcelain, white linen napkins, sterling silver cutlery and serving dishes, with a low arrangement of hothouse flowers. This was the lone meal of the day marrying American and French tastes: eggs, sausages, whole wheat toast, *pain au chocolat, croissants, madeleines*, fruit, *café au lait*, and fresh squeezed Valencia orange juice.

"Oh Mommy, I didn't expect to leave Anna before Christmas," Mary said, chewing a large bite of *madeleine*.

"Don't talk with your mouth full, Mary. How many times..." Abascal put a silver fork down lightly on a plate of untouched food. "Anna can take care of herself. And she's busy studying at the *Conservatoire*. Correct, Anna?" Abascal's bloodshot eyes bored into Anna's.

"Ah *oui, c'est bien*, Mary," Anna set down her *café au lait*. "Please don't worry. I would enjoy receiving letters about London. I would like to go someday to see it as well." Anna almost blushed, wishing she hadn't revealed that desire in front of Abascal.

"I shall have to force Mary to write. She's awful at it!" Anita said. "I'll write you a lot, I promise."

"Anita, lower your voice. My head...."

"Why can't Anna come with us?" Mary brightened at the idea.

"As explained, she's too busy with studies, as you both are well aware. And Anna, Madame Bouchard is here, of course. According to William's last letter, he has requested she find a woman to be your chaperone during your extended stay in Paris. Probably no longer than May, correct?" Abascal glanced sharply at Anna, and then looked down as if she knew something Anna did not.

How quickly Mrs. Abascal gets over headaches to make sure her point is firmly made. Anna lost her appetite. Going back as soon as May was no longer agreeable.

"In any case, the months will go quickly. And my, my, you'll have plenty of time on your hands. No more *soirées* once I'm gone, I dare say. *Quel ennui!*"

Now alone, Anna felt tempted to reach out to others living in the same household. It was tempting to be chatty with maids and Bouchard. Only then did she comprehend how apropos Abascal's final advice was in her precarious situation.

"You *must* maintain distance for the staff to be respectful to you as a mere ward and not a family member. And for goodness sake, do not associate with any men, married or single, outside of or in the flat if you want to remain under this roof. In Paris almost anything is permissible, but my brother won't tolerate that. You shouldn't forget your place as a distinguished ward of the Clark family.

"However, you aren't a Clark *and never will be*. You're merely a normal American girl who has had a streak of very good luck for a short while. But while you're in Paris, you must remember yourself at all times! Don't give the servants anything to gossip about, nor Madame Bouchard anything to report back to my brother, hmmm?"

After the new year began, due to Clark's Parisian patronage of the arts and his sister's notorious sojourn the year previous—which, it must be admitted, had given credit to the Clark name in certain social circles—Mademoiselle Anna La Chappelle was accepted into good society. From friends met at the conservatory, invitations and social opportunities arrived in greater numbers.

Clark's ward clearly needed a respectable chaperone to maintain the young lady's position in the polite society of the *haute bourgeoisie*. The chaperone would accompany Mademoiselle La Chappelle to all necessary appointments and lessons befitting a young lady of breeding. Bouchard and Pelletier went to work making enquiries.

January 1896
6, avenue Mac-Mahon, Paris

Amidst gentle flurries, a woman alighted from a carriage. With ladylike caution, Amélie Joséphine Isabeau de Cervellon made her way up to the fourth-floor residence. Once the butler admitted her through the tall oak doors, she was privately amazed to find a household fit for a king.

Cervellon was of average height and looks with a spare figure. At fifty-seven years old, she was the widow of a French army officer. Never having been a beauty, she had studied elegance. Thus elegance, in all its forms, became her religion and cemented a sterling reputation in an age such as the *Belle Époque*. For this reason, she was recommended without fail from one mansion or flat to another. For those who could afford to privately educate their daughters in the social arts, consistent success and an unimpeachable reputation put Cervellon in high demand. However, what she was after was far more than mere education. She was an *artiste*.

Cervellon paid minute attention to the finest points of conversational and social etiquette. Her spare wardrobe received the same attention: nothing but the finest. Ordering solely *haute couture*, she dressed herself in a manner which would put her without question in the uppermost tier of the *haute bourgeoisie*. At the *maison*, Cervellon worked directly with the house's *première vendeuse* to choose ensembles in designs and colors that abhorred trends and never drew undue attention.

Cervellon's perfect penmanship was a joy to behold. She made an art form of graceful feminine refinement. Never once had anyone witnessed her falling prey to a *faux pas*, even when goaded by envious acquaintances. To generous hearts, she seemed without vanity or guile, which she used to advantage when the need arose. Her conversation was discrete and peppered with wittiness which never trailed into vulgar sarcasm. She never cared to be the envy of others or the most important figure in the room. She was selective with locales and acquaintances.

The consistent holding back from society helped ensure Cervellon was guaranteed an invitation to everything worthwhile *Le Tout Paris* had to offer. Unusually, her reputation superseded her occupation as a mere chaperone.

Cervellon's one fault? She had no musical talent due to a tenuous upbringing with a high-strung mother, which she made a point never to mention. She had learned how to gloss over the fault quickly, turning the conversation back to the hostess. Most happily, that musical drawback did not matter in the case of Mademoiselle La Chappelle, already occupied with advanced musical studies.

After Cervellon's husband's unexpected death, perseverance was needed to recreate herself. Over many years, she gradually morphed into the most in-demand Parisian chaperone of well-to-do young ladies due to two things: A phenomenal success rate at converting the young lady into an elegant woman, and the young lady's ensuing offers of marriage. What she could accomplish in eighteen months was admirable. Given thirty-six months, a miracle! By the time Pelletier caught up with Cervellon, it was marveled she could increase the social value of a young lady merely by standing up with her at a ball.

Thus, Cervellon's plan worked brilliantly. Due to a mixture of talent and the requirements of the age, her career as a private chaperone to privileged young ladies was making her wealthy. When she met Anna, she calculated in about five years she would be able to live as an independent woman.

Bouchard had heard much of Cervellon's reputation in the *quartier*, and, uncharacteristically, came out of her kitchen office to personally greet the woman.

She escorted the chaperone into the red drawing room in order to look her over. Bouchard smiled as she departed. *Mademoiselle La Chappelle could learn a lot from this woman.*

Cervellon examined the well-appointed room with experienced eyes.

Living here would be very pleasurable. And it's so quiet. Will it remain so, I wonder?

Several minutes passed before she saw a beautiful young woman enter. In a flash, Cervellon realized this would be her last and best client.

What raw American material stood before her!

Wearing a simple, white blouse and long black wool skirt, Anna appeared serene and confident. Cervellon beamed with pleasure at the easiness of the coming task.

"Mademoiselle La Chappelle, it is indeed a pleasure! I have not yet met Monsieur Clark, but I have recently been hired by him through mutual contacts to be your chaperone, as you must know."

"The pleasure is all mine, Madame de Cervellon. I was expecting you. Please call me Anna."

She held out a graceful arm to an arrangement of Louis XV chairs around a low marble-topped table holding an overflowing bouquet of flowers.

"Do sit down."

Cervellon smiled broadly at the young lady's manners and correct French. "Thank you for inviting me to do so. It is the mark of an excellent hostess."

She moved purposefully but delicately towards a red and ivory damask gilt chair. Tea was requested. The two women regarded each other. With natural cunning and lightning quick observational skills, Cervellon surmised the situation.

This is no ordinary ward. This seventeen-year-old is being prepared for something. Whether for paternal love, a mistress, or wife remains to be seen. From what she had learned from the housekeeper, whispered social chatter, and this jewel-box of a flat, *this young woman had a chance to strike it big. If she so chose! And perhaps she will need all of my help to do so?* However, I would not dream of scaring off this new charge through being forward about the delicate household situation.

"I hope we can be friends, Anna. It is much easier to be so when we must spend much time together. If we can agree to treat each other to the best of our abilities, life will be pleasant. I always have an excellent relationship with my young ladies. And you are a lovely young woman who is an asset to any social situation or to any man..."

Cervellon smiled demurely and glanced down for a moment before continuing. Despite her best intentions, she couldn't help baiting the young American. *Would she divulge details about the relationship with her patron?*

"From now on, I want you to *always* regard yourself as lovely. *Tout le temps!* You see, Anna, I cannot help myself, I am always teaching!" Cervellon clasped delicate hands to a lace-covered breast.

From a tray recently set down, Anna handed Cervellon a gold rimmed teacup and saucer. Anna took a sip of tea as she considered what was being said. She liked this woman's sweet open manner and honesty. She was so different than Abascal it was humorous.

This chaperone will teach me far different lessons than those taught last year! How do French women simultaneously pull off elegance, wittiness, and dignity? Perhaps this new chaperone will help me with those matters?

※

In February, Clark wrote Anna he would be arriving the next month. He was planning an itinerary full of exhibitions, museums, and other cultural entertainments. He asked she arrange with professors to be absent.

I want you all to myself, my dear. And be warned, I am going to examine you thoroughly to see how much you have learned after all these months in Paris. Please indicate if you are pleased with Madame de Cervellon's service to you, as I hope she will be able to be a long-time chaperone.

As ever, W.A. Clark

Reading those words, all at once Anna was flustered and excited. She knew a visit would happen someday, but now she had a definite time.

Mr. Clark will be here in the flat in a mere five weeks! What is expected of me? Will we discuss my departure date?

The impending visit worried Anna as she lay down to sleep, which uncharacteristically kept her tossing. Suddenly, she was wide awake in the darkness, excitement and dread equally wrapped around her heart. *Will he ask me to leave soon? Will it be strange to be with him here? What will I talk to him about?*

Winter's damp, cold wind whined outside. In response, she snuggled deeper under the layers of wool blankets and blue satin duvet. The wooden shutters agitated against window casings. The rhythmic sound lulled her to sleep.

She dreamed she was standing in the middle of a vast gilded ballroom. She had forgotten how to waltz. Then she was in a young man's arms. He reassured, "You are beautiful, Mademoiselle La Chappelle..." They whirled around again and again. The familiar Strauss rose louder and louder. Suddenly, Clark's strong arms were about her, not a young man's hesitant ones. Clark pulled her close; she stared into his hawk-like eyes. Then they stopped dancing abruptly as if he were going to kiss—

Anna half-woke. *Kiss Mr. Clark? Why am I dreaming this?*

The day of Clark's arrival, she dressed carefully, putting on the 18-karat gold Cartier small hoop earrings and locket Clark gave her for Christmas. *What will he think of me now?*

When Clark arrived, Anna read alone by a fire in the library. Hearing the commotion of servants, doors, and a man's voice, she set down her book. She was unsure what to do. It was too far away to discern what was said, but it was clearly not the butler's voice she overheard. She perked ears intently. Several minutes passed.

She stood. *Should I walk to him?*

Anna moved a few steps across the thick navy and gold Aubusson rug. Suddenly, the door swung wide. Clark stood staring. He wore a three-piece black wool suit with a diamond pin on a red paisley silk tie. He had a determined look as his eyes sought hers.

Clark was old enough to be her grandfather, but his slimness, energy, and intensity of expression made him appear much younger. However, the way he was looking at Anna now was not paternal. He admired his young ward as she stood frozen, uncertain how to behave.

She's been waiting for me!

"My dear," Clark said in a soft voice, "Paris has done you well. You look marvelous. So grown up! May I kiss you a fond hello after such a long time?" He held arms out as he approached.

"Mr. Clark, how do you do? It's good to see you." Anna automatically stepped forward. Feebly hands raised and then lowered. Blushing, she could not recall a single thing Cervellon had taught.

Clark took the lead by moving to gently embrace Anna. His kiss was light; he didn't linger. She backed away awkwardly, engrossed in examining the rug's pattern. Even last summer she had felt little in his presence, but now something was different. Inexplicable, but she felt it. She longed to escape those eyes which seemed to observe everything.

"How was your trip, sir?" The question came out automatically. Too polite.

Clark seemed to understand, and to Anna's relief, he walked to the desk at the other end of the room.

I'm very pleased at her bashful behavior, more girl than woman. It indicates she's been with no man during all this time. I can trust Cervellon with these matters. The situation is as I desire.

"Oh, it was a fine crossing, a little rough weather. But fine. And now, I'm excited to be in Paris! We shall have to belatedly celebrate your eighteenth birthday. Tonight? How does that sound?"

Sitting in a tufted leather desk chair, Clark opened a long drawer. He removed stationery and a Waterford pen with a 14-karat gold nib. He was pleased no one had used the desk in his absence. *That Bouchard runs a tight ship.*

"That would be lovely, thank you," Anna said while sitting down.

Opening a letter while checking over an open appointment book his valet brought, Clark said, "Tonight, we shall dine out to celebrate you. Tomorrow, there are several important things I must do while here..."

Busy eyes and hands looked at papers. He checked the appointment book again, running a slim finger with a manicured nail down detailed columns of appointments made by Pelletier.

"I need to send some letters directly this afternoon... Tomorrow I will take care of some business in the morning. I have an appointment with an agent I must see to, and then after lunch, the fun can begin. We will start with several galleries and shops I must visit. I have other appointments of business, naturally, but those can wait for another time. Those would be too dull for you... I hope you will accompany me..."

Anna was surprised to see a gentle, questioning look in his eyes. *How can he think I'll turn him down?* She perceived how Clark went from jovial to serious with ease; she was momentarily confused by his manner. *But of course, I've never been alone in a room with him.*

With Clark safely seated behind the large desk, Anna relaxed. She saw the family resemblance in attitude and energy between Abascal and Clark. *Although I prefer his manner to his sister's...*

"As you wish, Monsieur Clark. I've asked for several weeks reprieve from lessons, as your last letter directed. I'm at your disposal."

"Disposal? My dear, pish posh, as the English say. It will be *fun*! But you sound as delighted as my secretary at all the work I pile on him! Now, I need to attend to some business. Leave me to these boring letters. We'll dine tonight and can talk then.

"Inform Madame Bouchard I would like to leave at seven o'clock this evening. Early, I know, but I can't get used to French eating habits. Invite Madame de Cervellon to dine with us."

Anna departed with a pounding heart. She went directly to her room to recover. She didn't want anyone to witness her reaction to Clark's arrival. Not knowing what to think, she pushed out confused thoughts and tried to read again. She then dressed for dinner and went to the music room. Several hours passed agreeably. In the musician's flow, her anxiety settled, and all was well.

Clark heard the soft, intricate notes of the harp and entered quietly. He had formally met Cervellon earlier in the day when he had called her into the library to discuss Anna.

Cervellon nodded, not wanting to interrupt Anna's playing. She noticed that despite being small in stature, Clark was handsome in white tie with a gardenia in the lapel. Bespoke tailoring and erect posture lended an air of superiority. *As he is a man, I know the ultimate objective. But will he do right by Anna?*

Cervellon looked over at her young charge, who was growing on her. If Anna wanted, Cervellon would do everything possible to win Clark's hand.

He's as rich as Croesus, that's clear.

Her American contacts informed that Clark possessed far more than Europeans realized. More importantly, he seemed to be genuinely respectful of and devoted to Anna's education.

This is an auspicious beginning!

Clark felt refreshed, remarkably well. Staying at his Parisian flat always delighted his senses. After Kate died, he never thought once of selling it. He sat on a blue velvet sofa adjacent to Cervellon's chair.

Charmed by the scene of the two women before him, Clark thought, *It's been too long since I've visited Paris!*

In honor of the master's presence, Bouchard ordered all the gas sconces and the central chandelier fully lit. The massive black marble fireplace had a healthy fire. Large flower bouquets scented the air. Lulled by the beauty of his own flat, Clark closed his eyes and became engrossed by the intricate flow of Félix Godefroid *Étude de Concert, Opus* 193.

Eventually, fingers halted on the strings as they struck a wrong note. Anna's forehead wrinkled in frustration, upset she had flubbed in the exact spot as yesterday. Then her head lifted in surprise at Clark's voice.

"My dear Anna, bravo! That alone was worth my journey across the Atlantic. *Merci!* How well you play!" He clapped. "Such an accomplished harpist you've become! I would like you to play for me every day I'm in Paris, if you would..."

"Of course, Monsieur Clark. It would be a pleasure. I'm in another world when I play; I didn't know you entered the room. Forgive me."

"Yes, I remember well from your letters. *Le musique c'est fantastique!*"

Clark raised hands to vigorously clap again, urging Cervellon to do likewise. She gamely followed along with the American enthusiasm.

After a week of nonstop running through Paris and the surrounding countryside, Anna reveled in their outings. Clark's manner never reverted to overfamiliarity; he took on the role of friendly father-figure.

With Clark at Anna's side, Paris opened wide. They visited galleries, boutiques, and museums, and attended concerts and plays. She was able to go places ordinarily she would feel too awkward or poor to be in. Clark had a passion for art and energy for everything. Each evening they went somewhere new. Many mistook them for father and daughter or a May-December union. Anna blushed and looked away. Clark paid no attention to the comments, merely concluding his business or moving rapidly on. He bought several paintings, a small sculpture from Rodin, and a recently discovered master drawing from the Renaissance, shipping everything to his warehouse in Vienna.

Then it all ended abruptly.

Very early in the morning a telegram for Clark arrived. Anna slept later than usual owing to heavy rainclouds cloaking the city. Drinking *café au lait* and picking at toast, she wondered when Clark would appear. Cervellon said nothing. The servants spoke in muffled tones.

Before she left the table, Cervellon whispered it was "something *grave*. Do not trouble him, my dear."

Anna practiced an assigned Bach piece. Over an hour passed before Clark appeared wearing a black wool overcoat and black silk top hat.

Anna's eyes widened in instant distress. *This is too early of a departure. Have I done something wrong?*

"My dear Anna, I regret having to cancel the rest of our time together... My son Paul has died." William stopped to compose himself, pain distorting his face. "He was sixteen and... my... my youngest son."

"Oh, Monsieur Clark!" Anna stood up. "That is upsetting news! I'm terribly sorry to learn of his passing. May I ask what happened?"

Clark adjusted his top hat and looked at his valet motioning behind him. "Paul was enrolled at a boarding school in Massachusetts. He developed a strep infection and it proved too much, the poor boy!... I will take the first ship to New York. Take care, my dear."

William gave Anna a kiss on the cheek. He left without a backward glance.

Anna was filled with unexpected dismay. She went to a window facing the street to watch the carriage roll away. She regretted she didn't have time to fully express how much she appreciated him.

Her chaperone came up behind to look out the window. "Such terrible news, the poor man! No parent imagines they will have to bury a child. I expected something terrible when the telegram came. Nothing good ever comes from that slip of paper." She lightly clucked her tongue.

While brushing her hair that evening, Anna realized they never discussed her sojourn in Paris. It was all one delightful activity after another with no talk of the future. However, the uncomfortable fact remained: Anna only had a few months left of classes.

What then? Perhaps Mr. Clark will send a ticket to return. Do I want to? I can stay if I want...

Anna went into the dressing room which smelled heavily of lavender. From the towering wardrobe doors hung multiple gowns airing out or ready to be ironed. Anna sank down on hands and knees. She pulled up the Persian silk rug and liner and felt for the edge of a loose wooden floorboard. Many years ago, a carpentry repair to get rid of wood rot had cut the long floorboard in sections. The small section Anna was prying up was not fitted correctly, and the space underneath provided a vault of sorts. Inside a locked metal box was her fortune. In the past half year, she had added one hundred fifty dollars.

I should be grateful, but I desire far more security than this money represents. How long will I be able to live on it in Paris...? Do I dare ask Madame de Cervellon for help...?

Several weeks later Anna held a short letter from home. In shock, she had read and reread it multiple times. Her mother wrote that her father died; the funeral in Butte had been small; there was no need for Anna to take the long trip back:

I have the boarding house for income. And we all know your dear papa did very little to keep the place running. It wasn't in his nature to do that sort of work. I will get by. Thank you for the money you have sent. It has helped a lot. Write to me often, as now I have to rely on your younger siblings to keep me company. We are all well. Do not be too sad.

Your loving mother, Philomene

Anna didn't consider her father a frail or old man. *He's dead? I wasn't able to see dear Papa one more time!*

Broaching the subject to Cervellon, her chaperone set down needlepoint and seized Anna's hands. "Anna, please permit me to speak honestly. Do you trust me to do the best for you in the situation you currently find yourself?"

Anna nodded, mesmerized at Cervellon's electrified expression.

"You've recently turned eighteen-years-old and are from a family who does not enjoy money or social position. Am I correct?"

"*Oui, c'est vrai...*" Anna felt embarrassed by the frank appraisal.

"*D'accord*, then please consider *all* your options before making a rash choice. I know you are grieving, as any good daughter would! But your father is gone, buried weeks ago."

Cervellon's tone softened, and she put an arm around Anna's shoulders as the girl wept. "As your mother has written, she is occupied with the other children and her business. Anna, if you left Paris now, to be with your family, you wouldn't have completed a full year of courses at the *Conservatoire*, nor would you be able to politely ask Monsieur Clark *if you could return to his Parisian household!* What if it escapes his mind, my dear? It could happen! He's a very busy man, with many relying on him.

"It's not for my employment's sake I'm saying this. I'm in demand as an experienced and knowledgeable chaperone. I've money, social position, and powerful friends."

Cervellon grasped Anna's shoulders. "Look at me...!"

Anna raised her head slowly, not wanting to listen. Her eyes were red and swollen.

"I beg you to take me seriously and consider your current standing in *this* household. If you leave now, there is an enormous risk you'll not be asked to return! Monsieur Clark is one of the wealthiest and most powerful men in the United States. I've done some asking around... Many others clamor after him, as we have seen even here in Paris! Do you not remember that *demimondaine* at Maxim's?"

Anna nodded dejectedly. How could she forget one of the most fascinating women she had ever seen? The dark-haired woman was an ageing beauty. At a nearby table in full view of Clark's gaze, the famous woman—in scarlet satin with a large spray of black feathers over the shoulder and in her hair—did little but stare at Clark, ignoring the fawning young lover beside her. Long black gloves highlighted slender arms lifting a cigarette holder to voluptuous lips. She wore signature jewelry she had had since youthful days with a Russian Grand Duke: a pigeon's blood ruby, sapphire, and diamond parure.

Anna could not know the famous *demimondaine* heard about the wealthy American from the restaurant's manager, who was tipped handsomely. Clark nodded his head slightly at the bold woman for a brief moment, otherwise there was no indication of interest.

Cervellon said, "Even now we have *no idea* regarding his return to Paris. *Rien!* It's almost the summer season when Americans book passage to France, but will *he* come? There is no word yet. You must be careful not to lose this delicate situation!"

Cervellon released Anna's hands and sat down beside the fire. Anna, forehead wrinkled with indecision, sank down beside. Her hands remained idle in her lap. At that moment, she wanted nothing more than to hug her *maman*.

"I want to say goodbye to my father... I can't believe he's already buried!" Tears rained down. Anna blew her nose loudly.

Cervellon waited some time before she began again in a soothing tone. "My dear girl, walking away from this opportunity for no other reason than to make a visit to a graveside in the back of beyond is not a sound idea. Please do not think less of me for saying this so bluntly...

"To leave Paris now puts you in a vulnerable position, and frankly, allows other women to move in on Monsieur Clark's generosity. He's a man, and a recent widower. Remember, you are *not* the only woman he is thinking of."

Anna's head lifted with surprise. She did not know how to reply. *What was she alluding to?* A bashful smile then spread across Anna's face; she smoothed her black wool skirt over drawn up knees. She sighed, dabbed at eyes with a handkerchief, and rose to go to the window. She parted the lace curtains to look down onto the street.

"I'll think about what you said, *merci beaucoup*. I realize it's meant kindly."

Anna heeded Cervellon's advice. With no change in her status, the years passed quickly and delightfully while the City of Light whirled decadently on around her. There was never even the merest hint from Clark during infrequent, random visits that she needed to quit his household. Now twenty-one, she had completed years of formal musical studies. She continued private harp lessons with Hasselmans, along with adding tutoring in piano, German, and Italian. She took a greater interest in the cultural arts.

Like many fashionable Parisians, Anna was swept up in art nouveau with its graceful forms and love of nature and innocence. But the fashion for *Japonisme* most captivated. She attended lectures, and frequented galleries, booksellers, and exhibitions featuring artists and works inspired by the burgeoning movement. For Christmas, her favorite present from Clark was a rosary of jade and pearl. While fingering the smooth, light green beads kneeling at the *prie-dieu*, she was touched he was paying close attention to her interests.

During these years, Clark visited France only once annually because he was too preoccupied with various projects, business ventures, and a Senatorial election. These visits to Paris were much like the first one. He treated Anna as his favorite ward, showering gifts of demure gold jewelry with semiprecious stones or pearls, hair ornaments, opera gloves, chocolate, and flowers. She played for him in the music room, and he disappeared for hours to work. When Clark was free, they made a mad dash through the city after concerts, fine restaurants, exhibitions, theater, and art galleries. Clark reveled in the chase of coveted treasures.

"You will have to come to see my mansion on Fifth Avenue someday. The blueprints are finalized, and I hope very much we can break ground soon. I'm very much looking forward to that, Miss La Chappelle! It'll be a handful of years in the future before the house is finished, at the earliest, to be sure, there is so much remaining to be done! The planning and execution invigorate. I feel like a young man of twenty-five!"

At the height of booming business ventures and developing political influence, Clark typically left Paris after a few weeks. He would travel on to Rome, Dresden, St. Petersburg, or London before returning to America. Anna was never invited to accompany him. He merely said a fond goodbye, kissing her on the cheek. He would not return for another six to ten months.

Nothing was ever seriously discussed regarding her return. Clark asked Anna if she was happy in Paris, which she assured with a delighted smile she was. And that was that. Cervellon advised Anna to say nothing, to do nothing but please him. Therefore, Anna remained throughout the years exactly as she had been upon arrival.

Broaching the subject with her chaperone one evening in late winter, Cervellon replied in a relaxed tone of voice tugging gently on embroidery. "Accept the situation as it stands, my dear. He seems content with you, more pleased than ever... However, prepare yourself for the day it changes, is all I will advise."

"Changes? Whatever do you mean?"

Anna kept eyes on her embroidery, which she participated in because her chaperone recommended it as a worthwhile, ladylike activity. Cervellon only smiled, waiting until the right question was asked before she explained further. A plan was brewing in her mind after more than three years of witnessing no change in Clark's behavior.

Several months later, while sitting in an enclosed carriage on a spring day, Anna was itching to talk. She turned her gaze to the busy street. They had spent the morning at Worth in fittings for summer gowns. Anna wore a yellow broad-brimmed hat over a bouffant updo. Her pale-yellow silk gown with black piping along the length of the skirt had delicate handmade lace falling from three-quarter sleeves.

Anna shifted on the carriage's leather seat, not wanting to make a fool of herself. She was uncomfortably aware she was now thinking of Clark as much more than a father-figure. She had begun to wonder at his private motive for sponsoring her at considerable expense all these years.

In the past ten months Anna had tried to accept young *beaux* who called, but she was unsatisfied due to obvious immaturity, lack of culture, or shallowness. She understood her life would diminish greatly if she were to accept a proposal. It wasn't merely the lack of funds, there was another quality Clark had in spades that the rest lacked. *Perhaps it has something to do with his massive energy or drive.*

As for the younger men, sooner or later they annoyed tremendously. One man even had the effrontery to say he was bored by the harp, leaving Anna incredulous he paid no attention to her preferences. Then fifteen minutes later he inquired if she were going to inherit anything from her "filthy rich patron." Anna sent him packing, along with anyone else who came calling.

I'm done with foolish young men.

It took many months of contemplation before Anna realized she was expecting Clark to come forward as other men had. But then she lost faith he even saw her as anything other than a ward. His polite behavior never varied, there was only a hint of strong admiration and attraction before he would look away. The situation had to change in Anna's favor, but overall, she was very unsure how to proceed. She wanted Clark to visit more often.

I know Mr. Clark is old enough to be my grandfather, but after all this time, I don't view him in that way. Mr. Clark is powerful, knowledgeable, in complete command of himself and his businesses. He takes care of everything, allowing me to live independently. And he's a perfect gentleman who makes me laugh. I adore my life with him in Paris; I want it to be secure.

The carriage stalled in mid-day traffic, and Cervellon pulled an impatient face. Gloved fists went up into the air. She normally betrayed no unladylike emotions, but traffic in central Paris frustrated.

"This imbecile driver is not adept at remembering to avoid the wrong streets at this time of day. You'd think he wanted to parade his horses in front of everyone. We should learn how to drive one of those new motorcars tearing all over. Then we could go faster! Imagine, at my age..."

Anna barely heard; her eyes were dream-like, fixated on inner thoughts. Normally she made fun of her guardian's temper with traffic, but today Anna's fast-beating heart drowned out her companion's conversation.

"Madame de Cervellon, if I...if I tell you something, you will guard it with the utmost secrecy, *oui*...?"

The older woman turned away from the carriage window and regarded Anna with interest. "*Oui, bien sûr!* You alone have my strictest confidence."

Anna traced the black piping on her gown with a gloved finger. "I.... I've been thinking... I would like to..." She hesitated, never having uttered the incredible words out loud before. "I care deeply for Monsieur Clark, and I would like to marry him," she said in a rush.

Anna froze with the emotional effort of forcing the words out. Now she could not take them back. Someone knew! The imagined, mocking face of Lizzie Abascal loomed: "You're not worthy to shine my elder brother's boots, much less be his *wife*!"

"*Oui*, I am aware."

Anna snapped out of the unpleasant reverie. "You are? How long have you known? Is it obvious? Am I being foolish?!" She clasped hands against her breast in nervous excitement.

"*Ma fille chérie, calme-toi*. I'm with you every day, and I've been your companion for many years now. I've known for quite some time. I can see your frustration Monsieur Clark has not come forward like other men have. As a woman, *je te comprends très bien*..."

"If you've seen it, has he?"

"No, I don't believe so. Not entirely. Otherwise, he would've come forward to claim his prize. I think perhaps he wants you to want him in return, as all strong men do. And secondly, most importantly, I believe he has been too preoccupied of late with plans for his grand mansion and with politics in the United States. Power is like a drug to many men of his caliber.

"And you must concede, you might not be the only woman in his life... Who knows who he is with when he is not visiting Paris, hmmm? It is his right as a male in our world, unfortunately. Have you considered that possibility?"

"That another woman might win him?" Anna's voice caught in her throat.

"*Oui.*" Cervellon looked straight at Anna, almost in challenge.

"I... That is so disheartening. How will *I* win him? I've no experience with men. Do you think I'll have to leave his household soon, then?"

"No, silly girl! I'm not saying that, nor is he. But are you considering his side of the story?"

"His side? Do you believe he thinks of me? Do you honestly think I have a chance then? Can you help me to win him?"

"*Bien sûr*! It will not be hard. Why do you think I've stayed with you this long...?" Cervellon waved a hand dismissively. "And I think he fell in love with you *quite* some time ago. Which explains why he is so patient (not a trait most men are good at). He merely needs a little nudge in the right direction. A widowed man like him, now a Senator for the United States, busy as he is. And perhaps busy in other ways..." She nodded knowingly. "You'll need to come forward during his next visit. No more wasting time!"

Anna's face lost its color, and her mouth went slack for a moment.

"But... that's in two months! How do I come forward, as you say, without being unbecoming? What if he rejects me?"

Her pretty mouth turned down at the risk. Cervellon chuckled softly and grabbed Anna's hand to squeeze it affectionately.

"Now stop being ridiculous. You're a beautiful young woman, accomplished and educated after all these years in Paris to be the *perfect* Madame Clark. Believe it! And I can teach you how to seduce him as a lady does. As a *demimondaine* does! Those American women will look like swine compared to you. The *demimondaines* always get their man. Any willing man is easy to seduce..."

Cervellon's gloved finger went up in the air, a pearl and diamond bracelet glimmering in the sunlight. "*Faites attention!*"

Her eyes darted over to Anna's intent face. "I don't think he'll marry you quickly, as he has already done that, you see. He has had respectability, married in a church, raised a family, buried his first wife a number of years ago. Now, as a widower, he always has beautiful and elegant women desiring him. Therefore, to win him we'll take into account *your* privileged position. You must approach him differently in his own household, coming in the back door of the marriage house, so to speak. And what of it?" She shrugged petite shoulders.

"Many women do it. It's your advantage in the game of love, and you must seize it if you truly want his love. This is France, you won't be looked down upon if you do it correctly, without losing your little head. And if so, you'll probably gain more respectability, not less. The gossip about your position in his household will cease. Your position in Parisian society will be established. And what do you have to lose, my darling girl? Do you want to return to Montana or wherever it is you will return to?"

Cervellon then smiled benevolently at her charge, knowing Anna would triumph. Her hand reached out to caress Anna's cheek. "Don't fear. He will love you in return, that I know! I've seen it in his eyes, in his patience all these years."

Anna felt riveted to Cervellon as the carriage swayed down a cobblestone street, under construction from the Metro being built far below ground. Cervellon shut the window against the dust.

"Therefore, are you prepared to be his lover first and wife second, *ma fille chérie*?"

"His lover!" Anna's eyes darted nervously around the carriage and then out the window to her right. That was a title she had not considered. *What would* Maman *say*?

"Oh, I hadn't considered that. Rather, I hoped to be married..."

"In a church? You can still be married in a church, perhaps with only a few guests though and with a baby at home. Wake up, my darling, idiot girl! What do you think he wants you to stay here for? All these years? He's not desiring you to remain his ward or to remain an innocent girl! He can see very well you're becoming a beautiful woman, cultured, and educated, a perfect wife for him."

Cervellon smiled at Anna's expression which altered between elation and doubt. "Anna, whatever happens, I'll help all the way to the altar, *je te le promets*. And if you get pregnant quickly, before we can get him to the altar, all the better! He will assuredly marry you then.

"He will need a wife to run that grand mansion he's always prattering on about. Mark my words, it sounds so enormous you'll be lost inside! It's all for his pride, so typical of American *nouveaux riches*. But back to the point, *oui*, I've watched him with you for *quite some time*. It will all work out as I say."

Cervellon leaned forward to resume rapping on the ceiling of the carriage with a parasol. "Pick up speed! The workmen can clearly see inside!"

To Anna, the conversation had been a revelation. But to her guardian, it was as if they were merely talking of what to have for luncheon.

"You're *sure* he will marry me someday? That if I come forward, he won't marry me first? Isn't that better in the eyes of the Church, that we marry first?"

Anna sat bold upright, suddenly tense at betraying her faith. How would she explain to Father D'Souza?

"*Bien sûr* that's what you want! I cannot say anything about what Father D'Souza would think. You'll have to deal with him during confession. I only know the kind of man Monsieur Clark is. And to catch him, you'll have to become his lover first. Otherwise, I believe he would've married you long ago.

"Remember he has adult children. What do they say about remarriage? What about his will? Do you think they want more heirs to dilute their inheritance? How are they influencing him? So, pray you become pregnant immediately! That will seal his heart's protection and pave the way for the respectability you desire."

<hr />

The seed was planted in Anna's mind, and after a few more long conversations over the next month, Anna became accustomed to this new way of thinking of love and marriage. Despite Father D'Souza's warnings and differing counsel, Anna sprang into action. Clark wrote he was upset he had had to resign from the Senate due to what he described as his enemies temporarily triumphing. That defeat spurred him to plan a long visit to Europe. What was supposed to only be a short visit in early July ended up being extended.

Anna was kept very busy, following all Cervellon's detailed instructions to the letter. She tried not to be confused by the lessons on flirtatious gestures, coy eye glances, and subtle movements of the body. She was taught how to properly offer a prepped cigar to a man during evening conversation, how to converse on subjects that drew him out, how to sit more elegantly whether playing the harp or sitting on a chair. They soon went back to Worth and reordered summer gowns to be cut in a more sophisticated way.

In the end, Anna's courage was emboldened by the altered gaze of Clark. After a week he was looking at her like a desirable woman. She could see the longing in his eyes, and how he allowed his hand to linger on the small of her back far more often as he led her into a dining room or a concert hall. He also grasped her hand more ardently when she was entering or exiting the carriage. This pleased Anna very much. She made sure to smile often, welcoming his touch.

By some miracle, Cervellon knew how to diminish herself to be present but absent from the room at the same time. Clark seemed to take little notice of her, which was unusual. She was an excellent conversationalist and knew how to draw powerful men out. Her trick was she did not fear them.

After a candlelit meal at home one warm evening during the second week of Clark's visit, they sat down in the gold drawing room. Cervellon soon said, "I have a small matter to attend to in my room. Please excuse me."

Clark stood as Cervellon exited. Sitting back down by Anna, he was quiet for a minute before remarking, "I'm quite taken with you this trip, my dear Anna. You've grown into a magnificent woman. I can't take my eyes off you. What have you done differently?"

Clark moved a bit closer on the long sofa. Anna softly smiled. She had been taught to say little when a man began to complement. She listened, waiting. Her heart was pounding in anticipation of his touch.

She wore a lavender silk and chiffon ruffled gown over a swan-bill corset. The gold locket he had given her the first Christmas in Paris was around her neck, and pearl earrings in her ears were his latest birthday gift. Her hair was curled and swept up in the full Gibson girl style so popular on both sides of the Atlantic. She flushed a little in the warm evening.

Clark's hand reached out to gently grasp hers as he eased alongside her. She returned the gentle pressure of his warm fingers. She dropped her gaze so lashes stood out against full, pink cheeks, then waited.

Clark raised an arm to gently kiss the top of her hand. "You are so beautiful tonight, Anna."

"*Merci,* Monsieur Clark."

"If you will, dear Anna, due to our close association that's lasted for years, I would ask you to call me William." He reached out a hand to caress her cheek.

Anna was pleased at the intimacy of using his first name. She looked directly into his eyes. She had never been this close to him before. She could clearly smell his cologne mixed with a clean, masculine scent.

"*Oui, avec plaisir,* William."

William's finger went under her chin while he very gently put a hand to her waist and pulled her closer. Deftly, he lifted her mouth to his. Anna was surprised by the softness of his lips surrounded by ticklish whiskers. His arms drew her closer in a full embrace as their kiss deepened.

At that moment, Anna understood there was no other man for her. She was ready to bear his children, to share a life together in Paris.

For the first time, Anna slept in the master bedroom with oak paneled walls and plum satin damask bed hangings and upholstered furniture. William was so entranced he ended up staying through the end of August. He didn't vary his routine; he rose early for a brisk walk and then a light breakfast before going into the library. He spent hours writing business correspondence and taking appointments until a late luncheon. Then William concentrated on Anna. The arrangement suited Anna perfectly, because she spent mornings attending Mass, writing correspondence, and practicing music.

For William's final night, he arranged a candlelight dinner with a menu prepared by his celebrated French chef: oysters, *foie gras*, caviar, turtle soup, venison with truffled potatoes, veal with asparagus, *fromages*, and chocolate mousse. Before eating, the valet entered to present William with a large square red box on a silver salver.

"And what's this?"

"For my beautiful darling, and because I adore your smile and your one blue eye." He leaned to squeeze her hand affectionately.

Anna smiled softly at the joke he always made about her differing eyes. They kissed.

"Thank you for a perfect summer in Paris. Please open it." He sat back with a pleased look.

Nestled on velvet inside the iconic box was a sapphire and diamond necklace and earrings. Anna stared, mesmerized by the rich blue of the stones and the brilliancy of the surrounding diamonds. She had no experience handling major jewels, much less wearing them. The set far surpassed anything he had ever given.

"Is all this for *me*?"

"And you will look lovely in it! Do you like it? I want you to have beautiful things to wear when we're together. Can I put it on you, my love?"

William moved behind to fasten the heavy necklace. Anna put on the dangling earrings. She leaned over to kiss William, arms tightly going up around his neck. She was at a loss for words.

"You're very welcome," William laughed. "Only don't strangle me or else you won't get any more Cartier! No doubt they will bankrupt me someday. I can't afford my ticket back to New York, I'll have you know... You're going to have to put up with me until I can have some more funds wired over..."

Chuckling at his own joke, William knew how ridiculous it sounded that he would ever run out of money. His copper mines alone were generating profits at such an astronomical rate that regardless how much he spent on frivolities, the next day the amount and then some would be replenished from merely one of the mines he owned. He could have bought Anna several royal parures fit for a czarina and the cost would only be a pittance compared to his overall assets. He would never be able to spend all the money he was making in his lifetime even if he tried. Although, from hard-won experience, he never openly discussed that topic with anyone.

William called to the butler. "Let's eat, I'm famished! *Bon appetit!*"

September 1901
6, avenue Mac-Mahon, Paris

Anna was stiff from traveling. She set down a beaded purse to open Amelia's first letter. It lay on a stack of correspondence piling up for weeks while Anna holidayed in Trouville. She frowned at the date, August 11.

Written weeks ago... Why wouldn't Amelia have sent it to the hotel address?

The unusual letter read:

My dear sister,

Rumors are rife around Washington and New York about Mr. Clark marrying soon. Our surname is used in the press frequently—although they report an Ada or Amy is attached to it—but speculation and gossip abound regarding several suitable women. No doubt someone with a big mouth in Paris has informed the American press you're still living at Mr. Clark's Parisian apartment.

What's concerning is the tenor of the gossip has altered in recent months, and in some circles, I have even been accused of being the object of his affections due to our shared surname. Me? I seldom see the man, as you well know. To escape the gossip, I'm planning on returning to Butte for the next six months. It has been decidedly not in my favor. I was rudely questioned by a hostess of a party recently attended, and

the next day an invitation was revoked. I cried, I was so upset! So, I'm escaping the
seething tongues for a time. You know how private I am with such matters. I never
discuss your arrangement with Mr. Clark, nor do I want to be accosted.

It's been a day since I last wrote. Not to alarm, but I have also heard from the
cousin of a distinguished Boston family that Mr. Clark has been wooing a young
lady there. As he is a senator now, it's whispered he's searching for a suitable bride
to ensure increased political power in Washington...

Are you apprised of any of this? Does it surprise? I don't write to upset, only to
warn of what is happening over here. Maybe you should come back for a visit? I'm
sure you will know what to do—please write soon.

As ever, your loving sister, Amelia

Anna thought back to when the last visit by William occurred. *Was it January*
or February...? We went to Madame Aubert's excellent dinner party before he
departed... Regardless, that was quite a few months ago... William had regularly
written all summer; she assumed all was normal.

When Anna walked in brandishing the letter, Cervellon was spraying rosewater
on her face while seated at a dressing table.

"What's bothering you, *ma chérie*? Did bad news come...? Oh, my hair needs
washing." Cervellon picked up a hairbrush to fix grey fly-aways.

"Amelia is alarmed by gossip about William, which is highly unusual. Will you
read this? I hardly know what to think!" Anna's face was stricken with female
intuition.

All is not well! Amelia is not prone to exaggeration when it comes to our mutual
benefactor.

After reading, Cervellon was silent for a moment, lost in thought. She rang the
bell. Soon her maid appeared. "Please inform Madame Bouchard I need to speak
with her."

After the maid left, Cervellon said, "How much money have you saved up?"

Anna was momentarily taken aback by the question, but immediately followed
her train of thought. "I can pay for first class tickets, hotel, and food for both of us
to go to America with no difficulty. I've saved up a small fortune from William's
generosity."

"Smart girl! Well done! I'll pay for myself, of course, Monsieur Clark is very generous with me as well. But I'll ask you to cover your own expenses. We should pack tonight and leave for Le Havre immediately, departing on the very next ship available. If you agree..."

Suddenly exhausted, Anna nodded before plunking herself in a pink slipper chair. She wrapped arms tightly around a pink silk pillow with floral needlework, smashing it into her upset stomach. She lowered her head dejectedly.

"Have I made a grave mistake?" Anna moaned.

"All is not lost. Sit up, my girl! Your posture is deplorable." Cervellon went over to the fireplace, her eyes locked in on the Venetian mirror above. She did not see her own reflection; her eyes saw only what needed to be accomplished.

"We'll rise to action immediately. There is a Latin proverb which states: 'If there is no wind, take to the oars.' Well, that's what we're doing now! I would write Monsieur Clark *tonight* that we're visiting America. That you miss your family terribly; that it has been too many years of absence; that it's all impromptu—a whim of a trip. Make sure he knows I'll be with you, as that ensures your return to Paris."

Thinking best on her feet, Cervellon began pacing the bedroom's length. It had been quite a few years since she had felt this roused. "Say nothing about the published gossip your sister has alluded to, *bien sûr! Rien!* We don't want to alarm or be silly females making assumptions. We'll divulge nothing we suspect.

"We'll simply travel to New York and then on to Washington D.C. to see for ourselves what the fuss is all about. It could be lies or journalistic fabrications, or it could be quite serious. Only when the truth is found out will we know how best to act!

"The fact of the matter is, in this delicate situation, we cannot merely wait here any longer for him to come to us. As Monsieur Clark has not visited in quite some time, nor has he informed you of any upcoming visit planned... and because his renewed Senate seat has been so terribly important to him and his pride... I believe there must be some merit to the whispers. American politics certainly function around a husband-and-wife team, as I've heard. There's all the entertaining, for one... Running a household set up for political prominence is no mean feat.

"And, as we well know, Monsieur Clark is *certainly* a man who adores women. Therefore, we will not delay in securing his immediate attention this fall." Cervellon stopped pacing to face Anna. "Never fear, *ma fille chérie*, this will work!"

Anna stood, straightening to her full height inches above Cervellon. "Thank you for clear thinking at such a time. I'm all nerves, good for nothing. I'll go play the harp for a few minutes to relax. Meanwhile, in my head, I'll compose the letter to William. It'll be written before we retire for the evening, I promise."

Several weeks later, the two women were at Washington's best hotel, the Arlington on Vermont Avenue. A mere block from the White House, the opulent hotel was built by the philanthropist William W. Corcoran. Its sumptuous suites, ballrooms, promenades, and restaurants catered to the rich and powerful. When government was in session, many senators and congressman made the hotel their home. If any dignitary, king, or president visited, he was advised to stay at the Arlington.

Cervellon delighted in seeing America, where she had not been for twenty years. She knew a few visiting European friends and the French ambassador and his wife. Since their visit was announced on short notice, Cervellon planned many cultural activities and accepted any promising social engagement offered. She suspected Clark wouldn't have much private time for Anna.

Anna put on a brave face when meeting others. She knew she must act as if nothing were amiss. She tried not to tense up when her name was unexpectedly linked with William's. It was unnerving to politely brush off inquiring questions into her private life in Paris as "Clark's ward." Very Parisian in her thinking and manners, Anna was unused to such intrusive questions. In Paris, the stranger enquiring would not be worth knowing.

She bristled at back-handed comments from much older women at crowded parties. Some spoke as if they knew her, which was unsettling.

"My dear Miss La Chappelle, how you've grown into a beautiful young woman. France has done you well! A hidden flower you are in gay Paris, hmmm...? So far from your country for *so long*. How long exactly has it been...?"

As Anna almost flushed with anger and averted her eyes—*Who is this woman?*—the overdressed, elderly hostess continued, "How long will you remain Senator Clark's ward? He surely has *no time* these days for such matters…"

The woman tittered into a splayed fan; her two companions followed suit. In a flash, Anna regained her composure.

"I hardly know, ma'am, perhaps we should ask him tomorrow at the Embassy Ball?"

She excused herself with chilly reserve. Caught alone and unawares, the rudeness was intolerable. *I must find Cervellon in all these crowds! It's time to leave!*

If Anna were in public with William or another member of the Clark family, then no such barbed comments were made. To her face, everyone was cordial and delighted to become acquainted. However, the tone of many conversations struck her as false. William introduced Anna to everyone in public, but she attended no intimate gatherings with him. For his part, William saw Anna as much as he could in either city; but both business and politics wooed him away far too often.

Cervellon, returning from tea with the French ambassador's wife, entered Anna's room. "It seems there is some merit to the gossip, but nothing has come of it. Many are still speculating. No one has any names. If I may ask, is he the same with you?"

"You mean in private? *Oui, le même…* He simply seems distracted, or rather, entirely absorbed by the dual challenge of politics and running his businesses with only spotty support from his sons. However, he's energized and completely absorbed in his new political role in ways I've never witnessed. It's neither bad nor good. However, it might drive a wedge between us… He gave me this last night before he left."

Lying on a satin double bed outfitted for royalty, Anna held up an emerald and diamond bracelet. Her eyes blankly stared at the flowered wallpaper. She could not delight in the gift yet because William was not with her, nor had he mentioned a word about marriage.

He's slipping away and my great sacrifice amounts to nothing. I've prayed and attended Mass... Mais, rien!

Cervellon suppressed a delighted cry. She reached to lift the stunning bracelet to the light.

"The perfect blue within blue in each green stone, so lovely! My, my, Monsieur Clark always knows the best pieces."

Setting the priceless bracelet carefully onto the nightstand, Cervellon sat down gingerly beside her forlorn charge. Anna's head bowed with defeat.

Softly Cervellon prodded, "What's our plan, *chérie?*"

"I realize now I love him dearly and I don't want to lose him," Anna mumbled. "*Oui... Je sais...*"

"He told me last night he's leaving in two days to go to Butte. He'll be gone for a long while... But with everyone around us no matter where we are, he didn't think to invite me! Of course, I know there are many eyes here watching, unlike in Paris. No one questions us there. The papers don't report on our actions. There are no nosey journalists on every street corner and train stain as there are here in America. It's hateful!"

Anna smacked a down pillow with a fist.

"He explained he has a lot of pressing business in Montana before going on to Los Angeles. That he wished he could spend more time with me, but he cannot stay on the East Coast right now. Normally, from what I recall from habits he details in letters, he'll travel in his railcar between cities, and then stay in Montana before returning to Washington D.C. He doesn't mention it directly, but Butte remains his home base."

Anna stopped talking for a long moment, then she slowly brightened.

"*Bien sûr*, Madame de Cervellon, *c'est fantastique*! You're brilliant!"

She turned to Cervellon with a hopeful countenance.

"*Moi? Pour quoi?* I've said *rien*."

"But you've given me the idea! We'll likewise follow him to Butte, for the winter. What do you think? You must say yes!"

"Well, then yes! Although I fear to go so far away from the coast in the winter. Montana is in the 'Wild West,' *n'est-ce pas?*"

Cervellon looked at Anna with trepidation, and they burst out laughing.

"I hate to admit, but I'm a bit afraid!"

"It'll be fine! And it's the perfect plan! We'll be freer there! Why didn't I think of this immediately? Amelia wrote she has several guest rooms in the apartment. It's only a few blocks from William's house. That way, I won't be too far when he's in town. And I haven't seen *Maman* in so many years... What a selfish daughter I am not to visit her as well!"

Anna gathered skirt and petticoats to bound off the bed. Her mouth broke out in the first genuine smile in weeks.

"It's an excellent plan," said Cervellon. "He knows you've family there, as does everyone else, so it's a perfect reason to trot along after him. Let's book train tickets in the morning, shall we? We'll write Monsieur Clark of our plans *en route*, not before, and we'll settle comfortably in 'Smokey Butte,' as you call it, for a few months. We'll see what that accomplishes in the way of love."

A handful of days later, Amelia whooped at the train station after they alighted.

"You've escaped those nasty journalists and gossiping hordes like I have. Bravo!"

Anna was overjoyed to be with family after so many years apart. It was also a relief to have William's undivided attention, despite frequent business trips away. They spent most evenings at his mansion. He would attend parties and events until late, and she waited alone. Philomene assumed she was living with Amelia, when in truth, she was only with her sister when William was out of town.

I'll confess to Maman *someday soon.*

After six weeks, it was well established William was content. Cervellon fibbed about a family reason to return to Paris immediately.

"It will take me some weeks to visit family in Alsace. I do apologize for the inconvenience, Monsieur Clark. You do understand the importance of family."

Clark assured them both it was fine for Anna to return sometime in the next month. "And why not include Amelia in the trip? I'm sure she'd be delighted to see Paris at the Christmas season."

Privately to Anna, Cervellon said, "America has been a lark, but I need to breathe properly. The air is *intolerable* here. How does anyone survive? *Non*, it is not healthy at all! I will see you and Amelia soon."

December arrived with mornings of swollen breasts and bouts of nausea and vomiting. Anna lost her appetite. She looked at Amelia—as inexperienced as she—"I'm a little frightened at the unknown prospect of having an illegitimate child."

"If so, we need to leave soon!"

"I can't face *Maman's* disappointment. I won't tell her!"

"Are you sure that's wise? What will you do when the baby arrives?"

"I don't know! I'll think of something."

Anna put a plain gold ring on her left hand and went to see a doctor in Deer Lodge under a pseudonym. That evening, William was called to Amelia's flat.

Brimming with energy from an evening with business associates, William said, "My darling Anna, this is unexpected! I assumed you would be too tired to talk at this late hour. I was surprised to receive your message. How are you?"

He took her hands and bent to kiss the tops of each.

"I'm well, William. I've some news I hope will make you as happy as it has made me."

"You don't appear happy." William looked at her curiously. "Alright, what is it?"

He bent to kiss her nose.

"I'm.... I went to the doctor today. I wanted confirmation... I'm pregnant. William, I'm carrying your child."

William wrapped his arms around Anna to lift her. He held her tight to cover conflicting emotions.

A baby by Anna, wonderful! I love her, more than I ever expected to. She's a joy. But what will I tell my children? What could this illegitimate child do to my political career?

He released her and looked into her face. He covered worries by smiling from the sheer joy of loving his progeny.

"That's wonderful news, my love!"

"I think so, too."

Tears welled up in Anna's eyes from the relief at the welcoming reception. She clung to him.

"Are you afraid? My Anna doesn't usually cry..."

"No, I simply need you to hold me."

They embraced for a long moment before she gently extricated herself to dab at wet eyes with the handkerchief offered.

"Don't fear, Senator Clark. I know this poses a significant problem. You already have enemies in Washington, and I don't plan to make the pressure any worse. I'll return to Paris to have the baby in seclusion. I don't want your political career impacted."

"My dear, at such a joyous moment must we speak of it?"

"Yes, because I don't want you to be concerned. I'm not a foolish woman." Anna lifted her chin with pride. "I know how society can be, and I intend to protect my child and his father."

"Ah, and that's why I love you!" William pulled her into his arms again. "I wish I could be with you at such an important time. A baby is wonderful news! I'll visit as soon as I'm able, but I can't say when. I've many irons in the fire at present. However, I pray all will be well."

"I love you, William. Please come to Paris as soon as you can."

She grasped his hand tightly, knowing it could be months before she saw him again.

"I promise, I will. Someday soon! In the meantime, I'll take care of you."

William kissed Anna and departed. As soon as he was out of her sight, he allowed himself to feel the deep agitation this unplanned event caused. He jumped into his carriage and rudely urged the driver on to his downtown office.

Damn the time, I've got work to do!

Sitting back in the carriage, he restrained himself from ripping off his top hat and smashing it to smithereens against the seat.

Remarriage is not part of my plans! This couldn't have come at a worse time! I'm really losing my head... Yet I've no time for a wife and second family at this, the pinnacle of my business and political career! She must *keep the child a secret!*

By the time William arrived in his office, he knew what to do.

It's the only way to ensure maximum privacy.

Within an hour, he sent several telegrams to Paris to get things moving, and then wrote a long letter of instructions authorizing the trusted Pelletier to full action.

When the La Chappelle sisters arrived in Paris weeks later, they discovered Cervellon had received an unwanted visit that morning. She reluctantly filled them in on the major change in plans.

Pelletier had arrived unexpectedly. Barely seating himself, he said, "Mademoiselle La Chappelle's health and happiness are being taken under the most careful consideration, I assure you. Every effort will be made to ensure she feels at home in a rented villa—"

"A villa? *Where* is this villa? Within a day's drive, I hope!"

Cervellon had inquired casually only because she was loathe to be far away from the city in the winter. She had no intention of going north.

"No, madame. The villa is located in the French colony of Algeria."

"What! Are you serious?"

Cervellon uncharacteristically lost her composure. Her normally sweetly animated face went still in concentration.

"Monsieur Clark wants Anna to give birth in *Africa*? In a mere colony? I cannot believe this! This is *outrageous*! You must be mistaken!"

"Believe it, madame. The matter has been in motion for some time now. It is entirely settled to Monsieur Clark's satisfaction. If you will allow me to explain, every effort has been made to ensure the future mother's safety and comfort."

Cervellon sat forward with great energy, needlework dropping to the floor.

"Well, those are pretty words when it's Algeria we're speaking of! The back of beyond! Decades of fighting and local protests." She shuddered. "A mere colony far away from Paris! Far away from everything and everyone! She might as well be sent to the moon to give birth! And it's Monsieur Clark's own child! Mademoiselle La Chappelle is not a pariah to be cast off!"

Cervellon's eyes fixed on the prim secretary dressed in a black wool three-piece suit and gold-rimmed glasses. Pelletier bore a nonplussed expression. She restrained herself from reaching out to slap him.

Pelletier continued in a smooth, bland tone, "The villa will be fully staffed by French-speaking servants. A private doctor, two nurses, a midwife, and a wet nurse will be on hand several weeks before the due date. Orders from the best Parisian and English merchants—medical supplies, infant clothing, what have you—will arrive within the next six weeks. It is arranged that Mademoiselle La Chappelle will be offered every luxury and comfort a new mother requires."

Pelletier paused, warily eyeing the woman who threatened to turn into a harpy.

"And for your safety, a small team of bodyguards will also accompany the party down to Algeria. Does that satisfy, madame?"

Cervellon rose from her chair as if to strike. A carefully concealed temper surfaced.

"*My* safety!" She pointed to her chest. "So, *I* must go to Algeria as well? Without being asked beforehand? I find this intolerable! I've not consented to this!"

"Are you submitting your resignation, madame?" He smiled expectantly.

Cervellon's eyes narrowed.

"No, Monsieur Pelletier, I am *not*! However, I don't mind saying that the idea of such extreme secrecy had never entered my mind as necessary. Madame Bouchard and her staff have never spread tales! It is common for men to have lovers in Paris. You know this perfectly well! Why all the cloak and dagger?"

"Then the matter is settled. You will leave in forty-eight hours."

Pelletier set down a package of tickets and paper bills. He rose to depart without looking at her or taking leave. As he exited the room, Cervellon held herself back from screaming an obscenity.

"We'll be leaving for Algeria very soon... And that my dear, is the extent of the information I'm privy to. I'm sorry."

Cervellon reached a hand to take Anna's limp one. Anna, already exhausted from the intercontinental journey while pregnant, grew even more pale and quiet. Amelia was the first to speak. She looked in confusion first at Anna then Cervellon.

"Africa! I know it's only across the Mediterranean, but, uh, no.... It's been a whirlwind of fun traveling to Paris. But the prospect of Africa is simply *too* overwhelming. Sister, your life is dramatic, I must say."

The next day Amelia departed for England while Anna and Cervellon directed packing for the extended trip. To deflect attention, they made a point to not leave the flat. Everything was kept on a strict need-to-know basis. In the predawn hours, they headed south to Marseille where they would board a ship to cross the Mediterranean.

Meanwhile, Cervellon did her best to lift Anna's flagging spirits. It was clear the withdrawn young lady had her suspicions now as well.

Were we both mistaken about the man?

On the train, Cervellon said, "A little mystery about one's whereabouts will hurt no one's reputation *if* one knows how to field the questions correctly. You shall be a surprise! You won't be boring, predictable, perpetually at home. Therefore, people will wonder where you went... All shall be well upon our return. In fact, in time you'll receive more invitations due to our foreign travels, not less. Mark my words!"

Cervellon nodded in absolute surety of how society thought underneath the façade.

"Is it such a terrible thing to him that I've fallen pregnant...? Is Algeria even safe...? If he loved me, how could he send me to an unsafe place to give birth?" Anna uttered an agonized cry, pressing hasty fingers over wet eyelids. "Oh, I hate these tears! All I do is cry like a baby these days!"

"Yes, I believe it's safe... Many French live there... It will be an adventure! We shall be more than fine. I cannot tell you what Monsieur Clark is thinking, however, at the moment, put *all such worries* out of your pretty head. Only pay attention to how well he is taking care of us. All is very well!"

Cervellon kissed Anna on the top of her head before opening a book to keep quiet a while.

Anna will detect falseness in my tone if I'm not careful.

August 13, 1902

Villa-sur-Mer, Cap Mâtifou, Algérie

Despite the enervating heat, twenty-four-year-old Anna had an easy delivery. Louise Amelia Andrée was a healthy, cherubic newborn with a small tuft of brunette hair. Anna made sure the surname Clark was written on the birth certificate.

Anna had never longed to have children, but now a mother, she was enraptured. While convalescing, she wrote William long letters explaining the joy of holding their daughter. She requested her sister and Cervellon should be godmothers.

Several days later, Cervellon sat drinking coffee with Anna in the cool of the early morning. "Are you going to race back to Paris now?"

"As a matter of fact, no."

Anna lifted her chin while smoothing the linen duvet. Like a queen, she sat in the center of an enormous canopy bed against white linen pillows trimmed with lace.

"That is *precisely* what William expects because of my initial letters of complaint. But Algeria has grown on me. And I want to make him wonder, frankly! So, I've no intentions of returning to Paris at the moment."

"I see! And so I'm captive here with you, is that it?"

A smile spread across her agreeable face.

"Absolutely not! Return to Paris if you please. But I will remain here, for awhile at least. William will not expect that. I want to make him squirm."

"That means I have to write to that awful man, Pelletier."

Cervellon's pleasant expression turned into a deep scowl and Anna laughed.

To her surprise, Anna reveled in the yellow villa facing the Mediterranean Sea. The well-designed house had dense stone walls protecting from the brunt of the scorching North African sun. Soaring ceilings, with rooms around a central courtyard open to the sky and deep awnings outside windows, created a cool interior. The Moorish style villa had over one hundred rooms. Local servants explained an eccentric Englishman built it in the first flush of French conquest, but never lived in it. It was eventually sold to a Frenchman based in Morocco.

A servant named Imane, a middle-aged Algerian woman wearing a voluminous white *haik,* became Anna's favorite attendant. Throughout the delivery, Imane dabbed Anna with a cool washcloth and hummed soothing songs. She had almond-shaped brown eyes lightly rimmed with kohl, a highly capable air, and endless patience with the newborn. Imane rarely spoke, and her limited French was heavily accented, but she doted on Andrée.

Anna respected Imane's soothing presence so well she worried about the widowed woman's future. "But what would Imane do in Paris? It would be too brutal, with motorcars bleating, crowds of people, and cold winters. I couldn't take her away from Africa's warmth. What say you, Madame de Cervellon?"

"*Je ne sais pas...*"

Cervellon lay with closed eyes on a chaise on a darkened balcony late in the evening. Wrought-iron lanterns cast geometric shapes onto the warm tile floor. She adored Algeria's quiet, cool nights.

"I shall leave her with money, so Imane can buy her own house. That's what I shall do to show my gratitude!"

"Write to William. He'll take care of it for you," assured Cervellon, waving a hand dismissively.

During the ten-month stay, the villa fostered rest and absolute privacy. For exercise, Anna walked around the interior courtyard or in the exterior gardens. Surrounded by one hundred acres of private parkland, it was situated on a high bluff commanding a spectacular view of the sea. Anna was delighted by the soaring arches, tall water fountains, colorful mosaics, and inner courtyard.

"This villa is *marvelous*," Cervellon sighed. "I assumed Algeria would prove despicable. But the weather has been beautiful! However, you've not spent any significant time in Provence, Anna. You'll have to come visit me there after I've purchased my farmhouse. I've one in mind, a special one, and I'm prepared to purchase it. I'm negotiating with the elderly landowner now. *She's* not so delightful, however. She keeps raising the price."

She frowned at the memory of the hard-bargaining woman and then laughed once she noticed Anna's eyes on her. She took a sip of lemonade, and then reached for a small piece of *tamina*.

"How lovely for you! But I didn't realize it was happening so soon. Does this mean you're leaving me?"

"Not for a bit more. Wait until I get my farmhouse settled. We'll see how things play out with Monsieur Clark. He's ready, I believe."

"Oh, you think so? Which explains why he has packed me off to Africa to give birth!" Anna gave a rueful laugh and shook her head. "He's not ready."

Anna looked off to the horizon as the sun set in another spectacular array of coral, salmon, and gold over the Bay of Algiers. She pondered for a long moment their two different life situations. It hadn't hit her with such force until this moment. She entirely depended upon William.

She suddenly longed to be in Cervellon's shoes. To be independent. She didn't like feeling unsure he would marry her in the future or, worse, might die before he acquiesced! Anna was troubled the most by living life under a small cloud of doubt. William treated her no less than a wife, even if Africa initially grated.

"You're the best friend anyone could ask for. What sort of housewarming gift would you like? You must give me some ideas. I know you abhor silly, nonsensical gifts."

"I'd like a few of these hardworking Algerian gardeners to come work for me... How they manage the roses in this heat, I cannot figure out."

"Consider it done! We'll have the bodyguards kidnap the lot, ship them north, and offer double pay to put up with your demands. Which, therefore, will make you the premiere gardener in the village as soon as the deal goes through. Anything for you, my dear chaperone."

Anna began laughing. Cervellon smirked and rose to stretch. She motioned for Anna to rise for their evening stroll.

In late October, they returned to Paris. Soon after, Anna was not surprised that an impatient William took the next ship across the Atlantic.

"My little plan worked, didn't it?" she said to Cervellon.

As soon as William arrived, he burst in with even more energy than usual. The aging butler was almost knocked down in William's zeal to see baby Andrée. He went immediately to the indicated drawing room.

"Where is my baby girl...? There she is! Of course, she's a lovely, lovely girl," he cooed. He rocked the infant in his arms. Rather than be offended he bypassed her, Anna was pleased at his fatherly enthusiasm.

William looked down at the tiny face. Dark blue eyes watched him with a serious expression. He reflected quietly, "It's been so many years since I've held a child of my own. This takes me back. My love, you've done well."

He reached an arm to draw Anna in for a kiss. She glowed with happiness.

"It's about time you notice me!"

"How could I not, my love? You're radiantly beautiful. And look at our daughter!"

"I didn't know I could be this happy." She gazed at the baby in his arms.

"It shows. You're more gorgeous than ever," William said, kissing Anna's forehead.

It had previously been arranged with the newly promoted Bishop D'Souza to have the baby christened privately with William present. Due to long-time patronage and Anna's devoutness in attending Mass, the bishop only required

Anna's confession. Having met William previously, the empathetic bishop did not press the obvious issue of the child's illegitimacy.

That night, Anna slept in the master suite, typically waiting long hours due to William working. She was restless but knew better than to bother him. *I detest when he's short with me.*

In the large four poster bed, Anna yawned and stretched. One hand went underneath the pillow on William's side. She flinched when hard metal brushed against her skin; she hastily withdrew her hand. Confused, she lifted the pillow. There lay a large revolver.

The chamber was full of bullets!

Is he going to kill me in his own bed?

Anna jumped up, put on a robe, and retrieved the revolver. As she was about to leave the bedroom, in walked William.

"Hello, my love, I expected you to be sleeping, but here you are ready to shoot me!" He lifted hands in mock horror.

"*Moi?* Shoot *you?* You're going to shoot me! What's this doing under your pillow, *s'il te plaît?*"

With wild eyes, Anna shook the gun. Her voice had a thicker Quebecois accent, not as refined as the Parisian accent she long cultivated.

"Careful, my pet! Please put the gun down." His eyes pleaded.

"*Non.* What does this mean?" She thrust the revolver forward.

"I can explain, don't be upset. It's a habit I can't shake from frontier days. I haven't told you most of those stories, but it was pretty rough, very violent. I saw plenty of good men die in dirty circumstances. I was threatened numerous times.

"I now have a fear of being ambushed at night. They come for you when you're sleeping, see? It almost happened to me, twice!" He put a hand out for the gun. "It's always been there, every night no matter where I am... This entire time... Put the gun down, my love, please..."

She paused, warily eyeing him. The hand that held the gun slowly lowered.

"So, you have no intention to murder me?"

William threw back his head and laughed heartily, his slender body shaking with laughter. Anna was taken off guard by his reaction. Then she began laughing at the ridiculousness of asking such questions. If he wanted to kill her, it would have been done long before tonight. Still chuckling, she moved to place the revolver on the side table.

"Anna Eugenia, your high spirits keep me entertained, which is why I absolutely adore and love you. Come here!"

Once Cervellon moved to Provence, Anna was the undisputed *chatelaine* of *6, avenue Mac-Mahon*. Motherhood boosted her confidence and altered her outlook. Bouchard learned to not cross the young mistress, whom she began pointedly addressing "Madame Clark" to urge the master along with his duty.

Anna willed herself to become a respected lady of sophistication accepted by all in the neighborhood. Only those with sharp ears could detect in her French a tone not quite native born. Her devotion to the Catholic Church protected wagging tongues from enquiring too loudly regarding her background. Like any self-respecting Frenchwoman, Anna did not stop to regard gossip. She kept her own counsel and surrounded herself protectively with cultural and musical endeavors.

From head-to-toe, Anna wore the latest season's *haute couture*. She frequented all the best *couturiers*, shoemakers, furriers, and milliners. William assured no bespoke creation of the season was out-of-bounds. As the years passed, he likewise grew her jewelry collection with Cartier and Tiffany's. He was turning everything Anna touched to gold. She possessed everything imaginable for a fine lady in 18 to 22 karat gold or platinum: jewel-encrusted bracelets, necklaces, rings, earrings, hair combs, and watches.

On Anna's desk and stashed in drawers were a plethora of solid gold items: Cartier fountain pen; Tiffany letter opener; safety pins; manicure set. A full-size, Tiffany toiletry case—a Christmas gift from William—was engraved with her initials on a solid gold plate.

Sometimes Anna received gold items as little gifts, and on other occasions Bouchard was ordered to upgrade things to enhance Anna's comfort and lifestyle. In time, the master bath's plumbing fixtures were switched to gold—to the absolute astonishment of the servants—and the copper tub in the master bath rejected in favor of a solid hunk of pink Carrera marble.

One afternoon while overseeing the cleaning of her mistress's bedroom, Bouchard counted another thirty-odd other gold items or jewelry now in Anna's possession. The housekeeper had never seen anything like it. *Monsieur Clark is a modern-day Midas...*

When Anna discovered she was pregnant again a mere half-year after giving birth to Andrée, she was delighted. The second pregnancy was as easy as her first. Due to not a whisper of rumors impacting his various interests in the United States, William didn't object to Anna remaining at home for the birth.

On a morning of a hard frost in the late fall of 1903, the labor began. The Christmas season approached, and William was due for another visit. Anna was pleased the baby would arrive in time. Overall, the experience was easier than birthing Andrée, despite a large loss of blood. Anna held the newborn boy with red hair on her chest for a few exhausted moments before handing him over to the nurse. She was elated it was a male.

William will be happy to have another son after the unexpected death of his youngest. I'll name him Paul Pierre Andrews Clark.

The midwife's strong hands massaged her stomach to expel the afterbirth, and Anna was given a sponge bath before soiled bedsheets were changed. She fell into an exhausted sleep. Only an hour later, she was awakened abruptly by noises and muffled cries. The nurse and midwife scurried around. The newborn Paul had turned an unnatural color. He gasped and struggled for breath; tiny limbs feebly jerked his distress.

"Oh no! It can't be! The wee thing!" said one elderly nurse.

The nurses' backs were to Anna. She could see nothing.

"What's happening?"

One elderly nurse turned with a reddened face and downcast eyes underneath a large lace bonnet.

"Madame, I... I cannot revive the baby."

"What do you mean?"

Anna struggled to lift her head.

"I'm so sorry, so sorry... I believe the baby has died."

"Died!" Anna croaked. "You *must* be mistaken... Give him to me!"

She extended a hand but lay helpless. With flagging energy, she ordered them to call for Bouchard.

"Call back the doctor at once!" Bouchard said, ordering everyone out before setting the swaddled body by Anna.

Anna was sickened by the blue face.

"No, no, no! This can't be happening! He was healthy..."

She lifted the tiny body, patting its back, attempting to get the baby to breathe or to cry out.

It was no use.

At first, she cried herself into a numb state; then, as energy returned, her grief swelled to enormous proportions. She was inconsolable baby Paul had died so soon. She longed for William. Only one-year-old Andrée, eventually placed on the side of the canopied bed by the nanny, caused her to alter dark thoughts.

Anna reached out to hold her little girl, overwhelmed with gratitude for Andrée's strong body and gleeful smiles.

"*Merci*! Thank you for bringing her to me. She is exactly what I need at this moment!"

Andrée's little arms clasped her mother's reclining body.

"I must look at the joys in life, not merely the sorrows."

William's visit over the holidays was over before Anna was ready to relinquish him. He left in January, and she cried from loneliness as soon as his 1903 Berliet 20CV Demi Limousine zipped away.

It's impossible for me to return now. My life would change for the worse if I were to go to America with a child and no public mention of a wedding.

Wiping away tears, Anna felt determined.

I'll never subject Andrée to that kind of prejudice.

By April, Anna was concerned because for weeks she had no letters from William. She was prone to imagine the worst. Soon a telegram jolted her further. Two sentences provided days' worth of intense worry:

I've been ill STOP Will write soon STOP WAC.

It was another week before a letter arrived in his own hand. It explained he had had mastoiditis; a high fever kept him in bed for weeks, including a hospital stay. He omitted confessing the worst: He had undergone two surgeries already.

Now in his early sixties, William's doctor and children were stressing full retirement. The newspapers enraged him by having a field day predicting his early demise. However, privately, William still felt poorly. He wanted to ensure his good health wasn't in jeopardy. Doctors urged the senator to take time off from working fourteen-hour days.

Therefore, I booked a seven-week cruise on the Mediterranean this coming month, and I would like you to accompany me. It will put the finishing touch on reenergizing my body after this unexpected ordeal. I am heartily sick of doctors and lying abed. I am too young yet for the sickbed!

With your lovely person by my side, I know I will be feeling tip-top in no time at all. I hope you will agree. As a mother, I imagine you will miss our daughter very much, my love. However, I need you at this time more than ever.

Yours ever in love, William

Anna was delighted at the prospect of a cruise from May through the third week of June. *We've never spent such a long stretch of time together under conditions of pure recreation and relaxation.*

With only 250 passengers and luxury accommodations fit for royalty, the cruise went on with weeks of sunny, mild weather. There were entertainments every evening, and day excursions to various famous cities and islands ringing the Mediterranean. Passengers assumed the intimate couple were a May-December pairing who were on their honeymoon. Accordingly, they were largely left to themselves.

Within days, Anna understood William had greatly downplayed the severity of his illness. She was alarmed; he wasn't as he was formerly, vital and in constant motion. Diminished, William appeared older. He was more apt to speak and walk slowly. He also needed naps, which Anna had never witnessed.

Despite the naysayers, William and Anna were well-suited. They had no trouble getting along or deciding how to occupy their day onshore. After weeks onboard, the steady sun, warm sea breezes, and regular meals energized William. To put weight back on, Anna urged him to eat a little more than he liked. She allowed him to relax, placing no demands other than well-timed conversations about getting married. William would resist, retreating to the men's lounge for hours. But the sulking soon passed, and he returned in a cheerful mood.

One night toward the end of the cruise, as they gazed at the stars while docked in Alexandria's harbor, William reached to take Anna's hand.

"I'm sorry for my stubbornness and pride. I love you, my darling, and want to marry you. I don't have a ring with me, as this impromptu request is coming from my heart not my head, but I'm now prepared to make you my wife."

"William, I don't care about another ring! You've already given me a dozen!"

Anna's arms went around his neck, and suddenly she could barely squeeze out a muffled "*Oui*."

"I think I heard yes, *mon amour*, correct?"

"*Oui, oui, oui!* Of course I'll marry you! I want nothing more than to be your wife."

Heart bursting, she kissed him. He returned her kiss passionately.

Then in a dry tone he remarked, "Well, I figured you would say yes... You've seemed very happy in my Paris flat all these years."

"William! Don't joke at such a tender moment," Anna lightly smacked his chest, her eyes glistening with tears. "I'm marrying *you*, not a flat."

"But it helps my case, correct?" he chuckled, never resisting an opportunity to become a blowhard about his wealth.

After eleven years, William trusted Anna implicitly. She was faithful and discreet. *I*

f not, ugliness would have reared its head well before now. I've experienced too many avaricious women to not discern Anna's integrity long ago.

"I want our union officially recognized to bring you to live with me in my new house in New York. I want a proper and perfect mistress of my mansion, and you will do splendidly, my dove. When the house is completed, perhaps in two more years. There is still much to be done to the interior, and like a fool I keep adding to the plans... Yet, I want it to be perfect!

"How does that sound, to be mistress of the finest mansion on Fifth Avenue?"

He gazed at her lovingly, tucking a stray brunette lock behind an ear.

"Well, I don't want to leave Paris. I'm very content there, as you know. But of course, I'll visit you in America and preside over any social gathering for as long as you need me."

Anna's mood turned somber at the thought of residing in New York.

A cesspool of modernity compared to Paris.

"I understand, and I wouldn't dream of tearing you away from France for good. However, I want my daughter reared as an American who knows her own country and language. I'm a senator in the finest country in the world!"

They rose, and his arm went around Anna's trim waist as they stopped at the railing to gaze upwards. The moon reflected softly on the waves lapping against the ship. The repetitive movement lulled the pair into quiet reflection.

What William neglected to explain was the conniving opposition to a second marriage he had suffered at the hands of his adult daughters. Preserving his legacy was paramount, yet it surprised him how much Anna was becoming key to his happiness. She made him feel virile and youthful, able to tackle head-on the cut-throat nature of American capitalism.

I'm confident the family dynamics will all work themselves out; my family life won't be disrupted for long.

On William's next visit to Paris that fall, the sensitive issue took some time to rear its head. First, the couple enjoyed attending the *Salon d'Automne* at the Grand Palais, a must-see in the art world. The couple went back a second day to take in all the latest *avant-garde* artworks. William said little, striding from one shocking canvas to the next. Anna conferred with him on perhaps adding to their art collection with several young artists.

"Sometimes, I rather enjoy modernism!" she said to William, who looked away in disgust.

The next day, William asked Anna into the library to sign a document detailing a one-million-dollar gift and rights to all jewelry, art, furniture, and other personal property she acquired during their union. She was not completely taken aback;

he already explained months earlier she would have no legal right to any portion of his estate.

What if William dies soon, and I'm kicked out by his children? Non, *I'll be alright. I've my personal money. I can always sell the jewels as well.*

Anna's hand hovered over the document in hesitation.

"Is there anything amiss, my love?"

"*Non,* I'm merely reading slowly."

I'll sign it, and hope everything works out in my favor.

Seated at his antique English oak desk, William tenderly observed his wife. With a lawyer as witness, he had spent quite some time explaining the purpose of the legal document.

"Don't fear to sign this, my heart. It's to placate my children because my second marriage is unexpected. I'll take care of you."

Months earlier, in July 1904, William made the official announcement regarding his second marriage and two-year-old daughter. The American press went wild. Speculating headlines abounded. In the Social Register, Anna and Andrée's names were immediately listed alongside Senator William A. Clark's.

It was almost too much to be borne for Mary Culver and Katherine Morris. Each woman had only recently discovered her father's altered status before the official announcement. Letters were immediately exchanged. A plan emerged demanding a legal agreement to safeguard the estate from their new stepmother, however much it galled to use that title.

The driving force behind the request was Mary and Katherine's iron wills. Charlie and Will Jr.—intelligent and cultured philanderers—were far too busy on the other side of the country enjoying life.

"Who are we to bother with berating Father for marrying a much younger woman?" The sons merely agreed to the necessity of a legal document blocking any financial interference with the estate.

Which is how William found himself in the presence of Mary and Katherine in the Navarro Flats library. He sat down in an overstuffed leather chair, regarding his daughters gravely, wordlessly. He had no patience being put on trial by anyone, least of all by the women in his family.

Mary began, "I had my heart set on living at your house on Fifth Avenue! We made such perfect plans, didn't we, Daddy? It has all been in place for years. I had such high hopes. But with your surprise second marriage... I will now have to completely alter my family's life! And that will be *most disagreeable* as all our expectations will have to be rearranged. But we were *so looking forward* to living with you, Daddy."

"May dearie, you already have a lovely house to entertain in," said William. "I think you can do without mine as well."

Mary's mouth turned down. She was almost hysterical on the discovery not merely of the second marriage, but of a half-sister less than two years of age! The existence of the child proved their father's virility, which came as quite a shock after his recent brush with death. The pile of inherited gold diminished before her very eyes.

What if there were yet more children? Mary stopped her tears with one look at her father's cold stare. Time for reinforcements and for blame to fall on Katherine, as well. She glared at her younger sister.

Katherine hesitated and leaned forward, her voice lowered to placate. "Yes, Father, please don't be discomfited at our displeasure. It is only from shock, you must understand. Forgive May and me... Of course, we are delighted we have a new sister..."

Mary always puts me in a bad light! What can I say more about our diminished inheritance?

Katherine Stauffer Clark Morris had been married only a handful of years to Dr. Lewis Rutherford Morris of Manor House. His was a prestigious lineage which boasted a signer of the Declaration of Independence. The Continental Congress had given the Manor House and acreage to the decorated family.

Clark was bursting with pride when Katherine became engaged in 1899 to such a member of the American aristocracy. He rewarded her accordingly with lavish gifts.

Mr. and Mrs. Morris had ambitious plans for the 1300-acre family estate in Butternut Valley of Upstate New York. The 6-bedroom, 5.5 bath colonial manor house was upgraded but retained its historical character of 1805. The small family—Katherine had only one daughter—spent summers and early fall at the estate. With the infusion of Clark gold in 1900—Clark's wedding gifts to the couple were: $3,000,000 in cash; a wedding for 6,000 guests costing over $1,000,000; and a honeymoon of a private yacht tour of the Atlantic seaboard and Europe—the estate grounds were soon elevated from a not very productive, rural farm to a teeming country estate. Mr. Morris all but retired from the medical profession to turn himself into the epitome of a country gentleman.

The Morris's master plan included many upgrades and new additions. Along with improved barns for livestock, the estate needed a greenhouse with potting shed, tennis court, and Annex building. The Annex's great hall with fieldstone fireplace and a room with bowling lanes would be used for entertaining large groups. A four-car garage was built to accommodate quarters above for chauffer, estate manager, and other key male personnel. Other smaller buildings would be erected for the numerous staff now needed. A kennel for breeding and housing dogs, and state-of-the-art stables spoke to the couple's expensive hobbies.

To beautify the landscape, a project was undertaken to build a dam to create a pond from Morris Brook. Other outbuildings to harvest, process, and transport meat, dairy, fruit, honey, vegetables, and flowers to other locales spoke to the prosperous nature of the enhanced estate.

Such prosperity was expensive. Katherine had need of protecting every dollar owed.

"This new marriage and knowledge of a child upsets only because it has been sprung on us without warning! Please forgive our emotion, because we have clearly been left very much in the dark regarding your personal matters. And that is not fair, Daddy.

"However, we love you and will support you. We want nothing but your happiness. This legal document will prove that your second wife is not a fortune-hunter. We beg you to consider the wisdom in providing us with that comfort. And the protection it will give us, the *rightful beneficiaries* of your hard-earned wealth, your children from our own dear departed mother, of whose beloved name I, and your granddaughter, bear..."

William looked from his daughters down to his lap. He traced the pant crease of a dove grey suit with ivory silk vest while feeling conflicting emotions of love and anger at their interference. It felt almost too low to bring up his first wife as if he had forgotten that wonderful woman. William knew Anna's heart, but his daughters were not listening.

He had long suspected his vast empire of mining, real estate, and businesses was at risk of being sold off the moment he died. *They must not sell the goose that lays the golden eggs. That lesson I was never able to adequately teach, and perhaps that was my fault.*

He knew he had been far too anxious to control his business empire to the exclusion of everyone else. To relinquish control would be enervating. Devastating to his self-concept.

It was implicitly understood what was at stake: The second generation of Clarks required every bit of that vast wealth to remain at the pinnacle of the American aristocracy of the industrial age in which they were born. *And I would not dream of excluding them from that birthright. I applaud them for their ambition. However, I feel I have provided more than adequately not only for my children, but my grandchildren and great-grandchildren as well.*

Since William alone was privy to all—he alone knew *all* his bank account balances, assets, stocks, and the overall value of holdings that made him the second richest man in America—*I'll take advantage of their willful ignorance.*

The following day William asked to be driven to a bank. He had never done business there, but recently he had heard positive reports. He went inside, and the staff began falling all over themselves to accommodate Senator Clark. He requested to see the bank's manager, impatiently waving away offered beverages and cigars.

The bank manager, Edward Cashton III, entered in less than a minute of Senator Clark seating himself in the oak paneled conference room. Cashton moved forward as if walking before deity. In his mind, he was in the presence of one. Cashton's head full of numbers swirled with possibilities of even greater figures, vast sums.

To do business with such a titan would honor me!

William brushed off pleasantries. He explained to the bank manager—wearing a navy blue three-piece wool suit and tortoise shell glasses—his purpose in coming.

"Mr. Cashton, will you oblige me by keeping this out of the press, whether now or in ten years?"

"We strive for that secure reputation with all our clients, sir."

"Excellent. I want to open a private account for my wife, Mrs. Anna Clark. I'll start by depositing one million dollars... Do you have a fountain pen handy?"

William set two leather-bound books on the polished wood table. Only the bank manager's lips visibly fluttered at the proposed initial deposit amount, the sole indication other than a deferential manner that he was aroused by fiscal envy. Money was the only god he worshipped.

Cashton almost forgot to hand Senator Clark a pen while dark brown eyes fixed themselves on the checkbooks.

The power!

William opened the first book; he wrote a check for one million dollars.

"I require two receipts of the deposit of this check, Mr. Cashton."

"Very good, Senator Clark. I will see to it myself."

The bank manager then witnessed William closing the first book and opening the second; he again wrote a check.

"I will now make a second deposit that will be kept confidential between you and me. I require *absolute confidentiality*, as I've already indicated. I require only one receipt of this second deposit."

Cashton momentarily lost all ability to speak as he looked down at the second check cradled in long fingers. It was for millions. The bank manager's fingers caressed the edges of the two checks, marveling at the absolute ease with which the man doled out such princely sums.

William then signed paperwork declaring Anna E. Clark as the sole owner of said account on the date of July 8, 1904. Ensuring his second wife's future security was a non-issue; it was now within his right as her husband.

He walked out of the bank with a spring back in his step. Now it didn't matter what his will stated. And, as William wasn't inclined to intimate conversation with his offspring, no one suspected what he had done until it was too late.

Months later in Paris, Anna was informed of the private account with millions in her name only after she signed the financial document cutting her off from any claim to the estate at his death. William wanted to test her to discern whether she trusted him. He looked benevolently at Anna as he observed the dumb-founded expression on her face ease into an incredulous smile.

"Oh, I thought I had lost out a little, but you have given me so much already, how could I expect more? And look how you've privately more than made up for the loss without upsetting any of your older children! How clever of you, *mon amour!*"

"You're now a very rich woman in your own right. As primary account holder, you have full access to the money in the account. No one knows of its existence but us and the bank. I recommend you not use the money, as I pay for your care, and willingly. Nevertheless, the fortune is yours. Keep in mind I won't replenish it if it's spent frivolously."

Anna went around the desk to sit on William's lap, gently yanking his bushy, whitening whiskers. She then put arms around his neck and heartily kissed his cheek. He chuckled at her playfulness, reveling in her caresses.

"Is that all I get for all this trouble? A mere kiss on the cheek?"

"William! You're incorrigible! What a legal mess I'll be in if any of your children find out! I'll become the wicked witch of France!"

"Oh, but you already are!" He chuckled. "But don't worry. They won't find out, I assure you, my love. They know very little of my business dealings because, alas, none of them is interested in taking over after my demise. They're too busy spending the money I make!"

William kissed her. "You're my legal wife now that we've been married by Bishop D'Souza. I've no intention of dying any time soon. You're stuck with me. Does that make you happy?"

"*Oui*, I'm happy! And for you, yes, I'm most grateful. What a wonderful life you've given me. *Je t'aime.*"

As he drew her closer, Anna rewarded him with a far better kiss.

Three months later, descending from the *Kronprinz Wilhelm* in New York harbor, Anna made her American debut as a married woman. She wasn't looking forward to the trip, and she missed her daughter as soon as they departed. Too young to travel, little Andrée had been left in Paris.

The newspapers dragged out the six-month-old story that Senator Clark's expatriate bride, the surprise second wife and mother of yet another Clark heir, had finally arrived on America's shores. Young, beautiful Anna thrilled the waiting journalists by appearing swathed in dark brown Russian sable from head-to-toe.

"Mrs. Anna Clark doesn't disappoint, boys!"

Instead of going to Navarro Hills, William ordered the chauffeur up Fifth Avenue. He jumped from the vehicle as soon as it glided to a stop. He reached out a hand to help Anna.

"It's several years from completion, because there remains a lot of detailed, interior work only the best craftsmen can do. However, I'm pleased with the progress thus far."

Anna glanced upwards. She felt momentarily dizzy. "How many stories is this house? Are you sure you're not building a hotel? Am I going to have to sit behind a front desk to admit guests?" Anna laughed.

William, absorbed in checking the detail on masonry work above, didn't hear. "In a moment, Anna..."

The façade was imposing, gleefully proclaiming its riches as each ornate story climbed higher up above the city skyline. Anna counted nine.

"William, dear, this is a palace not a home... And it's not completed?"

Her heart sank. The ornate mansion wasn't to her taste, but she knew William was proud. *I won't allow any complaint to disturb his pleasure.*

The tour took place on the lowest three floors due to many scaffolds, drop cloths, marble slabs, missing staircases, and large piles of materials and scattered tools. Workmen stopped and retreated wherever they went. The dust and the noise were overwhelming in some areas.

William raised a congenial hand but did not speak; his eyes roved the walls and ceilings in inspection. He then took a few minutes to speak with an architect and construction foreman over blueprints while Anna gazed around herself in wonder.

I can't imagine living in this house; it doesn't feel real.

While describing plans, William's head moved from side to side, taking it all in, arms waving, and legs moving ahead at a rapid pace. He talked incessantly about the overall design and purpose which kept enlarging. His expression grew serious, eyes sharp. He oversaw every detail.

"It's as if the house is directing me, my darling. Not vice versa. I'm merely the conduit for art to be born architecturally. I'm no painter or musician, but I can pay for superb architecture. I want this house to stand out. I want its four galleries to be the caretaker of some of the finest masterpieces in Western art. This house is destined to become one of the greatest jewels of New York City. My legacy..."

This driven side of William Anna had never witnessed in person. She knew it existed, but she had only seen him quietly engrossed in ledgers and paperwork. Until now, she had no idea how much William had invested both spiritually and materially in the building of his mansion.

It was the height of the season, and the Clarks were going to *Faust*. Many eyes would have glasses out at the Metropolitan Opera House at 1411 Broadway, roaming the audience looking for tidbits of gossip to pass along afterward. William paid dearly for membership with a seasonal box. He was planning on attending a business associate's ball before he went to his club later on that evening, but Anna begged off.

Seated at the vanity, she sighed audibly while a maid held out two couture gowns. Regardless of what she chose, she would outshine those around her. The attention she drew in public overwhelmed. Paris was accustomed to centuries of ostentatious glamor and extreme wealth. Europeans were cosmopolitan, less apt to gape. Not so the Americans.

I want to stay out of the limelight.

William whistled while strolling into the master bedroom's dressing room. He wore white tie with a white rose in his lapel.

"Don't attempt to hide, my love. I buy you these beautiful clothes and jewels so that you'll stand out. Choose the Doucet ivory satin with gold embroidery and wear the emerald and diamond set."

"Oh William, I don't want to make a spectacle of myself!"

"But *I* want you to..." He bent to kiss her forehead and departed, his mind on a deal about to close.

"Oh, it'll be too much..."

In Europe there were always others who eclipsed everyone else in wealth, rank, or sheer notoriety. But New York was different.

My husband is notoriously famous here... I'm treated as if I were a demi-mondaine. Before rising gracefully to dress, Anna moaned softly.

Several weeks after, Anna received a reprieve from social preoccupations when she was rushed to the hospital. That evening, William was at a men's only dinner at one of the four private clubs he was a member of. Upon returning to Navarro Flats after midnight, the butler stopped him at the door.

"What! My wife's in the hospital? Why the devil did no one send word!"

Not waiting to hear the response, he was back in the motorcar in a flash, experiencing uncomfortable associations of Kate's untimely death.

"For Pete's sake, drive faster, man!"

Hours later near dawn, Anna came out of surgery. The doctor said, "The operation to remove her appendix was a success. But your wife is sleeping now. Come back later."

William was crushed he couldn't talk to Anna, but after anxiously popping his head into the room, he retreated. Hours later, Anna smiled weakly as he entered the hospital room scented by many bouquets of pink roses.

"I'm sorry to have caused so much trouble!"

"Nonsense. I'm relieved you're well! The doctor said you need to spend two more weeks resting, but that you'll recover splendidly. Are you in pain?"

Anna motioned to her torso. "I'll most likely have a terrible scar. It feels dreadful."

William sat down beside the iron posted bed. "You're strong, my darling. All will be okay. Only don't read the newspapers for the next week. Your imminent death is being trumpeted from the housetops. The fools!"

"I'll miss May's wedding."

"Oh, that's no matter. The union will be of no account, mark my words. I'm not sure what I think about the man, nor of his conduct cavorting with a married woman. However, I've already talked to May about my displeasure. She insists on going through with the marriage. She'll receive no gift from me."

At the end of February, Anna had recovered sufficiently to travel to Washington D.C. for Theodore Roosevelt's inauguration to a second term as president. William wouldn't miss it for anything. They stayed at his mansion surrounded by dark woods in an historic district. Anna was amused the three-story house with tall white columns and a circular drive was positively plain and small in comparison to the one she had recently toured in New York.

On March 4, the day of the inauguration, the parade was stirring. The mounted Rough Riders surrounded Roosevelt standing in a landau with a few other politicians. Anna marveled at the patriotic American zeal in the boisterous crowds with their optimistic fervor. Roosevelt seemed to mirror the enthusiastic energy with a beaming smile, shining, chubby cheeks, and periodically raised hands in acknowledgement of the cheers.

"He looks too young to have such a powerful position."

William doffed his top hat as the president's landau rolled by. The two men with enormous frontier experience had had their differences, clashing on multiple issues dealing with how to best utilize America's vast natural resources.

"Looks can be deceiving!"

Anna still walked slowly and William observed her anxiously before lessening his robust stride. He took Anna's arm to steer her to the seats reserved for senators.

"The parade and swearing-in ceremony are being filmed for posterity, to be archived in the Library of Congress. Our seats during the ceremony are prominent, but not enough to show up on film, unfortunately. Nevertheless, I'm thrilled to be part of history."

"*Mon cher*, your patriotism is very evident."

"As it should be!"

The weather was cold but there was no snow. Anna wore a large black hat with black feathers and a Russian sable cape and muff over a wool gown. The inaugural ceremony was on a platform erected on the east front of the Capitol. The teeming crowds were electric, but dutifully silent during the swearing-in ceremony. Anna strained to catch a few words in the open air.

That evening, Senator and Mrs. Clark were invited to a large dinner party and then four inaugural balls in historical houses. To Anna's eye, everything was bland, white, and staid. After attending consecutive entertainments by her husband's political allies or enemies—Anna could not tell them apart—the houses, food, people, and conversation all blended into an amorphous mass. There was little originality, beauty, or irony.

Everyone was polite, but the longer she conversed or stood by others, Anna detected slight but incessant sniffs of disapproval.

"This *just* won't do. Oh dear, that man is the very definition of *gauche*," Mrs. J. Thomas Carson's grey head swiveled, and long diamond earrings swayed while observing Senator Clark waltzing with his young wife. She fluttered her feather fan.

"Cousin, how did he ever get elected as senator?" asked Mrs. Andrew Wright.

"Have *you* ever been to Montana? That's how he got elected! By the *rabble...*" said Jackson Everett Lee IV, in Washington solely for the inauguration. He would be on the earliest train back to Georgia in the morning.

Before the evening was over, an unseen curtain descended to shut Anna out. She sensed it intuitively.

Knowing many pair of eyes followed her movements, she deliberately and elegantly adjusted an arm adorned with a white opera-length glove and two, thick diamond bracelets to gently take William's arm. Anna kept close as they strolled out of the crowded ballroom. She leaned to whisper, never allowing her face to drop its mask of *La Gioconda*:

"My love, never leave me alone in these crowds full of vipers."

William covered her hand with his own. *My business concerns will have to wait to be discussed at another time.* "My love, you are 'the star to my wandering bark.' I won't forsake you tonight!"

Anna smiled broadly, making sure her eyes met no one else's. "Ah, my favorite sonnet!" *I won't give these people the satisfaction of knowing how terribly uncomfortable I feel.*

People might be able to sneer at her past, and question the origin of her French accent, but they could find nothing of fault in her present person, wearing a diaphanous blue chiffon Worth gown with tiny diamonds sewn in swirls. Anna glittered from head to toe.

One middle-aged political wife, whose multiple pearl ropes reached to her waist, noted to her elderly companion as eyes swept over Anna: "Impressive. No wonder Senator Clark is so besotted. If I hadn't known anything of Mrs. Clark's reputation previously, I would have assumed she were a member of the French nobility."

The first week of April, Anna was relieved to escape Washington. Ecstatic, she boarded William's private rail car for the multi-day journey west. In Butte, Anna was able to relax in private households and walled gardens, far away from the prying eyes of journalists and society's gossip.

The La Chappelle family met in the matriarch's lovely but much smaller house in the same neighborhood as the Clark mansion. William bought the house after Pierre La Chappelle died; he wanted Philomene—as grandmother of his daughter—to be lifted up in society, retiring from the boardinghouse for good. Arthur still lived with his mother. He had successfully passed his apprenticeship year; the young man prepared for law school.

Philomene said, "It's perfect for me and Arthur, my dear Anna. Please tell Mr. Clark again I'm very happy."

"I'm happy then, *Maman*, if you want to stay in Butte."

"*Oui, bien sûr*. Where else am I to go? To Paris, with you?" She clucked her tongue. "*Imagine! Moi en Paris...* I couldn't stand such finery. I want to stay right here, nursing my bad right hip. Everything has turned out well *pour mes enfants*, and my two girls seem very happy. *Je suis Mémé...*"

Philomene put both her hands up with fingers splayed in a gesture of acceptance. She smiled broadly, with several teeth missing. Philomene's large-knuckled,
calloused hands reached out to grasp both Anna and Amelia's soft, white hands.

Amelia hugged her mother and stood up to serve more tea. "Have some of
these delicious lemon bars, *Maman*. You're losing too much weight. Don't you
like your new cook?"

Looking over at Anna, Amelia knew Clark had recently hired the cook. Anna
nodded in tacit agreement to look into the matter.

"*Maman*, what a pretty house you have made this into. The garden is exquisite."

"*Oui, je suis trés contente dans ma maison, dans mon jardin*. I even enjoy living
alone, although I miss your father... Amelia, leave those doilies alone and come
sit down *avec moi*. I want to talk to my two girls together. This hardly happens...
If only you had brought *ma Andrée*! Why ever did you leave *ma petite en Paris*,
Anna? I would have her here *tout de suite*!"

The older woman looked plaintively at Anna, making her feel guilty.

"William and I had so much to do with traveling and the inauguration, I
couldn't possibly have handled a child during that time. Forgive me."

"Ah, *oui*, it slipped my mind." Philomene made a consoling gesture. "You
attended President Roosevelt's inauguration... I read about it in the newspaper,
but you were there! How important your life now is, *ma fille*."

"Oh, not really. William's life is important. I'm merely his wife."

"I don't accept that! A woman is always important. You'll learn." She nodded
while wagging an arthritic finger. Philomene asked a few pointed questions, as to
her consternation, Anna had omitted large swaths of her life the past few years.
But largely, she was so taken with a photograph of Andrée she didn't pry for long.

"When can you bring her to see me, Anna? *Ma petite est très beau*."

Anna noticed immediately her mother's *Québécois* came out now that
Philomene was relaxed and alone with her children. It reminded Anna of being
a very little girl in Michigan, before the move to Butte. Once the boarding house
was purchased, her savvy mother had quickly learned to use only English.

Two days later on a sunny morning, Anna wrote letters in the morning room. She expected Amelia and Philomene for luncheon. She stopped writing momentarily when she heard people at the front door, then voices approaching down the hall.

It's too early to be them. It's only half past ten.

Timothy Wallace, William's butler for many years, stood erect in the open doorway. He wore a black suit with black and white striped vest. He liked to oil back his hair and a trim his black mustache extremely thin.

"Mrs. Clark, you have visitors waiting in the drawing room. Shall I bring tea?"

"I'm not expecting anyone. Who are they?" Anna did not lower her voice as she looked up at the somber butler.

"Three prominent ladies in town have come to call. A Mrs. Allen T. Johns, a Mrs. Christopher Langston Scott, and a Mrs. Daniel White. Would you like tea, ma'am?"

"Tell them I'm not home, Mr. Wallace. And, in future, tell anyone else who calls who's not a member of my family I'm not at home. That will be all." Anna turned to continue writing.

Wallace hesitated. Upraised eyebrows indicated his confusion. *This is a first in my career. What is this woman doing? The gossip about Mrs. Clark must have the story wrong. No low-class woman raised in Butte would ever have the gumption to do what Mrs. Clark is doing. It's social suicide!*

Wallace nodded and shut the door to ensure his mistress would not have to hear the fracas that may soon ensue on her property. He retreated to the drawing room where he had deposited the group of women. With an impassive expression, he planned to state that his mistress was not at home in the blandest tone he could muster, but there was no need.

It was immediately apparent by the women's stunned faces, now huddled in a group, they had already overheard the damning words down the wood-lined hallway and through the open door.

The hearing ability of women, a truly remarkable thing...

Mrs. John's green eyes, opened startlingly wide like an angry cat's, glared at Wallace. She grabbed the gloved hand of her long-time friend, Mrs. White, and abruptly turned to depart the Clark mansion with a great swishing of satin skirts.

Mrs. Scott quickly followed the pair, her head bowed in social defeat while small brown boots shuffled forward.

In Chicago, a young journalist named Jonathan Walker received an interesting letter from his great aunt in Butte. She wrote with the scoop:

I thought of you immediately, Jon, on account of your career. I heard about the entire social fiasco first-hand. My best friend is the head maid who gossips frequently with Mr. Clark's butler, Mr. Wallace... I also found out Mrs. Clark is planning on leaving Butte. She will be at Hotel —— in Chicago by the fifteenth of this month, visiting for several weeks. You must try to interview her!

With all my affection and support, Aunt Madge

Accordingly, Walker spent the next day tracking down Mrs. Clark. His persistence paid off; he caught Anna in a magnanimous mood. She and Amelia were window shopping after lunching at a hotel restaurant nearby. A motorcar with a bodyguard trailed them on the curb. As soon as Walker approached Anna, a bodyguard jumped out.

The intrepid journalist spoke boldly, "Mrs. Clark, hello, my name is Jonathan Walker, journalist at the *Chicago Daily Tribune*. If you would allow my asking a few questions. Do you have a minute, ma'am?"

"Perhaps," Anna nodded watchfully at the young man in a brown wool suit and bowler hat. She held off the bodyguard with one gesture. The man loomed over the slight Walker.

Amelia looked aghast at her older sister, never knowing her to be willing to even acknowledge a journalist's presence.

Walker began: "You recently spent some time in Butte, Montana, correct?"

Mrs. Clark nodded, looking directly into his grey eyes. Walker fumbled. He had never attempted to talk to a woman so wealthy and famous, and he didn't expect her to acquiesce immediately. His grip grew slippery on the small pencil.

"Well," Walker cleared his throat, "through family living in Butte, I heard you received no well-born women into your fine mansion on Granite Street. I'm a little familiar with the town," he quickly explained. "Is that true, ma'am, that you weren't interested in society in Butte? Does that feeling extend to the whole of the United States, as you and Senator Clark have various houses?"

Anna thought for a moment. *This is my chance to give a warning to all those who would use my vastly improved, new social position to enhance their own. I want no part of empty friendships.*

The young journalist eyed the silent Mrs. Clark, eager to have a story when so many others had failed. He took a breath; right hand glued to a small notebook; entire body poised to write.

"Mrs. Clark...?" He nudged Anna, whose gaze followed street traffic.

"As far as society is concerned, I know nothing about it and care nothing about it. It has absolutely no charms for me."

"No charms..." He scribbled notes as he talked, eyes going from her to the notebook. "That is an unusual answer, Mrs. Clark. May I enquire what're your interests if society isn't one of them?"

"I'm domestic in my habits. I love family life. I like to read, study, and above all, to look after the interests of my little girl."

"What's her name?"

"I'd rather not say."

"Pardon me, ma'am. Any final thoughts on society people, Mrs. Clark?"

Anna was about to stride off but she hesitated. "I've been told society people rarely mean what they say or say what they mean. As for me, I always wish to say what I think, and I believe I do so. Good day, Mr. Walker."

With that Anna nodded to close the interview and looked back pointedly at the muscled bodyguard to ensure the journalist was cut off. She took Amelia's arm and moved away. Walker was so elated to have spoken with Mrs. Clark, he extended a grateful hand to the imposing man in a black bowler. His article expressing Mrs. William A. Clark's rarely heard opinions ran in the *Chicago Daily Tribune* the next morning. Walker's editor soon promoted him.

The story was snatched up by multiple national newspapers because it was that good: Senator Clark had married a firecracker of a woman!

By the end of 1905, Cervellon reclined in a chaise in her Provence garden reading her mail:

I'm delighted to announce I'm pregnant again. My belly is growing fast. The doctor thinks I'm four months along already. The baby must have been conceived in Italy last September. Perhaps I should choose an Italian name? Please plan a trip north.

In loving friendship, Anna

Earlier in the year, William had been convalescing from brain surgery, and Anna remained with him in New York. As soon as the doctors gave the go-ahead, the Clarks sailed for Europe. They took three-year-old Andrée to visit Italy. To Anna's delight, after they returned from Rome, William stayed with her until the Senate reconvened later in the fall.

On a cold day with bright sunshine, Anna lazed uncorseted in a peacock blue velvet gown in a chaise by the fire in the master suite. She put down a novel by Stendhal and requested to see her daughter.

"*Ma petite fille*, come here, please." Anna beckoned to Andrée.

"*Maman…*" Andrée beamed and ambled quickly over. The little girl leaned on Anna's knees, looking up adoringly. In the past year she had matured at a fast rate. Andrée had large light blue eyes, an olive skin tone, and long brunette hair held back with a generous white bow. Many stopped to admire the pretty girl when she walked in the park with her nanny and poodle named Claudette.

"Andrée, give me your hand." Anna put the small hand on her round belly.

"Why is your tummy growing, *Maman*?"

"I'm going to have a baby, my darling. There's a baby inside there. You're going to be a big sister! What do you think about that?"

"Let me think it over!" Andrée deadpanned with perfect timing, putting a small finger to one cheek while cocking head to the side.

Anna laughed at her precocious daughter. "Wherever do you learn such things, I wonder? I'll have to tell Papa about this one!"

On June ninth early in the morning, Anna's labor began. William was not present, but Anna joked with the ailing Cervellon—visiting for the birth and to see her doctor—that was not surprising, given his transatlantic history.

"Save him a box of cigars and a bottle of champagne!" Anna said in jest, briefly smiling in between contractions.

When Anna's labor pains became intense, Cervellon took Andrée out for hot chocolate and shopping. "We're going to pick out a new doll for the baby, which is going to be another girl, of course, because that's what I ordered. Girls are superior to boys! Never forget that, darling Andrée. And, if you are a very good little girl, you can pick out a new toy or doll for yourself, as well."

"*Merci beaucoup*! My sister will like my present," Andrée said with a serious expression.

Cervellon nodded at the child while coughing hard into a lace handkerchief. She held a thin hand to an aching chest. She listened to the child ramble as the motorcar moved slowly along the boulevard. They were headed to *Au Nain Bleu Jouets & Jeux* at *408, rue du Faubourg-Saint-Honoré*. She admonished the chauffeur in a sharp tone if he drove over ten mph.

"These damned motorcars are ruining Paris!"

Andrée looked startled at the outburst, then she giggled impishly. "You talk like Papa!"

After the birth, Anna was anxious for the midwife to leave the baby on the bed in a soft bassinet. She sorely needed sleep but wanted reassurance this third child would not slip from her grasp.

Running into her parent's bedroom an hour later, Andrée said, "*Maman*, is my little sister here?" Climbing up on onto the bed, her light blue eyes examined the newborn's pink face, swaddled in a white, cashmere blanket knit by Cervellon.

"Can I hold her now?" Andrée whispered.

"Not now, my darling. Let mommy rest and then you'll be able to hold her, alright?"

"*D'accord*. When will her eyes open?" Andrée pointed a tiny forefinger at the closed pink lids with blonde eyelashes.

"Soon. Mommy needs to rest now." The nanny collected Andrée while Anna turned her head to Cervellon. "Will you watch over the baby now?" She said, eyes already closing.

Anna had discussed names with William, but it was her idea to name the new baby Huguette Marcelle Clark. William liked the French names which set apart his second family.

Within four weeks, William was cradling the newborn in his arms and addressing Andrée. "While your mother is busy with the baby, I'll be in charge of organizing your fourth birthday party. And what a party we shall make it! We'll have a hundred balloons, a troupe of dancing dogs, and your birthday cake will be as tall as you!"

Andrée giggled while prancing in excitement. She clapped hands with glee before wrapping arms around his knee.

"Papa, watch me dance ballet!"

"William, you'll spoil her," Anna said while entering the drawing room.

"Nonsense. She's a Clark. She'll grow up *beautifully*. She's charming. Keep dancing for papa."

Directly after Huguette's christening, Anna insisted the family of four be photographed professionally. Holding Huguette, she sat proudly in an enormous navy blue hat with white ostrich feathers wearing a Worth navy blue wool skirt with matching bolero jacket and ivory lace blouse. Her serene face looked radiantly lovely. Baby Huguette bore the ivory *couture* christening gown Andrée had worn.

William and Andrée stood beside. Afterwards, Andrée had her photograph taken alone and then sitting beside her father.

Days before he left, William returned to the flat from being out all morning. He said, "My darling Anna, you're blooming, as usual." They embraced and Anna strolled with him to the gold drawing room. "I've some exciting news."

William halted to kiss her, and then drew back. "I've just been to see about a present for you."

"For me?"

"We're moving!"

"Moving? Out of Paris?" Anna went pale. *It can't be time to move to America!*

"No, nothing like that. These past months I've had Pelletier out looking for a flat. A larger one for our growing family."

Anna dark eyebrows rose. "William, I'm very happy here…"

"Of course, as I've been. But, nevertheless, it's time to move on. I've bought a beautiful flat at number 56, *avenue Victor Hugo*." He looked at her expectantly.

"*Victor Hugo* is in the more prestigious *seizième arrondissement*…"

"Yes! I've already ordered renovations. We'll be able to move in six months or so. Probably much longer as these indolent French workmen take so many blasted breaks. Are you pleased, my dove? It's my gift to our growing family, and to you."

"*Oui! C'est extraordinaire. Merci*, William."

Anna and William embraced as Andrée raced past holding a wooden horsehead on a short pole. The nanny began to rush over as William held her off.

"Ms. Browning, leave the child be. Anna, do we have that child in riding lessons yet? It's time to start!"

May 1991
Doctor's Hospital, Upper East Side, New York City

Beverly Hoskins was tired. She had worked a double the day before, filling in for a nurse who had a car accident. Now she dragged a bit on rounds. She groaned when the head RN approached.

"Sorry, Bev! Sick kiddo at daycare Tamara had to pick up immediately. You know how it is," said the RN. "The patient in 405B normally has a private nurse, but she's out for the afternoon. The patient requires minimal care. Easy case, but, I would advise to go slow. Lingering homeless lady syndrome, k?"

Hoskins nodded, "No problem. It's my specialty!"

"That's why we luv ya!" said the RN, who walked off scanning a patient chart.

With a sinking heart, Hoskins turned to go to the assigned room. Then she rallied. She was used to being stretched thin juggling different duties. *Nurses either accept that or they get out of the profession real fast. Maybe I'll get lucky and be able to sit down a bit if the patient is asleep.*

Halting in the hallway to massage her back, Hoskins then knocked discreetly and opened the door a smidge. On the hospital bed across the room was a slim, elderly woman sitting upright with hands folded in her lap. Large blue eyes in a sunken oval face stared straight without blinking. The patient was wearing a white nightgown with a white cashmere cardigan buttoned up to the neck, cashmere socks on her feet. Her skin was very pale with mottled brown spots, and the bobbed fluff of white hair framing her face needed a trim.

"Hello, Mrs. Clark, I'm Nurse Hoskins," she said from the doorway. "May I come in?"

Huguette regarded the unknown nurse. The dark-skinned woman wore mauve scrubs and had shaved off all her curly hair. She wore small, gold hoop earrings and had a warm smile.

Huguette nodded and said, "Yes, you may. Thank you for asking. Usually nurses barge in, as if they have a right to disturb me whenever they choose."

Hoskins smiled at the old woman's attitude. *Well, this is a hospital, not a hotel room, lady. New York is full of quacks, there seems to be a never-ending supply. Maybe I'll go back to Mississippi, like my auntie keeps asking. Take a nursing job there, be closer to family. Far fewer nutsos to deal with in Mississippi. Just racist ones, but those are a dime a dozen. In New York, you never know what sort of craziness is comin' at you.*

The veteran nurse had to make the patient feel comfortable before she could check vitals, make sure the patient ate a snack, and afterward take any pills prescribed. Hoskins retrieved the patient log to have a look.

"May I sit down and see how you've been doin' lately?"

"I'm very well, thank you." Huguette looked away.

"Okay, then!" Hoskins stood to move to the bedside table. "Look at that delicious cookie. And you have some milk to go with it. Does that sound good? Want to take a bite?"

"No. I've tried that kind before. Tastes like cardboard."

Hoskins tried not to laugh. *I think that too!*

She missed slow-cooked barbeques with fresh meat and homemade, seasonal fruit pies.

"How 'bout a drink of milk while we take your pills?"

Huguette popped two pills in her mouth and drank the milk through a straw. After months in the hospital, she was still grateful for the ability to drink and eat normally again. Her restructured lips were still tender, but overall, recovery had gone far quicker than Townsend had anticipated. She settled back on the white pillows propped against the mass-produced headboard. She lifted the remote to turn on the VCR to watch *Scooby-Doo.*

I wish I had the transcription to read with it, thought Huguette.

The nurse looked at the cartoon playing on the small box TV and then back at the elderly woman. *How'd she get a VCR in here? What did this old lady get out of watching this? Wouldn't she prefer "Days of Our Lives" or "Wheel of Fortune"? Everybody liked game shows, even cranky old men.*

"Want me to change the channel?"

"Oh no! This is one of my favorites."

Hoskins's eyebrows rose. *Strange... Too bad, since my soap starts in a few minutes!*

She crossed the room to throw away the uneaten cookies and rinse out the cup with detergent. She refilled the Styrofoam cup with cold water, popped in a clean plastic straw, and placed it beside the patient. She waited quietly on a side chair for a half hour, wondering how to politely get the patient to turn off the cartoon. Her attention wandered to her sore back and the desire to go home.

Abruptly, Huguette pressed a button, and the TV went black. She asked for assistance to get out of bed. As Hoskins waited outside the bathroom door, she recalled she also needed to get the patient to walk around the room for ten or fifteen laps of exercise.

When Huguette shuffled out, Hoskins said, "Mrs. Clark, before you sit back down, would you mind walking around the room with me a bit? I feel like stretching my legs..."

"Let me think it over!" Huguette said as she held up an aged forefinger in the air.

Hoskins was amazed. The woman's entire demeanor altered. Her face glowed; blue eyes came alive; a small smile animated her face upward. The patient then chuckled and lowered a thin arm.

Hoskins could not follow the long-standing Clark joke, and merely waited patiently.

"My normal day nurse says we're going to take a walk around Central Park, out there." Huguette pointed to the window, which she didn't bother to look out of.

"Central Park, one of my favorite New York City landmarks. Let's pretend we're down there in the fresh air, walking on the paths, shall we?"

Hoskins was also surprised at this sudden outburst of warm communication but willingly complied. They took repeated turns around the room, as the nurse held one arm out protectively, ready to steady the willow-whisp-thin patient.

The elderly woman walked slowly, naming landmarks and statues in geographical order with ease.

Hoskins always spoke in an easy tone used to soothe patients. She barely paid attention to repetitive small talk most days. Today might prove to be the same nonsense.

"It sounds like you're *very familiar* with Central Park. Can't say the same, myself. Honestly, I never go there. I work, go to the grocery, and then head straight home. There aren't enough hours in a day!"

"Never go there! I used to go there *every day*. After classes when the weather was fine. We had a large house right across the street. In the winters my sister and I would sled or ice skate. And in the summers, we would ride horses or bicycles, and have picnics with our friends. Flying kites on windy days was so much fun! One year my friend Susan had..."

"Hmmm..." Hoskins feigned attention. She winced as a shot of pain zinged down her right buttock and thigh.

It was common for patients to tell imaginative tales. She had worked in New York for many years; everyone knew Central Park was full of druggies, rapists, and homeless people. Each mayor promised to clean it up, but he only got so far.

I should be a novelist for all the stuff I've heard. People just losin' their marbles, that's all it is...

Hoskins experienced a wave of fatigue along with another pain spike. In growing discomfort, she scarcely noted the patient's ramblings. Then something stuck out; Hoskins couldn't help herself.

"Wait, did you say you had a house in Central Park? Where? There are no houses there..."

She looked down at the patient dubiously, wondering what the old lady would spin now. Huguette continued matter-of-factly while brushing aside frizzy white hair on her forehead.

"Not *in* the park, alongside it. There used to be many fine, large houses around it, and I lived in the grandest, the tallest one. My father made sure of that! He was a dynamo!

"There were always tall buildings and fine hotels, of course, but the high-rise apartments being built over demolished private houses began occurring after I was ten years old or so. It made my father furious. All that gorgeous architecture being razed as if it were nothing special. By the time I was a teenager, it was happening so fast it made your heart burst with the massive changes to the neighborhood.

"But, when I was a young girl, there were still many beautiful, private houses and townhouses up and down, oh, all over New York. Instead of a high-rise, you would have a lovely house taking up a city block. Now they've been replaced by skyscrapers."

"Right... Jackie O got involved, I saw that on PBS Newshour a couple of years ago. Said we're 'losing our sun and clean air' to skyscraper developers. Those were her exact words. She was right! Those developers are devils who don't care about normal people living in the city. I think she won. At least, temporarily. They'll be back."

Huguette doggedly tugged her captive listener along, back to strong memories which beckoned.

"As I was saying, one year a friend of ours had her tenth birthday party in Central Park. It was a glorious summer day. We played *all sorts* of games. I liked to play hoops. A troop of dogs did pet tricks with a clown who knew how to twist balloons into colorful animal shapes. There was a visit to the menagerie, of course. The monkeys were my favorite. I thought it was a perfect party...

"Would you like to see pictures?"

In order to sit, Hoskins readily agreed. She steered the patient back to the bed. The nurse was directed to a short bookcase by the window to retrieve a leather-bound photo album that was good quality but worn with age. The patient's hands eagerly reached for the heavy album. For the next hour, she opened to the first, well-worn page and began animatedly talking as she pointed out this or that detail.

Hoskins stifled a yawn. *Looks like a fine photo album, just very old. Where'd she pick it up, from an estate sale or antique shop someplace? She's too young and too poor to be in these old-time photos of rich people...*

Soon another nurse knocked on the door to relieve Hoskins. Huguette shut the album with a thud and eyed up the newcomer.

On the way out, Hoskins whispered, "Have fun..."

Arriving at the curved beige and mauve nurse station, Hoskins said, "Say, Monica, that Mrs. Clark in 405B is crazy as a loon. She has this old photo album and dreams up all these tall tales about livin' in a mansion on Fifth Avenue with gold faucets and like, twelve stories, and going down with the Titanic and playin' her violin on a balcony in a Paris castle before escaping the Nazis. She's somethin' else... Livin' on Fifth Avenue by a dumpster more likely!"

She shook her head at the absurdity, reaching to massage her back.

"Yep, everybody wants to be rich, even if they have to fib. My grasp of history isn't the best, I can admit, because science was always more my thing. Hence the job... But, isn't all that a *little too much* history for one person to go through? Probably!"

Monica Garibaldi gathered a stack of manila files and rose from a desk. "No, Bev, Mrs. Clark is not a bag lady like we thought. She's here on her own dime, believe it or not. Zero health insurance for *months* now, all cash! We checked with billing. I've met her lawyer, too... Schwann or something. He's the real deal."

Hoskins raised an eyebrow. "You pullin' my leg...?"

From across the station, a lead nurse with a helmet of permed black hair looked up from paperwork and said, "Bev, those tall tales she tells over and over in that photo album: It could be all true! I was so curious a few weeks ago I went to the library and looked up her father, Senator William A. Clark. He was—"

"Nah, nobody's been through all that! Ladies, I've heard *enough* for one day! That's just somethin' out of the movies. I'm beat and outta here for three whole days. See you later, alligator!" Hoskins turned away.

Down the hall, Huguette ate a Wonder bread bologna sandwich with limp ice-berg, carrot sticks, and cherry Jell-O before turning on the TV. She no longer felt like talking. The nurse got the message and sat down across the room with *People*.

Huguette watched *The Flintstones*, reviewing the well-known animation tech-niques. Her artistic mind scanned the rapid scenes; she knew so much she could have successfully joined the artists who developed the animated show without a hitch in production.

Thank heavens I never had access to television cartoons as a young child with no self-discipline. I would've rot my brain through watching day and night.

Huguette relaxed into the pillows, scarred eyelids growing heavy. She no longer had to think about how to care for her surroundings or physical self. The hospital staff took care of everything; she could finally consider projects again.

I wonder how my dolls are doing without me?

The hand-tooled, gilded leather photo album nestled by the footboard. Huguette's attention strayed from the cartoon to the album and back again; her eyes began seeing more of the past than the present. As if yesterday, Andrée stood before her asking to play Snakes and Ladders. Every beloved feature of her dear face was clear.

She had a great deal to share with her sister.

Scooting her spare form deeper under the covers, Huguette nestled under clean bedding. She desired to return to the halcyon days of playing in Central Park, her dear family living in their beautiful house across Fifth Avenue, and loneliness utterly unknown.

Huguette closed her eyes on the present.

July 1910

Château de Petit-Bourg, Évry-sur-Seine, France

The petite girl paid no attention to either the barking lapdogs or the women calling. After receiving counsel from *Général* Clark, she slipped through one of the library's elongated, open windows. Alighting down stone steps, she raced through the formal gardens generously surrounding the eighteenth-century limestone *château*. The nannies and governess dutifully urged decorum and modesty, but it fell on deaf ears most days.

The spirit of wild adventure was upon her. Cornflower blue eyes glowed with excitement; late afternoon sun shone golden on pale skin. Churning legs kicked up layered white linen skirts. Straw-like blonde hair stuck out from the woven hat—secured by a black ribbon— which soon gave up altogether trying to stay on its owner's head. As short legs pumped forward, the straw hat slid to crazily bob up and down.

The girl left the gardens behind and was now amongst grassy meadows imprecisely yet artistically dotted with ancient oaks towering overhead. In one tiny hand she triumphantly clutched the crucial missive from *Général* Clark, signed and sealed. Now, dangerously crossing enemy lines, she was headed to the battlefields to locate *Génèral Jeanne d'Arc*, who urgently needed the message.

In the girl's mind, she wasn't running across acres of meadow; she was riding a trusty black steed bearing her swiftly and safely to her *génèral* in the center of a medieval army. France was in peril.

Jeanne d'Arc is relying on me!

Lungs bursting, Huguette raced into the woods past the towering beech they used as a reference point. She gasped for air while leaning against a thickly knarled oak trunk. Then she bowed to Jeanne d'Arc.

"Ah, my trusted servant finally returns from the arduous and dangerous journey through enemy territory. I have been waiting anxiously for your return, my brave courier. Please leave us," Andrée declared with a sweep of her arm to the row of military advisors. In reality, a row of scrub pines on her far left.

Huguette gravely held out the military missive. Andrée took the scroll secured by a purple ribbon which *Génèral* Clark had created using his best paper. Arguably the more beautiful, the nearly eight-year-old Andrée was slender and twice as tall. She read the contents with an intense expression. Turning, she raised a long stick—in her imagination, a golden hilted sword—high in the air.

"*Excelent!* It is most useful information. We are ready for battle! *Courage!*"

"*Oui, courage!*" Huguette said, mimicking Andrée by holding aloft her own imaginary sword. She beamed with pride she hadn't messed anything up this time. Her wiser, older sister naturally took the roll of Jeanne d'Arc, one of the family's favorite heroines.

After a good while of such play, the two sisters began strolling through the meadow up to the *château*. They picked wildflowers along the way.

"Perhaps we can ride our ponies down here? Then the walk back won't take such a long time..." said Huguette halting. She slumped over then huffed, "I'm tired..."

"C'mon, lazybones! *Allons-y!*"

Andrée walked faster before beginning to skip. Huguette's petite blonde head popped up, her face bright pink.

"Wait for me!"

She began skipping before immediately becoming distracted by a patch of dainty yellow wildflowers. As she adjusted her straw hat, the little girl's eye noted it was the perfect color to compliment the Queen Anne's Lace already in her fist. She selected blossoms to pluck while bumble bees hovered amongst the grasses warmed by the afternoon sun. A plethora of songbirds darted in and out of the trees, and a chubby red squirrel chittered at his fellows amongst the thick, swooping branches of a beech some feet away.

Andrée halted and smiled indulgently. She could always convince Huguette to do things others could not. Her trick was not giving in to Huguette's stubbornness as so many others did. To distract, she almost always remained cheerful.

Andrée explained to Anna—with the world on slim shoulders—"Because, *Maman*, as the older sibling, when I become cross at how difficult Huguette can be at times, I feel obliged to be the example."

Andrée sighed profoundly. Anna suppressed laughter at her eldest's dramatics. "That's good, *ma fille*. I'm proud of you for being responsible."

She wondered if she were ever that serious at such a young age?

Non, I don't think so. There is a strong bond between them. I hope it means they'll help each other in life, as Amelia and I do.

While the girls strolled up through the meadow, walking along the dense tree line was a security team. Wool suits were tailored specifically to hide twin handguns in holsters alongside torsos; daggers were strapped to both shins, and interior pockets carried other weapons. In pastoral settings, the team wore brown tweed; in nocturnal, a black suit took advantage of no light. Both men watched until the Clark daughters' route back to the *château* was clear. Then they went in opposite directions to canvas the extensive forested grounds on foot.

After the daytime shift, several other highly trained, well-armed guards would begin patrolling the *château* grounds and roadways. William ensured his family was protected round the clock from curious neighbors, intruders, communists, socialists, unionists, journalists, thieves, and kidnappers.

As the sun waned, a balmy breeze caressed flushed cheeks. Glowing with health and happiness, both girls sported pink cheeks as they skipped merrily into the gardens. They abruptly met up with the group of women who had been waiting.

Skidding to a stop in the gravel, Andrée pulled a face before masking her annoyance.

Constance Browning, Andrée's English nanny and therefore the woman with the most status in the girls' retinue, clucked over them. Dust covered leather shoes; dirt smudges and burrs marred silk stockings and laces. It all perturbed. Huguette's nanny, Jennie Walter, obediently followed Browning's lead in every particular. Walter waited while Browning made a face that portended a lecture.

Each child held a warm handful of dangling wildflowers with a few trailing roots holding onto soil. Frances Whitechurch, the English governess, immediately looked away with distaste. If the bloom wasn't from the hothouse, she didn't want it near.

"There are lovely flowers already in the *château*, *must* we bring those weeds inside?"

The governess sniffed.

Huguette frowned, "They're not for you!"

Very accustomed to her youngest, brash pupil, Whitechurch looked away while sneezing harshly into an embroidered handkerchief.

"Huguette, you're being rude. Apologize..."

Andrée glanced up at the governess, attempting to smooth the situation lest *Maman* find out.

Huguette, unrepentant, stuck out a small, pink tongue at the tall woman who no longer faced the child's direction. Andrée clamped lips together to stop a giggle and averted her eyes. This governess was more boorish than the last. Whitechurch had an allergy which made zero sense.

"Who could be allergic to flowers?" they had asked *Maman*.

"That's quite enough, Mademoiselle Huguette. If you don't behave like a little lady, I will have to discuss the issue with your mother," said Browning.

The nanny's stern brown eyes examined the girl who, despite tender years, was quite the spitfire. On the whole, Andrée was intelligent and prone to complain, but more often sweet and even-tempered. Huguette had other ideas about most everything. The little one needed several reminders, and Browning was often after Walter to be stricter.

It's obvious which daughter takes after the notorious father.

Huguette's angry eyes gazed steadfastly at the ground. She scuffed a left toe in the gravel, suddenly uncomfortable by the disapproving attention from the circle of women.

"Girls, inside immediately. It's time to bathe and dress for dinner," ordered Browning while clapping hands.

She rose with a small heave from the carved stone bench. Before advancing with gusto, the head nanny smoothed an imagined wrinkle from a uniform of a heavily starched, white blouse belted at the waist above a black wool, floor-length skirt. In one large hand she carried a white lace parasol.

Browning was a middle aged, Cornish woman, and absolutely dedicated to her profession. She took it upon herself to be the lead amongst the women employed to care for the Clark daughters. She couldn't control little Huguette's tongue or Andrée's occasional bursts of whining, but she could control her charges' appearance. The Clarks were fastidious; they expected their daughters to always look and act their best. Browning well knew Madame Clark always took precise care to enforce this point on each new staff member.

"My girls are never to act spoilt or be slovenly."

The group made their way to a wooden side door of the *château*. Inside to the right, they ascended a gracefully curving, limestone spiral staircase. On the massive second floor, the nursery suite was on the opposite side from the master suite.

The maids had almost finished drawing baths with *Provençal* lavender and verbena soap in the black and white marble tiled modern bathroom. With help from the maids, both girls gladly stripped and sank with delighted cries into the warm water. They splashed and chattered in side-by-side, copper bathtubs.

"We're playing tonight, right, Andrée?"

"*Oui*. But don't make the same mistake you kept making during practice."

Andrée held her breath and slid underwater.

"Sorry! It's hard..."

Huguette pouted, swirling a hand towel in the bubbles.

Rising up out of the water, the girls' dripping bodies were immediately wrapped in white Egyptian cotton towels. As soon as they stepped onto the bathmat, terry-cloth slippers were put on, and the maids whisked them out of the bathroom.

In the girls' dressing room, wardrobes lined the walls with a round raspberry pink and ivory Aubusson rug. The wardrobes featured a great number of matching costumes. Dressing for dinner occurred even when their parents went out for the evening. If it were windy, cold, or damp, the sisters were clothed on an Aubusson rug in pale blue, apricot, and ivory in front of a pink marble fireplace in the bedroom. On those days, a small fire burned.

"I don't think a fire is necessary. I'm quite warm, thank you," Andrée usually said.

Browning always countered in a sharp tone, "In my opinion, there are many days requiring a small fire even at the height of summer. Damp is damp. And dampness leads to infections. Be grateful you have that luxury, Mademoiselle Andrée, for there are *many* who don't. It is my duty to protect your healthy constitutions from the virulent and dangerous germs present everywhere."

Still swaddled in the oversized towel as she emerged from the bath, Huguette ran ahead to leap onto her canopy bed and jump up and down. She giggled and pranced, easily evading Walter's arms.

"Come now, Mademoiselle Huguette. Must we always do this? Let's get down before Nanny Browning sees you this time."

Walker smiled and waited.

"But it's fun to bounce!"

"Hugo, get down..." Andrée said.

She put arms up to have a chemise slid on.

"Hurry, we need to dress to see *Maman* and Papa."

"*D'accord!*"

Huguette hopped to the edge and into Walker's waiting arms.

Andrée and Huguette shared a large bedroom with fifteen-foot ceilings and four windows overlooking the surrounding countryside. The pale blue *toile de juoy* fabric on the walls accented the apricot silk curtains. The *lit à la Polonaise* twin beds were festooned with yards of sky-blue watered silk with apricot silk lining underneath. The bedlinens were trimmed in handmade apricot lace, and the pillows and comforters made of the loftiest goose down.

At the foot of the beds were matching blue watered silk benches. Andrée's bench was spare, with only small pillows and a lone brown teddy bear sporting a green striped vest. Huguette's bench, on the other hand, was crowded with Jumeau dolls, two teddy bears, Peter Rabbit, and Humpty Dumpty.

The nannies oversaw the general order of the nursery suite. They enforced etiquette and decorum, keeping a critical eye on the children and staff. The team of women were responsible year-round for the girls' physical, mental, emotional, and educational needs. When the parents were away—which could be frequent depending on the season—it became clear how much the staff was relied upon.

In the world of the nursery, the schedule did not vary. After waking the children at eight o'clock to wash and dress, breakfast would be served at half past. The children were escorted at nine o'clock to the schoolroom by Whitechurch. On weekdays, the children were taught three hours of lessons: English, French, mathematics, science, and history.

The piano and violin were studied for one hour in the music room with the music instructor three days a week before the mid-day meal; the girls were then required to practice for one to two hours in the late afternoons. Drawing and watercolor instruction were given by an art instructor on the mornings they did not study music.

Lunch was eaten after one o'clock. Then, a nap or time to read was granted. On fine days, they would take a walk with *Maman* in the gardens.

A German tutor came on Tuesday and Thursday afternoons at half past three for one and a half hours of conversational practice and grammar drills. On Monday and Wednesday at half past three, a riding instructor came for two hours. On Fridays at the same time, a dancing instructor arrived to torment the girls. He aligned them in front of a room with large mirrors displaying every sagging arm and disinterested foot.

Educated year-round, there was little vacation time or lollygagging. From their tenderest years, Huguette and Andrée were continually impressed with the value of a first-class education. They knew no other option. On many afternoons, they witnessed *Maman* sitting with tutors in music, literature, or foreign languages. Meanwhile, Papa perpetually worked.

On Sunday mornings, Anna took them to Mass. William was far more sporadic.

As they prepared to depart, William would invariably say, "I'll attend the following week. *Au revoir*, my loves."

In the evening, Anna knelt at a *prie-dieu*, her daughters saying the Lord's Prayer beside her.

"Pray your father will find the time to attend Mass with us, *s'il vous plaît*."

"Please, *Maman*, can I also pray for tomorrow not to rain?" Huguette knelt on a velvet pillow, holding a rosary. "I want to go on a picnic!"

"I suppose..."

Anna closed her eyes while smiling, always amused at Huguette's spirit.

Andrée nudged Huguette.

"How silly! The Virgin Mary doesn't have time to worry about our picnics!"

"Shush now, let's be reverent."

Anna's head bowed gracefully and the girls mimicked her.

At the *château,* the Clarks were in a private world. Extremely few acquaintances—whether in the social, artistic, political or business realms—were ever invited. Besides Amelia, the La Chappelle family never accepted an invitation to visit—Philomene was terrified of crossing the Atlantic, "I'm too old for such adventures now!", and Arthur too busy setting up his law practice to take such a long voyage—and after a few years Anna stopped asking.

It never occurred to invite anyone in William's family. The times she had heard through contacts that William's adult children or the Abascals were in Paris, Anna made a point to stay away. She instinctively understood to never attempt to ingratiate herself. When his older children did join their family gatherings, it was always awkward.

⚜

That late afternoon, Anna stood at a tall bedroom window looking out on the meadow to watch her daughters playing far below. The house and grounds overlooking the Seine and the Sénart Forest was a view Anna never became tired of. She often expressed to William the wish to buy the *château*. The owner refused to sell.

She reflected on their first year renting. In the early days, before the girls were old enough to remember, they were so intrigued by the property they invited to dinner a local historian who came highly recommended. They requested he educate them on its history. It was stunning to realize how prestigious the property was, designed and used by high-ranking clergy and royalty since the early seventeenth century.

Amelia entered the sitting room to observe Anna gazing pensively out the window. "Well, here you are! I've been searching for you all over on the ground floor. How silly of me. Of course, you'd be up here. Ooof, I think I need to sit down after all those stairs..." Amelia chuckled. She moved to see what had captured Anna's attention out the window. "Oh, there are the girls. Don't they make a pretty picture?"

"*Oui*, they certainly do. What is it you needed, sister?"

"Oh, nothing in particular. Merely wondering if you've discovered any ghosts in this ancient house, that's all..." Amelia feigned a scared face before sitting on a jade silk chaise. "Didn't you mention Peter the Great has been here? Or was it Marie Antoinette? The Sun King...? I might get greys..." Amelia patted her dark brunette bun.

Anna laughed softly while turning from the window to sit beside Amelia. "Not Marie Antoinette, but other kings and queens, yes. Famous mistresses. But that's ridiculous. This *château* is too wonderful for anything like ghosts." Anna picked up needlepoint before commenting, "Oh Amelia, I'm very content to spend my days alone here while William is away. In fact, I believe it's what keeps our marriage happy. He has his business pursuits and politics in America, and I've my music and the girls in France. Don't be sad for me."

"I'm not sad for you, sister, but I do worry. Here all alone year after year in this old castle deep in the woods." Amelia shuddered. "I'm not as comfortable in France as you are. I enjoy visiting, but I could never imagine staying permanently... Will you ever return? *Maman* would like that."

"Are you guilting me? If I had my way, probably never. I've lived in France now for so many years it would feel odd to return. We'll see what the future brings. I'm determined not to think about it..."

Anna rose and held out a hand.

"Let's take a walk down to the Seine, shall we? It's so cool in the forest, it'll do us good."

Outside on the path underneath the trees, the sisters made a charming pair. Some assumed they were twins.

Anna said, "Will you consider me horrible for complaining about my good fortune?"

Amelia looked at her sideways. "Uh-oh. You must mean the New York mansion. I drove past before I boarded."

"And your impression?"

Anna almost winced. Her sister wouldn't mince words.

"All I can say is, good luck to you, sister, because you're going to need it in that place! It's over the top!"

Amelia hooted before apologizing.

Anna frowned. "I well know New York City's reputation with upstarts. I'm not looking forward to living there. William enthuses about it regularly. Last night, for instance. Instead of sleeping, he droned on about the frequent dilemmas with building and locating desirable materials, quality workmen, and so on. And one mustn't forget his obsessive arranging of the art galleries. He installed the most expensive organ in the city—costing over $100,000 if you can believe that—along with the quarantine tower."

"Oh, so that's what's way up there! I wondered... Well, a tower's a wonderful idea. I know where to go when a pandemic breaks out. But you don't sound pleased. That's not like you."

Amelia looked at Anna with a confused expression, adjusting her straw hat.

"No, I am! I *insisted* on the tower being fitted with a quarantine suite. There's too much sickness in the city for me to be comfortable with anything less."

Anna stopped underneath the deep shade to put down her parasol.

"I'm upset because I know the move back will disrupt our life in more ways than one. It makes me sad. I feel life there will never reach the perfection I now enjoy. I'll be required to relinquish so much to live back in American society."

"Does William know this? That you feel this way?"

"Oh, I've said nothing overt. It's not my place. I know he has his suspicions, which is why he doesn't press to relocate before the house is in the 'most perfect state attainable.' He even installed a Turkish bath to woo me over. Isn't that incredible?"

"Well, why didn't you say that before!" Amelia said. "I'm going to require an invitation merely to use the Turkish bath! Maybe I'll move in for good despite my husband's protests! You've got plenty of guest rooms!"

While Anna and Amelia finished their walk, the girls badgered the nannies to know where they would eat dinner. Several times a week the children ate dinner in the formal dining room. Tonight could be one of those nights, and the girls were excited. It was a treat, even if *Maman* was a stickler for etiquette.

Walking into their small music room, Andrée and Huguette wore identical white silk and lace *couture* dresses, whisper light for the warm evening. Large white bows adorned heads of shining long hair. On legs and feet were white silk stockings and white kid leather slippers. Delicate eighteen-carat Cartier gold charm bracelets and lockets with respective birthstones encircled wrists and necks.

After an hour of practicing instruments, the children skipped eagerly downstairs to join their parents and *tante* Amelia in the music room. Their mother's favorite room was decorated in eighteenth century gilded ivory boiserie. French doors were opened to cool, evening breezes from the darkened gardens. A Steinway, two harps, and a Stradivarius violin were set out attractively on one end while sofas and armchairs in ivory and red damask were available in groupings on the other.

When they entered, the girls hesitated because they heard *Maman* playing. Music rooms were always associated with loving memories.

"Encore!" William said, clapping as Anna plucked the final note. "Your mother is an excellent harpist, my dears. You put a spell on me, my love." William stood to help Anna to her seat while the girls kissed their aunt on the cheek.

Huguette was impressed by her father's praise. "Can I learn the harp too?"

"Oh, *ma petite* Hugo, you will need to grow taller first. We'll stick to your violin and piano lessons for now."

"But Andrée plays the piano. I can play the harp."

"*Bien sûr*! Playing the piano is a foundational musical skill. And you must improve before learning other instruments."

Andrée looked over the adult women and gushed, "You're both very beautiful!"

Anna's Doucet gown of jade satin and Amelia's Worth black silk satin complemented slender figures and pale skin. The girls presented each woman with a simple bouquet of wildflowers secured tightly with white ribbon. The bouquets couldn't compare with the enormous flower arrangements already in the room.

"*Merci beaucoup!* The wildflowers are *beautiful*. Exactly what I wanted!" said Anna.

She motioned for a servant to take the bouquets before guiding Andrée to sit down beside her and Amelia on the sofa. Huguette sat across in a loveseat with William.

"Now tell me what you learned, what you both did today. I want to hear everything."

The girls spoke about the difficulty of math lessons before reciting a poem recently memorized. Andrée displayed the Jeanne d'Arc scroll to *Maman* who read its contents.

"So that's what you were doing..."

"Shall we play a duet for you now?" said Andrée. She stood slowly, conscious of watching eyes, and walked towards the piano with head held erect.

Huguette hugged *Maman* before scrambling over to the violin. Despite a few wrong notes, the adults clapped.

"I'm sorry I messed up several measures," said Andrée, hanging her head.

"Nonsense, you did well!" said Amelia.

"Let's keep practicing. When we have another visitor, you'll play that piece again," Anna said.

Her daughters nodded in unison, knowing *Maman* never forgot about recital plans.

The family moved into the dining room. The evening meal of four courses was simple: *vichyssoise*, a small portion of roast chicken with new potatoes and *haricot verts*, *fromage*, and a berry tart with a dollop of *crème fraîche*.

"I want two!" said Huguette with greedy eyes.

"*Non*, we never have two servings. Only one. And hands off the table," admonished Anna.

After the meal, the group moved into the main drawing room. William stood patiently by the unlit fireplace. "I've an announcement to make."

He waited with a pleased manner while his daughters fidgeted in excitement.

"Tomorrow morning, we shall leave for Trouville. It's time we took some fresh air and bracing sea water for a change. I've rented a beach-front villa. Does this excite you, my dears?"

The girls leaped up, clapping, shouting simultaneously: "Hooray, Papa!"

They looked at each other and hugged, thrilled with the prospect of heading to the Normandy coast.

"Oh Papa, how ever did you guess that that's exactly where I most wished to go?" said Andrée.

"Let me guess. Is it because we went there last summer and had a fabulous time? And the summer summer before last last, and then the summer summer summer before the last last last, and the summer..."

Andrée laughed. "Stop, Papa! You're talking very silly. I *know* we visit every summer."

She grabbed his hand to swing it in gratitude.

William smiled down at her, resting a hand on her brunette head.

"Now I'll give you and Huguetty a hug because it's off to bed. We must rise early tomorrow. We've a long day of travel ahead. *Bonsoir, mes petites!*"

The girls hugged and kissed the adults before turning to meet waiting nannies at the door.

"How happy you make them," Amelia said from the doorway where she had gone to observe her nieces ascending the ivory marble central staircase.

"It's my pleasure. They are a joy to my golden years."

William smiled at Amelia before looking pointedly at Anna. "As are you, my beauty."

William reached to kiss Anna's hand while Amelia averted her gaze, always somewhat embarrassed how openly affectionate he was.

Weeks later, after many afternoons of swimming, both girls were tan. They now knew all the children who came down to the beach to play. Any holidaying newcomers were always accepted into the fold. Andrée was one of the ringleaders of coastal play.

Huguette's hair had turned platinum blonde and her fair skin was golden brown. One evening, as the family sat in the drawing room in the fading twilight, William looked them over with loving eyes. His sister-in-law had recently returned to the States, and he had a similar idea.

"Well, Andrée and Huguette, I hate to tear you away from your fun in Trouville, but I have another surprise in mind."

He paused for effect, enjoying the squirms of his eager daughters.

"Only tell us if it's a pleasant surprise, Papa, like coming here was!" Andrée said. She eyed him warily.

"What do you mean? Do I ever tell you unpleasant things?"

William grabbed at his heart and made a face of anguish.

"No, Papa, stop...!"

Andrée put down her book to climb onto his lap.

"We adore the sea! And, I'm not ready to leave. I've written a poem about it."

"Well... maybe you'll like this new idea?"

William's smile returned. "Can you make a guess?"

"Let's go to China! I learned about Han Kong today," suggested Huguette from the floor, where she was drawing a crab.

"It's *Hong* Kong," said Andrée, getting down from her father's lap. "Miss Whitehouse corrected your pronunciation this morning, remember?"

"Isn't that what I said?" Huguette looked crushed.

Andrée mimicked Whitechurch's prim head shake. "You need to pay better attention."

"I wanted to go swimming! Lessons are boring."

Huguette pouted while coloring the crab with a blue pastel.

"Girls, maybe someday we'll go as far away as that, but, for now, I'm too busy to travel to the Orient. I was thinking a little closer to family."

"Yours or Mommy's?" said Andrée.

"Both! How about we try another place, a faraway place, such as... America! It's the most beautiful and prosperous country in the world, and I want my youngest daughters to see it with me. Which means, in a mere three days we'll be departing on a White Star liner called the *Teutonic*. Doesn't that sound grand? What a name! From New York, we'll take a train ride to Butte. There you'll meet family. We'll stay at a special red house I built for my first wife, a *very* long time ago to you youngsters."

"Oh Papa, you had another wife? Oh, right, didn't I know that?" said Andrée.

Her eyes shifted to Anna with a worried expression. Huguette popped her head up, listening intently.

"Yes, my dear. She died well before I married your mother. Which is why you'll meet a few siblings in America on this trip, as well. They're my adult children."

"Adult children? That sounds strange... Oh yes, I forgot. We're going to America, *again*?" said Andrée, suddenly becoming animated. "I have seen Papa's large, red brick house, remember?"

"But you were so young, Andrée. You remember?" said Anna, eyes raising from needlework.

"I think I do... Does it have a lot of wood inside? And colored glass and long wooden stairs? I'll miss the sea, but perhaps we can go to the sea there?"

"We'll go to lakes! How about that?" William said.

"Huguette, wake up, silly! It's not time for bed yet. Do you want to go to America?"

"I *am* awake!"

Huguette stirred from a prone position on the rug. She rubbed an eye above skin flushed with a mild sunburn.

"*C'est vrai, Maman.* I want to go! How many dolls can I bring?"

"As many as you like, Hugo. But remember, there needs to be room in your trunks for clothing..."

When the family disembarked in New York, William was eager to display his daughters. Andrée had experienced the frenzy on previous trips; she smiled widely, not minding the attention. But it was new to Huguette. She slowed steps while descending the first-class gangway.

"Who are they?" Huguette whispered, looking first anxiously at Papa and then back toward the upper decks as if planning to bolt.

But William couldn't hear. Crowds of people with a lineup of photographers from all the major papers jockeyed for position. Some shouted; the first-class arrival area was mobbed. Two policemen waited for anyone to cross a line.

Poised expectantly at the end of the gangway, reporters had notepads in hand, desperately needing a reaction from Senator Clark fresh from a European summer. Even better, it would be a scoop to publish the first picture of both Clark daughters arriving for the first time from France.

In 1913, Eleanor Gates would have a successful Broadway play, "Poor Little Rich Girl," that capitalized on the zeitgeist during the last gasp of the Gilded Age. The press seized on the catchy title, bestowing the title Poor Little Rich Girls on multiple, über-wealthy heiresses. Subsequently, the lucky young ladies were idolized, envied, copied, or hated by readers. Journalists knew the average American male earned $750 annually, which paled in comparison to the estimated $20,000,000 fortune Senator Clark would leave *each* heir if he were to die that day. The American press would milk the story for decades to come.

Unfortunately for Huguette, her attention-seeking father kept heading straight toward the crowd.

"Senator Clark, are these your youngest daughters? Will you pose for a picture, sir?"

William fixed Huguette's straw hat to shield tender eyes from the sun. She clutched his hand while he squatted to her level for a few seconds.

"I'll explain what this is all about later. Right now, hold still and smile big while they take our picture. Daddy's here with you."

Huguette shrank to her father's side and instinctively lowered her gaze. Then she was whisked off to the Pierce-Arrow 66 Landau 7-passenger Brougham. It was a relief when the heavy metal doors closed.

People everywhere strained to look into the windows. Some of the photographers tried to take a picture of the motorcar. The bodyguards blocked both sides, and the chauffeur vigorously honked the horn. The vehicle eased onto the street. To part the crowd, policemen blew whistles and raised billy clubs.

"William, this is a circus," Anna waved tiredly at the scene out the window as the car picked up speed. "Even police are needed today! New York always exhausts me..."

"My dear, what can I say? You've married a well-known man. And the press is always looking for a story. You have to hand it to them. Nothing exceeds American ambition!"

"*C'est vrai*, but must we subject our daughters to it?"

"Good press is good business. Didn't you like having your picture taken, Andrée?"

"Oh, I don't mind, Daddy, but it scared Hugo."

William looked over at his youngest, bug-eyed and silent in a corner of the automobile.

"Huguetty, you'll like my train better. Trust me."

The Clarks spent the rest of the summer and all of fall in Montana. Huguette was delighted to meet *Grandmère* Philomene, who cried to see them. Both adored their kind *grandmère* from the first.

"Eat as many brownies as you want. Don't worry about what your mother says," said Philomene at the tea table.

Anna had dropped the girls off for the afternoon and Philomene let them do anything they wanted.

"We don't have these in France!" said Huguette, already on her second.

She was amazed to see multiple photographs of herself and of Andrée displayed on a table. She hopped down to go over for a closer look.

"*Grandmère*, how did you get these? Here I am in this one, and that one is Andrée when she was little. We've all these photographs, too!"

"Aren't you both precious! Your mother sent them to me, *bien sûr*."

"How come you never come?" Huguette said, approaching her grandmother and regarding her with a serious expression.

"I'm too old to travel to France, *ma petite*. I wish I could!"

Philomene delicately took little Huguette's hands in her own and smiled.

During the first few weeks, Huguette was a little overwhelmed hearing English all the time. She understood, but it disoriented. She would respond in French or say nothing. Sometimes she looked to Anna or Andrée for guidance. As the months passed, the girls' fluency in English rose quickly, but French was the dominant language whenever Papa wasn't around.

Huguette largely shrank from the attention of strangers in this new country. When someone approached, invariably she was with her father, who knew everyone. After greeting Papa, they would stick big faces down into hers, causing her to recoil. Americans talked louder than she was used to. In France, no one shouted the Clark surname in the streets or stopped dead to watch their motorcar drive past.

"Papa, everyone knows your name!" said Huguette.

"I don't seek the limelight. I'm too busy to seek after trivialities. If perchance a person knows my name, it's from reading the newspapers or having done business with me. That's all."

They were soon invited to Mowitza Lodge. William wasn't keen to go at first—"Will Jr. grandly calls it some fool Indian name, Mowitza. However, it's a mere fishing shack and too pedestrian for my tastes! The darn roads aren't even paved. We have to boat across the lake to arrive at the lodge!"—but was finally persuaded by Anna to accept. He was pleasantly surprised at what Will Jr. had created.

During summers not working as one of his father's lawyers in Butte, Will Jr. had been renting a fishing lodge forty miles from Missoula for his second wife, Alice, and son, Tertius. He eventually bought the lodge and accompanying cabins on 40 acres at Salmon Lake; expanding the property to buy another 17 acres on the east and 10 acres on the southern point. Will Jr. and Alice worked each summer improving the retreat to the tune of $400,000. Building materials had to be shipped to the lake and then rafted across. The log lodge and cabins were rebuilt or refurbished, bathrooms upgraded, and service and recreation buildings now had a bowling alley and shooting gallery. For lake recreation, boats, canoes, fishing equipment, and multiple docks were built new or added to.

A mountaintop tea house was constructed with a charming view of the surrounding countryside of Salmon Lake nestled within Seeley Valley. Taking guests needs into consideration, many wouldn't have the hardy shoes needed to hike the steep climb. The problem was solved by building a storage shed at the base. A shelving system of leather boots in a full range of sizes for both male and female guests was on one end with benches on the other. With proper footwear secured, guests hiked up to the tea house, arriving refreshed and ready to settle themselves on wicker furniture in front of large windows to take high tea.

Alice said to Anna, "It greatly adds to Mowitza Lodge's charms. I come here almost daily."

"Yes, what a splendid idea. I almost feel bad for the servants having to hike up, though!" said Anna, looking at the well-appointed table laden with sweet and savory dishes and several kinds of tea.

To Huguette, the Ponderosa pine, Western larch, Douglas fir, and deciduous trees seemed much taller and mightier than those in France. Everything was bigger and wilder, yet quiet. Huguette noticed *Maman* kept remarking on this. Climbing up to sit beside her mother on a cushioned wicker loveseat on the cabin's porch, Huguette wanted some clarification. The day was sunny, and the heat had lifted with a breeze off the lake. Anna removed a large straw hat to drink lemonade.

"Remember the wolves in the fairy tales Andrée reads?"

"*Oui, ma petite fille.*"

"Are they here, in these woods?"

Huguette's blue eyes were wide with possibility as they gazed out at the nearby forest.

Anna hesitated. The child had a point.

"Have you seen one?"

Smiling, Anna tickled her daughter to get her mind off the subject. It only worked for a few moments before Huguette returned to the topic.

"Will they jump out and eat us?"

"*Peut être*, but they're scared of us, too."

"Scared of me?"

"*Oui*, but don't worry. That's why your papa employs bodyguards. They will kill the wolf exactly like 'Little Red Riding Hood.'"

"But *Maman*, that's not what happens! She gets eaten!"

On long walks with her sister, Huguette's observant eyes noticed rich and interesting details. She hiked on slim dirt paths studded by jutting rocks or thick roots while pines swayed overhead. She liked the scent of the pine needles, and noticed in the forest underneath the trees, it could be wide open with no grasses or flowers. The sunlight was dappled, and the forest smelled alive and fresh.

"Andrée, there are too many bugs here. But there are no sheep!"

"Good point, I hardly ever see them."

Huguette also saw no formal rose gardens or *châteaux*, but lots and lots of vegetable gardens with small flower patches by small white or plain wooden houses in the dusty towns. There were no oceanside beaches with villas, and the train took days to get to Montana. Her family used motorcars wherever they went, but Huguette saw most people using a horse and carriage or a wagon like farmers. And at tea there were brownies with walnuts and sugar cookies instead of *brioche* and macaroons.

"Don't eat more than one small brownie, girls. You'll spoil your appetite. They're too rich!" said Anna in the teahouse one afternoon.

Andrée looked sheepish, suppressing a giggle. Several cousins sniggered behind hands at the amount already eaten.

"I wouldn't live in France if I couldn't eat brownies every day," announced Cousin Nancy.

"We've chocolate cake!" piped up Huguette.

Nancy shot back, "Not *nearly* as delicious as a brownie, sorry! America wins."

As the weeks passed, Huguette met many new relatives at Mowitza Lodge. She was told it was owned by her older brother, Will Jr., which confused her.

"*He's* my brother?" She was surprised at how large Papa's family was. "Why don't they visit us more in France, *Maman?*"

"Maybe they will in future?"

Anna then changed the subject, never saying anything of the burdens she faced.

I hope William's adult children accept me by the time my daughters mature into understanding family dynamics.

Huguette adored exploring. Her sister and cousins practiced taking photographs with the Kodak Brownie box camera. Huguette kept dropping it.

"Careful! *Maman* said we won't get another if we break this one!" Andrée warned. "Let me hold it until you want to take a photograph, *d'accord?*"

"*Je suis désolée.* I didn't mean to. But can't I hold it sometimes, *s'il te plaît, s'il te plaît,* Andrée? I like it so much!"

"Maybe next year when you're bigger. See, this is why I'm your older sister. I'm wiser and more experienced. Now, no fussing, Hugo."

"Okay, but I like taking photos, too. Don't hog it!" Huguette said in English.

"You must've picked up that vulgar language from Tertius. Don't say that in front of *Maman.*"

In early December, the family sailed back on rough seas with howling winds. They stayed in their suite, except for the one evening Anna roused herself from a short bout of seasickness to join William at the captain's table. The girls played games, read, had lessons in the private dining room converted into a classroom in the mornings, or played fetch with Claudette and other dogs on the promenade deck.

When left to her own devices, Huguette could typically be found in the stateroom she shared with Andrée. She would be standing next to the brass bed or by a blue velvet wing chair with several dolls. She spent a lot of time arranging and talking to them.

Andrée came over and idly took up one of the dolls to inspect its dress.

"Are you done yet? I want to play Snakes and Ladders."

Huguette looked up amidst a pile of exquisite silk doll clothes and dainty leather shoes. The afternoon before setting sail, William had taken them to Delmonico's on Fifth Avenue and 44th Street where they had had banana splits for the first time. Then William introduced them to FAO Schwarz.

The girls entered the grand toy store, eyes shining with rapture at the exclusive creations from floor to ceiling. Its size and scope dwarfed Au Nain Bleu in Paris.

"Papa, Papa! I can pick out a toy?" Huguette began hopping up and down, overcome with excitement.

"Huguetty, you can pick out several toys today! This is New York's finest toy store. Let's go have some fun!"

William's normal reserve vanished as he escorted his daughters to all the creative delights the famous store had on offer.

The original idea had been to select a Manhattan souvenir, which Anna was in favor of.

"Only one toy each, William," she whispered before departing with Amelia.

However, as soon as the girls stepped foot in the magical store stuffed with the most luxurious toys they had ever beheld, William relented. Multiple souvenirs were selected in short order. He couldn't resist indulging them, nor making a mental note to have new toys delivered for the new mansion's nursery bedroom. To start, while the girls admired a display of games, he quietly ordered the deluxe *Polichinelle* puppet theater. It would primarily be for the girls' pleasure—a surprise for when they soon moved in—but the theater would ultimately delight all his many young relatives and grandchildren.

Huguette admired her new talking and singing doll. It was sold with a recorded set of Italian lessons on small records to be inserted into a slit in the doll's back. When activated, it appeared the doll sang the recorded songs, stories, and phrases.

"Can Anastasia play too?"

"I suppose."

Andrée knew if she said anything doubtful about her little sister believing dolls could really play then Huguette would cry. And then there would be trouble with *Maman*.

When the White Star Liner docked at Le Havre, the Clarks boarded a first-class train. A chauffeured motorcar waited at the station in downtown Paris. Soon after, the girls were rushing up the stone steps to the beloved *avenue Victor Hugo* flat a short walk from the Eiffel Tower.

"We're finally home! Look at how beautiful! Let's go see it all!" whooped Andrée.

The girls raced through rooms with garlands, wreaths, angels, and a fourteen-foot Christmas tree in the main drawing room. Handmade, sparkling glass ornaments would be set off by tiny candles affixed to sloping branches lit on Christmas Eve.

"*C'est très joli*! Soon there will be lots of presents underneath!"

"*Ç'est vrai*? Like our birthdays?"

Huguette's eyes widened as her head went back attempting to take in the massive tree.

"*Oui*, like that. Only *better* because Christmas is the *most beautiful* time of the year! It's baby Jesus's birthday. Don't you remember last year?" Andrée said, gazing at several tall angels arranged on a green marble-topped table.

"*Non*, I don't..."

"Pick out a favorite ornament. Mine's Noah's Ark here."

Andrée pointed to the hand-carved, painted ark brimming with animals. Clutching a doll with the poodle Claudette at her heels, Huguette stood in awe. She was too enthralled by the notion of more presents and the profusion of decorations everywhere she looked to pick out a favorite ornament.

"Let's go write our wish list for *Père Noël*!"

Andrée grabbed Huguette's hand. Claudette scampered after, barking with excitement. Sitting at a nursery table customized for children, Andrée enjoyed being in charge while the governess was absent; she set out writing paper and pencils.

"Now don't ask for anything ridiculous, Hugo. We can't have another puppy. And we can't get a cat either. Cook is allergic." Andrée slid over paper.

"I want fish and another doll. Will *Père Noël* bring me goldfish and another doll that sings? And I want some colored pencils, like you have. Can you help me with my spelling?"

"*Oui*, I think that request is perfectly reasonable. Although, you have quite a few dolls already. You must have at least fifteen, my goodness! What about another toy or a game or some books? *Maman* won't allow fish, silly goose!"

"Books? *Non*, I want more dolls... Does *Maman* help *Père Noël?*"

That perfect Christmas was the first Huguette would remember many years later. At holiday parties and family meals, she delighted in eating *Montéli-mar*, chocolate truffles, *marrons glacés*, and *tarte au citron*. On Christmas Eve, Huguette couldn't decide between the gorgeous *ile flottante* and the decadent chocolate *bûche de Noël* with groups of meringue mushrooms which delighted all the visiting children's eyes. Huguette's concentrated expression of joy made William and Anna laugh.

"How about some of each, my pet? It's Christmas!" William suggested.

"She's going to get a stomachache... Huguette, *ma chérie*, we'll be attending Midnight Mass soon. It's such a beautiful service, and I wouldn't want you to miss it because you ate too much."

Huguette chose a slice of the chocolate roll cake, making sure a few meringue mushrooms were included. "I like the crunch!"

Returning from a dinner party and ball on New Year's Eve, William escorted Anna to the small red drawing room. It was a colder winter than normal, and despite the roaring fire, the spacious, tall-ceilinged rooms in the flat felt drafty. They sat close to the fire.

"Anna, I've built the finest, most modern house, not merely in New York City, but in the entire nation, I wager! It's one of my proudest achievements."

"Congratulations, *mon amour*. You've waited a long time for this dream to become reality."

"Yes! Which is why I now would like you and the girls to move in with me. Everything is ready for us."

"But you leave in three weeks..." Anna's expression fell as she gauged his seriousness.

"Yes! From now on we'll all to be together under one roof. Doesn't that please you?" William steepled hands together, leaning back in the wingback chair. His thoughts fixated on the objective at hand. "My business engagements require me to travel, but New York shall be our home from now on."

"*Bien sûr*, I'm merely taken aback... Forgive me, I'm not prepared for such a hasty departure..."

"You'll be able to return to Paris when it suits. However, we'll depart for America in three weeks. I want my daughters to be educated in the United States and to have a native command of English. They only speak English in lessons with their governess or with me. That's not enough.

"I want their French accents softened. I want them to develop a patriotic heart for our native land. That can only happen if they're educated in America."

"I'm a little sad. These past sixteen years have been a dream. I love France; it's my home now. Much more than the States..."

"I hate to disturb your happiness, my dear, but this is my fondest wish."

The butler appeared at the doorway with a telegram on a silver salver.

"Excuse me, Anna. That will be from my secretary in New York, and I must reply."

Anna stared into the flames, her mind racing. *What will it be like to live in a house that's more palace than domicile? In such a conspicuous house there will be no way to hide from prying eyes. Living there exacts a price I'll be forced to pay.*

On the last tour, the gargantuan scale of the mansion stood out the most. Numbers stacked up, pinning Anna down with their weight: 121 rooms over 9 stories, with 2 elevators, a Great Hall, and a grand central ivory marble staircase topped off with a tower overlooking the city. The basement had a large, in ground, swimming pool and a train tunnel linked up to William's railroad for private coal deliveries.

If William could buy Central Park to increase his acreage, I wouldn't put it past him! And worst of all, think of the sheer amount of time it will take out of my day to be mistress of a house that size... William will be off gallivanting across the countryside; I alone will have to bear the burden of maintenance. And I'll be far more removed from the girls' daily lives...

Anna had always enjoyed entertaining, but the flat was small in comparison. It would take a great deal more effort to get the details straight in such an ostentatious house that demanded world-class entertainments and meals. She made a note to hire both a formidable housekeeper and butler; the best staff for such a house were found in London.

Would Queen Alexandra be able to help?

Anna chuckled, rising to go into the bedroom. She knew better than to wait up for William.

The next morning after breakfast Andrée and Huguette were taken to the sun-filled, blue drawing room. William stood when his daughters entered. He helped them to a loveseat where they sat side-by-side, hands in laps. William began talking about moving. He didn't get very far.

"Papa, we recently returned from visiting America," said Andrée. "Aren't we going to stay in Paris until the summer? That's what we usually do. I like this flat; I don't need a new house."

"I don't think you quite understand me, little one. I want you and your sister and mother to come to live with me in New York."

"But that's not a nice city. It's not pretty like Paris. I think we should stay here." Andrée nodded her head decisively with Huguette copying her every move.

"Anna, please explain. I'm not getting through."

William stood up to pace.

"Children, sometimes it's necessary to do hard things in life. Andrée, your father and I want you to attend school in New York."

"Go to school? And not have a governess?" Andrée grinned.

"I want to go!" Huguette said.

"We'll still have a governess for some time. When you're older, Andrée."

"Will I like school? Is it like in books? Will I make friends?"

Andrée's eyes brightened. Huguette watched her carefully.

"We'll talk about that another time. I can tell you all about it because I did it as well."

"We'll visit France in the summer," said William. "We'll be at *Château de Petit-Bourg* again in June."

"Oh good! I can't imagine a summer without visiting the *château*."

"And if you study hard, I might rent a villa in Cabourg as well."

"Oh Papa, please! I long to play on the beach again!"

"*Moi aussi! J'adore Cabourg!*"

Huguette perked up because Andrée seemed satisfied.

Once again, the girls boarded another steamship to cross the Atlantic. After docking, they were all eyes as the motorcar turned into 20-foot bronze gates, went past a 12-foot Italian fountain, and halted under a massive portico. The chauffeur opened the door and William sprung onto the pavement.

"Welcome to your new home, my loves! All you see here is ours. Let's go explore!"

William held out hands for both girls to take before walking proudly up the steps; a double row of servants in matching black uniforms flanked them. The butler and housekeeper stood at the top beside the front doors opened wide.

"Welcome, Senator and Mrs. Clark," said the new butler, recently arrived from London. His thick English accent delighted the girls.

"Oh Papa, this is exciting!"

"Yes, Andrée, I think so as well. This has been your papa's dream. I hope you'll love it as I do."

For the day and night nurseries on the fifth floor, William created a beautiful suite with the bedroom the crown jewel. A hand painted mural of a vast forest—in every rich shade of green imaginable—enveloped the room. Within and underneath the trees and occasional meadows were painted profusions of colorful fairy tale characters, mighty stone turreted *châteaux* with moats, knights and ladies, kings and queens, thatched roof villages with a Gothic cathedral, forest paths to farming villages, animals, and mythical creatures of all kinds, and flowers, witches, wizards, elves, and gnomes. Scattered rivers, mountains, and deep valleys added visual interest. Each grouping around the walls represented a different fairy or folk tale, including all their favorites.

The ceiling was divided into two murals representing day and night: stars in a midnight blue night sky, with a large winking white crescent moon in one corner, and fluffy clouds in a blue sky with a cheerful, smiling sun in the opposite.

Tall shelves and chests burst with toys, games, dolls, puzzles, stuffed animals, and numerous books of both children's and youth literature. A five-foot-tall dollhouse occupied one corner with a rocking horse beside. A massive brown teddy bear with a red bow tie and plaid vest overflowed a child-sized chair.

The *Polichinelle* theater, with numerous puppets to choose from, immediately drew the girls over to exclaim over it. An art easel was erected near a table which had paints, paintbrushes, drawing pencils, colored pencils, pastels, and different types of sketch books.

The matching Queen Anne canopy beds had curtains of pale pink silk fringed with cascading ruffles of white lace down to the floor. The same pink silk was used on the duvets and curtains of the four large windows.

Apart from the beds, every piece of furniture in the bedroom was scaled down. By the bookshelves, a round wooden table with four pink padded chairs was perfect for reading. There was also a seating area by the fire with an overstuffed rose velvet loveseat and two rose velvet easy chairs and a tall, emerald-green Tiffany lamp. A silk Persian rug in tones of ivory, emerald, and rose covered the parquet de Versailles floor.

Initially, Huguette was overjoyed to have new wonders to explore, but hours later in the dark, she worried. The great house loomed; the richly carved mantlepiece leered; odd shapes lurked.

Beyond the bedroom were the schoolroom and other nursery rooms, she remembered. But then Huguette wasn't sure anymore because the house was very large and very unfamiliar.

And Maman *now sleeps downstairs… somewhere.* Maman *is too far away!*

One stormy evening shortly after their arrival, Nanny Browning wished the Clark girls a good night. She turned out the lights and closed the heavy, oversized door with a thud. Huguette jumped headfirst under the covers. Freezing rain pelted the large windows, and the wind howled. The dancing firelight made the fairy tale mural ominous in the cavernous room.

Huguette poked her nose out. "Andrée, are you awake?"

"*Oui*. We only just got into bed…"

"I'm scared! Can we go see *Maman*?" Huguette's voice was muffled.

"*Non*, we'll get into trouble. Are you under your covers because you're afraid or you're cold? I'm right here, you don't need to be frightened. You simply need to get accustomed to this new bedroom. Why not find a favorite flower or character in the mural?"

"I like the unicorn, but I'm scared to see a monster."

"There are no monsters in the mural or in our room. I already checked all the corners and closets."

"You did?" Huguette's voice had a hopeful note; she poked her nose out.

Andrée could see by firelight blonde bangs stuck out wildly from Huguette's forehead. "*Oui*. You look so silly right now; your hair always makes me laugh! How about I tell you a story to distract you from the dark?"

"*D'accord. J'adore les histoires.*"

"I've been reading *The Arabian Nights*, which you can read when you're older. It's much too advanced; it's from Father's library. In the book, Scheherazade tells a story every night to Blue Beard to save her life. He's a scary man. How about I do that with you? I'll begin a story but not finish it until the next night. Then I'll start another one."

"Who's Blue Beard? That's a funny name."

"I'll tell you, but you need to agree to not hear the ending tonight. Don't get upset, alright? Maybe by the time I'm done telling stories you will learn not to be afraid of our new house. I'm not afraid, so you shouldn't be either."

True to her word, Andrée began telling Huguette stories inspired by *The Arabian Nights*. Huguette no longer feared the lights going out. In fact, she grew to love hearing her sister's voice in the dark telling tales of exotic places as blue eyes examined the formations of the painted constellations. She thought the moon laughed at her sometimes.

When either grew tired, Huguette would invariably ask, "Will you continue tomorrow night?"

"*Bien sûr. Bonne nuit, ma sœur.*"

Lessons continued within the day nursery with an American governess named Henrietta Smithson. The only other real difference to their normal routine was the riding lesson. They were chauffeured several times a week to Durland's Riding Academy on West 66th Street. The girls eyed up the many other children mounting horses for lessons in the park. Once on their ponies, the riding instructor led them to Central Park's bridle paths.

The park turned out to be a wonderful place. Each day, it was filled with children and interesting activity witnessed from the paths or from the mansion's highest floors.

"Andrée, look, look! You can see sheep way down over there! In the meadow beyond the trees!" said Huguette from the tower.

"Well, there they are, hiding in New York!"

"It can't be that bad here if the park has sheep like France. Maybe I'll like it here?"

The house was a boon for playing hide and seek. The tower—far from the adults many floors below—proved an especially fertile place to be alone or to play loud games. They could escape Browning to rush upstairs to play and scream as much as desired.

Huguette was overwhelmed with heights, but Andrée was fearless. She climbed steep steps the moment no adult was around to impede. From the rotunda, she peered down at Huguette several stories below.

"I see you!"

"Andrée, you're so small!"

"You're too! You should come up!"

Huguette silently regarded her sister high above in the rotunda walkway. Andrée's long braids and oval face hung over the banister. "Come down now; let's keep playing!"

Central Park with its tall trees, waterways, statues, menagerie, and flowered paths became their favorite playground. They could see the house's tower from many points in the park. In winter, sledding, making snow angels, and ice skating kept them occupied. In fall, jumping in leaf piles thrilled, and in warm weather, walking Claudette on shady paths while observing wildlife an oft-repeated activity.

The most fun occurred while playing hoops, marbles, hopscotch, and tag with other children whenever Nanny Browning permitted. It was a rare day Andrée and Huguette arrived back at the house with grass stains and grubby knees from rolling down hills, but it did happen on occasion.

"Madame, I do apologize! I couldn't run fast enough to keep up with them when they had a mind to join the other children rolling down the hill again."

"I understand your concerns, Mademoiselle Browning, but allow the girls to enjoy the park. They will be warped if they grow up unnaturally sheltered away from other children. If they have completed their lessons, and if the activity is safe, I've no objections to a little dirt."

Browning didn't discuss her prejudices with Madame Clark. The girls' playmates were typically other well-to-do children living in the grand houses and townhouses from neighborhoods ringing the park. But they were forbidden from playing with any immigrant children who approached mid-game. Browning would quickly intercede, and without comprehending why, Andrée and Huguette were shuttled away.

Senator Clark's girls won't be polluted by riffraffs on my watch.

June 22, 1911
London

"Behold the most significantly historical day of the year, perhaps of the decade! King George V's coronation. I'm proud we'll witness it."

Anna mumbled her assent, distracted by checking over Andrée, Huguette, and Kate Morris. She sighed with pleasure at the girls' charming appearance, tipping up Kate's chin to kiss her cheek. Kate shyly took her step-grandmother's hand.

Andrée noticed the brilliant flash as her mother moved. "Ah, *Maman*, may I see the ring again, *s'il te plaît*?"

Anna held out the hand bearing a nine-carat cushion cut pink diamond ring. It was a birthday gift from William, who bought it at one of the finest jewelers in the world: Dreicer & Co. at 560 Fifth Avenue. The pieces made on site or curated by the Russian family from Minsk were as superb as those purchased at rival Cartier.

When William saw the rare pink diamond, "I knew I had to have it for you, my love!"

"*C'est un si joli rose...*" Andrée said, mesmerized while touching the large stone.

Huguette came closer, eyes raised earnestly to her mother's face. "*Maman*, this is my favorite ring! It's as beautiful as you."

"*Merci*! It's yours someday." Anna winked at Huguette.

"Are we ready to depart, ladies?" said William, pacing in nervous anticipation.

"Will we get to see the king and queen, Daddy?" said Andrée.

"Of course, you will!"

"Will we get to shake the king's hand?"

"Andrée, you never ask to shake a monarch's hand. If he extends his hand, then you take it. But otherwise, you wait patiently," said Anna.

"And the queen?" said Huguette with a serious look.

"It's the same rule for both."

"Well, I'll curtsy for King George and Queen Mary. I practiced with Monsieur Blanc when we had our last dance lesson. See?" Andrée executed a perfect curtsy, with Huguette and Kate immediately joining in.

William ushered them out of one of the Ritz London's finest suites. "Girls, we won't get close to the monarchs, but we will see them pass by. Now, let's depart. The King and Queen won't wait for us, and traffic will be horrendous!"

Over an hour later, the British gentry, out-of-favor nobles, wealthy UK merchants, and bankers with legitimate tickets were confused how an American family—their nationality was obvious, although very well behaved and certainly dressed grandly for the august occasion: "Such *lovely* girls…"—could possibly find themselves in *their* grandstand.

Lady Edith enquired of her companion, "Are they lost, perhaps?"

As a matter of course, nothing was done about the vexing issue. No one wanted a scene. And the American interlopers' tickets were legitimate, if listing an unknown baron's name.

"I think my father knew the baron's father, perhaps? The name rings a bell…" Sir Wilfred George Abbot said, shaking a long forefinger to jog a failing memory.

Lady Francesca suggested, "And perhaps the baron has American relatives…?"

"Yes, of course, that's it," pronounced the elderly Lady Agatha, determined to enjoy the day. *I'm pleased as punch I'm able to attend another coronation in my lifetime. Quite a special day to record in one's journal.*

Sir Jonathan Martin, seated high above Lady Agatha, nudged his bachelor brother while watching William settle into his seat: "Kicked us out of our colony but the fools can't resist coming over to pay their respects to the monarchy!"

His taciturn younger brother, wearing a morning suit at least forty years old, nodded very slowly up and down while rubbing a long, furry earlobe.

Arriving before the calvary could be seen coming up the parade route, an ancient member of the House of Lords, Lord Whitebury—in a mended morning coat and frayed top hat—was heard muttering, "Damn cheeky Americans!" Lord Whitebury had been told by a neighbor about the American family in attendance nearby, but was quickly shushed by his diminutive wife, Lady Eliza. She was sympathetic because their granddaughter was courted by an American heir to a newspaper fortune.

As with everyone lusting to attend, William burned to witness first-hand the crowning of a new king of the mighty British Empire. Newspapers from Bombay to Johannesburg to St. Petersburg to Buenos Aires would have detailed reports. *But if one could attend in person, so much the better.*

"A glossy feather in one's social cap, so to speak!" said William to his secretary.

Over twelve months previously, it was announced George V of the House of *Saxe-Coburg und Gotha* would be king-emperor due to his father's recent death. William read about it with growing interest in *The New York Times*. He grasped immediately that the coronation would be an historic event— with tens of thousands in attendance and royalty from all over the world—and an unparalleled opportunity to hobnob. Any excuse to showcase his wealth and power in front of such a discerningly exclusive, global audience pleased William enormously. Few Americans could afford to attend the coronation in the first place, let alone attend in high style.

"I missed the last coronation in 1902..." William mused at his desk with newspaper in hand. "It would be a social coup to attend next year!"

He turned to the business section while his shrewd mind whirled with potential plans.

William spent the next year networking and negotiating to get what he desired. Due to the unprecedented demand created by British and continental aristocrats, dignitaries from the global empire, and wealthy gentry and ordinary citizens all converging on London, business owners knew they had the upper hand. William generously tipped the head manager of The Ritz Hotel and paid over ten times the going rate to guarantee a reserved luxury suite.

Then he secured future invitations to dinner parties, balls, concerts, races, and garden parties to be held in honor of the newly crowned monarchs. The first day offered, he bought advance tickets to sail on the *Adriatic*, along with tickets to the exhibition at London's Crystal Palace.

Anna was none the wiser until eight weeks before departure. "Oh, William, I had no notion of attending the coronation. It will be a zoo in London! Whatever gave you that idea?"

On their way to Mass at St. Patrick's Cathedral, gusts of wet wind buffeted the car as Anna looked with exasperation at her husband. They were stalled in a long line of black vehicles inching their way up to the cathedral doors in the storm.

"It'll be the event of the decade, and we'll be there to witness history!"

"Ah, you'll be the death of me! I thought you were a little more keyed up than normal the past few months..."

"Yes, yes, I suppose I was. Should I apologize? I was busy securing the best tickets I could acquire. Which is why I tell people I married a woman so much younger than myself. She needs to be strong of heart to handle me!"

"Oh William, that's ridiculous. You never say such things..."

"I know, but I enjoy teasing you."

William straightened his black silk top hat in anticipation of exiting the car. He had more of a fascination for monarchy's power than Anna had. She didn't object but sighed to attend social events in London. She had only a few good acquaintances in that city.

"We'll have to call on Lord and Lady Warburton. It's been too long since I've seen Ginny. I suppose the coronation will be *very* grand, won't it? What would you like me to wear, my ermine cape and emerald parure?" Anna said, suppressing a smile.

"How about you wear that for solely me tonight, my sweet?"

"William, you're incorrigible. We're busy tonight, remember? We're seeing the Ballet Russe with Nijinksy. I'm most excited!" Anna clasped gloved hands in anticipation.

"I would prefer you to dance for me... alone."

It would take far longer and far more money than William bargained for to acquire five tickets for the first luxury grandstand alongside Westminster Abbey. The desired grandstand, one of fifty to hold record crowds, would be built especially for the coronation. Closest to Westminster Abbey, the best grandstands boasted padded seats and an awning to protect viewers from the sun. It would primarily seat low-ranking aristocracy, gentry, and politically connected attendees who were, alas, not as monumentally influential, or as powerful as the lucky thousands squeezed into Westminster Abbey. The abbey would be full to the brim with royals and dignitaries from countries and commonwealths all over the world.

Unbeknownst to the aristocracy of the great continental European empires, George V's coronation would be the last magisterial event they would attend en masse. Soon, the world would be plunged into war, eradicating long-standing powers forever; propelling many into exile.

For sheer survival six years after the coronation, King George V and Queen Mary would turn their backs on Prussian and Russian relatives by rebranding the House of *Saxe-Coburg und Gotha* into the House of Windsor. The carefully cultivated royal alliances created by George V's indomitable grandmother, Queen Victoria, in the latter half of the nineteenth century would be subsumed under the straining weight of altered public opinion.

The summer day of the coronation, the horrors and deprivations of industrial warfare were not yet upon the innocently cheering London crowds. The Gold State Coach and the numerous landaus drawn by horses lumbered past tens of thousands of working-class Britons happily thronging the streets.

The year previous, Clark fought hard. "I expect to sit in the best seat for commoners available! And that's the *first* grandstand! You telegram Pelletier now to go to London as soon as possible. He can pay whatever price demanded, but *I will be* sitting in that specific grandstand! It has a total of 200 tickets; find 5 of them for me!"

Clark swore and threw *The Wall Street Journal* onto an empty desk. He glowered at his newly hired secretary, John Evans, as they stood in the mansion's private offices.

"With all due respect, sir," said Evans, "Mr. Pelletier wrote yesterday the first grandstand was strictly reserved for those with English titles or landholders or some such connections. You've no choice but to look further down the parade route."

"Then invent me a title or buy a knighthood but get five seats reserved on the grandstand *I* want! Not one further down in no-man's land! I won't accept that! If I have to go to London myself and talk to the Prime Minister, *I will!*"

William stalked into his office and slammed the door. Evans winced at the resounding smack of wood. Senator Clark was a slight man, but one completely forgot that when he was passionately worked up about something. He was the most competitive, determined man Evans had ever encountered.

In the end, a mere seven weeks before the event, a middle-aged English baron with male-pattern baldness and full red lips—who was more interested in the gaming tables at Monte Carlo than cheering on the monarchy—sold his six grandstand tickets. He felt a small stab of conscience afterward for his long-suffering wife back home. Clarissa had been annoying with long letters of plans for some time. Those unanswered letters made it clear she thought they were attending the coronation.

Plans I cannot afford.

The baron sat languidly at a hotel bar in Antibes. With a flick of the eyes upon introduction, he easily discerned Monsieur Pelletier was nervous.

The man will agree to pay any price.

The baron coolly doubled the original amount. "And I want it in pounds sterling, by midnight."

Blue eyes smiling, he sat back and tossed a drink into his mouth. Before he could set down the crystal highball glass on the white marble-topped table, the Frenchman extended a firm hand. Mildly surprised, the baron shook it.

But will he actually come up with the money?

When Pelletier returned an hour later with 15,000 pounds sterling, the baron was stunned.

Who was Pelletier acting for?

The baron sat pondering awhile before downing the remainder of his drink. He dismissed the thought with the delicious realization he would be flush for the foreseeable future.

And then I'll win big and be able to buy back all the estate land sold off.

Nothing in life made the baron happier than Monte. With bad teeth, he flashed the first genuine smile in ages at the bartender and left to inform his valet to pack.

In the first grandstand on coronation day, other than a few rude comments and a number of turned heads, all soon settled down to enjoy English imperial glory parading past. From William's beaming smile throughout, one would have thought he was the Prince of Wales instead of the sullen, proud young man in the parade.

Andrée, Huguette, and Kate were impressed by the Gold State Coach. They sat up tall or moved to peek between bodies. Eager eyes grew rounder as the royals in full regalia appeared as if out of a fairy tale.

"*Maman*, how beautiful! I've never seen a gold coach before! I read about it in 'Cinderella,' but never imagined it could be real," Andrée said, clutching Anna's hand in excitement.

"Can we have a ride?" asked Kate. "It's pretty!" She was trying in vain to peer out between two stout bodies.

"I want to a be princess in a gold coach," Huguette said.

"We're Americans now, Hugo, we don't become princesses. Listen to me as your big sister, I know all about that. We would have to marry an English prince. But because we're commoners, that'll never happen."

Huguette thought for a moment. "I'm going to stay French. But maybe Daddy could buy a gold coach?"

"No, he has far more important things to spend his money on. And nobody would drive that around town, it's so slow. A motorcar is better, it's fast! Oh look, here come all the soldiers! Look!"

"Lemme see!" Kate was the near the same age as Andrée but not as tall. She could barely crane eyes over the plethora of top hats and giant swirls of feathers or bunches of flowers atop broad-brimmed hats.

William briefly lifted Kate to see the numerous commanders of armed forces on horseback, the Yeoman of the Guard, colonial and Indian calvary, and the Royal Horse Guards troop past escorting the Gold State Coach.

Anna, who had never before seen the English display their imperial might, said, "How impressive they all are in uniform. So colorful! And the horses are gorgeous!"

While the ceremony took place inside Westminster Abbey, the wait of over three hours seemed interminable. William took the girls for a walk; Anna explained a little of the lengthy ceremony of crowning the king and queen, the singing of the choirs, and the priests surrounding the almost nine-hundred-year-old throne; then they went to a nearby stand for a treat. Still, the hours passed slowly. The crowd of adults chattered on around them, some eating sandwiches out of wicker picnic baskets delivered by servants.

"Did you know your father is related to William the Conqueror?" Anna couldn't resist.

"*Ç'est vrai*, Papa? You've the same name as he."

"Who's William the Conqueror?" said Huguette.

"Your father!" Anna laughed, covering her mouth with a gloved hand.

"Anna, don't fill their heads with nonsense! Huguetty, he's an ancient king who built the throne that I'll take you to see tomorrow. And, no, my dear Andrée. Your mother's being mischievous, that's all. Girls, British coronations have been performed in this abbey since 1066. You're amidst history of one of the world's most powerful empires. I would have you well remember this day."

"Ah, here we are, at last!" said Anna, as the abbey bells pealed.

For fear of their dilapidated state, Westminster Abbey's ancient bells hadn't been vigorously rung since the last coronation in 1902. The joyful, deep noise set off a chain reaction of cathedral bells all across the region to indicate the king and queen had been crowned and were now leaving the abbey.

Those in the grandstands and the tens of thousands assembled poured out of pubs or rose to their feet and began to press forward along the parade route. Everyone shouted in unison, over and over, "Long live the King!"

The Clarks saw the carriages and mounted soldiers parade past in the opposite direction. When the king and queen went by for the second time, the girls were able to focus more on the occupants.

"Look, see Queen Mary's beautiful diamond crown! Now they are *really* king and queen!" said Andrée.

That evening as the sun set, boisterous crowds continued celebrating in pubs and in warm streets. Decorative electric lights were strung over all the principal buildings in the center of London. The girls' hotel suite was high up in the Ritz, and they had a bird's eye view of the revelry.

Nanny Browning closed the windows directly after tucking the girls into bed. "No need for your ears to be hearing that ruckus."

The girls immediately felt stuffy; as soon as the head nanny exited the room, Andrée was up like a shot. "C'mon, Kate!" Andrée pushed open the sash window for the breeze but was foiled within the hour by an angry Browning.

Once again, the girls were tucked in. Browning stood a moment at the door and saw with satisfaction the still forms lying on three twin beds in a row. She nodded and retreated.

Immediately Andrée snuck back over to the window to shove it open. She leaned out as far as possible.

"Hugo, Kate, come over!"

Now after midnight, Kate was asleep. Huguette tip-toed over. The night wind was cooling down; it brushed against her face and made the sheer curtains dance.

"Are *Maman* and Papa out there with all those crowds, *peut être?*" Huguette leaned over to look as far down as she dared.

"Be careful, *sœur*! *Non*, they are probably at an elegant party with friends. Oh look, the string lights went out! Too bad, they were *très jolies*..."

For the rest of the summer, Kate was allowed to remain with her step-grand-mother and two aunts, who were her own age. The girls often laughed about this relationship, although it bothered Anna.

"Girls, shush, please. We're all family; don't dwell on who is aunt and who is niece. Merely love each other and go outside and play. Enjoy France, for we'll have to leave before you know it."

"Oh *Maman*, I don't want to go back to Old New York!" said Huguette while rolling her eyes. She had picked up the expression somewhere months ago, and now said it constantly. She and Kate pushed a perambulator full of dolls and a tea set that clattered as they advanced on the chateau's stone walkway.

In Trouville, Huguette, Kate, and Andrée met the Villermont sons whose parents were renting a villa nearby. The girls met frequently to play on the beach with seven-year-old Etienne and three-year-old Henri. They were delightful playmates, allowing Andrée and Huguette to run the show. The group of five children soon became inseparable, and the congenial weeks by the seaside flew by.

When Andrée turned nine, Anna threw a party with the Villermonts included. Anna was interested to learn the family had aristocratic roots extending back well before the Revolution, which had irrevocably altered their fortunes.

"I very much enjoy learning about French history. How fascinating for you to know so much about your genealogy and heritage. I'm not so fortunate," Anna said to Naomi, *la marquise de Villermont*, while watching the table of young children eat cake.

"*Maman*," Andrée wrapped arms around her mother's waist, "I've never had such a beautiful birthday party. *Merci beaucoup, c'est extraordinaire*! I'm so grateful my birthday is in August so we can celebrate by the sea."

"What lovely children you have, Madame Clark."

La marquise de Villermont was too far polite to ask about her hostess's American heritage. For many, the obvious wealth and culture the Clarks enjoyed entirely smoothed over their presumed undignified past.

"I would adore having you attend our dinner party on Thursday next. We've a particular guest coming, a Marcel Proust, who is staying in Cabourg for the summer. My husband has been friends with Monsieur Proust for many years. You'll like him, I think. He's a writer. He would adore your harp playing."

"I would be delighted to attend, *merci*. Now Andrée, go attend to your guests like a good hostess. I think it's time to play pin the tail on the donkey."

Early December arrived too soon, and packed trunks piled up in the front hall of the *avenue Victor Hugo* flat. The weather was rough on the voyage back. The ship rocked uneasily on white capped waves, which made the girls laugh at unsteady legs on the long promenade deck. Snug in matching navy boiled wool peacoats and navy sailor hats, they walked Claudette in the sunshine on mild afternoons with *maman*.

Anna's exclusive behavior on Atlantic crossings taught Andrée and Huguette to be discreet with strangers. They did not seek to cause trouble, to meet new acquaintances, or to explore beyond the strict bounds of first-class. They were content to eat meals in the suite's private dining room and keep themselves apart from the ship's crowded public spaces and lower decks.

William was waiting at the dock in a heavy snowstorm. "My dear girls! I missed you all so much!" He squatted to better hug each little form.

He rose to give Anna a kiss, then quickly escorted everyone to the warm motorcar. At the house, an unsmiling Katherine Morris was waiting in the first floor's main drawing room.

"But Mrs. Morris, we were so looking forward to having Kate stay with us longer..." Andrée said.

"That's very kind; however, I haven't seen my daughter in a half-year. And look how much she's grown, my goodness! Father, thank you for your generosity and kindness. It was wonderful to include Kate in the trip to Europe. However, I must be going. We'll see you all soon for the holidays."

In less than two weeks, William's family would descend on the mansion to celebrate in grand style. He ordered a fifty-foot tree for the front hall, a fourteen-foot tree for the family's favorite drawing room on the third floor, and multiple nine-foot trees to be positioned throughout the house. He orchestrated the decorating, as aesthetics interested him a great deal. Before Anna and the girls arrived, William could be seen frequently walking through the house, inspecting, and taking notes on improvements or alterations.

On that first evening back, Huguette plonked down on the stairs between floors five and six and whined, "I'm tired of looking. Let's go play now..."

"Okay, but I wanted to see if there was another tree up here somewhere."

"I don't care anymore..." Huguette pressed a black boot against the railing.

"*Non?* Well, maybe there's something special to see"

"Girls, come dress for supper," Nanny Browning, who had been looking for her charges for quite some time, finally discovered them because the central, wooden staircase carried voices with ease. She peered up from the floor below. Constant hunts to find the girls in the vast house were becoming a bother.

Perhaps it is time to retire to Surrey. The senior nanny caught her breath while pausing on the staircase; she smoothed a starched apron in a habitual gesture.

"Nanny Browning, what's for dinner?" Huguette said while leaning over the railing, arms dangling.

"Child, do *not* do that! What if you fall to your death multiple stories below?"

Huguette and Andrée suppressed giggles. The railing provided all sorts of fun Nanny clearly had no notion of. They obediently withdrew.

"Nanny Browning, are there more Christmas trees up here? That's why we're looking," said Andrée.

"Heaven help me... I've no idea about decorations. I've not had a moment to inspect anything. We've only just arrived! Now come along." Nanny Browning hitched skirts, muttering about using the elevator more.

By Christmas Eve, Andrée and Huguette were delighted the families of William's four adult children and five siblings filled the house. Much extended family traveled from out West—using the Clark brothers' railway connections to save money on the trip—to stay for several weeks. Bedroom suites all over the house were occupied, which was unusual.

On the day of a large holiday party, the gaggle of boisterous children fed on each other's energy and somehow ended up running through the first floor of the mansion to go through the open doors to the *Salon Doré*. The darkened drawing room's walls were antique ivory and gold boiserie imported from France and lovingly restored to eighteenth century perfection. The gold damask furniture was pushed against the walls with parquet de Versailles flooring underfoot. Somehow, a game of tag began amongst the dozen or so children who comprehended the vast space as they would a gymnasium.

On the opposite side of the large room through a closed set of double doors, William was standing proudly. He had collected a group of family and business associates to show off his pride and joy. He paused for effect in front of the closed doors of the *Salon Doré*, giving a few facts to impress before he turned on the lights. Upon throwing wide the doors, the adults were astonished to behold a rambunctious pack of children racing and screeching and laughing deep within.

Tertius swiped at a passing cousin before yelling, "You're it!" in full view of his grandfather's reddening face. Delighted screams reverberated through the open space.

"Stop!" William thundered. "Children, *stop* running in this precious room. You know better, Andrée, to allow this. Now all of you, *out this instant!*"

"*Oui*, Papa." Andrée hung her head. It wasn't the first time she had been admonished to never run or play in the special room. The children filed out silently, eyes downcast. They quickly ascended the grand, white marble staircase to the upper floors in an effort to escape adult eyes and ears.

"Great, now what're we gonna do?" said Tertius.

"All we do is go up and down stairs!" little Thomas whined. He wore a red velvet suit coat and shorts with black patent leather shoes. He stopped to look upwards and then downwards. He shook his pomaded head. "It's so high I'm getting dizzy!" He plopped down on the wooden stair of the seventh floor, chubby knees rosy from the exertion.

"C'mon, Thomas! We're going to the tower," Huguette urged, offering a hand. She waited patiently for her cousin to rise.

"Let's take the elevator!" Matthew said with a daredevil grin.

"I've already done that twice today!" said Tertius, as he tugged on his boiled shirt front.

"Will we all fit?" said Anthony, a shy boy who felt claustrophobic in elevators.

The children looked at Andrée expectantly. They knew the elevator was not to be played with, but the temptation was there.

"Who cares? Maybe it'll get *stuck*!" Matthew said with a big, freckled smile.

Twelve-year-old Samantha was tired of the grandeur and had no intention of squeezing into an elevator with her cousin, Matthew, who pinched hard. It was becoming too much to bear that she did not live in the mansion. *My own house seems miniscule and boring in comparison.*

Samantha halted and whirled to confront Andrée: "My mother doesn't like your mother." Green eyes narrowed in challenge.

"Why? How unkind of you to say. That's not true. Take it back!" Andrée clutched her red and black velvet dress and backed down a step.

"No, I won't. I heard it myself. Your mother is an *arriviste.*" Samantha had scant notion of the full meaning of the term, but she repeated what she overhead in the exact tone of superiority. "And I don't care anymore about your tour. It's giving me a headache," she said with a petulant air, passing with a sneer as she descended.

Samantha stopped to look around, "Who's coming with me?" No one moved, and her eyes flared. She whirled to descend, the skirt of her green tartan dress billowing. "See you children later! *I'm* going by the *adults.*"

"Just take the elevator, dummy!" Matthew hollered. "Beat you down!"

He took off racing downwards past Samantha with Tertius at his heels, jumping three steps at a time while barely gripping the wooden handrail. Andrée and Huguette watched open-mouthed.

After the New Year holiday, the staff had little time to recuperate. Endless trunks of decorations needed to be taken down to one of the many basement storage rooms, while simultaneously preparing for the house's first grand public entertainment. Senator and Mrs. Clark were hosting a ball at the height of the season.

"This is precisely why I built this house!" exulted William as they prepared for bed. "I'm most keen for the special day to arrive!"

A month before the ball, nine hundred embossed invitations were sent out to the most important families from Boston to Washington D.C. A seven-course meal was planned for the most prestigious forty guests. Tours with art experts would be given in the galleries, an organist was hired, and an orchestra would play in the ballroom until dawn.

Only, the social triumph did not occur. Or rather, a ball occurred, but not in the manner William and Anna envisioned. Regrets poured in in such numbers the postman put them in sacks to be delivered all at one time. They had been posted a mere forty-eight to twenty-four hours before the party; some even arrived the morning of.

The housekeeper walked into the morning room with another stack of mail for her mistress. "Here you are, madame." She stood nervously, knowing what was happening but unwilling to bring it up directly.

"Every last one is a regret..." Anna looked up with a forlorn expression for a moment before picking up a card. "In public some have assured me of attending, but now here I have their apologies 'due to a previous engagement'," she read slowly before her arm lowered and the card tumbled to the floor. "I have opened enough to know what this is about. I don't need to open any more..."

She would not allow herself to weep but her lip trembled. "What will I tell my husband?"

It was too late to cancel, which meant that evening the humiliated couple stood bravely in the main drawing room shimmering in their best evening clothes. They wore polite smiles while greeting the pitiful number of guests who trickled in. The total was less than twenty percent of the nine hundred who had been invited. William noted almost none of Mrs. Astor's 400 had deigned to attend, and almost no one of any great consequence save business and political interests.

That evening, as the Clarks circulated amongst their few guests, the art galleries, drawing rooms, and ballroom were barely populated. Many table settings were swept away and the remaining reconnoitered; a massive amount of food went to waste. Hundreds of bottles of champagne and wines were never uncorked; cigars remained in boxes that would be returned. The orchestra wondered who they were playing for as the hours dragged on and the grand ballroom held only scattered waltzing couples.

The disaster would spread quickly around New York society, repeated in homes up and down the length of Manhattan for months. Edith Wharton heard about it, and, years later, reworked the monumental social snubbing at "Clark's Folly on Fifth Avenue" to include in a novel.

During the early hours of the morning, long after the last guests departed, the couple remained in dress clothes by the fire in Anna's sitting room. They were exhausted.

At last, William spoke. "We've been discarded publicly by the entirety of society, and such a thing is not recovered from."

"Oh, William, I don't care so much for myself, but for you I care a great deal. You've been looking forward to this period in your life for so long, and now it has been damaged irrevocably. I'm so sorry, *mon amour*."

"Don't pity me, darling. I should've known. I'm a seventy-three-year-old, arrogant fool. I know full well what these people are like. I've been around them for decades. We're not the first, nor the last, they will do this to. They're having their day scoffing. And I well realize the concept of Mrs. Astor's 400 is flagging in strength. In my lifetime, it's been like chasing a rainbow.

"I suppose now that I'm thoroughly routed, I must concede defeat. Perhaps try another tactic. We'll think of something, my darling." He raked a hand through thick, grey hair, and pressed aching eyes.

Anna sighed before saying, "What would you like to do with the rest of the season? I'm afraid for me, after this, I won't be comfortable attending the opera or the engagements we've already accepted."

William balled a fist and pressed it to a knee to stop himself from grabbing the brass tongs beside the fire and smashing it repeatedly against the marble chimneypiece. It had been a long time since he had felt such rage flare.

Their continued presence in society would fuel gossip and heap further damage to their tarnished reputation. His businesses would continue unabated, but he couldn't bear to see Anna suffer.

"I'll be damned before I hole up in this house like a humiliated rabbit!"

Within a week, the dilemma was resolved. Arthur sent a telegram: Philomene was dying of pneumonia. The couple boarded William's Pullman car, not returning for months.

"When will you come home?" said Huguette, clutching at her mother's skirts in front of the idling motorcar.

"I'm not sure. Be a good girl," said Anna, stroking her head, but thinking about other things.

"Tell *Grandmère* Philomene we love her!" Huguette waved goodbye.

They received a letter from Anna weeks later. Andrée read while Huguette sat close on the rose loveseat in the bedroom. The letter was neither happy nor long enough. It explained their grandmother had died, and the funeral had been small.

"You mean grandmother's gone? I won't see her ever again?"

"Yes, Hugo, she died of pneumonia. *Maman* must be very sad. Think how sad we'll be when she dies. That's how she feels now!"

"What's pneumonia?" Huguette began crying, and Andrée hugged her.

"Don't cry, Hugo, it's okay. Everyone dies at some point."

"*Non*, I'm never going to die!"

Time dragged as they waited. They always listened for news regarding either parent.

Huguette said, "Will she return before the snow melts? Spring's coming. Miss Smithson said spring starts March 21. I want *Maman* to be here to see it." She held Suzette while sitting surrounded by doll clothes on her bed.

Andrée glanced up from reading a book. "She hasn't said anything about coming back yet. I think she's at a resort in South Carolina right now. But it's going to be all right. Don't worry."

Andrée was worried though. *What could be keeping* Maman *away for so long*...?

For her thirty-fourth birthday, Anna spent ten days alone at a hotel spa on the South Carolina coast. She dreaded returning to New York. Only when Anna considered her daughters' feelings did she feel strong enough to return the third week of March.

William wrote from Los Angeles he would return east by the start of April. Mid-month he had tickets for Europe on a new ship.

It's called the Titanic, *the unsinkable ship, and she's a beauty! I'm quite eager to sail on her; it's a pity we couldn't book her maiden voyage. However, the second voyage isn't bad. Our departure date to Southampton will be the twentieth of April. My nephew, Walter Clark, and his wife are on the maiden voyage to New York. Lucky fellow!*

Yours ever, William

In the letter, he requested Anna to walk with him in the Easter Day parade after Mass at St. Patrick's Cathedral.

My husband can never resist peacocking for the masses. If I go, it will be our first outing in public since the ball. She dreaded facing photographers. *I'll accept what happens and hold my head high, no matter where I am. I must forget the past and move on with grace. Those people are not worthy of my time.*

Anna could almost hear Cervellon cheering her on from the grave.

April 16, 1912
960 Fifth Avenue, New York City

"Anna, terrible news!" said William, an untouched plate and coffee before him. Attention riveted to *The New York Times*, he began reading the front-page article aloud: "Titanic Sinks Four Hours After Hitting Iceberg."

"I'm stunned... In actuality, the *Titanic* was *not* saved as was previously reported. It's sunk! And it's sunk on the maiden voyage. What rotten luck! Dreadful news! A fiasco for the White Star Line; they'll take a major financial hit with this disaster..."

William took a drink before saying, "I hope Walt and Ginny are safe. I'm sure they are. Walt's a smart boy. But I'll immediately send word to my brother, Ross, in any case."

"Oh, that *is* terrible news..." Anna had been standing staring into space. She sat but didn't notice the butler pouring coffee or setting down beautifully plated spinach quiche and fruit. Anna mechanically unfolded a linen napkin.

"Oh William, I can scarcely believe it... I do feel sorry for all those who've lost their lives, poor souls... We've always had such good luck crossing. Nothing in the least threatening has ever happened. I can't imagine how terrifying it would be to drown out there in the cold water..."

Anna shivered at the morbid thought, then reached for coffee. William downed a sliver of quiche.

"I want to get to my office as soon as possible."

"But *we* would've been amongst the next group of passengers on the Titanic! Oh, William, the thought alone...! To have come so close to death... I do hope Walt and Ginny are all right." Anna's hand reached for William's. "Please send a telegram to Ross directly."

Putting down a gold fork on the Sèvres plate with the Clark crest, William took her hands in his. "Yes, my dear, I will."

William rose from the table and touched her shoulder. Anna smiled up at him.

"*Mon cher mari,* please let me know as soon as you hear back."

"Of course. And I'll also see to it that the White Star Line refunds the full price for the return voyage as soon as possible. Those tickets were more expensive than usual!"

The next day, William and Anna listened to Huguette and Andrée play a duet. They clapped and smiled in encouragement, but it was obvious something was off.

"*Maman*, what's wrong? You look sad tonight. Am I not making sufficient progress on the piano?" said Andrée.

Anna looked over at William who nodded. "*Bien sûr*, you're making progress! You both played wonderfully, *merci beaucoup*. Your father and I are sad about another matter. Come here, *mes bonnes filles*."

The girls obediently sat on either side, automatically leaning into Anna's slim body with affection. Huguette loved that her mother always looked and smelled lovely. She put out a small finger to begin tracing the diamonds in the bracelets dangling from Anna's wrists.

William moved over to the fire, looking grave in his black tuxedo. "How about you start, Mother."

Anna took each girl's hand and placed them on her lap. Her mauve silk gown with shimmering black lace overlay was soft. Huguette squeezed her mother's hand and put her head on her shoulder.

"Do you both know the *Titanic* sank a few days ago?"

Andrée spoke up first, "*Oui*, we talked about it with Miss Smithson. She showed us the newspaper. I read the entire article. I feel very sorry for all the families who lost loved ones."

"I think it sounds scary," said Huguette. "The ship was so big in the picture. Did they all drown?"

"No, they did not all drown. But many, many people lost their lives. It's a terrible tragedy."

"Oh, that's sad!" the girls said in unison.

"And we have lost a member of your father's family."

"Who?" said Andrée, looking from one parent to another.

"Your father's nephew and your cousin, Walter Clark."

"You mean he drowned?" Huguette's face looked stricken.

"*Oui*. But his wife, Ginny, was saved in a lifeboat. You'll see her when we visit Los Angeles."

"Oh, poor Cousin Walt! Oh, it's such a pity he's dead; now his wife is a widow. We'll write a condolence card to her today. Alright, Hugo?"

"Is our cousin down in the water now, *Maman*?" said Huguette.

"Your cousin Walter is in heaven."

Huguette watched her older sister suddenly take her hand out of Anna's and sit up on the edge of the sofa. Andrée looked very troubled. "Papa! Weren't *we* going to Europe on the next voyage of the *Titanic*? Wasn't it departing on the twentieth? Papa, isn't that what you said?"

"Yes, we did have tickets. We'll take another ship to Europe. And for the present, we're all safe and sound. Please don't worry."

"Wait! But there's something else! The celebration in Domrémy of the five hundredth anniversary of Jeanne d'Arc's birth! *Maman promised* we could attend! It's going to be so special. Papa, are we still going to be able to sail in time? It's on May twelfth."

Andrée looked from one parent to the other, waiting anxiously. William glanced at Anna who nodded. "I'll make sure to find another boat for you in time. I'm pleased you want to attend the celebration. I wish I could as well."

"If we would've been on the first voyage of the *Titanic*, instead of the second, that could've been us, then..." said Andrée in a grave tone.

Huguette looked at her sister whose light blue eyes gazed steadfastly at *Maman's*. Huguette shrank into her mother's side, whispering, "We were supposed to be on the *Titanic*?"

William knelt in front of Andrée, grasping shoulders with gentle hands. "Not at all! Let's not invent fantasies of danger, please, Andrée! I'll not raise hysterical women. Now, no more worrying. Off to bed."

"Papa, can we ride the elevator?" said Andrée, knowing this was a good moment to ask.

"Yes, yes, of course. Take it every day! Now it's bedtime!"

As May began, William escorted his family to board the *George Washington*. He hugged Huguette tight in the backseat of the motorcar.

"I will see you later in the summer at *Château de Petit-Bourg*, my little loves. Chin up, Huguetty! If I were to run around fearing life, then how would I have become so successful? If I can teach you anything, then it's to have courage and be grateful. We'll keep on living as we have been despite the recent tragedy. All will be well!"

Clutching *Maman's* hand all the way up the gangway, Huguette reluctantly boarded. Within twenty-four hours, she had forgotten any immediate fears of drowning because crossing the Atlantic Ocean was a familiar action. The anticipation of being in France for the summer was the perfect distraction Anna utilized before bed. Before Huguette knew it, they were docking in Cherbourg and soon after on their way to the five hundredth anniversary celebrations of Jeanne d'Arc in Domrémy.

On June ninth, Anna threw a birthday party for six-year-old Huguette. The girls wore matching pale pink linen dresses and pink kid leather shoes. Large white bows pulled back long hair. The Clark girls stood with their mother to greet guests. Etienne and Henri de Villermont, Pelletier's daughter, and other French, British and American girls and boys of the Clark's acquaintance were invited to watch a clown show and a *Polichinelle* theater performance with many puppets. After a triple tiered chocolate raspberry cake by Paris's finest *patisserie*, the children played games.

While clowns performed, the children laughed at the trained monkey perched on Huguette's shoulder. No matter what treat it was enticed with, the animal would once again nimbly cross the room to Huguette. He reached tiny hands to grab her arm and climb to her shoulder in seconds.

"I'll save you, Hugo. I'll get him!" said Etienne, moving toward her purposefully.

"*Non*, Etienne, don't take him! I like it!"

"I'm only trying to help you. What if he bites?"

"He's not bad. I'm fine. Leave me be," Huguette said while moving away from Etienne.

The movement caused the monkey to scramble onto Huguette's head where he undid her bow. These antics made the children laughter harder. Huguette stayed still to make the monkey comfortable.

"He knows you're the birthday girl!" said a short clown with a guffaw.

Huguette beamed with pleasure at the monkey's preference before it was gently extracted. She went to *Maman* to have her bow retied.

"No wonder Papa sometimes calls you his little monkey."

"Can I have a pet monkey?" Huguette pleaded with upward eyes while her mother's hands were busy with the bow.

"Certainly not. It's enough to enjoy the animal at the party. Now, attend to your guests."

The next day, Anna moved the household down to *Château de Petit-Bourg*. Andrée and Huguette were thrilled to be back.

"I like America, but France is my true home," said Andrée. "C'mon, Hugo, let's scope out any changes since last summer. I think I spotted one earlier with the new groom."

The girls soon connived to have the groom, or Jacques as he told them to call him, stop working in the stables to teach them how to ride his bicycle.

The next day, Anna was standing on the veranda looking at a row of potted red geraniums. She was soon surprised to witness Huguette race by on the gravel drive with a large grin and whoops of joy. The girl was quickly out of sight. Then Anna heard a shrill scream and a crash. Anna ran down limestone steps and rounded the corner of the long veranda.

"Are you hurt, Hugo? I see blood." Anna made a tsk sound with her mouth and requested a maid to come with warm water and a cloth.

"*Oui*, I banged my knee, ouch!" Huguette got up slowly, then she brightened. "*Maman*, did you see me? Did you see me? I was riding so fast!" She smiled widely and clapped scraped hands. "*J'adore les vélos!*"

"And how did you begin riding a bicycle? And one that big? How did I miss this crucial event in your young life?" Anna said before tucking her daughter's chin with a finger. She reached out with a handkerchief to staunch the bloody scrapes on Huguette's elbow and knees.

Andrée came running, leather boots kicking up the gravel, slightly out of breath. "Is it alright, *Maman*? Please don't be upset! Jacques taught us. It's his bicycle." She vaguely pointed to the stables behind where Jacques could normally be found.

"Well, if you both enjoy riding, I can order bicycles for you. It's good exercise. And it looks like this one has seen far better days..."

"You could come too, *Maman*. That would be fun! And don't worry, I'm not really hurt," said Huguette with a plucky nod.

After the newness of bicycles had worn off, the girls went in search of another adventure. That summer marked the first time they explored the tunnels underneath the *château*. A bodyguard, as curious as his charges, stepped forward to go. Browning flatly refused; she ordered Nanny Walter and Miss Smithson to attend. Anna only gave permission with the proviso a trusted male groundskeeper, Alexander Simon, accompanied the group.

"And everyone needs a lantern," Anna said.

The group descended into the dank cellars below the kitchens. The girls were quiet as they looked around at the chilly stone passages, rooms, and tunnels they scarcely imagined existed. Even further down, dripping water could be heard.

"I didn't know these were down here!" said Huguette.

Once inside the tunnel to the Seine, Andrée noticed the increasing stink of rot and decay. Huguette was remarkably unafraid, but she kept close. Andrée pestered for explanations.

"Has this tunnel been here all along and I never knew?" Andrée's imagination fired at top speed as eyes scanned the brick and rock walls. She held up the small lantern to see the ceiling. "It looks so old. What're the tunnels used for? Do we ever use them?"

Simon shrugged. "These have always been here. There are so many tunnels under Paris it's like Swiss cheese." The adults laughed with him. "We French like our tunnels..."

Guesses were made to explain that possibly the nobility who lived at the *château* for hundreds of years escaped to the river during wartime or to evade debt collectors.

Simon said, "Or perhaps the tunnels were left over from the Romans? We're only miles below Paris. The *château* stone foundations and grounds are ancient. Very, very old! The structure itself is much newer because it's been rebuilt. And the rivers are like roads, keep that in mind, Mademoiselle Andrée. The Seine has always had a lot of traffic, back throughout history.

"Many years ago, it was likely large shipments of wine, food, or coal arrived from the river. The boats could come right down from Paris and dock here. Then shipments could safely go up into the *château* via the tunnels and from there, on into the cellars by the kitchens. Deliveries could be easily guarded from bandits and thieves, I suppose."

"Bandits and thieves? Are they still here too?" said Huguette.

"Have you heard of the notorious *Château d'If*? *Non*? Well, look up that prison in Marseille. That's where a thief robbing a duke living in this *château* two hundred years ago might've ended up!"

Andrée nodded, fully intending to ask her father about it. Miss Smithson hastily remarked, "Really, Monsieur Simon! Do we have to fill their heads with this information? It's not proper."

Simon ignored the governess. He adjusted his lantern and drew up next to the girls. "With these tunnels to the Seine, the formal grounds above, which were enjoyed by nobility, would not be disturbed by the noisy comings and goings every day of tradespeople, pack animals, and wagons. Rich people never want to see us commoners sweating hard for them, you see!" Simon laughed heartily.

The group soon came upon oars and sailing equipment piled upon the stone floor by the rough, wood door. Simon unlocked it and moved aside the mass of creeping vines to allow the group passage. By the Seine there was an old dock and several decaying rowboats. The girls were relieved to be out but were fascinated with the new sensation of being underground. They immediately asked to return to the *château* via the same route.

***

At the end of July, Anna moved the family to Trouville. The villa had a beach house with a pier large enough to dock a yacht.

"We can go to the beach every day!" Huguette's little face lit up.

"Now come and sit down," Anna motioned with one arm while taking a seat at the round table spread with white linen and blue and white hydrangeas.

Facing the flower gardens, they were shaded from the sun by a pergola thick with flowered vines. It was very pleasant despite the heat. A summer lunch was served: gazpacho, chicken salad on Bibb lettuce, fruit salad, and sugared berries over thin merengue nests drizzled with cream.

"I'm signing you up with an instructor every afternoon for you to learn how to swim properly. In deep water."

"Swimming lessons, for us?" said Huguette. She put down her fork to clap.

"I think that sounds *much more fun* than practicing the piano, *merci, Maman*," said Andrée with a grin.

"Oh, I didn't say one replaced the other. You'll keep up with your daily music practice. The both of you."

The girls slumped down in chairs with mock frowns.

"No slouching! *Mangez votre salade de fruits.*"

The swimming lessons appeared to be a normal summer activity, but, in reality, it was the *Titanic* disaster which altered Anna's thinking. Similar to the one-hundred-foot-high quarantine tower suite designed to protect from any infectious outbreak, learning to swim well in the cold waters off the northern coast would ease Anna's maternal anxiety.

The day before, she spoke privately with the instructor. "The ultimate goal is swimming for long periods in cold, deep water. Andrée and Huguette are weak swimmers, at best. It's high time to remedy that. If the task takes several summers, Monsieur Richard, it's no matter. But my girls must not fear deep water nor the cold, in the least, you do understand?"

By his hearty handshake, Anna was reassured the local swimming instructor—who came well recommended—understood the end objective.

A week after Andrée's tenth birthday, William arrived ahead of Will Jr., Alice, and Tertius. Hearing their ten-year-old nephew's name, the girls groaned. Tertius was not a fun playmate. *Tante* Amelia's appearance the week before made up for it; she pleased Andrée and Huguette more than any visitor. *Tante* Amelia enjoyed swimming and bicycling, and, best of all, didn't have to obey *Maman*. She could sneak them chocolates.

As entertainment, William rented a yacht. The girls delighted in long days on the water, learning about sailing culture, and watching other sleek yachts in the Normandy harbors. It was a new experience to disembark miles away to eat lunch at a seaside hotel restaurant or stroll along quaint streets of an unexplored village.

For the children, such adventures instilled a profound appreciation of the beauties of nature. Adult conversation frequently commented on the colorful sunrises or sunsets, the weather, flora and fauna, and the varying colors of the water. Meals in the late evenings were eaten *en famille* at a table on the deck under a green and white striped awning. The freshness and quality of the seafood, fish, fruits, vegetables, bread, cheeses, and wines were noted.

Being with the adults on board was an exciting development for Huguette. "I like eating with *Maman* and Papa."

Ten-year-old Tertius hissed out of Grandfather's hearing, "What do you mean? Are you that much of a baby still? I eat with my parents every night!"

Huguette stuck her tongue out the moment Tertius looked away.

After the first course, William remarked, "You two seem to be having the time of your lives this summer. Your mother has told me about the swimming lessons."

"Oh yes, Papa! I think France is the most marvelous place in the entire world. We've learned how to ride bicycles and to float in deep water. And we explored the tunnels with Monsieur Simon! Did you hear? We're doing so many fun things!" said Andrée.

"What charming children, Anna," said Alice. Brunette ringlets and large diamond earrings shone in the candlelight.

Before Anna could answer, William took up her hand and kissed it. "My darling, you've never looked better. Will, doesn't Anna look remarkable this evening?"

Anna stiffened a little at the compliment made in company. She knew William ignored the chill in the air when his children were around. In fact, he might praise her even more.

Will Jr. had had enough wine to make him smile congenially. He steadied himself as the yacht rocked against a wave. Charlie informed him millions and millions were literally pouring in from the copper mines, alone, increasing their future expectations. Why then should he waste energy picking at the fact his father had begun a second family, with daughters treated like little American princesses? It drove his sisters wild, but, lately, Will Jr. was sanguine.

Bringing a Cuban cigar to mouth, he reflected, *It doesn't bother me in the least, and I like that.* He winked at Alice.

On days ashore, Andrée and Huguette saw much of Etienne and Henri. The Villermonts once again rented a villa nearby to ensure their sons played often with the Clarks.

Racing down to the pier, Andrée pointed, "It's there. See, Henri? With the French and American flags, and with the brown wooden sides? That's the yacht we ate dinner on last night. It was so beautiful on the water."

"It's enormous! I'd especially adore seeing it! Can we go now?" said Etienne, nodding enthusiastically.

"Andrée, can we go?" said Henri.

"Sure! But no sailing," Andrée said.

Huguette said, "*Oui,* we can go inside. But Papa said we would not sail today or tomorrow."

The children raced around the levels of the docked yacht before walking back down the long pier.

"Too bad you can't come sailing," said Andrée. "Let's go swim instead, Etienne."

"Sure!" The tall boy with dark brown hair and eyes was easy-going and acquiesced to any suggestion.

The children quickly went to nearby beach cabanas to change into swimsuits. Helping Henri, Huguette's tanned legs were soon covered with sand from building sandcastles. She brushed bleached blonde hair off a warm forehead. The four children assembled on the beach again to race down to the water to run and laugh in the surf.

"Watch us now. We can float and doggy paddle in deep water. We have lessons every summer," said Andrée.

"Teach me, too," said Etienne.

"Okay, you must relax first to float. Like this," said Andrée as she lay back in the shallow water.

Young Henri couldn't get the knack. Etienne and Andrée floated off chatting while Huguette spent a long time attempting to give Henri tips. Too soon, the Villermonts were called away by their nanny.

"*A demain*!" said Etienne.

At the start of September, William delayed his return. "The late summer weather is too gorgeous to hurry away from," he commented as the family traveled south to the train station near the *château*.

Soon after arrival, William stood on the terrace as his daughters zoomed by on bicycles. He began laughing and reached a hand to tip his straw hat. He adored their energy and verve.

"Wonderful! I'm so happy you both learned to ride. I'll have to tip Jacques. Please come up here, girls."

He put a hand in a white linen trouser pocket while waiting for them to climb the steps.

"Here you both are for a job well done."

He set a gold coin in each upraised palm.

"*Merci beaucoup*, Papa!" the girls chimed.

They immediately turned to go into the *château* and up the winding staircase. In their dressing room, Andrée pulled open the heavy wardrobe doors and bent to yank on the lowest drawer. In the back, behind folded linens, were fat piggy banks, Christmas gifts from *tante* Amelia. Andrée grabbed both and set them on the Aubusson rug. Huguette squatted and turned over one of the heavy pink pigs to wrench at the cork. They knew it didn't matter which they claimed because both pigs had equal amounts. A much smaller stash existed in their New York bedroom.

"How much do we have now?" Huguette stopped counting at forty.

"I count 120 coins in my bank. Which means we double it to make two hundred and forty total coins."

The math was too much for Huguette to follow, but she knew enough to chirp, "We're rich!"

"Not exactly, Hugo... But, we can always buy *Maman* a birthday present. If Father even lets us pay, which never happens. Now c'mon, let's put these back and go down to the tunnels again. It's creepy down there but I like it! Maybe if we go quickly, Browning won't see us!"

"How about we bury the coins in the tunnel?" Huguette looked very interested in the proposition. "Like we're pirates!" A devilish grin spread across her face.

"No, silly goose! We don't live here all the time, and what if someone else found them whilst we're gone?"

By mid-October, the girls resumed lessons with Miss Smithson in the New York day nursery. Along with tutors and frequent recreation in Central Park, they were kept busy. However, after the summer they had enjoyed, it fell a little flat.

Weeks later, after enduring the same routine of lessons, practicing music, and reading, Andrée woke up on a cold Saturday morning in November feeling peevish. She sulked into her mother's morning room. Huguette was already there, contentedly arranging dolls on a loveseat in a corner. *Maman* sat at her desk.

Andrée slumped into a tufted chair.

"*Maman*..." She said quietly, then waited, fidgeting. "*Maman*, are you listening?" Andrée spoke louder, scowling.

"*Oui, ma petite*... I'm occupied at present. What do you need?"

"Something to do. I'm bored! I don't want to read any longer. What can I do...?"

Anna looked up from writing a letter. "*Je ne sais pas*. It's a rainy day and we'll simply have to stay inside. What do you feel like playing? How about a puzzle? Please remember to sit up straight."

Andrée ignored the request. "A puzzle? Those are for children."

"I see. Are you not a child?"

Andrée didn't answer. She watched Huguette with an impassive face but frowned when her sister offered a doll. "*Non*, I don't want to play dolls either. *Maman*... I'm so bored!"

Andrée slumped further, a frown deepening. Several minutes passed. She bolted up. "*Maman*, did you hear me? I have *nothing to do!*"

The Waterford pen was set down firmly. Anna turned to face her eldest daughter. For once, she did not moderate her tone.

"Andrée, stop whining *this instant!*"

Both girls froze, staring at *Maman* with wide eyes.

"How ungrateful for one of *my* daughters to complain when she lives *in a palace!* Should we drive through the slums of this awful city so that you can see how other children live? Would you like to see the ragged clothing they wear and the miserable toys they have? If any? Would that make you more appreciative of all that *you* have? Now, go to your room this instant!"

Andrée fled and Anna resumed writing. Huguette held a doll for comfort while she got over the shock of *Maman's* anger. After a minute, she too left in search of Andrée. She found her at the round school table.

"I'm writing a letter of apology to *Maman*. I've behaved beastly." Andrée wiped away tears.

"Can I help?"

"*Non*, I must do this as it's my fault *Maman* is so angry."

Andrée had the idea to design an invitation to a musical recital in honor of their mother. "The idea is to say sorry because I know music will soothe *Maman's* anger like nothing else."

After changing into evening dresses, they went to practice. Anna arrived, radiant in a Poiret hobble-skirted evening gown in imperial yellow and ivory satin with purple satin rosettes gathered at the waist with long black ribbons. When the girls began playing, Anna was pleased, and all was forgiven. She then played a harp piece before they went into the dining room with one end of the long table set for three.

"*Maman*, do you forgive me for being ungrateful today?" said Andrée with a shy glance in her mother's direction.

"*Oui*, only remember how privileged you are in a world full of those who are not. Chew your food and wipe your mouth before you take a drink."

After the holidays filled with Clark relatives visiting, the winter dragged. Andrée had learned her lesson about vocalizing discontent. Instead, she kept a journal. She also wrote stories she would read to Huguette in the evenings. Sometimes Andrée would get swept up, standing on the bed and acting out parts of the story. This made Huguette in the bed beside start laughing. She adored the different voices Andrée used.

As soon as they heard the door handle, they knew what to do. Andrée was down like a shot under bedclothes. She shoved papers under the pillow and laid very still, holding her breath, while squeezing eyelids tight. In the nick of time, Huguette threw the quilt over her little head. Nanny Browning stood perplexed on the threshold, peering into the room where only the firelight played against the deep green tones of the mural.

I thought for sure I heard laughing, but there they both are, still as mice.

In mid-May, William was engrossed in Arizona overseeing his most profitable copper mine in Jerome and the eponymous town which he created. In 1913 the United Verde Copper Company transferred over 1,200 acres to the Clarkdale

Improvement Company. Clarkdale, the company town built on the banks of the Verde River to support an extensive complex of copper smelting, was the first master-planned community in the state, with William's railroad servicing it. The entire Arizona venture was wildly successful from the start, and William was behind it all.

Anna knew never to wait when her husband was wrapped up in business. She ordered the girls, nannies, governess, tutors, chef, maids, bodyguards, several dogs—and, indeed, anyone who could prove their usefulness abroad—packed up and off to Paris.

Once the all-important orders for *haute couture* were completed, Anna announced her presence in France by hosting a high tea. She followed up with two musical concerts and dinner parties for eight couples. Having reestablished herself amongst her Parisian social network, Anna felt free to pursue her main objective: Spending as much time at peaceful *Château de Petit-Bourg* as possible.

For Huguette's seventh birthday, she was pleased a new doll joined her collection. It was a Jumeau with brown hair, blue eyes, and a bisque face. Anna motioned for Huguette to come to her, whispering in her ear, "Your sister paid for that with her own money, please thank her."

"*Merci beaucoup*, Andrée! *Je t'aime.*"

Andrée gave Huguette's head a playful pat. "*Je sais*, I give the best presents!"

The next week Huguette and Andrée were walking through sun-dappled forest on a warm afternoon. Huguette was reflecting on her birthday party, a smaller affair than last year but nevertheless satisfactory. "Since we both have summer birthdays, we'll always be able to celebrate whilst in France."

"Hmmm, you say that every year... *Mais, La France* is the most wonderful country in the world...," said Andrée, smelling wildflowers.

After the walk, the girls leisurely took the winding stone steps to their bedroom. "*Maman* wants us to practice music for an hour. Afterwards, is it my turn to read *La Semaine de Suzette*?" Huguette had a hopeful look.

Several summers previously, Andrée had been given back issues from a woman in the local parish. After Mass, a woman approached Anna as she stood outside the cathedral with Amelia and Father Allard.

"Madame Clark, my name is Marguerite Colbert. May I suggest a magazine that is a good influence for young Catholic girls? If your two daughters are as full of activity as mine own are, the weekly publication will perhaps keep them agreeably occupied with stories and wholesome activities."

"Merci, Madame Colbert. I'm always searching for ways to keep my precocious girls entertained."

Anna ordered an annual subscription of *La Semaine de Suzette,* and it didn't take long for both Clark daughters to follow suit with a legion of French girls by amassing a collection of issues and snipping out favorite comic strips of *Bécassine* to paste in a notebook. Huguette played with the accompanying doll, Bluette, that came with the subscription.

Andrée paused and then began skipping up stone steps. "I think I'm done reading it, at least for now. *Bécassine* is very funny this week, so don't color on it or cut it out without telling me!"

Dutifully Huguette practiced her piano lesson at the same time as the more-advanced Andrée played the second piano. Then Huguette went straight to the library to settle down with *La Semaine de Suzette.* She read the magazine from cover to cover. She liked the stories and the comics, and always scanned the designs for Bleuette's doll clothes.

An hour later, Andrée popped her head in. "There you are! *Maman* is waiting for us, Hugo. *Allons-y!*"

"*Je sais...* I'm trying to get Bécassine's clogs right."

Huguette's pink tongue stuck out of her mouth for a moment as she concentrated. She didn't feel like playing music anymore nor did she feel like eating. She wanted nothing more than to be left alone to draw. She slowly began to rise only after she heard Andrée calling again, her black pastel crayon still moving.

"*D'accord*! I'm coming!"

Huguette looked longingly at the sketchbook before turning away. *There's never enough time to draw!*

August 1914
Château de Petit-Bourg, Évry-sur-Seine, France

"Anna! Anna!" William called while passing through linear drawing rooms. Striding into the music room, Anna sat at a gilded concert pedal harp, her hands poised.

"*Oui, mon amour*, what is it?"

"Most distressing news! I've received a telegram that Germany has declared war on France and Belgium. Ambassador Herrick could announce that all Americans are to evacuate France in the near future."

"Evacuate? Due to the threats from the Germans?" Anna waved a hand dismissively. "*Mon cher*, you know the long-standing issues we've heard discussed for years have little to do with France, in the end. And they will never get beyond French borders. It'll come to nothing, mark my words. Why should we interrupt our time here? It's been such a glorious summer. Let's be patient and wait until more than the ambassador makes a recommendation."

Anna looked over the musical score and began playing, which normally would've induced William to sit down. But he was restless, eyes seemingly admiring the lush gardens but in reality, seeing nothing. From frank talk in clubs in

New York and London, William was not sure he agreed with Anna. He returned to his desk deep in thought.

Leaving now would spoil our summer. Perhaps Anna is right. There have been so many years of peace that perhaps the threats will come to nothing. French borders are secure.

William soon received a second telegram. The United States government was sending a ship to Le Havre for stranded Americans. He and Anna had planned to stay quietly for a few weeks in the country before going to Rome at the end of the month. William cursed himself for not keeping a motorcar at the *château*.

"Damn my age, I need gold and to ascertain what other Americans in the city are doing. If I'm not back by supper, know I'm spending the night at the flat."

William kissed Anna goodbye and mounted a black horse. Flipping aside his suitcoat, he put a revolver in a holster. He and two armed bodyguards left at a brisk trot.

Upon entering Paris, William slowed his horse. Traffic was congested and disorganized. At the flat, he was disappointed in the pitiful amount of money in the safe, all small paper bills and checks. The servants reported refugees from all over Europe had been pouring into the city in increasing numbers every day, hoping Paris would be a haven.

Bouchard said, "Paris is so close to the border we're all at risk from the German threat. I've never seen such a commotion. All over the city, sir, hotels, and restaurants have posted notices that hours are reduced, or they are closing their doors. Even the markets have less food, and the *boulangerie* is cutting back on the number of breads offered. Prices have risen sharply. Parisians will not stand for this; they will revolt."

"Madame Bouchard, if you would be so good as to remain here, I will not leave you without orders or money. I'm getting my family to safety first, and then I'll return to help."

"Of course, Monsieur Clark. We will be fine. I've stocked up on dry goods."

William rode through the city. Overall, he noted the atmosphere of the once jubilant city was tense. Carriages and motorcars were piled with furniture, luggage, and somber people. Parisians with means were fleeing south or to country estates. Those who had nowhere else to go hunkered down in flats, attic hovels, and mansions.

Immigrants and tourists were astounded as the hub of Europe rapidly closed down around them. Once reliable and plentiful modes of rapid transportation were overwhelmed by demand or threatened by increasing military requisitioning. Healthy horses, trolleys, and delivery trucks disappeared from the streets.

William knew he would need a great deal of gold to buy his way to the northwest. He first went to see Pelletier; but the agent's office was shut fast, completely dark. The man had no doubt taken his family out of the city; there was no way to contact him. William then decided to go to the bank he had done business with for decades. He was stunned to be forced to stand in line like a common customer.

The pressing need to protect his family through clear strategizing kept him from pushing everyone out of the way. He suppressed the irrational demand he be acknowledged as a rich and powerful man.

It wouldn't have done any good.

The bank refused to deal with traveler's checks or foreign currency. It didn't matter that a good portion of those who stood in line were multimillionaires. It didn't matter who they knew at the top. The bank's response was stone-faced. The manager behind the counter shook his head firmly. As the crowd swelled menacingly, the small wooden doors slammed down one by one. A man's hand snaked out a side door to hang up a closed sign before quickly retreating.

The line of people went berserk, raising fists and shouting obscenities.

William pushed his way out of the crowd and mounted his horse to ride south. *Germany's declaration of war is unprecedented. I've never been through a situation that not only cuts me off from my money but thoroughly threatens the safety and well-being of my family!*

The second-richest man in America had long carried only petty cash. The Clarks had francs in their possession, but not enough to get them much beyond the northern suburbs of Paris during a crisis of unprecedented demand.

Energized by adrenaline, William trotted up the gravel drive of the *château*, dismounted, and took the stone steps by twos. Striding into the room, William's flushed face and wild eyes alarmed Anna.

"Paris is flooded with travelers from every corner of Europe, it seems. It's devolving into chaos, and the military has taken over trains, vehicles, trucks, horses, everything! We cannot rely on them. We'll need quite a bit of money to rent carriages or perhaps a motorcar, if we're lucky, to travel north. We're three adults, two children, plus all the servants... Oh my..."

Pacing, William made calculations. He ran a hand through thick, almost white hair. He abruptly turned to face his wife seated next to her sister.

"I'm terribly sorry, darling. I should've seen this coming. I'm afraid we're in a pickle, as the banks are refusing to cash any foreign traveler's checks. I'm a fool to have waited this long! I should've gone to Paris *immediately*."

"That can't be..." Anna feebly suggested, "Did you try another bank?"

"Yes, of course!" He then swore before he restrained himself. "I apologize for my rudeness... It was the same situation at *every* bank. Friends report the same. No one has anything to lend. They're using what valuables they have on hand to barter transportation, lodging, food. Most are fleeing as fast as possible."

Anna and Amelia stared, needlework lying in their laps.

"Everyone...? And the trains? We can handle third-class during an emergency. I won't complain," Anna smiled, trying to catch his attention.

"There's not even that! I'm afraid the trains are increasingly unreliable and unavailable. The military is disrupting the normal schedules to mobilize men, horses, and supplies to the border, as we speak! If what I've heard is correct, the first battle could be fought within a matter of weeks."

Amelia looked at Anna with alarm. "*Weeks?* William, I've some dollars and francs, but it's not a great deal. You can have it."

William nodded but waited for his wife to catch his meaning. It pained him to mention it. Anna merely gazed at him, waiting.

"My dear, I hate to ask... but, we'll have to sell... a piece or two of your jewelry to get up to Le Havre. I've learned the USS Tennessee will dock there to begin transporting Americans out of France. Then we can get to England and to safety."

Anna's face took on a pinched expression. She wasn't happy to give up jewelry bestowed at important moments. She could hardly believe her ears.

"Of course, if it's needed..." Then she held out a hand. "William, please come here. You're scaring me. Is it really that bad? Are we in trouble? Do we need to leave tonight?"

William went over to embrace Anna as she wept. "I'm sorry I've been distracted lately, my darling. Yes, it's serious, but we'll be fine as soon as we get to Le Havre. I know you don't want to, dear wife, but I promise I'll give you three diamond necklaces for the one it will take us to get to the coast."

Anna nodded and dabbed at tears. "It's not losing a necklace. Goodness knows I've enough. I'm afraid at the idea of war. I cannot believe it's come to this drastic step. And so quickly! What will become of France and our home?"

"I can't say. Let's hope the conflict will end soon. We should depart early tomorrow."

Andrée and Huguette had heard rapid hoof strikes on the gravel drive below their bedroom. It was an unusual sound at the *château*. They descended to the ground floor to stand quietly at the door, listening. The adults were so engrossed in conversation in the middle of the long drawing room they didn't notice. William and Anna therefore didn't cover up fearful anxiety or mask their speech.

Andrée turned to Huguette and smiled wide. "C'mon!"

They raced upstairs. The heavy banks were lugged carefully down winding stone steps.

"We can help!" the girls chimed in unison to adults who barely registered their presence. Arm muscles strained against the porcelain bank weighing down each pair of hands. Sticking out a pink tongue with blue eyes squeezed shut, Huguette plonked hers on the rug with a grunt.

William was seated in an armchair beside Anna. He looked at his daughters uncomprehendingly. They poured toys out at his feet.

"Not now girls!" William looked away in annoyance.

"But Papa..." Andrée whispered.

Something in her tone caught his attention, and William looked down to behold dozens and dozens of glittering gold coins piled up.

"Manna from heaven," Anna whispered with grateful hands raised to her mouth.

Starting up from the chair, William threw back his head in a hearty laugh. He abruptly hoisted Huguette in one wiry arm and took Andrée's hand to twirl around the room. The girls shrieked with laughter.

"My smart, brave girls! My wonderfully intelligent, generous girls! You've saved the day exactly like Jeanne d'Arc! Bravo, my little heroines! Now we can get to Le Havre without trouble, for who can resist gold, eh?"

That night, Anna instructed the girls to dress in their plainest clothing with a light coat and sturdy hat in case it rained.

"Leave everything behind you won't agree to carry yourself. We can only take one bag each. Huguette, *je suis désolée*, you may only take one or two dolls."

"Only two! How can I possibly choose two? I know I can carry at least four... *Maman*, will I ever see my friends again? I can't leave them here for the Germans!" Her upturned face forlorn; tears threatened.

"We'll come back soon. The war won't last long, don't worry."

The girls sensed their mother's unease. It helped *tante* Amelia was there; each girl could hold one of the women's hands as they moved forward uncertainly.

Once leaving the safety of the *château*, out on the open roads they witnessed what William had already seen. Everywhere, commotion. The routines of normal life altered. Motley groups of people traveling. Soldiers in navy blue and red wool uniforms marching in formation while wagons eased to allow passage.

The over 230 kilometer journey to Le Havre took days. City, village, and country roads were sometimes choked with masses of people or military. It was a traffic jam comprised of aging horses, creaky wagons, farm animals, well-worn carriages, and many on foot.

In the village, two sturdy wagons were the best William could find. Seated on the wooden wagon bed with only thin pillows and leather valises underneath sore bones, Anna was grateful they were on their way to safety. William sat on the box seat with the farmer; both knew a smattering of each other's languages. The farmer had a good sense of humor, and William chatted as if he were back on the American frontier selling eggs for five dollars a dozen.

Anna said, "It has meant so much to have peace and security in France after our hard-scrabble childhood. Yet, all of the sudden, my adopted country feels like a bewildering nightmare. I can hardly believe this is the same country I've lived in for nineteen years. In a mere twenty-four hours, our lives have been completely upended!"

"And this dusty road seems to be interminable and getting hotter by the hour," grumbled Amelia.

"Here, I will share my parasol with you," said Andrée, who otherwise said very little.

"Oh, that is kind." Then Amelia's happy expression faded as they came upon a more populated stretch of road.

Up ahead, other well-dressed women clutching children's hands and lugging bags, sometimes on foot, appeared in groups. Dogs shrilly barked and howled, which set off their own. Huguette reached to pet Claudette and Margot, a Pekinese puppy.

"The poor things! They've been vacationing apart from husbands," said Anna, shading her eyes with a lace gloved hand. "No doubt the men are working in America. Is it possible the husbands are somehow oblivious to the seriousness of the situation?"

"Oh, who knows," said Amelia, as she swatted away yet another fly.

Anna scanned the crowd.

How very fortunate William was at the château when war broke out! His travel schedule can be hectic; it was a blessing he was there at the precise time needed. What would I have done without him?

Anna looked at her younger sister, who was attempting to smooth frizzy hair underneath a straw hat.

"Amelia, I'm sorry you have to go through this, but I'm glad you're here. I've never looked forward to getting to England as I do now!"

"Well, I appreciate that, but I can't wait to take a hot bath back in the good ol' USA. And I really *like* the Germans. What're they thinking? Preposterous. Let's simply play Beethoven and all get along, shall we?"

"*Für Elise* is one of my favorite songs to play," said Andrée.

"Of course, it is, dear one. And you play it well. As soon as we arrive in England, I want to listen to you play while I take a bath all afternoon eating *les bonbons au chocolate...*"

Both nieces burst out laughing, while Amelia continued with a wry tone, "In the meanwhile, I'll be eternally grateful when we're crossing the channel and *out of this wagon.*"

To distract herself, Anna braided Huguette's hair. A woman suddenly approached their slow-moving wagon. With imploring eyes, she reached for the side. She was dressed in an ivory silk and lace gown with an overlarge straw hat with ivory veil. William greeted her.

"I beg you, fellow Americans, to help me."

William quickly assessed the woman, children, servants, dogs, and two mares. The forlorn group stood next to a formidable stone gate with a long drive extending behind. A pile of trunks and leather bags, dusty from being heaped on the side of the road, was nearby.

"Madame, you'll have to wait. Our wagons have too many passengers and luggage already. These old horses are not spry enough to endure pulling overloaded wagons. Do you have a man to send out to secure wagons?"

"Possibly, sir. I couldn't say. Will you take care of it for me?" said the woman absently while passively observing them trundling away. She lowered an ivory lace veil.

"Send a servant to the local village!" William called out.

He wasn't willing to stop a second time. Previously, he had argued with a woman with five children, many servants, and an even larger pile of luggage. She flatly refused to leave anything behind. After a friendly overture, the smile left her attractive face when her wishes were not met.

"I demand you relinquish one of your two wagons! I'm an American in danger, as well, Senator Clark! My family is from Boston, perhaps you have heard of them? The Buckinghams? Art Cabot Buckingham is my husband's name."

"I can't say I'm acquainted, Mrs. Buckingham. At the moment, I'm trying to relieve your distress in any way I can."

"Well! *Any* gentleman of good breeding would do *far more* than you're offering! He would readily give up his seat for a lady in distress!"

"Mrs. Buckingham, by all appearances you need far more than a mere *seat*. However, I'll not abandon my family to save your hide. If you need gold, I've some to give. If not, then we must be moving on. I suggest looking for transportation without delay. If none is secured, then abandoning your material goods would be advised. Worry about the lives of your children instead. You should be on the coast within days if you begin walking now, and from there you will find easy passage to England."

"*Walk* to Le Havre! You must be out of your mind!"

"Madame, walking for a few days will do none of you any harm. If I were in your shoes, it's how I would proceed. Good day to you!"

William doffed his straw hat and climbed up onto the wagon bench as the harried woman screamed an obscenity. After that failed attempt, he closed ears and eyes to imploring, stranded tourists. He passed out gold coins until he could give no more away.

The slow, awkward trip northwest to the coast was the first and last time Huguette and Andrée would encounter sub-par travel conditions. They had known nothing but the height of first-class accommodations, polite interactions, and white-glove service. Yet here they were, swaying along dirt roads in a farmer's wagon with little to eat.

"Hugo, isn't this a very unusual adventure?"

"*Oui*. How much longer? I'm bored of sitting. I've no new books to look at," Huguette whispered because *Maman* had fallen asleep.

"Papa said sometime tomorrow. Here, do you want my plum?"

To be thrown without first-class barriers amidst common people was highly unusual. Huguette and Andrée saw raw life swirling around them at a pace never before witnessed. It was exciting and disorienting at the same time. Both girls spent long periods merely observing. Occasionally, they saw formations of soldiers and officers moving to the front lines.

Women and old men on the streets or in a nearby wagon called out, "*Bonne chance, les braves!*" or "*Vive la France!*"

Meals consisted of ham and cheese on a baguette with a plum. They were in need of washing up, but it was thrilling to be outside when the stars came out. If an open inn could not be found, Papa sat down with them on quilts laid out on the grass to review constellations. The girls counted falling stars until eyes grew heavy.

When the USS *Tennessee* was finally in their sights, the irony of escaping France was not lost on Anna. Once on board, William was quickly able to cash a check from the gold the government had sent over to aid stranded Americans. After the ship pulled away from the coastline, he sat down on a deck chair beside Anna and Amelia.

"All is very well! We'll be in England shortly." He opened *The Times* with relish.

Anna and Amelia chatted while the girls played on the deck with the dogs. Upon arrival in Southampton, they took a train to London where William booked two suites at the Ritz. It was obvious his wife and sister-in-law had been through an ordeal and needed some time alone. The two moaned about not getting out of bed the entire next day.

To help, William escorted Huguette and Andrée to the British Museum and to Madame Tussaud's. They ate at the Ritz and went to Harrods for new toys. The girls begged their father to let them have dessert at a café inside the massive store.

"Now remember to not tell your mother what you are eating, my dears. For your sacrifice and bravery, I'm rewarding you most generously today with lots of treats and a ride on the revolving staircase."

The girls giggled while eagerly digging silver spoons into *crème brûlée* and *mousse au chocolat*. Afterwards, William watched indulgently as he let them go up and down the escalator several times. He felt years younger merely watching their gleeful antics and wide smiles.

The next day at breakfast in the suite William said, "Why don't we recuperate at the Royal Leamington Spa while we wait to see what happens with the war? I think we've all been through enough, and I feel a great need to 'take the waters,' as the British say. What do you think, my darling? Are you in favor of a British tradition? I think it's the perfect time to try."

"Yes, I think that sounds wonderful. Thank you, William. Give Amelia and me a day or two more to do a few things in London. Tomorrow, we would like to make our own trip to Harrods."

"Well, now, we've already been there. Right?"

William winked and Andrée and Huguette laughed delightedly.

"How about that, my sweet girls, are you up for another adventure today? I've some time this afternoon; we could go sightseeing."

"*Oui, oui*, Papa!" they chorused.

Life had begun to feel like a vacation because lessons had been postponed for days. By the end of the week, the Clark family and their retinue took a train northwest out of London headed for Royal Leamington Spa. As the British had done since 1784, and later Queen Victoria, they drank the mineral water in the Royal Pump Rooms and Baths. They booked rooms in the Regent Hotel, strolled along quiet streets to see famous Regency architecture, crossed Victoria Bridge over the River Leam, spent hours at the Turkish Spa, toured manicured Jephson Gardens, and enjoyed concerts and an occasional opera singer in the evenings. For exercise, they played tennis at the Leamington Tennis Club. The war was so new restaurants had not begun rationing. Meals and teatime were decadent. Thus, their nerves were settled in high style.

After several weeks, they returned to London. While William attended a business meeting, the women went to Paddington Station.

"Goodbye, Anna, my dear sister! What a summer vacation this has been, I must say. Coming to Europe is as dramatic as ever, but, in hindsight... I think I'll pass on next summer's visit. I can get a sore bottom from riding a wooden wagon at home any time!"

Her nieces burst out laughing. Anna shushed them but could not suppress a smirk. "Amelia, always full of comedy. I'll see you soon."

"Goodbye, dearest *tante* Amelia! I'll miss you very much!" Huguette gave a hug and kiss before the whistle blew. Gloved hands were soon waving eagerly as their aunt's beloved face appeared at a window above.

Less than three weeks after the Clarks boarded the *USS Tennessee*, the first battle of the Marne was fought thirty miles northeast of Paris. With German aggression thwarted, the city seemed safe for the immediate future. For a good time to return,

William watched the newspapers and talked with politicians at his London club. The refugee crisis passed, and while the reality of war sunk in, France settled down as much as possible. In late September, William and Anna risked a trip. The trains were running but on a decreased schedule.

Anna had not been in Paris since the previous spring. "It appears the gaiety and pageantry are all snuffed out."

She and William rented a down-at-heel carriage to view once busy boulevards, entertainment districts, metro, shops, and innumerable busy households now far quieter. If any bustling activity and large groups of trucks and motorcars were seen, it had something to do with the military. Cafés and bistros were peopled with quiet patrons; but many boutiques and restaurants were closed indefinitely. Farmer's wagons trundled to markets, people walked quickly past, rubbish was thicker in the gutters, and street dogs loped by.

The world-famous city of elegant *demimondaines*, proud aristocrats, international tourists, and *flâneurs* seemed to be no more.

Anna snuggled closer to William that evening in the flat's master bedroom. "The reports of developing trench warfare bother me. To think of poor French and Englishmen digging down in the dirt and shooting at the Germans from Belgium to France is intolerable."

"Yes, my darling, I agree," said William, his eyes closed as one arm cradled his wife.

"I can't fathom the greed driving this senseless war... I want to do something to help those poor men out there, fighting to save this beautiful country. We'll have to help the war effort when we get to New York."

"Yes, of course," William mumbled sleepily.

"I no longer feel safe here. I hate to admit that, but it's the truth. I want to return to England as soon as possible... And if the war lasts through the fall, I want to return to New York immediately. My darling, I must concede I'm grateful we've a house there. Think of all the poor people who've made France their only home who're now living in fear or exile. I pity them..."

Anna lifted her head. William was asleep. She lay awake another hour, considering her future.

Now flush with money, William easily hired a few men too old or too lame to fight. They salvaged from their residences what was most important. For an exorbitant price, paintings, trunks, and furniture were shipped to a warehouse in Southampton for the duration of the war.

Bouchard was given money to retire on. She informed the Clarks she would go to her sister's house in Medoc. "I'll lock up the flat when I depart."

In October, the Clarks sailed away from Europe, little suspecting how deeply the rhythm of their lives would alter. In New York, normal life resumed, and Anna rejoiced to attend concerts and the opera. But it never resonated like Paris.

The American government and public were debating whether to aid the war effort from afar or to beef up the military or to roundly condemn the imperialist powers thriving in Europe and stay apart. Amidst all the discussion, the fall season of entertainments and social events was underway. Austerity measures and rationing affecting many didn't touch the Clarks in the least.

Anna read newspaper reports how France weathered the German storm, and donated money to war relief measures. The Clarks used the Fifth Avenue mansion and contacts in the music and art worlds. Anna organized violinist Tourret to perform with a small chamber orchestra, selling tickets for five dollars. The collected money was given to Villa Molière, an overwhelmed military hospital in Paris. A second charity fundraiser was held less than two months later; an organ recital was performed with a male speaker on war at the front lines. Tickets were three dollars with proceeds supporting families of French soldier-artists.

Anna garnered attention for her public support of the Allied powers. William was pleased his wife's name appeared favorably in *The New York Times* reporting on prominent women hosting benefits.

"Look at my accomplished wife's name alongside the Astors and the Carnegies. This makes my day!"

"Oh William, don't take that so seriously. It's embarrassing to be named in the newspapers, as if I were striving for popular opinion. I would have as many charitable events as you allow to help out my beloved France. It doesn't alter my feelings one way or another if the papers blare each event from the housetops. I simply hope it'll raise more interest, and therefore, more donations."

"Of course, but positive press is not something to sneeze at. Goodness knows I need some more of it!"

The Clarks also hired expatriate artists looking for work. Pierre Tartoué was making a name for himself in America by painting flattering portraits while charming patrons and charging a small fortune. He painted Andrée and Huguette with such speed, both portraits were hung in the the third floor drawing room before the house filled with holiday guests.

"I'm *enchanted*. The portraits reveal the personalities of the girls so charmingly. William, are they not wonderfully executed? Girls, we should have you both painted every year, to document your growth into young women."

"I think that's a fine idea, Anna. I want your portrait done next. Perhaps mine as well..." William's focus went back to *The Wall Street Journal*.

"*Maman*, it's tedious sitting still for that long! Please don't say it will be annually!" Andrée rolled eyes and snapped a book shut.

"I wanted to watch him paint, and Monsieur Tartoué said yes. I like him!" Huguette patted the doll's head beside her on the chair and went back to drawing a still life of a crystal vase full of yellow roses. "Maybe I'll be a painter someday like Monsieur Tartoué? But I'd like to be a violinist, too. Andrée, can I do both?"

"Not a good idea, Hugo. Best to choose one." Andrée rose from a velvet loveseat. "Papa, did the new shipment of books come in from London yet?"

"Yes, last night actually."

"*Parfait*! I'm off to the library then!"

As Andrée skipped from the room, Anna bent over Huguette. "Well done, *ma petite*. You do whatever you'd like. Practice both arts until the way is clear to you, *d'accord*?"

"*D'accord, Maman... Merci.*" Huguette gave her mother a kiss on the cheek.

Against Anna's wishes, after the new year of 1915 began, William allowed the girls' portraits to be displayed at a top gallery. Attention from journalists viewing the fashionable portraits of the Clark heiresses was immediate. Photographs of the portraits were used in speculating articles about the richest girls in America living in a 121-room mansion worth millions. The articles appeared in prominent newspapers across the country, fanning the flames of public interest.

"Anna, don't be angry. Who cares what they say?" William set aside the newspaper she thrust in his face a moment earlier.

"I don't think it was a sound idea to display the portraits publicly. William, you went against my wishes!"

"Come now, it's fine. What can the press do, anyhow? They never really hurt us, do they?"

In mid-January, Andrée and Huguette were surprised by their governess, Miss Smithson. With wet eyes and wearing a traveling cloak, she came in as they ate breakfast. She said goodbye and departed. Instantly, the girls rushed through multiple long hallways and down two flights of stairs, bursting into the morning room without knocking.

Anna had forbidden any of the decorators to touch her suite. She alone co-ordinated with a French firm for the decoration of the walls and curtains to be in hung in either jade or ivory silk with Louis XV and XVI furniture covered in the same fabric. Impressionist art, priceless Chinese and Japanese porcelain, and jade *objects d'art* were placed carefully throughout the bedroom, rose marble bathroom, dressing room, office, morning room, and small music room. Anna never succumbed fully to the lures of maximalism, despite the excesses around her.

Seated at the Louis XVI *secrétaire*, Anna raised her head. "Has the governess departed already? I didn't mean for her to leave *today*." Anna put down a 14-karat gold Waterford pen. "Ah, well, it's no matter. Girls, please, you're panting as bad as Claudette on a hot day. It's unbecoming. Sit down and compose yourselves."

Anna waited while they settled on jade damask slipper chairs.

"As promised, your father and I've decided to enroll you in private school. You'll both start this coming Monday. Andrée, you'll be attending Miss Spence's School. Huguette, you'll be attending the Anderson School for Girls."

"Finally! *Maman*, you've made me the happiest girl alive! I'll have many friends now and leave the house for classes all day! I feel grown up already! I wish it were Monday!"

"Why can't I go to the same school as Andrée?" Huguette put her head on Anna's shoulder.

"In time you will. Your father thinks it best you attend a different school, to become your own person. Now stop pouting, you're too old. Andrée, to the harp, and Huguette, to the violin. A minimum of sixty minutes practice before it's time for lessons. To the music room, *allons-y!*"

Huguette's shy demeanor and introverted nature overlaid a well-educated, well-traveled, independent mind that paid close attention to detail. At the Anderson School for Girls, the parochial teacher made the mistake of not considering Miss Clark's recent European sojourn when she began her lesson.

A mere week after Huguette's first day, the class of twenty-five girls stood loosely around the teacher who positioned herself at the front black board. The self-conscious Huguette, wearing a blue wool dress, blue hair bow, and black boots, stood at the very back.

"Now class, I'm pleased to announce we'll be performing a skit."

The class instantly hummed and chattered with anticipation at the fun activity. An outgoing girl at the front eagerly raised her hand for the lead role, whichever that might be. The teacher almost forgot herself and smiled.

"Now listen, class, please. Listen…! This is a cherished annual school activity, and your first opportunity participating. I've a list of parts here…"

The teacher explained the objective and when they would perform the skit onstage in the auditorium.

"Based on hair alone, Huguette Clark will be perfect in the role of the German girl in our skit. How does that sound, Miss Clark? Would you like to be a *fräulein?*"

The teacher looked expectantly to the back of the group in a misguided attempt to draw her newest pupil out. Many pairs of inquisitive eyes sought out Huguette, who shrank, clasping hands nervously.

The teacher mistook Miss Clark's long silence for shy agreement. The efficient woman looked down at the list of parts on a brown clipboard and wrote Huguette's name in penciled cursive.

"That will do splendidly. Now class, shall we choose the part for the mother? How about Emily Wickens in that role?"

"No."

The teacher moved eyes from the list to the students. Her expression darkened. In a nanosecond, the students knew danger lurked. Everyone froze, eyes darting like rabbits, ascertaining peril ahead.

"What was that? Who spoke, please?"

"I refuse to play a German."

Huguette thought about her recent experience being threatened. Of fleeing her home in France. Her chin lifted and back straightened in an obstinate pose Andrée would have immediately recognized had she been present. Several girls whispered and giggles punctuated the group. The teacher looked stunned before eyebrows drew together in consternation.

"Shush! Pardon me, Miss Clark? You refuse to participate? And what is wrong? This is a delightful skit, and there is a German girl, Greta. Now come along and don't be difficult. We all must participate."

"I'll not perform in a skit that's about Germans, nor will I play a German girl."

Huguette's eyes remained fixed on the high wall opposite filled with multi-colored maps and lacquered oak-framed windows. The sun poured into the room that morning as the assembled girls were dazzled by how mature the new girl sounded. Struck dumb, eyes traveled from the teacher—a woman not known to be terribly kind even on good days—to Huguette's determined face and back again.

"If you'll not help with the skit, after all we've done to welcome you into our class and into our school, I'll have to indicate your disobedience to the headmistress at once. Do you understand the consequences, young lady?"

Huguette remained silent. Only the wooden floorboards creaked as a few bodies in the crowd shuffled to see better.

Quite surprised by the overt display of disobedience, the teacher marched Miss Clark out of the room. The class erupted with chatter as soon as the lacquered oak door shut.

That afternoon, William and Anna sympathized immediately with their daughter's feelings and comprehended their source. After the headmistress perceived the matter quite differently, Huguette was withdrawn. The next day, Miss Clara B. Spence was delighted at the story of the courageous Huguette.

"What verve your young daughter has, Senator and Mrs. Clark! I shall take pleasure in getting to know her."

Weekdays, Huguette and Andrée were chauffeured in a 1915 navy-blue Rolls Royce Silver Ghost at half past eight to Miss Spence's School on 30 West Fifty-Fifth Street. To form a well-rounded woman, deportment, etiquette, and manners in all social situations were emphasized. Large swaths of poetry and Shakespeare were memorized with lessons focusing on penmanship, elocution, Latin, art history, geography, literature, chemistry, and physics. Examinations were thorough and frequent.

Celebrities were featured at the famous school for New York's best and brightest young females. One year, the girls would be given a dancing class by Isadora Duncan, and during other years, famous individuals such as George Washington Carver and Helen Keller spoke during all-school assemblies.

The Clarks and Kate Morris were easily in the top five wealthiest students at Spence. They fit in well due to inherent sweet natures which never fell prey to flaunting privilege. In her weekly assemblies, Ms. Spence encouraged the pupils to be kind. The headmistress, a suffragist with exquisite manners who refrained from raising her voice, held progressive views, gave Shakespeare readings, and urged repeatedly: "Free your imaginations!"

Soon it was May and classes at Spence wound down. The young students buzzed about summer plans while standing before an open window.

A tall, spectacled girl with black braids named Jennifer Anne Lee said, "My family used to always summer in the South of France. But obviously this year that won't happen. I think my mother said we might go to Palm Beach. Has anyone else been there yet? I bet Florida won't be as perfectly peaceful as Provence. Too bad..."

"I've been to Palm Beach! You'll like it. The beaches are my favorite!" said Molly Atkins.

"Hugs, where are you going?" said Susan Foster, who only attended Spence because her maternal grandmother paid the tuition. She was in awe of the Clark's massive Rolls.

"Well, we used to spend the entire summer in France, too. But this summer I think my father is taking us to Montana again. Then we'll go to Los Angeles to see family and the Pacific Ocean, my favorite."

"That's so far! The train ride will be so boring and cramped with far too many people."

"No, we go out in a rail car only for us," said Huguette. "I actually like it a lot. It's very comfortable. My bedroom is pretty."

"Wait! You have a private rail car with your *own* bedroom?" said Molly with bulging green eyes. "My grandfather had one a long time ago, but my parents had to sell it after he died. They said it was too expensive."

"My father has had it for a long time. I don't know anything else about it, though..."

Huguette, uncomfortable with the sudden attention, feigned ignorance. She was relieved to sit when the teacher began class.

With Europe closed off to all but the bravest of tourists, new markets were created. William heard the islands of Hawai'i were quaint but beautifully idyllic. For July, he booked a steamship from San Francisco to Honolulu, and reserved the largest suite at the Moana Hotel on Waikiki Beach.

While the great ship docked in Honolulu, Huguette and Andrée stood pressed to the iron railing, eager eyes attempting to take in all the newness. They were entranced by the warm, humid air, tropical vegetation, and clear, startlingly blue and turquoise waters. The sight of hula dancers swaying to ukuleles far below caught their interest. Tourists posed to get a photograph with a dancer.

"Let's do that, too!" said Huguette.

As the Clarks disembarked, several women with waist length hair and grass skirts waited at the end of the gangway. The pretty women smiled, saying, "*Aloha!*" They held up slim arms to hang several *leis* around necks. The girls giggled at their father wearing several flower necklaces.

"What do they call these?" Huguette asked, fingering a delicate blossom.

"A *lei*," said the black-haired woman. "*Aloha!*"

"*Aloha*!" the girls chorused.

From that moment, Andrée and Huguette made a point to use the new greeting. At the hotel, they rode the elevator to the top floor's best suite. Upon entering the wide door held open by the butler, they headed for the balcony.

Huguette said, "I feel tiny looking out at the water. It's thrilling! We're on land but it feels like a ship!" She laughed with joy.

The Moana Hotel, or the "First Lady of Waikiki," was built on Kalakaua Avenue in 1901 on deserted, swampy beach front surrounded by taro fields and duck ponds. The luxury hotel catering to the burgeoning tourist industry had 4 stories and 75 guest rooms with high ceilings and cross-ventilated windows. The best suites had telephones and private baths. Extra-wide hallways accommodated large steamer trunks. Guests could entertain themselves in the restaurant, billiards room, saloon, library, and main parlor with the first electric elevator on the island. The lobby extended to wide, outdoor lanais and the Banyan Court looking out onto the gentle waves of Waikiki.

The hotel was the tallest building in any direction, and the top-floor balcony afforded an expansive view. The blue water was clear, and the waves rolled in with an unceasing, soft rhythm. From the busy dirt streets in the front of the white, colonial-style hotel, the girls understood many people lived in Honolulu. The popular, curved Waikiki Beach seemed to be in the heart of the city. It was lined with many flowered bushes and palms growing close to the water at some points. Small cottages and a few large houses were dotted amongst the tropical forest.

"Hey, what're all those people out there doing?" said Huguette, pointing to the figures on the waves below.

"That must be surfing. Remember?" said Andrée. "It's a new sport only Hawaiians do. Father says there are some beaches in California that do it a little too, but not as much as here. It looks hard... *Maman*, I can't believe my eyes! It's so beautiful!"

"*Oui*, a perfect paradise. I know we miss France, but how lovely to try something new. Look how pleasant this is, my girls."

Anna took two coconut waters from the silver salver held by the butler and gave them to her daughters. She took another in hand and sat down on a wicker loveseat beside a large bouquet of purple orchids.

"I think I could stay here for a long while," she said, closing eyes as she took a drink. She could feel her body relaxing in the air's perfect temperature. She opened an eye to wink at Huguette, who watched her. "This is very refreshing! Do you like it?"

Huguette took another drink of the coconut water before answering. "Delicious! I'm going to drink it *every day*! It must be very good for me. Now can we go?" she implored Andrée.

"Of course! I'll beat you into the water!"

The girls changed into matching navy-blue bathing costumes, and descended in the elevator accompanied by Browning and Walter, who fanned themselves furiously. Exiting the hotel's rear patio, the girls jumped onto warm sand and raced down to the shallow waters of Waikiki.

"This is heaven!" Andrée splashed Huguette and jumped deeper into the calm waves.

"This is so much easier swimming than at Trouville. I bet we can swim way, way out!" said Huguette, dogpaddling.

The girls played for as long as the nannies allowed. That evening in the hotel restaurant, the family ate *en plein air* by moonlit water. The gentle night breeze soothed the girls' sunburned skin. Away from the lights of the restaurant, tall torches were put at intervals into the sand to illuminate the beach for an evening walk.

At the Clark's table, a dazzling bouquet of vivid plumeria, hibiscus, gardenia, bird of paradise, and red ginger was in the center with a starched white tablecloth. Curious about local eating habits, William and Anna chose a meal based on traditional courses and fresh-caught fish and seafood.

In the next weeks, the family toured pineapple and sugarcane plantations, took a carriage ride on red roads to see the countryside, hiked to a waterfall high in a tropical forest, and ate a picnic lunch on cliffs overlooking the expansive Pacific. Every day the girls swam at Waikiki or hiked down the steep grade to Hanauma Bay holding a guide rope on a dirt road. Once deep inside the bay, they ran down to the gorgeously clear water to swim out. Holding their breath, they saw thousands of multi-colored fish, coral reefs, and huge sea turtles.

As soon as Browning and Walter were distracted by napping off the exertion, they took off with a friendly, local boy, Ekewaka, who had emerged from the tropical forest to eye them up. He learned English from helping tourists.

The girls followed his lead to walk a distance on the dark rocks off to the left of the bay, leading right out into the heart of the pounding waves.

"Can a shark get me?" said Huguette.

Ekewaka shook his head, wet black hair in his eyes, and grinned. "I help you."

The children laughed. Soon they heard adults frantically calling them back to the safety of the beach.

"Well, there goes the fun. Thanks, Ekewaka!" said Andrée, jumping nimbly from one wet rock to another.

In Honolulu, the girls purchased ukuleles and grass skirts, wanting to dance like the women they saw at a luau. They bought numerous postcards and spent the evenings writing to friends and family about their heavenly trip to Hawai'i.

The third week of their stay, William booked the twenty-four-year-old, locally famous Duke Kahanamoku. When the surfing lesson started, Huguette ground bare feet into the warm sand and looked up at the 6'1" black-haired man with a perfect physique.

She squinted blue eyes to see his handsome dark ones better. "*Aloha*, Duke! Did you really compete in the Olympics?"

"*Aloha*, Huguette! Yes, I did!" Duke squatted to Huguette's level.

"Was it in surfing?"

"No," Duke chuckled and tweaked her nose. "I wish! Maybe someday. No, I won for swimming. I won a gold medal in the 100-meter freestyle, and a silver medal in the men's freestyle relay."

"Was it hard to win?" said Andrée, eyeballing the longboard.

Duke Kahanamoku easily hoisted then jammed the wooden longboard upright in the heavy sand. "No, not really. I grew up on the water. It's my home. Very few can beat me in my home." He grinned, displaying even white teeth against dark skin.

"Will you go to the Olympics again, do you think?" said Huguette. She was wondering if Duke Kahanamoku were really a merman in disguise, he had so many muscles and moved on the waves like it was nothing. *I'll ask Andrée if he's a merman when we're alone.*

"Yes, little lady, after the war is over. And I will win again!" Duke grinned. "Now it's time for your surfing lesson. First, it's most important to have respect for the ancient practice of riding the waves and for the water itself..."

After two hours, Andrée was able to stand up with Duke behind her guiding the longboard, but Huguette was not able to handle standing on the moving, slippery board. On the crest of a gentle wave, Duke thought he would try something bold. Senator Clark paid him well, and he wanted to reciprocate. He easily hoisted Huguette up onto a muscled shoulder.

He is a merman!

A startled Huguette grasped the surfing instructor's upraised hand while they cruised to shore. Very quickly her face became animated with the sheer fun of the unexpected water ride.

Andrée stood clapping and jumping in the calm shallows, laughing at her sister's elated expression. "We'll have to tell Papa about this! He went inside the hotel and missed it!"

After sailing back to San Francisco, the Clarks stayed for several days while their excited mother shopped at Gump's on Post Street for unusual Asian *objects d'art*, porcelain, and jade. Anna selected a jade dragon and an eighteenth-century ginger jar.

Anna's hearing had begun declining. She asked the girls to help carry her new hearing aid, a small wooden box with an acoustic horn to amplify voices.

"Remember, Hugo, always touch my shoulder before speaking or raise your voice if I don't respond."

"I do remember! It's my turn to hold the box now." Huguette gladly took the box in her hands to follow along as *Maman* walked through Gump's.

From San Francisco, the family boarded William's private rail car to travel east to Mowitza Lodge. Will Jr. and Alice had been busy with upgrades and there was much to explore. They celebrated Andrée's thirteenth birthday with a large family party. The Clarks and their extended family and friends fished, swam, canoed or sailed, and ate frequent meals of fried trout or salmon with Idaho russet potatoes. On one memorable evening, they ate s'mores by a bonfire singing camp songs Tertius or Will Jr. taught. When Papa rose to teach one from his frontier days, Andrée and Huguette were aghast then delighted.

"Our dear little Papa can sing!" Huguette said to a smiling Anna.

The girls' Kodak Brownie box camera was in constant use on hikes in the fragrant forest surrounding Salmon Lake. On days it rained, Andrée and Huguette joined cousins, nieces, nephews, and friends to play ping pong or bowling tournaments. They laughed with delight when *Maman* played ping-pong against Papa. She lost good-naturedly.

Anna held up her acoustic horn. "Alas, we shall have to pay attention to the calendar more particularly, as you both have to report back by the middle of September. We can't be late! What would Miss Spence say?"

"I would explain I was filling up my creative store in Hawai'i in order to have more imagination for school," said Andrée. "She always falls for that. Can we go back to Hawai'i next summer, please, *Maman*? It's *almost* as wonderful as France. It's a good enough substitute in wartime, at least."

Huguette took up the horn. "I want to go back too, *Maman*. Please, please, please convince Papa for us!" said Huguette with eager eyes, nodding vigorously at Andrée.

"Well, I don't think it'll be that difficult. Papa enjoyed himself mightily. Now, let's open books and get some knowledge in our heads. We mustn't neglect our intellects in pursuit of pleasure. And it hasn't escaped my notice neither one of you has completed music practice today…"

In April 1917, William put down the paper at breakfast. "With America now entering the war, let's pray it ends very soon!"

"Oh, it must. Who can abide more?" said Anna.

"Have you informed the girls of the invitation to the manor?"

"Yes. They'll be leaving tomorrow. Both seemed very happy."

"Good. I'm pleased they'll have a wholesome Easter holiday at Katherine's farm. And we follow on the weekend, yes?"

"Yes," said Anna, wishing she could get out of the obligation.

At Morris Manor in Upstate New York, it was too cold to swim in the pond, but the girls explored the extensive acreage on horseback and foot. After months of being cooped up in the city, they were thrilled with the country atmosphere and the plethora of newborn animals.

"Let's go to the kennels!" said Kate. "Mr. Sharpe said a litter of puppies was born last night."

"Maybe we can take one home?" said Andrée.

Rushing into the house afterward, Andrée gushed, "Mrs. Morris, we adore seeing the baby chicks, lambs, calves, colts, piglets, goslings, and ducklings." She paused dramatically, with a finger to cheek. "Did I remember everything, Kate?"

"Yes, good job!" said Kate.

"Hmmm, I suppose it's all something of a wonder for you city girls. You'd think I were running a zoo," said Katherine, her mouth turning down slightly as she scanned her half-sisters standing before her. She sighed, as if it were all a bother.

"I've been told there will be a new batch of puppies. Perhaps they will come today? That should keep you busy."

"We saw them already! They're so cute!" Huguette said.

"Please, Huguette, lower your voice indoors. Now girls, my father will arrive this afternoon. I expect you *all* to be on your *best behavior* during the holiday. I want baths to be taken daily. No barn smells allowed at Easter dinner. I want no issues while Father is here, do you hear? No squabbling. Only well-behaved children.

"And we'll not be out exploring barns or the pond tomorrow getting full of mud, do you hear?" Katherine looked pointedly at Huguette.

Huguette was mortified. It was no fun to be cut off from the fun of being at the manor, but to be singled out was embarrassing. She preferred the barns to Mrs. Morris's table with fingerbowls of rosewater and disgusting aspic on salmon any day.

While her mother walked away, Kate whispered, "Don't worry, I know some fun games in the hayloft! Mommy won't find out!"

That summer, William and Anna rented an historic estate in Connecticut on the coast of Long Island Sound. The twelve-bedroom house was situated on fifty acres of parkland in an exclusive community. The weather was hotter and more humid than normal, and the Clarks could frequently be found lounging on wicker furniture in the deep shade of the wide green lawns. William hired an historian to lead them through the region for multiple days of exploring sites. They went yachting to view local coastlines teeming with bird life and to swim at remote beaches.

On the Fourth of July, the family watched the parade in Greenwich. They returned to the house to welcome hundreds of guests. Croquet was played on the front lawn, and that night William hired experts for a massive firework show. Under an enormous, white tent on the back lawn, tables groaned with trays of barbequed chicken, pulled pork sandwiches, cornbread with honey butter, cobb salad, lobster salad, potato salad, corn on the cob, numerous fruit pies, and chocolate desserts. The children insisted first on eating the fresh ice cream.

"I turned the crank the longest so I should get the first bowl!" said Huguette, dashing ahead to get in line. "I would like a big scoop each of peach and strawberry ice cream, please, Miss Violet."

"Why sure, honey, here you go," said Miss Violet, the house's longtime cook. She served the first of many children come running from all corners of the yard.

Anna walked up. "Miss Violet, congratulations. Everything tasted delicious. I'm sure without your aid our French chef wouldn't have been able to pull off the American menu quite so expertly. Girls, let's not eat too many treats," she admonished with a pointed finger before moving away.

"I'm going to have *three* scoops of strawberry," said Andrée with a determined look. "It's definitely too hot to eat cake, and last year I didn't have any ice cream at all..."

"Three scoops! What a glutton, Andrée," said Kate.

"Aw, no, honey, enjoy it," said Miss Violet.

The next day, after exploring a dusty garage behind the house, they spied a tandem bicycle. Shrieks of laughter—with occasional screams of anger or frustration—could be heard for several days as they cycled up and down the long gravel drive with a circular roundabout in front of the house.

At the end of the month, the fun died down a bit with Kate's departure. Before supper one rainy evening, Huguette and Andrée played a duet.

William rose from a leather armchair, clapping. "Well done, my talented girls. You're both improving to a marvelous extent. Now, in a few days we'll be departing Connecticut. First, we travel to Los Angeles to visit family. Then we will go north to Yosemite to tour the park, which, in my estimation, is stunning. I want you both to experience its beauty firsthand. How does that sound?" William looked expectantly at his daughters.

"Yay! We get to go out west! Finally!" said Huguette.

"Ok, it's decided. I'm *very excited* to see Yosemite! I've read John Muir's book. It's destined to be my favorite national park, dear Papa. It'll be my fifteenth birthday present from you and *Maman*, agreed?" Andrée said.

"I think I can second that, daughter."

September 1917
960 Fifth Avenue, New York City

A month after she turned fifteen, Andrée successfully hosted her first party for twelve at fashionable Sherry's at 44th Street and Fifth Avenue. That same week, she took the next step into maturity by moving into her own bedroom.

"There!" Andrée shut the door firmly. "I'm tired of Browning in my face every other minute. Now that I'm out of the nursery, she can't come in here any time she pleases!"

"Yeah, that leaves her to torment me," muttered eleven-year-old Huguette. She sighed. "At least you're only down the hall. It's not too far…"

"You're welcome whenever you need to escape Nanny. But just for that! When it's time to sleep, Hugo, you need to stay in our old bedroom. I *won't be sharing* my bed."

"You mean *my* bedroom now! And it's much bigger than yours!"

Lips trembled as tears threatened. Huguette fled.

With Andrée's persistent bid for independence, Browning retired to England. Walter didn't last long after that. The Vidal sisters, Jaquita and Margarita, stepped into the void. Anna sensed their potential immediately, and she milked their talents in painting, violin, and Spanish conversation lessons. Jaquita and Margarita quickly became companions to Andrée and Huguette at home and on vacations. Anna utilized their skills to practice Spanish, but also encouraged the relationship with her daughters which ensured time away for her.

The well-educated, South American women were in their twenties and full of playful mischief. In Waikiki the next July, Andrée and Huguette watched open-mouthed as the sisters flirted shamelessly with the handsome Duke Kahanamoku during surfing lessons.

"I can't believe Margarita actually made Mr. K blush!" marveled Huguette to Andrée as they bobbed in the calm surf.

Huguette looked over at the Vidals, who were supposed to be vigilant when the Clark girls were out in the water, but were under a palm smoking and talking.

"They're over the top sometimes." Andrée shook her head in pity.

"Do you think so? I like them! I think they're so pretty Duke couldn't help himself. They're far prettier than we are." Huguette put her head back in the water to pull her long, heavy hair off her forehead.

"Who cares? Hey, let's go ask them to take us out for pineapple ice cream," said Andrée. "And don't tell *Maman* this time!" She began swimming to the shore.

"Perfect! I can pay for all of us with my birthday money," said Huguette.

In mid-August, the Clarks and their retinue sailed back to San Francisco before boarding William's Pullman to head south to Los Angeles. After visiting both Clark and La Chappelle relatives, they traveled east to Arizona to tour Clarkdale and hike Grand Canyon trails. They then went north to Butte. Wearing white linen dresses, white silk stockings and white gloves, the girls donned thick canvas and leather hard hats to descend into a mine accompanied by their proud father.

"This is how safe the workings of my mines are! I entrust my own children to it!" said William to the assembled men in front of the four-man steel cage. "Make sure that quote is in the article!"

Huguette flinched as the steel door clanged shut, but she felt better holding her father's hand descending into the pit's darkness. Sporadic electric lights were strung up all the way down.

William shouted above the noise of the machinery. "What do you think, girls? Isn't this something! Look at that rock and earth! I love it!"

William inhaled before grinning. He looked with great satisfaction at the clanking, metal cage recently painted for his visit.

Huguette pushed up the ill-fitting cap to grin at Andrée.

"It's always an adventure with Papa!"

William's next plan was to visit the manicured Columbia Gardens, which they did every summer in Butte. They listened indulgently as he drilled oft-repeated facts.

"I built this sixty-eight-acre garden and amusement park in 1899 as a gift for Butte residents and their children. Isn't this marvelous?"

William had a daughter on each arm as they strolled past his prized begonias.

"Are these colors fabulous? The finest in the state!"

Flanking their diminutive father, they were almost his height. A photographer was planted to take their picture at a certain spot William directed him to. He wanted good press the next day, even if it upset Anna.

"It's wonderful, Daddy. I remember coming here," said Andrée.

She noticed a few young men beside a pavilion looking at her. She wore a large navy-blue floppy hat with an ivory and navy-blue drop-waist dress and white boots. She smiled before looking away.

"It's very kind of you, Papa," said Huguette, dressed all in white with long blonde hair loose. She squeezed his arm for emphasis, eyes only for him.

After a stay at the West Granite Street house, William insisted on spending time at Mowitza Lodge. He enjoyed the weeks of complete privacy guaranteed by the remoteness. As the girls signed the guest book in the lodge's front hall before departure, Tertius snuck up behind to peek over Andrée's shoulder.

"Paris? You're delusional!" His handsome teenage face twisted with scorn. "Not only are you awful at ping pong and can't fish worth a darn, you don't even know where you live!"

Tertius laughed cruelly with Jake, their cousin.

"What? Paris is my home," said Andrée, choking back tears. She would be mortified if the competitive boy saw her crying. "As soon as the war is over, we're going back."

"Well, last I heard, you've spent the past couple of years in New York, *dummy*."

"Don't call her a dummy!" said Huguette, a fist about to be raised.

At the commotion, Anna stepped into the hallway. "Huguette, please! Tertius, that will be all from you. Girls, are we finished? It's time to get into the motorcar. Tertius and Jake, we will see you again at Christmas if your parents decide to visit. *Au revoir.*"

Anna knew better than to expect anything but a polite nod from William's grandsons and grand-nephews. Physical affection was never given. As soon as Anna's back was turned to exit the wide front doors, the boys began making fun of her French-accented English. Only Huguette could hear.

"Don't forget your dolly, Hugo!" said thirteen-year-old Jake in a sing-song voice. The boys guffawed and smacked each other's backs.

<hr />

Earlier in the year, escalating reports of influenza and deaths were widely reported. Fear was rampant. Miss Spence's School ended classes weeks early, which initially elicited whoops of joy from the students. That is, until they realized the result was banishment to stuffy townhouses or lonely country estates. European travel was still out of the question due to the war and the influenza pandemic. William immediately whisked his family west where there were fewer people, and they could easily travel privately and safely.

Anna said, "I insist on physical examinations for everyone on a routine basis. I've ordered a large supply of masks for donning in crowded areas. If anyone had the least bit of flu symptoms, they will be quarantined until fully healed."

Andrée looked at the fresh white cotton mask given to her by a maid. "I'm tired of wearing these every time we go out."

"Nevertheless, they are vital to our health. Huguette, put yours on as well."

"Can't I wait until we've left the train?" Huguette looked at Andrée for support.

"My dears, on they go!" Anna's voice became muffled as she had her ladies maid tie the mask firmly behind her generous bun.

Upon their return to New York in late summer, life slowed down so much the teenage Clark girls were astounded. While Spence delayed classes until November, innumerable letters and postcards were exchanged to ease loneliness and to indulge strong desires for communication. Andrée and Huguette wrote daily letters to friends now scattered all over the Eastern seaboard.

With enthusiasm, Andrée declared her undying love and gratitude for: "The postman, who's saving teenage lives during quarantine!"

As the pandemic raged, non-essential entertaining ceased, and Huguette and Andrée had little to do beyond basic academic lessons. The Vidal sisters were asked to live off and on at the house to tutor or simply to have fun in the pool.

After Dr. Lyle gave the go-ahead, Kate Morris was allowed to come for weeks at a time, which Huguette and Andrée were ecstatic about.

"Oh good! Now we'll have enough people for a diving competition!" said Huguette with anticipation of winning.

Anything more was off limits.

"We'll be very cautious in the city until the pandemic dies down, girls," said Anna. "I'll not risk your lives for a bit of fun. We've all had loads of entertainment the past few years. Therefore, we must be sensible and safe now by staying inside the house until Dr. Lyle gives the all-clear."

"But I'm missing everything fun! *You* still get to travel."

"Andrée, don't use that tone of voice with me. Consider all those who are dying right here in this cramped city as they live in squalor and poverty. Consider all those who are fighting and dying, year after year, in this war, so far from family. Americans as well."

"Oh, you're good to think of others, *Maman*. Forgive me," Andrée mumbled, her brunette hair hanging in long strands from her bent head. "I'm sorry to be peevish, but I'm so disappointed! I don't like being cooped up in the house. I miss my friends very much... I thought when I was sixteen, I'd be having loads of fun."

Andrée reached down to pick up Henry VIII, snuggling against the Pekinese puppy's brown fur. She immediately brightened, "At least we have you to play with! C'mon, Hugo, let's go for a walk in the park."

"Remember your masks and *no talking* with anyone, even friends!" Anna admonished in a sharp tone before addressing the maids. "Tie the masks firmly and they musn't come off for any reason. Make sure the girls talk with no one.

They will come back to the house immediately if they do. I'm only letting them out for a half hour because it was prescribed by Dr. Lyle."

"Yes, madame," said a head maid before ushering the small group of staff and Clark daughters out of the drawing room.

A month later, what had amused years previously had long ceased to bring a smile. When adults weren't present or when their parents traveled for weeks on end, they did a good deal of staring out windows onto the busy streets below, daydreaming of escape. When academics, swimming laps, and music practice completed, there remained hours to wander around the mansion.

In the billiards room, they played pool with Kate or the Vidal sisters while remarking on the beloved six paintings of Jeanne d'Arc's life. Strolling through the galleries, they examined masters of Western art hung in profusion. In the girls' favorite room, the library, they admired treasures such as the Gilbert Stuart portrait of George Washington in their father's office while spinning in his tufted leather chair. They pored over a large collection of first editions, including: Walt Whitman's *Leaves of Grass*, with a promotional insert by Ralph Waldo Emerson, and Charles Baudelaire's *Les Fleurs du Mal*.

One rainy day, Andrée tried to play the enormous organ with hilarious results. Huguette sat beside trying to help while looking with bewilderment at the multiple rows of keys above and pedals beneath. Andrée pushed down hard on a few keys deliberately and held. A deeply sonorous resonance blared through all the floors of the quiet house.

The girls burst into amazed giggles.

"It's so much more powerful than the piano! I usually watch the organ players at work, so I think I can figure it out," said Andrée, continuing to press keys and pedals.

Too soon, the housekeeper came bellowing out of the elevator, "What *are* you girls doing! Turn that organ off this instant! That is not a toy!"

Andrée froze but Huguette made a run for it. She dashed to a nearby drawing room to duck behind a sofa.

One day in late October, during the free hour after afternoon lessons, the sisters were ambling through the tower rooms conversing in French.

"Will we *ever* have fun again?" said Andrée.

"It's strange to be up here now that we're so much older. *Maman* threatened me that if I'm naughty, she'll make me sleep up here until the pandemic is over," said Huguette, poking her head around the door into a small bedroom she remembered playing hide and seek in.

"Remember the night when Alex smacked his head on the bedpost, and everyone heard his yelp, so he ended up being caught by Jenny? That was hilarious!" Huguette laughed at the memory of the New Year's Eve party three years ago.

"*Oui*, I heard his sister died of influenza though. Poor soul..." Andrée paused in the tower's kitchenette, then did a twirl on the linoleum. Her brunette braids whirled, and the black skirt of the sack waist dress billowed like a tulip. "I should be ordering sparkling gowns and practicing waltzing to Strauss instead of doing nothing! Soon I'm old enough to be a debutante!"

Huguette looked at Andrée with amazement. "Do you *want* to be a debutante?"

"*Bien sûr*, Hugo. How else am I going to find a husband? I can't wait to be a mother. Father said I could be presented at Court in London as well. One of my classmates is considering finishing school in Switzerland. What about that idea? Should I?"

"That sounds like *a lot* of bother and nonsense. I *never* think of such things. Only *Maman* brings that up with you, not so much with me. I suppose I'm too young. I must marry though... It would please *Maman, je sais*..."

Huguette's blue eyes roamed the plain room. She did not care for the small flower printed wallpaper and heavy wood furniture. Moving to the window, she loved the perspective of tall buildings, rooftops, and trees dotting the straight streets and large park below. *I should come up here and sketch.* "Will you marry an American or a European? I want to marry a Frenchman and return to France."

"I'm not sure," said Andrée with a dreamy expression. "I only want my future spouse to be able to speak French. And all our children will speak French. Let's go down and ask for tea, I'm hungry." Andrée turned abruptly with Huguette obediently trailing behind.

On November 11, William bought many copies of *The New York Times* with the blaring Armistice headline to give away with cigars and champagne. He exulted to everyone, "The 'war to end all wars' is done! Thank the Lord!"

Wearing masks, Anna took Andrée and Huguette to Mass to pray in gratitude. Anna felt enormous relief; life could soon return to normal. Living in the United States had been a godsend in 1914, but she thought, *I'm very ready to resume life in France.*

Soon after the New Year, Andrée and Huguette faced scrutiny over their health and well-being. They stood awkwardly in the gym lineup. Everyone wore thin, white chemises. Many girls shivered in the cold air. Behind a curtained partition, a doctor with two nurses examined each student's posture and spinal curve.

"Please bend from side to side, gently, that's right. And now down in front, try to touch your toes if you can. Then up, and now bend a bit behind until you feel resistance. I'm going to feel your upper spine to your neck. And that's all, I need, thank you, Miss Clark."

Andrée went behind another partition to put back on her dress. She was shocked the next week when her parents received a letter informing of a scoliosis diagnosis.

"So that's why they made us line up like bare chickens and bend over and all that!" said Andrée with a frown.

"It's alright. It's only a light case. The doctor said with corrective exercise it won't trouble you much. No wonder you've always struggled with posture and form during your dancing lessons, *ma petite*. It's a pity, but all is well. I've already engaged the services of a professional to help you with the exercises."

Andrée looked troubled. "When will that be? All I do is take lessons upon lessons, it seems! Isn't going to Spence all day *enough*? Elizabeth Jones is sixteen, is done with tutors, and says she sleeps in until eleven all weekend long. Will I ever get that freedom?"

"Andrée, Elizabeth Jones is not my daughter. And I won't have a poorly educated or a lazy, ungrateful daughter raised under my roof. You know how your father and I feel about the necessity of tutors and of continual education. Your father built his business on that creed, as you have heard many times."

"*Oui, oui, Maman...*" waiving a hand dismissively at the oft-heard argument. "I've no free time, and when I do, someone is looking at me like I'm lazy or I need to do laps in the pool or walk the dogs or spend time with Huguette—who was very mean to me yesterday, by the way!—but really, *Maman*, you *know* I'm not lazy!"

Andrée stopped in reflection. "I think I simply want some time alone..." she said in a quiet tone of voice.

Anna put down the listening horn. "You've your own bedroom now, that's time enough alone. No complaining. And don't compare yourself to others. You're a Clark. Be proud of that. I'll talk with Huguette if she's being inappropriate."

"You spoil her." Andrée's dark eyebrows lowered.

"Andrée, are we discussing your needs or your sister's?"

"Alright, *Maman*... What time is the physical therapist coming?"

"Before school, three mornings a week."

"What! I have to get up even earlier than I already do?" Andrée hoped her mother's poor hearing prevented her understanding how bitterly she complained.

"Your attitude is uncalled for..."

Alma Guy arrived at quarter to seven on Monday morning. Guy diligently worked on helping her new teenage client to stretch and strengthen back muscles while elongating the spine. In the course of doing so, she began listening to chatty Andrée.

Guy was a little surprised how easy it was to get information out of the young woman. She soon realized her client would benefit from socializing in a freer environment with more normal surroundings. In Guy's opinion—which she freely shared with everyone at every opportunity—the ornate mansion was "like a prison!"

Now, the little sister, on the other hand, is a different breed of cat.

Huguette looked at Alma Guy with no desire to reveal herself. Guy noticed with disapproval that Huguette carried around a doll or two most mornings and wasn't inclined to speak beyond the basics. The younger sister soon avoided Andrée's suite altogether.

A month later, Guy asked to speak to Mrs. Clark, and was promptly taken to the morning room. As she followed the maid, she reminded herself not to stare at the unimaginable luxury that revealed itself in floor after floor and room after room.

The most beautiful house she had ever toured was the governor's mansion in Kentucky when she was twenty-two. *But this house dwarfs that by a mile!*

Guy entered the room, stopping herself with the instinct to bow in front of the attractive woman sitting at a gilded desk. She felt a little overawed.

Am I going to jeopardize my employment?

Anna held up a listening horn while smiling politely.

"Mrs. Clark, good morning. I very much enjoy working with your eldest daughter, Andrée. She is making progress with exercises. If you wouldn't mind my mentioning it, I've had time to get to know your daughter a little, hearing her wants and needs.

"Therefore, if you would be so kind as to remember that this is done with only goodwill on my part, I would like to introduce you to the Girl Scouts. Here is a brochure of what the honorable organization is about."

Guy stepped forward to place a brochure on the desk. Then she stepped back deferentially. "Your daughter, Andrée, would *greatly benefit* from a wider social circle and more engaging physical activities. Socializing with other intelligent young women, like her, bent on personal growth. Not to mention, learning valuable skills through what only the Girl Scouts can provide. In my professional opinion, it's highly recommended."

"Doesn't school provide all that?" Anna's pleasant expression darkened, wondering how indiscreet Andrée had been.

"Perhaps, but the Girls Scouts focuses on worthwhile physical and mental activities." Guy gestured toward the brochure.

"I'm worried it's an organization too democratic for the daughter of a senator," said Anna, eyeing the brochure warily. She did not pick it up.

In her enthusiastic wish to help Andrée, Guy forgot any initial reserve. *This pampered lady has no idea how stifled her daughter is. She isn't raising them, servants are!*

"Mrs. Clark, with all due respect—"

The door burst open before Guy could cross the line with Anna.

"*S'il te plaît, Maman*! Cynthia Colefax goes, and her father knows Papa. And Mary Whitehouse too, remember her? She came to my party at Sherry's. And you said you admired Mary's piano playing. It's a wholesome organization and I'll learn lots of new skills that I'll demonstrate for you and Papa, I promise!"

Andrée stood next to her mother while nodding emphatically with big eyes. She smiled at Guy. Anna looked from one to the other and relented.

For the first time, Andrée left the house for a regular activity Huguette did not participate in. Huguette had no interest in joining the Girl Scouts. Instead, she concentrated on practicing the violin and conversational Spanish.

Huguette dreamed of following in her mother's footsteps. She had heard about the conservatory for years. Her celebrated violin tutor, Monsieur Tourret, had also attended in his youth. She wrote her thanks for his expert lessons, expressing, "I long to attend the *Conservatoire de Musique* in Paris like my mother."

She eased frustration about Andrée's frequent absences through playing tricks or being disagreeable. She informed Andrée of the wrong time to meet up with either Jaquita or Margarita or stuck her tongue out at her sister's back. She hid in a window seat in an out of the way guest bedroom to read when she knew Andrée was searching for her. Several hours later, Andrée would look up in wonder as Huguette silently slid into her seat at the table in the night nursery dining room.

Andrée blurted, "Where have you been all this time? I've been looking for you for over an hour. I was so bored and lonely. *Maman* has been gone for days with *tante* Amelia, and I can't even find you to go on a walk!" She began eating.

Huguette shrugged, idly stirring lentil soup. "How was Girl Scouts?"

"Very fun! I wanted to tell you about it, which is why I was looking for you." Andrée ripped a piece of baguette and took a bite.

With downcast eyes, Huguette began eating, barely paying attention as her sister jabbered on. *I miss you terribly. I miss knowing you're nearby at all times.*

With different classes, different friend groups, and now the Girl Scouts taking Andrée away from home for hours each week, Huguette felt the distance mounting. It made her restless and unhappy.

That spring, Huguette's rebellion was literally taken to new heights. Unlike others in the past, the new American nanny was young and pretty. Francine

Campbell had a pilot boyfriend, which made Huguette's head spin with the possibilities. While Andrée had scouting events on Saturdays, the new nanny took Huguette to cafés and restaurants in forbidden neighborhoods. The boyfriend, Paul Smith, was always waiting.

Then came the day Smith mentioned his newly purchased yellow plane he was immeasurably proud of. He grinned at Campbell, who he saw as upper-class because of her employment on Fifth Avenue. Huguette begged to see the plane at the makeshift hangar at Floyd Bennet Field. Without hesitation, Campbell agreed. They squeezed into Paul's Model T and drove out of Manhattan to South Brooklyn.

Smith was easy to manipulate, and before long, Huguette was eagerly accepting his offer.

"Why, this is splendid! Nanny Campbell, I'll never forget this day! What a lark!"

Campbell was happy to please. She hoisted Huguette to reach the ladder. Huguette clambered up and squeezed into the back seat of the two-seater plane. She slipped on a leather bomber jacket, leather helmet, and goggles.

"Yeah, it's warm down here, kid, but you might get cold up there," said Smith.

"Too bad we don't have a camera with us!" Huguette shouted above the engine noise.

In her excitement, Huguette gave two thumbs up. Campbell waved enthusiastically from a safe distance. Then the plane fully roared to life and lurched forward. Huguette coughed at the fumes and then laughed with mixed apprehension and delight as they lifted off the ground.

It was pure pleasure to grip the canvas strap and lean her head over the metal side. The novel sensation of weightlessness while ascending into the air for the first time she knew she'd never forget. Then they climbed up and up to soar over the city.

She was breathless with the shock of the altitude, and sensing the temperature changes. She looked down, in awe of gliding over the labyrinthine boroughs of New York.

What a view! I love this!

Arriving home, Huguette took the elevator and strode quickly to Andrée's bedroom. She entered with a smug face.

Andrée set *Anne of Green Gables* on her lap. "Well, where've you been?"

"You'll *never* guess!"

Huguette gloated about the early birthday present from Campbell. But soon, a shocked Andrée confessed to *Maman*.

An hour later William returned home. Then all hell broke loose.

"What?" William thundered. "Am I hearing correctly? My youngest daughter was taken up in an open cockpit joyriding above Central Park today? Flying above the city with an inexperienced pilot?! Must I be at home every day to keep the lid on my own household?

"Fire that chaperone! Anna, fire that young woman *now*! This instant! Such a grievous error of judgement on her part cannot, will not, ever be forgiven! In fact, I want to speak with Ms. Campbell *myself*! She will receive no letter of recommendation from me!"

William barked at the English butler, James Edward Wood, to summon the nanny. Wood returned only a moment later to stand before William pacing the length of the library.

"It appears Ms. Campbell has left the premises, sir," said Wood.

"Well, go get her!" William swore.

In the smoothest voice the experienced butler could muster, Wood said, "Sir, I believe Ms. Campbell has already moved on some minutes ago, to—"

"What! I don't get the satisfaction of firing her *myself*? Hugo, did you tell her to leave?"

William whirled to face her, knowing his youngest was far wilier than she let on.

"*Peut-être.*"

Huguette sulked stone-faced in an embroidered wing-backed chair, as far away from her parents as possible.

William stormed about, shouting simultaneously at Anna, the butler, his secretary, and anyone else within hearing range.

Wood took small backward steps. *This is an issue for the couple to work out.* He smiled as soon as he softly shut the library doors, going directly below to see who else had been listening in.

"Hire a middle-aged, grandmotherly-type woman next time, Anna, not a young, single woman! And I don't care what Huguette wants or her excuses. She should've known better! What a foolhardy stunt! She's grounded for six months if not forever!"

William stomped to the tall, white chimneypiece to lean against the carved marble side, trying to cool down.

Anna looked over at Huguette sitting morose across the room.

"Come with me."

In the hallway, Anna halted.

"That is the angriest I've seen your father in *quite* some time. Do you understand the danger you placed yourself in? Airplanes are notorious for crashes. Fiery, life-altering crashes that happen in an instant. It was extremely foolish to fly with an inexperienced pilot. Go to your room now, Huguette. I'll talk with you later."

Huguette turned away, unapologetic. She couldn't wait to go to school.

On Monday morning, she met up with good friends before English literature. Huguette bragged with hands on hips, "Aside from surfing in Honolulu, flying was the most exciting, most thrilling thing I have *ever* done. Trust me, if anyone offers you a plane ride, go for it!"

"Wow, you're brave, Hugs!"

Several girls nodded enthusiastically. The bell rang, and the girls scattered. Huguette slid into her wooden desk seat, appearing deceptively demure.

In early May, Andrée was invited to Morris Manor. She would leave the last day of school with Kate, traveling upstate on the train, and wouldn't return until the end of July. Huguette was not mentioned, and the omission stung.

I shouldn't be surprised. It's obvious Kate and Andrée are closer because they're older. I'm left out more and more.

Huguette flopped down miserably on her bed. She looked around with distaste at the childish mural. *When is it my turn to move out of the nursery?*

On June 7, Andrée wrote:

Dearest Hugo,

I'm most sorry, dearest little sister, to miss your thirteenth birthday this year. I do hope that you have a spectacular day. Trust I shall be thinking of you and sending well wishes across the distance. Enjoy your party at Sherry's, you lucky duck! Write to me if the new Sherry's at the Hotel New Netherland is as elegant. I bet it's even more grand! I can't wait to have my own party there, too.

Kate and I are having a wonderful time! Morris Manor is as idyllic as ever. As you know, I always win at bowling! Kate had dozens of gutter balls.

We ride horses in the meadows every day, which is thrilling. We can go for miles and miles and it's all part of the manor. I wish Papa would buy a country house!

You'd be interested to know that two of Mrs. Morris's dogs recently had puppies. (The kennel has so many dogs now, more than our last trip.) It was so adorable to hold them. I got to name one! Jeanne for Jeanne d'Arc, of course.

We play tennis almost every day, and swim in the pond when it's hot. Remember how you always liked to go there? It's still wonderful. I'm sure Kate will have us both next summer and then we can all enjoy it together. Mrs. Morris says we will leave to take a houseboat up to Canada before heading over to Maine to meet up with you and dear Maman *and dear Papa by the end of next month.*

A new adventure—I've never been on a houseboat. All in all, everything is a vast improvement from dusty, hot Old New York!

Bisous, ta grand sœur, Andrée

The thoughtful Andrée had coordinated with Anna to present Huguette's gifts on the day of the party: a book of French stories, doll clothes, and Sherry's chocolates in a lavender tin.

Huguette petulantly tossed the letter to the floor. *I wish I were swimming in the pond and holding puppies at Morris Manor, too!* She slunk about the house, even uncharacteristically throwing herself in desperate boredom on the bed at one weak moment. *An entire week has gone by without seeing friends or doing anything fun!*

The weather was too rainy for a walk in Central Park, and she was tired of reading and drawing. In actuality, Huguette's free time was limited. Along with language, riding, art, and academic lessons, Huguette swam daily and imposed upon herself a strict violin practice. When she became inattentive, she rallied her spirits. *I want to please* Maman *by becoming an expert violinist.*

That summer, the Clark's European friends assured it was not time to return to France; the arduous recovery was still underway. Instead, Anna followed advice to go north to Maine's unspoiled beauties. The Clarks rented a six-bedroom, white clapboard house with several fieldstone fireplaces and guesthouses on the grounds of a resort on Rangeley Lake.

Ten days after her birthday party at Sherry's, Huguette boarded a private train car. She cast a weary eye around. Typical of her mother, "Who would invite the next-door neighbors to vacation with us...," mumbled Huguette, there were a lot of people coming to Maine.

Tante Hanna La Chappelle, her spoiled six-year-old twins with blonde ringlets, Anna and Paul, and their servants had come from Montana. The fastidious and diminutive Madame Adele Marié, *Maman's* new social secretary, hovered in the background. This habit greatly annoyed Huguette when she wanted to have a private conversation with her mother. Marié didn't get the hint, and what was worse, the woman was French. It was impossible to hide anything. When Anna announced the well-educated Marié could easily provide academic lessons in place of a formal governess during the summer, Huguette was dejected.

Along with the Vidal sisters to provide language, music, and art lessons, there were multiple maids and bodyguards, the French chef, the butler, Mr. Wood, and three Pekinese: Henry VIII, Margot, and Mops. The dogs adored Anna and were attuned to her every movement with vigilant black button eyes.

Huguette walked down the length of the private car to scoop up Mops before taking a seat at a table with Margarita and Jaquita, who always cheered her.

"I bet you miss your *hermana mayor, sí*?" said Margarita. "When will she come to Maine to be with us?"

"Not soon enough!" Huguette patted Mops's head before idly picking up a card to toy with. "They're taking a houseboat to Canada and then maybe at the end of July she'll come."

"A houseboat! *Qué fantástico...*" said Jaquita who made a silly face attempting to make Huguette laugh. "You don't look like you think so, honey."

Huguette shrugged while scowling at the jostling crowds on the platform. *Train stations are always so obnoxious.* The first warning whistle screamed.

"*Pues, no te preocupes, Señorita* Huguette, we're going to have a *fabulous* time, too. Before you know it, Andrée will join us!" said Margarita, blowing Huguette a kiss. She picked up playing cards and carefully repositioned herself with back to Mesdames Marié and Clark.

"*Vamos*, let's play poker, okay?" Margarita whispered, winking.

Jaquita rolled dark eyes good-naturedly, before squishing closer to create a human shield.

To collect her hand, Huguette set Mops onto the seat. "I'm going to win again. I hope you two have money this time..."

At Rangeley Lake, Huguette was able to sleep in until eight o'clock. She luxuriated in bed, breathing in fresh, cool morning air coming through the open sash window. After dressing, she went downstairs to the dining room.

In the summer, Huguette liked to eat a light breakfast of *café au lait*, toast with black currant preserves, a small omelet, and fresh strawberries. She didn't linger at table. She went immediately to the library to study mathematics, science, and history. Afterward, she joined everyone for luncheon on the shaded veranda.

Anna raved about the view down to the water at each al fresco meal. "Hanna, isn't this a gorgeous resort, *n'est-ce pas*? The trees are majestic! I'm very content we decided to come up to Maine. *Quelle magnificence*! I think it's admirable so many are doing their best to preserve and defend the United States's natural beauty. Listen to me, I sound like a senator's wife all over again."

"Oh yes, Anna E., I feel relaxed already. This was a perfect choice of a resort."

"And I'm so pleased, as well, that you and little Anna and Paul have come to spend part of your summer with us."

"I'm most grateful for the invitation," said Hanna, setting down a lemonade glass. "Butte does not have this cool weather, as you remember. Arthur would like to build a house in Los Angeles someday. Any location other than Butte!"

Directly after finishing the onion soup, *salade niçoise*, lobster salad, and strawberry tart, Huguette waited fifteen minutes to be polite before excusing herself.

She left the older women to race upstairs. With eager movements, she slid into a navy bathing costume laid out on a chair. Then she rushed downstairs and out across the lawn to the pier, diving into the cool water with relish. After swimming, Huguette lay soaking on a thick towel. She luxuriated in hot sun on wet skin. The rays were so bright her eyes ached when first shut.

I've all afternoon to swim or take a long walk or bike ride or take photographs or talk to the turtles and the ducks. No Spence and no city. We'll be here until August. Then who knows what fun Papa will spring on us? This is the life! If only I didn't have to spend the morning studying! I wish I could sleep in until nine or ten o'clock. That won't happen, but maybe if I go back by myself, I can squeeze in that luxury before school starts?

Sometimes *Maman* didn't want to leave wherever they visited, and, presently, *Maman* looked very content. Huguette calculated the odds were good this year to be alone at the house with Andrée before school began.

The days sped by. She relished every outdoor activity, whether it was bird watching, hiking, or trotting a horse from the resort stables down quiet country roads. After being outdoors all afternoon, she would play the violin or the piano, sometimes helping little Anna with scales. In the evening, she performed musical numbers with *Maman* after the family dinner. Then Huguette practiced the violin before reading in bed.

Because the resort house was much smaller with only three floors, after Papa arrived, he would sometimes catch her.

"What? My girl still up reading, hmmm? Isn't it awfully late for you?"

"I take after you! You're up reading at all hours yourself."

"*Touché. Bonne nuit.*"

At the end of July, Huguette went to the station to eagerly scan for a familiar form to alight from the train arriving from Canada.

"Andrée, *bonjour! Bonjour!*"

Huguette waved an arm high and shouted above the crowds of travelers and servants lugging leather satchels and trunks in every direction.

"Andrée, *ça va?* I'm overjoyed to see you!"

Huguette embraced her sister.

"*Oui, ça va bien. Et toi?*"

She hugged Huguette back and kissed her cheek in a rush of emotion.

"*Très bien!* Aren't you happy to be in Maine? It's not nearly as fun without you around. I'm *so happy* you've come to join us."

"*Oui, je suis très contente!* I missed you, as well. I think you've grown taller since I last saw you, silly goose! You're catching up to me and *Maman.*"

"*Je sais!* It's about time!"

They walked to the motorcar chatting while Marié and a bodyguard followed. The Clark sisters were oblivious to the stares in their direction. Standing out in the lineup of vehicles and carriages was a new black Rolls Royce Springfield Silver Ghost with burgundy canvas and wheel spokes. A chauffeur in black suit with brass buttons and black driving cap stood at attention, waiting for his young passengers.

"I had a wonderful time at Morris Manor, though. Kate says hello. Did you get all my letters? *Maman* did nothing but send the usual telegrams. It was frustrating to only receive detailed news from you. Is Papa alright?" Andrée said as they settled themselves along the burgundy leather seat.

"*Oui,* but he already left... So did the Vidals."

Huguette looked over cautiously, sorry to break the bad news.

"*Ç'est vrai?*"

Andrée's expression deflated.

"For some reason I was under the impression Papa would still be here when I arrived... *Maman's* telegram was vague, and you didn't mention it."

Andrée sighed.

"He had to go to Arizona, you know how it is."

"*D'accord, allons-y!* I'm anxious to see *Maman.*"

With Andrée's arrival, the rains and damp weather picked up. The girls had been driving a horse-drawn racing buggy along quiet lanes for the past two afternoons when they were doused with a strong, mid-afternoon storm.

"Well, it certainly rains enough in Maine!"

"Andrée, we should head back. I hear thunder."

"Didn't it storm last night, as well? My goodness, this state is a wet one."

Andrée steered the gentle mare back in the direction of the house, arriving a half hour later with water completely soaked through straw hats, linen dresses, and gloves. Hair and clothing were plastered to bodies, and leather shoes sloshed while walking to the door. They immediately made puddles on the wooden floor of the wide front hall.

"Upstairs to change, the both of you, before you catch some awful cold I don't want any part of!" ordered Anna.

The next morning at breakfast, Andrée was listless and complained of a headache.

"Why don't you go lie back down?" suggested Huguette.

She took a bite of tomato quiche before remarking, "I bet it was getting wet yesterday that did it. Maybe you picked up a flu bug?"

"Oh, you sound like Señorita Jaquita, talking like that. It's merely a little headache, that's all. I have been tired this past week. I'm having too much fun this summer; I need to slow down a bit..."

It was a warm day with on and off rain showers, and the family stayed inside or sat on the wide veranda that wrapped around half the house. Andrée complained of a worsening headache and fatigue.

"*Ma petite fille*, why don't you lie down? I think a long day in bed will do you wonders. You're obviously not up to sitting out here with all of us."

"Maybe I will..." Andrée mumbled with eyes closed and head back.

When Anna recollected the events of the following days, she felt severe remorse not reaching to feel her daughter's feverish forehead at that moment. She was amidst conversation with Hanna and not focusing whatsoever on Andrée's complaints.

She later confessed to Amelia, "It seemed so harmless, as if she were merely ornery from too many rainy days and too much travel."

The older women, engrossed in cards and conversation, didn't notice Andrée massaging the back of her neck. Rising with glazed eyes half-closed, she walked slowly out of the room.

Huguette's alert eyes followed.

Andrée seems in a daze...

The next morning at breakfast, the maid announced, "Mademoiselle Andrée wants to sleep longer."

"Thank you for informing me." Anna turned to Hanna. "I'm glad. A restorative rest will do her good. She'll feel much better tomorrow..."

Anna sipped coffee before remarking on the beauty of the morning.

"How about we take a ride into the next town to see if it has anything interesting to see? I heard there are a few small landmarks and a pretty church. I'm feeling adventurous."

"Anna E., you have the best ideas. I'm game!" said *tante* Hanna.

Huguette excused herself as the two women decided the day's itinerary. She went to visit Andrée, who was barely awake with flushed cheeks and a sweaty forehead.

I'm usually the one who's sick in bed with an earache or something, not her...
She closed the door softly.

At dinner, Andrée didn't appear again.

Smoothing a linen napkin over her gown, Anna said, "It's just as well she stay in bed. I think she overdid it with the Morrises. I blame them. Perhaps it was too much to go to Canada on a houseboat, and then come here directly afterward? She's overstimulated and fatigued."

Tante Hanna agreed while helping her son cut venison. Huguette ate but felt uneasy. With Andrée sick in bed, Rangely Resort wasn't as fun anymore.

The next morning, Huguette woke to commotion. People were talking outside her door.

Something in urgent tones about... telegram... Dr. Lyle... immediately.
Why is that necessary?

Then she remembered. Throwing back the light duvet and sliding out of bed, she stood still on the circular red Persian rug.

Feeling strange all of the sudden, Huguette didn't want to open the door...
It isn't my fault I haven't helped Andrée.

Huguette tiptoed over to crack the door. Across the generous landing, several maids carried a white basin and a stack of towels into Andrée's bedroom. Huguette then saw an unknown, tall man in a blue linen suit with a stethoscope come into view. He leaned over a chair at the table to dig in his satchel.

That isn't our doctor.

She opened the door and stepped out. *Maman* was standing to the far left in the wide hallway with an expression of terror. Despite the warm morning, gooseflesh rose on Huguette's arms.

"Get dressed *immediately*. You're returning to New York this morning! Get back in your room and shut the door!"

"*Quoi...? Pour quoi?*"

"Immediately! Do as I ask!"

With crazed eyes Anna instructed a maid to pack a trunk with only the essentials and have it carried to the waiting motorcar. Huguette shut the door and began dressing.

Without eating or speaking with anyone, fifteen minutes later she slid into the backseat of the Rolls. Marié followed. She tried not to fuss at the abrupt departure, but she fidgeted so much out of anxiety Marié soon turned to her.

"Don't worry, Mademoiselle Clark. Your mother does not want you to be in the same house as your elder sister. The local doctor thinks she has a contagious illness. When Madame's physician arrives, we are hoping for a better diagnosis. In any case, it is wise for you to be quarantined from your sister. Once Dr. Lyle arrives, all will be well."

Marié reached over to pat her hand, but Huguette snatched it away. *I'm not a child!*

Huguette rarely looked at or spoke to Marié during the trip back to New York. *I'm headed back to crummy New York in the midst of summer vacation!*

It was unprecedented. She ate little and hugged her favorite doll at night trying to sleep on the train. She prayed for Andrée's recovery. She even repented for last year's poor behavior.

And this year's, as well. If only I could take back how unkind I was! I should go to confession.

Arriving at the house, Huguette slunk past assembled servants with only a small nod. She didn't ask for anything. In fact, it felt supremely strange to be the sole Clark occupant of the giant mansion. This was a first in all the years it had been her home.

Taking the elevator to the music room, she sat down at the piano to be in a spot Andrée had last been in. She looked at the music still laid out that her sister had played before leaving. Huguette began one of Andrée's favorite songs.

It's too cruel! I've only had a few days with her this summer!

The house seemed to echo, trapping her alone within oppressive depths. Huguette started to cry; she didn't understand why she was sad. She went to her mother's darkened bedroom to kneel on the *prie-dieu*. She wasn't sure she believed with faith like *maman* and *grandmère*, but she tried.

Hours later, the housekeeper knocked on the bedroom door. Huguette bounded up and snatched the telegram off the silver salver before asking the woman to leave. But it wasn't the message she expected. It wasn't a summons back to Maine, that all was well. That her summer was recovered in all its sunshine glory.

It was unimaginably worse!

The terse, black, typed words on cheap yellow paper blurred as she swayed in pain. Unbelievable words searing her soul.

Huguette stumbled backwards into bed. She rocked back and forth and back and forth surrounded by the forested mural of fairies and gnomes and castles and smiling sun Andrée used to make stories about. Time stopped. There was only the fading light in the large room.

She turned face away from any servant who came to the door. She said nothing as electric lights were switched on and a tray of unwanted food placed on the low table by the loveseat. A maid came to the bed, holding out water. Averting eyes, Huguette took the glass and downed it in one go.

Hours later, with eyes gummed shut from crying herself to sleep, Huguette was startled out of sleep to see the same maid enter the room.

"Leave me alone! Go away!"

The maid, Jennie Briggs, who was somewhat new, could not comprehend the French volleyed at her. But she understood the language of grief. The door was softly closed, and the housekeeper alerted.

In a daze, Huguette slid to the floor. The crumpled telegram was soggy and illegible in her clutched hand. Without any forethought, she rose to go down the long hallway and across the landing to her sister's bedroom. She crawled under the cheery yellow and pink chintz quilt to give herself up to spasms of grief, crying jags, and a growing loneliness.

Days passed.

Anna arrived in New York wearing a plain black silk gown with a long black lace veil obscuring her pinched face. She spoke quietly to the English housekeeper, Betty Smith, but did not acknowledge the remaining staff who had assembled. She was exhausted. Without William to support her, she had spent the past week arranging for a casket; having the body photographed; preserving a lock of hair; ordering express travel arrangements; and escorting her eldest daughter's remains from Maine to New York.

The housekeeper informed Anna where to find Huguette. "She wanted nothing to do with us, Madame. I do hope you understand. She is in quite a state. I can't tell you when she last ate a good meal. She touches nothing," said Ms. Smith.

Anna took the elevator up to the fifth floor. She went to Andrée's room and opened the door. The sight of her last remaining child tore at Anna's heart. Huguette was curled in the fetal position with a forlorn face and empty eyes. She rolled over immediately.

"*Maman*," voice cracking from days of non-use, "is it true? Is she really dead? Please tell me she's not."

Anna nodded, unable to speak for a moment. She took a breath while sitting down. "Yes, she's gone."

"Then I've lost my best friend! I can't believe dear Andrée is dead, and *I never got a chance to say goodbye*! I will never, ever have a friend as dear as my older sister. I can't bear she's gone forever. Please help me, *Maman*, I don't know what to do without her here with me! I can't bear this!" Huguette sobbed in great gusts of painful emotion.

"*Ma petite, je sais, je sais...*" Anna rocked Huguette in her arms, tears coming so fast that eyes stung and voices caught in raw throats. "I feel the same. We all loved Andrée, our dear angel. She was such a special girl. I can't believe she has departed so soon... I miss her very much. My heart is breaking as well.

"But trust she is with God and we will see her in heaven. Please have faith, *ma petite chérie*. You're all I have left now!"

After holding Huguette for awhile, Anna gently guided her out of bed. She opened the door. To the maids waiting in the hallway, Anna whispered, "Draw a bath and get a black dress and shoes."

William arrived in the early evening. He requested Huguette come down and have supper with family who were beginning to assemble. Huguette obeyed, walking numbly past scurrying staff preparing to care for the large number of guests. She sat obediently in the formal drawing room her father held court in. She chose not to enter the room next door that held the casket already surrounded by a sea of white roses, lilies, and daisies. Deliveries were coming so thick the housekeeper had trouble recording them.

Andrée's funeral was held off until the twelfth of August. William and Anna wanted as many family members in attendance as possible, hoping both sides had sufficient notice.

To Huguette, it was all a blur of nothingness. She withdrew further into herself when faced by crowds of unwanted family and strangers. She couldn't speak, shying away from anyone attempting conversation.

It's Andrée's birthday tomorrow, August thirteenth.

"She would've been seventeen, the darling girl. To die so young!" a relative from Montana said.

Anna nodded, holding a lace handkerchief up to red eyes. Her hand trembled as she set a gold-rimmed cup on a saucer. "I wanted to honor her birthday."

I'll never celebrate another birthday for my sister!

Others seemed hostile; she rose to return to Andrée's room, desperately wanting solitude. Anna soon dispatched Kate Morris to lead Huguette back downstairs. Kate put an arm around Huguette's shoulders as they descended in the elevator. Anna motioned them over.

"Try to stay with the family, Huguette. They have come to support us, and we should acknowledge that. They'll leave soon enough and then we can be alone to grieve."

Every morning Huguette allowed the maid to dress her all in black. Her long blonde hair was braided with a black satin ribbon. She then dressed a favorite doll from Andrée in black silk. Huguette clutched the doll, whether during family meals, the musical concert given in honor of Andrée, or at the funeral service held in the house with a boys' choir singing with the pipe organ. Afterwards, the procession slowly drove behind the casket encased in a horse-drawn glass box with a profusion of white and pink roses.

At Woodlawn Cemetery, Huguette stood between eighty-year-old William supporting himself with a cane and forty-one-year-old Anna who had left her listening box in the motorcar. Huguette didn't cry as she stood mute, watching the casket withdrawn from the glass box and born aloft on male shoulders.

To outsiders who knew nothing of her or of the close relationship with her elder sister, she appeared strangely withdrawn and stone-faced.

"*Adieu, Andrée. Je t'aime*," Huguette whispered as the casket disappeared through the bronze door. Only William could hear.

November 1919
Paris

Per Clark standards, the British passenger ship was down at heel, but not terribly so. "It's tolerable," William commented.

The train soon pulled into the familiar Paris station where a vehicle was waiting to take the couple to *La place de la Concorde* and the *Hôtel de Crillon*. At first, Anna—who partook of all Paris's splendors without pause before the war began—was stupefied.

Where is the Paris I knew?

The downgrade in quality for everything imaginable, obvious lack of service, and inconsistent staffing, were disheartening. Familiar places William and Anna had enjoyed many years ago now offered diminished services with subpar food and wine. An elderly waiter became disoriented, jarring the table and spilling wine on the patched tablecloth. To anyone who had experienced a city which had surpassingly entertained royalty and dignitaries from countries all over the world, it was sobering.

In the motorcar afterward, Anna said, "If only Balzac were alive to write of Paris today, what would he choose to focus on, *mon amour?*"

William smiled slightly with tired eyes; he looked out at the scattered lights of the Champs-Elysées streaming by. A fatigued William was having trouble sleeping well. He didn't want to admit anything to Anna.

"Do you not agree that anyone who had known the previous heights of this famous city would be stunned?" said Anna.

"Quite right. However, let's keep in mind that the war is only very recently over. Give it some time."

America endured some impacts with the Great War, with casualties and the returning wounded among the gravest problems. Europe was a different matter. Culturally, politically, and socially, the changes were bone deep. The architectural beauty of Paris was not altered, but the long years of war had ravaged the effervescent spirit of the city.

There were many of the nobility and *haute bourgeoisie* who clung to the old ways like they would a miracle-granting icon, shunning threats to beloved tradition. But huge swaths of society had seemingly moved beyond, morphing into something overtaking Paris like a densely humid thunderstorm. The zeitgeist of modern culture at the cusp of the twenties galvanized many of the lower and working classes, artists, entrepreneurs, and expatriates. They flourished with the freedom.

Two days later, the Clarks motored down *avenue Victor Hugo* with excitement mingled with trepidation. In the neighborhood, the shine was off everything. Once glorious flower beds were now little more than muddy patches with weeds; trash collected in corners, and paint peeled off shutters and metal railings. The many prosperous neighbors, who had come and gone all day long in decades past, were scarcely present. The horses were not as fine fleshed and the motorcars not as brilliant and new. The international character of the city, at least in the upper classes of the *seizième arrondisement*, was altered, as well.

"Perhaps they've not yet returned?" said Anna.

"I imagine they're still on their estates or in exile, waiting for Paris to regain her former glory, my love."

The economic damages to France from such a massive loss of manpower were incalculable. Overall, manners, speech, clothing, and lifestyle were not as formal or deferential. It made Anna and William pause slightly before they decided to tacitly move on. Instead, Anna saw people on *avenue Victor Hugo* in worn but good clothing who had been shaken up or damaged in one way or another. Grief over the millions of men who had perished was palpable, especially to Anna and William.

The eighteenth-century building slumped with the years of neglect. Walking inside, the interior had been damaged from what appeared to be a leak in the roof above; the marble hallway was dusty and stank of urine and stale air. Apparently, other owners had not yet returned or were disregarding the state of affairs in the hopes someone would scrub it up someday.

In the flat, thieves and squatters had taken advantage. Without anyone to oversee the property, locks had been picked. The majority of the remaining furniture and moveable parts of the flat had been carted off to sell or barter, or, perhaps, burned in the blackened fireplaces. A Chippendale leg stuck out from a pile of ash as evidence of someone trying to keep warm the previous winter.

"Well, now I know why Pelletier didn't want to go into details... Hmm, what can I expect after abandoning it five years ago?" William said while pushing aside newspapers and rubbish with his cane. "This is a bit like what the first flat I bought in 1880 was like. However, at that time, I think it was in better shape!"

He laughed heartily. "Katherine and I bought it from an old countess. You should've seen her, Anna. A relic from the eighteenth century! What a sorry, pitiful sight she was... Over one hundred years old pottering about in decrepit rooms stuffed with broken-down furniture."

William strolled into the next drawing room, shaking his head. His breath came out in clouds in the frigid air. A five-foot mirror on the wall above the marble chimneypiece caught his attention. The glass was shattered beyond repair by some projectile. Perhaps a bottle of wine, whose green shards they now stepped over on the dirt-encrusted floors.

"I do believe I purchased that antique mirror in Venice for quite a large sum. And now behold..." He raised his cane to the ruin.

"Things can be replaced or repaired, William. Don't fret. Although Bouchard would roll in her grave about these scratched floors..." Anna wrinkled her nose at caked on dust and debris.

"It's the principle of our home being ransacked by ignorant strangers that goads!"

"They must've been freezing, William. Have pity. Didn't Pelletier say the Germans flooded the coal mines in the north? What were people to do in the winter? Poor things…"

Later that day with Pelletier, William spoke about the nuisance of restoring the flat.

"Despite the problems, Monsieur Clark, the economy is healthier each quarter. But it will need another year, at minimum. At least prices are low all around. Well, for Americans they are low."

"Correct, but if the quality is low due to insufficient manpower and skills, then I'm not interested in investing years of time and effort. This will be the second time I've had to restore a flat from the bottom up! And at my age, is it worth it? How many years in your opinion until France recovers her former glory?"

"Monsieur Clark, I beg your pardon," Pelletier bore a proud but humble expression, "France has not lost her glory!"

"I do apologize, my good man! I should say, Paris. When will *Paris* recover?"

"It will take time, but already work has begun. I would recommend you restore the flat— regardless of the challenges or the time required, you know I will oversee everything to the best of my abilities—and then see what the market is doing at a future date."

Pelletier filled William in on France's challenging situation. Coal was in short supply and would remain so for another few years. Inflation plagued the franc, and the government had overwhelming war debt and social challenges. Many widows, orphans, and disfigured soldiers, *les gueules cassées*, were seen in all villages and especially in Paris. The city's population had swelled with the unfortunate and poverty-stricken looking for aid; they would require adequate, affordable housing.

Anna noticed she was no longer the most fashionable woman in the room. In fact, she felt invisible in outdated gowns and hats over a bouffant updo. On both sides of the Atlantic, wearing new clothes when so many in England and on the continent were fighting the war was seen as extremely poor taste. Even if new fashions were available, women denied themselves. Anna had followed suit.

With a disappearing clientele and greatly reduced orders, the great *couturiers* had been forced to close or move out of the war zone. The tradition of Parisian *haute couture*—with thousands of workers creating bespoke creations by hand—was severely impacted. Money to buy the clothes was a problem for clients; finding enough skilled workers and financial backing after a five year hiatus were greater problems for *couturiers*.

The fresh fashion breezes came from young women of all classes who were stepping out in shorter dresses cut simply with lighter fabrics. Hair was bobbed above the shoulders and topped with a small hat. And most brilliantly, corsets and restricting undergarments were shunned completely. The women looked modern and appropriate in a way Anna appreciated immensely.

For the first time in her life, off to the hairdressers she went. The shingle cut most fascinated, and she took the plunge despite being middle aged.

I'm determined to be modern. And I'll begin by getting rid of all this hair!

Two days later, when she emerged from Chanel at *31 rue Cambon* with shorn hair and newly outfitted, William chuckled good-naturedly. She wore a black and white, shin-length silk dress with matching coat, two ropes of long pearls, heeled Mary Janes, and a small-brimmed black hat.

"What a fashion-plate for a wife I have! My love, you're as beautiful now as when you were young. In fact, you look ten years younger. Give me a kiss, *s'il te plaît*!"

Anna leaned to comply before reaching to tentatively touch the hairdo which brushed the nape of her neck. "Do you *really* think it's becoming? Tell me truthfully, William..."

"I think everyone will suspect I'm your father, more so now than ever..."

"*Mon amour, merci.* I feel so much lighter! It'll take some getting used to, but it'll look beautiful with all the new dresses and gowns I ordered. Madame Chanel is very helpful and ferociously *chic*. Ah, it's wonderful to be in France again!"

"I might as well be attending a boarding school!" Huguette fumed to dolls arranged on her bed. "It's been a month since they've been gone!"

Huguette had begged to be included in the trip that fall, but her father refused.

"It's healthier for you to continue on with your studies. I don't want you getting behind."

"But Papa! I'll be here alone!"

"Huguetty, this trip is for your mother. You know how much she still grieves. Your Aunt Amelia is here for you while we are gone, probably through December. Now no complaining. Off to your dancing lesson."

Spence was not as fun, and even the holidays quieted down after Andrée's death. Coming home from school one day, Huguette learned her father was there from the housekeeper.

"He is? And Mommy?"

"I'm sorry, miss, your mother did not return today."

Huguette's expression fell. "Thank you," she mumbled.

She went immediately to the library to question her father. "Papa, she can't possibly miss Christmas with us!" Her mouth gaped in shock.

"I'm afraid so, Huguetty. She has a number of engagements and is enjoying Paris. We'll not complain to her, do you hear?"

"Yes," she grumbled, kicking a red leather Mary Jane against a low velvet ottoman. "She only seems happy when traveling."

"I'm aware of that. We'll accept it with grace." William gave his youngest a stern eye before rising from his desk. "I'll be eating at my club tonight. Take care not to stay up too late reading."

Completing the school year successfully was Huguette's primary duty; her feelings soared while distracted with friends and then sank when alone. She took solace in practicing the violin and swimming daily in the pool. And when the best time of year arrived—the almost four months of summer vacation—she could instruct maids to put everything imaginable in trunks. The delicious rush of anticipation to get out of "horrid Old or should I say New, New York,"—as she liked to joke—hit every May. Anywhere *Maman* wanted to go, Huguette was more than happy to acquiesce.

"Only don't leave me alone!" she pleaded.

During the summer of 1921, fifteen-year-old Huguette said, "Mama, I insist it's my turn to bob my hair. I'm tired, tired, tired of my long hair!"

"Are you sure? Once you cut it, it will take several years to grow back."

"*Oui, Maman*. With a bob you'll be able to see my new pearls so much better. And you've had a bob for years. May I then have a portrait taken with my violin?"

"Yes, I suppose it's time for a new one this fall. You've grown at least another inch. I would like you to wear your pink dress, it's so becoming. Now come along or we'll be late to Amelia's," Anna said while putting on white gloves.

"That's fine. I like that dress. I want a serious photograph though, as I am a serious *artiste* bound for glory!" Huguette threw arms out and waited for a reaction. "In all honesty, *Maman*, I do want a serious photo with my violin."

"Come along! I've another surprise for you. Or should I say, your father and I do." Anna smoothed her linen skirt before sitting down in the Rolls.

Huguette hopped in. "Well, what is it?"

"How about a two-month trip to Honolulu...? I've asked the Vidals to accompany us. Your father will come later."

"Hooray! This will be the best birthday! Thank you ever so much, *Maman*!"

With Jaquita and Margarita, Huguette asked for a third round of surfing lessons with Duke Kahanamoku on Waikiki Beach.

"I remember you and the gorgeous Spanish sisters!" Duke said while giving Huguette a playful pat on the head and looking appreciatively at the dark-haired beauties. He grinned. "Want another ride on my shoulders?"

He had been forewarned not to mention Andrée's absence.

"I rather think I'm a bit too tall for that these days. Do your best with me, Mr. K. I'm rather hopeless. But I enjoy surfing!"

"Please call me Duke."

"Alright. You can call me Hugo!"

She tore down the sand into the calm waves and kept going until she was waist deep. Duke smiled and grabbed the long board before trotting after her.

Apart from surfing, Huguette still adored anything coconut, from desserts to drinks. She and Jaquita bought grass skirts and ukuleles, which instantly reminded her of Andrée. She tried not to cry.

It was easy to be happy with the extroverted Vidal sisters. At night on the beach, they sang with a guitar. During the day, Margarita liked to dress Huguette up in native costumes or evening gowns and take pictures.

"*Qué bella*, Hugo! Vamp it up! Let's see you be as sultry as a film star!"

"Me? Not really..."

After Hawai'i, the Clarks moved on to Southern California to spend months at a villa named Bellosguardo overlooking the Pacific Ocean.

"I'm very taken with this area, William. Once one experiences the heavenly weather and wonderful light coming off the ocean, it becomes a sanctuary of sorts. At least for me..."

"I agree, my darling," he said, seating himself beside her. "I've only just arrived from Los Angeles and already I feel more relaxed. I'm pleased this house was available to rent. Damn fine Italian villa, this is."

"*Oui*, I can hardly convince Huguette to come up from the beach. She says it's almost as wonderful as Waikiki. Imagine that..."

When Spence resumed mid-September, Huguette invariably returned very tan. Envious classmates eyed her up, wondering which exotic locale she had visited.

"Well, *she's* not stuck at boring granny's estate in Newport, is she?" pouted Tabitha Leonard. She leaned over her friend's desk. "Hey, Hugo, did ya see any film stars in California?"

"No... My parents don't pay any attention to Hollywood. And it's not by Santa Barbara."

"What about you? You could go."

"Tabby, I'm fifteen," Huguette said while seated at a wooden desk. She opened her geometry textbook to the day's lesson.

"Exactly! The perfect age to become a film star. I read about it all the time!" said Tabitha. "You can lie about your age. Your career will be longer." She nodded as if it were her plan.

The older Huguette became, the more she only spoke to others on a need-to-know basis. Anna had given this tip the night before her daughter returned to New York. Huguette entered Anna's bedroom at Bellosguardo and climbed into the double bed. Her mother was looking through magazines propped up on jade silk pillows. She placed the magazines to the side before snaking an arm around Huguette's shoulders.

"Now that you are a young woman and will be attending Spence alone, unfortunately, but also happily continuing to socialize with more friends as you get older, I want you to be aware of something. Many girls will be watching you. It's human to want what we can't have. And you, *ma petite fille*, have *far more* than other girls. Even privileged Spence girls. So, make your friends very carefully, and tell no one about your private struggles and problems.

"It's a shame, but there are many who only pretend to be on your side. Vet your friends *carefully* and with patience. You know how I value my privacy; I want you to begin to do the same. To be discreet is to be happy. 'To live happily, live hidden.' Learn that lesson from the poem you memorized, Huguette. I'm sure I don't have to stress never to discuss me or your father to anyone outside of our family."

Huguette listened intently, accepting her mother's wisdom. As the months went by, she thought deeply about the warning to live hidden. It was an interesting notion; one she liked. Many friends seemed to be chasing after life in the opposite direction.

***

The next summer, it was her father's turn to give advice she would always remember. Seated on Bellosguardo's wide veranda at sunset, they watched the colors change over the ocean.

"As you are now sixteen years old, there is something important I wish to speak to you about. Anyone who wants to escort you at dances and parties," and here William paused, his hawk-like eyes boring into hers, "is after your money."

"I've no money. It's your money, Papa."

Huguette felt uncomfortable but riveted by the emotion emanating from her father. William paused before patting her hand reassuringly. Then he sandwiched her hand between his, pulling her closer.

"Listen well, Huguetty. You'll inherit a vast fortune from me someday soon. And then a second fortune when your mother dies. I've made sure she's a multi-millionairess to protect her from my adult children. Share that information with *no one in the family*. It's for your ears alone!

"I won't live many more years. Therefore, it's my paternal duty to protect you from the many, many different types of fortune-hunters you'll encounter. You'll see it with *beaux* and with female friends. Allow no one to get too close unless they remain *completely independent* of your largesse. Most people are wolves in sheep's clothing. Keep in mind: *Unless the man himself comes from great wealth*, it's a certainty he wants your money, not you! Most men are like that, I'm sorry to admit."

"Oh Papa, that can't be true—"

"Listen to me! I'm not being harsh; I'm telling you the facts. I love you dearly, as you know. Choose wisely or *stay away from marriage altogether*! It'll no doubt bring you great unhappiness."

"But you and Mommy are very happy..."

William paused before he said something which haunted her the rest of her life.

"Huguetty, no one will love you for yourself."

"No one?" She looked at him with pure incomprehension. It didn't seem possible. She had always been loved.

Her father turned his attention to the fading light over the ocean. "Remember I said that. You'll thank me some day."

No one, Daddy? Ever...? I'm to be alone forever?

She felt pinned by a great, smothering weight. Then, the feeling became a sinking deep down inside, drowning her in its depths. Huguette's eyes sought the Channel Islands on the far horizon, where she wished she could swim to escape her present reality.

I'll live safely out there like a hermit.

Feeling profoundly shaken, she went to bed that night with a downcast heart.

Papa is so knowledgeable about life, about people, about everything! He must be telling me the truth. I just don't want to hear it...

Huguette learned to put on a type of armor to get through the lonely months of the academic year. Socially speaking, she was as busy and in demand as any young lady could expect. She wasn't part of the most popular set, nor was she as popular as Andrée had been, but that was all right with her. Despite fun times with friends like Larissa Turner, Carolyn Storrs, and Jessica Montrose swimming in the basement pool or parties at Sherry's, there was no one she confided in.

Her dolls listened to her confessions and watched her cry amidst unrelenting loneliness. Her daily routine of music, swimming, and reading became a salvation.

At a quarter to nine on weekdays, Huguette forced a small smile with teeth recently altered by a long round of braces. With straightened teeth, bobbed hair, couture clothing, and a tan, she looked the picture of health and prosperity stepping out of the Rolls. Huguette was far more elegant and self-assured in private; in public she preferred to fly under the radar. She automatically adjusted facial expression and body language; she went inward instead of projecting outward.

Academically, Huguette always did well. She suffered through Latin and labored in sewing class to craft infant clothing despite not ever imagining what kind of a mother she would be. Elocution was a challenge as her French-accented English annoyed.

A frequent refrain was, "Try again, Miss Clark!"

Huguette's native intelligence and life-long education allowed her to sail through most classes without needing to study. The curriculum was designed to challenge enough but not too much. It was an inevitable fact precious few students planned on university studies. The undercurrent in the oldest classes of the Upper School was perpetually about: "Who has a beau? Is he a decent kisser?"

In the library one afternoon, Patricia Foster picked on an easy target. "I heard you're going to Sarah Lawrence in the fall, Jessica. Why on *earth* are you doing that?"

"Well, Patricia, for one, I love literature. I plan on studying Shakespeare." Jessica Montrose put a monogrammed bookmark in a novel before setting it down.

"Four more years of school? And no men in sight? You've got to be kidding!" said Patricia, hiking up a leg to ostensibly adjust an already perfect silk stocking. The abrupt movement allowed everyone a good look at slim legs.

"Once I'm out of here, I'm done," said Patricia with a flippant attitude. "And, now that it's becoming a *must*, I'm going to chop off my hair! My cousin in London got the shingle cut even though her dragon of a mother wasn't pleased. It's about time I take the plunge! Then I'm off to find Valentino!" Patricia tossed a long, brunette braid.

"And how!" said Janice Madsen, who delighted in being a sycophant. "My father only let me cut my hair after I waved 'Bernice Bobs her Hair' in the *Saturday Evening Post* enough times in front of his oblivious face."

"Good for you! And Pat, never mind these girls. They're merely a pair of wet blankets." Theda Brown looked pointedly at Huguette and Jessica. The older group of girls laughed loudly and moved in unison down the library after more sympathetic listeners.

Huguette glanced over at Jessica who shared her table. Jessica looked annoyed as she gripped a pencil and stared hard at an essay. Huguette ducked back into *Pride and Prejudice*, but her concentration was ruined; instead of reading, she began thinking.

I don't want to go to college either, but I understand Jessica's strong desire to do something other than get married at twenty after a year of being a debutante... Girls like Pat puzzled her. *What exactly are they rushing after?*

Huguette preferred to spend time with her parents or pursuing personal interests. She attended concerto concerts, the theater, the ballet, and the Metropolitan Opera where her father kept a box. With Papa or *tante* Amelia, Huguette saw new exhibitions at the Metropolitan Museum of Art and toured art galleries. For the library—still her favorite room in the mansion with its sixteenth century mantlepiece from a Normandy castle, armed knights standing guard as andirons, and stained-glass windows from a thirteenth-century Belgian abbey—boxes of leather-bound books from booksellers in New York, Paris, and London arrived monthly.

"Huguetty, if you take so many up to your room, perhaps I should ask for two of each title! However, I'm pleased you're a reader. In all seriousness, you'll enrich your life greatly through broad reading of all genres. Don't make the mistake of solely reading novels."

"Well, I read novels for English class, Papa, but I like to read many things." Huguette shrugged, returning the books to a nearby table.

A new challenge presented itself. Spence's music teacher passed around flyers for auditions for a prestigious youth orchestra. From hard-earned prowess, Huguette became first chair violin amongst 110 talented youths performing in the American Orchestral Society. The teenagers fondly called it "Mrs. Harriman's orchestra."

Mrs. Mary Williamson Averell Harriman, a billionaire widow and philanthropist, was the founder, president, and financier. Anna was thrilled for her daughter's accomplishment. She donated money and attended every concert given.

"I can't believe it's been eight whole years since I've been to Europe, Papa! 1914 to 1922, incredible!" Huguette linked her arm through William's as they walked the ramp to the first-class deck.

"Yes, it's high time you were back. Now that the land and beaches are cleared of explosives, I feel it's safe enough."

Huguette turned her head to glance back at the reporters below, shouting for any famous person's attention they caught a glimpse of boarding that afternoon.

"I'm very happy to leave them behind as well! *Maman*, it'll be wonderful to spend the summer in France."

"I'm glad to hear it. Now, let's get settled and then rest our eyes before we have to dress for dinner. Remember, we're at the captain's table." Anna smiled at Huguette before greeting a passing acquaintance.

Huguette's face scrunched up. "Must we? The first night?"

After the dinner ordeal ended, Huguette snuggled gratefully underneath the ivory lace down quilt. She reveled in the remembered feel of the massive ship as it hummed and powered through the Atlantic waves. It instantly reminded of other nights when she was a little girl, remarking on the sound to Andrée in the next bed.

"Silly goose, Hugo, you can't hear anything much. Papa said this big ship is state of the art. I'm tired now, let's go to sleep." Andrée turned away, grabbing a pillow to cover her head.

"But I can hear it. You can't?" said Huguette. She leaned to push the fringed curtains aside, craning neck upwards. "And there are so many stars out tonight!"

"Nanny Walter is going to come in any minute and scold you. *Again!*" came the muffled words from under a down pillow.

Coming out of the reverie, Huguette whispered to a doll, "We're finally going home! After all this time away, France is in our sights at last! If only dear Andrée could have come with us. She never made it back to France... We miss her so very much!"

The Clarks first traveled to London, staying at the Ritz. Anna and Huguette ordered riding clothes and boots, all to be shipped to New York. William went to Anderson & Sheppard on Old Burlington Street, and to Hawkes & Co. at No. 1 Saville Row, to order bespoke clothing, shoes, and hats. At night, they attended various entertainments, and during the day, bought antique furniture and paintings at shops bursting with recent acquisitions from beleaguered estates.

Crossing the Channel a few weeks later, the Clarks stayed at the *Hôtel de Crillon*. Huguette was starry-eyed with memories, and liked feeling she was in the heart of the city. Exulting in speaking French at every opportunity, she willfully eschewed English. She reveled in the familiar food and treats from *patisseries, chocolateries,* and *boulangeries*.

They visited Anna's favorite bookseller and William's favored art gallery, but Huguette, accompanied by Marié, went to Au Nain Bleu alone. She indulged herself in her passion, carefully looking over all the handmade treasures to make her selections. The attendant started to protest a young woman affording the extensive haul before Marié gave him a look of death and demanded the bill.

"William, have you noticed how energized Huguette is by France? She's now a young woman and I cannot help remarking on the change in her. She misses Andrée so, this trip has done a world of good for her," Anna remarked before bed.

"Yes, she's been quite the cultural maven. She has asked me to get tickets for every show, concert, or exhibition at the Louvre, *Musée du Luxembourg*, and the *Muséum national d'histoire naturelle* that I'll agree to. The next month will not be restful with all the tearing around she wants to do."

William chuckled to himself at the thought of his youngest excited by France. "It's about time Huguette showed some signs of enjoying life again."

The next day, he wanted to pay his respects to veterans. The afternoon was quite hot as they made their way to the Arc de Triomphe. They purchased roses from a street stand to lay at the Tomb of the Unknown Soldier. Huguette found it profoundly moving to consider all the remains that could not be identified at the end of the war.

"I've been reading about the war, Papa. It must have been so terribly awful to have died in front of German machine guns or in the miles of muddy trenches."

"Yes, Huguetty, I'm grateful you understand their profound sacrifice. May we never forget!"

William stood before the monument with head bowed; Huguette put her arm through her father's. Her attention was drawn to how thin his frame felt, how short he suddenly appeared. Despite daily, rich meals, he hadn't put on weight. Paler than normal, he didn't mind the heat. His inherent energetic nature covered the frailty.

When *Maman* invited Huguette to couture appointments, she was in heaven. For two days, they were kept busy ordering. Ten days later, they attended the final fitting. Huguette was suddenly very interested in ordering fashionable clothing from Chanel, Lanvin, and other elegant *couturiers*.

"It's not like it used to be, so grand, colorful, and dripping with jewels and embroidery, but it's still a wonderful, luxurious experience."

"I remember the ornate gowns you used to wear when I was little. You were so beautiful, *Maman*."

"*Merci, ma petite.* I hope you'll appreciate *haute couture* and always dress well when you're a woman." Anna patted Huguette's hand. "And, someday you can take your own daughter to order *couture* as well."

The next day they toured the *avenue Victor Hugo* flat to check on the delayed progress of final repairs. While her parents conversed with workmen in the grand drawing room, Huguette walked through rooms swirling with dear memories no matter where she looked. Despite the cosmetic changes and lack of furniture, she felt as if in a dream.

If only Andrée were here with me now. How happy she would be! Huguette's eyes filled with tears.

"Huguetty, come along now!" William called from the hallway.

She hastily wiped away wetness before leaving the former nursery bedroom. "Papa, is it not possible to visit the *Château de Petit-Bourg* someday?"

"We've some time before luncheon. It's not far."

Soaking up every detail wherever they went, her eyes scanned familiar boulevards and city landmarks with avid interest. South of Paris, when the car turned on the well-known road, Huguette's heart beat faster. She leaned forward to catch the first glimpse of the *château*.

"Ah, there it is! There it is! Even more beautiful in real life than in my memories! How I long to go inside."

"You know that's not possible," said Anna.

"*Quel dommage*! Father, is it not for sale? Can you buy it?" Huguette asked in a voice full of longing.

"I would if it were for sale...but it's not," said William. "The new owner is adamant he will not take offers. I've tried various ways, but it's to no avail. In fact, if the man sees me on the grounds again, he might get out his gun!" William chuckled. "Good thing I brought my men with me..."

"So, I cannot even get out of the car?" whined Huguette, gripping the door handle in eagerness.

"I'm afraid not, Huguetty. Driver, turn around before we're shot at."

"Oh, William, please!" said Anna. "Huguette, sit back like a lady."

***

The Clarks went on to Italy, reveling in its history of the arts. They took a break from hotels to rent ancient palaces with soaring ceilings, enormous carved wood beds, five-hundred-year-old portraits of the Madonna and Child, and sculpture that hearkened back to a glorious past.

Huguette practiced Italian—upset when a word or phrase eluded her—and sought out bookshops to ship Italian texts home. Flipping through her mother's old red *Baedeker*, she said, "Daddy, there is so much to see in Florence alone, I'm despairing. I know I'll miss something important!"

"Huguetty, what a provincial tourist you're becoming. These cities have been here for many hundreds of years, and they will still be here when you're an old lady. You've plenty of time to see everything!"

On a Venetian canal two weeks later, Huguette quickly averted eyes away from a gondolier who appeared romantically ferocious. He serenaded with songs of unrequited love. Throughout the singing, she examined the dirty water or the ancient crumbling foundations. Anywhere but at the dark-haired singer's eyes boring into hers.

When she stepped out of the gondola, the gondolier clasped her hand fervently with a fawning smile. William stepped forward to glare at the Venetian who backed down with hands upraised.

Huguette would return to Spence to report on the incident. *Finally, it's my turn to have something romantic to tell!*

As they walked across a busy piazza, she moved closer to Anna to whisper, "*Maman*, I can already hear Grace Morris, with both hands clasped to her chest, sighing the usual, 'How romantic, like a moving picture but in *real* life!'"

"Hmmm, ridiculous... Hollywood is not where a woman should get her information about men," said Anna as they moved through the crowd.

"Oh, I know. It's just that this trip is so different than before. There was that young man who was staring when we stepped out of the salon in Paris, remember?"

"*Oui*, a handsome Frenchman. He reminded me of Etienne de Villermont."

"Oh, Etienne? I haven't seen him in years. I wonder why we didn't visit."

"The family's in Lyon for the summer. He's growing up to be a tall, handsome young man."

Anna winked at Huguette.

"Stop, *Maman*. We were mere playmates!"

When traveling in Europe, Huguette experienced first-hand the importance of sartorial elegance to both her parents. In the States, neither made much of an effort to shop for clothing nor did they discuss it. But in Europe, *quelle difference*! It was part of the itinerary in all major cities. In Milan alone, the Clarks ordered bespoke shoes, furs, cashmere shawls, and a variety of leather goods.

From Milan, they boarded a private rail car to travel north to Oberammergau in Bavaria. William had planned this part of the trip as a gift for Anna.

Walking along the train's narrow passageway to the dining car, Anna said, "The Catholic Church has recently granted a *Missio Canonica*. The Passion Play is performed on outdoor stages only once a decade, starting in 1664. Imagine! However, it has been delayed for two years due to war-recovery efforts. This is our big chance to see the important, historical work which won't be performed again for another eight years."

Huguette, trailing close behind, protested, "But... but we are now headed for enemy territory and, strangely, as tourists. *Maman*, Germany! The *Oberammergauer Passionsspiele* may be historical, but geographically-speaking, it's morally questionable."

"Not so." Anna turned and laid a hand on Huguette's arm. In a soft voice she said, "The war is over, and so should our rancor be. We must choose forgiveness over vindictiveness and shunning of our fellow human beings, regardless of their crimes. It's my express wish we attend the *Oberammergauer Passionsspiele*, and that we shall."

William arose from the table to look at them expectantly. "I'm famished! We've walked a great deal today, which is wonderful exercise. The food will taste even better. Isn't that so, my love? I've ordered us to start with *bouillabaisse*, then *salade de tomates, coq au vin* and whatever dessert Huguetty prefers. I was considering the *blanquette de veau* but decided against it."

A waiter pulled out Huguette's chair. While seating herself, she said, "Daddy, what do you think about going to Bavaria?"

"What about it?"

"Daddy, the Germans!"

"Well, in that light, I understand your concern. However, the Armistice trumps all. It's been years of peace and rebuilding. Justice and moral right prevailed. We must move forward, Huguetty, resuming our lives. Don't forget, but also, don't dwell on it either, my dear."

Huguette's eyes went from one parent to the other, searching for a hint of support. She looked temporarily disappointed but squelched feelings which would lead to complaining.

"Attending the Passion Play and donating a princely sum afterwards might get me into heaven when I die. Don't change your mother's mind!"

"William, please don't make such jests..."

Huguette smiled wickedly, "Don't worry, Daddy, *Maman* makes up for *any* spiritual deficiency you or I possess."

"You little minx! But," William looked at his wife, "that she does. Saint Anna we shall dub her!"

"I'm going to leave if you both don't stop at once. You'll spoil my appetite."

Anna lowered eyes to place a linen napkin over the fine fabric of her Chanel gown. Huguette saw she was holding back laughter.

In early August, Anna and Huguette returned to the *Hôtel de Crillon* while William traveled home.

"It's just like old times. Me alone in France."

"I'm with you, *Maman*! Don't forget about me!"

Now that Huguette was old enough to comprehend mature subjects, Anna couldn't resist regaling Huguette with stories of her youth. Huguette took her mother's arm during long walks in the Bois de Bologne, thrilled to be hearing what her mother was like when young.

"Mrs. Abascal was your first chaperone!" said Huguette, aghast.

She had only seen her ferocious aunt on her father's side a few times during family parties in Los Angeles. The woman had terrified.

"*Oui, oui*... I was seventeen and very gauche, and Madame Abascal let me know it every day."

"I bet that was awful..."

Huguette shook her head in pity.

"Hmm, I survived. Then I was with Madame de Cervellon for years. She was a wonderful woman who died before you were old enough to know her."

"*Oui*, I don't recall... Tell me more about the *Conservatoire de Musique*, *Maman*! Did you really meet Debussy?"

The first week of September, Huguette tearfully sailed home accompanied by Isabel Sandré, her new French chaperone, and her maid while Anna remained in Paris.

"I'll be home before you miss me, *ma petite!*"

"*Maman,* have a wonderful time but I already miss you so much. Please write a proper letter instead of sending telegrams." Huguette reached to hug her again.

"*D'accord.* Now off to board, or you'll be late."

That academic year there was one major difference which Huguette was pleased with. Her nieces from San Francisco—Agnes, Patricia or "Patsey," and Mary—enrolled as boarding students.

Unlike Huguette, her nieces had prominent members of society on both sides. Their beautiful mother, Cecelia "Celia" Tobin, was heiress to the Hibernia Bank fortune. Their Irish-born, multi-lingual maternal grandfather, Richard Tobin, was raised in Valparaíso, Chile. In 1849, Tobin came to California with his father and brother, studied law, and, ten years later, began the Hibernia Savings and Loan Society. Tobin married, and being a progressive man, insisted all six children were educated in elite Catholic private schools. His two daughters, Agnes and Celia, studied the sciences and mathematics along with poetry and languages.

Celia adored her intellectual older sister, Agnes, naming her first-born daughter after her. Agnes Tobin was a poet and classical translator who lived in England. Her associates were writers such as William Butler Yeats—who referred to her as America's "greatest poet" since Walt Whitman—and Joseph Conrad, who dedicated *Under Western Eyes* to her.

Not a scholar like her sister, Celia was still far more educated than most women of the age. She had wit, style, and grace; she was also a skilled equestrienne, polo player, and an accomplished pianist. These skills Celia would cultivate in her three daughters, and, years later, use to influence Anna as well.

Celia's modest wedding to widower Charles Clark occurred on August 4, 1904, at her widowed mother's mansion at 1021 California Street in San Francisco. Two years later it was leveled by the 7.9 earthquake and charred to bits from three days of ravaging fires. In the wedding party, all Celia's supportive siblings stood up with her. Ethel Barrymore was a guest. A traditional wedding breakfast was provided before the newlyweds departed for Charlie's mansion in San Mateo.

True to form, William was too busy with his own affairs to attend despite being pleased at the Tobin's prominent standing in San Francisco society. He wrote to inform Anna of his eldest son's remarriage; he expressed hope Celia's desire for a large family would keep Charlie in line.

Directly after the wedding, the newlyweds went to Paris. The thirty-year-old, brunette Celia was painted by premier portraitist of the *beau monde*, Giovanni Boldini, at his studio at 41 *boulevard Berthier*. The newspapers made sure to include details that the Tobin-Clark union had not only the Hibernia fortune but also $25,000 a month in spending money from Charles Clark's stake in his father's most lucrative copper mine, rumored to bring in $1,000,000 monthly.

While Anna lived in Paris the two women hardly saw one another, but eventually, Celia would get along well with the discreet Anna.

At dinner in Paris months after the wedding, William confessed, "I'm glad he chose such a sensible woman from a solid family, but I worry about my son's private proclivities."

"Oh, I don't know. Charlie is always respectful to me, and there's no gossip about him. His bride will no doubt do him good. When will we meet her?"

"I couldn't say at this time, unless you want to entertain them here. They'll be in Paris later this fall, but I cannot come again until Christmas."

"I might consider that, if Charlie agrees. After all I've heard, I'm curious to meet Celia."

"Yes, Charlie raves about her piano playing."

Anna would not meet Celia for another year, but she was pleased to discover Celia's intelligence and passion for music. Over the years at Clark family gatherings, the two women played many duets.

After four children and years of patience, Celia found marriage to Charlie Clark intolerable. As William feared, Charlie was a man who, despite loving music and fine living, also philandered, drank, and gambled constantly. Having no father to rely on for advice, Celia attempted to avoid a scandalous divorce. She was incensed that after all her entreaties, her father-in-law ignored her. Rancor built up for both Clark men. By 1922, there would be no way to save the marriage.

"William, I don't like to interfere, but if Celia is determined to live in England for the time being, then we can offer to take care of your granddaughters. They can attend Spence with Huguette." Anna looked forward to spoiling her three step-granddaughters.

"This divorce is a headache I don't need right now! I'm angry with Charlie for not being the man I raised him to be!"

William's hand slapped the table as he swore. Anna and Huguette flinched.

"I'm sorry I lost my temper, my darlings, but I have had it with my son! I'll deal with him privately." William took a deep breath before saying, "Anna, I've no squabbles with my granddaughters going to Spence. Huguette, are you ready to be an aunt?"

"I think it sounds fun!" Huguette smiled at the thought of having family at school again.

"Then it's settled. I'll write to Charlie to arrange the trip. Huguetty, I warn you: You'll have more responsibilities watching over the three youngsters."

"I can manage, Papa. After all, they'll be boarding, correct?"

"Yes, that I'll insist on. I don't want to return home to a chorus of yapping females."

"So, this is our fate," said Agnes the week before classes began. "To be at boarding school while Mother takes our brother with her to England..."

Agnes bore a stoic expression. A pretty, fifteen-year-old brunette, she was passionate about musical studies. Huguette liked Agnes because it reminded her of Andrée when they performed together.

Huguette hosted her nieces at Sherry's that afternoon, explaining the importance of being familiar with the restaurant many at Spence swore by.

"I adore it when Grandma Anna sits on his lap and pulls his whiskers!" said Agnes. "And Grandpa merely laughs!"

"She does that from time to time," said Huguette with a wry smile. She took a bite of sandwich.

Patsey said, "Grandpa Clark took me to FAO Schwarz and told me I could buy any toys I wanted. Daddy and Mommy never let me pick out exactly what I want and then offer me more. But Grandpa *always* does. I got a horse and stable set."

Mary looked up from spooning potato soup into her small pink mouth and nodded seriously. "Yes, I love Grandpa and Grandma Clark very much."

Huguette reached over to give her youngest niece a hug. "You're sweet, Mary."

Huguette had her own problems that school year. Instead of resuming the normal routine at the Fifth Avenue mansion, on the day she arrived in New York, she was delivered to a 4-bedroom suite at the 15-story Ambassador Hotel at Park Avenue at 51st Street. The hotel was built in 1921 and advertised its pied-à-terres for "patrons of art."

Upon arrival, Huguette sent a telegram. "I want my complaints to get to Papa as fast as possible!" she said to Sandré.

In answer, William sent a letter apologizing for the inconvenience and gave her a financial lesson on out-of-control New York taxes.

On Sunday evening after dropping her nieces off at Spence, Huguette laid on the hotel bed with the letter that gave no good news. She rolled her eyes and tossed the offending papers to the side.

"This is ridiculous! I'm living in a hotel suite for the next few months? What's wrong with Papa? He has enough money to pay extra taxes!"

Huguette scowled and then addressed a black-haired doll in a yellow silk dress which lay against the pillows. "Of course you agree with me, Veronica! Papa is a cranky old man who isn't thinking about his daughter's comfort!"

She looked around the luxurious but unfamiliar room with unsatisfied eyes. "Now how am I supposed to swim in the mornings? This is too much. I feel cross!"

Huguette dragged herself off the bed for violin practice. The maid had laid out the violin on a small table by a music stand in the corner. She didn't analyze the feeling of loneliness in the strange space, which she didn't like because it made her feel weak.

What she couldn't express was her impacted family life, and now, being cut off from her past life with Andrée. Huguette couldn't see Andrée in the unfamiliar hotel suite; she had no memories here. The lack intensified longing.

Maman *in Paris for weeks more perhaps, and Papa out West for who knows how long...* Huguette ran a finger down the bow. *Maybe I can still get into the house to swim?*

Then she remembered Papa had written: "The house won't be opened until mid-November, and not a day before!"

He probably figured I'd want to use the pool! Huguette attempted a new piece, playing for a while before whirling to address Veronica. "I'm left here alone with the dull Madame Sandré. This is unfair!"

Setting the Stradivarius violin to shoulder, she drew down the bow with force, breaking a string.

April 1923
960 Fifth Avenue, New York City

"Huguette, come, I'd like you to meet someone," said Anna, motioning to her daughter who stood sipping a drink by an oversized silver punchbowl.

Huguette blanched and averted her eyes. *Maman* was standing with the Polish painter who was the handsomest man she had ever seen!

Earlier in the party the man had looked straight at her and smiled. She froze with fear at the attention. By the fluttering reaction of the women in the room, she knew she wasn't the only one who thought him highly attractive.

Huguette made her way through the crowded drawing room to stand with downcast eyes beside her mother.

In French Anna said, "This is Tadeusz Styka. He's come from Paris to exhibit work at the Knoedler Gallery. Monsieur Styka, this is my daughter, Huguette."

"Delighted to meet you, Huguette," Styka extended a long-fingered hand. "Please call me Tadé."

Huguette looked up at the tall painter with blonde hair and kind, hazel eyes and forgot to speak. Only the knee-jerk reaction of politeness had her extend a hand.

She was amazed how wonderfully smooth yet powerful his hand felt gently gripping hers. Her cheeks flushed.

"Monsieur Styka will be doing all our portraits. Isn't that wonderful?"

Huguette's eyebrows raised and her mouth went dry. *I'll have to sit with him for hours!*

"My daughter is artistically talented, Monsieur Styka. She's been drawing since she was young. She's had some tutors, but none of your capability. If you ever find the time while you're in New York, perhaps you could give her lessons?"

Styka looked Huguette over with interest. "Ah! I thought there was something different about you. Are you a painter?"

"Oh no! But I... I would like to learn oil painting." Huguette felt her cheeks grow warm again. She wanted to flee.

"I'll consider it, Madame Clark. Thank you for trusting me." He bowed slightly before beaming another warm smile.

Styka was lavishly admired, and like all popular portraitists, knew how to make patrons look their best. The Clarks quickly became his most important clients, eventually commissioning almost two dozen portraits.

Months later, standing in his light-filled studio at 222 Central Park South, Huguette said, "Will you be able to paint Andrée accurately from photographs?" She cocked her head dubiously.

Styka immediately comprehended the challenge. "Well, well, well... My new little friend doubts me already!" He pointed the paint brush at her. "You shall see, Mademoiselle Huguette, that I shall faithfully render your dearly departed sister to the *very best* of my abilities. And if your *maman* is satisfied with my talent, why are you expressing doubts, hmmm?"

Styka shifted his palette as he regarded the young woman.

"Pardon, I didn't mean to be rude. I'm merely intrigued by the process as she's not here to stand in front of you, a living person, as I am doing at this moment... And, frankly, you must do your best, *bien sûr*, because dear Andrée is very special to all of us. You mustn't fail. I will let you know if the features are done correctly."

Styka shot Huguette a perturbed look. The young heiress normally modeled silently. *For all her shy looks, she certainly can lay it on the line.*

Despite the large age difference, Huguette was drawn to Styka and his playful eyes that missed nothing. He was well dressed, cosmopolitan, an accomplished artist, and best of all, spoke French like a Parisian. He charmed the entire family, like he did everyone everywhere. Within months, the painter was dining *en famille* in New York and staying long periods at Bellosguardo.

That summer in the coastal light, Styka painted while Anna and Huguette played golf, took private tennis lessons on the estate's courts, or swam at the private beach. Styka would take a break to go horseback riding with Huguette far down the beach.

Despite the extended Clark family clamoring, William did not consent to retire like most octogenarians. It was much easier on his packed schedule to visit Anna in Santa Barbara. Soon, he began making excuses to spend more time at idyllic Bellosguardo. Styka was able to complete multiple portraits.

"I've precious little time to sit for you, so you better paint fast, young man!"

Anna's favorite was hung in the front hall of the villa. William's white hair glowed in the painting as he sat in a chair gazing at his viewer with challenge in his eyes.

"I stop and admire the painting of Papa all the time. You've done an admirable job of capturing his personality," said Huguette during tea.

"Finally, some praise from my harshest and youngest critic!" said Styka, stubbing out a cigarette. "It's about time." He smiled indulgently.

Sitting under the pergola one September evening alone after Huguette was sent back to New York, Anna and William gazed out at the ocean.

"My love, I don't know how much longer I'll live."

"It upsets me to talk about that, let's not..."

"Anna, listen, please. I want to provide for you for your remaining years. The other properties are for my children, as you're aware. However, I've purchased Bellosguardo for you alone. It's my final gift for being the most wonderful wife. How grateful I am I took you on as a talented but ignorant ward all those many years ago in Butte!" He chuckled.

"Don't speak of me as an ignorant ward. I know I was. And it was ages ago!" Anna waved a hand dismissively but there were tears in her eyes.

"But what a wise, talented woman you became, my love." He reached out to take her hand.

"Bellosguardo is for me, William?" Her eyes searched his. She was used to lavish generosity but receiving the oceanside property was unexpected.

"Yes, I'll write to my lawyer tomorrow to redraft my will. This property will be included as a gift to you as my beloved second wife."

"It's perfect, *mon amour*." She leaned to kiss William.

Satisfied, he sat back, gazing at the emerging night sky. The breeze was gentle off the ocean, and they could talk for another hour before retiring.

How I relish this time alone with Anna!

A new passion supplanted the violin. The violin made her mother happy; oil painting made Huguette happy.

During Saturday morning lessons in Styka's well-lit studio, Sandré sat faithfully in the foyer with a book while Huguette disappeared inside. She began to learn about brushwork, techniques of form, composition, perspective, and light. She was interested in mastering how to mix her own oil paints.

"Well, for that my little student, we might wait a bit. It's not as easy as it looks. In time, alright?"

Styka instructed how to set up the pallet, how to mix the small dabs of color to maximize the shade range, and which brush to select for the desired effect on canvas. She worked diligently on whatever he asked in the first twenty-four months.

"Now it's time to step up. *You* are the artist. You choose the subject!" Styka shouted from the small storage room off the studio as he sorted framed canvases.

"*Cher maître*, what if I'm unsure of a proper subject?" Huguette sat before a looming, empty canvas, which made her sigh.

"Then *keep* thinking!" she heard from the other room.

"One of my dolls...? Or, or... something Japanese? I adore their culture. It's so refined, beautifully controlled. How about a still life with fan and cherry blossoms? Haven't I already seen that done...?" Huguette said to herself, slumped on a wooden stool.

She felt determined to learn to paint as well as her teacher. *But am I fooling myself...?*

Styka strode into the studio holding a medium sized canvas. He took one look at his young pupil and knew the problem.

"What image came into your head first?" he said, putting the canvas against a large easel.

"A blonde Jumeau doll with brown eyes."

"As a serious artist, is that what you want to portray?"

"Not really," Huguette sat up straight, conscious he was observing. "She's merely one of my favorite dolls. However, I won't choose that subject if you don't want me to..." She looked away, instinctively feeling she should only choose sophisticated themes.

"I want you to learn to choose worthy subjects. To feel confident in your choices. What was the second image you saw?"

"A Japanese still life, with a patterned fan, a sprig of cherry blossoms. Simple but elegant forms. An empty, neutral background."

Styka nodded, gesturing with long arms at the canvas. "It has been done, but let's see what you as an artist do with it. Begin!"

On the morning of January 12, Huguette stood on a low stool with a seamstress altering the hem of a bridesmaid gown. "*Maman*, I'm not sure... I feel overwhelmed with everything. Do I have—"

"You *must* go through with it, everyone will be there. It's already been discussed as one of the toniest weddings of the year, imagine that. Our little Kate... Now, let's think of her because she's relying on you as family and friend."

"Andrée would've been the bridesmaid, not me!"

Huguette's blue eyes implored as she grabbed heavy yards of mauve silk satin trimmed with plum velvet, lace, and seed pearls, pulling the fabric awkwardly.

"And this ugly bridesmaid gown!"

"Stop at once! The hem is not finished. You might hurt it! Kate's mother selected the gown, so say nothing!"

Anna helped the seamstress by reaching to smooth folds in the skirt. "Never mind the style. Put on a smile and that silly, silly hat I tried to tell Mrs. Morris was too much and walk serenely down the aisle. As you were shown yesterday. You'll do beautifully!"

Anna patted Huguette's arm and stepped back to admire her.

"But John Paul is so tall and gangly. He tromped on me during rehearsal, twice! And I'll have to dance with him at the reception, too!" Huguette pouted, crossing arms.

Anna reached to gently uncross her daughter's arms. "And if John Paul does it again, you'll not forget to smile. Disguise his awkwardness with your grace as you float beside him." She smiled brightly while lifting arms to demonstrate.

"You sound as if *I'm* getting married..." Huguette scowled.

"Someday..."

Anna winked and then immediately indicated to a waiting maid to alter a section of Huguette's bobbed, marcelled waves.

"Make sure you hold your bouquet correctly. Don't let it droop! And chin up, up, up! Smile..."

She swept from the room waving a jeweled hand, French perfume wafting in her wake. Huguette turned her attention back to the long gilt mirror.

To the reflection of lined-up dolls on the bench behind, she declared, "Listen up! I don't know if I'm ever going to get married!"

The seamstress below glanced up in surprise. Huguette blushed and eyebrows lowered in annoyance of herself and everyone.

Today's going to be a long one. She sighed and shifted a quarter turn to accommodate the seamstress.

Miraculously, John Paul Howard Ward III didn't trample on Huguette's satin heeled feet once. She was relieved to be on the fringes, as most guests' eyes during the ceremony were on the lovely, twenty-two-year-old bride. Katherine Elizabeth Clark Morris wore a *Maison Lucien Lelong* wedding gown with real pearls, handmade lace, and a fourteen-foot veil—paid for by her maternal grandfather—to wed John Hudson Hall in front of hundreds at St. Patrick's Cathedral.

After the long ceremony, Huguette stood with the other bridesmaids as they waited for photographs to finish. She took off a glove to anxiously bite cuticles because she knew *Maman* wasn't around.

"I think he's a little creepy, don't you, Jackie?" said Samantha Hesse, Kate's best friend. Her dark eyes were haughty as she tilted the brim of the large hat to look, vainly trying to catch the older man's attention.

Tall with broad shoulders, slicked back black hair, and black mustache, Huguette's bodyguard in black tie canvased the interior of the cathedral and the exterior steps abutting the busy street. He never seemed to look in their direction.

"Well, I think he's kind of a looker, if you ask me. Hugo, why does your father always insist on bodyguards?" whispered Jacqueline Boehm, her eyes on the man.

Huguette shrugged and lied. "Beats me."

She watched Kate beside John standing awkwardly before the altar with stiff smiles. *I'll miss her when they move away.*

"You *must* be a target for kidnappers!" gasped Samantha, as if suddenly solving a mystery.

Huguette averted her eyes. *Why is Sam always so obnoxious?*

"Yeah, that's probably it! So sorry, Hugs," said Jacqueline, feeling chagrined she had brought up anything to do with kidnapping danger. She tried to change the subject. "Think we can get him to talk to us?"

After the pictures, the large group of young men and women dutifully followed the bride and groom to pile into a lineup of Rolls Royces. They were driven to Times Square to the Hotel Astor, an eleven-story *beaux arts* edifice with a mansard roof. Heading up to the ninth floor, the reception with over 800 guests took place in the Large Ballroom decorated in the Rococo style of Louis

XV adjoined with the Small Ballroom decorated in the neoclassical Louis XVI manner. The dance band "Fred Rich and his Hotel Astor Orchestra" played until well after midnight.

Huguette snuck away to sit with friends. The tableful of girls—exquisitely dressed in chiffon, silk, and satin, with immaculate, shining hair and a few brave ones with rouge on lips and cheeks—largely sat out the dancing. They were plagued by awkward shyness or chubbiness or a plain face. To cope, they giggled; indulged in cake; jealously rated the gowns of more sophisticated women; and swayed to popular songs like, "I'm Always Chasing Rainbows" and "Everybody Loves My Baby."

When the song "It Had to Be You" began, a frustrated Eleanor Dorsey burst out, "We'll never get asked to dance sitting way over here! It's obvious the boys are intimidated."

"I don't mind in the least, Ellie" said Huguette, tapping her feet to the beat and watching the packed dancefloor.

Several minutes passed with no young men in sight. "I should go to the other side of the ballroom," said Eleanor. The girls ignored her.

"Oh good! 'Linger Awhile' is playing. Anyone wanna dance with me?" asked Eleanor's twin sister, Gertrude. Huguette shook her head as Eleanor rose to go with her sister.

Every now and then, Huguette would pop head up, searching, and there *Maman* would appear in between guests strolling past. At her table, *Maman* would be talking and laughing, perpetually at ease. Huguette knew how well her mother masked true feelings. She also knew better than to expect Papa to attend.

Hours earlier on the street outside the church, Papa had congratulated his granddaughter and promptly returned to work. His wedding gift of $200,000 made up for the absence.

"Finally! School's out, and we're headed home!" said Mary, settling herself onto a burgundy velvet train seat with a view. William's daughter and three granddaughters traveled west in a private train car with accompanying staff.

"We can't get to California with its blue sky and palm trees soon enough! I'm going riding as soon as we get to Bellosguardo!" chimed in Patsey, setting down a stack of leather-bound books.

"I wish Mommy could come earlier...," said Mary, who slumped against Agnes.

"Sometimes I'm not with my mother either," said Huguette. "Don't worry, Mary, we're going to have a cat's meow of a summer. We'll swim and sunbathe and play croquet on the lawn that's as big as a football field. And think of all the fun your mother and Paul are having in England. She'll be in Santa Barbara before you know it."

"I suppose so... You know I always lose at croquet," said Mary, straightening up with a grin. "But I like it!"

"We'll also golf. How about that?" said Huguette, enjoying the feeling of being a big sister.

"Let's do *everything*!"

"She'll wear you out with her demands!" said Agnes, flicking a finger lightly on Mary's upturned nose.

A week later, Huguette stood in the hot sun on the veranda in her swimsuit, holding a beach towel in one hand and Mary's hand in the other. She whined, "But *Maman*, we've only just arrived..."

"What has that got to do with it?" said Anna, sitting underneath a large umbrella at a white wrought iron table. "I've met quite a few prominent members of Santa Barbara, and I would like to welcome them to our home tomorrow night. A jazz band is coming up from Los Angeles. Won't that be fun? After you're done swimming, we can all practice the latest dance steps."

Agnes and Patsey cheered, but Huguette mumbled, "It'll only be loads of strangers crowding the house..."

Anna ignored her. "And tomorrow night we'll eat delicious Lobster Newberg and Chicken à la King."

"That sounds delicious, Grandma!" said Patsey.

The next evening, put out by the overflowing crowds in every room and out onto the veranda, William ate nothing. He fussed about a few movie stars who had crashed the party—"They're beneath our dignity, Anna!"—and the loud jazz band.

"Merely a pack of obnoxious instruments competing with each other instead of harmonizing. This isn't appropriate music!"

"Oh, *mon chéri*, it's modern. And it's *expected*. We should strive to please our guests. Besides, I kind of like the frivolity of jazz music." Anna smiled while putting up jazz hands, swaying a little to entice William.

"I'm not impressed!" He swore under his breath.

The wailing of the saxophones drove him wild. Disgruntled, by half past eight he shut himself up in the library. Sitting at his desk in a tuxedo and gardenia in the lapel, his white hair glowed in the lamplight.

"Huguetty, go have fun. Leave me be."

She kissed her father on the cheek and shut the library's double doors behind her. She turned in surprise to see a few guests attempting to glimpse the notorious tycoon. A bodyguard stepped in front of the doors.

Unbeknownst to William, his habit of moving about town had attracted attention. It wasn't the frequent haircut and shave that was unusual; it was *how* Senator Clark arrived. Leaving Bellosguardo's curved drive down the cliff and passing through tall iron gates, two identical Rolls Royce Silver Ghosts motored slowly along Main Street. Onlookers watched vehicles chauffeured by drivers in black suits pull up along the curb in front of the toniest barber shop.

"One Rolls is for Senator Clark, and the second Rolls for multiple armed bodyguards!" said one astounded man sitting on a bench nearby.

During the party, Huguette was chicly dressed in a sleeveless, black Chanel gown, gold Mary Janes with a demure heel, and gold beaded headband. Feeling awkward, she attempted to keep up with trendy jazz dancing. She stuck close by her nieces off to the side of the ballroom or in a corner of a drawing room.

Falling back into a chair, Huguette said, "I think I'll sit the rest of the night out, Agnes! I've never been very good. Ask my former dance instructor!"

"I'm having a ripping good time! Where's Grandpa? I want to show him this new dance step."

"He's retreated to the library, put out by the noise. Don't bother him."

"Well, then I'll go and show Grandma!" said Agnes.

"She'll like that. I think I see her talking to *tante* Amelia. Over there!" said Huguette, as she pointed through the crowd to the next room.

"Hugo, come have some Floating Island with me, please. It's my favorite!" implored Mary.

"*En français?*"

"*Je voudrais île flottante, s'il vous plaît!*"

"*Très bien*, Mary. *On y va!*" Huguette took the girl's hand and headed to the dessert table.

By July, Huguette was free to do as she pleased. Her nieces had returned to Hillsborough and the days quieted down. At tea towards the end of the month, when her mother reminded her father that Tadé Styka would be coming the next day, Huguette's eyes widened with mingled excitement and nervousness.

"I didn't know you expected him. How long will he be staying?" She tried to keep her voice casual as she set down her teacup. *I haven't seen him since last winter.*

"I think he's only been back in the States for a few weeks. He's coming to spend the month of August at Bellosguardo. How pleasant for us! William, you'll sit first, of course," said Anna, motioning for the table to be cleared. "Then Huguette, you need to stay out of the sun a little. You're getting too brown. You'll sit second, *d'accord?*"

"I like being tan, *Maman*. It's fashionable now."

Anna nodded. "It's simply hard for me to get used to, that's all. I worry about your skin getting leathery like a farmer's."

Huguette immediately went to her room. She sat on her twin bed biting cuticles, staring into space while her heart pounded. *Monsieur Styka will be here a whole month!*

Ten days later, Huguette stood on a canvas tarp in a room with large windows converted into a temporary studio. Huguette watched Styka's hazel eyes examine her as he painted sitting down, one slim leg extended forward.

After some time in silence, Styka addressed her in French. Slowly, while one hand worked the brush on the canvas without ceasing, he said, "Mademoiselle Huguette, you're changed for the better. I think the constant sun, relaxation, and turning eighteen has done something for you... *non?*"

He stopped painting to smile flirtatiously. She blushed.

Averting eyes while clearing her throat, Huguette lifted her head to announce, "You're breaking my concentration through talking, Monsieur Styka. Papa said this portrait has to be *excellent*. Let's keep working!"

Styka smiled wryly, his brush again moving rapidly.

Huguette began her final year of Spence feeling a prisoner in the Ambassador Hotel suite. She crossed off the months to graduation. In the meantime, she kept busy with studying, playing a final season in Mrs. Harriman's orchestra, and taking Spanish lessons with the Vidals. *Tante* Amelia took her out at least once weekly. The attention somewhat made up for her mother being absent.

Anna and William remained at Bellosguardo until early December. Once at the Fifth Avenue mansion for the approaching holiday season, Huguette knew something was different.

She walked into Anna's dressing room demanding, "Why are there far more family members present than I ever remember? What's going on?"

Anna thought for a moment how honest should she be before she rose from the dressing table. "Well, your father is the head of the family, and he deserves respect and attention." She adjusted a pearl necklace in the mirror before scooping up a black silk cloche hat. "Now, let's go down and see if everyone is ready to leave for the concert. Go get your gloves and hat."

Huguette likewise noticed a change in how the family communicated with Papa. Large groups milled around while he sat in a favorite wing chair by the fire or at the head of the table. The fire blazed away, the eight-course meal seemed endless, and, as usual, the wood-paneled room was festooned with pine garlands punctuated with red velvet and gold bows. The altered attention and heightened conversations around the table made Huguette scrutinize her father with fresh eyes. She wondered about his longevity.

On the opposite end, Anna smiled politely and looked beautiful. She was quiet because it was difficult following the quick turns in conversation due to further hearing loss. Few in the family made concessions, and Huguette was too far down the table to help. Anna bore it patiently, eyes betraying nothing of the frustration she felt.

While eating, Huguette held Cynthia wearing a tartan dress. She ignored a red-headed, snub-nosed cousin sitting across the table. She hadn't seen Stephen for years. He was a student at Harvard Law and looked like a gentleman. Until he began speaking.

Squinting dark blue eyes at the doll while draining a gold-rimmed goblet, Stephen motioned impatiently for more wine.

Leaning over, he whispered, "When are you gonna give up that childish habit, cuz?"

Stephen's full lips drooped like his eyes. Huguette looked directly at him without answering.

He hasn't changed much since we were children...

Stephen's mother overheard and shushed him, which caused a few stifled laughs at Huguette's expense. No one was brash enough to draw William's eyes this far down the table.

Huguette took a small bite of cranberry compote and shut out the talk around her. She observed the long table brimming with four large silver candelabra, and several overflowing red rose, white lily, and evergreen flower arrangements. The butler shooed *Maman's* three Pekinese out. People conversed as they took elegant bites or sips of wine, except for Will Jr. and Tertius who always inhaled their food.

Charlie and Katherine laughed and attempted to continuously draw William into conversation. He looked pleased but with tired eyes as Mary, seated on his right, urged him to eat more.

"No, May, I've had enough."

"Daddy, you're skin and bones. Didn't the doctor say you needed to put on more weight?" Her round, needy eyes appealed to nearby siblings for aid.

Huguette felt left out of the real meaning of the conversations humming around her. *What do they know that I don't?* With a presentiment she would never sit for a Clark holiday meal in this room again, she shivered.

Huguette missed painting lessons with Styka that winter. After his stay at Bellosguardo, she discovered he went down to Los Angeles. Anna didn't explain to the innocent Huguette that Styka was spending time with gorgeous actresses like Pola Negri. He had painted her a few years earlier, naked but for a brown sable covering her front while a long pearl necklace hung suggestively down her bare back. The scandalous portrait was displayed publicly in 1923, and a good friend, Amanda Storrs, dutifully reported back to Anna on the sensation it created.

Seated with William in a drawing room of Bellosguardo, Anna said, "I assure you the painter is merely flirtatious. Styka would never truly pursue our fey daughter after cavorting with the likes of Pola Negri. Huguette's not the kind of woman he is attracted to. Mark my words." She patted his withered hands.

"I hope you're correct, Anna! I've already warned Huguetty about men after her fortune. I *don't approve* of the painter for our daughter."

"Never fear, *mon amour*. He's too independent."

Soon after the New Year, Huguette skipped into her mother's dressing room at 960 Fifth Avenue while Anna sat having her hair done.

"*Maman*, Monsieur Styka sent my favorite: red roses!" Huguette's eyes glowed; she buried her nose in the fragrant petals.

"How kind of Monsieur Styka. What did he say?"

"He wrote we'll resume lessons as soon as he returns."

"Did he say when? I should invite him to dinner."

Huguette hummed with happiness while inspecting the roses as if he picked out each one. "He says he's finishing up work in Los Angeles. It won't be long." She turned and went back to her room to ensure the roses were set by her bedside.

The next month, William returned from out west ill with a cold. Huguette knew it was serious when he didn't emerge for work. The house was unusually quiet when she returned home from school.

Mary called Anna to check on her father's condition; she had plans to marry her third husband on the twenty-eighth of February. As Anna put down the receiver, Huguette glanced up from her book.

"Mary's adamant but William won't be able to attend." Anna sighed. "The doctor says the cold has developed into pneumonia. She would do well not to expect a party and publicity for a third marriage, in any case!"

"Are we going?"

"No. She wouldn't want us there without your father. And I'm not leaving your father alone. He's quite ill."

"May I see him today?"

"Wait until before dinner. He's usually awake then. Asking for *The Wall Street Journal* to be read to him. *Cet homme!* When will he ever rest? He'll work himself to death…"

In early March, those words echoed in Huguette's head during the vigil around William's bedside. When she entered her father's large, wood-paneled bedroom with red velvet curtains, she saw Mary and Katherine were already present wearing black silk dresses. Across the wide room by the windows, Will Jr. and Charlie stood talking quietly together. No one looked at her.

Once settled in a chair by *Maman*, Huguette's attention was riveted to her father. William lay unconscious against the full, white pillows of the massive carved canopy bed. His normally energetic frame looked shrunken, as if he were already dead. The minutes passed. Huguette heard soft conversations. A priest entered the bedroom to pray over her father. She heard weeping and more whispering.

The hovering doctor put a stethoscope to William's chest. He checked the pulse. Then he softly stated, "Senator Clark is dead."

Huguette held her breath, stunned at the thought her beloved, strong father was gone. It didn't seem possible. She saw her mother's head bow and the effort not to make a sound as she sobbed. With tears stinging her eyes, Huguette reached out to take her hand.

The New York Times ran a front-page obituary of Senator William Andrews Clark detailing his accomplishments. Huguette sat alone in the library by the fire, repeatedly reading the headline, "Ex-Senator Clark, Pioneer in Copper, Dies of Pneumonia." She hoped no one would find her there.

Deliveries of hundreds of floral arrangements, including from President Calvin Coolidge, stunk up first-floor drawing rooms. All day Huguette had avoided both the overpowering smell and the casket placed in the *Salon Doré*.

Her eyes scanned the article, taking in well-known facts and traits, but wondering at the tone of awe. *It's a strange feeling to read about dear Daddy in the newspaper when the man I've known is different from the one portrayed.*

The funeral took place at St. Thomas Church with Dr. Ernest Stires presiding over the hymns they had sung five years previously for Andrée. There were hundreds in attendance, but only the immediate family was allowed to witness the interring of the casket in the Clark mausoleum at Woodlawn.

"He's finally joined his Katherine," said Anna as the bronze door was shut.

Huguette looked with a worried expression at her mother. "Is that alright with you, *Maman*?"

"Oh, yes. I've long ago accepted that. How I miss your father now, though! I've many years left without him."

Anna reached for Huguette's black gloved hand for support as the two avoided locking eyes with William's children and grandchildren all around them.

———

"I will not begin until all of the heirs, and I do mean *all*, are in this room. We shall wait," said the lead lawyer.

Mary huffed over to a tufted leather chair and sat down beside her new husband. "Why wait for that child?" she hissed.

"Shush, you're acting like a child yourself," admonished Katherine.

A minute later Huguette, clad all in Chanel black with a white lace collar, darted into the library and sat beside Anna. While listening to the will read, she was somewhat dumbfounded to hear figures she had never considered before. Along with half-siblings, she would inherit a fifth of her father's massive fortune, and a fifth of the proceeds from the sale of the Fifth Avenue mansion and auctioned contents.

High valuations of the Clark estate were estimated at $250,000,000 in an era when a middle-class man earned $5,200 annually, and $.38 bought him a decent lunch. As one of William's five children, Huguette would inherit $50,000,000.

The lawyer met with her privately after her older siblings departed. "There is more your father wanted you to be apprised of upon his death. Let me explain. Until the age of 21, your annual allowance, Miss Clark, will be approximately $90,000. Your father made provisions to protect you at such a tender age from fortune-hunters.

"As his youngest heir, you will receive three portions of your inheritance at set intervals. These begin at 26 years of age until 33 years of age. Do you understand?"

Huguette nodded, eyes glancing at the papers set before her. The enormous figures were neatly listed as if she knew what they meant. She clasped hands tightly together in her lap at the oak table in the library, not wanting to meet the lawyer's stern eyes.

Oh Daddy, why did you have to die?

The true impact of the staggering numbers meant little at the time. Huguette had zero conception of want. However, she was pleased to learn her mother would inherit $2.5 million; all jewels, instruments, and paintings received as gifts during the marriage; the contents of the Paris flat; and the California villa Bellosguardo.

Some of the Clark will details were leaked because wealth-worship was rampant. Speculations were commonplace about how many hundreds heiress Huguette Clark could now spend daily.

Billions from selling to the Allies had enriched many Americans. Debt soared due to ramped up speculation and increasing extravagance on the part of Wall Street and city dwellers. Any heiress was good copy any day of the week, but some soared above the rest. To an incredulous public, Huguette's fictional daily life as a spoiled rich girl—replete with elegant illustrations portraying her as a vapid, ideal beauty—spending tens of millions with glee sold an Everest of newspapers.

From coast to coast, newsmen went into high gear commenting on the young heiress's astonishing fortune:

"The Baby Copper Queen Inherits Big!"

"Miss Clark is a poor little rich girl if there ever was one!"

"Any beau will be in the swim with that GOLDfish!"

Huguette was aghast reading about her fictional life. Soon after the funeral, at breakfast at 960 Fifth Avenue with her mother's side of the family, she fumed, "This is outrageous! How perfectly embarrassing! Can you stop it, *Maman*?"

"*Ma petite*, you must realize you'll always be a target. It won't ever change." Anna shook her head, putting down a croissant.

Hanna looked embarrassed while *oncle* Arthur leaned forward to say, "I'm sorry, Hugo, but it's a fact of life you must come to terms with now that you're coming into your inheritance."

"But why do they have to write about me as if I were a nitwit heiress?"

"You're not the nitwit at this table," Arthur assured. "She's sitting on my left."

Huguette smiled for the first time in days at her brilliant uncle poking fun at *tante* Amelia. Anna looked at her younger brother gratefully.

"Well, this proves your immaturity after all, little brother," said Amelia with a straight face. "Hugo, the healthiest way to cope is simply to turn a blind eye and continue on with your life. I never read those ridiculous articles spreading gossip and falsehoods about your family, and neither should you. Now, aren't these eggs benedict to die for? I've heard nitwits adore them."

"I've lost my appetite..." said Huguette.

Anna's siblings left that afternoon, and after almost two weeks of entertaining, the women gratefully sat alone in front of the fire. Anna began quietly crying again, mostly out of relief. That day she had submitted paperwork to withdraw her right to be an executor of the will.

"It's been very difficult to maintain my dignity while experiencing barely concealed hostility from William's older children." Dabbing eyes with a handkerchief, she continued: "Excuse me a little self-pity tonight... I'm crying tears of relief as well. Bellosguardo was a final gift from your father. I'm overjoyed... It will be our sanctuary. How're you feeling?"

Huguette pulled a robe around her closer. She wiggled toes in terry cloth slippers out to the warmth of the flames.

"I'm glad everyone's gone, but now I miss Daddy. It's as if he's off on another trip and will be back in a few weeks. But no, not this time..."

June 29, 1925
Bellosguardo, Santa Barbara, California

Huguette's eyes snapped open: She was falling! The room was in violent motion!

The walls shook and groaned strangely. Glass crashed. Muffled shouting.

Dazed, Huguette staggered up, arms stretched out. Attempting to reach for the sliding bed, she stumbled. The herringbone wood floor moved in waves beneath bare feet. Her stomach lurched from the unnatural movement.

Then it was over. The floor lay still; all was silent.

Shouts rang out from the first floor as Huguette gingerly stepped over chunks of fallen plaster coating the floor like sugar. Shards of broken glass and porcelain peppered the halls on the way to *Maman's* bedroom.

"Are you alright, *Maman*? It must've been a big earthquake!"

Huguette was pale, blonde hair akimbo. She wore nothing but a yellow silk nightgown. Anna sat in the middle of a Louis XV double bed, askew by several feet from the wall.

"*Oui, ma petite fille*. I'm alright. You look frightened. Are you hurt?"

"Not really. I was shaken clean out of bed while sleeping! Ha, what a lark! It was a little scary, but really something! I'm quite alright. At first, I thought it was a nightmare, but then it just kept happening."

Huguette clasped trembling hands together while she sat on the side of her mother's bed. Suddenly, she became aware of small cuts on tender soles. Blood oozed out in droplets onto the jade and ivory Aubusson rug.

Anna laughed nervously. "Wasn't that frightening! Everyone warned me about California, but that was certainly the biggest earthquake I've ever experienced. My bed moved this way and that!" Anna moved arms to and fro, wafting faded Chanel N°5. "It's a wonder I'm still in it!"

While Anna slipped on a blue satin bed jacket over a nightgown in anticipation of talking with servants, there was an urgent knock. The housekeeper stepped in the room, dressed in a long robe with grey hair in braids.

"Is everyone alright?" said Priscilla Ebert, clearly not calm herself.

"*Merci,* Ms. Ebert, come in, come in. We're fine."

"Oh, thank heavens! My, what a shocker! My heart is still racing!"

"Let's all have a moment to calm down. Give the staff time to dress and eat breakfast. Then, inspect the house and the grounds to report all damages to me. With an earthquake that big, there could be significant damage. We'll leave immediately, if so. I want a complete report before lunch, *merci beaucoup.*"

Ebert's eyes fell on Huguette's red-smeared feet. "Ah! Miss Huguette is bleeding!"

"What! Are you hurt? You said nothing!" Anna leaned over to grasp Huguette's hand.

"Oh, I hardly realized, I'm so shook up. It's merely a scratch from some broken glass. I need a Band-Aid or two." She had no desire to go to the hospital with an overanxious mother.

"We're calling a doctor," said Anna, throwing back the duvet.

Later on, after hearing reports, the damage was extensive enough to trouble. Anna was assured by the estate manager, "Despite the 6.3 earthquake which damaged or destroyed 85 percent of downtown buildings and killed 13 people, Bellosguardo is still livable and safe, ma'am. There will be no need to sleep out of doors tonight like so many other residents in the area."

"Oh my, we certainly were lucky then. Those poor people! Please send a message to the mayor about donation collections. My daughter and I would like to help."

Anna authorized structural repairs and new windows, but put a pause on further improvements. She thought the villa was fine; however, *it's never quite been to my taste. Maybe this event will have a silver lining?* As she listened to the estate manager and housekeeper discuss repairs over the next few days, a far better idea germinated in the back of her mind.

The long period of mourning drew to a close; pressure in various ways bore down. Very eager to sell—despite the will stipulating William's widow had three years to vacate—Mary and Katherine began a campaign to sell the house immediately. As inheritors and family members, they could enter whenever they pleased. Availing themselves of that privilege, they showed up unannounced with real estate agents, would-be buyers, and art and antiques dealers to gather offers.

Faced with the reality of life without William, Anna toyed with the idea of returning permanently to Paris. *With William gone and so much altered post-war...the notion does not strike as a safe one. Perhaps in a few years?*

On an abnormally cold day for October, Anna, Huguette, and Marié bundled up to view an apartment five blocks down at 907 Fifth Avenue.

The building's manager, James Monroe, explained, "This is *the* finest apartment available in the city at the moment, Mrs. Clark." He deferentially nodded a pomade-slicked head to usher in the small group.

"This luxury apartment is replete with windowed, generously proportioned rooms which will allow you, your daughter, and guests to enjoy the grandest views over the park. It's an excellent view of the city skyline which very few hostesses in the city can boast! For the entire floor, 12E and 12W—which the previous illustrious tenant enjoyed—it is $30,000 annually. For 12W alone, $12,000 annually."

Moore waited expectantly, monitoring Mrs. William Clark and her daughter for some confirmation they would spring for the entire floor. He knew it wasn't a question of affordability; rather, were the apartments prestigious enough for the widow stepping away from the largest mansion on Fifth Avenue? In the face of Mrs. Clark's nonplussed expression, Moore put on his game face and urged the small party along.

Walking briskly, gesturing, and talking seemingly without taking a breath—Moore drilled luxurious facts: "This twelfth-floor apartment has 14 gracious rooms with 11-foot ceilings, herringbone floors, stone door surrounds, linen-fold panel doors, and ornate mouldings in the Louis XVI style. It commands in total over 100 feet of Fifth Avenue frontage.

"Upon stepping into the foyer, guests look down a 37-feet long, 12-feet wide Jacobean gallery with paneled walls and ornate gold chandelier. There is a 20x24 drawing room with fireplace; and a 23x16 dining room with fireplace. Along here, there is a 12x13 study, and over here, Mrs. Clark, a 9x14 breakfast room." He gestured for the women to walk inside.

After mere glances into the kitchen and staff quarters, Moore spent considerably more time trumping up the virtues of the private living quarters with two bedroom suites and two guest rooms. Moore looked expectantly at his client. The taciturn daughter opened a closet in the hallway. The social secretary shadowed her mistress while Mrs. Clark looked out each of the master suite's windows.

Moore waited patiently before inhaling to relaunch his pitch. "If you consider—"

"Follow me, please." Anna went down the hallway and back into the gallery.

The party scurried after. Anna scrutinized the foyer paneling, touching the grooves.

"I would like to take out the existing entryway to the bedrooms in order to install a hidden door, here, in the paneling to the right of the front door. The hidden door will be controlled by a touch spring mechanism with the door handle and lock located on the other side. I've seen it done in European great houses. If done with skill, it cannot be located by someone unfamiliar with the premises."

Moore's thick eyebrows raised high but soon dropped to soothe: "I'm sure that can be accommodated in your lease terms, Mrs. Clark. A clever addition."

That winter Anna and Huguette remained at the house because 12W, 907 Fifth Avenue was busy with workmen, carpenters, painters, and a decorator. A long list of minor repairs and refurbishments was handed over by Marié.

Mildly shocked, Moore said, "But Madame Marié, I assure you the apartment is pristine!"

"Mr. Moore, would you like Mrs. Clark to reject your lease terms?" Marié's small grey eyes widened with the threat. Her French accent became sharp. On an errand for Madame Clark, she could become quite demanding.

"Oh no. No. I mean, yes, yes! Ms. Marié, that will be fine."

Moore had begun to sweat. He needed that apartment rented immediately. The diminutive woman in front of him smiled, but it did not reach her eyes.

New paint, wallpaper, curtains, and rugs were ordered for all the rooms. Wall-to-wall carpeting was installed for the bedrooms: cream for each except Huguette's suite. She requested cerulean blue. The bathrooms were to be fitted out in the latest technology with marble tubs and other luxurious touches. The kitchen and staff rooms were left as they were, including Marié's room.

The first Saturday in January, Anna and Amelia took Huguette to *L'Aiglon* at 13 East 55th Street. The French-Italian restaurant had been a favorite of Anna's since it opened in 1919. After ordering, Anna looked pointedly at her daughter.

Amelia smiled softly while averting her eyes. *I know what's coming next. I wonder how Hugo'll take it? One never quite knows what my little niece is thinking.*

"Huguette, it's time we discuss your debutante season."

"*Pour quoi?*"

"Because you're nineteen and graduated."

"I, uh... I haven't really given it much thought. I've been too busy." Huguette toyed with a goblet. *Soupe à l'oignon* was set before her. "Can we postpone it a bit longer? Perhaps until the fall? I don't feel ready." Huguette's eyes darted from her mother to her aunt, then down at the cheese covered bread floating on the soup. She bobbed it with a silver spoon.

The sisters exchanged a look. Amelia's expression urged: *Keep going!* Anna didn't want to press. After a long moment, she said, "Huguette, if you're not going to take a bite, put down your spoon. Do you want to wait until you're twenty, then?"

"Well, what're we doing this summer...?"

"You won't come out then, that's a bad time. Everyone's summering out of the city... Stop twirling the goblet, *s'il te plaît*."

Huguette rolled her eyes. She struggled to keep anxiety down; she hadn't realized her hand moved on to the goblet. She wiped wet fingertips on a napkin. "I would like to know if we're going to California or Europe, that's all. It impacts my plans." Huguette smiled congenially but her eyes were wary.

"I've decided on France for the summer. Is that agreeable? And are you going to share your plans with me?"

"*Oui. Tante* Amelia, can you come?"

"No. Thank you for offering. Bryce hates it when I leave for long periods. That's alright by me; I've seen Europe enough. But aren't you changing the subject?"

"*Peut-être...*"

"When you're ready, Hugo," said Anna, "we'll discuss your debutante season. Understand I won't forget. It's important you're properly introduced into society."

In the late spring, Anna and Huguette sailed to Le Havre and took a first-class train to Paris to stay at the Ritz. Huguette's debutante season approached; therefore, visits to couture houses to select fall wardrobes were non-negotiable. Anna continued to be a stickler with sartorial matters. After hours of help from the stylish *vendeuse* at each house of Chanel, Vionnet, and Lanvin, Huguette learned what was most becoming as a young woman on the marriage market.

With both Marié and Sandré present to take care of details and logistics, along with Pelletier out of retirement to assist Clark's widow one final time, Anna eventually undertook the disagreeable task of dismantling 56, *avenue Victor Hugo*. She sent out much to be sold. Her favorite items—Louis XV and XVI furniture; a *coiffeuse* of French marquetry and parquetry William bought in 1895; Impressionist paintings; the matching set of Louis XV porcelain-mounted Vernis Martin mantle clock and two twin light candelabra with chinoiserie figures bought in

1901; and an ancient, 12x15' Flemish tapestry—she had crated up and sent on to New York.

"I cannot believe I'm doing this today..." Forlornly, Anna looked at the empty drawing room with gilt boiserie. "This hurts my heart more than leaving the house on Fifth Avenue. I wonder what they're going to do with the flat?"

Huguette knew who her mother was referring to. Ownership had not left the family; Anna was simply not allowed to reside in it any longer.

Anna wistfully examined details of the room which, after many years of absence, felt comforting. "Here is where I was a young wife and mother; where you were a baby... Right here on this very floor you learned to walk!"

"How charming, *Maman.*"

"*Oui,* I suppose. It feels so long ago now... Another world entirely. I don't know what would've happened to my life without your father. He gave me *everything.*" A sweet smiled played on Anna's lips.

"I wish dear Papa and dear Andrée were here with us now..." said Huguette with a pained expression.

Anywhere in France and especially now, in the flat where she was raised, bitter-sweet memories of Andrée and Papa swirled. Huguette struggled to express to anyone, even to *Maman,* how much she missed her sister. She thought about Andrée daily. Some fleeting memory of walking in the Bois de Boulogne, or a conversation they had had in the Fifth Avenue nursery, or hiking in Yosemite, or sitting in the rose garden at the château.

Huguette moved to step out onto the balcony. She longed for fresh air. Breathing deeply in the mid-morning stillness, her eyes fluttered shut for a moment. With dawning recognition, she looked about herself. "Is this the balcony where I played the violin?"

"*Oui!* How precious you were! I cherish that photograph. Your earnest little face, trying so hard to please. Your little hands poised just so..." Anna paused before the open window.

"Did anyone stop below to listen? I couldn't have been very good."

"*Bien sûr!* You had several admirers."

Anna moved on to London where she shopped for antiques. Soon after, the Clarks boarded the Cunard Line's *Berengaria* bound for New York. The ship proved to be delightful despite being crowded with over 700 guests in first class alone. Huguette was annoyed the palm garden, tearoom, grill, and promenade decks were packed with passengers no matter the hour. Excitement swirled in public rooms whenever wealthy and attractive society siblings Vincent Astor and Alice Astor Obolensky, with celebrated husband Prince Serge Obolensky, were nearby. Anna and Huguette avoided such people. They typically requested a small table in the dining room well away from crowds.

Anna never thought of going near the dance floor or pursuing acquaintances; she was only interested in urging on her daughter. *Perhaps one of the good-looking British heirs would distract Huguette away from certain American males less worthy?*

"Huguette, what about Lord Balfe's son? He was charming yesterday when we bumped into him on the promenade deck."

"Henry? Oh, I suppose so. But, he's not really my type."

"*Quoi*? What is this, *type*? You either like him or not. I thought you preferred blonde men."

Before she could answer, a tall Texan with a dark mustache approached. Huguette recognized him from the day before; he had told a funny joke at luncheon and had been kind. She thought she remembered his name was Tom Jones. Anna looked up in surprise as Jones offered a hand to Huguette.

Wanting to silence her mother, and feeling a little daring, Huguette took it. *Maman said I need to get ready to be a debutante! Isn't this what they do? Dance with all sorts of men?*

Jones took Huguette in his arms and said, "I couldn't resist asking the prettiest American heiress on board to dance."

They twirled, and Huguette stiffened a little at the label. "Oh really? I couldn't imagine who you mean."

Maybe this was a mistake!

"Why, you're the Copper Baby, if you don't mind me sayin'. I saw your little photograph in the paper years ago." Jones chuckled a pleasant, deep-throated laugh.

"I'm what?" Huguette was put off at his impertinence. It had been a number of years since she had heard that moniker said to her face.

This must be the type of man Daddy warned me of! Why did I agree to dance?

"Do you mind my sayin' so, darlin'? You're famous. You and your mother were so sweet when I met you yesterday, I thought I'd try to get to know you a little better." Jones chuckled again as he twirled her. "Are you eating at the captain's table tomorrow? I'll be there."

"I'm not sure. I'd have to ask my mother..."

"I'd be mighty pleased to see you again, little darlin'." Jones smiled down at her, his big mustache moving comically.

Huguette was grateful the song ended soon after. For the rest of the trip, she and Anna ate meals in their suite. Several days later, descending the gangway, Huguette thought she heard her name being shouted with a Texan twang from above.

"Don't turn around. Don't acknowledge that man!" said Anna as they hurried forward.

These days, the Clarks were horrified to be recognized in public. It was even worse when approached. Some attempted to ingratiate themselves or pump for personal information. Soon after such encounters, details of their appearance or activities were written up in the society pages of New York, Palm Beach, and Los Angeles. "The widow Mrs. William A. Clark and heiress daughter, Huguette Clark, lunched at the fashionable hotel..." The smallest details about the wealthiest heiresses—Huguette Clark was in the same boat as Doris Duke and Barbara Hutton—were normal fodder.

Huguette eschewed all but the unavoidable invitations. Her art took prominence. She practiced music, or, if Styka were in town, she had a lesson in the morning. Then she ate lunch with Anna and returned to her canvas of the moment. Donning a smock, she set up an easel on a canvas tarp to protect the carpet of a guest bedroom. She adored the views over the park or down the long avenues lined with tall buildings. Manhattan grew ever taller; the urban perspective never failed to interest.

Word of Huguette's return to New York spread via word of mouth and news-paper copy. In a week, resting on her sitting room's chimneypiece were a dozen embossed invitations.

"Well, I certainly have something social to do every day and night of the week," she moaned at breakfast with Anna.

Huguette took a bite of spinach quiche and ran a finger down *New York American's* Cholly Knickerbocker column describing the activities of the most *fêted* debutantes and the eligible males ostensibly chasing them.

"I've two new books I've barely cracked because I can't find the time. At this rate, I don't have to come out because everyone is already inviting me to their parties!"

"Nonsense, you'll have a proper debut. And, naturally, you are wanted... Enjoy it!"

After discussing Huguette's debut with Amelia, Anna decided to avoid an evening party that might attract a lot of gatecrashers, press, and attention. Host-ing a modest gathering during the day would be best.

"To allow Hugo to get used to the attention, let's say," said Amelia, almost as if she had read Anna's mind. She poured more tea and took a cookie.

"Just so!" Anna nodded with vigor. "I'm more interested in having her come out in Paris. That will be a bigger party. But say nothing to Huguette!"

"*Rien!*" said a mocking Amelia, smothering giggles. "What a to-do this will all be. I'm glad I've no children."

"Oh Amelia, you don't know what you're missing! Now, who shall we invite?"

Huguette's American debut luncheon occurred on Sunday, December 5, in a private room at Pierre's at 290 Park Avenue. She wore a modest black and white Chanel silk dress with a Tiffany pearl necklace to be presented to the small num-ber of guests. Everyone knew everyone and the luncheon went off quietly, even disappointingly if one were looking for excitement. No one suspected Anna's bigger plans for her daughter the following summer.

The next morning, snow descended in fairy flakes while Anna sat in the break-fast room staring out the windows. She sipped coffee and opened yesterday's *New York Times*, hunting for the article showcasing her daughter. The planted article brought desirable attention.

I hope an eligible bachelor or two will take notice.

At her daughter entering, Anna looked up, smiling brightly. "Good morning."

Huguette greeted Anna while smoothing her brown wool skirt to sit down on a Chinese Chippendale chair. She stifled a yawn while spooning out scrambled eggs from a silver bowl held by a maid. Anna showed Huguette the article.

"I'm glad we chose to run that photograph. It's flattering. Are you pleased?"

Huguette quickly scanned it, then shrugged. She took a drink of *café au lait.*

"Me, one of the debutantes of the season? My, my, that's a lark!"

"Isn't that wonderful? Soak up the attention. Remember, it isn't forever..."

Huguette leafed through another newspaper mentioning her debut. "Written by some Cholly Knickerbocker-type, I suppose? He's everywhere and nowhere."

"I think the article is respectful, not much gossip or speculation. We should be grateful."

"Well, let's hope it's the last one for the season. *One* is enough... Monsieur Styka is going to tease me horribly."

From winter into spring, Huguette complained privately but dutifully whirled on the party circuit. She couldn't help but enjoy the frivolity. To be surrounded by good friends and handsome males such as William Gower and Thomas Blanchard made her giddy with the attention. Huguette ate luncheons at Sherry's and joined Spence alumnae at a theatrical review at Pierre's. Parties of all kinds were held in hotels, private residences, or at Long Island estates. Huguette never stayed well into the evening unless she was with Anna or had enough dance partners to distract her from bolting.

"I think I enjoy the hours of getting oneself spruced up far more than the actual party itself," Huguette confessed to Suzanne Ferguson as nearby couples moved limbs wildly to the raucous jazz. They had been sitting out the dancing for a full hour.

"I agree with you! Although this dance isn't so bad. The band's good! My, my, my... Isn't her silver beaded dress pretty?" Suzanne pointed discreetly to a woman nearby.

Huguette nodded, feeling anxious. The jazz band began playing a slow set.

"I think I'll slip out early tonight."

William Gower appeared out of nowhere. He said hello and offered his hand to Huguette. She mouthed "Sorry!" to Suzanne before following him onto the dance floor.

As they began dancing, Huguette asked nonchalantly, "How've you been, Bill? I haven't seen you for a while."

Gower perked up that Huguette had noticed his absence. "I had to take care of a few things for my father at the bank these past few weeks. It's been busy lately, lots of business. I had to make a few trips out of town as well. There's been virtually no time to socialize."

"That must be a good thing, all that business?" Huguette offered.

"Of course, yes, yes, it is! My father is pleased."

Gower then spun Huguette, who grinned with pleasure. He could dance better than he could hold an interesting conversation. Suddenly, a couple who had had too much to drink jostled them. Gower looked over his shoulder with annoyance, moving Huguette away. She was impressed his dancing kept up with the music.

"Say, want something to drink? How about we rest a bit?" Gower looked down at Huguette who nodded her head. He steered her off the dancefloor and they sat down at an empty table.

After fifteen minutes, Huguette fidgeted at an awkward lull in the conversation. She stood up. "I need to leave now. It was nice to see you, Bill."

"May I walk you out? I can call for your driver."

The Rolls headed Uptown while Huguette sat next to an exhausted Sandré. Huguette let thoughts linger on Gower. *Is he interested in me?* She enjoyed the attention, and he was nice, but she wasn't sure how she felt. Now and then his breath smelled of a combination of alcohol and cigarettes, which she didn't like. And his eyes wandered to others, which she also didn't like.

Alas, Bill isn't nearly as thrilling and well-mannered as Styka. Well, no one is...!

Months later, during a walk in Central Park, Huguette observed trucks lined up on the curbs of her father's house ready to cart off what had sold. A few windows—looking like gaping, eerie black holes—had been knocked out to easily pass items down to street level. A long canvas shoot was affixed to a huge fourth story window to slide unsalvageable materials to a massive metal dumpster. Outside the main gate, a reporter in a trench coat interviewed a man in a black suit.

Huguette stood riveted to the horror of seeing a beloved house dismantled. She returned crying to 12W. In the drawing room, she sat in front of Anna so her mother could clearly hear.

She raised her voice: "I... I can hardly believe it. It's almost as if Daddy is dying again. He would've been heartbroken if he knew my older siblings voted to sell it without living in it or enjoying it within the family for at least a few years more."

The dogs sniffed Huguette's ankles, then resumed panting. She leaned down to pick up Henry VIII.

"*Oui*, he would be *very* disappointed. That house was a long-cherished dream, and they all knew it."

Huguette wanted to express the even deeper hurt the rooms she had shared with Andrée would soon be demolished. That ache was inexpressibly deep. Her throat constricted before the words emerged.

"Let's put it out of our minds," Anna said. "It does no good to dwell on the past, for it will not return. How about we plan our next trip to Bellosguardo or Europe? How about a cruise in the Mediterranean? I did that several times with your father, and it was *marvelous*.

"We simply won't look up the street any longer. It's too distasteful. No more walks in Central Park until next year!"

They stayed in town long enough to attend the late April wedding of Huguette's friend, Grace Cuyler, to Count Albert de Mun de Paris. *The New York Times* ran an article detailing as much of the lavish proceedings as could be scrounged up: "One of the most notable weddings of the spring" at the Lady Chapel of St. Patrick's Cathedral.

Anna hoped Huguette would be swayed by the romantic grandeur of the wedding. *How I would love to see her married like this! The Cuylers have such style!*

Huguette was silent throughout. She congratulated her long-time friend, Grace, and moved on to the reception with Anna. After the meal, a young French marquis related to the groom soon stepped forward to ask Huguette to dance.

That was kind of Grace, thought Anna, witnessing the interaction.

Huguette was charming, but obvious to those who knew her best, she mostly enjoyed speaking French with an educated, native speaker. She had hardly seated herself back beside Anna before Gower loomed out of the crowd. He approached their table with a polite nod to Anna.

Huguette smiled shyly, pleased. *Bill never fails to ask*. She immediately raised her hand to be taken gently by Gower's.

Anna nodded agreeably while the pair moved off, their figures swallowed by the crowd within moments. *This isn't the first time the Gower boy has approached Huguette; he seems to be everywhere this season. He's nice enough, unfailingly polite. Tall, good looking, Princeton graduate... But his father is an employee. William Gower has to work for his living; he isn't on Huguette's level.*

As far as warm-blooded young men went, Anna perceived Gower might expect too much from her fey daughter. Huguette didn't seem to have as strong an interest in the opposite sex as normal girls had.

The closest Huguette comes to that is the crush she's had on Tadé Styka all these years...

Anna repeatedly steered Huguette away from any notion the painter would make a good mate. She lectured, "Artists make perpetually bad husbands. They are inherently selfish and are surrounded by the most beautiful women in the world. The man in question could be seventy and have a thirty-five-year-old wife and an even younger mistress. In your case, you'd be financing the entire affair *and* his career. Don't put yourself in a situation to be hurt!"

Anna was grateful Styka was living mostly in Paris these days. *A separation to cool Huguette's interest is ideal. But I'll have to watch William Gower more closely...*

After the Cuyler wedding, Anna hatched a clever idea. She rang up Amelia.

"Huguette will debut in French society the same week as the Franco-American charity ball at the Ministry of Foreign Affairs."

"Why then?" said Amelia, reaching to switch off the radio program at her Park Avenue apartment.

"Because many Americans and Europeans will be in Paris. The ball is very well attended. It'll be a cinch to fill my guest list with desirable attendees."

"Very clever, sister. But what does Huguette say?"

"You're going to help me figure out how to tell her, so she agrees."

"Oh, really...? Does that also mean I'm going to Paris in June?"

"*Oui!*"

That summer, twenty-one-year-old Huguette received a fair bit of attention for her elegance, vast wealth, impeccable French, painting, and musical skills. Some whispered she was a "rare bird," but acknowledged the heiress simply "danced to her own tune."

At lunch in Paris with good friend Lady Virginia "Ginny" Warburton, Anna said, "Frenchmen adore my daughter because she's fluent and well educated. I think this gives her more self-confidence around them. But so many are not the right sort of man I desire for her. There are fortune-hunters lurking who would simply suck her dry and ultimately abandon her. William warned me endlessly."

The amiable pair sat in the afternoon light streaming through the skylights of the restaurant in *l'Hôtel Majestic* on *19 rue Kléber*. It felt like old times because Anna met Ginny at the *Conservatoire de Musique*.

"I couldn't agree more. I shall help you weed them out!" proclaimed Lady Warburton.

"I want Huguette to be around suitors who are at her social level. This is daunting, Ginny: To marry off one's daughter without her father alive."

"You do well to expose Huguette to the good amount of quality suitors in Europe. Are you going to present her at Court?"

"I don't think so. At least, not at this time. It seems impossible to suggest that Huguette will ever get over her shyness enough to even consider the notion. At the moment, she'd sail back to New York without me if I were to suggest it!"

"Oh, pish posh. I can't imagine a young, pretty girl with all her accomplishments being so uneager to show herself off..." Lady Warburton shook her head before reaching for a wafer topped with caviar. "Have you tried these? They're delicious."

Anna set a wafer on her plate and pressed on with the subject at hand. "My daughter is a sensitive artist at heart; I doubt she'll ever change. Perhaps she gets that trait from me... Heaven knows it isn't from her father!"

"There's plenty of fish in the sea, as they say. You worry too much, Anna."

"Probably," Anna sighed. "Before the summer is over, I only long to go to Bellosguardo for a lengthy visit. Ginny, if you're ever on the West Coast, you and Lord Warburton are invited. It's *heaven on earth*, I assure you. The Pacific Ocean tranquil, the weather perfection."

"*Merci,* Anna. I'm most grateful; I will certainly remember that kind invitation. I know little about California. It's terribly far away, rather like India. Although what comes out of Hollywood is deplorable. You don't invite actors to parties, do you?"

Anna chose the triple gilt-edged Grand Ballroom at the Ritz for Huguette's Parisian coming out party. Twenty-four guests were invited for supper in a private dining room; five hundred more from across Europe and the United States were invited to a ball to last until dawn.

Huguette felt inexplicably full of confidence in a bespoke Lanvin gown with layers of gold beads, gold satin heeled sandals, and two long ropes of natural pearls borrowed from Anna. On the packed dancefloor, she was in Villermont's arms during the hit song, "My Blue Heaven."

Villermont said in French, "This is a smashing debut party, Huguette. Anna still has the touch."

"Etienne, whatever do you mean? This is all my genius, of course." Huguette's smile faded as Villermont pulled her in closer.

He's even resting his chin on my head!

"I think I know you better than that, my old friend," said Villermont, pulling his head back to look down at her. "In any case, you two are throwing one of the best debuts I've been to in some time. Ah... this song is one of my current favorites... I could dance to it all night long..."

Villermont twirled her before she noticed he kept glancing across the room. He said after a long moment, "Say, who *is* that blonde chap over there who keeps staring at us? The tall one with the brooding eyes? He looks bothered by something. Couldn't be on my account. I don't know him!"

Huguette looked in the direction Villermont pointed. "Oh, that's Bill. William Gower from New York. He's a friend."

"*Oui*, he does strike one as American. If you don't mind my saying, he stands out in a gauche way."

"Oh, Etienne, be nice. Bill's a good guy. You'll like him. I'll introduce you later."

Carolyn Storrs sashayed over, momentarily leading her man. "Well, hello, love birds. Darling Hugo, you *do* look divine this evening. Which is appropriate, as the night is yours. Etienne, don't you agree with me?"

Carolyn rushed ahead without waiting for a response from Villermont whose English was not up to speed. "Anna does know what she's doing, Hugo darling... Isn't this party fabulous? Wish my mother were as clever! Coming out in Paris is a *coup*!" Carolyn smirked. "Are you pleased with yourself?"

"Yes, but I have no idea why! You know me, always a wallflower."

"Oh hardly. You'll beat us all someday! Mark my words!"

"You do exaggerate, Carolyn. I think I'm simply very happy to be in Paris."

"Well, in any case, you look smashing in that Lanvin! I'd like to borrow it!" said Carolyn before draping herself elegantly across her dance partner's shoulder.

At that point in the evening, Huguette was a bit delirious; she was relieved the grand entrance was over. Her knees had nearly knocked together before the double doors opened onto the crowded ballroom. A horrible flush spread down from cheeks to chest. What got her through was the front row of familiar faces. Villermont, Anna, *tante* Amelia, Carolyn, and other friends urged her on during tenuous steps forward while the orchestra played. At precisely the right moment, Anna saw her hesitation turn to fright and stepped forward to escort Huguette down the center of well-wishers.

"*Merci, Maman!*" Huguette had whispered.

When the clapping subsided, Gower immediately asked for a dance. "You've never looked more beautiful," he whispered in her ear.

His hot breath tickled, and she almost burst out in nervous giggles. But she did like the way his arms held her protectively. By the third song, she glanced quickly over to where her mother was sitting. *Was* Maman *watching?* She knew she shouldn't dance with Gower more than twice.

"You must allow for all the eligible men to have an opportunity to ask you," Anna had admonished in the elevator earlier. "There are several young men I would like you to pay close attention to."

Huguette allowed Gower to move her through the crush of dancers. Avoiding the men her mother had eagerly introduced her to, she clung to his familiarity. After all the night's demands, it was too much to make conversation with one stranger after another.

"Are you going to Santa Barbara this summer?" Gower increased the pressure of his hand on Huguette's lower back.

His touch was like a hot water bottle heating her spine. Huguette lost her ability to speak. She wasn't sure she wanted him to get any closer even though he looked attractive in white tie. *I do admire Bill's all-American handsomeness.*

After Gower looked expectantly down at her, she remembered to reply. "We plan to be at Bellosguardo by the first of August."

"May I visit you? I'll be in Los Angeles that week."

All this traveling exerted tremendous pressure on Gower's budget. Paris put him solidly in the red. He wasn't sure if he could get time off work or borrow yet another five hundred dollars. *However, maybe if I told Father I'm thinking seriously of a law degree? And maybe too, if I add in my intentions toward Miss Clark, it wouldn't be an issue?*

"Of course, Bill! *Maman* likes to give a big party during Fiesta Days. I'll be sure to send you an invitation."

Huguette covered up anxiety at his physical proximity by smiling before ducking her head. Her right hand felt warm and moist in his grip. Gower was relieved. He relaxed, knowing he was making strides. He held Huguette close while he could.

To Huguette's relief, after the party they went to Cabourg.

"I'm going to do nothing but eat berries and paint after the last few weeks of craziness!" she said while stretching in the early morning sun on the ocean-front terrace. It had stormed the night before; behind her, there were whitecaps. "Perhaps I will stay here *all* the rest of the summer, *Maman*." She sniffed the air, enjoying the freshness of the wind.

Anna looked up from harp music she planned on practicing after breakfast. "Are you serious...?"

"*Non*! I'm merely relieved to be far away from the social whirl. I needed this break to recoup my nerves." Huguette popped a berry into her mouth, the tangy sweetness all she needed at the moment.

"Oh, your nerves!"

Huguette ignored the comment, recrossing her legs before jiggling a sandaled foot. "Did I... Did I, uh, mention that Bill will be coming to California as well?"

"Will he?" Anna feigned disinterest, keeping eyes on the musical score.

After eating a few more berries, Huguette continued, "Is it alright to invite him to Bellosguardo, for the party during Fiesta?"

"If you want him there, of course. You don't need my permission. Why don't you give me a list of friends you would like to include."

"I... I wasn't sure you would approve. He's not the sort of young man you were hoping I would be taken with, is he?"

"Well, no, no he's not. I think there are discrepancies between you that you should pay attention to."

"Yes, Mummy, but I *really* like him. I feel comfortable with Bill. I've known him ever so long now. He's familiar and he knows all my friends. His father worked for Daddy. And his French isn't *that* bad."

"His schoolboy French is passable," said Anna. "Only be sure to make a wise decision before agreeing to a serious attachment with any young man, *d'accord*? I would prefer you invite at least a half dozen friends, not solely Mr. Gower. And don't discuss the Biltmore ball with him. I want you to have an entire night with fresh dance partners, do you hear?"

"Are we going to the Biltmore ball? I haven't given it a thought."

"*Oui*, it's the night before mine. I'm so taken with what Reginald Johnson has designed for the Biltmore, I could move in tomorrow."

After the earthquake, Santa Barbara had rebuilt itself with architectural flair. The new hotel's Spanish Colonial Revival architecture followed suit. The hotel had oceanfront views on "America's Riviera." Enchanted, Anna would support the Santa Barbara Biltmore for the next twenty-five years, preferring to stay there if for any reason she felt it was too much work for the staff to open up Bellosguardo.

"Huguette, are you listening?"

"*Oui, Maman...*" She sighed, picking up a spoon for yogurt.

"You'll wear your new Chanel silver and white gown and there will be no Mr. Gower invited. It's too bad the Villermonts aren't traveling to the States this summer."

"*Pour quoi?*"

"I think Etienne is quite interesting, very dashing. Let's keep our eye on him, shall we?"

"Oh *Maman*, he's like a brother..."

"We'll see about that."

In Santa Barbara later that summer, Anna welcomed the middle-aged Dr. Gordon Lyle and his young wife, Larissa with their children, Sam and Luna, for lunch. Her private physician and Huguette's long-time, good friend deserved special treatment.

"Come every day, Dr. Lyle. We might be gone, whether out and about in town or down in Los Angeles, but never mind our absence. Enjoy the ocean at our beach. No pesky crowds to deal with such as are by your hotel."

"You are most kind, Madame Clark. We'll most certainly take you up on that generous offer," said Dr. Lyle. Larissa beside him beamed.

"My pleasure. Sam and Luna will enjoy it, I'm sure," Anna smiled wide at the children. *Hopefully someday soon I will be a grandmother!*

As if on cue, from around the corner of the house Gower and Huguette appeared leisurely walking a gravel path. Joining the gathering under the pergola, Gower said nothing. He appeared stiff in a seersucker suit and straw boater. Huguette affectionately hugged Larissa hello before sitting next to her beau at the white wrought-iron table. Drinks arrived, and the conversation shifted. Gower appeared content to listen.

Later on that afternoon in the music room, Larissa held Luna as Anna selected music.

"William Gower must be serious about Huguette to have taken the trouble to come all the way out to California. Didn't Huguette tell me he was also at her debut party in Paris?"

"*Oui*, he was..."

"And Huguette is off saying goodbye to him now?"

"*Oui*... Mr. Gower is returning to Los Angeles," said Anna, sitting before a Lyon & Healy Louis XV Special concert grand harp in 23-carat gold. One of her most prized possessions, William had given it as a Christmas gift.

"And..." Larissa said, "does Mr. Gower's attention please you? Forgive me if I'm being nosey."

Anna said nothing while slipping a 15-carat diamond ring from off her left hand before playing. Larissa admired the cool flash of the inner brilliance of the diamond against Anna's scarlet lacquered fingernails.

Larissa picked up on Anna's mood. "Ah, I understand perfectly. If you don't mind my saying, he's not in Huguette's class. And she needs a livelier man, as well; she can be reserved too often."

"Wise words, Larissa. We'll have to see what Huguette thinks. She has told me nothing about a serious attachment. Please influence her if she talks to you."

"I'll get the truth out of her! Huguette usually confides in me at one point or another. I'll ask her to lunch sometime. Leave it to me!"

Larissa sat back reveling in the harp's soothing tones. Her daughter fell asleep in her arms as she thought about her old friend. *Huguette is lovely if at times very difficult to read. She was the same when we were young. Not like Anna at all, who's discreet but warm and open with her emotions if she knows you.*

Anna stopped playing. "If she does say anything at all, tell me, Larissa, *s'il te plaît*. This is too important. Distract her to other worthier male attention, if she'll listen."

"*Bien sûr*, Anna!"

Larissa knew Huguette may not take kindly to the intrusion. *Andrée took after Anna. Who does Huguette take after?* She wondered about the differences whenever she examined the numerous family portraits hung around Bellosguardo.

Back in New York for the fall social season, Huguette felt more relaxed and mentally prepared. Gower was usually among the crowd and always had something complimentary to say. She began to search for him more and more as the months passed. She felt confident he was singling her out.

By the winter, Gower asked Huguette to dinner and the theater.

It's fate: we know all the same people; Bill's father worked for Papa; we never lack for conversation. Always curious about other's experiences, Huguette liked to hear about his Princeton days and eccentric family members on his mother's side.

"About a decade ago or so, maybe I was thirteen?, I went with my father to see Senator Clark. What a kingpin he was! Perpetually working, doing deal after deal. My father admired him immensely. I probably met him another dozen times." Gower took a large bite of roast beef sandwich.

"Oh, that makes me very happy to hear. Dear Daddy was a wonderful man!"

Huguette beamed with pleasure while poking a fork into chicken salad nestled on a cantaloupe bowl. She barely ate; alone at a table with Gower made her feel a little jumpy. She noticed he had no trouble devouring his food. Departing the restaurant, Huguette was sorry he was going out of town for the weekend.

"Yep, it's time to visit my crazy Aunt Petunia in Philadelphia. Remember her? The one who has plants growing in all her sinks and bathtubs? My mother demands I come."

"Oh stop, the poor lady! Leave her and her plants be!" Huguette laughed.

Gower grinned and moved closer. "I'll see you at the Thompson's next week Thursday." He took a risk and slowly bent to kiss Huguette's cheek before guiding her into the Rolls after Sandré.

Huguette was a little flustered but looked up sweetly through the window. She waved a final time. As the vehicle eased from the curb, she thought, *I wonder how I'd feel if he'd kiss me?*

While dancing at the Thompson's party two weeks later, Huguette babbled on about the importance of Parisian *haute couture*. "However," Huguette said after Gower complimented her for the dozenth time, "only if one prefers elegance over flashy glamour, of course."

"I prefer *you* every time, no matter what kind of gown you're wearing. You're a dish and I want a bite!" He playfully champed teeth at her.

"A dish? Bill, are you hungry, by chance?" Huguette said. She could smell alcohol on his breath; she turned her nose away.

"For *you*, yes!"

Gower laughed and squeezed her waist with one hand. He pulled her closer, but she resisted. Huguette stared off across the ballroom with a frozen smile.

Bill sometimes goes too far with the teasing and groping and drinking.

It was unknown, overwhelming territory. Friends warned about brash tactics of certain young men about town.

Is he taking advantage of me? She abruptly wiggled away and walked off the dance floor.

Gower stood alone for a moment, arms out, blinking in confusion. *What did I do?*

Two couples flanking him burst out in cruel laughter. He blushed to be the target but went rushing after Huguette anyway.

"Hugue... Miss Clark... Did I offend you? I apologize most sincerely if I did."

"I only wanted to sit down a moment. I felt a little overheated all of the sudden. Could you get me some water, please?"

She smiled politely but did not meet his eyes. She couldn't say why, but the night was ruined.

It's his forward comments or his alcohol breath or how much time we spend together now... or something!

She watched Gower's departing figure with relief. A conversation at a charity luncheon a few weeks previous came to mind.

"They seem to try *anything* to get a girl to take off her knickers," Annabelle Harrison had relayed in a vehement tone, obsessively straightening new blonde bangs. "I heard that one girl was taken to the stables during this big party at the Falworth—"

"That's *enough* of that talk, young lady!" Mrs. Arthur Harrison III proclaimed in a loud voice. The six-foot tall woman towered over Huguette and Annabelle from behind.

Annabelle twisted her shoulders, protesting, "You said it to me your—"

"I said *no* such thing, Annabelle Anne. I apologize, Miss Clark, if you think we discuss such vulgar matters in our household. Now, please excuse us. We are taking our leave."

While Mrs. Harrison marched around tall ferns in ceramic vases beside their bench, both girls immediately jumped to their feet as if twelve years old. With one white-gloved hand, Harrison pulled her squawking daughter down the hotel hallway's black and white checkered floor. Huguette witnessed the forced departure.

I wish I could've heard the entire story.

Snapping back to the present when Gower reappeared with drinks, Huguette put a polite smile back on.

It's a pity, because I probably could've picked up tips on how to proceed with Bill. Who else can I ask that I trust? Larissa?

Always self-accepting, Huguette knew she would never be the femme fatale in a red beaded gown or chasing after the limelight trailing a white fox stole and heavily rouged lips. However, what exactly would happen when the event of taking advantage occurred was something she remained a little puzzled about. Lately, she had felt no desire to stay locked in Gower's arms when they embraced at the end of an evening. When he talked with friends and sneaked long draughts from the flask in his suitcoat, it usually spelled trouble.

"As soon as Sandré isn't vigilant, out come the octopus arms," Huguette relayed to Larissa.

"Oh yes, and those can be a challenge! Thankfully, my husband never stooped to that. I probably was the more forward one."

"So you liked kissing him?"

"Oh yes!" said Larissa.

After deserting Gower on the dancefloor, Huguette avoided him for weeks. It did nothing but enflame his desire. Eventually, she agreed to go to lunch. On his best behavior and very sober, Gower was dashing in a new camelhair overcoat and navy blue suit. It felt like old times.

Perhaps I was overreacting? It's quite nice to have a handsome beau.

After escorting her home, Gower ignored Sandré to slowly inch closer—monitoring Huguette's reaction every millisecond—before he kissed her lightly on the lips. To the experienced Gower, it felt like nothing much, but to Huguette, she was deeply moved.

Inside her bedroom, Huguette addressed Jumeau *bébé triste* dolls lined up on an upholstered bench. "Listen up, everyone, I think I'm in love!"

A month later, after several more successful dates and a few more kisses, an emboldened Gower phoned Huguette.

"Would you go on a walk with me in Central Park this Friday? I'd like to ask you something."

Huguette was too clever not to grasp his meaning. She dressed carefully. Then she began wondering if she might be mistaken. She paced and chewed off her lipstick until Gower arrived with chocolates and red roses. Strong feelings built up inside her chest and she was speechless for a moment before accepting the bouquet.

This must be love.

Talking amiably while strolling for over a half hour, the day seemed normal, and Huguette calmed down. Suddenly, on a quiet bridle path surrounded by leafless trees with Sandré trailing ten feet behind, Gower took off his fedora and went down on one knee. In one large, trembling hand he held out a Tiffany's ring with a one-carat oval diamond encircled by sapphires. He avoided mentioning his grandmother loaned him the money for the most expensive purchase he had ever made.

"Huguette, will you marry me? I think we make a great pair, and there's no other girl for me but you. Please say yes, darling, and make me the happiest man. I promise I'll work on my French!"

Gower looked earnestly up at her, his nose red from the cold. *This has to work!*

Huguette blushed, then giggled softly while putting a leather gloved hand over lips before nodding. Quietly, she said, "Yes, Bill, I will."

The much-discussed event was finally happening! *Now I will be able to announce my engagement, too. I won't be a debutante who sits too long on the sidelines! If not Bill, then who?*

Gower rose as she removed a glove for him to slide on the ring. She then tilted her head so the brown felt brim of her hat wouldn't bump as he bent for a chaste kiss.

The mouse-like Sandré burst out with a little shriek of joy. "*C'est l'amour!*"

Huguette glanced back, wondering why her chaperone was crying.

After hearing the news, Anna said, "I'll announce it when you're absolutely sure he's the right man for you."

"I assure you I love him!"

"Are you entirely aware of William's character and of the kind of future he wants?" Anna ignored she was obviously vexing her daughter.

"I'm only aware that I love Bill and am happy with my choice. *Maman*, aren't you happy for me?" Huguette was crushed.

"I'm only trying to guide you. I worry William Gower won't be a proper husband in the long-term sense. He lacks some... backbone, shall we say. Besides college, what are his claims to be a proper husband? He doesn't have any money or property of his own, for one. He won't inherit a fortune."

"Everyone can't be like Papa! Bill's a graduate of Princeton and is very nice. You don't seem to approve of any man I like! I only know of all the young men of my acquaintance, it's him I'm thrilled by."

Anna nodded with a small smile before saying, "In any case, I'll wait a while before I announce the engagement."

"Why, *Maman*? Waiting won't change my feelings! Why don't you approve?"
To hide angry tears, Huguette sprang from the chair and raced out of the room.

Anna sighed. *This isn't going according to plan. If I push her to deny him, she might elope or refuse to marry anyone and then I'll have a mess on my hands.* She went to Huguette's room to apologize.

A month later when Huguette was out, Anna invited Gower to see her. They talked in the drawing room. Gower wore a grey pinstripe three-piece suit and sat on a sofa incessantly petting Henry VIII to cover nerves. The dog stretched, grunted, and soon began snoring.

Anna wore a mauve and ivory geometric patterned silk dress by Schiaparelli, and Tiffany four-strand natural pearl necklace with matching bracelet and earrings. Mops and Margot slept at her feet. After a few minutes of small talk, she broached the subject foremost on her mind.

"I understand the predicament you're in. I too married up, shall we say. Huguette's father provided handsomely in order to make me as equal to him as could reasonably be expected. Therefore, I was a wealthy woman in my own right during my marriage. Now, I want to do something similar for you."

Anna looked pointedly at Gower and waited for a reaction.

Gower blinked and hesitated, unsure of Mrs. Clark's meaning. *Was this a trick of some kind?* At the mere hint of money, he became excited. Heart pounding loudly, thoughts zinged around his brain: *Mrs. Clark makes me nervous! Is she paying me to marry Huguette? Did I oil my cowlick properly? Are my shoes shined enough? I'll be able to pay off the ring much earlier than I figured!*

Beads of sweat ran down his sides. His wool suit felt entirely too warm this close to the blaze.

"I propose a gift of one million dollars upon your marriage to my daughter. This isn't given to make you feel less than. Please understand: It's done with concern for the class discrepancy between you, if you'll forgive my frankness.

"As a married couple, it's important to begin on somewhat equal footing. As that isn't possible in Huguette's most unusual case as an heiress," Anna looked sharply at Gower, "then I shall be generous to relieve some of the pressure you may feel."

Gower's mouth went slack. He didn't hear much after "one million." It was an astounding sum. *And we're not even married yet!*

He squeaked, "Mrs. Clark, I, uh, I don't know what to... I wasn't expecting this... I'm not marrying your daughter for her money!" His unblinking blue-grey eyes were opened fully round, as if protesting his innocence before a jury. With flushed cheeks, he looked impossibly young.

Did she really just say one million?

Anna waited a moment for the young man to collect himself before she dug in harder. "Please comprehend that Huguette's money will *not* be freely available to you upon marriage unless she gives the go ahead *after* the age of thirty. I warn you now, she's a conservative spender. She knows the value of money and has never been extravagant, regardless of the gossip in the papers.

"However, with my gift you'll be able to keep up in the meantime, shall we say. And if you're careful, paying attention to our financial advisors, it'll continue to grow. Do you understand me, William?"

Gower swallowed hard; cheeks and ears flamed pink and palms slicked with sweat. The way she said his name felt like a dagger. "Yes, Mrs. Clark."

Anna's tone turned cheerful, "Good! Please call me Anna." Her gaze settled on Henry VIII slumbering against Gower's long, muscled thigh. "Do you like dogs, William? Huguette and I adore them."

June 2004
Upper East Side, New York City

Colton Shepherd took the stairs by twos up out of the subway. He inhaled deeply to clear the acrid smell of mass transportation out of his nose. In less than ten minutes, long legs covered the short distance to 907 Fifth Avenue. Entering the pre-war building via the service entrance, he rode the elevator up to the eighth floor. He walked the parquet floored rooms of 8W and 8E on autopilot because the appearance and jumbled contents of each had not altered since the first day he completed this tour.

That was desired. No one had lived in the apartments for many years; all Shepherd was scanning for was water damage, theft, or any other undesired disturbance to report.

As a male employee, his daily presence at 907 Fifth was a bonus. Shepherd had heard the story multiple times from Boss. Before he began working for her, the apartments had remained quiet and closed for so long watchful eyes were alerted to the absence of true security. Someone knew there was no one watching fat bank accounts and expensive art. Once Boss didn't return from the hospital, thieves hatched bold plans. One involved cashing a blank check at a seldom-used bank account for hundreds of thousands of dollars, and the other involved an old ballerina.

Shrewd eyes ascertained 8W should be targeted first. Anna Clark's Degas pastel had been off the market for so long, it would pass as an inherited piece. The 1875 Degas, *La Danseuse faisant des pointes*—purchased for a discount after the 1929 Crash from the Impressionist art gallery, Durand-Ruel and Sons on 12 East 57th Street—was worth a mint.

The Degas ballerina was plucked from the wall.

Sequestered at the hospital, Boss was not advised of the theft for months. Once her lawyer took the frantic call, "Mr. Schwartz sprang into action desiring immediate permission to call the police and FBI to begin an investigation. But I refused!"

"You refused? I don't understand," said Shepherd.

"Neither did he!" Boss laughed. "Let me explain."

That day in the early nineties, Schwartz stood up in excitement, the phone pressed to a pink, fleshy ear. "There'll be a sensational international investigation into the crime. I warn you, Mrs. Clark, you'll need to give a statement. I advise you to prepare yourself for an onslaught of major media companies wanting interviews. It's necessary, however, in this instance. The painting has historical importance. Not to mention the value alone!"

"Mr. Schwartz, calling the police or media never entered my mind. I abhor publicity and attention, as you well know. That would be worse than the missing Degas! This is a private matter, and I'll retrieve the stolen artwork *privately*. I've the purchase receipt from the art gallery in my files. Please make a note of it having left my possession for insurance purposes and then communicate that *privately* to the *proper* art authorities in this city, including Paris and London. That way the piece can be watched out for when it is eventually sold on the open market."

"But that could take *years*!"

Schwartz's voice squeaked when he was upset. He felt suddenly stifled in his office. To be pussyfooting around when millions were at stake was beyond his middle-class upbringing. *I need a walk, some fresh air.*

Uptown, Huguette sat bold upright in a hospital bed. "Mr. Schwartz, I realize that. I *will* retrieve Mommy's Degas. Good day."

Schwartz eventually discovered the Degas had been sold to a prominent family in Kansas from a legitimate New York gallery. The current owner vehemently claimed his innocence and threatened legal action. To keep it quiet, a local museum had to play diplomat. They would accept the pastel as a "donation" from the original owner in order to turn around and donate it to the outraged, supposedly legitimate owner to be rehung back in the spot it had occupied for years in the man's mansion.

For the fourth time in a decade, Boss lost out on millions of personal wealth and sentimental property to thieves. She kept all matters in private hands and out of the media, but at a high cost.

"Once again, Mommy's property had to be sacrificed. Such a pity..."

***

Whistling jauntily, Shepherd scooped up collected mail before riding the elevator up to 12W. Entering the darkened gallery, he switched on a light which revealed the line-up of dust-covered chairs and tables pushed against walls with gilt framed oil paintings and a Flemish tapestry. Without ogling the antiques and art—which he did plenty the first few months—Shepherd turned right and reached out to spring the concealed door leading to the bulk of the rooms he would need.

Going through, he set down mail on the chair in the hallway placed there for that purpose. *Anywhere else, I might lose it in all these piles and boxes and stuff. And then wouldn't Boss be ticked! Can't lose her new mail.*

Performing the same walk-through of the top-floor apartment, albeit this time stopping to admire the view over Central Park—acres of verdant trees gloriously bursting in the late spring sun—Shepherd thought about Boss's to-do list.

Every day it was somewhat the same, but the order and the intensity changed. The projects changed. Most people complained about their bosses; he had never found occasion to complain about his. Earlier that morning, while cradling the Nokia, Shepherd scrawled the list of demands with a free hand on a notepad he always carried.

Boss called daily, at all hours. A mobile was a must.

Wanting to please, Shepherd felt distracted by urgency. He hadn't expected to be called to the hospital. Normally he went weekdays, but today he was supposed to be at 8E organizing tax papers. Yet Boss had changed her mind; everything on the list she now wanted delivered before lunch.

That means I only have three hours. Better get a move on!

Shepherd landed this job because, as a young man in the seventies, he had volunteered with the donation of Christmas gifts to an orphanage in Greenwich Village. Boss undertook the project annually, and after learning his father had a few sons, she asked for help. His family, who worked for Boss first in all her apartments via Shepherd Construction, became more involved each year.

Every December, Shepherd looked forward to the project. His family first unpacked hundreds of toys from Au Nain Bleu—which he couldn't even pronounce then: "Doesn't this lady know what Toys 'R' Us is? It's so much betta!"—before wrapping (Boss liked to do the dolls herself), labeling, and repacking the gifts to be taken to the truck waiting below. The project took a few evenings and one Saturday morning, at least, but the sizeable tip was much appreciated. During all that time, Shepherd never met her.

The first $5,000 check stunned; Shepherd carried it around for a week before cashing it. But he needn't have worried because every year without fail he received another. Then the orphanage project stopped for some reason in the late eighties, and he lost contact. Shepherd was hazy about the details, but sometime in the early nineties, when Simone Pierre called, that's when the association picked back up. Boss remembered him from all those years ago volunteering. Only then did he return to Fifth Avenue to work part-time.

Gradually, she needed him every day. He morphed into a full-time personal assistant, going to the hospital daily. Only at that point was he permitted to talk to Boss face-to-face. Some weeks he worked over forty hours, receiving more and more trusted assignments. Now he ran the entire show out of 907 Fifth Avenue.

"I can't do without you, my arms and legs!"

"Yep, you're the Boss!" Colton would always joke back.

Every time, she broke into peals of laughter. Her high-pitched, French-accented English distinctive as she rejoined: "Imagine! Me, a boss! Nonsense!"

Colton's Christmas bonus now was a $30,000 check. His salary was also generous, even for the city.

"Don't wake me up from this dream job," he said half-asleep to his wife lying next to him. "It's saving my back! I hope we're putting enough aside because this sweet gig won't last forever..."

First, I'll do the books. That's easy.

Shepherd went to the room which had once been a bedroom. It was now a book-lined office, of which there were two in 12W. The bookshelves Shepherd studied were stuffed with novels and volumes on history, biography, literature, science, photography, and art. But the ones he was after she had owned for a long time.

They would be on a shelf somewhere over here...

Before Mrs. Clark's eyesight began deteriorating, Shepherd unboxed frequent deliveries of books which he would take by armloads to the hospital. Attempting to find a suitable place in the study's cramped bookshelves in each apartment was another matter. Which was why one now had to maneuver past stacks of books piled on the floor. Storage space was at a premium, with some rooms completely overtaken by boxes, projects, dollhouses, and shelving full of art supplies, photographs, a myriad of doll accessories and doll furniture, and out-of-date cameras and tape recording equipment. Boss made no move to return to live at the apartments, which had given Shepherd the freedom to spread things out in order to find them easier.

Glancing at the list, Shepherd hunted around. His eyes passed over the old sex manuals at the very bottom of one bookshelf. The dust cover edges were flaking off in brittle bits. When he first encountered them, he was surprised for a moment. *Why would anyone read these...?*

He had leafed through one in curiosity, the cover creaking apart from decades of nonuse. The volume from the fifties amused; it was scientifically anatomical with chaste illustrations. *Boss must've had troubles with her sex life, maybe? How could anyone understand human intimacy from reading these dry descriptions? If there ain't chemistry, folks, no textbook's gonna help...*

He never mentioned finding them, figuring it would embarrass Boss. Getting back to business, his eyes raised and he saw what he was searching for amidst a plethora of Eastern titles. He grabbed *The Hidden Flower* by Pearl S. Buck—her favorite novel—a thick book on the Edo period of Japan, and several books on imperial families of Europe and Asia. Then he moved into the dining room.

Shepherd carefully unboxed the recently arrived Japanese summer palace. He double-checked to make sure all the tiny parts were included before he set it up on the dining room table. A time-consuming part of the job was meticulously photographing dollhouses from every possible angle, even creating what could be called story boards with the photos. For this particular palace, Boss wanted an array of imperial figurines posed in the courtyard with tiny bonsai trees. He had to go and find the appropriate historically accurate figurines in one of the storage rooms, ending up in 8E to collect a long-unused box.

From the exertion, Shepherd began sweating. It could be a strain to attempt to see what she would. If he didn't get the photos right, he would be right back here this afternoon documenting the miniature palace and posed figurines all over again.

And I hate messing up!

The palace had already been sent back and forth twice in the past eighteen months. Boss said, "I'm particularly keen to ascertain if the artisan followed my instructions for alterations and additions."

She was always extremely particular on presentation and technique, adamant every detail had to be historically accurate.

She shoulda worked for a museum. She'll probably scold me about using the dining room table. Sorry... needed the space.

With the hardest task completed, Shepherd locked up. On a whim, he went to pick up treats at a French bakery. Laden with bags, he entered the hospital room with a big grin on his bearded face. Huguette's face lit up when she saw Shepherd's large frame in the doorway. Then Nurse Price gently tugged his sleeve and quickly shut the door on looky-loos in the hallway.

"Ah, Colton, how lovely to see you! And with *cadeaux pour moi, merci*! You do a fine job, young man. Ah, and you have brought *pain au chocolat* and *brioche*. How thoughtful!"

Despite his fifty-one years, Shepherd almost blushed. Pleasing Boss had become an unexpected part of a most unusual job description. If he confessed to friends she had had a ticket for the second voyage of the Titanic and surfed with an Olympic champion in 1915 in Hawai'i, they wouldn't believe him. If he further confessed that he changed Barbie clothes, organized a slew of doll accessories, and photographed dollhouses, they might think he had lost his marbles.

But in New York, hey, one could make a pretty decent living being the assistant to a perfectly healthy, fantastically wealthy, elderly woman living in the hospital.

"It all smells heavenly! We shall save it for afternoon tea."

Huguette gave Price the bakery bag, then she stretched brown-speckled hands out eagerly for the stack of mail. "Did it come? Did it finally come?"

Shepherd knew what she was after. He grinned, watching as she flipped through the stack. Her enthusiasm at the age of ninety-eight amazed him.

Boss cheered, holding aloft a glossy Theriault's hardcover catalog with a bisque doll wearing a lace bonnet on the cover. All the remaining mail slid down scrawny legs, landing askew. Price immediately rose from a chair and began tidying up the thick pile, moving it to a side table.

A skeletal forefinger with an unpolished oval nail stabbed the cover. "I'm most anxious to bid on this wonderful *Jumeau* from 1891!" She opened the catalog and made a gleeful squeak. "Look! It includes the original *Letter of a Jumeau Baby to Her Little Mother*. Wonderful!"

Shepherd nodded. He couldn't appreciate the antique doll pictured but knew how passionately his employer collected them. She owned many, many dozens of such French bisque dolls, including many other types from Germany, Japan, and America.

He tried to explain to his wife: "I've lost count. There's got to be well over a thousand, maybe more. There's an original Barbie from 1957, if you believe that.

Our nieces would have a field day with the Barbie collection alone. She's got all the special holiday ones. The entire lot has to worth over a million, easy."

"How's that possible? How can old dolls be worth over a million dollars? Like, who would spend good money on that stuff?" his wife said, her eyes disbelieving as she drove the inherited Volvo 740 wagon to their cabin upstate.

If he only concentrated on the dolls, Shepherd could spend days and days organizing and cataloguing that collection alone. Once, while unpacking a newly acquired doll, he wondered, *Are antique dolls considered an asset?*

He eyeballed the Jumeau *bébé* in his hands, a frilly, lacy, doe-eyed creation from 1888.

Huh, who can say? Boss is crazy for them though.

For the upcoming Theriault's auction, it was routine the best dolls would sell for tens of thousands. Boss, represented by her lawyer phoning in, would be the highest bidder. She authorized up to $100,000 every time, which made Shepherd's head spin. There was no contest. Regardless of the steep climb from bidders around the world, Boss was the victor. She never lost.

But, as with anyone searching for the thrill of competition and conquest, Shepherd knew Boss would lose interest soon after. The antique *Jumeau bébé triste* in its handmade costume and dainty leather shoes and hand-painted face would be carefully removed to 12W to join its fellows or be given away. Shepherd had seen the routine so many times he figured he could time the sequence of events.

Once a few years previous, when Boss was in an excellent mood and had given him a bonus, he had felt brave enough to thank her for unfailing generosity which provided him with enjoyable employment.

She simply blinked, saying in a surprised tone, "Why Colton, don't thank me. It's dear Daddy's money, not mine!"

Then Boss returned with intense interest to her favorite game laid out on a bed tray: solitaire. This action meant Shepherd was dismissed. He left the hospital feeling bemused, wondering about her past and the massive amount of money she had wielded throughout a very long life.

What in the heck was that like? To give away thousands like it was nothing but a piece of candy!

Boss's phrase, "dear Daddy's money," rolled around in his mind for the next twenty-four hours.

December 14, 1927
907 Fifth Avenue, New York City

Anna formally announced the engagement between Huguette Marcelle Clark and William MacDonald Gower in *The New York Times*. Several major newspapers blared out the news along the lines of: "Princeton Grad to Marry Heiress." The press planned to squeeze this so-called love story for every revenue-enhancing drop of ink. Columnists immediately speculated on the coming society wedding and the success of the marriage.

"Gower doesn't even graze the stratosphere the Clarks inhabit!" insisted one newsman to his chain-smoking editor in a Midtown office.

During the morning perusal of periodicals, Huguette avoided all such articles. "As if they know anything about me or Bill, for that matter!"

"Don't let it trouble. Avoid the society pages until after you're married. Then the attention will slow down to a trickle."

That same week, the newly engaged couple attended two holiday parties thrown by family friends, the Storrs, at the Ritz-Carlton Hotel at 46th Street and Madison Avenue. A chief promotional feature of the fifteen-story hotel from its opening in 1911 touted the Ritz's: "perfection of service which has characterized the foreign hotels" and "the comforts of a country house" in the city.

The Ritz-Carlton's capacious dining room—with a live orchestra—led into successive areas. Famously, there were the elegant Palm Court; Pall Mall Room; Smoking Room paneled in oak; third floor exterior Roof Garden with green and white striped fabric ceiling and massive hanging baskets of pink roses; Crystal Ballroom with tented canopy, fabric draped walls, and crystal candelabra; and the interior Japanese Tea Garden, which was a favorite of Anna's circle. A five-story pagoda, statue of Buddha, and tiny Japanese village along a live stream with dwarf pines, firs, laurel, and lilac delighted those taking tea under the pavilion alongside the gurgling stream.

Mr. and Mrs. Frank Vance Storrs and their vivacious daughters, Carolyn and Anne, had been frequent patrons of the Ritz-Carlton for years. For their first party that season, Amanda Storrs selected décor for the hotel's Grand Ballroom with the theme of a southern garden laid out underneath a Lindberg miniature plane hanging from the ceiling. Masses of potted trees, green plants, and flowers of every variety were flown in. A large ice sculpture of a pilot stood amongst a plethora of refreshments.

At such a popular party, the crowd was thick with friends. A dozen young men in white tie huddled around the newly engaged young man.

"Look at you, Gower! Headed to the chopping block already, eh?" the red-headed man took a hasty swig from a flask. Forbidden alcohol dribbled on his boiled shirt. "My old man's on my case, too!"

"When's the big day then?" said a black-haired man with the physique of a boxer, who reached for the flask.

"I dunna know, this summer probably," said Gower.

"Never would've guessed you would've landed such a lady!" said a short young man named Ruddie Gerber who slapped Gower on the back repeatedly. Gower's expression darkened.

Gerber, in expertly cut white tie, then turned to Huguette, standing un-comfortably six feet away. She wore a silver Poiret couture gown and Cartier diamonds, smiling shyly as the young men talked for the past fifteen minutes. He eyed her up, putting a stubby-fingered hand to chest.

"And may I introduce myself as your fiancé's best friend? How do you do, Miss Clark? I'm Rudolph 'Stud' Gerber II." He extended a hand and suppressed a guffaw. "I also might be zozzled! Has anyone informed you that you look stunning this evening?" He drew up closer. "Is my pal Gower treating you well? If not, I'm available to take his place."

He wiggled eyebrows at Huguette, who immediately stepped away to cut the conversation off.

I think I've had enough of this! She motioned to Gower and whispered, "I'm going by Carolyn. See you later."

Three nights later the couple attended a second party hosted by the Storrs, this time in honor of their youngest daughter, Anne. The Grand Ballroom was transformed into a vast jungle with live monkeys, parrots, and a stuffed tiger peeking out of abundant foliage with the waiters in monkey getups serving coconut and pineapple-themed drinks. A full orchestra played for a packed dance floor.

"This drink is delicious. It reminds me of something I used to have in Hawai'i," said Huguette.

"Right, that was Mummy's intention. She adores Waikiki," said Carolyn.

"Oh, that's right. She wants my mother to go with her one of these days."

Carolyn didn't respond while downing her third glass of champagne smuggled in by her date. Her scarlet mouth turned down. "Hey! Have you shown me the ring yet? I don't believe you have. Lemme see..."

Huguette held out her hand, and Carolyn burst out: "Did he forget his wallet?" Hoots of laughter followed.

"Oh, stop it before someone hears you! It's dainty and *just fine!*"

"Sure. Does Bill realize that he could've simply raided one of Anna's jewelry boxes for a diamond much bigger than that little thing? Did you tell him you used to have gold faucets in your bathrooms and a pool *and* a train in your basement? Seriously, Huguette, does this man realize your background?"

Carolyn was drunk but she looked sober for a long second as she gazed into Huguette's eyes. Huguette looked away.

"I uh... I haven't discussed anything to do with money with Bill. It isn't the right time. And I didn't know him well enough when we were young to have him over."

"Sure... Sure it's not the right time. Honey, when will it be? After the marriage? Are you sure he loves you? Remember what your father told you?"

"Don't bring that up here!" Huguette hissed. "I wish I hadn't told you!" Her mouth turned down petulantly.

"Well, too bad!" Carolyn took another sip of champagne. "My memory's that of an elephant's. It was years ago, but I remember *very well* how upset you were when your father said no one was going to love you for you. I love you for you, but that man over there?" Carolyn pointed to the group of young men. "I'm not convinced. So, Hugo, how d'you know after such a short time that he loves you for you?"

"You're drunk. I'm not discussing this."

"I'm not so drunk I can't discuss reality. I'm trying to protect you."

"I'm leaving."

"Hugo, stop being such a baby! Come back!"

Carolyn shook her head sadly at her friend's retreating back. The gorgeous brunette was only alone for a second before an eager man emerged from the crowd.

After New Year's, Amanda Storrs arranged with Anna to honor the engagement with a night more in tune with Huguette's character: A dinner party in a private room at their favorite hotel, the Ritz-Carlton, followed by a Broadway show. After eating, the group headed out to see the new hit musical "Rosalie" with music by George Gershwin and Sigmund Romberg, and lyrics by Ira Gershwin and P.G. Wodehouse.

Huguette was grateful not to have to endure another night of wailing jazz, crowds, and friends drunk with smuggled-in booze.

"Isn't this a perfect way to celebrate, Bill? I do enjoy any music the Gershwins write," she said as they drew closer to the bright lights of the marquee of the New Amsterdam Theatre at 214 West 42nd Street. She felt warm and safe with Gower at her side, far away from the party scene.

"Of course, dollface. I agree."

Gower's eyes glanced at his fiancée swathed in an ermine coat with massive collar and cuffs. She wore red lipstick and a thin sparkling silver and crystal headband around shining blonde bobbed hair. She looked innocent and pretty. He was proud to escort Huguette, one of the most discussed debutantes of the season.

My fiancée is so famous she's written about routinely in the papers all over the country! He marveled at that, and that he, William Gower, had caught her.

The only concern came from the lack of physical contact. Some girls were so forward they turned him off. But Huguette was almost too girlish.

If only she'd return my kiss with some type of passion one of these days, Gower thought as a crease formed between thick eyebrows. *But she always shrinks from anything more than a peck. She's not that young; I can't be the first man to have kissed her...*

While the chauffeur eased the Rolls under the marquee, Gower looked out into the stalled traffic in front of the theater. It was going to be a packed house. He enjoyed being a part of the exalted crowd Huguette moved in.

Because face facts, buddy, without her I'm practically a nobody.

The only issue Gower could readily acknowledge had to do with their differing views of night life. He enjoyed the never-ending round of parties his fiancé seemed to want to escape. More and more she shunned their crowd. He couldn't fathom why.

We're young, rich, and in love. Why waste it on going home early?

Without divulging anything, for the past six weeks Gower dropped Huguette off at 907 Fifth Avenue—by midnight or earlier depending on Huguette's head or nerves—and returned to the party alone. He would stroll in, invariably yanking on the collar of his boiled shirt. Then, taking a good pull on a silver flask, he reached for whichever eager girl was handy and danced madly. Prohibition had only increased his father's generous cellars and intensified the parties since university days. Gower would stay awhile before corralling male friends to head to the *real party*: the Cotton Club on 142nd Street and Lenox Avenue in Harlem.

It excited him to learn about the history of the Cotton Club from a friendly bartender. He became fascinated by Owney Madden and watched for his appearance on weekends. An English-born gangster of the Gopher Gang—raised in the dregs of Hell's Kitchen, sent to Sing-Sing for manslaughter in 1916, and paroled in 1923—Madden quickly built the Cotton Club into a premier nightclub with risqué musical revues and an extensive drinks list. The club had a notorious ability to avoid police interest.

A whites-only club during Jim Crow, a legion of the era's most talented colored and black musicians and entertainers such as Duke Ellington, Adelaide Hall, Cab Calloway, Louis Armstrong, Ethel Waters, and Earl "Snakehips" Tucker were well compensated but only allowed onstage. A $2.00 minimum cover fee on weekdays for food and drinks ensured the club attracted only wealthy customers such as William Gower.

Whistling a Duke Ellington tune, Gower rounded the rear of the vehicle to offer a hand to Huguette. He already well understood there were some things—such as frequenting the Cotton Club late at night—a man never divulged to his lady. He leaned to kiss the top of her head. He still hadn't figured out why she perpetually looked at him as if she were about to blush from his attentions.

Huguette gently took the offered arm, "What're you whistling, Bill? I've never heard that melody before."

"Oh, it's nothing. You wouldn't know it, baby..."

The couple headed to the theater doors opened by valets with several flashbulbs popping in the cold air and onlookers crowded on the sidewalk to watch.

The next month the engaged couple was honored by long-time family friends, the Clarkes, with a party for eighty guests featuring a small orchestra and lavish catering in a super-luxury apartment at 999 Fifth Avenue.

Two weeks before, Gower looked from the embossed invitation in his hand up to Huguette and then back down again, his expression doubtful.

"You know Lewis Clarke, President of the American Exchange National Bank?" For a moment, he felt disoriented with disbelief. "*How* do you know such a man?"

"Why, I've known him since I was young. We used to vacation at his New Jersey villa. He's been like a second father to me the past few years."

"You're joking... Why don't I know this?"

"I couldn't say," said Huguette, shrugging nonchalantly. "The Clarkes are a wonderful couple. Mommy has them over to dinner on occasion. You'll like them. Don't be nervous."

"I'm not nervous!" Gower said with a worried look.

Lewis Latham Clarke was a descendent of a signer of the Declaration of Independence, board member of many organizations, and member of the Metropolitan Club of New York, the Piping Rock Club of Locust Valley, Long Island, the Spouting Rock Beach Association of Newport, Rhode Island, and the United Hunts Racing Association. At Clarke's side that evening was his equally pedigreed wife, Florence Marguerite, who perpetually wore a smile on her plump face. Despite innate shyness, Florence was a formidable hostess who had taught Anna a thing or two.

Similar to the Storrs, President and Mrs. Clarke were also parents of two daughters, Florence and Augusta, who had attended Spence alongside Huguette and Andrée. Like Carolyn Storrs and Larissa Lyle, Florence had been one of the girls who had truly mourned with Huguette when Andrée died.

For many years, the Clark family had visited the Clarkes at Villa Fiorenza on "Millionaire's Row" in Elberon, New Jersey. The oceanside villa was part of an exclusive summer resort developed after the Civil War as the second-best option for wealthy families who could not muscle their way into Newport.

Lewis Clarke, a fourth-generation bank president, and his father, Dumont Clarke, had been long-time business associates of Senator Clark's. Lewis Clarke had remained for years a principal advisor to growing the wealth of the Clark women. In fact, Clarke would be key in preserving their fortunes from the coming stock market crash which would soon cripple the nation. All eighty high-society guests that evening instinctively comprehended this key financial relationship, never needing to waste a moment's thought on why Mr. and Mrs. Clarke would pay such marked attention to Huguette Clark.

For once, Gower had the sense to leave the flask at home. He tried to keep cool when introduced.

"President Clarke, it's a *great* honor—"

"William Gower, pleasure to meet you. Congratulations are in order."

"Thank you, sir, President Clarke, sir."

"You're in banking yourself, I've heard from Anna."

Lewis Clarke looked the young man up and down. *How could Anna have allowed Huguette to choose a husband who isn't listed in the Social Register? He's good looking, but rough around the edges and obviously inexperienced. Not a solid choice for Huguette.*

"Yes, sir, yes, I am. Not up to your level yet though, sir." Gower laughed nervously.

Clarke looked thoughtful; he clasped arms behind his back. "But you're too young to be at my level, dear boy." He gave Gower a stern eye. "Understand that I started at the bottom, an office boy in 1889 for my father. Had to work my way up for over twenty years, like the best of them!

"Son, put in the time in your career now while you're young and strong. And take good care of Huguette for us, will you?"

Clarke looked pointedly at Gower, who nodded vigorously. Gower's mind went blank except for the most ridiculous thought: He wanted to ask about the fabulous parties put on at Villa Fiorenza. A few well-connected Princeton friends boasted about them, but he had never managed an invitation.

Maybe Huguette can get us one this summer?

Villa Fiorenza was a year-round estate which disregarded the long history of merely summering in Elberon. Seven presidents had made the resort their summer home of choice before the winds shifted to attract businessmen of the early twentieth century. Until the railroad was laid in 1870, Elberon was an exclusive enclave. Like many upper-class Eastern Seaboard communities in the nineteenth century, one arrived by boat or yacht.

With a certain social set fleeing hoi polloi arriving on trains, another arguably more powerful moved in. By the beginning of the twentieth century, the Guggenheims, Loebs, Bloomingdales, and Seligmans had as much or more money than WASP families in Newport or Southampton. They gladly sailed into Elberon to form their own oceanfront community, razing uninsulated, multi-story, wooden houses with wrap-around porches and turrets—now very *passé*—to build grand estates made of imported stone and brick.

Gower stood a moment alone before Huguette rescued him. She took his arm and whispered, "There's someone I'd like you to meet. I think you might have met her at one of the Storrs's parties."

They walked towards a beautiful young woman with a smile that could not conceal her mischievous nature. "Bill, this is my good friend, Florence."

Gower eyed up the blonde woman, barely able to conceal his interest. "Nice to meet you." Gower shook Florence's slight hand. *No, I'd remember this one!*

"A pleasure. Huguette, you must be very happy with such a handsome fiancé," said Florence with flirtatious eyes.

"Oh, I am! Thank you!" She took Gower's arm. "Your father and mother are so kind to do this for us."

"Yes, of course. You know Father adores you and Anna. It's the least he could do after all these years of friendship."

Gower seized his opportunity for enhanced social capital.

"Florence, I've heard about your beautiful estate in Elberon."

"You mean the parties?" She laughed and toyed with a diamond and pearl necklace. "We Clarkes like our parties... I've heard some tall tales that *probably didn't happen* at Villa Fiorenza, I will have you know. But! I have better ones when my parents are abroad."

She winked at Huguette.

"Really?" said Gower.

This girl's incredible.

"Hugo, you should come one of these summers. Every time I try to invite you, you're already off to Santa Barbara or Paris."

Florence pouted with a small shake of the head.

"Oh, I know. Mommy and I adore California. Didn't you have a good time when you visited?"

"Yes, Mother and Father almost bought a villa there as well. Remember? But it would've been entirely too much to have houses on both coasts. Mother isn't feeling the best these days."

Huguette looked concerned.

"I'm sorry to hear that."

"No matter, she'll pull through. Let's talk about something more fun. Have you chosen the *couturier* for your wedding gown?" said Florence, taking Huguette's arm and moving her away.

Starting in 1915, after Anna and William began taking investment advice from President Clarke, the Clark family was invited to Villa Fiorenza. Huguette and Andrée were happy swimming, sailing, and playing tennis with Florence and Augusta, perpetually joking to their parents during each visit: "We're really cousins due to our identical surnames, Clark and Clarke!"

Anna enjoyed the wide-open feel of the resort town of Elberon, with strong ocean breezes wonderfully cooling even on the hottest of days. She was amused by the quaint aesthetic of copying Normandy with many "Villa Norman" examples that still survived. During one visit, when Anna casually suggested buying a summer cottage designed decades ago by the prestigious Manhattan architectural firm of McKim, Mead & White, William adamantly refused.

"There are too many damn Republicans for me to relax!"

In early March, Gower was again awed by Huguette's world. In a ceremony at the Corcoran Gallery of Art at 17th Street and New York Avenue in Washington D.C., he witnessed President Calvin Coolidge cut the cord of the new William Andrews Clark Annex. The president turned with a big smile to play up to the crowd before offering his arm to Anna, who was turning fifty but appeared years younger. President Coolidge and Anna led the procession into the new wing designed by architect Charles Platt. The $700,000 cost was donated by the Clark family.

Directly behind, Gower walked with Huguette and a crowd of Clark family members.

"Baby, are those your older siblings?" Gower motioned with his head at the middle-aged group desiring to be as close to the president as possible.

"Yes," Huguette whispered. "They're jealous that Mommy, as Daddy's widow, is getting the lion's share of attention because we all paid for the annex."

"I've never heard you discuss them before. They're decades older!" He looked mystified.

"Oh yes, I was born when Daddy was an older man. We're not close because they treat Mommy coldly. But never mind. This is too happy of an evening to even give them a thought!"

Huguette steered him away. Over the next hour, she eagerly showed favorite pieces in the bequeathed collection. Her fiancé looked around incredulously at the nearly 200 objects on display.

While touring the seven rooms, he weakly probed, "Your father gave all this to the museum? This all fit in your *house...*?"

"Oh yes, and more that's probably stuffed in storage rooms or sold. There was so much that the Metropolitan Museum refused it all as too onerous. Which lead the family to choose the Corcoran."

Huguette beamed, her eyes avidly taking in the beauty of the exhibits. "Isn't all this art grand? I adore it. I wish Mommy and I could have kept a few more things. Andrée and I used to play in the *Salon Doré* and get scolded. Monsieur Styka gave me lessons using some of these paintings. I've so many memories merely looking at these pieces! It brings me back to my childhood in a heartbeat..."

She animatedly drew Gower's attention here or there, tugging his hand. He had never heard her speak so passionately before. Entranced by the alteration in her person, he followed her lead. This tactic allowed stories to pour out. He hoped it was a sign of good things to come.

Five months later on August 18, Huguette and Gower were married by a Catholic priest in Santa Barbara with Larissa Lyle as matron of honor and Luna as the flower girl. The reception luncheon with thousands of roses, orchids, and a small orchestra was held at Bellosguardo. Wedding photographs were taken on the lawns under the clearest of blue skies. To honor her father, Huguette wanted the bridal photographs taken next to William's portrait by Styka. She desired little fuss, apart from a fashionably short, *Maison Lelong* bespoke gown with headdress and cathedral length tulle veil, a Cartier wedding band ringed with 32 diamonds, and a white rose bouquet with trailing ivy.

In the late afternoon, Huguette and Gower climbed into Anna's wedding gift: A green 1927 Rolls Royce Phantom I with silver door handles and black leather top. Mr. Armstrong, the full-time chauffeur, was seated at the wheel outside the cabin. The car would be transported on the train for parts of the journey to arrive in a timely manner at San Francisco.

The newlyweds planned to take a few days to explore San Francisco before boarding a steamer to Honolulu. A second car trailed the newlyweds with masses of luggage, valet, ladies maid, and Sandré, Huguette's social secretary now she was a married woman.

At a San Francisco hotel, Gower took care of all the details, selecting the honeymoon suite with a double bed instead of twins. Huguette felt nervous because Gower seemed excited to be alone with her. She said she was hungry, so they went to a late dinner in the hotel restaurant and danced a few songs. They rode the elevator up at one o'clock in the morning.

As soon as Gower embraced her to kiss, she wiggled free. "Oh Bill, it's been such a big day. I'm exhausted. Can we sleep?"

Gower quickly responded, "Of course, baby! I'm sorry, *Mrs. Gower...*" He smiled, trying in vain to catch her eyes.

Huguette went to change in the bathroom. She chose a modest full length silk nightgown with peignoir. Avoiding Gower, she slid into bed without turning on the light. She remained on the far-right side, pulling up the sheet as far as possible. Her eyes were wide open. It was still warm in the room despite the breeze. He reach over to turn out the bedside light on his side.

Huguette didn't dare twitch or change sides. *What if I accidentally brush my leg up against his? Will he mind? I can't believe I'm in bed with Bill right now...!*

Gower said goodnight. *Perhaps this is best.*

He sighed and turned on his side away from his wife, immediately falling asleep. Huguette lay awake another hour before she got out of bed to fetch two dolls from a Louis Vuitton suitcase. She set them up on a chair on her side of the bed and then fell asleep.

What Gower thought was a one-off became routine for the next few days, then also in the steamer to Honolulu, and in the honeymoon suite at the Moana Hotel. Finally, late one night after amiably talking and laughing in bed, Gower gently drew Huguette into his arms. Before she could voice excuses, he softly kissed her. He didn't let go, and slowly she began warming to him. When he attempted intercourse, Huguette cried out in pain and pushed him away.

She scrambled to the edge of the large bed so fast, she accidentally slid off. The silk nightgown pooled in smooth folds around her on the floor as she blubbered unintelligibly.

"Did you just say you want to return home?"

Gower was stunned. It felt like someone doused him with Artic water. He yanked back on blue cotton pajama bottoms, losing all desire to touch her.

Huguette sniffed.

"Yes, yes, that's what I mean. I want to go home!"

She pulled knees to her chest and cried for ten more minutes before Gower could induce her to move.

"Don't worry, I won't try anything again! Good grief!"

He threw himself down, grabbed a pillow, and turned his back to her.

The next morning, Gower eyed up the dolls watching him from across the room. He moved out onto the balcony to smoke.

She's obviously completely uninformed about physical intimacy in a marriage. This is far more difficult than I ever imagined. It's going to take some time. I figured Huguette would relax now that she's my wife. The sexual constraints we've been under all our lives should go out the window! She just needs to relax!

At all costs, Huguette avoided discussing the issue but continued treating her husband as respectfully and cheerfully as ever. It was strange to Gower, as if she didn't blame him but wanted nothing physical either. During the day she was pleasant; she didn't mind kissing and affectionate hugs. But sex was not yet on the table.

Gower was surprised to discover an iron core within his demure wife that refused to relent to any entreaty. They were due to leave the next day. After hearing about the islands for years, he was bitterly disappointed he had only spent a few days in Hawai'i.

"Hey, Hugo, dollface, come out here."

She put down a hairbrush and came out to the balcony.

"Yes, darling?"

"Try this," Gower said, extending a cigarette.

"I tried that years ago in school. I coughed so hard it was ridiculous."

"Sure, but you're an older, sophisticated woman now. My wife! Try it..." he grinned at her then took a deep drag before extending the cigarette in her direction.

"You won't laugh?"

She gingerly took it, eyeballing it, then him.

"Nope. Smoking settles my nerves. It will for you too."

He winked. She took a drag and burst out coughing.

"Try again, dollface."

After an hour she had the hang of it. They went out to dinner that evening, both smoking.

If only I could induce her to drink more. That'd be the ticket to get her to relax! But Huguette always stopped at one glass. Come to think of it, I've never seen her drunk!

They rose from the table for a walk on dark sand illuminated by torches. It was so mild, ocean waves could barely be heard. Gower fantasized about making love on the beach.

"Have you changed your mind?"

"About what?"

"About wanting to go back to California tomorrow. I'd like to stay."

"We've had a nice day, Bill, but I must insist. I want to return to Bellosguardo as soon as possible."

Gower turned around, knowing she would follow. He escorted her back to the suite, and then left without saying a word. He stayed out until three in the morning. The next morning, he boarded the ship with a hangover and slept all day. When he woke up, he saw the dolls staring at him again.

Less than a week later they arrived at Bellosguardo with a visibly brightened Huguette and a confused Anna.

"Why, hello, you two... I'm very surprised to see you back so soon... You've only been gone—Is everything alright?" She stood in the front hall, looking at both Huguette and Gower by turn. "Why was the honeymoon so...?"

"*Maman*, everything is very well! We merely missed you so! And we decided that Hawai'i is nice but not as nice as Bellosguardo. Right, Bill? So, here we are!" Huguette embraced Anna.

Annoyed with his wife's fibbing, Gower greeted Anna with as few words as possible. He took the stairs by twos, his valet following. He planned on a few rounds of golf.

I need to get away.

Huguette was content to be back on her own turf. She was happy with her marriage if her husband wasn't pressuring her.

Gower kept hoping Huguette would warm up to him. *It's just a matter of time... Meanwhile, I feel like quite the man about town with a fat bank account, a valet who caters to me, and a chauffeured Rolls at my disposal day or night.*

Until late September, propelled by Gower's zest, the newlyweds played golf, attended polo matches, and ate lunch at the country club. They went to Los Angeles to attend museum exhibitions, film premieres, concerts, and parties. They visited family. With Gower in charge, most nights they dined out at fine restaurants and danced well past midnight. They attended every invitation extended, which puzzled Huguette.

"Bill, we don't have to go merely because we've received an invitation. As you'll discover, there's no shortage of parties around here. You might tire of them as I have."

"Not a chance, my girl!" Gower took her in his arms to do a dance step before quickly twirling her. She was left breathless in the drawing room while he went out to take a tennis lesson with a pro instructor.

A few nights later driving home from a party after one in the morning, Huguette yawned before sleepily remarking, "The Pattersons are such a nice couple. It was an enjoyable evening... I think we're busier now than when we were engaged."

"Isn't it fun?" Gower winked, then fished the flask out of his jacket.

"I'm playing in the golf tournament tomorrow. We should leave by nine in the morning."

"Oh, I, um... wanted to have a day for painting. I'm terribly behind. I recently wrote Monsieur Styka—"

"Listen, baby, it's important to me that my wife is there. All the other wives are coming to watch." He eyeballed her while uncapping the flask a second time. "You've plenty of paintings. Just choose a couple off the walls. Simple! That way you don't have to work on anything new and we can go out more."

"No, that's not how it works..."

Huguette didn't hear anything in reply. She glanced over at her husband, head back and mouth open. He began to snore.

In the fall, Anna stayed on at Bellosguardo while the newlyweds returned to New York. Huguette wanted to paint, and Gower wanted to pursue an expanded night life. A wedding gift from the Clarkes awaited their arrival.

"How lovely! A tray engraved with our initials and wedding date. Won't this display nicely in the dining room?" Huguette lifted the hefty sterling silver tray for Gower to see, but he wasn't looking.

He went to the window, his back to her. "Maybe I could work for President Lewis Clarke someday..."

"Do you want to go back to work? You don't need to. Although, I'm sure he would give you a job if asked." Huguette handed the tray to a maid.

Gower turned and put hands up in a pleading gesture, "Doll, don't say anything if you see him! I want to handle it. I'll think about what position I might like. In the meantime, I'm quite busy having my portrait done, you know..."

He smiled and jauntily began walking to the gallery.

"We'll hang it in the drawing room," said Huguette, following him. "He does such beautiful portraits. Bill, may I come today to watch the progress?"

She stopped herself from expressing it had been too many months without seeing Styka. Gower whirled around.

"No, you can't come and watch me! That'll make two of us doing *nothing*."

He bopped her nose with a fingertip. Huguette flinched.

"You'll just have to wait your turn like everyone else to see the final product."

"Tell Monsieur Styka that I'll see him in two days for my lesson, then."

Huguette's soft voice trailed after Gower already striding away.

Anna returned to 907 Fifth Avenue to take up residence in apartment 8W. It had undergone a thorough restoration and redecorating, with another concealed door created to access the bedrooms. Huguette either called or went down at least once daily.

During the day, Gower was content to do low-key activities at home. He read newspapers, an occasional history book, or listened to baseball games and boxing matches on the wireless. Every evening, Gower wanted to be out broadcasting his wealth. He sorely missed going to the Cotton Club, among other unmentionable venues. In an effort to make the marriage successful, he deliberately cut his wings. He kept hoping Huguette would come around and be a proper wife.

When will it not be merely me making all the concessions?

Gower didn't complain when his wife insisted maintaining separate bedrooms, which didn't surprise him. He felt defeated. He desired nothing but to be physically close, but Huguette pushed him away so effectively it was as if they were brother and sister, not man and wife. He had little idea how to handle his new bride.

At least I won't wake up to creepy dolls staring at me!

That winter into spring, to avoid Gower's pressure, Huguette absorbed herself completely in painting or practicing music. She also went shopping. She spent over twenty thousand dollars on Cartier jewelry and a gold cigarette case. A Steinway was purchased for the drawing room to replace the one Anna had moved with her down to 8W.

Huguette then converted one of the guest bedrooms into an art studio, fully equipping the room akin to Styka's style. Gower could find her in there all hours of the day and night; she seemed obsessed. With Styka's guidance, Huguette was eagerly preparing seven paintings for an exhibition of her work at the Corcoran. The life-sized "Nun Walking in Snow" among those chosen to display.

In the late afternoon at the end of winter, Gower opened the door to the studio. He looked around at the orderly mess of a serious artist. His nose wrinkled at the unfamiliar odors of turpentine, linseed oil, and oil paint. He waited for her to speak to him. Nothing.

"Hey doll, it smells like a gas station in here!"

Gower waited for a reaction. Huguette didn't turn around. Her back stiffened and she dabbed the brush too firmly, ruining the fine black line.

He always says that. It's so tiresome! Now I'll have to redo that smudge.

Ramming fists into trouser pockets and leaning against the door railing, Gower said, "Baby, are you coming?"

Huguette set down the brush and said, "I would enjoy going to the Miller's party, as I explained previously, but I *must* finish this painting for the exhibition. There's so much work left to do. I can't stop now. I have a deadline. I'll write them a note in the morning to explain my absence."

"It looks great, Hugo. It's *perfect*. Can't you let it alone and take a few hours and come with me, like I asked? Like I've been asking for months? I'm tired of explaining to everyone where my wife is! It's been over two weeks since we've spent any time together, baby! Maybe three!"

Huguette turned her head only in profile. "If I didn't have the exhibition coming up so soon, then I would attend. Please be patient with me, darling. This is an unusual time, and it's *so important* to me."

"What about me? Don't I matter?" He glared at the back of her head before slamming the door shut.

Huguette flinched. *I hope the servants didn't hear that. The exhibition is next month. He knows that. He said he knows how important this is to me. He said he cared...*

She picked up the brush again, deliberately pushing away worry. She was determined to get the colors of the facial shading done perfectly before Styka saw it again.

At the end of April, Styka sailed back from France to accompany the Gowers and Anna to Washington D.C. Entering the drawing room of 12W, he was dressed in a Saville Row black and white pinstripe suit with purple paisley silk cravat.

Styka greeted Huguette first, kissing her on both cheeks. "My dear Mrs. Gower, I've never seen you look so grown up and lovely before," Styka said, leaning to brush lips on her hand. "Marriage and an exhibition are doing wonders for you."

"*Merci beaucoup,* Monsieur Styka. How very good of you to come." Huguette was thrilled to see him after a long absence. Styka was as magnetically handsome as ever.

I get to be with him for the next few days!

"And how could I possibly miss my star pupil's first exhibition? Hmmm? That is not possible." Styka shook his head while softly clucking his tongue. "It's my pleasure, my darling Mrs. Gower, to accompany you to the party tonight in your honor." He switched to English, "With Mr. Gower's permission, of course."

Gower nodded curtly, averting eyes to mask flashes of intermingled anger and jealousy. *I feel like an idiot when this man is around. I don't even know what he's saying.*

Styka moved to kiss Anna, and after a few minutes of pleasantries, it was time to leave for Penn Station. Styka offered an arm to Huguette, and they walked out of the room talking animatedly in French.

Huguette hasn't looked at me once since that painter arrived! I might as well be chopped liver! Gower collected himself for a moment before turning to his mother-in-law to offer an arm.

That evening, the private party at the Corcoran and the next day's public opening of the exhibition were a resounding success. Despite the attention, Huguette felt protected with Styka and her family around her. She thoroughly enjoyed herself.

Styka proved to be an invaluable aid for her debut as a serious painter into the art world. Before the event, he coached her, and, as Huguette told Gower afterward, "His advice was spot-on!"

At breakfast in the hotel restaurant the next morning, Styka said, "And how well everything went off. Mrs. Gower, you performed marvelously! I've never seen you so animated in a room full of strangers. Did it kill you, though?"

He leaned forward with eager interest, a small smile playing on his lips. Huguette smiled back, not wanting to admit how difficult it had been.

"Not at all. I thought the entire experience lovely. And I can't wait to head to Paris to do it all again."

"Well, the details on that one are still in the works. It won't be this year. However, I'm pleased you came out of your shell for the sake of your art here in America. And, all in all, journalists and critics were respectful and even complimentary in the reviews, so I needn't have worried."

Styka began cutting into an omelet. After a minute, he gazed expectantly around.

"And where is Mr. Gower this morning? Done in by your marvelous debut?"

Huguette put down her *café au lait* with a clatter.

"He uh... oh, he's coming in a little bit. We're supposed to go on eating without him."

She wasn't sure if her husband would show. He was still in bed when she left. She pushed Gower out of her thoughts to concentrate on the reviews.

Anna congratulated her, pointing out the most favorable report.

"Read from here to here!"

Huguette complied and said, "Monsieur Styka, after years of lessons, it's highly gratifying all the hours of toiling away are paying off. I've only you to thank!"

She wanted to throw arms around her painting instructor. Styka, seeing the adoration in her expression, looked away before replying.

"Oh, not so! You've worked very hard, especially the past five months while I've been largely absent. You deserve all this praise and more!"

He smiled generously, eyes seeking out primarily Anna. Just then Gower arrived with puffy eyes, already chain-smoking. Styka examined the stone-faced, young husband.

"Isn't that so, Mr. Gower?"

What a strange young man for Huguette.

"What did I miss?" Gower grunted.

He stubbed out a cigarette while waiting for coffee to be poured. Before the waiter retreated, he lit a fresh cigarette.

"Your wife's reviews. They're marvelous! You must read for yourself…" said Styka, nudging the folded newspapers across the table.

The man acts like he's still in college!

Gower didn't move to pick them up. He waved vaguely in his wife's direction.

"Oh, right. Congratulations, doll. I certainly know how hard you've worked!"

He pushed aside the scrambled eggs and sausage set down in front of him. He inhaled deeply from the cigarette before craning his neck to ascertain who was in the dining room that morning. Styka and Anna exchanged glances across the table.

Huguette kept reading the same paragraphs over and over, entranced by favorable articles.

For the first time, I feel like a serious artist.

The Corcoran exhibition gave her confidence to agree to two more future exhibitions. She was deliriously happy for weeks, but Gower appeared worse by the day. Ever since their return, he had been going out nightly. He no longer asked Huguette to accompany him and slept until noon.

Huguette didn't say anything, allowing her husband to "sow his wild oats. Isn't that what they call it, *Maman?*"

Anna checked her temper. From across the table at 8W, she looked at her daughter curiously before replying, "I couldn't say. I never once saw your father inebriated."

Two weeks later when Gower appeared in the doorway while Huguette ate lunch, she noticed he was freshly showered and dressed in a brown wool suit and silk tie.

"Hello, Bill, it's been some time since we've eaten together. I'm pleased. You look nice. Do sit down." Huguette gestured to the empty place beside her. "The pea soup is delicious!"

"No, not today."

"You're not hungry? Have you eaten anything? You really should—"

"No, I'm not hungry. I don't plan on eating."

"Are you still hung over?"

"Probably. Who cares? Baby, I've got something to tell you."

She looked up from spooning soup, uneasiness creeping over her. His tone of voice was odd. When she did nothing but gawk, Gower's temper flared.

"Leave it all up to me, fine! Well, here's the truth: I'm leaving you! I've begun an affair with another woman because I can't stand this sham of a marriage we've got going on here."

"Sham of a marriage...? What? Bill, I... I thought you were happy. I thought we loved each other... Whatever can you mean?"

Gower said nothing as he stared fixedly out the window, both hands shoved in pockets.

Huguette blurted out, "You've been with another woman!" Her face crumpled with dismay.

Gower's eyes narrowed and he pointed a long forefinger at her. "Here's the unvarnished truth! I do love you, or at least I *did*. But now I'll be very happy *away* from you. You're driving me crazy!

"Right now, I feel miserably guilty and very angry. I wanted our marriage to work, I really did! But you seem determined to keep me as your brother or best friend or whatever it is that's in your little head. It's delusional!"

Gower gesticulated wildly, eyes roving the room, spittle flying. "At the end of the day, it all amounts to a husband in name only!"

"Delusional...? We married less than a year ago and you're already not in love with me...?" Her blue eyes implored him to take away the pain.

"Then after the pretty little wedding, that was it! *Nothing* for me!"

"Oh, I see. This is about *that*..." Huguette voice trailed off as she looked down, clutching hands, not wanting to continue.

"Yes, it's about *that*! I didn't sign up for this kind of a marriage! I thought you were normal!"

Huguette flinched, then began weeping. Gower's shoulders slumped a moment because he didn't want to hurt her, but he had been hurting himself by staying. Hiding behind anger was the only thing giving him courage to leave.

"Bill... you're... seeing another woman? Who is she?" she wailed.

He leaned forward to white knuckle the curved back of the Chippendale chair. He restrained himself from hurling the antique against the wall.

"For cryin' out loud, it's *not all my fault*! Who cares who she is! Don't you care about *me*? I can't handle being your brother or guy pal! I can't handle not having sex with my wife for the next fifty years! Because guess what? I'm not your brother! You care about your dolls more than you care about me!"

To calm down, Gower trained eyes on one spot on the Renoir opposite. *Dad told me when my wife drove me nuts and I wanted to kill her, count to ten. One...two...three...*

Gower hadn't meant to be this forthcoming. It wasn't in his nature to be loud or violent. His wife's stricken face and sobs stopped him from shouting yet more hurtful things, even if truthful. He knew now after months and months of trying she couldn't handle any of it.

Huguette shuts me out. She lives in her own little world, and I'm done trying.

A minute or two passed while she cried, face buried in her hands. The longer Gower stood silently the more uncomfortable he became.

In a quiet tone, he said, "I've got to go now. I'll see you around sometime... I'm going down to talk to Anna. Don't follow me."

"What?" Huguette's head popped up, too late. "Are you leaving me now...?"

She heard only loud footsteps echoing down the gallery. Then the front door slammed.

Mind whirling, she felt light-headed. Her skin was clammy, and her heart raced as she gripped hands together while restraining herself from making any more noise.

Where did he go? To talk to Maman. *She'll help us.*

She sat numbly at the table for the next quarter hour without touching the second course of baked fish and steamed vegetables as she waited for his return. She then rose and went blindly up the gallery, headed to her husband's bedroom.

Maybe Bill returned? I thought I heard something...

Gower's valet packed multiple Louis Vuitton suitcases and trunks laid out efficiently all over the room. The slight man folded cashmere argyle socks and silk ties as she stood in the doorway a moment, hoping he might divulge information on Gower's plans. The valet ignored her.

Retreating immediately, tears overflowed as she locked her bedroom door. Grabbing Suzette, she lay on the bed with the doll cradled in her arms. She expected her mother to come, wanted her to come, but Anna didn't. The room gradually darkened.

For several hours, Huguette listened for sounds of Bill's return. When her maid knocked on the door, she told her to go away. She eventually slept.

At the warm grey light of earliest dawn, Huguette woke up startled, as if coming out of a nightmare. The streets below were still and silent. Open windows allowed cool air and the faintest twirp of birdsong to come up from the trees.

Yesterday's events raced through her mind in a jumble of vague impressions as she rubbed at gummed eyelashes and grit in the corner of one eye. She lay back on the pillow and remembered.

Bill's gone... What am I going to do...? Maybe he's going to come back today... He'll come back!

The pain came in waves, and tears bathed red eyes. "Who is she?" she blubbered out loud to no one. "Bill's left me for another woman..."

It was too unbelievable. *We're supposed to be newlyweds... Maybe he came back while I slept?*

Huguette felt a rush of hope. She rose immediately to go down the hall.

The door was open, the bed pristine, shades and curtains open to the first blush of sunrise. She checked the dressing room, smelling Gower's cologne in the air. Her hands went up to her mouth in agony at the truth: Rows and rows of forlorn hangars and several scattered shoe trees in a corner. Bare walls. Bare shelves.

Everything's gone! All his clothes, shoes, everything!

She went to the bathroom. It too was empty. Toiletries, combs, and bathrobe missing.

An hour later, Anna knocked. Huguette rose with stiff limbs and unlocked the door. Anna glanced at her daughter's disheveled hair and yesterday's clothing.

"Wash your face, get dressed, and come talk."

William's been good enough to tell me the truth, but I need to hear it from Huguette. What a pickle she's in.

Fifteen minutes later, a more presentable Huguette went into her sitting room and closed the door. Both women were avoiding the servants from overhearing any more details than they already knew. The conversation was carried out in rapid French; voices never raised. Despite a nosey ear pressed to the thick door at one point, nothing more could be ascertained.

"Is it true, what he told me?"

"What did he tell you?" Huguette looked shrunken in the overstuffed chair. She pulled her blue cashmere cardigan more tightly around her torso while pressing knees together. She had to steel herself from trembling.

"I won't go into details or explain how angry and frustrated he's become. It's not my place to interfere. In short, he's leaving you for another woman because you won't be a proper wife."

"A proper wife? I was kind to him. I love him." Huguette began weeping, hands shaking.

Anna said nothing, knowing she could not push Huguette too far too fast.

"Did he confess he likes to look at other men? Did he?" Huguette said, her eyes becoming wild for a second. Her hands moved to tug and twist a handkerchief.

"What do you mean?"

Anna didn't divulge what she suspected. *Could my daughter have been the unwitting victim of a homosexual fortune hunter desiring a beard? She's so innocent it could be possible. But then why would he complain she didn't desire him?*

"Sometimes I...when I was with him, especially when we were alone and he wasn't paying attention, I observed him looking at young men. The waiters or a man at the bar, someone on the polo field. I was bothered by it because he never looked at me with the same interest. It was very obvious..."

Huguette looked down, not meeting Anna's steady gaze.

"If he's inclined to be with men, well... But! Have you considered he might have forgotten about men if you were to love him like he's asking?"

"I do love Bill!" Huguette paused in frustration. "We always had a nice time together, and we only just married. He's humiliating me. What do I tell our friends now?" Huguette fell silent. Then she brightened. "Money's terribly important to Bill. Do you think if I were to give him another million, he would return? Could you ask him?"

"*Another* million for that man? Do you mean to buy his love?" Anna's eyes narrowed. "You shouldn't have to offer *another cent more* than I've already given!"

"Then what should I do?" Huguette gasped. The idea of Gower's desertion ate away at her. "How will I face everyone?"

"I cannot tell you what to do. I'm not his wife; he's not my husband. I never had any problems with your father; we had a wonderful relationship. What I will say is that if you don't submit physically, you will neither keep him nor ever hope to bear his children. Is that what you want, to have neither husband nor children? To have me never be a grandmother?"

Anna gave her a pointed look. Huguette's made a small cry and looked away, crossing her arms. Anna waited a long moment before continuing.

"What a sad life we'll both have... You, no children. Me, no grandchildren. Perhaps William would forget about others if he had *you* to please and love him."

Huguette froze at the memory of being with Gower in bed. "I don't know, I don't know... This is all very hurtful. I was uncomfortable," she confessed, eyes riveted on the blue carpet.

Anna paused, watching her daughter wipe at a swollen pink nose, before rising from the sofa. "When you have it figured out, and perhaps after you talk with William again—he's most likely at his parents' apartment on Park Avenue—only then we will discuss this topic again. I won't tell a married daughter of mine what to do."

Anna paused at the door. "It's high time you grow up, Huguette."

Huguette burst into fresh tears. *We're still newlyweds. I can't believe this is happening to me...*

To escape the hot gossip oozing around town that Gower squired another woman, Huguette fled west. She knew what everyone was saying because she had long heard it said of others. It was unbearable to be part of the gossip lineup.

I wonder what he'll confess to friends. I hope he's discreet!

It had been weeks since she had talked to her estranged husband. He remained immune to requests via letter and telephone to join them at Bellosguardo.

"Maybe Bill will come back soon...? And then all will be well, and no one will be the wiser. I want to hope for the best despite his silence. I'm going to give him time."

Huguette smiled at words of hope spoken out loud. She looked out over the ocean as she sipped coffee.

Anna sighed. "It's been months of no communication. I believe you're dealing in self-deception. But, I won't discuss it with others, no matter who they are. Frankly, I don't want to get involved with wooing your husband home. That's your job if you want it."

"He'll come back, *Maman*. Give him time."

For Huguette's twenty-third birthday, Anna soon took her to Honolulu on the *Malolo* out of San Francisco. The days during the five-week trip were hot and sunny, which Huguette relished. The brilliant colors soothed, occupying her artist's eye. She spent many happy hours sunbathing on Waikiki or painting underneath a cluster of palm trees in a garden. She captured the sunset or the exotic flora on canvas, finding the rainbow trees the most pleasing. As the tranquil days moved on their natural course, the striking colors of the flowers against an ever-changing ocean and sky were a never-ending delight.

She wrote to Styka: *Oahu is such an enchanting island with scads of artistic inspiration.*

Absorbed by painting, Huguette almost forgot about the gossip awaiting her return. Seduced by island life, she rarely thought about Gower. She felt calm and centered concentrating on the task at hand, completing five paintings with two more in progress. She slept better than she had in months.

"I regret to say it," said Anna at dinner, "But the growing popularity of Honolulu as a tourist destination is a becoming hindrance to what I've always enjoyed about Hawai'i."

Huguette set her buttered taro roll on a bread plate. "It appears they're overtaking everything. Just today I was annoyed on the beach because it was packed with children and nannies. People everywhere!"

"Yes. And in the evenings, unfortunately, we hear far less Hawaiian music and far more jazz. It's a shame." Anna shook her head in disappointment.

As Huguette needed to paint with great concentration, the gawking tourists with their obnoxious behavior, shrill laughter, and shouted conversations late into the evenings were taxing. The noise carried straight up into the hotel balconies of the Moana Hotel. Some nights, the raucous honking and screeching of cars until after midnight on the newly paved Kalakaua Avenue below kept them up. Huguette wrote again to Styka to complain about a Hawaii overtaken by trendiness.

And to sum it all up, my dollar bills are ironed, and the change cleaned before it's put back into my purse by the maid. It really is too much! I preferred Honolulu when it was more primitive. I suppose I should say that I'm lucky to have seen it like that many years ago thanks to my father's intrepid ways.

Affectionately, HC

The Clarks returned to the sanctuary of Bellosguardo. Within its gates, there was no unpleasant news or bothersome tourists. The East Coast talk about the Gower split passed by; the Stock Market Crash passed by (Lewis Clarke sent a telegram to Anna to assure all was well); and still they remained quiet by the Pacific.

"New York is at its loveliest in the fall. I hate to miss all of it," said Anna while seated at afternoon tea on the veranda. "I'll have my maid begin packing, if you'll do the same."

Huguette quickly calculated the months of absence. *Had enough time passed to avoid the talk of Bill leaving me?*

"I've received word Monsieur Styka will be there. He's decided to spend most of the year in New York. Isn't that wonderful news? I'm anxious to take up regular lessons. I've sent him five new brushes with my last letter. He has an exhibition in Chicago in January and confessed he needs to get busy."

"That was kind of you. And it's good news he'll be in New York far more this winter. He's such wonderful company. I'll make sure to include him at my next dinner party." Anna patted Huguette's hand. "And speaking of lessons, I'm going to start up with a new harp teacher, as well. From Julliard. I can't wait to begin!"

Anna quietly celebrated the holidays with a dinner party for twelve one evening and the next week, a concerto concert for the New Year. At some of her mother's gatherings, Huguette made only a flash appearance or stayed longer to play the violin after dinner. When small talk began in earnest, Huguette slipped out using the back servant staircase instead of the elevator. The new move drove Anna wild.

Nevertheless, it was easy for the protective Anna to obey Huguette's wishes for privacy. She immediately changed the subject whenever a hint of Bill Gower floated past. When an acquaintance became too nosey, Anna froze them out. The Clark's intimate circle learned to hint at nothing, eliding the young man apart from addressing Huguette as "Mrs. Gower."

For the Clarks, it was a simple process of elimination: Life went on as it always had.

To escape the worst months of winter, Anna insisted they return to Bellosguardo. Then it was back to New York for the first glorious days of May with pink budding trees all over the neighborhood. Huguette loved to inhale their delicately heady scent on long walks in the park. Right before sailing for France for the summer, Huguette went to Durand-Ruel and Sons to scoop up at discounted prices: Monet's *Les Trois Peupliers* and *Nymphéas, temps gris.*

Huguette stood before the paintings in an ivory Lanvin dress, diamond bracelets and brooch, and ivory cloche hat. Anna came up alongside, as fashionably turned out. The gallery manager watched the mother-daughter duo with fascination. He motioned for his assistant to stay in the storage room.

After several minutes of silence, Huguette gestured at the paintings. "Ah, nature... I adore Monet's dreamlike eye. I think these two will look splendid in my drawing room, don't you think? Or, perhaps this one from the waterlily series of 1907 for the dining room..."

She pointed with a gloved finger to *Nymphéas, temps gris.*

"You seem to have your father's eye. And you're smart to take advantage of the reduced prices. My, my, so unusual..." Anna whispered. "However, I wish you would choose a painting or two that have a bit more modernism or dash to them. Although, I say that, and yet, I adore Impressionism as well." She shrugged. "It reminds me of my youth. Such innocence and beauty. They're both lovely, *ma chérie*. You're buying quite a bit of art these days..."

"Yes, isn't it splendid? Father would be proud!"

In the back room, the manager was agog Mrs. Gower chose not one, but two spectacular paintings. "And this when people are still doing away with themselves because they've lost everything in the Crash!" hissed the thin man as he and his young assistant prepared the canvases for delivery.

"It boggles my mind how Mrs. Gower escaped financial ruin when it seems as if everyone was leveled at once. It's one thing to read about the Clark wealth in the newspaper and quite another to see it in action at such a time!"

The purchase of the paintings gave Huguette a lift. She departed the art gallery with head held high.

It's exactly as dear Daddy would've done: If one has a little extra money, then spend it on appreciating assets. And the best art, he always said, has an exquisite rate of return on one's original investment. Well done, me! I can't wait to show them to Monsieur Styka.

Huguette didn't have the moxie to simply show up wherever Gower was living. It never crossed her mind that she merely needed to seduce him back. After some months, he finally wrote a short note of apology sent with a dozen roses. Not a word of reconciliation.

Uncharacteristically, Huguette burned the note. She wanted no reminder of the pain, and the note explained nothing. She knew she would forgive in time because he hadn't been cruel, but it was too fresh right now. She wasn't surprised to hear he had done the same for Anna.

"It was a nice note, very apologetic. William indicated he has had a great loss. It's too bad. Would you like to read it?"

"*Non, Maman, merci.* I'm through with thinking about Bill Gower."

April 1930
Reno, Nevada

Upon the Clark's arrival in Reno, the locals were gobsmacked not by the presence of celebrity or fame in their midst—after all, Reno was notorious for quickie divorces for the wealthy and well-connected—instead, what truly made heads turn was how the Clarks operated.

Absolute exclusive extravagance.

Huguette had Arthur La Chappelle's Beverly Hills law office arrange maximum privacy for all the Reno proceedings. To gain residency, the entire top floor of the six-story Riverside Hotel along the Truckee River was booked solid for over three months. The hotel bill alone would amount to over $7,000.

The Clarks arrived forewarned and forearmed; the Riverside Hotel had an international reputation. The hot spot divorce locale was watched round the clock by the likes of: the Associated Press, *New York Daily News*, the United Press, the International News Service, and *The Sacramento Bee*. That hot summer of 1930, exclusive copy on the Gower divorce would be at the top of the list. Newsmen were on high alert for sightings.

Despite the Riverside Hotel designed for prolonged stays—with corner suites laid out purposely with kitchenettes and connecting rooms for children and servants—two suites were insufficient if one had no interest whatsoever being seen in the public hallways. *Oncle* Arthur worked his magic, and special permission was granted to the Clark's chef to use the hotel's kitchen. The suite's kitchenette was *entirely* inadequate. Anna and Huguette didn't plan on ever being seen dining in public in the backwater city.

"I feel as if we have royalty in our midst!" the hotel manager said, bemused by the Clark's lifestyle. "I've never seen the like in all my years..."

"We probably will neva see 'em, which is a cryin' shame as they's so famous and rich and all!" wailed a maid. "These towels are fer 'em, but my orders are to give 'em to their personal maid only, who's always waitin' fer me. I'm not to enter beyond the service elevator!"

Bleached blonde curls bounced as the hotel maid swept away with a stack of perfectly folded white towels.

On the top floor of the Riverside reigned only peace and tranquility. A lap dog barked now and then, and classical music could be heard, but all in all, it was serene and well-ordered. Every day during the quiet months of forced residency, Anna played the harp in a bedroom converted to a music room or played bridge in the suite's living room with Mesdames Marié and Sandré. Huguette preferred reading or painting in her suite.

Once a week or so, the Clarks left the hotel early in the morning to avoid pesky journalists. They went on chauffeured day trips with a stuffed picnic basket. Lake Tahoe was only twenty-two miles away, albeit on roads that could be unreliable or so rough they caused flat tires. They liked to see the forests, and the local historical sites that featured the gold rush, the pioneer trek west, or the westward expansion. It reminded Anna of William's stories. They also enjoyed the stunning vistas of the Sierra Nevada mountains. Huguette took photographs to see if anything could be turned into a painting.

Despite the interesting landscape, in late July the days dragged.

"Well, if we were gamblers, in this ridiculous 'Biggest Little City in the World,'" said Huguette, "this would be a *much* more fun experience... But, gambling has never interested me at all. Ah..., if only we could go to Bellosguardo for a week, a mere seven days, to escape the desert heat and experience the fresh Pacific air, now wouldn't that be nice?"

She took a sip of lemonade with mint, and rolled an ice cube around in her mouth even though she knew Anna would give a disapproving look.

"*Oui, bien sûr, ma chèrie...* But we're here to do an important job. Let's look forward to August and our double liberation: your divorce and our escape from Nevada."

Anna shuffled a deck of cards.

"Oh *Maman, tu es si drôle...* I too look forward to our liberation. I apologize for having to divorce my husband in this manner. I never wanted to be scandalous and yet here I am! Turning twenty-four and *already* a scandal."

Anna smiled without looking up, "*Oui,* here *we* are. I'm not sure I want this behavior to continue in future, however. Let's pick out a man who's on more solid footing next time, shall we?"

"I don't even want to *talk* about men right now!"

Huguette waved hands in denial while making a face of dread. Then she picked up "The Kreutzer" to practice. She kept the telegram sent from Europe in 1920 tucked into the case: "Darling... bought you the most wonderful violin in the world." During this time of seclusion and waiting, the Clarks relied heavily on musical talents to uplift spirits.

Largely absent from the social scene on either coast for over a year, Huguette noticed in her forwarded mail there had been a major drop in correspondence and invitations.

It doesn't matter. Once I get this divorce over with, it'll all smooth out. I'll be able to pick up where I left off and resume my life.

However, the next day she sent a telegram to nudge Styka in France. He hadn't replied to her letter sent weeks ago.

"Oh, he's probably vacationing at some gorgeous villa and not even reading his mail, but I can't help myself! I want to know if he'll be in New York this winter," Huguette said with a plaintive note.

She held out a hand to the Swedish maid—oblivious of the French language—who painted Huguette's nails scarlet.

"Why're you worried? You sound needy, which isn't like you. Sending him multiple communications might run the risk of perturbing. He indicated he'll be in New York in October. Leave it be," Anna said, while fixing Margot's folded over ear.

Margot's rheumy dark eyes looked up at Anna before she put her head listlessly between paws. Mops rolled over and sneezed.

"The heat is so hard on them, the poor, elderly things," Huguette said. Henry VIII lay at her feet, panting continuously. "August can't come soon enough!"

On August 11, Huguette woke with nausea and fear gripping her innards. Only the strong desire for freedom from the shame Gower had heaped on her urged forward movement.

She dressed carefully in a couture dove grey summer skirt suit, bespoke Italian open-toe heels in black leather, with a dove grey cloche hat. She wore a Cartier pearl necklace, bracelet, and earrings. She dutifully arrived early for the quick court proceedings which declared divorce on the grounds of desertion and infidelity.

The lawyers from her uncle's firm took care of all communication with the court, and Huguette sat primly at the table beside them. Anna and Marié sat directly behind, and Huguette knew the formidable Armstrong waited outside the doors, arms crossed protectively.

Gower did not appear, which Huguette counted on. She had received a letter from Larissa Lyle; the gossip was Gower and his mistress were in France.

"If only *I* could be on the Riviera right now instead of measly Reno," Huguette ruefully told Anna on the way to the courthouse. "Isn't that so like Bill?"

"Oh, the Riviera is gorgeous but entirely too full of people. It was much more pleasant twenty-five years ago or so when I first went with your father."

Huguette paused in thought before asking, "What would Daddy think of all this?"

"Your father?" Anna turned her head to Huguette as the Rolls glided to a stop. "At the first sign of trouble, he would've strung William Gower up by his scrotum. There never would've been a divorce."

Huguette burst out in shocked laughter. "Mother, how crass!"

If only Daddy were alive to help me with this.

As soon as the gavel rang down, the mother-daughter duo was up and out of the heavy wooden doors with Armstrong's impressive height and broad shoulders fending off the crowd. The chauffeur threatened to deck anyone with a camera.

The Clarks went straight to the station to board a private rail car bound for Los Angeles then Santa Barbara. There would only be a one-hour delay before departure. Huguette didn't mind. She finally felt like she could breathe.

Now officially a divorced woman bearing her maiden name once again, Huguette smiled through tears of relief. She missed Gower's friendly nature and companionship, but not the stress he had brought into her life.

I think I can live without him. It wasn't meant to be.

Huguette removed hat, heels, and gloves before stretching. On the tufted chintz couch, she put stockinged feet up and rested her head. She was emotionally exhausted. Upon arrival at Bellosguardo, she knew she would feel like kissing the ground.

No intrusive journalists could follow up the steep cliff beyond the gates. No demanding, needy, fawning men could come to bother. No one could access the beach, lawns, and gardens unless invited. Gossip, shame, and humiliation were held off somewhere below on Cabrillo Boulevard.

That's what I'm doing: convalescing. And now, I'm finally free to do as I choose. How lovely!

With head and heart cleared of the past, Huguette began preparing paintings for her second exhibition. It would be held at *Robinot Frères Salon* in the spring of the coming year. Huguette was nervous. The Parisian art crowd's opinion meant more.

After painting all morning, Huguette joined Anna to swim or golf at the Valley Club of Montecito. They had been members at the premier golf club since its inception the year previous. Although she chided Anna—who was the one who got her interested in the sport in the first place—Huguette enjoyed it. They both took lessons, but Anna devoted endless hours to mastery. She could easily outplay Huguette, Amelia, and Arthur.

One afternoon, after returning from a round of eighteen holes, Anna breezily suggested, "Why don't we go to Honolulu for a spell?"

"What a wonderful idea, *Maman*. I want nothing more than a coconut drink and a dip in Hanauma Bay."

"Then it's settled. I'll have Madame Marié take care of the travel details and we should be able to leave soon. Doesn't Hawai'i sound like heaven after months spent in a miserable state like Nevada? Your father loved the desert but as for me, not so much. Alas, plumerias and hibiscus cannot grow there, so, it's off to Honolulu *tout de suite*!"

October 1931
House-on-Hill, Hillsborough, California

"I'm looking forward to viewing the completed house," said Anna. "It's too bad it's such a foggy day. I can't abide Northern California for this reason."

Huguette pulled her chinchilla coat closer to ward off the chill seeping through the windows. The Rolls Royce Phantom I mounted the forested hilly roads of Hillsborough with ease.

"How did Celia come up with the house inspiration?"

"From what she's told me, while the girls were at Spence she was touring England with David Adler. She studied Tudor architecture, eventually returning to Hillsborough to commission Adler to design her vision of a Cotswold Tudor estate. She must've spent a fortune hiring Syrie Maugham as her decorator. The woman does nothing but spend money."

"Patsey told me the best feature of the house is being surrounded by endless acres of forested gardens. Olive trees, sunken gardens, ponds. She's ecstatic there is a huge stable. How beautiful it must be," said Huguette, sighting the wrought iron gates. "I think we've already arrived."

The cobblestone drive led to a square motor court before two stories with peaked roofs. The entry belied the expansiveness of the house tucked and folded ingeniously into the hillside. The luxury Tudor-style residence was only recently completed for $1,500,000. It would prove to be Adler's masterpiece, offering Celia and her children decades of restful solitude.

English interior designer Maugham, the "White Queen," brought in Chinese wall hangings, English hand-carved oak paneling, paintings by Van Dyck and Sir Joshua Reynolds, and her signature blending of pale neutrals offset by green. Maugham urged Celia to fill the house with the most expensive French and English antiques and paintings she could afford. The celebrated library had long green velvet curtains, and would, in future, be described as one of America's one hundred most beautiful rooms. Celia's high-ceilinged white and green bedroom was designed for an exquisitely modern woman. It was immediately photographed for a national magazine.

Anna had seen the write up about Celia's bedroom and was very curious about the rest. Soon after, Anna and Huguette were invited for a weekend.

Walking through the hand-carved door, Anna said, "*Bonjour*, Celia! I feel as if I'm in the English countryside." The women kissed hello.

"Welcome to House-on-Hill, my new treasure!" said Celia, wearing a cherry red Mainbocher dress.

Anna looked down the gallery. "I adore the black and white tiles. How gorgeously done. Celia, this house is going to be stunning, I can already tell."

"Thank you. I hope I won't bore you, but the tiles are laid end to end without mortar. I appreciate the optical illusion it gives." Moving down the hall, Celia said, "I know you'll want to see the crown jewel first, as both you ladies adore music. I don't think I would've invited you so soon if you didn't!"

Celia's high-pitched laughter and clacking heels filled the gallery.

Anna later remarked to Huguette, "This is the happiest I've ever seen the woman. Her marriage to Charlie really did her in for a long time, unfortunately! He must've been terrible! I know she held a grudge against poor William, but it wasn't his fault. He didn't want to become embroiled."

"I don't blame him," said Huguette.

Upon entering the 55-foot music room with layered shades of cream, white, and ivory, a 15-foot ceiling, and antique parquet de Versailles flooring, Anna was greeted by her step-granddaughters. Anna then looked around with admiration. Her eyes soon fell on the prominently displayed Boldini.

"Oh Celia, how exquisite! I wish I would've been clever enough to have one made all those years ago in Paris. It's too late now!"

Anna laughed.

"You're always so impressively stylish. Two steps ahead of everyone!"

"Oh, you do flatter, Anna."

Celia put hands together and examined the portrait.

"That was another life altogether," she said soberly with a faint smile. "Weren't we lovely way back when?"

Anna decided to distract her.

"I insist on a detailed tour if you wouldn't mind?"

"Of course, I would be happy to." Celia smiled once again, and turned to address the young women. "Girls, would you like to come?"

"No, Mom, we're going to play before dinner," said Mary who turned to join Agnes and Huguette at one of the two Steinways.

"We'll only be gone for a bit. Then I'd like to hear you all play."

Celia gestured to Anna to follow. While walking through the 35,000 square foot mansion, Celia pointed out key features and design elements.

"It's all very intricate work. Due to the depression, the plan was to involve as many workmen and artisans onsite as possible."

"And how long did construction last?" Anna said, very curious to soak up all the details.

"Oh, a good two years. It's not for the faint of heart!"

"And did you find the extra cost burdensome?"

"Oh no, I would do it again in a heartbeat. I had so many of the men thank me for the extended period of guaranteed work. It was very gratifying," said Celia with a hand to heart. "I've been so blessed, it was the least I could do to help."

After a half hour of touring—including a walk through the carmel-colored, wood-paneled room designed to mimic the card room on Celia's favorite ocean liner—she led Anna into her airy bedroom.

"And here is the famous bedroom for the queen of the manse," said Anna. "You're daring to have it photographed. I couldn't imagine! And the cut pile rug is by Marion Dorn?"

"You remember your details!"

"I'm not nearly as modern, but I admire your taste. It fits beautifully. This house is a masterpiece! Well done! I've been seriously considering redoing Bellosguardo for awhile now. You've given me ample food for thought in what I want."

"I'm happy to hear that. I would love to see what you decide on for a remodel."

"Actually, I would like to rebuild from the ground up. House-on-Hill is such a vision with so many historical English references. Perhaps you wouldn't mind helping me sort out my vision for a French-inspired Bellosguardo?"

"Oh, I would be delighted, Anna. Building houses is one of the most wonderful legacies one can leave one's children."

"Hmm, yes, I've heard that before."

Over the course of the next eighteen months, the Great Depression deepened with newspaper and radio programs reporting escalating hardships. Frequently, the Clarks were amongst the most generous at charity events or when donations were called for.

During a charity match at the Santa Barbara Polo Club while riders thundered past on Fleischmann Field, Anna said "Despite the nuisance, I think it's time to build a new house. We can stay at the Biltmore while Bellosguardo is transformed. How does that sound?"

"*D'accord, Maman*, I'm sure whatever you decide will turn out to be splendid. You have beautiful taste. Have you been conferring with Celia?"

"I have. She's been most inspirational. But my vision is more French."

"House-on-Hill is lovely, but you want something more like a *château, peut être*? I'm happy to contribute money to the cause. I can certainly give you anything required to cover the *palatial* studio that I expect," Huguette said with a wicked grin. Her eyes flicked from Anna to a particular player.

The dark-haired polo player who had caught her attention was Alejandro Gael Herrera Medina. Heir to a massive fortune from numerous sugar plantations and cattle ranches, Herrera had abundant means to travel the globe with a fleet of ponies playing polo almost professionally. The splendid command of his horse and the powerful swing of the mallet with a muscled arm at precisely the right moment had many watching with admiration. The athlete stood out even amongst the best players on the field.

"Isn't he fabulous? He was at the Amundson's party last Friday, remember? He's Argentinian, from Buenos Aires, I've heard. I'd like to paint someone that alive. Maybe I should brush up on my Spanish instead of all the Italian lessons I've been taking!"

"Hmm, *oui, il est très beau...* I confess I'm surprised to hear you admiring a handsome man. You've been so quiet lately, I thought you had sworn them off." Anna waited for a reply but her daughter said nothing. "By all accounts, that actress over there is after him."

She discreetly indicated an attractive young woman standing across the field dressed all in fashionable white: knee-length dress, heels, hat.

"In any case, if you're paying attention to my plans, I've met regularly with Mr. Clarke. He's advised me on solid investments which have been lucrative. I'll be fine covering the entire cost of construction myself. *And* your studio, *bien sûr.* I know better than to forget to inform the architect about that requirement."

As the players shifted on the field and went racing past once again, Huguette quickly set a thin slice of baguette with *paté* onto a plate to cheer with the crowd. "Isn't this an outstanding match?"

"Perhaps you should discuss your requirements with Mr. Johnson, as well? To ensure the studio has all you require. And have you met with Mr. Clarke in the past twelve months? I think you're plenty old enough to do that on a regular basis yourself. Your fortune requires attention."

"Can't my lawyer and accountant meet with Mr. Clarke? I can read the reports and make a decision afterwards. Oh good, they scored again!"

Attention on the field, Huguette began clapping. The crowd cheered loudly. Herrera—standing in stirrups and raising a mallet in triumph—raced his pony across the field. A number of local players were clearly not pleased with the man's athletic prowess.

In a planning meeting with Reginald Johnson, Anna set her amplifier on the polished wood conference table. She said, "I want a house constructed of the finest quality materials and technology available today that is quake-proof *and* beautiful. I also require as many human hands as possible to reap the benefits of a steady paycheck. Don't cut short or rush anything, as I'm sure the project will take some time. Many artisans will be required to do the intricate work I want.

"You see, I have some experience with building grand houses from my late husband..." Anna smiled at the memory of William's mania.

"And you *shall* have a beautiful house, Mrs. Clark," said Johnson in a loud tone of voice while leaning forward. He looked down at the amplifier, hoping he was being clear. "Bless you for doing this. I might be stretched stylistically with this project. You've had quite the education, it appears!"

With no budget constraints, it would be a dream project for Johnson. He grinned broadly, eager to take on the commission.

"And what a site to build on: A 24-acre, hilltop property with 1,000 feet of unobstructed, oceanfront views to maximize. It has the capability to be the finest house in the region!"

A month later Anna returned to look over blueprints. Johnson spoke while indicating with his finger the areas he referred to. "I'll raze the 25,000 square foot structure from 1903 and build a slightly smaller, 22,000 square foot house here. Construction will take about 36 months, if I calculate correctly. I'm pleased the views will remain unobstructed and private, largely thanks to the 31-acre bird refuge situated here."

Johnson grinned, taking his finger off the map. "I bet the city didn't appreciate all the constraints."

"My daughter donated money to create the refuge, named for my deceased daughter. And of course, Huguette made a point to guide the city. The refuge is strictly off limits to any touristic interests."

"That was wise. Consider, Mrs. Clark," Johnson then pulled over another map. He pointed, "The refuge is here... the view of the Santa Ynez mountains, the bordering cemetery here.... and the nearby town of Montecito. These landmarks and natural borders all ensure exclusivity and privacy. The property value will only increase in time."

"As it should! My husband well-knew a prime piece of property."

The new Bellosguardo would be an elegant oasis. Following Anna's vision, Johnson designed the completed structure to be unabashedly formal: A French-inspired villa with parquet de Versailles floors, marble fireplaces in rich hues, and tall ceilings with antique chandeliers. The 16-inch walls were constructed of reinforced concrete sheathed in 3-inch-thick Indiana limestone. U-shaped, with 27 rooms and 13 chimneys, there were bedroom suites for mother and daughter, and 4 guest bedrooms with ensuite baths. The dining room, library, and *bureau* all displayed unpainted ornately carved boiserie from Sherwood Forest whose 167 panels originally graced William's dining room on Fifth Avenue.

The grandest space—to indicate music's place of prominence in the Clark's lives—was the acoustically perfect music room. Their instrument collection was on display: several Steinways, Stradivarii violins, and multiple Érard forty-seven string double action concert harps in the Gothic Revival style. For card or chess players, a game table in a corner of the room was meant for hours of entertainment. Anna studied how to improve her bridge game; it had become competitive with circles of female friends on both coasts.

Looking over a list of Huguette's specifications, Johnson designed a two-story artist's suite oriented toward the back of the right-hand wing. The ground-floor studio with plain oak-pegged floors featured excellent natural light with a seventeen-foot ceiling and an enormous rear window facing the gardens and mountains. A second window on the right gave a view out onto the lawns. In order for the painter to be accommodated throughout long workdays, a kitchenette, half bath with silver leaf ceiling, and a large loft closet for storing art supplies and canvases were close at hand. A private staircase accessed the bedroom suite directly above.

The suites for mother and daughter had a sitting room with marble fireplace, dressing room with book-matched bird's eye maple, and bathrooms with marble tubs and swan or dolphin gold fixtures. Anna chose a double-sized bathtub made out of a solid hunk of pink Carrera marble flecked with gold. For the bedroom and sitting room, she chose jade silk damask for the double bed's upholstered wood frame, curtains, chairs, and down-filled chaise. From the bedroom, she could enter an acoustically perfect, small music room or walk out onto a balcony with expansive views of the ocean.

Reminding her of the water, Huguette selected blue for carpets, bed, curtains, and furniture upholstery throughout her suite. She had views of the rose garden and the ocean. For her doll companions, she commissioned twelve petite Empire-style chairs.

At the front of the house on the motor court, a large, botanical mosaic had been hand-laid with white, grey, and black beach stones which never failed to charm guests. The chauffeur was instructed to direct delivery trucks to the rear entrance. Anna was concerned heavy, oil-spilling trucks had the potential to crush or crack the stones.

To look its best, Bellosguardo required 20 gardeners, 2 painters, 2 plumbers, a French chef, an English butler, a housekeeper, and team of maids. The service area of the mansion was extensive. There was the kitchen in which the French chef was deity. The housekeeper and butler took care of the staff and the house. The architect made their jobs easier by planning for a: pantry, butler's pantry, meat locker, pastry room, tray storage room, flower room, laundry room, staff dining room, houseman's office, housekeeper's office, and butler's office.

"It's quite an experience to be invited to Anna's American *château*," said Styka at a dinner party in 8W. "Any dirty item from your journey is immediately washed and pressed. The bed turned down every night, made up with new D. Porthault linens the next morning. The latest bestsellers, plus international and domestic newspapers and magazines laid out. If I'm hungry? A basket of fruit is nearby or I can ring for a tray. Waterford pen, Smythson stationery, and stamps in the desk. The bathroom is full of the softest towels known to man, and toiletry items for any grooming ritual. I could go on! I prefer staying at Bellosguardo to the Ritz, I assure you."

Styka put a cigarette to his mouth and inhaled deeply. He continued with a wry smile, "And I always gain weight. Even as a younger man doing the family's portraits... with the chef's talent, being on a diet while visiting Bellosguardo is *not* recommended!"

"Don't blame me for your gluttony!" Anna said, laughing while sitting down on the sofa by Amelia and Bryce.

Amanda Storrs twirled the ice in her cut crystal glass. "Anna, the house reminds one of how Europe was *before* the war. Of course, that was by design."

"*Oui*, that was my intention. I'm pleased you both enjoy Bellosguardo. You must come again soon."

By 1937 with Bellosguardo completed, the Clark's routine was cemented into annual tradition. They wintered in New York, sailed to Europe for late spring and fall trips, and summered at Bellosguardo. Occasional visits to other locales were sprinkled in whenever the mood struck. Regarding Bellosguardo, the Clark women followed their whim. Any season of the year, Anna would nudge Huguette and they would hop on a private rail car at Penn Station to head out. As rail technology improved, arrival in Santa Barbara occurred faster and faster, which meant they would sometimes hardly give notice before arriving.

As soon as apprised by the chauffeur who was called to collect the women at the station, or if by chance they were lucky and Marié alerted them from Los Angeles, Bellosguardo's housekeeper and butler bellowed for all staff to report. To meet Anna's standards, numerous rooms required immediate freshening. Everyone raced around wildly tearing off innumerable dust covers, opening windows, plumping pillows, arranging flowers, vacuuming.

"Did you bring a white glove? Go get one if you haven't got it," said the head maid rushing up the stairs with two junior maids following. Meanwhile, the housekeeper would dial up the local grocery, "I need an immediate delivery of Bibb lettuce, lamb, shallots,..."

The English butler, Mr. Morton, would wave to the chauffeur from the front door, "Drive slowly, good man!" before scrambling to oversee the setting of the dining room table with flowers, Baccarat crystal, and gilded china.

Then Anna and Huguette would arrive, leisurely easing themselves out of the Rolls and walking up front steps, all smiles and cheer—with several Pekinese at their heels—none the wiser their spontaneity was quite a chore.

Mr. Morton breathed hard from rushing to the front door. He calmed himself before saying, "Good day, Madame Clark. How was your journey?"

"Oh, hello, Mr. Morton. I do hope you're well. The trip was fine. I wanted to inform you I plan on hosting a dinner."

Anna eased off gloves and hat, handing them to a maid. Young, petite Pekinese raced past, barking excited greetings. Henry VIII was so beloved, before the dog died he had been immortalized with Anna holding him in a portrait by Styka.

"Tonight, ma'am?"

Mr. Morton eyed her nervously, hoping he wasn't sweating. Shrill barking pierced tender eardrums as the dogs returned.

If only madame would stop acquiring small breeds...

"Oh, no. The party's tomorrow, seventy-thirty. For ten. My step-granddaughters, Agnes and Patsey and their husbands and mother, Celia Tobin Clark, and the marquis Etienne de Villermont will all be arriving tomorrow. And oh yes, my sister, Mrs. Turner, and her husband, Bryce, as well. They will arrive first, late this evening."

"We'll prepare a room, madame."

Anna walked down the hall towards the library, the dogs and Morton following.

"I want the Turners put in the guest room by mine, as usual. Please inform the housekeeper I'll be in the *bureau. Merci!*"

Since returning to New York a divorced woman, Huguette ignored her hurt over Gower by nourishing interest in the attentive but elusive Styka. Winters with late morning painting lessons up to four times weekly were a cherished season.

Styka remained the perfect man, in Huguette's opinion; his aristocratic air only added to numerous attractions. She was drawn to his illustrious European heritage, and privately wished she had the same high-born blood. Without anyone explaining, Huguette understood she had the right money, the right culture, and the right connections—even a fashionable figure and looks—however, she lacked a prestigious bloodline.

The hours in his studio passed too quickly.

"Despite my full social calendar—watching Patsey Grey compete in horse shows or visiting family, for example—I'm a lizard lazing about in the hot sun at Bellosguardo. However, in the city I'm reborn, a workaholic. All because of you, *cher maître!*"

"Oh, I see what I've become now. I'm the one to blame!" said Styka, mixing paints at a table in a corner. "Just to remind you of my latent talents... See that drawer right there?" He pointed with a mixing knife covered in carmine. "It holds a great deal of dimes from every time you've lost a bet, my dear Mrs. Clark. And I believe that jar is *plum full* at the moment..."

Huguette laughed, putting a hand to mouth as she watched him from a stool in the center of the studio. "You're too clever for me." She sighed with pleasure to be with him, examining the large canvas in front of her. "I think this must be my fifth painting this winter."

"That's good! If only the economy would improve enough to organize another exhibition in Paris. If not, I'll have to live off that dime collection."

"Hmmm... New York reinvigorates me! As do your lessons... Imagine, I've shown my work at three exhibitions thus far."

"And there will be more..." Styka worked azure with a mixing knife. "New York is unique. I feel subtle shifts from London to Paris to New York. Painters always discuss the difference in the light, but for me, it's likewise the culture and the language that influence my work."

Styka assumed his pupil was an experienced woman; he felt free to book nude male models. During 1933, he had enough free time on his hands to set up a canvas to capture his star pupil painting a muscled male posterior. Styka tinkered with it before finally allowing Huguette to see the painting.

Before noticing Styka's devilish grin, she blushed a little to see herself on a canvas beside a nude man. "Monsieur Styka, *you* are incorrigible! Is that how you see me?"

"Whatever can you mean? This is a chaste work! The local cathedral has asked to purchase it," said Styka, wondering if she would finally display some anger.

His European sensibilities longed to crack open Huguette's girlish, even prudish, reserve that remained like an old coat despite her divorced status. But he didn't want to be responsible for the consequences; he was too independent to burden himself with such a wife. She could provide materially enough to make him a king, yet his romantic spirit valued freedom more.

Depending on the season of the year, he could be somewhat torn. Money was always an issue. Despite baiting Huguette a little, he never wanted to do anything that might jeopardize a wealthy client during such constrained economic times.

"It's well-done, nonetheless." Huguette put her nose in the air and said imperiously, "I'll buy it. If only to hide it!"

"Ready to part with a painting of my favorite, my most gifted student hard at work in my studio? Not paying attention to seductive distractions? Never!"

"Hmmm, we shall see about that." She grinned back at him.

Huguette departed wanting to dance down the steps. Her chaperone wouldn't have approved, nor would Anna. All these years later, Anna held fast to dissuading her daughter from making another mistake. Amanda Storrs, now that her husband's health was failing, was frequently escorted by Styka about town. Amanda confessed all the gossipy tidbits to Anna, who was titillated but didn't want her daughter involved.

Commissions for portraits trickled in, which was disturbing. Even Europe felt the pinch from America's depression. Styka desperately needed the Clark's social capital to make up the difference.

"I even allow you to have key hours of the day for good light that, for a lesser client, I would've turned down flat."

"*Cher maître, merci beaucoup!*" Huguette's eyes did not hide their adoration when they were alone in his studio.

Then came the day Huguette would never forget. The lesson was over; she was wiping brushes at the sink when the doorbell rang. Soon she heard a young woman's high-pitched laughter. Taking up the canvas and giving Sandré a large tote, Huguette walked in the direction of voices.

Standing in the foyer was a tall, striking woman with black hair and light blue eyes. She had the type of unforgettable face Styka adored capturing on canvas. The young woman was dressed beautifully and animatedly talking.

She's here for a lesson too?

Huguette frowned slightly; in a snap she became the older woman wearing brown tweed and sensible shoes. She knew Styka was always with such gorgeous women—in fact, on two or three continents—but it was her first time coming unexpectedly face-to-face with the competition.

Uncharacteristically, Styka paid almost no attention to Huguette's departure. She was rapidly introduced to "Miss Foster, a fashion model." Throughout, Styka and Foster stood face-to-face, oblivious to anyone else. Huguette passed into the outer hallway and the maid shut the door on the scene.

Looking at the closed door, Huguette felt an immediate pang in her heart. *I've never before witnessed Styka so taken with a woman. What could this mean?* Despite all the nights he had squired her around Manhattan, such an interaction had never happened between them. *His eyes were riveted on Ms. Foster.* Tears sprang up and she took a deep breath to control herself. In the car, she averted her face from Sandré; she did not want *Maman* hearing about this.

The loss of hope was soothed by Styka's continued attentions and never hearing about Ms. Foster again. He was almost always available to eat dinner at Anna's. Afterwards, he played a game of bridge or listened with admiration to their playing. Together, they went to concerts, art galleries, plays, and fashion shows. Styka frequently accompanied them to Penn Station, always giving chocolates and corsages before they boarded. Huguette nursed hers to make the delicate lavender orchids last as long as possible.

Even *tante* Amelia fell under Styka's spell, inviting him to celebrate Thanksgiving. "After all, he did such a wonderful job painting me, I feel indebted for life!

Bryce thinks the portrait is better than his favorite photograph. He wants another one but balks at the price you paid. Would you like more tea?"

"*Non, merci*. Styka commented how much we look alike now," said Anna.

"*Oui*, isn't that funny...? But you've been here for twenty minutes, and you haven't told me a thing about your evening with Edward." Amelia settled back in the chintz overstuffed chair. "I want all the romantic details, *s'il te plaît!*"

Anna had recently begun dating Edward Bowes, the famous radio personality of NBC's staple show, *Original Amateur Hour*. Major Bowes, the proud master of ceremonies, began the hit program at Radio City Station in 1934. Anna was delighted to meet Bowes at a charity ball.

"I do very much admire your nurturing of young talent. Well done! My daughter and I love the catchphrase 'The wheel of fortune goes 'round and 'round, where she stops, nobody knows.' We say it to each other at the oddest moments. It always makes me chuckle. And my daughter sometimes sends in postcards to vote."

"Thank you, Mrs. Clark. I'm gratified to hear you say that. May I sit down to join you at your table? Do you mind? I'd like to continue talking."

"Why, of course, Major Bowes. It would be a pleasure."

"Please, call me Edward." He gave Anna a smile and took her hand in his large one to kiss it. He smelled of aftershave and peppermints.

Anna was a little surprised at Bowes's marked attention. Many months later at lunch she said, "I think you should be aware I've no intention of every remarrying. Nevertheless, I do very much enjoy your company, Edward."

"Anna, that's foolish. I'm a wealthy, widowed Catholic man who enjoys music, cards, and fine art. What more can you ask for?" Bowes splayed large hands as if it were a given. "We're perfect for one another!"

Within a year, Bowes was so crazy about Anna he bestowed both a five-carat yellow diamond ring and an autographed, framed photograph. "What more do you need? A ring and me. It's fate, sweetie."

Anna displayed the photograph in her Fifth Avenue music room and wore the diamond every day. But she did not relent.

On Thanksgiving that year, Amelia looked with satisfaction around the table laden with Tiffany china, crystal, tall silver candlesticks, and flowers in her Park

Avenue dining room. Bowes was charming and Anna cheerful. Huguette was seated by Styka, and since both were reserved, they fit well together. To Amelia, it was readily apparent they made a nice set of three couples. Amelia knew her sister would be a hard sell for Bowes, but it was high time Huguette settled down with a man who could understand her ways.

"Who knows, Bryce," said Amelia while spreading Pond's cold cream on late that evening, "perhaps Mr. Styka will come around one of these years and marry Huguette? How long has he been acquainted with the family now? Oh heavens, so many years. And think of it! They're both artists, both *wonderful* painters. He speaks French, lives on and off in France, tells the most divine stories about eccentric clients... He's so funny."

She dabbed at eyelids. "It could work! It's *very* obvious to *me* she's in love with him..." Amelia wiped off cold cream with a cotton ball while looking at her husband in the mirror's reflection.

Bryce rested his bald head back on pillows. "He's not in love with her. Trust me. *Stay out of it*, busy bee. You know how your sister feels."

He scowled and moved to turn off the bedside light. He didn't want his wife's feelings hurt when Anna gave a dressing down.

❧ ⚜ ☙

On a routine basis, Styka took Huguette to the theater or the opera. They saw *Carmen* and *La Bohème*. Wanting to expose his pupil to the seamier side of life, Styka escorted Huguette places she would never have gone alone. She took in all the newness, frequent socializing, and late nights without a murmur of complaint. They attended the showgirl extravaganza *Folies de Femmes* at the French Casino on 7th Avenue and 50th Street. The cabaret show began in Paris, went to London, and then played in New York in the summer of '36. Another evening, Styka took Huguette with his brother and sister-in-law to see a Hindu dancer at a top venue.

Naturally, Styka sought after all the hot spots where New York's elite swarmed. It was good advertisement. Wearing white or black tie as was called for, with a white gardenia in the lapel, the dapper Styka enjoyed the stares. Even better, exclusive venues not as apt to admit him or give the best table, fell all over themselves when Mrs. Huguette Clark was mentioned. Her name opened any door, granted any desire. As soon as they were seated at the toniest restaurants, complimentary champagne and caviar arrived with white glove service.

Styka's interests varied, and they ranged all over the city. Any given evening he might select a movie premier, Broadway play, or concert. He frequently escorted Huguette to his favorite cabaret, Versailles, on 151 East 50th Street. While they ate, continental reviews were performed by showgirls three times a night. Desi Arnaz with Cuban flair led the house orchestra for the thronged dance floor before he moved on to Hollywood in 1939; Judy Garland and other celebrities sang; Edith Piaf came from France.

After a show or the theater, Styka would frequently select dinner and dancing at the Rainbow Room at 30 Rockefeller Plaza at Rockefeller Center in Midtown. To reach the sixty-fifth floor, they took one of the eight new express elevators on their first visit.

"Gee, this is the fastest elevator ride I've ever experienced!" giggled Huguette, placing a gloved hand on stomach as she whooshed higher than ever imagined.

"*Oui*, it's really something, isn't it? Good thing I haven't eaten anything yet!" Styka said.

Once in the restaurant, the sparkling lights of New York laid out below enchanted. "It's so much better than the view from my apartment," she murmured so quietly only Styka could hear.

"There's an observation deck, if you want to go up."

"Maybe later," Huguette said, as they walked into the restaurant with flattering indirect lighting. "I'm hungry."

Powerful and wealthy heads turned like swivels to observe the handsome couple escorted to a choice table. Guests such as the Whitneys, Auchinclosses, Kennedys, Astors, and European royalty dined in the lofty Rainbow Room's air conditioning.

While slicing rare meat, a balding man with deep jowls indicated with his head. "You see who's being seated over there? That painter is a clever man. He'll catch that Clark heiress one of these years. The little lady has more money than she knows what to do with. I read she receives $500,000 a year. A pity.

"Consider, what does she know? Money like that should be invested in *my* businesses. In any case, for some lucky chap much younger than I, she's ripe for the picking."

One of the balding man's dinner companions replied, "If so, he'll be set for life!" He swore. "What she's got is better than my trust fund, boys! I need a fresh infusion!"

"Hold your horses, if he doesn't get around to the deed soon, maybe I'll take a stab at it!" said a widower with a full head of white hair and a perfectly cut tuxedo.

Rude laughter went around the table of the three men dining on Roast Prime Ribs, Roast of Ontario Beef, *au jus*, and Yorkshire Pudding.

When the Ziegfeld Follies tour was announced, Styka bought advance tickets. After the celebrated show, they walked out into the crowded, red velvet lobby.

"Wasn't that marvelous? The Nicholas Brothers' tap dancing is superb. The way they can move!" said Styka, shaking his pomaded blonde head in admiration.

"Yes, it was wonderful. And no wonder Josephine Baker is a hit in France. She has such a voice," said Huguette, holding a mink with a silver clutch. "I'm so glad we came."

On the packed street, they entered the Rolls idling on the curb to head to *La Maisonette Russe* at the St. Regis Hotel at 2 East 55th Street. The 18-story *Beaux-Arts* style hotel with a limestone façade was built by John Jacob Astor IV. That night, Russian-born aristocrat Prince Serge Obolensky, Vincent Astor's former brother-in-law, was also at *La Maisonette Russe*.

The prince stopped to greet Styka warmly and they fell into conversation about mutual acquaintances. Despite a beautiful woman on the prince's arm, Obolensky brazenly scanned Huguette from head-to-toe. He smiled as soon as he caught her eye. She lowered her gaze to take a nervous drag on a cigarette.

As soon as Obolensky left, Styka said, "Well, well, well, you must look very fetching tonight. The prince could not keep his eyes off you."

"Oh stop! That's ridiculous. The woman he was with is ten times better looking than I." Huguette did not want to discuss men with Styka.

"*Peut être*. But he wasn't staring at her... Let's dance, shall we?" Styka stubbed out a cigarette and offered his arm.

Huguette had spent a good deal of time and money attempting to appear more attractive and sophisticated. She studied how to act nonchalant, as if she were out on a regular basis with men such as he. Using Styka as her guide, Huguette went with the flow wherever they went.

Styka was the epitome of a cosmopolitan companion. Middle-aged but appearing younger, he possessed a world-weary spirit. To Huguette, the artist had seen and done everything; popular and sought after, he knew everyone. It was a dizzying experience to be out with him. People stared. Huguette felt eyes raking over every aspect of her appearance. Some whispered rudely; some tried to draw her out; some ignored her. The majority of women blatantly flirted with the attractive, single painter as if she weren't standing beside him.

It was a whirl to Huguette, who only went to these glamorous places because she was escorted by Styka. For anyone else, she would have turned them down without a thought. The high-profile Versailles cabaret or the Rainbow Room was never the place to go to avoid attention, nor was she entirely comfortable. But when asked, she gladly donned a bias-cut white or black satin gown, slipped on Cartier diamonds, swiped on red lipstick and mascara under penciled eyebrows, and grabbed a chinchilla. Off she went, wishing he would touch her one of these nights.

Huguette knew she was attractive, but only passably pretty. New York was thronged with stunningly glamorous women seeking a way to get ahead. Huguette's response was to include in her twice-annual couture orders far more sophisticated evening wear than she had ever worn. Anna raised eyebrows a little when the latest slinky Jean Patou was unboxed in Huguette's sitting room.

"My, my, aren't we the seductress in *that* bias-cut black satin gown. At least you've the perfect figure for it."

"Isn't it lovely?"

Huguette ran a hand down the satin, loving the feel on her skin. She reached for the new bottle of Joy *parfum* sent along with the order and dabbed numerous times on her wrists and neck.

"I suppose that's for a night out with Monsieur Styka? I think you've put too much perfume on." Anna sighed, and after a moment, rose from the sofa. She didn't want an argument to start.

In the mirror's reflection, Huguette watched her mother depart. She took another good look at herself before slipping off the gown and passing it to her maid. They had been out so much in the past twenty-four months, Styka had seen all of her gowns. She didn't regret the bold move.

When out, Huguette conversed mainly with Styka. With acquaintances or strangers, she could be politely standoffish or blatantly ignore someone she felt threatened by. Despite her introverted nature, *couture* gowns, Cartier, and Russian sables spoke volumes. Everyone in the nightclub or theater knew who Tadé Styka was escorting that evening. And how much she had in the bank.

For cash-strapped Americans dreaming of a better life, reports—whether fabricated or truthful—of how much cash one of the wealthiest heiresses in the country commanded on a daily basis were still fodder. Some Americans reminisced how easy life had seemed in the twenties when money was abundant. Coveting eyes tracked Huguette across night clubs, restaurants, dancefloors, and opera houses. Scheming, watching, waiting for a break.

Some nights, Huguette could almost feel the hands reaching to snatch at her. *It's Daddy's wealth they crave.*

She could sense a fortune-hunter like a fox tearing through foggy, early-morning woods vigorously pursued by hounds. And when confronted brazenly, she learned to be wily and nimble-footed. Worst case scenario: She played possum.

"If you don't mind my saying, Mrs. Clark, they're like circling hyenas! Some nights I wonder if I should serve as your bodyguard," said Styka at a table in the Versailles nightclub.

"Oh, that reminds me of Papa. Don't you remember all those bodyguards?"

"*Bien sûr*! And now I comprehend your father's worry," said Styka, shaking his head in disbelief at the rude behavior.

Men would continually attempt to separate Styka from Huguette. He couldn't leave their opera box to smoke; a stranger would slip in while he was out. At a party, a man would commandeer her attention, all but running her into a corner in an intense effort to hypnotize with his charm. On the dancefloor, a stranger would cut in. Styka would acquiesce, not wanting a public scene at what was a perfectly normal thing to do.

Huguette would be frantic, her face immobilizing into a frozen mask. She would dance stiffly and mutely with some European count in white tie or a handsome playboy. Avoiding eye contact, she easily sensed the man's angry frustration when she refused to comply to flattering entreaties.

The count probably does have a castle somewhere, but no money to live in it!

When the song ended, Huguette fled to Styka's table. Under such circumstances, he always stood waiting, one hand in a pant pocket with a cigarette dangling from his lip. If the count or actor or politician wouldn't desist, they would leave. Huguette apologized profusely once they reached the privacy of the vehicle.

"Nonsense. Say nothing, Mrs. Clark. It's abominably rude behavior, and it upsets me these types of men are so presumptuous."

Huguette hesitated before asking, "Mommy always says to live happily, one should live hidden. Do you believe that?"

"*Oui*, I do. Anna is a wise woman. I'm a social creature, as you well know, but I long for private time as well. I imagine it's quite difficult to incessantly read about oneself in the papers. All those fabrications and intrusions into one's private life..."

Styka's hazel eyes looked gently over at Huguette who was forlornly wrapped in black mink in the far corner.

That was the closest Styka would come to discussing Huguette's life circumstances. He well remembered the portrait completed by his predecessor: A petite, blonde girl in a blue and white striped dress seated on a garden bench. Blue eyes in a winsome face, the girl cradled a favorite doll. When Styka examined the early portrait hanging at Bellosguardo, it seemed as if it were from another world. A world of charm, grace, and respected boundaries.

She has lost that innocence forever. Her wealth could destroy her someday.

They stepped out of the elevator and stood outside 12W's door. Sandré opened the door and waited.

Styka said, "The good thing is, you recognize the fortune hunter's lack of manners for what it is. You're a wise woman who takes after her mother. I admire you. Until next time!"

He kissed Huguette's gloved hand and turned to reenter the elevator, the bronze doors closing on his handsome face.

The fleeting feeling to reach out to kiss him one of these evenings struck; but Huguette could never muster the courage. When she eventually discerned he was also squiring the younger Ms. Foster, that squashed the desire into a lump deep inside.

I'll wait.

The next day, Styka sent a rose bouquet. Huguette had received many over the long years of close acquaintance with the painter. As usual, his flowers were placed in a choice spot in her bedroom. Except now the crimson blooms made her want to burst into tears.

For Styka, the platonic relationship with Mrs. Clark dangled like a golden carrot. In weak moments, he wavered. Despite knowing she was attracted to him, he held back due to his own romantic creed: Under no circumstances would he give in and marry a woman he didn't love. He was no fortune-hunter, and she inspired no passion.

Thus, to the loyal Styka, it was simple. *We'll remain good friends and fellow painters for life.*

October 1973
907 Fifth Avenue, New York City

The Irish housekeeper stepped into the dining room of 8W and softly cleared her throat. *Mrs. Clark startles so very easily!*

The rubber and leather beige nurse shoes Cynthia O'Henry wore entirely cushioned footfalls. The shoes were the only concession to modernity. At the age of seventy-two, O'Henry continued to dutifully wear the black cotton maid's uniform with starched, ruffled white apron.

"Mrs. Clark...?"

"Oh! Yes, Mrs. O'Henry, what is it?" Huguette's head jerked up from a card game laid out on the dining room table's glossy surface. *Her daughter must be here.*

"Sorry to disturb, but my daughter, Karen, has arrived. As you requested, I'm letting you know..." O'Henry hesitated a long moment to ascertain if Mrs. Clark were going to change her mind. "We'll be waiting in the kitchen. As soon as you have a moment."

"How nice Karen is able to visit today. I'll come now." Huguette carefully placed the cards down.

O'Henry noticed, as her sixty-seven-year-old employer rose from the table, Mrs. Clark had changed into a finer dress. A flowered lavender chiffon with a belt. O'Henry had picked the dress up from the drycleaners many times, and knew it was a favorite. She was pleased by the small gesture.

A half hour earlier, as Huguette stood adjusting the belt in the floor-length mirror, she immediately heard *Maman* remark as if she were standing behind in the doorway: "A chiffon dress in those colors in October in the city? I would change if I were you."

Well, I don't feel like following the rules today. I've a visitor coming and this is one of my most becoming dresses!

It had been a favorite since ordering it from *La maison Jean Patou* in 1950. That trip to Paris had been particularly wonderful, with fabulous couture collections and other delights shared with *Maman*. Huguette remembered it fondly.

I would like to go to Paris, but I don't want to go alone. Bill said he'd like me to visit. Maybe I should? It would be heaven, I'm sure. We'd have such fun!

Another memory surfaced as Huguette ran a hand down the skirt to straighten a fold. "Oh, you'll wear that Patou dress right out!" said *Maman*, this time from her deathbed. "Go put on another one I haven't seen a hundred times." Anna closed her eyes and waved a blue veined, emaciated arm in Huguette's direction.

Huguette had remained seated. *I'll wear what I want.*

She moved to the vanity to put on gold and diamond clip earrings before smoothing a curl beside her ear. She typically wore a modest gold necklace with a geometric or flowered Cartier brooch in diamonds and gemstones. She looked at her hair with satisfaction. Yesterday the traveling hairdresser from Kenneth Salon had freshened the champagne dye and trimmed the bob of curls she favored for years.

Maman *approved of that, at least.*

"Oh, you've tried a new hairstyle. It suits you. Curls are always becoming. If only I could rise from this bed and do something with what's left of my hair. Oh, dying is awful, *ma petite*. Don't fall for it." Anna sneezed hard, which set off coughing spasms.

Huguette cheerfully handed over a fresh handkerchief. "You're not going to die soon, *Maman*. Let's talk about something more pleasant."

O'Henry knew her mistress was a creature of habit, which made her job easier. The light strokes of rose rouge and lipstick, the classic red nails, the spritz of Joy, the gold and diamond jewelry, the ancient *haute couture*, the bespoke Italian heels. It was a uniform. However, O'Henry had the disagreeable task of filling in whenever the manicurist did not come to the standing weekly appointment with the hairdresser. She would look at the bottle of Revlon's Cherries in the Snow and sigh.

My shaky brushstrokes always mar it.

Then Mrs. Clark would wrinkle her nose. "Oh, that won't do. Take it off and try again, please."

At least Mrs. Clark was unfailingly polite. That was more than O'Henry could say for other Fifth Avenue employers who thought nothing of screaming in her face for the least infraction.

O'Henry darted to the side as Mrs. Clark rose from the table. O'Henry then picked up the silver salver that bore the remains of sardines on Saltines on a porcelain plate. Frequently she arrived in the mornings with a few bananas and a liter of milk, and every trip to Winter's Market or Gristedes, she stocked up on pantry staples: a sleeve of sardines packed in olive oil and two boxes of Saltines.

Heaven help me if I ever run out of Mrs. Clark's lunch! I'd be out the door even in a blizzard.

Mrs. Clark hesitated and gave her a look. O'Henry realized what she wanted. She quickly moved to walk first down the hallway.

I wonder how long it's been since she's seen someone face-to-face besides myself.

With a free hand, O'Henry reached to open a swinging door with half-moon brass plate. She was grateful Mrs. Clark chose to spend most of her time during the day in 8W. It had far fewer items and boxes and projects in it, which meant easier cleaning. Which was preferable, because her mistress had her frequently stepping out to withdraw cash from Chase for errands to FAO Schwartz for dolls or to Bloomingdales for stockings.

Lunch was basic, but for dinners, Mrs. Clark wanted baked fish or chicken with a dessert. Once or twice weekly, O'Henry would return from errands with a freshly baked *tarte aux pommes* or a *mille feuille*. She was surprised she enjoyed the desserts as much as her mistress, who always urged, "Eat it up!"

It was a frequent chore to organize dolls, accessories, and dollhouses, trying to dust in between and around the haphazard piles some rooms in 12W were choked by. In the early days, O'Henry had once rearranged the order of the boxes and piled up dolls, attempting to make it more appealing. It landed her in trouble.

So, Mrs. Clark does know what's here! I should respect her method.

Some days O'Henry would spend more time washing and ironing delicate doll clothing than she would linens and clothes. She was extremely careful with the doll clothing and jewelry made by Dior, Patou, and Cartier. Mrs. Clark had spent an hour one day telling her all about those treasures, and how long it took the French design houses to get the order right.

"I wanted them to use original eighteenth century fabric, you see. And it wasn't immediately available. They had to hunt the fabric down from the correct *atelier*. It was an intensely interesting procedure. I'm quite proud of the result!"

O'Henry had nodded as if she understood. In reality, she contemplated little about Mrs. Clark's quirks or life choices. O'Henry liked the woman, but professionally, she aimed solely at fulfilling her basic duties. It was the best placement she had ever had, even if it was with an eccentric mistress.

The first day working for Mrs. Clark, O'Henry was stunned to discover she would have not one, but *three* large apartments to care for.

"Mrs. O'Henry, did you hear me? I asked you a question." Huguette paused from writing out a list of chores.

"Yes, yes, Mrs. Clark... Forgive my silence. I heard you. I'll have duties as well in 8E *and* 12W. I'm simply surprised, ma'am. That's a first for me. I've never had to clean more than one apartment. You own three in this building?"

O'Henry's lined face devoid of makeup was slack with disbelief. *Why would she need three if it's just her? It boggles my mind to consider how much that must cost!*

"Oh, is it? I suppose I don't think about it... Is it too much?" Huguette put down the Waterford pen to face her new housekeeper with kind eyes. She was genuinely concerned the woman would balk at the work required.

Oh dear, will this work out? She seems perfect, and I don't want to go through the hassle of dealing with the hiring agency again!

"Well," said O'Henry with a concerned expression, "it depends on what you would like done in each of the apartments, ma'am."

"I bought 8E for privacy; I don't ever live in it. 12W is for my art projects, sleeping, and sometimes entertaining. If I have a visitor, I usually entertain in 12W's drawing room. I never have overnight guests these days. Don't worry about that.

"But I do go between 12W and 8W; they'll require the most work. However, *I don't tell anyone about that* because I like to keep my doings private. Can you remember? It's very important to me. When anyone calls, please remember, Mrs. O'Henry, to keep that information solely between us. I might have to pick the phone up in another apartment, you see."

O'Henry paused. "So, to review, I won't be deep cleaning 8E each week like I will 12W and 8W?"

"No, I don't suppose you will. But since it's just me, 12W and 8W don't get that dirty. You'll manage fine. If there are any issues, I can hire a part-time maid as well. I want 12W always ready to receive guests."

O'Henry thought the entertaining comment odd as the months passed into years and the front doors remained locked tight. *No wonder she doesn't need a butler...* It didn't appear her mistress ever entertained anyone in any of the three apartments.

The phone was used daily, and mail came in stacks, but she never had to open the door to any of Mrs. Clark's friends. *Maybe she's not up to entertaining these days?* But then it became clearer that what Mrs. Clark said she did and what actually happened were not the same. Besides workmen or a delivery boy or the Christmas volunteers in December, almost no one was admitted in all the years O'Henry worked at 907 Fifth. And precious few seemed to have the direct phone number to 12W or 8W. Mrs. Clark made many outgoing calls, however.

Updated in the sixties, O'Henry appreciated the renovations to the eighth floor. *Jeepers, it'll be a nuisance to work in 12W's kitchen.* When she first saw it, she was taken aback by the old appliances and overall antique appearance of everything. Then she was taken aback all afresh by *what wasn't there.* She stood alone in the center of the large room, gawking...

A woman with all that money and she can't be bothered to help out staff by purchasing new appliances every twenty years or so? Is that too much to ask?

O'Henry told her friends about the ancient kitchen, but they scarcely believed. "What woman doesn't want a brand-new Frigidaire?" said her best friend wearing a pink geometric scarf around pink and yellow curlers. "Are these ready to come out yet?" Her friend reached a hand to pat the dry curlers itching her scalp.

Early on Sunday mornings a group of O'Henry's friends sat around her Formica kitchen table with coffee, powdered sugar donuts, and cinnamon coffee cake. The women had all worked as maids on the Upper East Side at one point in their careers, and they liked to comment on "the crazy ways of the rich."

O'Henry rose to undo the pink scarf, saying, "Mrs. Clark can afford to do anything. Yet she does so little! She's a sweet shut in, fearful of leaving the building. With crime everywhere on the streets, how can I blame her?"

"Maybe you could buy her a new fridge with the fat Christmas bonus she gives you every year!" said her neighbor in a raspy smoker's laugh which filled the small kitchen.

O'Henry's expression said, "Can it." Still grinning at her joke, the neighbor picked up a stained ceramic mug of black coffee to take a drink.

Once O'Henry realized she was the only full-time worker, she began to worry about her vulnerable mistress. She worked six days a week but never lived at 907 Fifth Avenue. But it was Mrs. Clark who worried about her.

"You can't possibly go home on public transportation all the way to the Bronx every night. I won't hear of it. It's not safe for a woman. You'll take a car home through Carey Car Service. I'll pay for it."

Perks of the job... The aging O'Henry gratefully sank into the leather back seat to nap a bit before returning home to Wally and making dinner. She eventually worked reduced hours with two part-time maids picking up the heavy cleaning.

It worked out because the demands were low. Every year, Mrs. Clark begged her to delay retirement another twelve months.

As O'Henry passed into 8W's kitchen with Mrs. Clark trailing her, she smiled encouragingly at her youngest. *Despite her quirks, she's a fair employer. I hope Karen makes a good impression.*

O'Henry's daughter, Karen, stood by the white Formica counter drinking a glass of water. She was in her mid-thirties and wore her long strawberry blonde hair in a ponytail. She was dressed fashionably in a tan and orange Fair Isle sweater pulled down over a brown corduroy skirt with knee-high brown leather boots. Karen quickly put down the glass and plastered on a smile.

"Mrs. Clark, this is my daughter, Karen Lockwood, who was able to find the doll you've been looking for at Madame Alexander's. She's worked there for five years now. I'm very proud." O'Henry beamed with obvious dentures.

"Hello, Mrs. Clark."

Karen waved a hand awkwardly with a freckled smile. *Should I extend my hand? Would she even want to shake it, being a recluse and all?*

"Nice to meet you, Karen. I wanted to thank you personally for locating that particular doll for me," said Huguette. She stood five feet away and kept hands at her side. "I've been searching unsuccessfully for over six months. And look, you found her so quickly. You're the doll sleuth, I believe. I'll remember that in future."

Huguette smiled with genuine pleasure. The young woman had been able to locate the desired American doll in mint condition. Huguette assumed it was sold out, and she would have to wait until it surfaced at auction.

"Oh, it's no trouble. None at all! I'm happy to be of use to *somebody*." Karen twirled her ponytail and laughed loudly.

O'Henry knew Karen was referencing her troubled marriage. She hoped Karen wouldn't say a word more to Mrs. Clark about it. It would only upset her employer. O'Henry had tried to explain what an honor it was to be invited.

"You should feel special because she doesn't permit hardly anyone to see her. She has never talked with a stranger in person for as long as I've worked for her. And that's years now!"

"Then what does she do?" said Karen, leaning against the mirrored wall of the elevator.

"She'll talk on the phone, pass notes under doors, speak through the door, yes. But this? Requesting to meet you? Unheard of!" O'Henry shifted a paper bag of groceries in her arms. "Maybe it's because you're a younger woman and not a male? Mrs. Clark seems to avoid males... At least, I've never seen her deal with one face-to-face. Well, besides Dr. Pierre, of course. But he's the only one. Can't say I blame her. Anyway, Karen, sweetie, be on your very best behavior."

"Ma, I'm not a kid!" Karen rolled brown eyes as the service elevator halted on the eighth floor.

After a long moment of silence, Karen wracked her brain for something to ask. "Mother says you have quite the doll collection, Mrs. Clark. I wonder if it's better than Madame Alexander's?"

"I imagine hers is quite wonderful as well. Mine is suited to my personal tastes, which are international. Antique French mostly, one could say. But I love Barbies, too. There are always more treasures to pursue. Have you ever heard of Theriault's? They're marvelous if you're interested in antique bisque dolls as I am." Huguette sighed. "It must be such a pleasure to work at Madame Alexander's Doll Company. How lucky you are!" She suddenly had an expectant look, as if to urge Karen to talk more about it.

Karen didn't particularly care for the job but decided not to give her mother a heart attack by broadcasting that. She glanced over at her mom who was looking with a strange expression at Mrs. Clark.

"Oh, it's uh, fine... The dolls are really pretty. And so expensive! The top-of-the-line dolls or the custom ones, I mean. Which is groovy, if you've got the money. But they're thousands. Which is *a lot* of bread! But I like it okay and it pays decent. Good bennies."

At the mention of money, Huguette dropped her gaze. It struck her as odd how freely some people spoke of money. *It's rather vulgar.* She was at a loss how to respond.

The conversation stalled. O'Henry figured Mrs. Clark would make a run for it.

"How long have you collected dolls?" Karen plowed on, oblivious to Mrs. Clark's hesitation.

Huguette looked startled by the question, but offered thoughtfully, "Oh, I couldn't say. Probably since I was a child. I've a picture of myself as a very little girl sitting on the porch of my father's Butte house, surrounded by many dolls and Humpty Dumpty. All my treasures of the time. It's one of my favorites..." She wore a dreamy expression for a fleeting moment, before the wary rabbit face returned.

O'Henry had never seen the picture described. She wondered where it could be in the stacks and stacks of books and leather-bound albums scattered throughout all the apartments. She had so much work, there was no time to dawdle looking at pictures.

"Karen, I have to go now. I've something important I must attend to. But thank you again for locating the doll. I'm very pleased with it."

"You're so welcome, Mrs. Clark. I'm willing to help locate any doll you gotta have. I can use my employee discount. Bye-bye!" Karen waved cheerfully.

⚬   𝚿   ⚬

A week later, Huguette reminded O'Henry of an impending visit. "Etienne Villermont is coming to see me next week Thursday. It's on the calendar. At one o'clock for luncheon."

"Oh yes, Mrs. Clark, I remember. I've been buying things we need. The flowers will be delivered on Wednesday. I can buy most ingredients the day or two before. I'll buy the shad roe and oysters the morning of for the best quality."

"Well done! He's finicky about his food. Nothing but the very best for him... Do you think we'll manage with that new hot roller set I recently purchased? And could we give me a manicure?" said Huguette, looking down at chipped nails with a sigh.

"Yes, whatever you require." O'Henry saw the excitement on Mrs. Clark's face. "May I ask, ma'am, is Mr. Villermont a good friend?"

"Oh, yes! I've known him since we were children in France! He's as dear as a brother to me."

O'Henry nodded. *That explains why then!*

"Then I'll do my best to make sure everything goes smoothly during the luncheon. Would you like me to hire a server?"

"Yes, of course. I should have thought of that. *Merci.*"

Huguette hosted the luncheon for Villermont in 12W. She didn't want him in 8W commenting on Anna's things, *poking about like he owns the place*. She paced nervously in front of the drawing room windows before he was announced.

"My dear Huguette, look at you! As lovely as ever!" Villermont said, his eyes scanning her as he crossed the room.

Over five years since she had last seen him. Huguette became a little flustered at his height, at the way he strode purposely toward her. He kissed her warmly on both cheeks.

Villermont stepped back, warm hands on her shoulders. "This is the pink polka dot dress you wore in your latest Christmas photo, *oui*? I like it very much. Everything you wear is beautiful."

Their conversation was carried on in French. A mystified O'Henry stood for a few moments in the gallery eavesdropping. She had never seen her mistress so animated. *Even if I can't understand a lick of French, it's obvious he's special! Wonders never cease.*

"Etienne, how good of you to make time for me. It's been some years, hasn't it, since your last visit? Do sit down."

Villermont settled himself on an embroidered wingback chair. He patted the arm. "If you ever wake up and this chair has disappeared, you'll have to come to France to get it back!" He winked while crossing long legs in grey tweed trousers.

"Oh, Etienne, you've always preferred that one. It was one of *Maman's* favorites as well. How is everything with Elisabeth and your daughter? Did they come to New York this time?"

"Oh, they're fine." He waved a disinterested hand. "Marie is busy with school. Neither came this particular visit, but perhaps in the future. Would you like to meet them? It would entail a visit to France..." He baited her knowingly.

"Oh yes, that would be lovely. I long to go to France again! And to meet your wife after all these years. From her letters, I feel she's my friend, too."

Villermont pretended to believe her. "They would like to meet you as well. Elisabeth especially wanted me to thank you for the generous Christmas gifts the past few years. The money has helped enormously with raising our daughter. Maybe I should use it to buy myself some hair?"

He put a self-conscious hand up to a receding hairline.

"Oh, Etienne, you're as handsome as ever. And it's my pleasure! One must take care of one's children. I only wish they didn't outgrow the wonders of Au Nain Bleu so quickly! How long will you be in New York?"

Huguette smiled, completely at ease with small talk with such an old friend. Drinks were served before he answered.

"A week more. Elisabeth doesn't want me gone too long. She's bedridden so often these days. It's heartbreaking. Our neighbor is kind enough to care for her while I'm gone. Ah! I won't worry about that now! There is always so much to do and see in this marvelous city! Elisabeth really has no idea the kind of life I left behind to return to France, now does she?"

Huguette pretended to comprehend his meaning. "New York has many pleasures, but it must be heavenly to live in the French countryside. So peaceful."

Villermont didn't want to think about France. He leaned forward, almost reaching out to touch her knee.

"Come out with me! At least one evening, *ma chérie*."

Huguette shifted her body and uncrossed legs to put feet squarely on the vast Aubusson rug.

"*Peut être*. I've been meaning to make more of an effort to go to the opera or see a play."

"What have you seen lately? I miss the theater here!"

"Oh, I... I really can't recall at the moment. I've been waylaid by a little cold recently. I need to get back in the swing of things."

She glanced down, taking a drink for something to do.

"I'm sorry to hear that. You're well, *oui*?"

"Perfectly, *merci*."

"I would feel awful if you were ill and I were distant, across the Atlantic. You're too far away these days, Hugo."

He looked into her eyes, waiting. She was at a loss for something to say. O'Henry entered to inform luncheon was served. With relief, Huguette rose.

After several hours and five courses later, she fibbed and said she had another engagement that evening.

Villermont talks entirely too much! I'm exhausted from listening to his stories.

"Can I see you in a day or two? How about we go out to a wonderful restaurant? I'll ask around."

He stepped close, looking down into her eyes.

"I'll have to get back to you, Etienne. This is a busy time. Thank you for coming today. It was as lovely as ever to see you."

Villermont took Huguette in his arms in a warm embrace and kissed her forehead. She allowed it but stepped back as soon as he released her. Then he was gone, and she began devising excuses.

Sitting in 8W's library the next afternoon, Huguette was dwarfed by an enormous bouquet of red roses. The card read: *Cher Hugo, I can't wait to see you again. Let's have fun in New York like we used to! EV*

Huguette heard the phone ring and waited to know who was calling. *If it's Etienne, I won't pick up.* Mrs. O'Henry stepped into the room.

"Dr. Olivier Pierre on the phone for you, ma'am."

Huguette reached eagerly for the brass and polished wood receiver. "Dr. Pierre, *salut!* Thank you for getting back to me today. There's an urgent matter I need to discuss with you."

"Are you well? Should I come for a visit?"

"I'm quite well, thank you. It's Victoria who's in need of your services."

"Victoria? I'm not acquainted with—"

"You will be, Dr. Pierre. She's in serious need of repair. I can't bear to box her up and send her air mail to Au Nain Bleu. Are you familiar with that store in Paris, on *rue Saint Honoré*? Boxing Victoria up is too horrible to contemplate. Would you mind doing the honors? I have another appointment and cannot possibly go. There will be a plane ticket for you, Dr. Pierre, and another for Victoria. She would find the trip most amusing."

Huguette held the phone expectantly with a smile, knowing he would come through. Dr. Pierre stood at the desk in his home office on Park Avenue clutching the orange Bakelite phone, eyebrows raised in surprise.

"Forgive me, did I hear you correctly, Mrs. Clark? You want me to take one of your dolls to Paris for service?"

"Yes, Dr. Pierre, I would do it myself, but I cannot go this week. It's impossible with my schedule. And Victoria needs to be seen by the experts as soon as possible. Will you go in my place? I'll purchase two first-class Air France tickets on the day you indicate."

A long silence. Pierre pressed eyelids shut for a second while shaking his head. The heights of delusion unnerved him. *What a waste! A first-class ticket for a doll to go across the Atlantic... Yet Mrs. Clark is healthy and, I suspect, has a high IQ. She's harming no one. I will indeed deliver the doll to be repaired, but Simone will occupy the seat next to me. Mrs. Clark will be none the wiser.*

"I will be free by this Friday."

"*Merci beaucoup*, Dr. Pierre. Victoria thanks you as well! I'll have the tickets delivered tomorrow. Good-bye."

Fall 1938
Midtown, Manhattan

A young woman—frustrated once again to be out with three "old biddies in the family"—slouched at a table for four. Dramatically penciled eyebrows and pouting red mouth seemed to drag her long face downward even more. A strapless gown barely hung on her awkward frame. Hearing buzz behind, she turned to observe Huguette Clark and the marquis de Villermont escorted through the restaurant. She had read all about the woman in the society pages.

"Now why would *he* choose her? I mean, apart from her *millions...*"

Beside the young woman, the squinting eyes of a middle-aged bottle blonde scanned Huguette Clark wearing a black lace Chanel gown and diamonds. Gentle waves of natural blonde hair gleamed in a long bob; fashionably pointed nails painted scarlet stood out against a black satin clutch. The tanned woman looked every inch the über-wealthy, successful heiress.

A tall, attractive man with wide shoulders and brunette hair dressed in white tie walked beside her. He had one hand protectively on the famous woman's lower back for a moment. The handsome couple, escorted by the *maître d'hôtel* to a choice table off in another section of the restaurant, didn't look over in their direction.

The bottle blonde's attention went back to her food. She took a bite of meatball, and said while chewing, "Well, she's not as beautiful as Barbara Hutton by a long shot, who I saw last year at Musso & Frank's in Los Angeles, I think accompanied by a famous actor, but I really couldn't say. I never pay attention, as you know...

"But! Huguette Clark is very elegant. Her Chanel gown is *très chic*. Notice that despite her mother's grand house in California, she steers clear of Hollywood when her beau are concerned."

A pointed look directed then at the bottle blonde's young niece, who glared back because of the jab.

The bottle blonde continued, "As far as Huguette Clark's heritage... Well, a tangled web of long-time, French associates, that's for sure. Wouldn't it be nice to have such *caché*...? Maybe it would get me somewhere!"

Self-deprecating laugher. Raised black-penciled eyebrows and furrowed brow exaggerated wrinkled skin coated with Max Factor Pan-Cake Make Up. "Although frankly, I've never heard a good enough explanation as to *how exactly* she knows the marquis."

The bottle blonde's emaciated, elderly aunt with yellowed teeth spoke up after sitting silent for the past half hour. Her low voice rasped: "Through her mother's family. Her mother, Anna Clark, is Parisian, high born but not titled. I believe the family lost everything with Napoleon's defeat. In any case, it all occurred eons before the Great War." The elderly aunt waved a black Bakelite holder with a French cigarette above an untouched plate of food. "I lived in Paris many years ago. I've heard *all* the talk."

The young woman squinted, her mouth ajar, elbows on the table. She sniffed, "The Great War? Why would you call a war 'great'?"

A plump, middle-aged woman in a puce lace and velvet gown beside the elderly aunt nodded vigorously with one hand grasping a bread knife smeared with butter and the other a yeast roll.

"That makes sense, Mother. Anna Clark fits the part *very well*. I saw her once, at the opera. She was up in her box, all alone... I felt sorry for her."

The plump woman moved on to her water goblet, leaving a candy pink lipstick ring on the edge. With mock horror, the bottle blonde across the table put a hand with a jewel on each finger to her ample bosom.

"My dears, don't *I* fit the part as well? Don't leave me out!"

Tittering laughter floated above the din of the hotel restaurant's crowd.

The facts of Anna's true story were known by an extreme few outside the bounds of high society. In mid-October, the hit film, "The Sisters," was in theaters. Huguette was a fan of Bette Davis and went to see it one afternoon with Anna and Amelia. That evening, Huguette went out with Styka, which Anna was grateful for. She didn't want her daughter to hear the conversation with Amelia.

Sitting down to an early dinner at a quiet French bistro on the Upper East Side, Anna and Amelia displayed conflicted emotions.

Amelia confessed with a frown, "I had to go see it. I read the novel the movie is based on. There are far too many similarities for Mr. Brinig from Butte to have invented on his own."

"No, Brinig used us as inspiration, that's for sure," said Anna. "I was in his mother's class, you see, in Butte before I went to Deer Lodge. She would've known who you were as well. Her name was Sasha Turner before she married Tom Brinig, a local man. In any case, I think I remember Sasha tried to keep in touch after I left, but I wasn't interested in continuing the friendship.

"Unfortunately for us, Sasha must've been envious of our family's good fortune as it related to William. I'm sure she heard all the gossip and described it in detail to her son years later. What a terrible twist of fate Brinig turned out to be a novelist!"

Amelia's mind whirled, trying to think of who could use this against them. "It's not very obvious... How many suspect our connection to the book and the film?"

"Who knows? The film isn't that closely related, but for anyone who's heard the gossip from Montana about us, it's a snap to put together... How old do I have to be before the slander and gossip about my life die down?" Anna looked distressed.

Amelia reached to take her hand and said, "Sister, it's my life too... We must stand firm and say nothing. Discretion always wins the war."

"Quite right. But there's something else I haven't told you... A manuscript posted from Butte arrived at both my lawyer's office and Huguette's. It was meant for us. I should say, it was meant for everyone. It was an inflammatory, damaging biography of William and his entire family. It horrified me; painting me as a scheming woman who cared nothing for William but for his money. It takes the truth and twists it into ugliness. The book is an abominable mixture of facts and slanderous gossip even worse than what Brindig has used. Far worse!

"The book accused me of infidelity and Huguette the spoiled fruit of it. He says William didn't care for us, only for Andrée. I wept afterward. Huguette refused to leave the house for weeks after she read it."

"Who wrote it? Why didn't you tell me immediately? How did I not hear of this if it upset you both so much?" Amelia said, concern furrowing her brow.

"A man by the name of Mangam, Will Jr.'s friend and William's long-time secretary in Butte. I never met him, of course, but over the many years Mangam worked for William and Will Jr., he had access to quite a bit of personal information. Who knows what he overheard and witnessed?

"Not being a principal player, and having some axe to grind, Mangam misunderstood and misrepresented what he did know. Then he invented the rest pursuing some vendetta, always presenting the family in a damaging light. He even wrote that Huguette wouldn't sleep with William Gower."

"How did he find *that* out?"

"Oh, Charlie or Will Jr., most likely, relayed the story while drunk. They don't care about us, as you know... I'm sure William Gower talked about it with his male circle, too. Word gets around, unfortunately for Huguette..."

"How come I know nothing about the book? Was it not published?"

Anna shook her head. "I wrote to William's children, who agreed with me it would cause a scandal for us all. We instructed our lawyers to buy up all copies and destroy them. I think you were out of town with Bryce then. In any case, I have tried to forget about it..."

In order to forget her unrequited passion for a man in love with another woman, Huguette threw herself into a close friendship with Villermont. He had been in the States some months, and, working hard on his English, was very popular on the party circuit. It seemed he cashed in on his aristocratic heritage; he'd been working plumb jobs in New York while spending vacations and weekends visiting multiple grand houses.

Anna put down the society pages, which listed Villermont's name and another young heiress's. "You might lose the chance, Huguette. Another woman is going to snatch him up. I wouldn't let that happen if I were you. Etienne is a good man."

"Why of course he is... I've been preoccupied with my lessons, and we've been busy lately. He and I keep in touch now and then. And it's been such a disruption all these years to have Bellosguardo under construction. Now that it's finished, perhaps Etienne could be invited more?"

Taking her daughter's cue, Anna invited Villermont to Bellosguardo for several weeks each summer. She wanted him to see how lovely Huguette had become, and Bellosguardo was the perfect backdrop. How could he not be impressed?

Anna spoke endlessly to Amelia how overjoyed she would be to welcome such a trusted, pedigreed man into the family. She wanted nothing more than her daughter to fall in love.

It's best if Huguette is wooed away slowly from her Styka fantasy.

However, it soon became obvious, Villermont was playing the field as handsome young men in demand typically do. Despite faithful visits during Fiesta Days and other socially opportune times, the marquis's head had been turned too much by all the attention in America. He was unfailing polite and attentive—even doting on Huguette—but for months afterward, he disappeared.

"Etienne favors a social routine far more ambitious than Huguette will ever follow. And it appears he's now linked with Emily Davis," said Anna to Amelia and Bryce on the veranda one morning in Santa Barbara.

"The Davis girl? Oh, the dark blonde with the large nose. But why do you say that? Huguette's been turning over a new leaf. Look how much she's out and about with Styka in New York lately. She's almost a social butterfly."

"Hardly, Amelia! And you know perfectly well that Styka is not the right man. I've told you a hundred times. Etienne is *far more suited*, and he would be faithful. But he's being pursued all across the country, and now with this Davis girl..." Anna clicked her tongue. "The society pages and gossip attest to his popularity."

"Has Etienne been to Bellosguardo this summer?"

"Yes, he only left two weeks ago."

"Well, then, what's the matter?"

"Because we won't hear from him for months. He all but forgets Huguette is alive until I jump up and down again. She won't pursue him either."

The back-and-forth situation lasted quite some time. But, suddenly, for some reason unknown, Villermont seemed to have a change of heart. He corresponded with Huguette more; flowers arrived regularly. On an upcoming visit to New York, he asked to see her alone on a Saturday evening for dinner and dancing. Anna was pleased Villermont was possibly ramping up his wooing.

And even better, she's allowing it!

Like Styka, Huguette thought of Villermont as a man who had it all. He was tall, attractive, a French marquis, and appreciated the arts. Infinitely better, they had known each other since childhood. He was vetted in an even more personal way than Gower.

Oui, I should allow Etienne to be my beau. I mustn't let him get away... Huguette sat staring into the vanity mirror, psyching herself up before Villermont arrived. She forced herself to stop daydreaming. *I must see things for how they really are! He's not changing his mind about Ms. Foster.*

With Villermont, it was a cinch to fall into an expected pattern of romantic interest. *I'm attracted to Etienne, and I can see myself possibly married someday.* Then, Huguette's mind went blank. Her thoughts turned to the painting she was sketching out. She picked up a comb to fix a wave in her hair.

That night, when Villermont held her in his arms while dancing, or gently took her arm, she enjoyed his touch. She smiled and had no trouble accepting small advances. He was suave, far more careful than Gower had been. He smelled attractively of cologne and scented hair pomade. Even better, there was no evidence of a flask hidden in a pocket or eyes scanning a good-looking bartender. Like Styka, Villermont could bring Huguette completely out of her shell by reminiscing for hours about her father, sister, and childhood summers on Trouville and Cabourg beaches.

The next day at a luncheon at the St. Regis, Huguette said, "Oh Etienne, how I love these conversations! You're the only one who indulges me. It seems like a dream now, my childhood in France..."

Huguette wore a faraway, gentle smile. "I long to return to live in Paris, but *Maman* is very reluctant. I'm not sure why... I think the war greatly altered her view on living in Europe long-term. She says Paris is still lovely, but the perfect life she had there with my father is gone for good. She wants to look forward."

"That could be," Villermont said. "There are many who prefer the United States, for many reasons. Even with economic problems, America seems to be more alive than France. France is so tradition-bound. Here, I feel free! Although, for me, ultimately, I think I'll return someday. Do you see that in your future?"

Villermont's eyes searched hers. Huguette dropped her gaze to the plate recently set down by a white-gloved waiter. Arranged nicely on the embossed hotel china were a thick steak sandwich cut into quarters and *pommes frites*. Villermont had invited her to a luncheon celebrating Lady Decies's departure for Europe. The room was crowded with friends and well-wishers.

The Baroness Elizabeth de la Poer Beresford, or Lady Decies, recently married for the third time, knew Villermont's family. She was a society beauty whose first husband commissioned a portrait by Boldini in 1905. The week before, Lady Decies had run into Villermont in the lobby of the St. Regis, white hair poking out from under a black veiled hat, wearing a five-strand pearl choker and large jeweled rings on arthritic fingers.

"Oh, my dear Etienne, you *must* come to my little *soirée*, here on Tuesday at one o'clock. Before I sail. Bring a pretty friend. I shall see you there. *Adieu!*"

He leant to double kiss heavily rouged cheeks before she disappeared into a navy-blue Alfa Romeo 2900B Lungo Berlinetta.

"How do you know Lady Decies?" said Huguette, before biting a French fry in half.

"My father's good friends with her husband, Baron Decies. He's an amazing man. Gold medal polo player in the 1900 Olympics and Second Boer War veteran." Villermont lowered his voice. "Unfortunately, he's confessed privately to my father he's trying to get rid of her! Apparently, Lady Decies is *quite* a handful."

"*Ç'est vrai?*" Huguette scoffed at the idea the overdressed, aging woman could be so hard to live with. "The poor woman! Isn't she an author? I should read one of her novels."

"Going back to our previous topic, will you ever return to France?" Villermont's eyes implored.

"Return to France? Those were my halcyon days... Imagine! Me living in Paris again! I quite like that idea, but I'm not sure at this time. I want to be with *Maman*. That's important... She's over sixty now. As you know, she loves to visit, but with talk of another war, Etienne, I don't think so. Mother avoids instability like the plague."

Huguette eyed up the steak sandwich, knowing she wouldn't be able to chew it elegantly. She opted for another French fry.

"*Oui, oui, bien sûr.* I should've known. You're most loyal. It does you credit."

Villermont picked up his steak sandwich, determined to keep extolling France's virtues. As he took a bite, he thought, *I'll have to try another tactic.*

Several mornings later, while eating yogurt with berries in Anna's breakfast room, Huguette was dismayed. Skimming through Walter Winchell's "On Broadway" column, it read: "Mrs. Huguette Clark will wed Mr. E. de Villermont this summer... And won't that be a blessed union for *le marquis*! She can finance his nonexistent chateau in France."

"Oh my, however did he find out about that? This is embarrassing!"

"I saw that. Pay no attention. Go to the comics, maybe."

"I must read it. Look at what he's saying! Winchell seems to have more idea of my relationship with Etienne than I do! How can I go out after this?"

"That's his job, *ma petite*. And Winchell is known for going overboard. Maybe you should show it to Etienne when he comes for supper tonight?"

"*Maman*, imagine! How forward!" Huguette put the paper down forcefully.

Anna sipped coffee before answering in an innocent tone, "Well, you told me that he asked you to marry him..."

"*Oui!* And I'm still thinking about it."

Huguette reached for her *café au lait*. The article stung. She had been out with Villermont quite a lot the past few months.

Journalists always watch for those patterns; I shouldn't be upset.

"Stop thinking, *ma chérie*, and say *oui, oui, oui!* Etienne is delightful and well suited. I wholeheartedly give my consent."

Anna winked before taking a small bite of toast with black currant jam imported from France.

"Don't rush me. I must think on it. I'm going to my painting lesson. Are you still planning on a lesson with the Julliard teacher?"

Anna dabbed her mouth with a napkin before placing it back on her lap. "Mr. Packard? Yes, he's marvelous. He's reinvigorated my harp playing. Come down at seven o'clock; I told Etienne to be here at half-past. Wear something becoming."

Huguette rose from the table, gave her mother a kiss on the cheek, and ascended to 12W via the nondescript cement service staircase. She thought about seeing Styka soon. Her heart fell.

Last week she had been contentedly working on a still life with blue vase and white hydrangeas. Styka was giving advice and going about his business in the studio, per usual, discussing how war disrupts art markets.

"Just when artists are getting back on their feet, and then this! I can hardly believe how serious some of the reports are."

Styka returned to scan the paints Huguette mixed, instructing her to alter one of the shades of blue with a dab of grey. Then Ms. Foster burst in, immediately interrupting their quiet comradery.

"I'm sorry I'm early, darling dear. I couldn't wait anymore! You don't mind, Mrs. Clark, do you?"

As Miss Foster approached Styka with outstretched hands and a beaming smile, Huguette's quick eye noticed on the woman's left hand a large diamond and platinum ring.

Abruptly, Huguette stood up, almost knocking over a canister with brushes. Face pale, chest constricting, she blurted out, "Oh, oh, I uh, that's fine. I forgot I had to go just now. I've another engagement I failed to mention. Silly me!"

She shoved supplies willy-nilly into a canvas tote, not waiting for the slow Sandré. Styka moved in her direction.

"Are you sure? Is there anything amiss?"

He noticed she was uncharacteristically leaving thirty minutes early. Miss Foster looked deflated. Her beautiful eyes went from one to the other uncomprehendingly, frustrated at her lack of French.

"Oh, no! Of course not!" Huguette paused a moment to collect herself, gripping a handful of paintbrushes. "However, I really must be going. *Merci beaucoup!*"

Huguette went directly home to lock herself in her bedroom. She kicked off heels and clenched fists to pace the blue carpet, weeping.

I'm such a fool to hope Styka would never marry and we could just go on with our relationship!

She felt despondent, canceling her next two painting lessons over the excuse she had a cold.

As the months passed, she didn't discuss the ring she spotted on Foster's hand. The truth came out much later at one of Anna's dinner parties. Seated around the table were Amelia and Bryce Turner, the recently widowed Amanda Storrs, and Edward Bowes.

"It's to remain private, my good friends, but yes, yes! I'm engaged to Miss Darlene Foster. I've known and loved her for quite some time now and I'm very happy."

Polite clapping from around the table as Styka nodded with a pleased smile. "Say nothing, as there is no wedding planned as yet and I'm trying to keep it out of the papers for the rest of my life! We shall see about the business of a wedding date another day, *oui*?"

Styka grinned, avoiding Huguette's eyes.

"A toast to Monsieur Styka's engagement!" Anna lifted a crystal flute of champagne to her guests around the oval table.

Huguette complied. A pleasant social mask obscured true feelings.

Hours later as Amelia departed, Anna whispered, "I know she's upset now, but it's just as well. And perfect timing! Etienne has been talking of marriage!" Anna squeezed Amelia's hand in eagerness.

May 1939
Flushing Meadows-Corona Park, Queens, New York

"I'm eager to see the World's Fair today! Don't forget, Mrs. Clark, it's the Dawn of a New Day," said Styka with raised eyebrows as looked out the window at the crowds entering the open-air Marine Ampitheatre.

"Me, too! I've been looking forward to the show all week." Huguette, admiring his gift, minutely shifted the purple orchid corsage on her wrist.

"I've heard reports this is the second-most expensive World's Fair. I paid twenty cents for us to view 'The World of Tomorrow.' That seems like a bargain ticket to me!"

The Rolls then glided to a stop and Styka helped Huguette out. They headed to a VIP entrance of the amphitheatre decorated in Art Deco style to watch Billy Rose's "Million Dollar" Aquacade. Male and female synchronized swimmers and Olympic gold medalist divers such as Eleanor Holm performed alongside a specially engineered, lighted water-curtain in front of the stage.

Referred to as a "man-made Niagara"—260-feet wide and 40-feet high—8,000 gallons of water a minute pumped through the water-curtain. Ted Royal led the orchestra throughout the water show for an audience in the thousands. At times, the applause and raucous cheers were deafening.

"Imagine, diving from that great height!" said Huguette, tipping back her head adorned with a purple Claude Saint-Cyr felt hat to take in the spectacle. She had stopped clapping only because her hands ached.

As they exited, she said, "The water ballet swimmers were my favorite. I could see that show again. Maybe I should bring *Maman*?"

"I bet she would love it... Would you look at that." Styka's hazel eyes were riveted on a futuristic grey-blue display up ahead. They went inside to view small black and white RCA TRK-12 television sets playing.

Styka shook his head at the latest technology. "Did you hear that NBC televised the opening ceremony?"

"Yes, I read about it. How peculiar! How ever does it work? I'd like to know."

"These must be an unimaginable luxury for average Americans accustomed only to entertainment from books, radio, and theater... Hey, let's go see ourselves on television!" Styka suddenly looked like a little boy with a new toy.

"Oh, must we? All these people."

"C'mon, Mrs. Clark! We're viewing the World of Tomorrow, I'll remind you."

They stood for a moment with a few others watching their images on the grainy black and white screens. Everyone slack-jawed, shaking heads in wonder.

"Is it a trick?" a young woman whispered beside Huguette.

Her friend pointed, "No, look over there at that display. One of the televisions is clear, to convince Doubting Thomas's of the inner-workings, I guess."

For two hours, Styka and Huguette made their way through enthralling booths and displays. On the ground, crowds surged everywhere before they reached the comparatively sedate Italian Pavilion's second floor restaurant and nightclub. The menu featured insalata Caprese, fresh pasta with pesto, and white truffle lasagna.

Styka ate with relish. "Eating such wonderful food, I feel like I'm back in Italy. It makes me long to visit. Alas, with the troubles Mussolini has caused, I shall not be going any time soon. A pity, is it not?" He took a bite and discreetly scanned the room for anyone he knew.

"Oh, yes. Italy is such a gorgeous country. It's been too long for me as well, at least seven years. When I was young, we used to visit often. Father was always after Renaissance treasures."

"I think tourism has been way down ever since the Spanish Civil War influenced Italy's politics. I fear for Europe. We shall see what the summer brings for political scheming." Styka noted with a shake of his blonde head, not a hair out of place, "Remember the Great War began at the end of summer."

"That's right! We hardly got out of France in time before the First Battle of the Marne. You've heard the story, I believe."

"Yes, indeed. Your father told that story at least three times. I did paint his portrait numerous times, you recall..." Styka winked in jest because William ordered almost a dozen portraits. "The bravery by you and your older sister enchanted him."

The next month, Anna invited Arthur and his family up from Beverly Hills to celebrate Huguette's thirty-third birthday at Bellosguardo. Surrounded by the heat and quiet, Huguette desired only to swim at their private beach. Anna would join her, and they spent hours sunning themselves on the hot sand. Huguette painted little, spending the days reading, taking photos, and drawing.

Villermont arrived at the end of July for Fiesta Days. Initially, Huguette was excited to see him every day because he was a wonderful companion. But it faded fast.

"Being more serious than we are right now won't do for me, Etienne. I love you, as always. You've always been dear to me. Since we were little! But I'm unsure I want to remarry... I like my life as it is. I'm busy with *Maman;* I couldn't leave her. She has her activities and I have mine. You know, all the things I enjoy. I do what I like when I like, and that suits me fine." She shrugged.

For the past half hour, Villermont sat slumped on a towel in the sand. Huguette wore a white swimsuit stretched out partially in his shadow. Both were very tan from lying out at the peak of the sun's powers. When it got too hot, they would hold hands and go racing into the surf. Laughing and soaking wet, they would emerge out of cool waves to fall down on oversized, red and white striped towels.

"I've no intention of taking you away from your beloved mother. I want you to know that. Who knows better than I that special relationship? Henri and I have been friends with you through so many years."

"*Oui, cher* Henri. Tell him to come, *s'il te plaît*. I'm grateful for you both! He should visit more often. Wouldn't he love it here in the sun…?"

Villermont nodded, sensing she was good at distracting him with charming nonsense. Returning quickly to his point, "Hugo, I'm so happy with you here. I can't imagine being with anyone else. I want to be here with you always. Don't you feel the same? I feel we're well suited. You know, I've said it a hundred times, *mon amour*."

"And I love you too, Etienne. But I don't want to get married just now."

"Later on, then, Hugo? Will you change your mind? How long should I wait?"

He took her warm, dry hand in his and brushed off sand. He kissed the top of it, wanting to move on to her lips but he knew that would ruin the moment. She preferred to be touched very gently and chastely, or not at all. Huguette shaded squinting eyes with her other hand.

"I can't say… I would never ask you to wait. I'm not telling you to run off and ask someone else, but I can't agree to an engagement right now."

"*D'accord!* I will quit badgering you. However, I won't forget, my brown beauty!"

He changed his mind and leaned in to kiss her softly on the lips. Huguette briefly kissed him back.

"Put more oil on my back, *s'il te plaît, Monsieur le marquis de Villermont. Ta reine te commande.*"

"*Avec plaisir, ma reine et mon amour.*"

Villermont departed three days later on the morning train. At the al fresco lunch, Anna was hopeful.

"Did Etienne say he's coming back? He's not far away, after all. Long Beach is just around the corner."

"Not in so many words…"

Huguette flicked her fork through niçoise salad. "We had a good time. He's always such fun. We know we'll see each other in New York. Henri might visit, too."

Huguette averted her eyes from Anna's direct gaze while drinking piña colada.

"Did he bring up marriage?"

"*Oui, Maman...*"

Anna put down her fork in concentration, hopeful for details. Huguette looked at her and shrugged.

"We discussed it a little. Everything is alright. But I don't want to discuss it further."

"You didn't say no?"

"Correct, of a sort. Now can I enjoy my salad without an interrogation?"

Anna took a bite, thoughts churning. *Of a sort...? What is this willful daughter of mine thinking? She could lose him!*

Anna's clever eyes surveyed the gorgeous view.

I'll throw a series of dinner parties in New York to keep Villermont coming regularly. Amelia can be called upon to do her part as well. If Huguette won't help herself, then it's my job to help her. What is she going to do after I die? Live all alone? No, I won't let that happen.

The month of August passed in delightful repose. Huguette reveled in the freedom afforded when one was not called upon to be a hostess. Then came the September day when she ambled downstairs intent on a walk in the warm sunshine. The radio was blaring, which surprised her.

Huguette walked into the library. "*Maman*, what are you—"

"Listen!" Anna's sharp, urgent tone stopped Huguette in her tracks.

The male announcer reported Germany had invaded Poland. In return, Britain and France declared war on Germany. For a long moment Anna's brown and blue eyes fearfully bored into Huguette's.

"Not again!" Anna moaned, hands clasped.

The last time Huguette had seen that much apprehension on her mother's face was during the first harried day of the evacuation from France in 1914. She sat down gingerly on a chair. They listened for a half hour before Anna motioned Marié to switch off the radio.

"I cannot believe this... War in Europe... a second time... And Germany *again*! The devils!... If they have invaded Poland, then France is threatened. This is retribution for the first war. For the Treaty of Versailles. I remember your father explaining it to me. Oh, I wish he were here! I don't know if I can bear this alone..."

Huguette felt chilled from the grave tones of the program host. Her feelings were complicated as all memories of war came from childhood. She didn't know what to think. A tension headache suddenly manifested itself and she put a hand to a throbbing brow. Anna stood and moved to the window.

"Well, that changes the plans for our next trip to France. I propose we stay here for another month, at least. Let's see how this develops. I don't want to rush back to the East Coast if there's war across the Atlantic."

"Whatever you think is best, *Maman*. I'm content to stay here. I regret our fall trip to Paris, though. I was looking forward to it."

August 10, 1941
Santa Barbara, California

Huguette gave Villermont a quick hug. He looked wistfully down at her, taking a gloved hand to kiss it. "I don't want to say goodbye, Hugo, but I know I must. I wish we weren't parting like this."

"Oh, please, Etienne, not again. It's my final decision. But I'll see you in New York sometime soon, *d'accord*?"

She hugged him a second time, and then stepped several feet away. Villermont took the hint, picking up a Louis Vuitton suitcase. Once up the metal steps, he turned to give a weak farewell wave. Huguette cheerfully waved back. He moved inside the first-class car, and she darted away through the crowd.

What a tiresome time I've had with Etienne the past two weeks! He seemed more desperate, as if he merely tried a little harder each day, I would acquiesce sooner or later. He misjudges me completely.

In the back of the Cadillac moving along East Cabrillo Boulevard, Huguette wondered what *Maman* and *tante* Amelia had said privately.

No doubt they egged him on! I'm sure Maman *would think it adorable for me to marry a marquis...*

Only two nights ago she and Villermont had been strolling through the rose garden well after midnight. *Maman* busied herself with several hundred guests while an orchestra performed on a dais on the lawn. Huguette had enjoyed his close attentions all evening. They danced multiple sets together and became overheated. He suggested a walk; the space away from the crowds came at a perfect moment. In the nocturnal party atmosphere, she fancied herself feeling something akin to love.

Simultaneously, the fleeting desire crossed Huguette's mind to walk like this some evening with Styka. Her imagination could picture it effortlessly; her heart beat a little faster.

But it's been years since he's been to Bellosguardo.

Her heartbeat slowed. She focused back on Etienne, feeling pity. She smiled with a guilty conscience.

Etienne's such a nice man. So good to me!

Villermont reached to gently take her hand. The cool breeze off the ocean soothed warm skin. They fell silent, strolling amiably in the darkness, talking little. Within fifteen minutes, there were no other couples in a secluded section of the gardens. A cloud went over the moon, obscuring the path.

With that cover, Villermont pounced.

Huguette was bent back in his fervor to kiss face, neck, and chest. His fingertips pressed into the flesh of her bare back which the sleeveless lavender chiffon dress revealed. She felt revulsion at the wet touch of a tongue slid between lips. She yanked her head away.

"Hugo, *mon amour*. Have I waited long enough? Please say you'll marry me!"

Hot breath at her ear. Huguette had never been kissed so passionately. Villermont seemed to have lost control.

"Let me go!"

She shoved him and scampered off in the direction of the back of the house, only slowing when she encountered guests on the paths. Ignoring any entreaties to talk, she headed immediately up to her bedroom. Villermont pursued, knocking repeatedly.

"Hugo, forgive me! I can't help myself! I'm in love with you. I'm in love with the idea of marrying you. I love being here at Bellosguardo. I can see our lives here! Can't you? It was such a romantic moment. You looked so beautiful in the moonlight...

"Forgive me! You know I'm a romantic fool! I'm terribly sorry for upsetting you, *mon amour... Ma cher, s'il te plaît...*"

He waited an hour. The door remained shut and no sound came from within.

The next day, Huguette stayed in her double-floor suite, taking all meals alone. She took advantage of Anna's prowess as a hostess to automatically make excuses for her prolonged absence.

Huguette alternated amongst varying stages of processing the romantic encounter. Guilt and shame at perhaps leading him on—*What was I thinking to be walking alone with him so late at night?*—to revulsion at a man's tongue in her mouth to pity: *Oh poor Etienne, I've rejected him once again. I hope he'll forgive me.*

It was Villermont's last day. Without Huguette, he moped. Anna did her best to amuse, finally packing him off for a mid-afternoon eighteen holes with a local friend.

Early the next morning, Anna strode into Huguette's bedroom and stood gazing at her daughter reading the comics. A breakfast tray with empty coffee cup, bread plate with crumbs, and a single pink rose in a crystal vase rested on a table beside the twin bed. Huguette returned the gaze, expressionless.

It's obvious she's upset with me, too...

Suddenly she was a little girl deserving a scolding. She shrank against the down pillows.

Anna said in a quiet tone which barely concealed anger, "The marquis's train departs in precisely one hour. He is our long-time friend and a very eligible suitor. As you decided on neglecting him for the *entirety* of yesterday, you'll do your part and escort him to the station today. Get dressed at once!"

Anna gave Huguette a look of death and departed. Huguette threw back the down-filled duvet and stalked to the dressing room. To her annoyance, a young, Irish maid was waiting with an outfit picked out by Anna.

How many people in the house know my business?!

After ruining the first pair of silk stockings by jerking on them, Huguette dressed in a Jacques Fath blue linen suit, white silk blouse, and pearls. She shoved feet into tan leather pumps and grabbed the matching blue hat and clutch, and small white gloves held out gingerly by the maid, who looked awkwardly at the floor. Her employers seldom argued.

Anna left Huguette alone all that day and the next. By the third day, she called her daughter into her suite's sitting room, making sure no staff were around before shutting the door.

"Sit down."

Anna waited, knowing whatever she said at that moment was too little too late. *Nevertheless, it must be said. For my own sake if not for Huguette's.*

"It's my duty as your mother to guide you. Do you accept that?"

Huguette nodded while crossing legs. She nervously jiggled her top foot. Anna observed her daughter for a long moment, allowing the tension to build.

"Obviously, from your behavior the past few days and from his hang-dog appearance, you've told Etienne you will not marry him."

Huguette nodded, feeling uncomfortable with her mother's stern tone. She had heard it before, but rarely directed at her personally. Anna pointed a jeweled index finger.

"You have made a terrible mistake. Do *you* realize you have made a mistake?"

"No, *Maman*, I haven't made a mistake."

"And how is that? How is it you think—as a divorced woman of thirty-five with no children—telling a fine man you won't marry him, you have *not* made a callosal error in judgement?"

Anna's stony expression made Huguette want to cower. But the way her mother described her made her furious. In self-defense, she lashed out.

"Would you have me marry a man I merely like, not love, because you *pity* me?"

"I suppose I *do* pity you. I wouldn't have you be alone and childless. I wouldn't be without grandchildren. Yet here I am, not a grandmother by my own biological child. At this rate, I never will be!" Anna put a hand to her forehead in silence for a moment. "What will you do when I am gone? How will you face friends and family alone?

"Your father's family isn't exactly forthcoming with love and attention, and Katherine Morris, as your sole surviving sibling, pays us no attention. My side is no better. Amelia has no children and Arthur's two children aren't successfully reproducing. Therefore, as an old woman, you will most likely be completely alone! What will people say about you? Oh, I know I'm hardly one to talk, but I still kept within the bounds of society. I played their game when it comes down to it.

"You, on the other hand, are going off on a tangent *all by yourself*. A completely avoidable tangent at that! You cannot act as if you aren't a grown woman, Huguette. You need to face up to what life is really about. I'm telling you this for your own good! Before you are left out in the cold. Alone!"

"I refuse to marry a man I esteem highly but am not romantically in love with! You and *tante* Amelia have been forcing me and Etienne together for some time now. I beg you to stop!"

"Forcing you?" Anna's eyes narrowed.

"Yes! You've invited Etienne so many times I think he *assumed* I was going to marry him! He made a pass at me the other night. Never has he acted so brazen, as if I were going to bed with him that moment. I will not stand for it any longer. I told him in no uncertain terms I had no intentions of ever marrying him or any other man ever again!"

"If he made a pass at you then he's acting like a man *in love*!" Anna threw up her hands. "What more can you ask for? What more do you need?"

"Well, it's a problem, because I do not love him the same! And it makes me uncomfortable to be grabbed and kissed by a man I'm not sure I want to be grabbed by!"

"Do you want to be no better than a divorcée? *Le marquis de Villermont* could eradicate that stain in a second!" Anna snapped her fingers. "No one would discuss your first marriage or reference it ever again. A good man of quality and breeding gives a woman so much in today's society. I should say, he gives her everything! I fear the gossip about you if you don't remarry soon."

"I don't care what people say about me! I might never remarry."

"Do you mean that? Do you really...? What am I to do with you then...?" Anna's voice faltered.

"Do with me? I'm happy living my life! You need to stop pitying me, *Maman*!"

"True, I should... But a man who is in love with you is far better than no man at all!"

"I don't believe that."

Huguette averted her eyes, blonde eyebrows drawn down tight. Her mind made up; she hated being forced to do anything. *After Father's warning, I went on to be humiliated by Bill. It'll never happen to me again.*

Anna sighed, waving a hand at her. "Etienne deserves an apology. Write and invite him over when we return to New York."

"I won't do that."

"Why ever *not*? You will lose him to another woman! He has plenty after him, I know!"

"Good! They can have him!"

Huguette sprang from the chair and fled.

For the next two days, Huguette secluded herself in the studio. Anna wanted to cool down herself. It was so unexpected to quarrel, quite outside their normal communication pattern. She even had a mind to return to New York early, but that wasn't palatable until at least mid-September. Instead, she went down to Arthur's 5-bedroom, 7-bathroom Spanish-inspired mansion at 1004 Roxbury Drive in Beverly Hills. Arthur and Hanna built it in 1932 after his law practice began making serious profits. Arthur not only lived in a tony neighborhood laden with film stars, directors, and producers, he represented his neighbors in court.

Anna left a note she would return in a week. She needed to think, to pause in the long quest to erase the embarrassing divorce and get Huguette remarried as soon as possible.

Obviously, it's too late... She saw the same steel-like decision in Huguette's eyes she had observed in William's when he was worked up about something. *Huguette will have to find a man on her own or it won't happen at all. No children for her or grandchildren for me to enjoy. No husband to love and spoil her, to be companions with. Who will take care of Huguette after I'm gone?*

Huguette was grateful for the reprieve; she needed solitude to regain her equilibrium. She turned down all requests to socialize, obsessing what to say to *Maman* when she saw her again. To keep herself busy, she worked on a new painting, and took a trip to Marsh and Company to personally check on an order. She played tennis daily, booking a local tennis ace for lessons.

When Anna returned from Beverly Hills, they embraced in the front hall. "I'm sorry, my dear, for upsetting you. Forgive your mother. I'm only trying to do what's best."

"I know, *Maman*. I'm sorry, too." They embraced again.

Anna gave her purse and hat to a maid and took Huguette's arm.

"Let's go sit on the veranda with some tea and cookies. I want to enjoy the delicious breeze. The train was stuffy."

Huguette smiled and moved closer to Anna: *All is right once again.*

When Villermont wrote he was sailing for France, she didn't reply.

In early December, the Clarks returned to Bellosguardo. Anna said to Huguette, "California is a far more pleasant prospect to sing 'Oh Come All Ye Faithful' than during a blizzard on Fifth Avenue, wouldn't you say?"

"Absolutely. I won't miss the snow. Let's stay through January."

"Well, we'll miss the Wilson's New Year's Eve party if we do that."

Anna smiled and took a drink, admiring the decorated fir tree in the drawing room. Suddenly, there was commotion at the front door. The butler came in with Mr. Hoelscher on his heels.

"Madame Clark, I would advise you to turn on the wireless."

"Whatever for—"

"We've been attacked by the Japs!" The estate manager was in such a rush he forgot to remove his fedora.

Over an hour later they turned off the radio. Drawn faces, eyes downcast. No one spoke for a long moment.

"I can't fathom they're talking about Honolulu..." said Huguette. "Hawai'i is too beautiful to be bombed. All those friendly people!"

Anna called for Marié before saying, "I'm going back to New York as soon as possible!"

Early the next morning, Marié was packed off to acquire first-class tickets. Incredibly, she returned empty-handed. Not ten minutes later, Anna stood at the telephone, uncharacteristically attempting to make travel plans. Marié stood faithfully beside wringing small hands.

"Miss, I heard you, yes, but this is *unacceptable*. I want to leave on the next train to New York. I don't care about the hour of day or night. I would prefer it if available, but under the circumstances, I don't care if it's not first class. I have a lifetime rail pass as the widow of Senator William A. Clark. That's Clark, yes, Clark... I've never previously been denied a ticket."

Anna paused, listening intently. The volume was so loud Huguette could hear the woman on the other end saying no repeatedly. Anna felt a strong desire well up inside to demand instantaneous service.

Instead, with a choked voice she said, "I see. Thank you." Hand trembling, she placed the receiver down on the brass cradle.

"And... what did they say?" squeaked Marié, even though she had heard word-for-word.

"All the woman kept saying was, 'All tickets are sold out as of today. Due to the number of travelers leaving California, Los Angeles rail travel is completely tied up for days... Call again tomorrow.' It's enough to drive one mad with frustration.

"Madame Marié, you will go to the train station early each morning until we can secure tickets. Huguette, we might have to drive down to Los Angeles if that doesn't work. Best to be as close as possible. We must get away from the coast!"

"Is it because everyone fears an attack on American soil?" Huguette looked horrified as the idea dawned. "That means us! We're on the ocean!"

It was crushing. The country Huguette had revered for many years was now the enemy. Japan's culture, history, and arts had thrilled ever since she had been old enough to explore the Japanese room at the Fifth Avenue house, then, as a teenager, the Asian galleries and stores bursting with imports in Santa Barbara and San Francisco.

Like her mother, she had turned into a collector of jade *objects d'art* and Japanese dolls. She was proud of the graceful Japanese room at 12W Anna had commissioned. Her library contained several shelves on Japanese history and its arts. But, with the successful attack on Pearl Harbor, a love for culture and the past meant nothing in the present theatre of war the Pacific had recently blazed into.

The butler announced Hoelscher. The women were seated in the drawing room with dazed expressions, unsure about the next step.

"Madame Clark, an infantry regiment is being brought up to the beach sometime within the next several hours. They'll take over and put a post at the beach house."

"Must they? I suppose that makes sense... For how long?"

"The military cannot answer that, Mrs. Clark."

"Of course, yes, yes, it must be done. I want to help the war effort, as I always have in my life. It's simply disconcerting it's on my property!"

"I understand, Mrs. Clark. I... I wanted you to know I've volunteered to be the Civil Defense Warden. My house will be the district headquarters. I'll have to divide my time between this job and that one."

"Of course, of course, Mr. Hoelscher. We all need to do our part. Thank you."

Anna looked down with a furrowed brow, immediately comprehending many of the men employed on the estate would volunteer or be drafted. Bellosguardo would have to keep up with the changes now America had entered the war. It clearly was time to close down areas of the house and retrench.

Oh my, we're in the war as well. A second world war... How terribly troubling this all is.

Hoelscher nodded—relieved his boss had taken the news so well—and said, "Good night, ladies." He turned to leave, putting on his fedora while exiting.

With a sinking heart, Anna watched him depart. "This is incredible. I have the U.S. military camped out in front of the house!" she moaned. "I don't want to be this close to the conflict...! Oh, William, what would you've done?"

Huguette's ears perked up at the mention of her father's name. She wondered how often *Maman* thought of Papa. Many things reminded her of both him and Andrée. Preferring to keep these wonderings private, only sometimes did she mention memories. It was a subject seldom broached despite the impossibility for Andrée not to be present continually, as portraits and busts graced both of Anna's residences.

During the next week, the attack on Honolulu and America entering the war consumed much of their time. They read the various newspaper reports and listened to radio broadcasts for hours. They couldn't tear themselves away; the topic grasped with complete absorption. The amount of information available via radio, magazines, and newspapers was greater than it had been in the first world war. Now the enhanced ability of communications spread details, conflict outcomes, national reports, and military decisions from various nations far more thoroughly than previously.

Huguette reflected on their first trip to Honolulu. "Remember, *Maman*, we walked on the beach at Pearl Harbor? Papa had wanted to see the mighty ships and naval drills. That was twenty-six years ago, when the naval base had only occupied the region for sixteen years."

"*Oui*, I remember how excited your father was to tour it," Anna's eyes looked dull but her lips curved into a gentle smile.

"I'm amazed they let us see what we did."

"No one told William no!" Anna's eyes came alive, and she burst out laughing. "How I miss him!" She began to weep.

Huguette watched her mother take out a handkerchief. She thought back to what she had seen as a young girl. Pearl Harbor had been a happy place then, full of American zeal, the harbor bustling with naval activity in stark comparison to the traditional ways of the native Hawaiians. However, now, with the brutal Japanese attack lasting two hours, thousands dead, and oil fires belching black smoke into the air from the destroyed warships, the former peace and contentment of the island harbor were destroyed.

"This has never happened before in our history, *Maman*." Feeling chilled, Huguette wrapped arms around herself.

"*Oui, c'est vrai*. Not in the United States. It greatly concerns. Your father and I have always retreated to America for protection. But now? Where do we go? There is *nowhere else safe* to go!" Anna's mind whirled: *Either coast is a threat. Asia and North Africa are threatening. Europe is in shreds once again.* "It's too awful to contemplate."

"We should return to New York soon."

"I agree, but we'll have to wait. Procuring tickets doesn't look like it will happen soon. They'll not budge, regardless of the amount of money I offer." Anna dabbed at wet eyes.

From upstairs windows and balcony, the Clarks watched the beginning activities of the army officers who arrived to turn Bellosguardo into a war zone. Young men in uniform carried post diggers. Their orders were to put posts in the ground at regular intervals all along the cliff line. The Clarks would later learn each post had a time clock which ensured sentries made rounds.

Next, the soldiers were busy strewing barbed wire in long lines along clifftops and beaches. Then the Santa Barbara Cemetery adjacent to Bellosguardo's grounds was taken over by an even more serious military lookout with artillery, searchlights, and numerous soldiers. Round the clock, sentries patrolled beaches below.

On the West Coast, it became American's objective to hide from Japanese submarines lurking off the coast to spy on naval ship movement. A blackout was ordered from Northern Washington to Southern California. Wartime changes were enacted at sunset: blackout curtains closed, streetlights turned off, and only a vehicle's parking lights used. For the children, Hoelscher reported, boxes of government-issued steel helmets and gas masks arrived.

To help with medical supplies, clothing, and food, Huguette sent money to American and European war charities and Pearl S. Buck's United China Relief Fund. Anna bought war bonds for the staff, a $1,000 for a family and $75 for a child. For Hoelscher, Anna went one step further, providing the estate manager with a .45-caliber pistol, a rifle, and $10,000 in cash in case of evacuation.

Swimming or walking on the beach was impossible with the constant presence of soldiers and menacing barbed wire strewn out in either direction as far as the eye could see. Huguette was dismayed to be observed whenever outside. She was even more upset to learn current orders for Japanese imports from Marsh and Company were put on hold indefinitely. A few projects, such as commissioning dolls from *The Tale of Genji* and one painting, had to be put aside.

She began losing the drive to create. The studio sat empty.

Entertainment, sporting events, and social schedules were severely curtailed or stopped altogether. The normally robust crowds thinned dramatically. Restaurants, the Biltmore, and the country club were far quieter. The Clarks likewise stayed at home, sequestered. It took until the end of January before they were successful in acquiring enough rail tickets for themselves and staff for the long trip back to New York.

The day the Clarks departed, Bellosguardo's contents were put under dust covers. Curtains drawn; valuables locked away. The estate would run on a skeleton crew for the next eighteen months. Hoelscher sent regular reports. A barbed wire check point on Cabrillo Boulevard was set up, and government passes were issued in late February after a Japanese submarine surfaced and fired shells at Ellwood Oil Field's storage tanks. The attack wasn't successful, but people up and down the coastline were in near hysterics. The mainland attack occurred a mere ten miles west of Bellosguardo.

"How grateful I am we made it out in time! I don't know when I'll want to return," Anna told guests at dinner at 8W. "The relief to be away is immense."

"I can't imagine what you went through," said Amanda Storrs, a hand to heart. "You were so close!"

After dinner, as Anna played the harp, Styka looked over at Huguette seated to his left. The normal cheerfulness was present only when one directly talked to her, otherwise her eyes appeared troubled. Her white Chanel gown was from many collections ago. He thought she had lost too much weight.

In any case, Huguette's not looking her best.

After Anna's performance, Styka requested his favorite Bach violin concerto. "Mrs. Clark, it has been many months. I would so enjoy it this evening!"

"Oh, I couldn't just now. I wouldn't do it justice. I need to practice a little more, then I will play it for you the next time you come." Huguette's eyes darted nervously around at Anna's guests.

"I won't forget. And what about resuming your painting lessons?" said Styka. "It has been far too long. Since last fall, I believe. You're neglecting your talent, my dear."

"Oh, and that as well. Don't I have a lot to do?" Huguette smiled. "*Mais oui, cher maître,* I'll come soon..."

Huguette's anxiety only increased after hearing from her lawyer and accountant regarding government taxes increasing during wartime. She felt she had to economize. Couture clothing and painting lessons she took a hard look at.

I think I should go down to two lessons a week.

After days of Styka not hearing a response, Huguette finally came; however, her normal concentration flagged. After ascertaining she wasn't quite herself, Styka graciously allowed her to leave without mercilessly teasing like he would've done previously.

He later confessed to Anna, "I'm a little surprised she lets the world get under her skin so thoroughly."

"Yes, don't discuss *anything* about the war. Help me out by simply focusing on painting."

Huguette was preoccupied with spiraling, fearful imaginations. She read constantly about Occupied France.

Repeatedly to Anna she confessed, "I feel consumed by what Japan has done to the United States. I'm dismayed at the government's response to the second attack in California."

All Japanese Americans living on the West Coast were rounded up by authorities and housed in internment camps in out-of-the-way locales; a "necessary precaution" against an enemy threat. Before the war ended, ninety-four percent of Japanese Americans in the continental United States were detained against their will.

"All those poor people," Huguette said during dinner at 8W. "Some have lived here for several generations and look how we're treating our own citizens. It's not their fault the Japanese government attacked us."

"Arthur has lost his Japanese cook in Beverly Hills. Mr. Muto and his wife were interred ten days ago."

Huguette set down her sterling silver fork and knife on the Tiffany plate. "You're not serious? How long did he say they had worked for him?"

"Oh, I'd say going on twenty years, at least. It's a shame. He has no idea when to expect their return. Thankfully, they'll never lose employment with my brother."

"Well, at least there's that. That poor, sweet couple! I hate to think they will not be at *oncle* Arthur's the next time we visit! No one can make miso soup and seaweed salad like Mr. Muto. He taught me to use chopsticks... Can you imagine being rounded up like traitors with no rights?"

"No, I cannot. The Mutos were sent to a camp in Cody, Wyoming."

"Heaven forbid, such a desolate place. I pity them." Huguette picked at the *sole meunière* and *pommes vapeur* without ingesting anything more.

"I pray every night this war will end soon. How can anything be worse than what we went through in the Great War? It's unfathomable," said Anna. "I'll go to Mass again tomorrow. I feel more at peace there. Will you come with me, *ma chérie?*"

"No, *Maman*, not right now."

Overall, life in Manhattan was quieter. Huguette had little desire to be a hostess. Her chef had quit, citing boredom. No matter. The housekeeper and head maid pooled knowledge to cook simple meals for the unfussy Huguette, who, in any case, mostly ate dinners at 8W. For breakfast and lunches, Huguette preferred small, light meals. The baked goods she requested were easily purchased at the local French bakery; Winter's Market on Lexington Avenue made deliveries of groceries. The servants learned it was no trouble scaling back work at 12W.

With the war, it was preferable to keep entertainments in one's home. Social ostentation or display of wealth was frowned upon, regardless of social strata. Only the most exuberant of extroverts complained but were hushed by the majority supporting the war effort. Many had European friends and family who were slogging through a third year of rationing and war deprivations. At Anna's latest *soirée*, an observant Huguette overheard conversations which unnerved. Some of the guests arranged in small groups and couples around the drawing room couldn't resist conversing openly of the topic on everyone's mind.

Mrs. Sarah Harding, from 7W who sometimes accompanied Anna on the piano, spoke up: "Oh yes, my British cousin on my mother's side informed me quite some time ago even the great houses of Chatsfield and Blenheim are taken over by the wounded or military intelligence, or something of that nature. All those gracious rooms dusty and shut up except for spaces large enough to create offices or hospitals of sorts for the wounded soldiers pouring in from the continent.

"Consider the vast change! I cannot, I confess. I was there as a young woman, and those were the most beautiful palaces, I dare say. Simply stirring to my soul."

"Mrs. Harding, that *really* is not new information. Must you bring up such things? It's too much for me... I'm old! I want to imagine Britain as grand as it used to be," said Laura Green.

"Do forgive me, Mrs. Green, but I cannot out of good conscience avoid it. Consider that France, Belgium, Luxembourg, and Holland all fell to the Nazis like dominoes! It's shocking, I tell you. A swastika draped over *l'Arc de Triomphe*! Who would have imagined after the bravery and triumph of World War I? And now? The Nazis a stone's throw across the Channel from Britain! Are they next...? Are *we* next?" pouted Harding, who was still sore plans to move to London had been foiled.

"Oh, now that our boys are in the war it will be over very soon, mark my words. Let's talk about something less shocking," said a third woman, a Mrs. Kay Carter, Anna's long-time rival at bridge.

At the mention of Nazis in Paris, Huguette felt a frisson go down her back. *The Germans never made it to Paris during the first world war. What's gone wrong?*

Suddenly, she couldn't stand to be at the party. Rising without meeting anyone's eyes, she slipped out of the room to the kitchen and then up the back stairs. Only Anna and a few maids marked her departure.

"There the young Mrs. Clark goes. How long she stay this time, maybe an hour?" said a maid, wiping off a kitchen counter while shaking her head.

With a stern eye, the butler put finger to lips before picking up a loaded silver salver to make drink rounds.

May 1942
907 Fifth Avenue, New York City

At 12W, the doorbell rang unexpectedly. The butler was perturbed because he hadn't received advanced notice from the doormen, which was highly unusual. When he opened the door, he understood why. He led the visitors into the drawing room and hissed at the maid, "Fetch Mrs. Clark at once!"

The maid went through the hidden door in the gallery, and then rapped softly on a door. Her mistress was sitting on a stool at a sunny window loading film into a camera.

Huguette glanced up with the camera in her lap, annoyed at the interruption. "I don't have an appointment with anyone. Why on earth did you admit them?"

"I couldn't say no to the butler, Mrs. Clark! You know how he is!" The maid backed up against the closed door with a frightened expression.

"Why ever not? Who is it? Why are you acting so strangely?"

"Some real serious men, ma'am. I was afraid of 'em. I peeked in the drawing room. Dark suits and such serious faces. And they want to talk to *you*!"

"Men in dark suits...?"

"One showed a badge to Mr. Thompkins, ma'am."

Huguette rose, setting aside the camera. "It sounds like the police. Why would they want to talk to me...?"

The maid shook her head with wide eyes. Huguette gave up on the maid's idiocy. She automatically pulled shoulders back and ignored an uneasy stomach. On the way to the drawing room, she put on the social armor learned long ago at Spence: head held high; ramrod straight posture; tuck in stomach; Mona Lisa smile; and, at all times, a quiet tone.

Grey fedoras in hand, two tall, thin men with conservative haircuts and clean-shaved faces wearing charcoal grey suits, white oxford button downs, non-descript ties, and black leather brogues stood in the drawing room. They looked uncomfortable surrounded by Louis XV antiques, Impressionist art, and heavy silk curtains pulled from generous windows displaying Central Park. The men appeared very out of place, as if middle management had come to the boss's house for a routine business meeting. If Huguette hadn't already been on alert, she might have been tempted to smirk.

She walked a few feet into the room. At once, in a neutral but serious tone of voice—betraying no emotion—one of the agents spoke.

"Mrs. Clark, we're here from the Federal Bureau of Investigation. We're sorry to disturb without attempting to contact you first. However, with the sensitive nature of the conversation we need to have with you, and with a war on, we felt it necessary to come to your home to talk face to face as soon as possible."

"You're from... the Federal Bureau of Investigation? Am I supposed to be familiar with that agency, sir? This is highly irregular. Can I have you discuss this issue with my lawyer? He—"

"The Federal Bureau of Investigation is part of the United States government tasked with conducting counter-intelligence operations against Axis threats along with internal security threats from enemy countries. Mrs. Clark, we're interested in the years of close communication you've had with our current enemy, the country of Japan..."

Huguette was stunned. She recollected Bryce Turner discussing the FBI last year. He distrusted their methods; it was rumored Americans were secretly wiretapped. In nanoseconds, she understood the full implication of this unannounced visit.

She was under investigation.

Will I too go to a camp?

Automatically, Huguette invited the agents to sit down because her legs suddenly felt weak. Sinking down with relief in the closest chair handy, her heart raced. She realized she was holding her breath.

I'll pass out if I don't breathe.

Without waiting, one recently hired agent began firing off questions, remaining on his feet with legs spread in a power position. The other senior agent likewise remained standing, tacitly pulling out a small notebook and pencil. He observed his partner's performance and the woman in question. The agents were merely two of thousands in the rapidly expanding bureau. This was not their first meeting that day with civilians suspected of spying.

Nausea and dismay gripped Huguette as the agent drilled her. She was barely able to answer coherently. When Anna queried her later on the specifics, Huguette had zero recollection.

"It was all I could do to constantly keep my wits about me. I felt pressured, mistrusted, even though the agents betrayed no feeling. They never wavered in what they were doing, ferreting out my suspected wrongdoing."

The FBI came back three more times during the next six weeks. The agents were not always the same, although the sartorial choices and vocal tones remained identical. During the final visit, yet another unfamiliar pair brought recording equipment. This frightened Huguette far more than the notebook had.

She stared hard at the unfamiliar metal equipment spread out on the coffee table. Normally she was delighted by technology, but not when it was being used against her.

Now she would be on record, word for word.

Who else will listen to these recordings?

Each time it was the same routine. Identical words of introduction. Questions she failed to answer to their satisfaction. And then more questions which had the same intent but were worded differently. Different variations on the same theme.

Huguette's intelligence immediately picked up the psychological patterns meant to confuse. To trick into confession.

They think I'm a spy!

Prying questions about how many languages she spoke. About her childhood. About her wealth. About her ex-husband. And especially about anything which could drum up associations with Japan:

Have you ever been to Japan, Mrs. Clark? Do you speak Japanese? List the names of all the Japanese associates and acquaintances you know as of today. Do you ever intend on visiting Japan someday? Has anyone from Japan ever visited you in the past or since the war began? How long have you lived in California?

How long has your uncle, Mr. Arthur La Chappelle, employed native Japanese servants, Mrs. Clark? How often do you associate with them? How often do you import Japanese products from the Marsh Company in Santa Barbara? Do you sell your Japanese artwork? Do you offer any aid to or support the country of Japan in any way at this time, Mrs. Clark? Have you ever been asked for any information sensitive to the United States government from a Japanese associate in Japan or in the United States?

Huguette answered everything to the best of her ability. She repeated herself. She retold the same story of her long-time interest in Japanese art and culture. She offered to show collections of Japanese dolls, jade sculptures, and paintings, which they turned down. She was at a loss as to how they could think she would betray her country.

Is it true, Mrs. Clark, that you were not born or reared for the first five years of your life in the United States? Is English your first or second language? Do you hold allegiance to the United States or to France? We understand your father was a United States Senator from Montana, is that correct? Do you have any current political associates in Washington? Do you associate with or give donations to any socialist or communist organizations at this time? Are you or have you ever been a fascist? Do you sympathize with Marxist principles? Have you ever been a member of a communist or socialist party? What is your current political party, Mrs. Clark? Has your party affiliation ever changed?

The FBI agents stood or sat rigidly on the ivory damask sofa, intently listening, taking occasional notes. Bland, nondescript, young or middle-aged faces that revealed not a shred of emotion. The agents refused to alter their set procedure for any social niceties.

They think I'm a spy!

During each interrogation, Huguette went through the same agonizing routine. She smiled like a Jumeau doll—a frozen smile with wide blue eyes—clenching sweaty hands in her lap, knowing she wasn't convincing.

I'm not guilty of anything!

Yet somehow it wasn't bad enough that the agents ever asked her to leave.

What will happen to me if I have to leave with them?

With the same dispassionate expression, the agents departed down the long gallery hung with world-class art and a sixteenth-century tapestry. Huguette was at a loss how to deal with the experience of personal interrogation. She felt like she was in a cheap film endlessly replaying.

They think I'm a spy!

And then abruptly, the torture ended. The FBI did not return. But by then Huguette was a mess.

She had lost over twenty-five pounds and wasn't sleeping soundly. The nightmares continued. She woke up to delusions of looming male faces in the windows or high up on the ceiling, watching her on the bed below. She hadn't gone to a painting lesson or practiced the violin in many weeks. Despite Anna's frequent phone calls, nothing could induce her to come down to 8W. She sat dully, with a book or a newspaper on hand, staring into space. Sometimes she burst into tears, especially if Anna came over.

"Oh *Maman*, I can't handle another visit. I don't ever want to see those men here again... Can we go to Bellosguardo to get away?"

"Hugo, please stop crying, *ma chérie*. This is unseemly. You've been told they won't return; the investigation is done. And they can come to Bellosguardo as easily as here. The FBI is everywhere. But, cheer up, we both know you are *not* a spy. What a silly notion! Will you not laugh at it?"

"You want me to laugh? *Maman*, they're coming back! I don't want to be here when they do!" Huguette wrapped arms around herself and began rocking back and forth.

Anna reached out. "Stop! There is nothing more to concern yourself with. It's time to be grateful it's over and rejoin normal life. I don't believe you've bathed all week, nor have you changed your clothing. This cannot go on. I will make a call for a hairdresser to come tomorrow morning.

"And look at your chipped manicure, my goodness, Huguette. You need to do something productive to take your mind off of your worries. Clean up. You're coming to dinner."

"Yes, *Maman*. I should..."

But Huguette didn't move, her haunted eyes looking over at Anna plaintively before flickering around the room and then back down. She picked up the book, opened it at the bookmark, and then closed it. She stared at nothing before beginning to rock back and forth again. Anna knew Huguette had no notion of going anywhere.

Was she even listening? She's becoming a wreck!

She asked quietly, "When is the last time you've eaten?"

"I ate breakfast."

Anna checked with the butler, who said his mistress had not eaten a full meal in weeks.

"She'll pick at her food, but that is all, madame."

Anna knew Huguette had not left her apartment either. She had never closely monitored her daughter's schedule, as Huguette liked to spend days sequestered happily. Huguette was not an indolent woman, and she had always been content spending large amounts of time alone. That didn't surprise Anna, either; she and William were the same.

The women lived separate lives despite residing close together. But it was Huguette's practice to come to visit Anna multiple times a week, if not daily, and talk on the phone multiple times a day. But now that wasn't occurring unless Anna rang. She was getting asked by friends where Huguette was these days.

Something is terribly wrong.

She returned to 8W to phone Amelia.

"Will you come stay the night with her? She asked for you. It's awkward for me to watch over her because she fusses about it."

That night, Amelia put Huguette to bed with a glass of warm milk. She sat with her for a half hour, reminiscing about Andrée mothering Huguette during the beautiful parties and holidays at *avenue Victor Hugo*. Hours later she was awakened by Huguette screaming. Amelia gave Huguette a sleeping pill, which knocked her out for the next twelve hours.

In the morning, Amelia went down to 8W. Using ornate silver tongs, Amelia selected buttered toast from the silver toast rack.

"When she wakes, we'll drive to a sanitarium in New Jersey. I've already discussed it with the doctor."

"I don't know if that's the best step."

Anna took a small bite of plain yogurt.

"Anna, this is beyond us!" She looked up from spreading marmalade. "If you can't make a decision, then let me. What harm will it do? She'll have excellent care and be monitored by doctors specializing in nervous breakdowns. I know this is best. She simply can't handle what's happened to her."

The toast crunched thickly on Amelia's first bite.

"Oh really? Listen to what you're saying. She can't handle life despite being a grown woman of thirty-six... We've been through bad times in life and haven't fallen apart! We're all going through the war and not having a nervous breakdown! The FBI came, yes, and how unfortunate they misunderstood her interest in Japan. But that is over now. I've told her a dozen times. She won't listen."

Amelia dabbed her mouth with a napkin before speaking.

"Be patient. A complete removal from New York will no doubt help her healing process. I've discussed the FBI with her, too, but it is as if she is expecting them to return any day. She cannot calm down."

"I realize, Amelia, but I'm not comfortable with the idea of admitting her into a sanitarium." Anna looked at her sister, tapping the linen tablecloth. "How elegant to withdraw from troubles and pain and discomfort while the rest of the world is at war! She wants to be protected from the world. As if that were possible!"

"Anna, please..." Amelia gripped Anna's hand. "She must have lost thirty pounds already. She's nothing but skin and bones. She's not sleeping, not living life normally. She's clearly not in a sound mental state, which worries me. She needs to be seen by a doctor specializing in mental disorders, not merely your private physician. She had a terrible nightmare last night."

"She's not your daughter... I *want* her to be healthy, of course! To be happy, to be married someday. You know this... Perhaps... I... feel some guilt because this is *my* fault she is so delicate!" Anna pressed a hand to mouth, fighting back tears. "Am I a bad mother? Am I the reason why she can't cope with life?"

"Don't blame yourself, Anna dearest. This is unfortunate, but it's not your fault. I believe it is the FBI investigation that is to blame. Not you. However, we must do something very soon to intervene in this downward spiral she's on."

"You're the wise one now, little sister. Will you come? That way it will seem more normal. Like we're on a day trip." Anna brightened.

"*Bien sûr*. Let me finish my breakfast and I'll call Bryce."

Uncomfortable with the need for a sanitarium, and desiring to protect Huguette's reputation, Anna concealed what was happening from everyone but the Turners. She stayed at a hotel in a small city nearby while her daughter was being treated at an institution surrounded by hundreds of acres of woods. She visited every afternoon. It took eight weeks before Huguette was discharged, still underweight but with a far calmer aspect and no talk of the FBI or the war.

Amidst the Clark's prolonged absence, Styka quietly married Darlene Foster.

Anna said to Amanda Storrs while they dined at *L'Aiglon*, "Finally! I never thought that man would do it, but he has. I would bet he made the decision due to the war."

Storrs ruefully laughed. "Hmmm, I agree. It's too bad though... He was always a *wonderful* companion, so elegantly attired, so gentlemanly, taking me out whenever I wanted. Alas, now he has a wife, that era is over for good!"

Anna forbore informing Huguette, not wanting to interrupt her daughter's convalescence. When Anna did broach the subject at breakfast days before she knew painting lessons were to be resumed, Huguette was silent. Huguette set down her *café au lait* and picked up a fork to push around scrambled eggs.

"You're not saying anything. Aren't you pleased?"

Huguette looked up with empty eyes. "*Bien sûr*. I'll send a wedding gift this week. I knew it would happen someday..."

She looked at the sliced rye toast and eggs, suddenly not hungry. A wave of pain enveloped her heart.

He's married!

Anna motioned for the maid to clear her plate.

"Monsieur Styka is over the moon she's pregn—"

Huguette bolted out of her chair.

"Sorry, *Maman*, I just remembered I forgot to make an important call. Now I'm late! I'll be back down for dinner."

Huguette kissed Anna's cheek and fled.

At first, it was excruciating. Huguette entered 222 Central Park South after a long absence, hauling a large leather portfolio to conceal paintings from onlookers. When the door flew open, it gave a moment's pain to encounter a broadly smiling Mrs. Darlene Styka.

Darlene's cheerful voice rang out, "Oh hello, Mrs. Clark! It's been a long time. How are you these days?" She wiped flour off dusty hands with an apron. "You've caught me baking up a storm."

Huguette stood looking at her mutely. *Doesn't she know I'm on a no-talking cure? Does she expect me to reply?*

She nodded and went down the hall to the studio.

Now he's a permanent duo. Once the war ends, there'll be no more outings together.

The moment Styka saw her, he began acting like a mime. She laughed softly as first he performed the classic hitting a wall routine. He searched for a way past the glass barrier, then put a finger to one eye to indicate a tear. Spinning around, Styka mimed an entire routine of introducing a new student to the studio, all in complete silence with outrageously dramatic gestures and expressions.

Huguette good-naturedly brushed him off by setting her canvas on the waiting easel. She deliberately pointed to the partially completed painting and then waved him over to begin the critique.

As the months passed, Styka remained attentive from afar. He sent bouquets of flowers. At Christmas, he gave Huguette a new palette of Sitka spruce commissioned from the Steinway factory. In small ways, he was continually urging her to paint. Her love of art remained, but the strong interest to paint waned.

Since the mid-1930s, air travel became more popular despite cold, unpressurized cabins and frequent accidents. For years, acquaintances bragged to the Clarks about the speed and efficiency of United Airlines or Transcontinental and Western Air using the Douglas DC-3 aircraft which carried up to 32 passengers. But the Clarks stubbornly clung to the traditions of the past. They made the long and familiar train trip as comfortably as possible. A private rail coach with opulent sleeping and dining quarters took them from one end of North America to the other in a few days.

After eighteen months of exile on the east coast, Anna wanted to return to Bellosguardo. On the train, she sat with Huguette in the private lounge.

"Goodness, train travel is far safer. I can't imagine squeezing up into one of those airplanes. It must be like sardines in a can," she said while observing the Midwest's forests and agricultural fields stream past.

"I've heard on long flights they have cots. Doesn't that tempt you?"

Huguette said with a smile, looking up from the latest issue of *Vogue*.

"A cot! Imagine! It would be like camping during the expeditions Will Jr. always bragged about."

At Bellosguardo, all seemed normal despite wartime alterations. Anna forgave a lessening of services and less-than-stellar gardens in the name of patriotism. From her balcony, they used binoculars whenever a ship was spotted.

"Despite the victory of Midway, the threat of an enemy submarine lurking beneath the waves is ever-present. Will we ever feel relaxed at Bellosguardo again, do you think?"

Huguette shrugged and put a protective arm around Anna's shoulders.

"Let's go inside. The sun is so hot today. Now that I don't have much of a tan, I can really feel it."

When the chef complained about the lack of quality ingredients, Anna had Marié make enquiries into real estate. As soon as it was clarified Mrs. William A. Clark would be the purchaser, the owner of the agency, Tom Carlyle and his top seller, Fred Jackson, came without hesitation to Bellosguardo. Together in the *bureau*, they looked over available properties. Anna was pleased to discover amongst the offerings a nearby ranch of over two hundred acres, on the market for ten months.

"Is there a reason it hasn't sold?"

"No, Mrs. Clark. It's a fine ranch in the Santa Ynez Valley,' said Mr. Carlyle. "Which might be the problem. As you know, there's a war and credit is hard to come by, even for well-to-do folks. The asking price is high, and I don't believe this particular seller will come down much, if at all."

Several days later in the car, Anna said, "It's only twenty-two miles from Santa Barbara. I feel it's imperative we should have a retreat of sorts, away from the coast. And I want to ensure access to plenty of food and fresh water in case of invasion."

Huguette turned her head from watching the passing scenery. "Oh, you are wise to do that. Although I don't want to think of an invasion. My goodness, what a horrible word!"

"One must always prepare for the worst. Your father taught me that. Since we are not entertaining much at all, or spending much money, for that matter, I've decided to invest those funds into property. I think it's a splendid idea. I feel better already!"

"So, have you purchased the ranch? Why're we going?" Huguette was amused. "It thought it was only a casual look-see today."

"My lawyer has the paperwork. I'm simply taking a good look in person before proceeding. And I want your opinion."

Huguette knew it was a done deal. *If Maman is troubling herself to see the property up close, she has made up her mind.*

Soon the Cadillac passed underneath the wrought-iron gates. Huguette's eyes immediately traveled up to read "Rancho Alegre" posted high atop. The car quietly purred underneath on its way up the long dirt road leading to the house constructed out of field stone. The ranch turned out to be an unspoiled property in the mountains.

The house and swimming pool fed by a mountain stream were nothing much. Two stories, a handful of bedrooms and bathrooms, and a lodge-like great hall with a gigantic field stone fireplace.

"It's no matter, we'll only live there under duress," said Anna. "I'll simply update all the bathrooms, plumbing, kitchen, and roof, those sorts of basic things."

What interested Anna more was the food production capabilities and natural streams. The gardens, orchards, and large meadows with long dried grasses were surrounded by forest. She wanted her chef to have access to fresh vegetables, meat, and dairy. The ranch was able to feed not only humans but a variety of animals. Once they peeked around the perimeter of the pig pens and chicken coops—because Anna was not going to step one well-shod foot closer—she wanted to know more.

"Mr. Jackson, is it dangerous at all? Do the wild animals come up to the house?"

Jackson, a jumpy real estate agent in his late fifties with an amputated leg, Sears pinstripe suit, and black fedora, was at a loss. As a rule, he never stepped foot in the country. A nearby ranch hand was called over to answer the question.

Jimmy Jones tipped a sweat-stained cowboy hat back to squint at her. "Yes, ma'am, there's quite a bit of wild animals 'round these parts. You've got mountain lions, but them's shy. Coyotes, an' snakes is everywhere. Coyotes might come up ta the house if they're des'prate 'nough. We certainly hear 'em howlin.' An' snakes… Eagles an' hawks love ta eat 'em if yer ever ridin' through these hills an' lucky 'nough to see 'em swoop down an' grab one!"

Jones took his dirty leather gloved hands and squeezed, as if he were the eagle. "An' then that darn eagle flies off like nobody's business with a raw lunch that's still awrigglin' an' ahoppin' in its beak! It's quite a sight to see, ladies!"

He laughed heartily, revealing missing teeth. "Heck, snake tastes mighty okay over an open fire, that's fer darn sure."

Huguette was highly amused—she had only seen cowboys in films—but for Anna, it was a little too much raw reality.

I'll tell the chef he or Hoelscher will need come up to the ranch to oversee things. Anna nodded curtly.

"I appreciate the information, but I've no intention of becoming a ranching woman and riding wild through the hills."

Anna looked at Jackson, her mouth a displeased, thin red line. Jackson almost missed the cue.

"It's imperative to make this sale!" Carlyle had said before Jackson left. The ranch's owner, publisher Thomas Storke, pressured the agency to unload it at top dollar. Assuming the ladies would be pleased by the dramatic information presented by the ranch hand, Jackson discovered his error. He sprang into action.

"Thank you, Mr. Jones, thank *you*! That will be *all*. But, we appreciated the *bird's eye view* into local wildlife on the ranch."

Jackson winked knowingly at Anna while slapping Jones on the shoulder. Huguette had a tiny smile on her lips at the pun and the incongruity of the cast of characters, but Anna retreated a few steps away. She turned her back to examine the trees ringing the meadow and Figueroa Mountain.

"My, how lovely the forest is up here. All those oaks and Coulter pines."

"Ladies, if you don't mind, follow me over to the barns and stables," said Jackson in his booming voice. "We'll only take a moment in there for you to see how well-kept everything is. There are a few horses worth taking a good look at. I wouldn't dream of taking up too much of your time with more stories, however. They would be, you understand, your employees if you were to purchase the ranch."

"Yes, of course, Mr. Jackson," Anna said. "But I'm more interested in speaking with the overseer."

Jones, in dusty dungarees with a soiled, red handkerchief looped around a sweaty neck, leaned back with a brown leather boot against the wooden fence. He smiled wide at the younger woman in a fine buttercup yellow dress and hat.

She's a real pretty blonde. He nodded respectfully before putting back on his well-worn cowboy hat.

Huguette focused not on his looks, but that he was missing at least three teeth. *The man probably isn't past the age of thirty. If* Maman *buys this ranch, we should offer dental care for employees.*

Huguette quickly turned to catch up to her mother going to the barn and stables, commenting quietly in French, "What a peculiar man!" Privately, she thought, *I wonder if Andrée would still be living today if we had been born under these rural circumstances? She would've turned forty-one this month...*

Anna was pleased, and, on their return, rang her lawyer to go ahead with the purchase. With the ranch secured and aflutter with long-postponed plans to meet with Marcel Grandjany—her celebrated harp instructor—she soon desired to retreat to New York's security. At breakfast the morning of her departure, Huguette requested to stay on. An hour later, Anna stood with an Italian black leather purse and white gloves in hand while she eyed her daughter. Outside the front glass doors, the chauffeur in black uniform stood in readiness next to the idling vehicle.

"Are you very sure you don't want to come back with me?"

Huguette nodded. "I need some rest, and Bellosguardo is perfect for that. I don't feel like being back in New York just yet. Is that okay, *Maman*?"

"*Oui, c'est bien*! I'm only concerned as your mother... Are you feeling all right? You'll be alone here."

"*Oui*, don't worry about me, *s'il te plaît*. I enjoy being alone." Huguette embraced Anna.

"Alright then, *ma petite*, I won't. It's simply not like you... However, a little bit of independence from your mother is probably best."

Anna smiled in an attempt to encourage her daughter to talk. She waited, but Huguette only looked at her. Anna slid on gloves and adjusted her hat.

"Come back in a month or so. The rest and sunshine will no doubt do you wonders. You've got more color in your face now. It's becoming.

"Keep in mind we've a number of important social engagements this fall. I don't want you to be absent for too long. And recall the Stykas had their baby girl. We need to send a bouquet. Will you take care of that for me?"

Huguette nodded. "I will today, *Maman, bien sûr*. And like a dutiful *marraine*, I'm also ordering a baby basket from Au Nain Bleu."

"Wonderful idea! Put my name down as well. Amelia and I'll visit the Stykas in several weeks or so. When his wife is up to it. Goodness knows she won't want us barging in too soon. I remember those days...! I'll let you know how it went if you're not back. *Adieu, ma petite!*"

Anna kissed Huguette before descending the stone stairway with a view of the ocean stretching out to the Channel Islands and the horizon. Her busy thoughts already dwelled on upcoming social obligations.

The motor soon faded completely as it disappeared down East Cabrillo Boulevard. Huguette stood in the sun on the front steps. She could faintly make out the gentle waves shushing on the sand below the cliff. She inhaled deeply, reveling in the clean air. Squinting at birds flying high above, she held a hand to shield eyes from the glare.

Who wants to rush back to New York when there's all this beauty to enjoy? Maybe I'll go for a swim later?

The maid waited in silence until her mistress stepped back inside the foyer before shutting the doors. Huguette went to the *bureau*. Then she rang for the housekeeper.

"I need flowers to be sent to this address in New York, with a card congratulating on the birth of a baby girl named Wendy." Huguette handed an address to the housekeeper.

"I want only light meals, you know my preferences. No entertaining will be going on for the next month or so of my visit. There's no need to buy large quantities of food or supplies or open up any guest bedrooms. I plan to live quietly. That will be all. Thank you, Ms. Wilbur."

The petite housekeeper nodded while saying, "Mrs. Clark."

Only far down the hall did a smile break upon her lined face. *As if I need a reminder the younger Mrs. Clark won't be whooping it up with a houseful of young guests while her mother is absent!*

Huguette rose to go to the studio. She stretched neck and arms. *I already feel lighter.*

Since the hospital stay, both her mother and Amelia had been hovering with questioning eyes and patting hands. It seemed Anna was afraid to leave her alone. It was hard on both of them.

Huguette looked around at various projects, including a half-finished painting. Feeling energized, she had no desire to sit or be inside. She took up a camera, checked the film, and spent hours photographing meticulously decorated rooms and manicured gardens. She assiduously avoided any scene including military paraphernalia or barbed wire. She wanted no visual reminders of the harsh war years.

Her ears appreciated the lack of police or ambulance sirens. She occasionally halted to breathe in another draught of sweet, Pacific air. The wonder of no smog or car exhaust always soothed.

I feel healthier here.

In the studio, she removed the film to be developed and carefully put away the camera. That was a task she alone performed.

She slowly ascended to her sitting room. Normally in the late afternoons she would be out swimming or playing golf or maybe at a garden party with *Maman*. But with the ongoing war, those long-standing routines were on hold. She figured she would read awhile. She was in the middle of *Dragon Seed* by Pearl S. Buck, and *Maman* had given her the bestseller *The Robe* by Lloyd Douglas. Books were an easy topic of conversation to fall back on at parties, Anna always advised.

A half hour later, instead of finishing Buck's novel as planned, Huguette meandered into the bedroom. She put the novel aside to lie down on the bed. The windows were thrown wide to catch the soft breeze. Stretching luxuriously, she purred with contentment.

To be alone at Bellosguardo for the next four to six weeks at least. This is perfection...

Deep in her subconscious, there was the hunch the FBI could not find her behind Bellosguardo's exclusive gates. In the war fought inside her mind, her own country had become the enemy.

As soon as eyelids fluttered shut, Huguette fell into a deep sleep.

September 10, 2001

Doctor's Hospital, New York City

At almost half past eight, Hannah Price scurried down the hospital corridor with plastic bags looped around an arm and banging against her thigh. One tiny hand clutched a Nokia 6160 while she eyed the exact hour on the digital screen. She knew if she were even a minute late her employer would begin calling; she had already spoken to her twice today. Earlier that morning, Price's young daughter—after a rare forty-eight hours together—threw a tantrum at the front door as she attempted to leave.

Not a good way to start a seven-day work week.

Price knocked once and waited until the night nurse opened the door. She knew to never barge in without announcing herself.

"Good morning, Mrs. Clark! It nice to see you!" Price waved cheerily as Nurse Nelson grabbed her bag and exited.

"Good morning, Hannah! It's very nice to see you. The weekends always drag when you are off two days. I'm *very happy* you are back. Now the day can properly begin." Huguette smiled cheerfully, clasping hands in front of her with delight.

"I need to see my children, too..."

Price felt torn. She wanted to excel at her profession by acquiescing to Madame Clark's incessant demands for attention, but she desired more family time. She went to the counter to busy herself with the coffee machine and small fridge, unloading the bags. She turned to hand Mrs. Clark *café au lait* in an I heart NY ceramic mug.

"I brought croissant for breakfast and chicken soup for lunch."

"Oh, thank you! That's very kind. You'll have to help me eat the croissant. I don't know if I can manage. They make them so large now, it's rather ridiculous."

Price—an immigrant from the Philippines who had married a New Yorker—had little experience with French baked goods. She remained silent. She learned years ago to let the patient talk, which was a green light of kindness to Mrs. Clark. The nurse's personality was one which had no desire to question beyond practical topics. Chief amongst any topic of importance: the welfare and promotion of her family.

Huguette busied herself with the breakfast tray. She then asked with genuine interest, "How are the children, Thomas, Annabelle, and Samuel?"

"They good. They say I work too much, you know. Annabelle cry a lot when I leave this morning. That why I almost late."

Huguette chuckled. "Well, you're *very* important here. Tell them you're needed here *just as much* as home. Will your husband bring them to see me soon? I'd like to hear about their school year beginning. I always *adored* the start of the academic year. Such a wonderful feeling of anticipation."

Huguette took a delicate bite of croissant, wiping buttery fingers on a paper napkin.

Once breakfast was completed, Price took away the breakfast tray and went about the usual morning routine. She kept an eye on Mrs. Clark as the patient went into the bathroom alone to wash up, then brush teeth and hair. Afterward, they made laps around the room and stretched. Easing Mrs. Clark back into bed, the TV was turned on at the same time a newspaper was handed over. The nurse then had a moment to look over the day's schedule. She saw one appointment that could cause problems.

"Remember Martha Townsend coming today."

"Who? I don't recall authorizing that."

"She Dr. Townsend's mother. She come in one hour."

"Oh, now I recall. Why did I agree to it...?"

"He a persuasive man."

"Quite right. It can't be helped then."

Sixty minutes later there was a soft knock. The nurse opened the heavy door a crack to make sure Mary Townsend was alone. She knew Mrs. Clark would protest if there were two or more people wanting access. She suggested to Dr. Townsend some time ago it was best to deal with her employer one-on-one.

"And maybe your mother work better than you. Mrs. Clark like women. Men, it depends."

"Interesting! She's always respectful to me." Dr. Townsend looked with questioning eyes at the private nurse whom his patient clearly favored above everyone.

"She respect you! She just don't want to be pressured by a man. She in charge, not you."

"Oh, I see... Well, if you could help get Mrs. Clark to agree to a donation to the hospital, then I would be *most* appreciative."

He nodded to Nurse Price as if he were the one who could give her a promotion. Knowing better, the nurse ignored the hint. She would help the hospital because it lowered any personal medical bills, and, if administration were happy, then Mrs. Clark wouldn't be kicked out. Her job security was paramount. Thus, it benefitted both the doctor and the nurse to get Mrs. Clark to donate in the near future.

"Send your mother. I too see if I can persuade."

Which is how, on a warm, bright Monday morning the second week of September, Martha Townsend found herself in the unenviable position of requesting a massive donation out of her son's most elusive patient.

"Just be yourself, Mom. With your killer charm, you'll be successful. You're the best fundraiser in New Jersey, right?"

Between appointments, Townsend stood in his office rallying his mother's spirits. *She has to be the ticket!*

"And keep in mind, Mom, we've concluded this patient has a probable net worth of over seventy million. So don't feel bad, okay?"

"Son, when do I ever feel bad? I have to go, the driver's here."

Martha Townsend, a seventy-five-year-old retired lawyer, clicked off the Handspring Treo. She was dressed in a navy St. John suit, Ferragamo heels, and a Hermès silk scarf with pearls twisted around to hide a sagging neck. Normally avoiding the city, she dutifully went to aid her son's career.

When Martha entered, Huguette looked up from *The New York Times*. "Hello, Mrs. Townsend. We've been expecting you."

"Hello, nice to meet you, Mrs. Clark. Please call me Martha."

She extended her hand which Huguette ignored. The woman smiled graciously, looking cheerfully from Huguette to the nurse.

"My son has told me about you, as his long-time patient, and thought it would be nice if we were to meet."

"Alright. Do sit down. Did you have a hard time getting to the hospital? I know the traffic can be awful. Did you take the city bus?"

Martha smiled at the odd question. "No, I was driven here from New Jersey."

"New Jersey! That's quite a distance. I hope you have another errand in the city."

"Of course," Martha lied.

"Have you lived in New Jersey long?"

"Most my life. I think it's a fine state."

"I've been a few times... I prefer Connecticut and Rhode Island. Where do you like to go in New Jersey?"

The conversation went round and round, with Huguette asking one inane question after another. A half hour passed, and Martha was no closer to her true objective of wrangling money out of this patient. She began to feel a trifle impatient.

There's no way this woman is worth tens of millions... Mark is mistaken. It's time to end this.

"Mrs. Clark, you seem content here. Are you happy with my son's medical care?"

"Oh yes, Dr. Townsend is wonderful. He visits me from time to time. And see my skin cancer scars, how well they've healed? One can hardly refer to them as scars." The woman pointed first to withered lips and then to eyelids.

"Ah! I'm happy to hear that! And are you happy with the hospital itself? With the level of care, the amenities, and food available?"

"I suppose so. It's fine."

"You don't sound very pleased. That's too bad. Perhaps there's something we can do to raise the level of care. I myself am a generous donor to the hospital. Have you ever considered doing likewise? We donors do a great service to the hospital and the surrounding community..."

Martha's commanding tone of voice gradually lost momentum as she watched in growing disbelief while Mrs. Clark ignored her to search amongst folds of blankets to retrieve a remote. The elderly woman's finger activated the VCR. Jaunty music immediately filled the room. Silly voices rang out: "Fa la la la la, la la la la..."

"Have you ever watched this episode? It's delightful," said Huguette.

Martha recognized it only because of her grandchildren. Several minutes passed in sheer boredom: *And why are we watching the* Smurfs? *Is she going to respond...? This is ridiculous! Am I supposed to just sit here until it ends?!*

Twenty minutes later, Martha had had enough. She slipped the chain of the black quilted Chanel handbag on her shoulder and quietly stated, "Excuse me, Mrs. Clark, I've another appointment. Good day."

Huguette did not turn or say anything while Martha Townsend exited. She trained eyes on the animation based on the Belgian comic series written by Peyo. She found solace in mentally recording patterns of movement and familiar stylistic flourishes and themes that reminded of her childhood in France. She adored the eighteenth-century opening credits of forest with castles, villages of mushroom cottages, and the tiny, sweet Smurf characters persecuted by the evil wizard. Everything else was put out of mind as unimportant.

The next morning, Huguette woke to a smiling Nurse Price. Her thin hair was smashed on one side of her skull and spiked on the other.

"What time is it?"

"It about half past eight. You slept wonderful! You normally up like clockwork at half past seven. How about I brush your hair, and then I get some coffee."

Once hair was tamed, Huguette said, "I would like the newspaper, please."

She pulled on a blue cashmere sweater before reading the comic pages first. Then she called Simone Pierre. There was a busy signal.

"This is the fourth time I've tried. Why on earth can't I get through? This has never happened... Let's watch my morning program instead. I'm sure they'll fix the phones momentarily."

"Sure thing!"

Nurse Price pointed the remote at the TV. She rapidly clicked the channels until she landed on "Good Morning America." Something was off. The typically vivacious hosts were anything but. They weren't smiling or joking or talking endlessly about the fine early fall weather.

The hosts looked bewildered, even scared. Something about an airplane hitting a building in the Finance District... And then the image of the burning Twin Towers was displayed. Both women's eyes were riveted to the screen: It was like watching a horror movie playing out in one's backyard.

Huguette put a hand to mouth and mumbled, "Something terrible is..."

"What going on...?" Nurse Price's eyes widened at the grey smoke billowing out of the skyscrapers. She paused mid-task in the center of the room, hands slack.

"Someone's attacked us! New York is under attack!" Sitting up straighter in the hospital bed against multiple pillows, Huguette uttered small cries of dismay.

Then came the gut-wrenching collapses of the towers. First at 9:59a.m. and then 10:28a.m. Huguette merely squeaked in fear at each incomprehensible image, clutching blankets or reaching for the phone which was perpetually dead. They heard raised voices in the hallway but didn't open the door.

What was occurring was a mere six miles away.

"Don't open that door for anyone!" wailed Huguette. "We're under attack!"

She tried the phones repeatedly while viewing the live footage. "I well remember Pearl Harbor, but the difference was we didn't see the attack live! Afterward, we heard the radio broadcast and the horrific details. Hannah, you try to get through on the phone for awhile. I need a rest."

Huguette passed the beige receiver to Price who dialed Pierre's number. When that wasn't successful, Huguette switched to a number outside the city.

"Try Wendy in Massachusetts. That should work."

For the entire day, Huguette watched all the commentary and replays of the collapse of the Twin Towers on multiple channels. She listened to every talking head. Frustrated at the fits and starts of the phones, she kept calling Wendy Styka, Simone Pierre, and Colton Shepherd until she got through.

It's imperative to check up on everyone I love!

As soon as she knew they were safe, the calls ended quickly. Simone Pierre she called about every two hours.

"Simone, what do I do?"

"We can't do anything. Stay there. We're safe. The police and firefighters will protect us."

Mollified, Huguette hung up. She unmuted the TV and watched until late into evening. When Nurse Nelsen attempted to follow the normal routine, Huguette brushed her aside.

"I'll go to bed when I feel like it! I'm going to watch the broadcasts until they're done."

CNN and Fox News were a boon, as the talking heads endlessly rehashed—for weeks on end—every detail of press conferences, video footage, stock market plunges, and President Bush's speech that was tantamount to a declaration of war. Senators railed against Bush or insisted on supporting him. Round-the-clock CNN financial commentary on volatile global stock markets played day and night.

Huguette normally watched the markets obsessively as soon as she discovered those channels on cable. Now, she watched for the economic fallout of the attack on the Twin Towers. Keyed up for weeks, Huguette lost interest in everything which normally kept her cheerfully occupied.

"I insist on knowing what's happening. What *could* happen next!"

While she watched the 24/7 networks, she didn't eat much. She drank water only when the nurses pressed. When they weighed her, she had lost five pounds.

Price said, "Mrs. Clark, this not okay. You must eat or I take away the remote. I mean business."

"No, please don't do that. I'll eat. I think Bush is trying to give us a hint we're headed into World War III. This is unbelievable! Hannah, I remember both world wars. It's really something to live through. There are economies and deprivations. America however has been spared for so long. Until now! Americans' lives will change someday soon, mark my words..."

If Huguette were too worked up, Nurse Nelson cut a sleeping pill in half and dissolved it in warm milk before she turned down the lights.

"Thank you, that was lovely."

Huguette handed back the mug and bowed her head. She softly repeated from memory the Lord's Prayer in order of the languages she learned it in: French, English, then Spanish. Thinking of dear *Maman*, she added a line to bless the United States:

"And I pray there won't be a third world war. Amen."

December 1945
907 Fifth Avenue, New York City

Anna picked up the polished wood and brass handset to dial. By her side was her step-granddaughter, Agnes Clark Albert, visiting from San Francisco. Anna winked at Agnes who started chuckling.

Agnes shook her head. *Some things never change...*

She was reminded of an incidence at Bellosguardo long ago, well before it was rebuilt. A much younger Anna had perched on Grandfather's knee gently tugging on bushy whiskers. Anna had mercilessly teased Grandfather before he tickled her. Anna uttered playful shrieks before she was silenced by his passionate kiss.

Playing a croquet game on the lawn below the veranda, Agnes and her sisters stood in awe. Only Anna got away with disrespectful behavior. And then that kiss! They forgot not to stare as a side of grandfather was revealed they didn't know existed.

The girls knew their mother, Celia, detested both their father and grandfather. After Grandfather died and their father, Charlie, gave up interest in them, their relationship with Anna filled a breach. Anna and Huguette had made a point to send gifts to all the grandchildren, while occasionally attending Patsey's horse shows or polo matches and Agnes's concerts with the San Francisco Symphony.

To Agnes, Bellosguardo was like a second home. She thought it a pity her mother and Anna, having so much in common, were not closer.

Anna's vivacious voice trilled out, "Huguette, *bonjour, ma chérie.* Will you come down...? *Non?* But I have a surprise for you. And your niece Agnes is here. She'd like to say hello..."

Twenty minutes later, Huguette entered the drawing room dressed for a party. She wore a black silk dress with fat red polka dots, gold jewelry, and red and black leather bespoke pumps. She reached to give her niece a hug.

"Agnes, it's been too long! I'm happy to see you. Did you come alone?"

"Yes, the children are with their nanny. I'll only be gone a week."

"I didn't come down last night because of a little cold, but I feel better today." Huguette sat down with a smile. "How're your mother and siblings? Everyone well?"

"Oh yes. Mother is redecorating bedrooms at House-on-Hill, and Patsey is up to her eyeballs in children and palominos at the ranch. Mary is with Mother, I think, and Paul, who knows where he is these days. Off exploring Africa or something."

"We should make a visit to see Celia, soon," Huguette said. "It's been too long; I would love to play in her exquisite music room once again." She looked over at Anna, who sat quietly waiting. "Well, *Maman,* what is it now? I was in the middle of painting a fan. I can't quite get a yellow shade to mix properly. I probably smell of turpentine."

Huguette examined her scrubbed red hands self-consciously.

"Ask Monsieur Styka for help; I'm of no use in that arena. I want you to look over there."

Anna pointed to the far wall. Huguette's face fell and she shook her head. Anna said nothing, keeping her finger trained on the spot. She smiled in expectation, and Huguette rolled eyes playfully. Huguette turned her head a smidge and perceived the empty wall out of peripheral vision. Then she turned completely.

"And what did you do with the *horrendous* Cézanne?"

"I sold it!" Anna exulted.

Huguette gazed with wide blue eyes at the two women for a few moments.

"You've had that painting forever! I'm quite surprised... Whatever was the reason? I don't believe for a second it was my complaining about it. Agnes, don't take her word for it!"

Agnes blurted out, "Oh Grandmother, if you've had the *Madame Cézanne* since you were young in Paris, maybe it was a mistake to sell?"

"Sell...?"

Huguette was mystified.

"*Non, je ne regret rien*. We still have the other Cézanne to enjoy. And since Huguette was a girl, she has detested *Madame Cézanne in a Red Dress*. She's always had an artist's eye, knowing exactly what she liked and didn't like. It was the first Cézanne I acquired; it used to hang in our Paris flat in the red drawing room. Huguette would wrinkle her little nose at it. Ah, that was so long ago... But for years she hasn't wanted to come into this room because she detests it so.

"I believe now with the end of the war, it's time to spread goodwill. I want to celebrate musically! To encourage musicians to keep beautiful music alive in this precarious world. Therefore..." Anna paused with a triumphant smile and looked pointedly at her daughter. "I sold it to pay for four Stradivarii for Robert Maas. I promised him I would fund his next quartet, and I have!"

She looked absolutely delighted with herself. Huguette settled back, crossing arms in righteous judgment.

"Well, I won't miss the painting one bit! I'm ecstatic it's gone. I'll even donate one to replace it...!"

They laughed before Huguette said, "Agnes, did you accompany Monsieur Maas last night?"

"Yes, I did. It was wonderful."

"I wish I would've come, then. What did you play?"

"Several of Bach's sonatas. It's such a joy to play Anna's Steinway concert grand," said Agnes whose long fingers played with a gold necklace.

"Yes, mother's is newer. What, you purchased it about five years ago?"

Anna nodded. "*Ma petite*, with *Madame Cézanne* gone will you come down more often for parties?"

"*D'accord, Maman...* you've won!"

"I believe I have!"

The famed Paganini Quartet with four Stradivarii instruments would debut on October 30 at the Library of Congress's Coolidge Auditorium in Washington. Maas and the other musicians played three of Beethoven's string quartets to standing ovations, the Clarks amongst the appreciative audience. The next month, the quartet performed Bartók and Schumann at one of New York's top musical venues, Town Hall's auditorium at 123 West 43rd Street.

Establishing themselves in Los Angeles, the Paganini Quartet visited Bellosguardo on occasion to indulge themselves in Anna's generosity. After luncheon, they practiced for hours in the music room. Occasionally, out of deference to Anna's patronage, Huguette, Anna, or Agnes Albert were invited to play. However, normally, the Clarks sat on the outskirts to avoid disturbing the quartet's intense practice sessions.

Due to her close association, Anna was able to hire the Paganini Quartet on multiple occasions while other hostesses in the region—desiring some of Anna Clark's panache—were given the run around. She featured the quartet at parties, seated above the lawn on a new, specially constructed dais. While guests milled around chatting or admiring the stunning sunset over the Pacific (*Mercifully with the barbed wire long gone*, thought Huguette), waiters circled with laden trays and faultless concerto music played in the background. Once the sun set, Japanese lanterns were lit on paths and veranda steps.

Anna's parties became well-known for refined culture. Tycoons and politicians knew it would be the perfect night to network, secure donations, or close a deal.

Before traveling abroad, the Clarks waited until France regained its footing. In the late spring of 1947, they felt confident to book passage. Anna well remembered the terrible aftermath of World War I which lingered for years; she expected to find the overall appearance and quality of services down. However, she was pleased. France, like the United States, robustly emerged from the deprivations of the Second World War. There were still privations, but a wonderful spirit of renewal hung about Paris.

Choosing adjoining suites at the *Hôtel Ritz*, mother and daughter immediately dove into the familiar comforts of the French culture and language. Huguette, ecstatic to be back, felt a zest lighten her step. The Clarks reacquainted themselves with friends while visiting boutiques, bookstores, museums, and galleries. In the evenings, when not attending a dinner party, they chose tony restaurants and entertainments. When the temperatures rose, friends swayed them to rent a villa on the coast in Marseilles instead of Normandy.

"Give it another few years to recover properly," urged Naomi, dowager marquise de Villermont. "Who knows what one could uncover on the Normandy beaches! Some Nazi gift left for some poor soul, I dare say."

Villermont looked at Huguette across the wide table in his mother's formal dining room. "Don't stay away from Paris too long."

Huguette smiled but it was Anna who responded.

"Oh, never fear, dear Etienne, we will see you again."

Like many fashionable women hungering for Parisian *haute couture*, the Clarks were eager to visit Christian Dior at 30 *avenue Montaigne* to see the *"Corolle"* spring-summer collection, dubbed the New Look by American fashion editors. The feminine shape with rounded shoulders and a wasp waist atop a full skirt comprised of yards and yards of opulent fabric impressed scores of women. The soft femininity replaced the boxy, wide-shouldered look which nodded to the fabric-conserving, military fashion of the war years. Anna was particularly pleased at the return to traditional elegance.

The Clarks soon chose Christian Dior as their top *couturier*. The Bar Suit for daytime wear was a must-have. Sagging, well-worn wardrobes were boosted by orders which grew quite long. For softer, more accessible ensembles, they went to Jean Patou and Jacques Fath. Chanel they now avoided, as close association with the Nazis made her a pariah in the Clark's well-connected, European circle.

Early in the visit, Huguette went to lunch with Villermont at a bistro near the Eiffel Tower. Afterwards, she requested to drive slowly past *avenue Victor Hugo* to fondly point out her childhood home.

"But of course, I remember the flat. How could I forget about the adorable monkey at your birthday party or the Christmas party when we drank the alcoholic punch and threw up?"

Villermont chuckled, then put an affectionate arm around Huguette's shoulders.

"Well, I don't remember the spiked punch, that must have been only you. But oh, yes, the monkey. Why, of course you were there!"

Huguette smiled before bending forward to rummage in her leather handbag, ostensibly looking for a lipstick while deliberately squirming away.

* * *

Weeks later, the Clarks visited *Château de Petit-Bourg*. Driving up the familiar, winding road late one morning, the driver pulled to a stop at the end of a weed-choked gravel drive.

"I can drive no further, Mesdames Clark. Would you like me to turn around?"

He adjusted the black driving hat, white mustache thick above his lips. Staring ahead with round eyes and raised eyebrows, the women didn't acknowledge him.

There was no *château* to be seen, only blackened limestone and charred timbers. In the back seat, the Clarks sat stunned into silence for a long moment.

"Why... Whatever happened?" Anna sat tall with a dismayed expression. She craned neck to see, hesitating to leave the vehicle. "It's gone. Completely gone!"

The chauffeur from Burgundy with a false left foot from World War I immediately comprehended. More Nazi atrocities scarring his homeland. He sighed while exiting with a grunt. He opened the squeaking metal rear door, figuring it would be best to say nothing to the Americans.

Speechlessly, Huguette stood, eyes riveted ahead. A cherished home had vanished. While a sudden gust of wind whipped past and swayed the encroaching branches of the forest, her eyes moved rapidly to take in the scene. The drive was familiar. Even the trees overhead felt familiar.

But then ahead, where the great *château* should stand in all its elegance, was...nothing. Ruins.

The Clarks stepped carefully on the overgrown drive. Eyes searched while mouths remained closed. The *château's allée d'honneur* of chestnut and lime trees stood forlorn, needing pruning. They observed overturned urns and statues covered with prickly vines and lichen; a long portion of the lower limestone terrace remained intact, teasing by recalling past beauty. A few rose bushes somehow managed to grow and bloom within choking weeds.

And most distressing of all, stretching the length and breadth of the former house's proud structure: blackened, mangled ruins disintegrating for years.

"*Bonjour!* *Mesdames*, be careful!" A young man shouted in French while running up the meadow's long slope, waving a brown cap. "I wouldn't recommend getting much closer. It's not safe!"

A sheepdog kept pace nearby, stopping to pant while keeping a vigilant eye on the herd down in the meadow.

"My name is Jean-Luc Beaufoy. Forgive my shouting," the shepherd said while panting. He leaned against a walking stick.

"*Merci*. My name's Anna Clark, and this is my daughter, Huguette."

"Pleased to meet you both. Are you wondering what happened, by chance?" Beaufoy wiped a wet forehead with an oversized, stained handkerchief.

The Clarks nodded in unison, aching to hear the story. Beaufoy scratched absently at a patchy brown beard, and replaced his cap. He gestured to the ruins with his walking stick.

"The *château* was a favorite of high-ranking Nazis. I heard from a local cleaning woman the officers marveled how modernized the bathrooms were in comparison to other *châteaux*. Many high-ranking officers resided here. All throughout the war, huge parties! But, when the tide turned, the retreating commander ordered it burned. About August 1944, maybe. A few soldiers sat guard to ensure the blaze continued unchecked."

The young shepherd's eyes scanned the charred rubble; he shrugged shoulders with defeat.

"The locals tried to save it, but it was too dangerous to approach while the Nazis were close. You understand? It's our history too, or was... By the time the villagers were able to come, it was *trop tarde*..."

Beaufoy shook his head at the loss. "Now no one comes here. I use the meadow for my sheep."

"What could you all do in such a situation? Absolutely nothing. How terrible for the townspeople. My husband, believe it or not, was the man who ordered the bathrooms modernized well before the first world war. Consider, if he hadn't done that, maybe the Germans would've moved on elsewhere...?"

Anna gave a rueful laugh, eyes scanning the blackened foundations extending deep into the earth. "How excruciatingly awful to see this! It was such a perfect *château*. I absolutely adored it...! We tried to buy it on many occasions."

Huguette thought, *If Daddy owned it, the Nazis would've still burned it down.*

In vain, Anna's eyes sought for any part of the structure which might still be recognizable. Tears welled. She knew the retreating Germans destroyed buildings, but she didn't imagine it could happen to the *Château de Petit-Bourg*. When she envisaged the new Bellosguardo, this *château* had been her private inspiration.

Wordlessly, Huguette turned. She had heard enough. She stumbled back to the car, wiping angrily at tears. The chauffeur opened the door of the 1947 black Delahaye 148. Huguette ducked her head and darted inside.

All the houses I've lived in with Andrée are destroyed! Only the Paris flat remains, inaccessible...

Overcome with loneliness and grief, Huguette slumped in the back seat. Anna gave the shepherd a tip and returned to the car. At the engine's roar, the sheep bleated and raced en masse into the far reaches of the meadow against the forest where Huguette and Andrée played *Jeanne d'Arc*. Beaufoy went tearing after, his dog nipping stray hindquarters far ahead.

At the age of seventy, Anna observed the direction modern, post-war culture was headed and was not pleased. The increasing casualness and superficiality of society perturbed. She trained eyes firmly on the past with its traditions of excellence. Despite advanced hearing loss, soothing, concerto music remained her preferred genre. High standards and strict etiquette were her watchwords, traditional French foods and *haute couture* her quotidian lifestyle.

Huguette, on the other hand, doted on technology. She spent much energy and funds keeping abreast of new inventions that delighted artistic sensibilities and distracted from niggling loneliness. She bought Land Cameras by Polaroid and television sets. Once she convinced the reluctant Anna the bulky, metal and plastic box with black and white transmission had some enjoyable programs—because Anna loved to laugh and be entertained—Huguette bought a television for her as well.

Anna and Marié warily watched the deliverymen unboxing it at 8W, with Huguette overseeing.

"I've decided on a television only for here, in my sitting room for now. I'm not sure I want one at Bellosguardo. I'll have to think about it."

"It'll be fine in our sitting rooms there," Huguette said, knowing her mother loathed technology's lack of aesthetics.

Afterward at dinner, Anna said, "Telephones are bad enough, then radios, gramophones, my voice box... Now a television set, too? You're spoiling my appetite for this delicious Pavlova, *ma chèrie*. I'll say, however, it's *marvelous* to be able to raise the volume on these devices."

Huguette smiled as she put a spoon through the crunchy merengue of the Pavlova and watched the berries and sweet juice make a small pink river on the flowered Sèvres dessert plate. She found it difficult to sit with her mother watching television; the volume was turned up far too loudly.

Eager to spread the wonderfulness, she moved on. The Stykas were gifted television sets that summer. By the next year, Huguette, after learning it was unaffordable in France, sent money to the Villermonts. Etienne sent profuse thank you letters and cards, urging her to visit again. With an aging mother and declining postwar fortunes, he wouldn't be returning to New York in the foreseeable future.

Darlene Styka likewise wrote to urge her to visit Wendy. But Huguette hung back. She saw her goddaughter occasionally at lessons, but rarely formally visited. She preferred the Stykas to bring the girl to 907 Fifth Avenue. To make up for the lack, she sent tens of thousands of dollars, boxes of toys from Au Nain Bleu, and air conditioning window units for the family to bear hot days in the city.

As the years passed in a predictable, secure whir of set routines, Huguette's social life shrank further. In her forties without much reflection, she began happily withdrawing into a self-created world which consumed much time. The remaining hours were devoted to Anna and Amelia.

Even *cher maître's* role altered. In the late forties and early fifties, Styka was hardly seen in the Clark's circle. The frequency of Huguette's painting lessons dwindled dramatically. Instead of painting, Huguette went to exhibitions and joined the Santa Barbara Museum of Art. She subscribed to the newsletter on contemporary and Asian art. She followed photography, subscribing to professional journals. She spent a lot of time taking endless photographs of easily accessible subjects: Central Park through the seasons or Bellosguardo's grounds. Like a professional photographer, on the back of photographs she noted the camera settings, opening, floodlight, number of seconds, and the date.

Dolls continued to fascinate. She purchased only top-quality ones or commissioned new. She was particular and did her research, never hurrying. The overall design, fabric, and face of the doll had to be the absolute best. She didn't purchase a nineteenth century doll simply because it was a *Jumeau bébé* or any twentieth century Barbie, but because each was made in the first round of production and was close to or at mint condition.

The nineteenth century dolls and automata she selected stood up, with rigid torsos. Many featured a musical act, which spoke to her own talents. These dolls were not for holding or carrying around. Huguette placed them as a standing display around private rooms, in a dollhouse, or seated in custom chairs lined along the gallery. If, at a later date, she found a replica excelling the one in her collection, she gave away the lesser doll to Wendy Styka or to a staff member with grandchildren.

She spent many happy hours studying for and dreaming up doll houses or *tableaux* for her collections. She loved Japanese ancient nobility, samurai, and European fairy tales. The fairy tales recalled a lost world. A world which could be comprehended and controlled. They also recalled happy moments in the nursery listening to dear Andrée telling of Rumpelstiltskin, Cinderella, Rapunzel, and Sleeping Beauty.

Whether commissioning from Au Nain Bleu or working with craftsmen from multiple countries, Huguette made a point to elide unpleasant aspects of the original tales, of which there were many. Sitting at her desk with a penciled list of project reminders, she would ring up Rudolph Jaklitsch, an immigrant artisan in Queens.

After giving requirements, Huguette said, "Yes, that's right, I'm well aware. Let me restate: When the prince kisses Sleeping Beauty, I want the *tableaux* to end. Do you understand?"

"But, but, but Mrs. Clark... That cuts out *half* the story! You cannot do that!"

Balancing the black Bakelite receiver on his shoulder, the balding artisan took off greasy, black-rimmed glasses to rub strained eyes.

"I'm well aware of the story, Mr. Jaklitsch. But that's what I require. Thank you." She hung up.

Jaklitsch knew Mrs. Clark would most likely call back in one hour, and then a second and third call with yet *another* so-called "small request" which threw his process off kilter. He entered the kitchen talking a familiar refrain.

"Whenever Mrs. Clark knows the day I'm working on her commission, she has a tendency to pester."

Sitting down heavily at the Formica table, Jaklitsch glanced at a plate piled with boiled sausage, onion, and potato. He wearily shook his head before raising watery brown eyes to look over at his wife, Agnieszka, busy at the stove.

Jaklitsch said, "If she didn't pay so very, very handsomely, this woman would drive me bananas and I would fire her!"

Agnieszka Jaklitsch stood ladling boiled beets into a bowl. She was delighted with her husband's profession because she cashed the enormous checks. It was a dream to save up for a nicer apartment while purchasing whatever she desired at Sears.

Shaking a wooden spoon in her husband's direction, Agnieszka said, "You keep Mrs. Clark happy, Rudolph, if it's *the last thing you do*!"

With Cold War fever gripping headlines and conversations, Anna had new worries gnawing during quiet evenings. She called Huguette down to breakfast.

"Here, have some *madeleines*. There's a new bakery in the neighborhood my housekeeper found. *C'est parfait*."

They ate for a few minutes before Anna broached the topic foremost on her mind.

"I'm concerned about the talk of a nuclear war... The Russians are terrifying me. You know, *ma petite*, I've the ranch and Bellosguardo for retreats, but what property do you have in the country? Do you think it's time you bought one, too?"

Huguette readily agreed, respecting her mother's foresight. She likewise read news reports threatening nuclear war. To Anna's relief, Huguette moved ahead that day, contacting her lawyer and accountant. Everything was put into motion to make a major purchase.

Real estate agents came to 8W to meet with the Clarks and present suitable options within a three-hour drive. Soon, a top property—a white-brick mansion built in 1937 with 9 bedrooms and 11 fireplaces—was chosen, and they were on their way to New Canaan, Connecticut.

It was unspoken throughout the tour, but Huguette easily ascertained Anna wanted her to purchase the house.

Anna whispered, "It could serve as a bomb shelter of sorts; close enough to the city to easily drive to during a time of need."

"I think I like it, *Maman*. I'll name it *Le beau château*."

"I do too. It's charming. Very rustic, I dare say... Where will you put your studio?"

"I'm not sure. Off the master bedroom, perhaps? Towards the rear?"

"Hmmm, just so. Altogether, I think it's quaintly elegant, but easily remedied. And it's your first house. Isn't that exciting? Are you going ahead with it?"

"Yes! I think I will..." said Huguette with a proud tilt to her chin.

The Clarks moved down the gravel drive to speak with the lawyer. He went to talk with the waiting real estate agent while the Clarks drove off in a cloud of dust.

Six months later, they returned to walk through the renovated but empty 14,266 square foot mansion at 104 Dans Highway. This trip, the architect, his assistant, the firm's suggested interior decorator, the real estate agent, and Huguette's lawyer were all present. The lawyer and real estate agent conferred about further acreage for sale, bringing the total up to 52 acres—which Huguette was keen to acquire—in one of the most exclusive communities in the country.

Anna reminded the lawyer a caretaker would need to be hired to live in the red-brick gatehouse. "To protect the house and property while my daughter's away. It would work out best if he were a bachelor."

To cover her daughter's awkwardness around strangers, Anna brought up possible décor schemes, fabrics, and further alterations. At first, the uninvited decorator was salivating to snap up these wealthy clients and possibly do another residence or two for them.

These people always have multiple residences.

He rushed to ingratiate himself. He was soon chagrined to discover it was the daughter—not the voluble mother—who had purchased the house.

Oh, that mute woman there owns the house? She'll never do a thing!

The decorator tuned Anna out, figuring it was all a waste of time.

Huguette was overwhelmed with all the decisions needing to be made before the twenty-two-room house was livable. In her element, Anna fired off suggestions and color schemes, effortlessly seeing possibilities. She frequently called Huguette over, who would nod and mumble something before turning away, not wanting to talk in front of the assembled men.

The group went into the empty master bedroom with a huge window.

"I adore the carved paint brushes going up the stairs!" Huguette said, content she had found one detail to latch onto.

The interior designer thought the idea gauche. *And carved in that trendy shade of wood!*

As far as *Le Beau Château* was concerned, after the second tour neither woman stepped foot onto the property again. Despite Anna's fears, the house was never utilized as a bomb shelter, and Huguette barely gave it a thought as the decades passed.

A bachelor caretaker was indeed found. He grew old in the one-bedroom, red-brick gatehouse. It guarded the start of the long, peaceful drive through many quiet, forested acres teeming with wildlife. Most mornings, he enjoyed walking through the acreage.

No one ever came to the gate to be admitted unless they were landscapers or handy men. No one ever strolled with him in the woods.

Every four months he would wax and polish the extensive hardwood floors in all the empty rooms. In the fall, he set the heat at sixty degrees, and turned it off in the spring. He routinely checked on the foundation and the roof. From time to time, he recommended repairs by calling the penciled number on a yellowed scrap of paper held fast with a chipped Santa magnet to his 1949 Frigidaire.

By the early eighties, he sat at his regular café eating breakfast before overhearing talk amongst a table of grey-haired women. He sipped coffee at a barstool as he tuned into the voices behind.

"I've heard the owner of that mansion on Dans Highway is a woman whose fiancé died at sea. She was so heartbroken, she could never face moving in alone. And so there it sits, empty and rotting away all these long years. Truth is stranger than fiction, that's for darn sure, ladies."

"I feel sorry for her, then!"

"Oh, me too, me too..."

The bachelor paid for his coffee and eggs, and then returned to the red-brick gatehouse. Getting out of his battered Toyota pickup, he said to himself, "Not that I know much either, but that sure ain't it!"

If any bold youngsters knocked on windows or attempted pranks during summer boredom, he shooed them off good-naturedly. Without fail, his modest salary was paid monthly. After a chaotic youth, he shook his head at life's sometime unexpected providence and peace.

In his early eighties, when he began seriously considering retirement, one day a friendly journalist came knocking. It had been so long since anyone bothered about him, he figured it couldn't hurt to show the guy around a little.

What're they gonna do, fire me after 57 years?

March 1952
Bellosguardo, Santa Barbara, California

A telegram arrived. Huguette read and reread it:

Tadé had stroke STOP Unable to communicate or move STOP Need to move to MA house from LI STOP D Styka

Huguette went in search of Anna, who was looking over estate paperwork in the *bureau*.

"Terrible news! Tadé has had a stroke! Can you believe it?"

Anna stopped writing.

"Oh, how distressing! They've been vacationing on Long Island this summer, correct?"

"Yes. It appears they're still there. However, there probably isn't adequate medical care. She should take him immediately back to New York instead of their house in Massachusetts."

"Let's wire money. No doubt that's what she's after. His commissions have been declining in recent years. I know he's been concerned from a few comments he's made."

"Oh? He never mentioned it to me. I'll wire over $10,000. I want the best care possible given!"

The painter spent the next year attempting to recover speech and fine motor movement. Months later, Darlene wrote from Cuba:

We've got to move on to Miami tomorrow because the medical care is better. My husband's made such little progress. He's tried, but all in vain. His latest painting remains unfinished. I don't know what we'll do. His career is most likely over.

Huguette reread the letter.

"I should send another check. I can't bear to think Monsieur Styka is in this position. I hope Darlene's doing all she can to get excellent medical care."

"That's good of you. I'll send money soon, too," said Anna as she put on a black hat. "I hate to hear about him suffering, the poor man..." She kissed Huguette goodbye. "I'm off to Mass. I'll pray for Tadé. See you at tea this afternoon."

Huguette turned to go down the hall to her studio. On autopilot, she drifted into the storage room. Assembled paintings of every size and subject and hue were stacked up. Almost all Styka had commented on or supervised. Many he had guided in some major way.

In a flash of memory, Styka stood before her in the Central Park studio as a vibrant, younger man. His thin face was tanned, and his blonde hair bleached platinum from summer months in the south of France. She was a self-conscious eighteen-year-old in her artist smock, beginning a new year at Spence, struggling with the human form. She saw Sandré peek her head in the door behind Styka.

"Mademoiselle Huguette, look at that leg. What's it doing?" Styka pointed at the canvas with a penciled figure on it, eyes dancing playfully. "Is it behaving like a *proper leg*?"

Styka looked from the canvas back to Huguette, wonderfully expressive hazel eyes mesmerizing her.

"The leg? It's, uh... it's... Can you show me what you mean?"

She blushed because he was standing so close.

Styka immediately moved off to position himself like the figure in her sketch. He froze, making his point with an awkwardly positioned leg in grey tweed trousers. Huguette giggled at the obvious mistake.

"Oh, now I see! *Merci beaucoup,* Monsieur Styka. I need to move the leg like so and position the knee this way, *oui*?"

Where is that painting? Do I even have it anymore?

Huguette put a forefinger to chin, closing her eyes to visualize the contents of storage rooms in multiple residences.

I can't say. I'll have to look for it. It probably wasn't good enough to keep! He might never be able to paint with me again... I can't bear to think that... Why haven't I had lessons lately...? When he recovers, I'll start a new painting and schedule a few lessons.

The next week, as their train pulled into Penn Station, Anna said, "Imagine, I never used to mind it at all... And now look, quite the pathetic woman of seventy-four who only wants to remain in one room every day! I'm disappointed in myself; nevertheless, Huguette, I don't know if I can keep making the trip to California. My limbs are so stiff afterward."

Anna gazed out the window at the crowd. A train whistle blared. She stood up, leaning on a silver-topped ebony cane.

"I'll need you to help me down the steps. My knee won't cooperate today."

Huguette raised her voice, "*Bien sûr, Maman,* it's no trouble."

"I'm sorry we've only gone to Bellosguardo twice in the past year. I know you miss it."

Huguette put an arm around Anna's frail back and eased her down the first step.

"Yes, but I don't want to go without you. It wouldn't be right to leave you alone in New York."

Anna took another step before grimacing.

"One moment, one moment! I need to wait before I attempt another." Anna breathed heavily. "What did you say?"

With a slightly louder tone, Huguette repeated, "I said we'll go home and put on our pajamas and watch a program on TV with popcorn. How does that sound?"

"Wonderful. Only I'll probably fall asleep!"

Anna chuckled, displaying yellowed teeth elongated from age.

The next afternoon Huguette sat down at the card table in 8W's drawing room.

"I've received news from Etienne that he's married a woman named Elisabeth. Isn't that interesting?"

Anna shuffled cards.

"Hmmm... At the age of forty-nine he finally decided to get married. My, my, he certainly carried a torch a long time for you!"

"*Maman*, please, why do you..."

"*Pardon*? Speak up, *s'il te plaît*. You know it's the truth. Now do you regret turning him down?"

Anna gave a pointed look and dealt the cards.

"*Non*. As with Bill Gower, it wasn't meant to be. Although, I do care for Etienne far more than I cared for Bill. I believe Etienne to be the better man."

"Just so... As long as you're happy with your life, I cannot say a word." Anna made a dismissive motion. "Are you ready to play now? I've a marvelous hand!"

Should I tell Maman *Etienne said he was 'split emotionally'?*

Earlier in the day, Huguette sat at an antique *escritoire* holding the tissue-thin air mail stationary, wondering at that phrase, reading it repeatedly.

Is he devoted to me...? What would Father have counseled me to do all those years ago when Etienne asked me to marry him...? Is he talking with me because he's after money...? I really can't say...

After many months in New York, Huguette attempted to convince Anna to summer away from the city. In 8W, Anna played the harp while Huguette sat on the sofa, fretting about a broken violin string.

"Well, if we don't go to Bellosguardo because it's too far, where would you like to go?"

"I haven't thought about it. I don't want to be seated in a car for hours on end. It bothers my knees." Anna reached to rub kneecaps.

"Perhaps we should consider plane travel? It would be much easier on you," said Huguette while examining the broken string.

"*Non, merci*!" Anna shuddered, then vehemently crossed herself. "There are too many crashes for me to agree to that. It gives me gooseflesh to even contemplate!"

"*D'accord, Maman*, I'm not sure I'm too wild about getting on a plane either. We'll stay in New York until you feel better."

"How about you go on to Bellosguardo? I hate to think you're keeping yourself cooped up because of me."

Anna's eyes were intent on Huguette, who was busy with the Stradivarius. She eased herself up and shuffled to a chair next to the sofa.

She's far too comfortable being alone these days She invites no one over, never has any parties.

"Oh, me and my nerves are very much soothed by the routine of shuttling between my apartment and yours. My nerves informed me last week that they've had enough of racing around here and there from one city or continent or coast to another like I've done *all my life*. It's rather a treat to stay still and work on projects." Huguette sighed. "I can be over-stimulated by the world, I've come to realize."

"Oh, your nerves..."

"Ouch! That hurt!"

Huguette put a lashed finger to soothing lips.

"Stop fussing with it! Why don't you simply send in the Strad to be serviced instead of bothering with it?"

Huguette nodded and rose obediently to make the appointment.

When Maman *feels better, we'll venture out together again.*

The next summer, Huguette opened a letter from Darlene to read the woman's hurried scrawl. *I wish he would write one of these days,* she thought while walking down the cement back stairs to 8W, letter in hand.

Sitting down to tea in Anna's drawing room, Huguette said, "Darlene says Miami isn't working out. She's transferring Monsieur Styka back to their country house. Should I call?"

"Of course. Don't you want to speak with him? Perhaps they can come for dinner in a month or two?"

Huguette went to make the call and returned with a much slower step less than ten minutes later. Anna looked at her expectantly.

"Your tea is cold. What did he say?"

Huguette moved to the window. "It was as if... as if... He wasn't himself. He wasn't on the phone two minutes."

"*Pardon?* I can't hear you when your back is to me. Was he tired? What did he say?"

She turned to speak, raising her voice, "That he would be delighted to come to dinner! But I have a feeling we're never going to see him again..."

Huguette stared down at the streets below, her thoughts troubled. She tuned out her mother.

Photographing the glorious, late summer trees of Central Park one afternoon, she took the dreaded call.

Her mind went numb. Like an automaton she spoke the socially-acceptable words of consolation.

"He died earlier today... At Mount Sinai Hospital... That's terrible. I'm very sorry, Darlene, for your loss. Yes, of course I'll tell my mother. Thank you for calling to let us know. It's a tragedy he's gone so soon."

With a tremulous hand, Huguette hung up. She stood a moment, frozen.

He's dead.

Her chest suddenly felt painfully squeezed. With labored breathing, she slowly went to 12W's studio. She stared numbly at canvases along the walls. Memories encased in each threatened a searing deluge of tears. Retreating, Huguette locked the bedroom door. Curled into the fetal position, she pressed a down pillow over her mouth to absorb sharp sobs of grief. With the tears, years of suppressed love oozed out.

There's no man to replace him! I love you, Tadé!

——————✦——————

Several weeks after the funeral, the Clarks paid a condolence visit to Mrs. Darlene Styka at 222 Central Park South. They didn't stay long.

Nine-year-old Wendy held a Jumeau doll. "This one was for my birthday! *Merci,* Madame Clark."

Wendy, with brunette pigtails and black ribbons, wore a black and white smocked dress, black patent-leather Mary Janes, and lace edged white socks. Huguette examined her face.

She takes mostly after her mother, doesn't she…?

"Isn't she precious?" said Huguette, observing the little girl. "I can tell you're very bright."

I'm going to go home and order her a new doll.

"The poor thing has lost her father…" whispered Anna, seated beside Darlene on the long sage green davenport.

"Oh, and I have lost my Tadé!"

Darlene sobbed for a moment into a handkerchief. Wendy moved to sit next to her mother, putting a consoling arm around her shoulders. Anna reached to pat Darlene's hand.

"It's hard to be a widow. I've faced it, too. But you must be brave for little Wendy." She smiled at the girl. "Think of all the good years you had."

"Yes, yes, I must. Thank you for the reminder. I will somehow!"

Darlene's beautiful face was pink and wet with tears. She rose to walk them to the door. Huguette almost smiled with relief. She turned to Wendy, who stood forlornly by the davenport.

"Be a good girl. Say a prayer for your daddy in heaven. He was a special, special man. I'll send you a gift soon."

"Another gift?"

"Yes, *ma petite*, from the most beautiful toy store in the world. Just for you, because your *cher maître's* daughter."

Huguette stopped talking to control tears.

"Thank you, Madame Clark."

Wendy reached to hug her godmother. She would always remember that day not only because of the grief, but also because it was the last time she saw her *marraine*.

In the car, Anna remarked, "Monsieur Styka was comparatively young. I confess I'm surprised I've outlived my brother, Amanda Storrs, and now, Tadé. Such a loyal friend to our family." Anna sighed. "Three gone this year alone. How depressing! I never expected to outlive so many..."

Anna paused, turning her head. She could only see Huguette's back and part of her profile as she stared out the window like a lost soul. *This has been happening far too often.*

"What's the matter? Are you feeling unwell?"

Huguette was startled by her mother's brusque tone. She sat back so her mother could clearly hear.

"Yes, yes, quite all right. I'm only concerned for little Wendy. I'll have to be a good *marraine* now."

She told the white lie and put on an appeasing smile. Seeing Anna was satisfied, Huguette's eyes flicked back to the window streaked with rain.

I'm relieved the condolence visit is over. I can't bear seeing the studio again! I don't want to ever go back... I can't believe he's gone!

***

Weeks later, Anna began the New York season in style. She regretted missing last year's charity ball put on by *Les Amis de Versailles*. Attending this year's event to benefit Versailles was a must.

The "Garden Terraces at Royal Château" themed ball would be held on October 28th in the Starlight Room of the Waldorf Astoria. Situated perfectly at 301 Park Avenue, the towering, limestone-covered 47-story building was the world's tallest hotel. It was dubbed New York's "unofficial palace" because of the über-luxury, exclusivity, and sheer number of celebrities and power-players inside at any one time. The Starlight Room—or Starlight Roof if one wanted to call attention to the state-of-the-art retractable roof which opened high above diners—was one of the most elegant locales in the city.

On a call up to 12W, Anna said, "I bought the best table available! It's such a pleasure to donate to Versailles, such an historically important palace. I've invited Amelia, and Agnes and her family. Her girls are so beautiful, they will be dancing all evening. Celia and the others sent their regrets."

Huguette hesitated before replying, "I'm not sure I want to go."

"Nonsense. It'll do both of us some good to get out. We've been far too quiet lately. I'm sending Madame Marié out on errands tomorrow. Consider what jewels you'd like her to retrieve. *Salut!*"

The line went dead, and Huguette sighed. She set the ivory and brass receiver on the cradle.

Maman sounds so excited. I can't refuse. She'll be so happy attending.

In preparation, traveling hair stylists from Roger Vergnes Salon at 36 East 57th Street were booked in advance. Anna insisted on having her hair done there when she discovered Monsieur Vergnes also styled the Duchess of Windsor's hair.

The Clarks spent one rainy afternoon going through accumulated Dior gowns, debating the merits of which bespoke design would be the most appropriate for the event. Marié was the packhorse who bought Estée Lauder and Elizabeth Arden lipsticks and matching nail polishes, perfumes, gloves, silk stockings, girdles, and skin creams at Bergdorf Goodman; delivered satin shoes to be cleaned or repaired; and collected furs from Bonwit Teller's climate-controlled storage.

Pre-ball, Anna mustered the energy to offer drinks and *hors d'oeuvres* for those who had been asked to sit at her table.

Anna sat queenlike in a turquoise satin and lace Dior ball gown with an aquamarine, peridot, and amethyst necklace and earrings, with a drink in hand. Bobbed white hair sleek with hair spray. Amelia sat beside in a black velvet Dior ball gown with a diamond necklace.

Anna said, "Let's plan on arriving a bit late, shall we?"

"Along with everyone else!" said Agnes in her husband's ear.

Agnes turned to see Huguette walk into the room wearing an ice blue silk satin Dior strapless ball gown, white opera gloves, and diamond necklace, earrings, and bracelet.

"Huguette, how lovely you look! I never buy couture but seeing you and Anna tonight makes me want at least one gown."

"Oh, Agnes, thank you. Your red velvet gown is beautiful. Very becoming. And look at your girls, both so pretty tonight."

"But it's off the rack." Agnes laughed, knowing she would never spend thousands on a single article of clothing.

Agnes's girls thanked Huguette and moved to sit down near Anna and Amelia. The outspoken, older sisters were amusing to the younger generation.

An hour later, it was obvious it would be a packed house. A parade of well-groomed guests ascended to the nineteenth floor of the Waldorf Astoria. Far below in the marble lobby awaiting any opportunity, crashers lurked. The nightclub was decorated with thousands of flowers and statuary, and the Starlight Orchestra played all the hits with a male singer stepping up to the microphone from time to time.

After over forty years in the city, the Clarks knew vaguely of or were well acquainted with a good number of attendees. While maneuvering between tables and conversing groups, Huguette kept eyes busy looking at everything and nothing. With a faint smile, she avoided other's eyes.

"I've no plans to be a social butterfly. Please don't make me, *Maman!*"

"I won't *make* you *do* anything. I only hope you exert yourself a little. Dance! Have some fun!" Anna had said on the drive over.

Once inside, Anna advanced across the ballroom smiling like the grand dame she was. She graciously nodded her shellacked and glittering head to anyone in her vicinity, responding only to those who merited attention.

"*Bonjour*... hello to you... Hello! So lovely to see you... *Salut, oui*, we'll talk later..."

Throughout the menu of classic French dishes, Anna's table received curious glances. It wasn't common for one of the richest mother-daughter duos in the city to appear at such a fashionably public event. Unlike the sedate Clarks, the hundreds of guests busied themselves with networking, preening, and gossiping.

With respect to the exalted position the Clarks inhabited, a fence of veneration extended around Anna's table.

They were whispered about as untouchable members of the Old Guard, rather like Consuelo Vanderbilt-Balsan. So wealthy, well-connected, and cultured, the Clarks never overstayed their welcome and carefully chose which select events to attend. These social tactics over a lengthy period launched them into legendary status. They floated over New York instead of plodding on gritty streets below.

Those guests who wished to remind the Clarks of long-time associations and alliances—or to have some of the fairy dust rub off—advanced cautiously, feeling out the welcome. Besides enviable *haute couture*, furs, and Cartier jewels, the Clarks gave away little. They behaved with the utmost decorum.

It seemed Anna held court. Anyone wishing to speak with someone at the table went straight to her first. Anna, who had left her cane at home out of pride, almost never rose. Only the young Albert daughters regularly left to dance.

Ostensibly on their way to the powder room, but, in reality, desiring a rare glimpse up close, one impressionable young woman—wearing a Chez Ninon gown and costume jewelry—whispered in her cousin's ear.

"The Clarks are *very* Old Money, you know. From Europe. Titled ancestors. Not *nouveaux riches* like some people here... Think of the van der Luyden's in *Age of Innocence*. Make sense?"

Her naïve cousin, nodded, wide-eyed.

Onlookers remarked how much Anna and Amelia resembled one another. Huguette's absent eyes and faraway expression were also noted. She didn't dance and was seldom seen conversing. Every now and then, she would be approached.

"Huguette Clark, is that you? Remember me? Jennifer Becker? I was Jennifer Norris then, one year below you at Spence."

The woman wore a cautious smile, one hand clutching her ruffled, salmon pink, ball gown.

"Oh yes, hello Jennifer. How are you?"

I don't remember who she is!

"Please call me Jenny. Can I call you Hugs? Remember that? Everyone called you Hugs. I thought it was an adorable nickname. You were so friendly." Jennifer tittered with nervous laughter, wrinkles creasing middle-aged skin. "I think they called you Hugo too..."

"Yes, yes, they did. That was a very long time ago. Is it Mrs. Bocker?"

"No, Becker. Jennifer Becker. You might remember me as Jenny Norris. I was a year underneath you before I transferred during Upper School to..."

The woman prattered on. Huguette allowed the conversation to fizzle out and the woman took the hint by skittering back into the crowd. She sat back with relief.

What time is it? I want to go home.

Agnes leaned over so Anna could hear. "Did you get your raffle tickets?"

"Raffle tickets? Please..." In dismissal, Anna waved a gloved arm with an amethyst and diamond bracelet. "Don't be ridiculous! I'm not interested in publicly vying for material objects. *Jamais*! I've donated money and that's sufficient."

Agnes looked hopefully at Huguette. "Do you have raffle tickets?"

"No," Huguette said. "None for me either. You go ahead though."

"There are two tickets to a New York Philharmonic concert I want to go to. I must win them!" Agnes said with a hopeful expression. She nudged her taciturn husband.

Huguette said, "That sounds worthwhile. I thought it was all cheap pearls and nonsense. *Maman*, did you hear what she's after?"

"*Oui*, and under no circumstances am I going to squeeze into two seats next to hundreds of strangers with who knows what germs packed in around me!"

"She usually buys up dozens of seats around us so that we sit alone."

"Well," said Agnes with raised eyebrows, "that must do the trick charmingly. It's a trifle expensive for my tastes, however..."

During the raffle thirty minutes before midnight, Huguette watched in horror as one woman seemed to have a meltdown because someone at her table won a coveted pearl necklace.

Why anyone would be attracted to such an activity is beyond me.

Agnes whispered, "Despite the fun earlier at Anna's party, you seem downcast sitting here now amidst the frivolity."

Huguette looked at Agnes before lowering her eyes to hide tears. *It's been six weeks since he died. I didn't want to go out yet.* She took a breath and shrugged shoulders.

"The night's dragging a bit. Is the music grating on your nerves as well?"

"No, I think it's lovely."

Agnes began humming. Her husband asked her to dance when "Stardust" played. When the couple returned, Anna indicated she needed help rising. Huguette smiled with relief as she gathered her full skirt to stand up.

Finally, Maman has had enough! Let's go home!

Life slowed to a crawl as cycles of seasons passed in ordered regularity outside the spacious windows of 907 Fifth Avenue. The women now owned their co-op apartments, and the city grew up around them. The Upper East Side became the center of Huguette's life as Anna's lack of mobility confined her more and more to 8W. Bellosguardo remained in dust covers; Rancho Alegre's harvest donated; and *Le Beau Château* entirely out of mind.

To capture the changing urban landscape, Huguette converted another guest bedroom of 12W into a Central Park viewing room of sorts, with a series of Rolleiflex cameras mounted on tripods from the Willoughby-Peerless camera store. She routinely upgraded the equipment. The Rolleiflex's telephoto lenses had the ability to zoom in on people far below. She took photo series at all times of the day or night and in all weather. Children playing games of tag; couples conversing while sitting on benches; a man jaywalking to get to the park; birds collecting under a water fountain on a summer day; streetlights shining through a blizzard on Christmas Eve.

She would then examine the photographs to draw movements and expressions, or a particular tree as it grew and morphed with the seasons. As Styka urged when she first began lessons in her teens, she never stopped studying human movement. She didn't, however, attempt another painting.

Anna called Bellosguardo staff regularly. She made promises to come, only to break them. Couture shows were seen at the French Consulate on Fifth Avenue, not in Paris. To enliven life at 8W, Anna splurged on a Renoir, *Jeunes filles jouant au volant*, and a new harp. Huguette brought down her latest prize, the museum-worthy Stradivarius, *La Pucelle*, and they practiced pieces to perform at occasional dinner parties.

Until finally, the years of no dinner parties began.

One morning while lying in bed, Anna became agitated. A long arm lifted from the ivory duvet.

"Huguette, stop reading. Stop reading! I don't want to hear anymore. I want to talk to you. This is very important. *Écoute bien*. I want to die in my own bed."

"*Oui, Maman*," Huguette closed *Paris Match*. "You've told me many times. I haven't forgotten."

"I should only die in a hospital as a last resort. I do *not* want to be taken to an elderly sanitarium. No matter what, promise you'll keep me here as long as possible! I want to die privately!"

Huguette said in a loud voice while clutching her mother's limp, bony hand, "*Je te le promets*. But please stop talking about dying. You're *not* going to die any time soon. I can't bear to lose you."

"*Ma petite fille*, everyone must die. I'm sorry you'll be left alone—I tried to avoid that all those years ago—but I can't live forever."

Anna sagged with exhaustion against piled up down pillows. She began coughing.

"Take a sip." Huguette carefully held a straw to Anna's thin, purplish-pink lips. "I can't bear to discuss it. Let's talk about something more pleasant."

Anna coughed into a handkerchief, ignoring her daughter. *We've argued about it too much already.*

"A new nurse begins tomorrow." Huguette put a hand soothingly over the layered lavender and mustard-colored bruises on Anna's forearm. "I've fired that nasty Ms. Brown. I can't believe how rough she was with you. It still makes me angry. I'm so sorry I didn't catch her sooner!... Mrs. Ruiz will be here by dinner... We're having shad roe, doesn't that sound delicious? Should I read or turn on a program? Or maybe you'd like me to play Bach on *La Pucelle* for you again? *Maman...?*"

Anna slept. Huguette rose to call her aunt.

"If we're both here, maybe it'll induce Mother to stay alert for as long as possible? Will you come to live here for a while?"

"I can't come this week. I've got my husband's children visiting. I'm busy planning with the chef as we speak. You do understand?"

Amelia put a weary, dark-mottled hand to temple as she stood in the kitchen of her Park Avenue apartment, wondering how much she could get away without her husband becoming angry.

"But I will come as often as I can. Sweetie, are you taking care of yourself?"

Huguette suddenly recalled the widowed Amelia had remarried a lawyer, Thomas Semple. Huguette readily accepted invitations to see her aunt but routinely made excuses when the invitation included Mr. Semple. Without Anna as a buffer, Huguette felt uncomfortable.

"Oh, how silly of me! Of course, you can't leave poor Mr. Semple all alone. We'll manage."

Huguette is acting odd. Anna is rarely herself these days. She's bedbound, sleeping endless hours. Eating almost nothing. Her heart has an irregular rhythm medication does little to fix. Her mind wanders in and out of the past.

Amelia was always shocked when Anna suddenly began talking as if they were young. Sometimes Anna thought William was alive, and she would ask to speak with him. Then the next hour she would be fully alert with a strong grip, wanting to get out of bed to play the piano.

"Tom's kids leave Saturday. I'll come Sunday to visit. Huguette, please let the nurses take care of Anna. You go home and get some good rest. You need it."

The next morning, Dr. Pierre arrived for Anna's daily check-up. Huguette hovered and interrupted him repeatedly while Anna was barely conscious.

"What more can you do for my mother, Dr. Pierre? I'm concerned she's uncomfortable. Is there any more medical equipment I can purchase, or something more you need?"

"I think we're fine in that department. Mrs. Clark, I'm sorry to report I believe your mother's life is drawing to a close... I'm doing all I can for her, but you must prepare yourself."

"*Prepare myself?* Dr. Pierre, you aren't giving up on my mother, are you? How can you say such a thing! She's too healthy to be near death."

Huguette's anxiety rose with his resigned look.

"Is there a surgery you recommend to aid breathing, or a new medication for her heart? Anything at all? I'll pay for whatever treatment you devise. Please, spare no expense at preserving my mother's life!"

"I'm indeed very sorry... There is no treatment for the normal course of mortality. Your mother's life is ebbing away, and you *must prepare yourself.* There is not much else I can do for the elder Mrs. Clark besides make her as comfortable as I can. I'll continue to visit daily."

Dr. Pierre took up his leather bag and walked out of the bedroom with Huguette at his heels.

"What surgery do you recommend? I recently read an article about an advancement—"

"Again, I *do not recommend* any further treatment beyond the course we have been on."

Dr. Pierre paused in the gallery. *This woman is exasperating!*

"My mother cannot die right now. Maybe I should get a second opinion?"

Huguette's eyes went wide for a second with the threat.

"If that is what you wish."

Dr. Pierre regarded Huguette without flinching. He had worked for the Clarks for eight years; he knew both women well.

This irrational reaction by the coddled daughter is no surprise.

He began examining her.

Psychologically, at the moment, she's hanging by a thread. Her mother's death might push her over the edge. But, of course, I cannot be too blunt; she might stop talking to me altogether.

Pierre cleared his throat and said in a measured tone, "Mrs. Clark, whatever you decide to do, I'm here to support you. I've cared for you both ever since Dr. Lyle retired and moved to Florida. Your mother has lived a long life. She confessed to me months ago she is ready to go."

"She said that?" Huguette's face was stricken. She turned away, eyes downcast. *How could I not trust Dr. Pierre? Maman trusts him implicitly.*

"As *your* doctor now, when was the last time you took a walk or went outside? You could benefit from some sunshine."

"Oh, I couldn't say! I've had a little cold. And I had the flu before that for a few days. And I've been so preoccupied taking care of Mommy..."

"I recommend exercise and fresh air. Go to the park and take a thirty to sixty minute walk every day."

"Yes, yes, of course, Dr. Pierre. *Merci.* Do what you feel is best. I know my mother is in good hands. Please forgive me."

Huguette's manner turned sweet and pliable once again while walking him to the door. Soon after, Anna lay unconscious; the nurse couldn't locate a heartbeat. Anna was rushed to Mount Sinai Hospital in a bleating ambulance.

A frantic Huguette urged the chauffeur: "Don't lose that ambulance! Stay close behind!"

Anna was revived and Huguette's spirits lifted. However, two days later, the doctor explained there was nothing more he could do. In the hospital lobby, Dr. Pierre sat with Huguette for an hour as she agonized. With a heavy heart, she followed her mother's wishes: Anna was transferred back home.

Anna Eugenia La Chappelle Clark died the second week of October 1963. Her obituary appeared in *The New York Times* in the respective section reserved for prominent deaths. Friends and acquaintances on two continents took note. At his villa outside Nice, Gower read the obituary with interest during breakfast in the garden's dappled sunshine.

I should write a condolence letter today. Poor Huguette will be bereft. Can't imagine how she'll cope without her mother.

Watched over by Amelia for the first several weeks, Huguette went numb. Anna's apartment filled with bouquets and extra staff to handle the entertaining required. Marié was given her last assignment: Arrange the funeral according to Anna's specific instructions. Particular emphasis was placed on the hymns played.

Huguette cried alone in her study or at night. Insomnia loomed and dark circles formed under restless eyes. To outsiders, she seemed fine. Activity was a salvation. On autopilot, she had the maid buy multiple copies of the paper, clipping the obituary out of each one. She made many phone calls, replied to condolence cards, and examined the menus for the required entertaining.

She was surprised to read Gower's letter. *But then he always did respect* Maman. *Imagine, seeing him after all these years!*

Before and after the funeral, Huguette and Amelia hosted the family gatherings and reading of the will in 8W. Huguette bravely assured the doubtful Amelia—who was also weakening and not feeling her best—she could handle the required entertaining. But once the drawing room filled up, Huguette fled to 12W to recoup. Amelia was left alone with the guests until Huguette reappeared near the end of the party, explaining, "I had a little headache, forgive me."

During the Requiem Mass, Huguette's mind wandered to countless ceremonies in many other cathedrals sitting quietly next to the devout *Maman* draped in a black lace veil. In later years, she recalled *Maman* perversely repeating she looked forward to being laid to rest with William and Andrée. This happened with greater frequency after she was bedbound.

"I never think of such things! *Maman*, how can you say that?"

"But Huguette, it's the normal course of life. And half my family is in heaven. I want to see them! It's very simple." The prone Anna moved frail hands as if to push Huguette away.

"I want to live a long life. And I want you to live a long life too. You're too young to die."

"You keep believing that. I'm an old woman in her eighties with a faltering heart, an erratic mind, arthritic joints, lost hearing, oh, who knows what else! But," Anna smiled and paused, "*I know I'll see you in heaven*. Don't worry. Have faith, *ma petite fille!*"

At Woodlawn, Huguette stood close by Amelia in front of the Clark mausoleum. The late morning was bright with warm breezes gusting around them. In a continuous procession, imperial yellow leaves merrily floated or spun their way down to the cut green grass at her feet.

Despite her pain, Huguette noticed the air smelled clean and sweet. *How* Maman *would've loved this October day, so pretty and sunny...*

Huguette's eyes were riveted on the ritualized performance as soon as the polished wood casket with long brass handles and a white rose blanket was slid out of the hearse and hoisted onto male shoulders. They carefully carried the casket past the small crowd of onlookers, up the steps, and through the bronze door. It was lowered to waist height and slid into its appointed spot in the marble wall on the left-hand side. Then the rectangular bronze door bearing Anna's engraved name was shut and the men filed out.

Huguette's heart skipped a beat when she saw the casket disappear. Maman *is really gone!* She reached for Amelia's gloved hand, not registering how frail it was.

Flanked by Amelia and Father Williams, Huguette ascended the steps. A few other family members followed to observe the priest saying a final prayer. Not everyone could fit by the altar, so they squeezed before the door.

When the priest finished, he and Amelia stepped out, and Huguette was alone. Her red-rimmed, swollen, blue eyes ran over bronze plaques reading and rereading the names of her father, sister, and mother. She had no words to describe the hollow ache of loneliness.

It's just me now!

She turned her back to face the altar. Black, Italian leather, kitten heels scraped the stone floor. The sound was amplified in the small space. It felt chilly in the mausoleum.

After Amelia's gentle nudge, Huguette stepped out, putting a handkerchief to mouth to muffle a sob. With a dull thud, the massive bronze door commissioned by her father in 1893 was sealed by a cemetery worker. Huguette looked back one last time at the mournful figure of Katherine Clark watching over the inhabitants' remains before she allowed Amelia to take her arm.

Huguette barely recognized Father Williams who stood waiting at the end of the staircase, but she knew Anna had known him well. Amelia had called the elderly priest to give Last Rites. The priest was frightening when he appeared in the bedroom, as if he were Death himself. Huguette looked on, disbelief and horror at viewing the sacrament performed over Anna's unconscious, shriveled form.

Maman, *what will I do without you?*

A few remaining family members shook her limp hand. "Thank you for coming." Then they drifted off, black limousines easing down slim cemetery roads. Huguette, silent in black hat, overcoat, and gloves, stayed put. Wet eyes traveled over the many multicolored funereal bouquets and wreaths. The sun shone warmly through the shedding trees.

As if this weren't one of the worst days of my life! That mausoleum contains all I hold dear...

"It's such a gorgeous day. How Anna would've loved it," said Amelia, wearing sunglasses and sniffing deeply. "Smell that! Oh, so fall fresh!"

"I thought the same..." Huguette whispered.

"I've only been here a few times, but every visit I'm struck by the elegance of the Clark mausoleum. I know Anna admired it as well."

"But it also makes one sad. So sad! I don't like coming here. Every time I do, someone very precious to me is gone..." Huguette sobbed again.

Amelia put a thin arm affectionately around her niece's shoulders and squeezed. "I'm sad too. I loved your mother very much, and I've lost my best friend. But life must go on, Hugo! Remember, sweetie, Anna wants you to be happy."

Huguette took a deep breath before she nodded. Amelia echoed her mother's sentiments in all things. She took one last look.

Adieu, Maman...

Huguette allowed Amelia to steer her back to the Rolls where Semple was chatting with the chauffeur. During her lifetime, she would never return to the Clark mausoleum; instead, a standing order of two dozen white roses was delivered weekly.

November 1963
1030 Fifth Avenue, New York City

Eighty-eight-year-old Katherine Clark Morris rang up her daughter, Kate Hall. "The poor thing is a lost cause. But, she is, after all, my half-sister. And now all alone. I can't in good conscience not try to make *some* sort of effort..."

Katherine had never cared for Anna, "but for Huguette, that odd thing... I will make an exception."

"Oh Mother, she's not. Stop. She's just marching to the beat of her own drum. She always has."

"Well, make sure she doesn't march too conspicuously in my drawing room, alright? Arrive early, by two o'clock, Katie dear."

On a wintery Friday, Katherine welcomed Huguette and a dozen female Clark family members to a late luncheon at her Fifth Avenue apartment. Afterward, they would attend a concert at Philharmonic Hall.

When her deferentially smiling, faded blonde half-sister minced her way into the drawing room—"At minimum a half hour late and wearing a green satin Patou gown *at least* twenty-five years out of fashion!"—Katherine's painted-on grey eyebrows raised. Her eyes shifted to her sixty-one-year-old daughter as if to say, *Can you believe it?*

Katherine, still in robust health, wore a simple, knee-length, ivory silk Givenchy dress with a twisted pink ruby, lapis lazuli, and diamond Van Cleef & Arpels necklace. Ignoring arthritis, she rose from the sofa as elegantly as she could muster. She lightly embraced and air kissed her half-sister.

"Huguette, how *lovely* to see you. It's been *too long* since you were here. Come in and sit down. I'm glad you've come."

"Thank you, Katherine, I'm pleased to be invited. Hello, hello..." Huguette said in a squeaky tone, nodding politely to each of the dozen women of varying ages, all beautifully coiffed and jeweled creatures.

From family ties, Huguette vaguely knew everyone there. She sat down by Kate Hall. The social mask etiquette demanded was firmly on her soft-fleshed face. She attempted to conceal the anxiety and depression brought on in spades by Anna's death. Nor did she reveal Dr. Pierre had her on sleeping pills. Instinct soon hardened the mask.

Most of them don't care about me. It's the money they're interested in. They probably want to know the details of Maman's *will.*

"How are you? Everything okay?" Kate said softly. "We haven't talked in so long. And I didn't get a chance to say much at the funeral."

"Oh yes, quite all right, thank you, Kate."

Huguette nodded agreeably, not wanting to talk there.

Kate's the only one I trust.

Kate whispered, "Let's go out for lunch sometime soon."

"Alright, that sounds fun. I'll call you."

Staff served *hors d'oeuvres* and drinks while polite inquiries were made about Anna's passing and the recent funeral. Eventually, a bold woman openly broached the topic only commented on in whispers.

"Now that Anna has passed, will you stay in New York, dear, or go to California?"

All eyes on Huguette. She squirmed under the pressure.

Bellosguardo was well-known, even if the oldest in the group had only been invited to a large, anonymous party thrown during Fiesta in the mid-twenties. "But that was years before Anna redid the entire estate, sealing it off from less-deserving family members," said one woman several minutes before Huguette arrived.

The unspoken consensus was: *Wouldn't it be something to be* chatelaine *of one of the most prestigious oceanside estates in California?*

Huguette's heart raced at the unwanted attention.

"Oh, I... I think I'm happy here. After all, I've spent most of my life in New York."

How can I return to Maman's *house when it will only make me cry more?*

To have something to do, Huguette took a sip of what the butler offered. The liquor seared her throat. *So strong!* She set it immediately down on a glass table.

"If you don't mind me asking, will you sell Bellosguardo? It's got to be simply too much for one person to manage," said an elderly woman with a dyed black pouf updo.

Huguette didn't know where to look.

"I can't imagine... What a thought!"

She giggled nervously before taking up her glass again. She remembered how strong the alcohol was and set it back down.

This would be a good time to take out a cigarette and ignore them all, if only I still smoked!

"Pardon my frankness, it's just my way, but it must be a *great burden* to have such a large estate on one's hands when you've two apartments now in New York?" The pouf updo woman gave the hostess a pointed look. "Selling is such a pain, but it'll make you money!"

Knowing laugher and nodded heads punctuated the group.

Huguette mumbled, "I can manage."

Conversation stalled as minds tallied the millions in cash, real estate, art, and jewels Anna must have left her socially inept daughter. Cold eyes minutely observed. A few women exchanged glances, reading each other's thoughts: *The immature, mouse-like Huguette will never manage life in the city, or another inherited fortune, without Anna's guidance.*

Huguette's heart hammered in her chest.

Why are they staring?

Awkwardly, she attempted to change the subject. Her voice rose as eyes darted to Mrs. Morris.

"I'm looking forward to the concert program!"

"Oh, yes, dear, we're all looking forward to it. Aren't we?" Katherine said, smiling broadly. *Maybe this was a mistake...*

After two hours of small talk, the group transferred to the dining room for a meal of: Avocado Pear *Belle Aurore, Poulet à la Estragon,* grilled tomatoes, mushrooms in herbs, *Baba aux Fraises, demi-tasse.* Afterward, they rose to follow their hostess.

"We'll meet in the lobby, alright everyone?" Katherine Morris said in a commanding voice. Her long, cherry red nails stood out in high relief against pale fabric and skin.

Each woman slipped on a mink or fox coat, exiting singly or in pairs. A few tried not to gawk as Huguette was helped into an ankle-length, Russian Barguzin dark sable. If her gown was disappointing, the coat was not.

In the back seat of a rented Cadillac Fleetwood limousine, two middle-aged first cousins enjoyed the advantage of being alone to gossip on the drive over to the Upper West Side.

"Seeing Huguette after all these years does not inspire confidence in her abilities, does it? She'll *never* be able to manage the Bellosguardo estate. *What* was Anna thinking? Who knows what will happen to Huguette's fortune? She'll lose it somehow! The dolt's probably sitting on piles of money. More than any of us..."

"Anna's California estate is spectacular. I know Kate has visited, probably far more often than her mother, of course, but she'll not say a word. She's always defended Anna. Celia Clark and her children, too, come to think of it. But otherwise, not too many others that I know of. At least to the new estate. To the previous villa, yes; but that was merely an average one..." A hand waved impatiently. "In any case, Huguette will sell Bellosguardo for a song or do something foolish due to incompetence. Mark my words!"

"How much money was left to her by Anna and William, I wonder?"

A long fingernail tapped on the arm rest.

"Somehow, all those many decades ago, Anna ended up with a *far larger share* than Katherine and her siblings originally agreed upon. Her lifestyle after William died spilled that secret! So much for pre-nuptial agreements... *Don't* mention the subject to Katherine! It still rankles."

A smirk while Elizabeth Arden lipstick and powder compact were drawn out of a black silk clutch.

"And little Huguette receives everything now, from *both* parents, I suppose..."

The fingernail stopped rhythmically tapping.

"Every bit of those millions! I haven't heard anything *factual* about it, of course. But with everything considered, and my standing in the direct family line, at the end of the day, it doesn't seem fair!"

The faux gold compact snapped shut.

Huguette stepped onto the curb in front of the vast courtyard still under construction at the evolving complex of Lincoln Center for the Performing Arts. Built atop the ghetto neighborhood of San Juan Hill where "West Side Story" was filmed, the vast urban renewal project—displacing thousands of black, colored, and immigrant American residents—would soon be a gorgeous home for American arts.

While the sun waned behind thick cloud cover, Huguette hesitated a good while beside the chauffeur. She stood disoriented by streams of people striding to and fro. Her keen eyes noted clothing, grooming, and behavior were far more casual and rougher than imagined. On television, it was safe to observe street scenes, but it was quite another experience to inhale the dirty concrete and exhaust fumes; to hear up close the non-stop clamor of the traffic, screeching tires, taxi horns, and piercing police sirens; to feel the cold air hit cheeks and ruffle hair; to view humanity swarming impersonally.

Aiming at Philharmonic Hall, Huguette scampered forward with a gold Dior clutch clenched under a sable-clad arm to ward off thieves. Once inside, Huguette was clearly taken aback by the very tall, all metal escalator.

I don't recall they moved quite this *fast... It's positively racing!*

She hesitated so long, in a flash she was at the bottom with the group almost up to the lofty upper floor. Kate Hall waited patiently behind.

Huguette warily scanned the grey metal teeth of the escalator ascending mercilessly. The teeth steps menaced with relentless movement that would chomp at her flesh.

"It's a quick, never-ending loop of a staircase powered by electricity," she heard Papa explain in Harrods.

As if a little girl again, she stood gazing up at him, wondering how the moving staircase worked. Back then she had no trouble pouncing aboard with glee.

But now, this feels strange.

Holding her breath, Huguette hopped onto the metal step and rose higher. Long Cartier diamond earrings swayed as she put a hand to heart. With the force, Huguette leaned back, and Kate protectively put out a steadying hand.

They zoomed up.

"I'm sorry. I didn't mean to make such a fuss. I think my heel got caught."

Kate smiled at Huguette's white lie, letting her play the little games she had always played. It was obvious her aunt was completely overwhelmed by modern life.

How long has it been since Huguette left her apartment or went out alone? She's so loyal, she probably spent years caring for Anna. Not much time for a normal life.

Once settled in a plush seat, the familiar atmosphere and tradition of the theater soothed.

"Isn't this magnificent!" Huguette gushed.

She bore a wide smile as she swiveled her head in wonder at the 2,200-seat auditorium. She was unaware her niece had attended opening night featuring Leonard Bernstein the previous fall, and many New York Philharmonic concerts thereafter. Huguette had only watched the televised live concert on CBS.

"What a marvelous job they've done. All the woodwork is stunning! *Maman* would have loved to see this!"

"Yes, but it's not as acoustically perfect as it could be. Anna wouldn't have liked that," said Kate, eyeballing the program. "There were issues with building, of course. Couldn't have it any other way in New York!"

"Oh, now that you mention it, I do recall. There were several articles about that..."

After the house lights lowered, Huguette relaxed and enjoyed the program. In the lobby afterward, she thanked Katherine Morris for the invitation and waved politely goodbye to the group. Then she gratefully retreated to the safety of her familiar chauffeur standing at the curb with the warm backseat beckoning.

Huguette was exhausted. *I can't return home fast enough!*

The next day she sent an effusive thank you note and a bouquet. After it was sent out, Huguette dithered about the wording while watching the evening news.

I hope my thank you note indicated my gratitude but didn't suggest that I don't intend to ever go again! I wouldn't want to be rude.

By the spring, Huguette was aflutter with studying the latest makeup techniques—"I can't possibly wear that much black eye makeup with false eyelashes!" she wailed to an astonished maid—and writing requests to Jean Patou for slimming dresses and slacks. She cursed herself for spending a winter of self-indulgence eating teas laden with *brioche*, Gaufrette biscuits, and Twinkies. She was ten pounds heavier than normal, and both men were coming to New York in the near future.

Tomorrow begins a diet of fish, broth, and vegetables!

Since Anna's death, Gower had been consistent with letters and telegrams from France. Huguette was content to be friends. *Only Etienne keeps up the ridiculous pretense we're young lovers still.* Villermont was all flirtation, chocolates, and flowers. She permitted him to come to 12W on occasion, but she kept him at a distance.

Six weeks later, at Gower's favorite Upper East Side bistro, they sat at a table well away from the popular section.

"I figured you'd like to eat in peace."

Huguette cut into asparagus.

"That's kind of you, Bill. This is a good spot. Thank you."

"How have you been now that Anna is gone? Again, I'm sorry she passed."

"Oh, I'm fine. I'm so busy these days." Then she whispered conspiratorially, "But I daydream about returning to France."

"Do you?" Gower's grey-blonde eyebrows raised. He downed his drink. He motioned a waiter for another. "I suppose that makes sense. You grew up there."

He speared *pommes frites* with a fork, eating with relish.

"I should visit soon, shouldn't I?" Huguette looked at Gower for confirmation. "It's been so long since I've seen the French Riviera where you have your villa, I probably wouldn't recognize much. Has it been built up, Bill? Losing the Old-World elegance?"

She took a delicate bite of chicken in mushroom sauce, discreetly examining him after all these years. Intent on his meal, Gower didn't notice.

"I think it's improved since we were young! If you decided to come, you can stay with me. You might have to share a bed with Snoopy though," Gower smiled indulgently and glanced up. "He loves women!"

From across the table, Huguette's eyes took in the aging Bill.

He's losing his hair, and I'm not used to his glasses, but he looks slim and healthy. Handsome still... I wonder what he thinks of me?

Huguette put down cutlery and dabbed her mouth with a linen napkin.

"Oh, I would like to meet Snoopy. But probably not in my bed! Thank you for the invitation, that sounds tempting. I'll consider it."

She smiled, picturing herself in Nice for a moment.

That was Maman's *favorite city in the region.*

Gower paused, stopping himself from asking if she meant that.

She's become so squirrelly!

He speared another French fry and changed the subject to TV shows they watched in common.

In March 1968, Huguette roused herself for one more Clark funeral. Kate Hall died within months of being diagnosed with cancer. Attending made Huguette skittish; she went back and forth for days.

It's my duty to acknowledge the close childhood bond. Andrée would want me to go...

The morning of the funeral at Saint Patrick's Cathedral, Huguette made a beeline to sit in the back. The usher headed her off, insisting he was ordered she should be escorted to the front. She reluctantly obeyed, sensing vigilant eyes as she advanced up the long middle. Once seated in the wooden pew behind the Hall and Morris families, Huguette looked over at Katherine Morris's proud profile.

The old woman has outlived her husband, her only daughter, and all her siblings save me. And I don't count for much... I pity her.

To Huguette—scooching as far as possible to the other side of the pew to avoid the frequent coughing and sniffling all around—it felt like another world to recall Kate had married at this altar in the twenties.

I was an uncomfortable bridesmaid while dear Papa and Maman *looked on from the very pew I now occupy.*

After the Requiem Mass, Huguette joined the queue. Despite avoiding people's eyes, she was waylaid by older relatives wishing to introduce her to their children and grandchildren. She disliked being stared at as if she had appeared out of thin air. The amount of handshaking expected was distressing.

I must wash my hands as soon as I arrive home!

Once the required conversation with Katherine took place, Huguette made her way to the door, repeating to everyone attempting to waylay her, "Oh, hello, yes, nice to see you, as well. Well, I really must be going... I have another appointment and cannot chat. Good day!"

She stepped out into heavy flurries, grateful her chauffeur knew enough to be waiting first in line. Driving up to 907 Fifth, she slipped within the safety of the bronze doors and was never seen by anyone in her father's family again.

The next year, Huguette could not face *tante* Amelia's death with the same courage. She attended the funeral but nothing else. She was bereft at losing another dear friend and intimate family member.

"I knew my aunt all my life, and now she's gone, too," said Huguette on the phone with Wendy Styka before she remembered herself and changed the subject. "Oh, never mind me! Your life is far more interesting and exciting than mine. How's Darlene these days?"

"Mom's fine. She says hello. Mrs. Clark, uh, I was thinking... How about we have lunch this week? I can come into the city any day it's convenient for you. Any day, actually..."

Wendy wound and unwound the extra-long telephone cord while standing in her mother's farmhouse kitchen. She was eager to see the godmother who had generously sponsored her entire private school and then university education.

"I would like to thank you in person for all you've done for me, y'know, all these years. You've been a terrific godmother. But I haven't seen you since I was a little girl! I feel funny about that."

Wendy scrunched up her nose, waiting for the excuse.

"Oh, that's not necessary, dear. I know you're grateful. We talk all the time, it's alright. And I've been ill lately with a little cold, but I'm all better now. Now tell me again about what you're studying for your master's at Brown. What're the course titles?"

Huguette donated Rancho Alegre and took Bellosguardo off its forty-eight-hour watch for good.

It's unthinkable to face seeing Bellosguardo alone right now. But maybe I'll go next year? I'll call beforehand.

She discussed her wishes with the housekeeper, Fiona Baker. "It would distress me greatly if anything were altered in my absence, you do understand? I want it to remain precisely as my mother designed it. Precisely as she left it."

"Yes, of course, Mrs. Clark. May I ask, since it's been quite a few years, when might you be considering a visit? The staff would certainly like that, you know, to see the house being opened up and enjoyed once again..."

The housekeeper trailed off, mystified by an owner who ignored such a beautiful house. Hired in 1957, she understood why Anna Clark was unable to manage a visit.

But the daughter? Why, she's only a little older than I am, probably.

"Oh, I couldn't say! I've been very busy in New York. And, well, the thought of coming without dear *Maman*, you understand, is so distressing to me at this point in time. Please remember my instructions, Mrs. Baker. Good day to you."

The housekeeper whittled down the staff by releasing nonessential positions or not rehiring when an employee retired. During the next twenty-five years, Baker became aware of ridiculous gossip in Santa Barbara related to the estate. She informed Mrs. Clark who dispatched a lawyer.

Jack Hurlburt flew out first-class to LA and drove up to Santa Barbara to spend a day riding the trolleys. He listened to tour guides divulge the mysterious story of the French family who had disappeared or of the orphaned heiress who hadn't set a foot on the haunted estate in thirty-five years. The lawyer dutifully wrote down the details, and then hopped off in downtown to buy up all the postcards with aerial photographs of Bellosguardo.

"I'll pay double or quadruple, whatever's required." Hurlburt stood with hundreds of dollars of cash in hand, requesting the shopkeepers contact him when more were printed. "I'll pay for those too. And if anything changes, call me. Here's my card."

Before flying back to New York that night, Hurlburt destroyed all incriminating postcards. This routine had to be repeated on multiple occasions, but Mrs. Clark never had him do anything more.

"Do you want me to reach out to the city council to cease the tours? We can sue the city or the tourist businesses for libel," Hurlburt said on the phone from his Manhattan office.

"Oh no, that's too distressing to consider. I don't want the attention!"

Once Bellosguardo was buttoned up, Huguette turned laser-like focus to 8W. Preservation of Anna's world was paramount. The long-term project would cost $78,000 to be returned to "just like Mommy." Translation: At its zenith in the thirties.

Normal wear and tear and years of neglect during Anna's elderly years had put a decided damper on the luster of the apartment. Parquet floors, marble, and tiles were dull, cracked, and scratched; silks were fraying and faded; paint and wallpaper needed freshening up; and the bathrooms and kitchen had seen much better days. Anna's preferred agency, the venerable French & Company, undertook the refurbishing along with replicating Anna's bedroom for a nonexistent occupant. All antiques and damask fabrics were to be sourced from France. Even the exact antique lightbulb had to be hunted down by the exasperated decorator.

"No detail should be altered from the original unless strictly necessary," Huguette wrote before sliding the paper under the door.

The decorator would pick up the note, scrawl his reply, and slide it back again under the closed door. That level of privacy became legend.

"In the many years I've worked with this particular client, I've never seen her face-to-face!" The famous decorator enjoyed regaling less well-heeled clients with the story of extreme exclusivity. "You know someone is of the upper crust when they don't want to deal with anybody! When she knows I'm coming, she retreats to another apartment she owns. In the same building, you understand."

Once workmen departed and the pitifully few staff remaining retired to bedrooms, Huguette descended cement steps to a darkened 8W. Using a set of blueprints and scaled drawings, she walked from room to room making notes and inspecting the work. She kept detailed track of progress or examined an antique replica. If something wasn't done to satisfaction, she rang the agency the next morning. And she would keep calling until it was done exactly as required.

"I have a few things I would like remedied at 8W, 907 Fifth Avenue, please."

The decorator would receive the detailed message from his secretary and shake his head in wonder.

"Mrs. Clark's never shy when it comes to demanding the best..."

In Huguette's mind, the overall plan was to move down to 8W once the renovations were completed. But due to one delay or setback after another—or perhaps due to her procrastination at the bother and the lack of staff to do the work—that wouldn't happen until the early eighties. There was always a water leak in the ceiling, or a plumbing or radiator issue somewhere. Huguette was in no hurry—time was not regarded—despite the deep desire to be as close to Anna's memory as possible.

The plan was not to occupy Anna's bedroom or even a guest bedroom nearby. That would disturb the authenticity. It suited Huguette more to adjoin two maid's rooms in the servant's quarters and install a kitchenette across from a plain twin bed. Anna had never stepped foot near this area, but her daughter had no such qualms.

If I were to live there, it makes perfect sense. I'm not disturbing Maman's *space, exactly as originally designed. Occupying a maid's room, I'm out of the way yet close enough.*

To assuage loneliness and occupy the endless hours, Huguette turned more and more to television. Since the late fifties, she had been enchanted by cartoon animation. Exclaiming with delight the first day she saw a televised cartoon by chance, she became fascinated by voice-overs and animation.

If only they had these when I was young! Imagine, how astoundingly clever! We only had comics and puppet shows... Oh yes, how could I forget? I remember Cher Maître *took me to "Snow White and the Seven Dwarves" at Radio City Music Hall. Such a wonder! That was in 1937 or '38. Now who could have imagined cartoon programs coming on television all these years later...*

She took up the *TV Guide* on the side table beside her easy chair and searched for more cartoons to watch.

I don't want to miss an episode!

Soon, there were notes listing the viewing schedules of such favorites as *The Flintstones, The Jetsons*, and *The Adventures of Rocky and Bullwinkle and Friends*.

It didn't take long before Huguette obsessed over how cartoon animation worked in conjunction with background music, sound effects, and dialogue.

There are all these moving parts that coincide delightfully.

By the early sixties she purchased a two-inch quadruplex videotape recorder, boxes of tape wheels, and animation guidebooks to study the techniques frame by frame. By 1975, a Betamax and, soon after, a VCR worked brilliantly and much faster.

She wearied the patient O'Henry with constant requests to transcribe cartoon dialogue and tape episodes.

"Never mind the ironing, I need *Scooby-Doo* recorded from this date to this." Huguette handed the *TV Guide* over with showtimes highlighted in yellow.

"But I usually do the doll clothes on Thursdays, ma'am."

"Put that to the side for now. I'd like a transcription of every episode. The dialogue is clever, don't you think? I find it fascinating how they move the faces just so to capture normal speech patterns. That will be all, thank you, Mrs. O'Henry!"

Huguette also watched the new PBS and *The Dick Cavett Show*, writing to Gower particular, clever lines or episodes he must watch out for. In her enduring enthusiasm for American TV, she sent him 37 boxes of tape wheels (she had kept O'Henry busy for the past 6 months laboriously copying). Gower hadn't a clue how to declare it for a bewildered, deeply suspicious customs agent who demanded Gower come down in person.

The accompanying telegram read:

Cher Bill thought it would be nice for you to watch some American TV for a change STOP I hope you enjoy the programs as I do STOP Affectionately H Clark

Huguette also became entranced by sophisticated, romantic BBC miniseries like *The Forsyte Saga* and *Poldark*. In 1980, she developed a crush on Richard Chamberlain portraying John Blackthorne in a silk kimono in *Shōgun*. She went through a stage of purchasing Betamax then VCR tapes of favorite miniseries and foreign films—especially Japanese—out of glossy catalogs. She built up a film library. Instead of boring her, she was soothed by the lineup of favorite, familiar films watched repeatedly.

It was during this period of intense viewing that she began having dreams of Bellosguardo. Each version of the dream was roughly the same. She was young, walking through beloved rooms appearing in full detail with rich colors. She stopped before her favorite portrait of Andrée in the music room, painted by the man she loved. She then went out to the impossibly green lawn with towering palm trees, eyes searching for the brilliant blue of the Pacific Ocean sparkling in the sun. Whales spouted offshore as a warm breeze caressed her face and bare arms.

Then she saw what she was searching for. He stood underneath the shade of a pink flowering tree, dressed in off-white linen trousers and white linen shirt with a brown leather belt and Huarache sandals. He gazed out at the water. She approached and he turned with a warm smile, looking into her eyes.

A young Styka enveloped her in strong arms and kissed her deeply.

Huguette woke up with a start, deliriously happy. She touched withered lips with tentative fingertips with short, unpolished nails.

I wish I could fall back asleep to continue the dream!

Amidst all the artistic endeavors and television playing, dust covers shrouded antiques in unused rooms. Sterling silver in cabinets and on side tables tarnished. Crystal chandeliers, sconces, and large windows dulled with the build-up of microscopic debris in the air. Impressionist paintings and Chinese porcelain remained where they were placed decades ago, with only Huguette's eyes to admire them if she even thought to pass through the room on occasion.

Crowding her desk, mushrooming on tables, and tucked away in numerous cardboard boxes in unused rooms were stacks of papers, magazines, photographs, brochures, newspaper clippings, recipes, documents, receipts, address books, notebooks, and letters. It was a veritable hive of activity with very little tossed.

Not exactly a hoarder, merely a preserver. Huguette had the knack of an archivist. *Maybe I'll need to look up this bit of information or this list or that financial document someday?*

Frequent water leaks from aging plumbing—that 907's population didn't want the bother of fixing—menaced the troves of paper, books, art, and photos. It was easier for everyone involved to do a patch job than tear up familiar rooms which had been a comfort for decades. Huguette understood while still looking with horror at bulging paint and spreading water stains. The damage was repaired, but, as a result, nothing gleamed and shone like it had when Anna was alive. Everything sat back and sighed through the decades of monotonous, peaceful quiet echoing through the many rooms of 12W and the entire eighth floor.

By the eighties, several part-time maids got away with the bare minimum: A casual sweep of a feather duster; a sprinkle of Comet in toilet bowls; pushing an ancient Hoover around. Trays shoved through a pass-through in the dining room wall held scanty meals. If one apartment was occupied by staff, Huguette retreated to another.

The word recluse never crossed her mind, but she shunned all human contact. All sorts of avoidance techniques became second nature in the quest to curate a solitary life.

All this meant—apart from the telephone and letters—she communicated with no one face-to-face aside from Dr. Pierre's periodic visits. She had no choice with him. He suspected her increasing tendencies and began insisting on seeing her in person. He didn't mind turning up the heat.

"Or I'll quit, Mrs. Clark, I'm warning you."

"Oh please, don't do that! Alright, alright. I'll come into the room this time. I'm sorry to trouble you. I know I need to safeguard my health. A checkup is foundational, Mommy always said."

"Quite right. Wise choice, Mrs. Clark. I'll be there tomorrow morning early, about half past seven. I'd come now but I'm headed home to watch President Nixon's resignation speech. The scoundrel."

"Do you think he'll resign, then? What a debacle he's been involved with. Shameful. *À demain!*" Huguette hung up.

Phone calls, letters, and visits from Gower and Villermont tapered off. Gower died in the mid-seventies—he instructed his valet to send immediate word of his death, knowing Huguette would worry—and Villermont in 1982 after many years of decline. Soon after, Dr. Pierre had a heart attack which plunged him into an unwanted retirement.

As was her wont, Huguette began calling over to 1075 Park Avenue to check on Pierre's progress. She spoke daily with his wife, Simone, a warm Frenchwoman who had oodles of patience. Over the months, the two discovered they had much in common; the calls increased to morning and evening check-ins.

After Pierre died, Huguette sent a large check and bouquet; she did not attend the funeral. She called the evening of to check on her friend.

"I hope I'm not being a nuisance. It really was impossible for me to attend today, I'm sorry. How was it, Simone? Did you at least enjoy seeing your family?"

"*Ah, oui, oui,* it was as lovely as can be expected. And Olivier would have been happy, too. And now, I'm a widow. Ah, life is so strange."

"I agree... Dr. Pierre was a wonderful man. A wonderful doctor. He'll be missed."

"Ah, *oui, merci beaucoup!* So many patients came to the funeral, or called as you are doing, to express their appreciation for Olivier."

"How wonderful to hear that!"

"Madame Clark, your friendship means a lot to me, as well," said Simone. "I will never be lonely with your daily calls!"

Simone earned her friend's loyalty by sending flowers and French baked goods over on a routine basis. She took Huguette's daily calls with aplomb.

"It keeps me busy to talk with you! We can take care of each other in our old age! It's providence."

With a phone buddy, Huguette's outlook improved. Apart from reciprocating gifts and sending generous Christmas checks, she made no move to see her friend in person.

"I've been so busy lately. I'll have to get back to you about that. When I get over having the stomach flu."

"*D'accord*, Madame Clark. Drink hot lemon ginger tea. It's delicious! And keep my invitation in mind for when you've recovered. I would adore seeing you for lunch some time. I know a great place!"

Simone was well versed in the avoidance tactics and eccentricities of her husband's wealthiest client. By the nineties, when the skin cancer rose up and manifested itself painfully, she got serious.

"I will make a list of soft foods and high-calorie beverages to be delivered from Winter's Market. How much weight have you lost?"

"Well, quite a few pounds. But I'm alright. I was getting chubby."

"No, it's not alright at our age to lose weight like that. Madame Clark, if you don't mind me saying, you must eat well."

Despite Simon's influence, it took months of cajoling for Huguette to agree to see a doctor.

"*C'est parfait!* I know just the man for you," Simone said. "Dr. Mark Townsend is a colleague of my husband's. He comes to see me from time to time. He will come to examine you in your apartment. He's wonderfully kind and capable. Please consider it."

"I'm not sure. I miss your husband."

"Well, he's not coming back after all these years..." Simone chuckled before saying in a serious tone, "And Madame Clark, you are in pain. Tylenol has stopped working! Your voice is more slurred than normal. I feel terrible you've no medical help. Let's take care of our health together, shall we? I'm here for you, my friend."

"I'll consider it. *Salut*, Simone."

May 24, 2011
New York City

On the front page of *The New York Times*, the headline captured the interest of those following the MSNBC story: "Huguette Clark, Reclusive Heiress, Dies at 104." Eighty-six years earlier, the paper had done the same for her father.

Absolute privacy cultivated at any cost was shattered. An unbelievable story centering on American history, an inherited Gilded Age fortune that had not been frittered away, unoccupied real estate, possible elder abuse, and estate wrangling by distant relations swept through the media. Photos and internet articles spread the news so efficiently that within weeks there was as much, if not more, public interest in Huguette Clark as there had been at the height of her divorce trial over eighty years previous. Americans continued to be as mystified by the Clark's privileged lives as their great-grandparents and great-great grandparents had been.

Young and old New Yorkers in stuffy studio apartments in Lower Manhattan reading *Curbed NY* on Smartphones were stunned the mysterious heiress owned not one but *three* massive apartments in an Uptown co-op. In the Financial

District on a lazy Saturday up on the fifteenth floor, a typical conversation could be overheard:

"Yet she lived in *none* of them? Like, for decades? I *literally* cannot imagine! The apartments are like *all massive*. Why would you choose an icky hospital room? That's cray-zee!" squealed one twenty-four-year-old analyst before grabbing a handful of Fruit Loops and eyeballing Netflix on a laptop.

"Lemme see those floorplans again. Pass your phone quick!" The blue-haired roommate stopped scrolling Instagram for a second to ogle the unimaginable real estate. "I'm so jealies..."

Huguette was cunning enough to live a life so fantastically private it was unfathomable to the Social Media Generation. She went viral in the twenty-first century: "Last Remaining Gilded Age Heiress Dies!" Google algorithms reported over a hundred million hits. Major media outlets jumped on the fantastic American story and impending court battle even before Huguette Clark was laid to rest in a copper casket in a space recently etched out by engineers underneath her mother. Woodlawn completed the internment before opening hours to keep lurking journalists out.

All this attention alerted publishers. Multiple biographies in the works would be best-sellers. There was obvious public interest in this almost-forgotten, once-powerful family, and throw-back of a woman born near the end of the Gilded Age.

To stoke international attention, various high-fashion publications profiled the Christie's auction of the last remainders of the Clark jewels. Plucked from a bank vault last accessed in the mid-forties were: a 9-carat fancy pink cushion cut Dreicer & Co. diamond; a 19.86-carat emerald cut diamond; and—prized by collectors—a strand of Tiffany natural pearls. Bids soared due to the pink diamond and pearls. Those two rare items alone ensured it was the second-most valuable jewelry auction in the United States in the last decade.

The next step was to auction off other valuables such as paintings, antiques, and Stradivarii instruments not available on the market for a hundred years or more. Top auction houses brought in record profits. Despite contemporary design trumpeted on a global scale, bidders seeking Old World extravagance poured in from Dallas, Cairo, Tokyo, London, Sydney, Moscow, and Singapore.

The estate estimated Bellosguardo was worth $100,000,000, but it wasn't on the market due to the trial. One of the wills stipulated Mrs. Clark wanted the mansion used to create an art foundation. The Manhattan properties were listed for a total of $55,000,000. Billionaires put in all-cash offers on all the prestigious properties. Über-wealthy eyebrows around the globe raised as they considered the benefits of creating a massive apartment out of 907 Fifth's eighth floor. The co-op board began to sweat at the unwelcome idea of a Middle Eastern billionaire with a gigantic family turning the exclusive building into sometime akin to Dubai's New Money culture.

Old Money and the Gilded Age were in the zeitgeist. Directors and producers discussed the possibilities; a few years later, the rights of one biography were purchased, and teams of writers, directors, and producers began considering how to turn the incredible story into a feature-length film or streaming series.

The Clarks pursued lives most postmodern people with a streaming subscription thought of only as a Julian Fellowes or Shonda Rhimes production. But not *real life* to ordinary folks slogging away at day jobs wondering what to DoorDash for dinner.

No one had ever *really* lived that way, right?

On a sunny spring morning, a series of rented cars pulled up at 907 Fifth Avenue. Listed in the case for the probate court were over a dozen distant relatives from William Clark's first marriage. All petitioned a chunk of Huguette's portion of the original immense fortune. It was unclear to many what Huguette Clark had intended with the remainder of the almost billion dollar fortune she had inherited in 1925.

Perhaps there had been somewhat of a relationship with one of their grandparents over eighty years previously, but who could remember? If Huguette were alive, she wouldn't have recognized anyone. They wouldn't have recognized her either, as no one in the family had seen *tante* Huguette in person. A few possessed a yellowed family photograph or two to go by. *Tante* Huguette was a child or a young woman in the photo. Several of their deceased grandparents had last seen her at a funeral in the sixties was the best they could muster.

Once assembled, the motley group of distant relations of Senator William A. Clark was escorted up the elevator. It took multiple trips to accommodate everyone.

The doors were flung open to reveal rooms upon rooms. Heads shook in wonder. Bass Weejuns and Easy Spirit pumps tread over unwaxed parquet de Versailles floors. Lacquered heads looked this way and that at high-ceilinged rooms emptied of valuable contents. The spaciousness and gracious architecture spoke of a bygone era.

"I wish we could've seen it with all the furniture and paintings. This isn't attractive at all! There's nothing of interest," pouted a middle-aged woman interested in maximalist décor.

"Oh, look! The views of Central Park... Simply heavenly!" said a perky redheaded woman to her disappointed second cousin. Eyes scanned the famous park below.

Nearby, an elderly woman dressed in a black Armani suit nodded repeatedly and waved a large hand holding a cigarette. The tour forbade smoking, which is why she was standing as far from the guide as possible. "I'd open a window but..." She shrugged. "It's always been one of my favorite views of New York. I must have green, you see. You seem rather impressed, however. New to Manhattan?"

With a malicious smirk, she squashed out the cigarette with a Louboutin heel and sauntered off.

The redhead felt out of place. These people were distant family, not really her scene. *I'm beginning to understand why Huguette went her own way. Maybe I'll withdraw my suit...*

In the end, it was the sheer *space* of the three co-op apartments which was commented on the most. Absolute luxury.

"Pardon me? All this square footage in New York City and she chose to live in a *hospital*," an elderly woman quipped in her husband's lowered ear. She wore head-to-toe Loro Piana; 18 carat gold hoop earrings swayed as she shook her head in denial of the strangeness.

The husband rubbed his thick nose abstractedly, while simultaneously standing on tiptoe rocking slightly back and forth. His watery, blue-green eyes darted here and there, calculating the price of the square footage. He was impressed.

And why did we never visit this relative...?

A tall woman with a blonde French braid and draped Hermès scarf looked over at the mention of hospital life. The woman, with a disagreeable habit of eavesdropping, nodded excitedly. "I agree!"

The wife narrowed eyes at the blonde woman to ward her off, then turned to her husband. She patted him lightly on the chest.

"Oh, I know you're bored, but we *had* to come. I can't wait to talk about the tour at the club. Beth Anne will be positively jealous."

Adjusting a Prada purse on an emaciated shoulder, the wife stepped away, determined not to miss a room. Her husband ambled silently behind.

The small crowd of distant family members peered here and there. Comments were overheard:

"It's a time capsule. Almost laughable if it weren't so grand."

"Oh my, oh my, *major* renovations... And don't I know about those! This will be *eye-wateringly expensive* for some hedge fund manager, no doubt. His gorgeous wife occupied for months and months with renovations, profiled in *Architectural Digest* in record time, no doubt. I read this stuff all the time." The woman waved a hand dismissively.

Up ahead, someone gasped, "A wood paneled Japanese room! Gorgeous!"

"Look at this kitchen from 1915, *un.be.lie.va.ble!* It belongs in a museum. A relic!"

"Oh, this is ghastly. Imagine having all that money and never renovating. It's beyond me..."

"I wonder how long it will take Christie's to go through her valuables. Isn't that intensely interesting? I always think so... I would be quite good at a job like that."

The most outspoken woman, with a blown-out champagne blonde bob and matching silver Tiffany cuffs on each thick wrist, spun around in the throwback kitchen. "You see everyone, what did she do here? Nothing! She lived like a hermit with all this wealth and then took off to a hospital room for decades! She had to have been touched"—she tapped her temple for effect—"or... manipulated by staff or something. It's *too incredible* to be believed! Anna Clark was the one who ran the show, it's obvious.

"When Anna died, it all stopped cold. So, people, who was in control if Huguette wasn't competent?" Dark blonde eyebrows raised in challenge.

"This will require so much money to renovate. It's not worth it!" said one portly, balding gentleman. He had recently flown in from Zurich, leaving his Portuguese wife at home for what would be a quick trip only. He took off a grey pinstripe suitcoat, then reached to shake out an ironed handkerchief to dab a protruding forehead. He felt stuffy.

Let's cut the tour short and go to Jean-Georges.

For all their talk of what was and was not needed, not one person on the family tour had enough money to bid on even the smallest and least impressive of the three apartments. Not one distant family member had the millions it took to buy property on Fifth Avenue on the Upper East Side in the twenty-first century. And add to the property cost tens of thousands of dollars in maintenance fees, taxes, insurance, and renovations. The total increased so fast it was prohibitively expensive for all but the super-rich.

"And here we are, in what was the main studio of Mrs. Huguette Clark," announced the guide in a pleasant tone. She had walked ahead, ignoring the plethora of rude and ignorant comments peppering the tour. "We've placed easels displaying Mrs. Clark's oil paintings. Some of these paintings were first displayed in galleries and the Corcoran in the 1920's and 1930's. There is a notecard below indicating the information we have thus far.

"They are wonderful examples of the talent of the former owner and long-time occupant of these illustrious apartments. As you realize, oil painting is more challenging than watercolor. We hope displaying Mrs. Clark's artwork will add to the historical provenance, and, at the least, will add artistic pleasure to the tour. Enjoy."

The black-clad, young woman backed away, letting the family in closer.

Geishas in kimonos, vases of flowers, Fifth Avenue at night, a portrait, and other still life paintings stood before them. Educated eyes scanned the paintings, some of which were "quite good," remarked a short man wearing a Brooks Brothers navy suit and polka dot bow tie.

"Nonsense," said an elderly woman in a vintage Burberry trench who had been quiet up until now. "They're mistaken," she said with a toss of curly, grey hair and a widening of brown eyes rimmed in kohl.

Her index finger with a French manicure pointed with certainty. "My grandmother was an astute woman. She saw Huguette Clark when she was young. She always remarked Huguette was off somehow, overshadowed and protected completely by her mother. Clearly, she was incapable of such fine work as these. Anna Clark probably purchased them from Tadé Styka, Great-Grand Uncle Clark's portraitist, ages ago. And because it's ancient history, the real estate agency has concocted this story to sell the apartments faster. If anyone knew, my mother knew!"

Several mature heads nodded in agreement. They likewise had heard the family stories, which became myth passed down at holiday gatherings. Behind the repeated stories in all the branches of the far-flung Clark family was a certain coveting air: Huguette had never been right in the head, from the get-go. And, together, Anna and Huguette had gotten away with so much wealth after William's death it was positively unfair. Wild stories of Anna secreting away boatloads of cash and jewels before his death were even whispered by relatives up until the fifties.

The assembled adults examining the paintings had witnessed parents struggle to retain the meager value of trusts. Mansions had to be sold or downsized. Only the oldest family members in the group knew a few authentic details from the first half of the twentieth century.

"But these women had so much it was obscene!"

"How else had Anna Clark afforded to build an oceanfront mansion she barely invited anyone in the family to? And it's still there! I tried to see it a decade ago. I was turned away. A direct Clark relation—which I can prove!—and I can't even get my foot in the door!"

"How had they done it?" It was some wizardry of Anna's or of her financial manager, surely not of Huguette's compromised ability.

Outside on the street, the Clark descendants air kissed and grasped hands in mutual hope and moral support for the probate case to not drag on.

"Maybe we'll see each other in court!" said the outspoken woman.

"Let's hope our lawyers know what they're doing!" quipped a tall, bald man before easing carefully into a Lincoln town car.

The bald man's life was a sham of debt; he required at least five million from the estate. William Clark was his great-great uncle on his mother's side. Before his mother, Buffy, died ten years ago in bed in Palm Beach, she revealed the mystery of "*tante* Huguette."

"She has no children and must still live alone in New York after all these years. It's incredible to be so long-lived, but there's a good chance she's lost her faculties completely. It's always been said by my parents *tante* Huguette had unbelievable wealth, and then inherited even more from her mother's hoarded millions. Of course, Huguette never spent anything because she was slow, you understand. Anything valuable she had, came from her mother."

"So, you move in on that inheritance, son. *Tante* Huguette never responded to my Christmas cards, but maybe you'll have more luck. Go visit her. Don't give up!" she urged, stretching out bone-like fingers to grasp his meaty ones.

Which is how the bald man came to research the family connection, becoming one of the principal characters who gathered the family at the Corcoran. They were ostensibly celebrating the Clark name and contributions to the art institute. Privately, they were sounding out the possibility of an inheritance. He was mystified when repeated attempts to contact *tante* Huguette through her attorney went nowhere.

"I'm not used to being rebuffed so thoroughly, Mr. Schwartz."

"I understand, sir, but there's nothing more I can tell you."

For some reason, in Huguette Clark's place, Joshua Schwartz and his wife attended the family gathering. All that was communicated to the family was Mrs. Clark was pleased by the venue choice.

"Oh, isn't that *wonderful* the party will be at the Corcoran?" Huguette gushed to Schwartz several months earlier. "You must attend in my place, as I have another engagement that day."

"Mrs. Clark, I'm not sure they—" Schwartz shifted in his office chair while typing, the black plastic receiver pressed against one ear with a thick shoulder.

"I insist on it! Take your wife. You must see Daddy's treasures! Let the organizers know I'll pay for the catered meal but be sure to give away *no other information regarding me*, is that clear? Thank you, Mr. Schwartz."

The line went dead. Schwartz sighed as he hung up the phone.

I don't want to go to this Clark shindig!

May 24, 2011
Beth Israel Medical Center, New York City

The ancient woman in the ICU hospital bed was bone thin, mostly blind, and deaf. She lay under a raspy, thin sheet and white cotton blankets. Pink carnations and roses in a red glass vase—sold in the hospital flower shop four floors below—stood drooping on the bedside table with wheels. A white Styrofoam cup with long, white plastic straw and remote were the only other objects on the table. The TV on the wall stand high above the bed gave out light but the sound was muted. A sweaty Nadal beating his opponent in an international tennis tournament played on the screen.

The patient was clothed in the uniform she had worn for the past twenty years: a hospital gown and layered cashmere sweaters. The woman held tenaciously onto life while a whisper of air crept in and out of exhausted lungs. A heartbeat was barely perceptible to the attending physician.

Despite an obvious decline, the patient had kept wits about her these past few months. To the doctor's astonishment, she could understand long-time caregivers with little trouble. She seemed to ignore him. However, it was agreed the end was near.

The frail creature ate and drank almost nothing, and an IV drip in an emaciated arm replaced a formerly sound appetite. She slept most hours of the day or was awake but unmoving, eyelids fluttering and lips sometimes moving as if in conversation. No words could be heard, and she did not raise her head for anyone. For her long-time caregiver, she would smile gently with paper-thin, blue lips, then mouth the words: "Hello" or "I love you."

No visitors were allowed but then again, no one had asked apart from the lawyer. Price explained to hospice staff that practice had been standard operating procedure per the patient's wishes so long it shouldn't be perceived as a red flag.

"Shouldn't we alert her family? There's *got* to be someone."

"Not to worry. It all okay. I take care of it," said Nurse Price.

The petite veteran nurse slumped awkwardly in a beige pleather chair between the hospital bed and the window with beige blinds shut. Her dark head with a few squiggly grey hairs bobbed now and then, and she snored lightly. She had finally fallen into an exhausted sleep in the darkened room with softly shushing and beeping monitors. Despite the familiar surroundings, living round-the-clock at the hospital for over three weeks was taking a toll.

Price's elderly patient had been declining physically at a snail's pace. It was a *miracle* the woman had lasted this long; the end could come at any moment. Earlier in the day, several nurses had begun thinking of plans to maybe bring in a few balloons and cupcakes to celebrate the patient's birthday.

"Will she even know we've gone to the trouble?" said the floor's RN.

"Oh yeah, she still there. She pay attention. I know, she communicate tiny bit every day," Price said, nodding emphatically.

"There's no way she'll last another two weeks. Until June 9?"

The RN examined the death-like stillness of the woman's body, the bruised flesh of the emaciated hand with a smattering of brown spots and an IV. She shook her head and moved closer to the bed.

"One can never tell with Mrs. Clark! Time you leave now."

Price held out a protective arm.

The anticipation of the patient's expected demise had kept Price on alert for days. The strain ultimately led to uncharacteristically falling asleep on duty. Physically and mentally, she simply couldn't tolerate the vigil any longer. She suffered from fatigue and missed her family terribly. For the past week, she struggled to stay awake to perform routine checks in the dead of night.

In any case, had the nurse awoken to check on the slumbering body curled into the fetal position, she would not have witnessed what next transpired.

Only two weeks shy of the ancient woman's one hundred and fifth birthday, the appointed hour finally came. She received a visitor she had longed for.

For a lifetime, even.

Huguette woke to a familiar voice softly calling. She knew that voice. It had been an eternity since she had last heard its welcome tones. But she knew it! Her heart fluttered in anticipatory excitement.

The voice got louder as if it were approaching. She thought the voice said her name. Huguette stirred, opening eyes and raising head to look toward the sound. She saw nothing but murky dimness. Disappointment.

She strained to see or hear something. There was only darkness. And then the sound once again.

It was her name!

In an instant, Huguette's eyesight cleared. She perceived a bright, white light growing in intensity. The light had a radiating warmth, as if it personified love. She was stunned by the cessation of loneliness which welled up within. A great, calloused weight sluffed off. With her whole being, she desired intensely to move toward that light.

Her name was called out a little more loudly. A vague figure advanced out of the center of the light. The figure revealed itself to be a young woman who stood without speaking at the end of the hospital bed, gazing solemnly at Huguette.

She caught her breath, frozen in joyful anticipation.

Could it be...?

The young woman appeared exactly as recollected: pale blue eyes framed by dark lashes; skin with a slight olive cast; long, dark brunette hair; and a soft smile on a thin-lipped mouth. The woman emanated a peaceful serenity and maturity beyond her youth. In particular, there was a light of knowledge and deep patience in her eyes that riveted Huguette's attention.

Entranced, she studied the beloved face. It evoked memories of a perfect life out of reach for far too long. Eyelids closed tight and snapped open again.

Am I dreaming?

The young woman remained silent while being examined. But then she switched to an expectant posture, as if waiting for something important to happen.

Huguette's spirit rose from the bed.

"*Bonjour*, Andrée!"

"*Bonjour*, dear Hugo. Are you ready to leave with me? It's time."

Andrée stretched out a hand.

"*Oui!* I've been waiting for *so long*. I can hardly believe you're finally here!"

Huguette walked a few steps forward. She paused a moment with a questioning expression.

"*Ç'est vrai?* Can I *finally* come with you now?"

"*Oui!* That's why I'm here, *bien sûr*."

The women were now the same height, wearing white cotton lawn dresses. Long hair pulled back in combs and two differing shades of blue eyes fondly regarded one another. Quick, light steps in tandem took them back into the heart of the light.

"*Maman* says you are being stubborn to live to be so old. Tell me, why did you hang on for so long when you knew we were waiting?"

"*Je ne sais pas*... I was having a good time. I suppose I was making up for all the years you lost! Although, I missed you *very much*."

Huguette linked an arm through Andrée's as they used to do ages ago during the soft summers of the French countryside.

"Dearest Hugo, I missed you, too. *Allons-y!*"

Select Bibliography

Aldrich, Jr., Nelson W. *Old Money: The Mythology of America's Upper Class.* New York: Alfred A. Knopf, 1988.

Boucher, François. *20,000 Years of Fashion: The History of Costume and Personal Adornment.* New York: Henry M. Abrams, Inc., 1987.

Brown, Liz. *Twilight Man: Love and Ruin in the Shadows of Hollywood and the Clark Empire.* New York: Penguin, 2021.

Colette. *Gigi.* Trans. By Roger Senhouse and Patrick Leigh Fermor. New York: Farrar, Straus, and Giroux, 2001.

Dedman, Bill and Paul Clark Newell, Jr. *Empty Mansions: The Mysterious Life of Huguette Clark and the Spending of a Great American Fortune.* New York: Ballantine Books, 2013.

Fussell, Paul. *Class: A Guide Through the American Status System.* New York: Touchstone, Simon & Schuster, 1992.

----. *The Great War and Modern Memory.* Oxford, UK: Oxford University Press, 2013.

"Gigi." Directed by Vincente Minnelli. Performances by Leslie Caron, Maurice Chevalier, and Louis Jourdan. MGM, 1958.

Gordon, Meryl. *The Phantom of Fifth Avenue: The Mysterious Life and Scandalous Death of Heiress Huguette Clark.* New York: Grand Central Publishing, 2014.

Mangam, William Daniel. *Biography of Copper King W.A. Clark and his Tarnished Family.* Butte, Montana: Old Butte Publishing, 2007.

Martin, Clancy. "Living Doll." *Town & Country Magazine,* June/July 2012. P. 46. [Author's first brush with the story.]

McAuliffe, Mary. *Twilight of the Belle Epoque: The Paris of Picasso, Stravinsky, Proust, Renault, Marie Curie, Gertrude Stein, and Their Friends through the Great War.* Lanham, MD: Rowman & Littlefield, 2014.

Stuart, Amanda Mackenzie. *Consuelo and Alva Vanderbilt: The Story of a Daughter and a Mother in the Gilded Age.* New York: Harper Collins Publishers, 2005.

Theriault's. *The Doll Collection of Huguette Clark: From Childhood to Centenarian.* Annapolis, MD: Gold Horse Publishing, 2020.

Acknowledgements

Firstly, I need to thank my creative writing students who were involved vicariously as I worked on the first draft. Their participation and struggles with their fiction in our discussion workshops helped me in my own writing. They were the first to read and comment on early drafts of chapters of the novel. The teacher gratefully learned more than her students.

Secondly, I want to thank the handful of readers who slogged through the first draft of the completed manuscript. Their insightful comments, suggestions, critiques, and questions helped to form the much-improved final draft.

And lastly, I want to thank my parents—authors and publishers—for rearing me in a house in the country full of books, ancient and modern history, PBS, BBC, films, dogs, family dinners, and computers. The early word processors and Mac computers of my youth were rarely used for gaming or for homework or other quotidian pursuits, but rather for writing and publishing nonfiction and fiction texts.

Made in the USA
Las Vegas, NV
08 January 2025

16038109R00308